As you Like it

Also of Interest

The Tragedie of Romeo and Juliet:
A Frankly Annotated First Folio Edition
(Shakespeare; annotated and with an Introduction
by Demitra Papadinis; McFarland, 2010)

As you Like it

A Frankly Annotated First Folio Edition

WILLIAM SHAKESPEARE

Annotated and with an
Introduction by Demitra Papadinis

McFarland & Company, Inc., Publishers
Jefferson, North Carolina, and London

Library of Congress Cataloguing-in-Publication Data

Shakespeare, William, 1564–1616.
As you like it : a frankly annotated first folio edition / William Shakespeare ; annotated and with an introduction by Demitra Papadinis.
p. cm.
Includes bibliographical references.

ISBN 978-0-7864-4965-1
softcover : 50# alkaline paper ♾

1. Fathers and daughters — Drama. 2. Exiles — Drama.
I. Papadinis, Demitra. II. Title.
PR2803.A2P25 2011
822.3'3 — dc22 2011007677

British Library cataloguing data are available

On the cover: *Rosalind*, 1888 (Robert Walker Macbeth); background text from Act I of *As you Like it;* ribbon © 2011 Shutterstock

Manufactured in the United States of America

McFarland & Company, Inc., Publishers
Box 611, Jefferson, North Carolina 28640
www.mcfarlandpub.com

For Jay Papadinis

Acknowledgments

This work would not have been possible without those who have shared a long and perilous journey through the uncharted waters of performing Shakespeare's early texts in the early manner, including Evan Alboum, Brian Allard, Collin Biddle, Amanda Bruton, Jim Butterfield, Jennifer Brown, Kacey Camp, Kim Carrell, Craig Colfelt, Lawrence Cranor, Jarel Davidow, Natasha Giardina, Bill Green, Christine Kahler, Bill Kincaid, Andrew Kirtland, John and Kate Kissingford, Michelle Kovacs, Jenifer Kudulis, Natalie Lebert, Christopher LeCrenn, Alan Milner, Alexander Richard, Dave Robinson, Elizabeth Ruelas, Karen Sternberg, Melinda Stewart, Justin Tyler, Jean Ann Wertz, Alan White, Jonathan Wolfe, Michael Yahn, and many, many others.

Contents

Preface

As a director and producer, I long ago stopped using edited, modernized versions of Shakespeare's plays because: (1) they obliterate essential meaning and reduce performability by altering spelling, punctuation, and lineation; and (2) the annotation provided is either inadequate, inaccurate, or both. For these reasons, among others too numerous to list, I began to prepare my own scripts exclusively from the First Folio of 1623, and, in the process, launched my own investigation into the signification of the dialogue. The resulting scripts are not only faithful to the original but also fully elucidated and practical for use in performance. I hope the reader finds them entertaining, enlightening, and useful.

D.P.
New Hampshire 2011

"When *I* use a word," Humpty Dumpty said, in rather a scornful tone, "it means just what I choose it to mean — neither more nor less."

"The question is," said Alice, "whether you *can* make words mean so many different things."

"The question is," said Humpty Dumpty, "which is to be master — that's all."

— Lewis Carroll, *Through the Looking-Glass*

Introduction

Forthright Footnotes (or, putting the "count" back in "country")

The purpose of this book is simple: to make obvious that which should be obvious in Shakespeare but which has been muddled through centuries of editorial interference, the standardization of spelling and grammar, and repressive social mores.

Take, for example, the word "count." In both modern English and modern American speech, the "cou" in "count" rhymes with "cow." By contrast, "count" was formerly pronounced identically to the first syllable in "country" (as is evident from early spelling variants of "count" as "cunte"; and of "country" as "cuntry" and "cuntrie"). So when, in Act I, scene iii of *The Tragedie of Romeo and Juliet*, *Lady Capulet* says to her daughter, "By my count / I was your Mother, much upon these yeares / That you are now a Maide," it should be clear that "count" does not simply mean "reckoning."[1]

Such linguistic details are not inconsequential verbal flourishes; they are vital to the life of the characters both on the page and in performance. Sadly, such details are continually overlooked or omitted. Most Shakespearean annotators would never dream of expounding on such lewd, deplorable, filthy language — probably for fear of getting the venerable Mr. Shakespeare kicked out of school. After all, if the "n-word" is enough to banish Mark Twain from respectable classrooms, how can William Shakespeare hope to survive when he drops the "c-bomb"?

Shakespearean editors abide eternally in the Never-Never-Land of the seventh-grade classroom. The trouble is, of course, that the rest of us grow up — and read, research, produce, direct, and perform Shakespeare's plays in the grown-up world. Nevertheless, most grown-ups still use the same jejune scripts and footnotes prepared for twelve-year-olds and thus remain unwittingly trapped in a pre-pubescent Shakespearean universe. Quite simply, it's way past time for the Bard's hormones to kick in. It's time to put the "count" back in "country."

If we seek to fully understand Shakespeare, we must accept that neither his world nor his works are PG-rated. Whereas denizens of the 21st century consider theatre an elevated and refined art form, to the Elizabethans it was common entertainment no more elite than sports are today. The theatres, banished from the city limits of London by the prim city fathers, set up shop in the suburbs across the Thames. Here they competed in close proximity with other "low" entertainments: brothels, bull and bear baiting rings, cockfighting, taverns, gaming houses, and bowling alleys. Sex and violence were as prevalent in Shakespeare's time as today, and the theatres had to serve up healthy doses of both in order to keep their doors open.[2]

The abundant nearby "naughty-houses" operated openly (if not strictly legally) under the protection of some powerful patron and featured a smorgasbord of services rivaling anything that can be found nowadays. Whether in the market for male or female companionship, one need not have looked far. Equally accessible were the bull and bear baiting pits, where spectators could enjoy a bloody life-and-death battle between the chained, tormented animals and savage dogs and perhaps even win some money by betting on the outcome.[3]

Public executions provided an afternoon's entertainment free of charge. Hangings were most common, but occasionally one might be treated to a burning, beheading, or drawing and quartering.[4] These spectacles also boasted the added attraction of real human blood; for use in their mock murders and duels, players were limited to whatever animal entrails could be found that day at the local butcher shop.

Given such competition, it is small wonder that Elizabethan plays are filled with perverse gore and carnal glee. However, from the blandness of most footnotes, one would think Shakespeare's plays about as boisterous as a game of Parcheesi, as is the case in the following exchange between the *Clowne* and *Maria* in Act I, scene v of *Twelfe Night, or what you will*:

> *Ma.* ...my Lady will hang thee for thy absence.
> *Clo.* Let her hange me: hee that is well hang'de in this
> world, needs to feare no colours.

In typical sterile fashion, most footnotes tersely proclaim that "fear no colors" is proverbial for "fear nothing" with a further pun on "collar" meaning noose. Such prim and proper definitions completely ignore that fact that a man who is "well hung" is genitally well endowed, and that "colours" is a pun on "culls," common slang for the testicles. Therefore the submerged witticism of the line is that a well-endowed man need never fear rivals in (physical) love. The *Clowne* shortly revisits this theme with the quip "Many a good hanging, prevents a bad marriage."

Some passages that seem like pointless jabber take on new weight if bawdiness is factored into the equation, as in Act IV, scene iv of *The Taming of the Shrew*:

> *Biond.* I cannot tarry: I knew a wench maried in an
> afternoone as shee went to the Garden for Parseley to
> stuffe a Rabit, and so may you sir: and so adew sir, my
> master hath appointed me to goe to Saint *Lukes* to bid the
> priest be readie to come against you come with your
> appendix.

True to form, on the subject of stuffing rabbits with parsley, most footnotes either maintain an obstinate silence or expound in a copious non-sequitur describing in minute detail the ingredients of Elizabethan cookery.

Instead of red herrings, red flags should immediately be raised by the words "Rabit" (which bears the same connotation as the modern "beaver") and "stuffe" (identical in sense to "fuck," as in "Get stuffed!"). No word is ever arbitrary in Shakespeare, so the next logical question is why the girl is looking for "Parseley" as opposed to any other herb. Parsley has a long folkloric association with both pregnancy and its prevention. Inserted vaginally (or, in the vulgar, "stuffed into a rabbit") it was thought to induce abortion.[5] The young lady in question was apparently "in trouble" and about to take matters into her own hands when the groom showed up to make an "honest woman" of her. In light of the fact that *Biondello* is arranging an elopement, his innuendo is far from innocuous.

As early as 1947, logophile Eric Partridge attempted to rid Shakespeare of his undeserved reputation for decency with his watershed work, *Shakespeare's Bawdy*. Ever since then, many fearless explorers have plunged themselves into the jungle of Shakespeare's language in an attempt to map his metaphors. The problem is that they have chosen to publish their discoveries solely in the form of scholarly lexicon, essay, or thesis. As a result, the only people who ever read their work are other scholars working on yet another scholarly lexicon, essay, or thesis. The information just never seems to trickle down into the footnotes that are so conveniently at hand and to which most readers solely refer.

The footnotes accompanying this text do not claim to excavate every nuance of a word or to find *the* interpretation of a passage, but they do provide possible explanations not commonly found elsewhere. Hopefully this annotation will serve as a starting point for the reader to launch his own investigation, which is in no way difficult: all that is required is patience, a good dictionary, and an open mind.

Yes, Shakespeare's poetry is beautiful, but his works boast a salacious genius, shameless audacity, and crude vitality that is all-too-often expunged. Instead of condemning Shakespeare's language as archaic and difficult, we should just take off our blinders and accept that *Pistol* says exactly what he means when he states that his "cocke is up." And no, *Romeo* is not describing a shoe rosette when he refers to his "well-flowered pump." The prudish and faint of heart should probably just steer clear of Shakespeare altogether, but the rest of us have a choice: continue to look at Shakespeare only from the neck up, or take down our pants and hang on for the ride.

"Filthy Plaies and Enterluds"

Shortly before a young William Shakespeare set out to pursue a theatrical career, God-fearing Puritan (and all around fun-loving guy) Philip Stubbes attacked "filthy plaies and enterluds" for luring people in with the irresistible bait of "bawdry, wanton shewes, & uncomely gestures" (*Anatomie of Abuses,* 1583). Stubbes was certainly not alone in his view that playhouses were an express elevator that would take players, playwrights, and playgoers directly to Hell: the venerable City of London had already kicked playhouses out of its precincts, banishing them to the Bank-side[6] in 1576.

Such was Shakespeare's success in this thoroughly disreputable line of work that by 1633 he was posthumously singled out for attack by William Prynne (also a God-fearing Puritan and all around fun-loving guy). In *Histriomastix,* Prynne expressed disgust that such vile, corruptive matter as plays "are grown from Quarto to Folio" and that "Shackspeers Plaies are printed in the best Crown paper, far better than most... Bibles." Prynne's buddies in Parliament agreed that plays were worthless at best and dangerous at worst. The "Ordinance of the Lords and Commons concerning Stage-plays" issued on September 2, 1642, forbade the public performance of plays for "too commonly expressing lascivious Mirth and Levity."

Evidence indicates that Shakespeare was anything but a goody-two-shoes. His wife, Anne Hathaway, was three months pregnant when they married. His *Sonnets* suggest that he simultaneously carried on extramarital affairs with both a married woman and a younger man. In 1596, a certain William Wayte took out the equivalent of a restraining order against him because he feared "he stood in danger of death, or bodily hurt," from "William Shakspere." A telling illustration of Shakespeare's personality, although apocryphal, involves his rivalry with fellow actor Richard Burbadge over the sexual favors of a female fan. On March 13, 1602, barrister John Manningham records the following anecdote:

> Upon a tyme when Burbidge played Rich. 3. there was a citizen greue soe farr in liking with him, that before shee went from the play shee appointed him to come that night unto hir by the name of Ri: the 3. Shakespeare overhearing their conclusion went before, was intertained, and at his game ere Burbidge came. Then message being brought that Rich. the 3.d was at the dore, Shakespeare

> caused returne to be made that William the Conquerour was before Rich. the 3.

So just how did this bad boy from the Bank-side become such a bastion of respectability? Certainly it was through no fault of his own. John Hemminge and Henry Condell, two of Shakespeare's colleagues, preserved the Bard's "filthy plaies and enterluds" in all their down-and-dirty glory in the First Folio of 1623. Things soon changed. By the time the Second Folio came to press in 1632, everyone who had played a major part in the publication of the First Folio was dead. This minor point did not, however, prevent printer Thomas Cotes and publisher Robert Alcott from independently making thousands of "corrections," thus launching the time-honored editorial tradition of making "improvements" to Shakespeare's plays based on absolutely nothing but sheer opinion and personal whim.

By the early eighteenth century, the integrity of Shakespeare's text was already in the coffin, but that didn't keep publisher Jacob Tonson, Jr., from driving in a few more nails. In 1721 Tonson hired Alexander Pope for the purposes of "correcting and Writing a Preface and making Notes and Explaining the obscure passages in the Works of Mr William Shakespear." Pope possessed the excellent qualification of being in no way connected with the theatre, so he seemed an ideal choice.

The esteemed Mr. Pope understood that Shakespeare was a mere player and playwright and thus could not be expected to write plays properly. In his preface, Pope denounced the plays' "great defects" of "mean buffoonery, vile ribaldry, and unmannerly jests of fools and clowns." However, Pope magnanimously forgave Shakespeare, because he understood "that Stage-Poetry of all other is more particularly levell'd to please the *Populace*" and that Shakespeare was therefore "obliged to please the lowest of people." As any self-respecting elitist knows, obliging the lowest of people is a great impediment to making highly cultured and inaccessible Art. Obviously the Bard needed a facelift, and Pope had the scalpel ready. He got right to work making the plays ... well, less like *plays*. His endeavors were certainly successful; he removed much of the tiresomely entertaining "ribaldry" and made the scripts much more "mannerly."

Shakespearean editing reached an all-time low in 1807 when siblings Thomas and Harriet Bowdler published their "Family Edition" that removed "those words and expressions which cannot with propriety be read aloud in a family."[7] The verbal carnage was so ruthless that the Bowdlers have the dubious honor of adding a new word to the English language: "bowdlerize," which means "to expurgate (a book or writing), by omitting or modifying words or passages considered indelicate or offensive; to castrate" (*Oxford English Dictionary*, 2nd Edition).

Unfortunately, Shakespeare's manhood has yet to be restored. Modern

Shakespearean editors fall right into step with the snobbish Mr. Pope and the pious Thomas and Harriet. They both (a) "correct" the text based on nothing but speculation; and (b) change, remove or ignore any passage that would make the volume unacceptable in a seventh-grade classroom. These so-called improvements certainly do clean things up; it is of seemingly no consequence that they also render the plays nonsensical and deadly dull.

The First Folio, by its own report, is intended for the enjoyment of the "Great Variety of Readers, From the most able, to him that can but spell." Despite the allegations of Mr. Pope *et al.*, the truth is that we, the lowest of people, simply have no need for a middleman to interpret what Shakespeare *meant* to write. We can go directly to the source to see for ourselves what he actually *wrote*. No matter what one's previous exposure to Shakespeare, no one should be afraid to consult Shakespeare's early texts. Far from being sealed, sacred works whose mysteries unfold themselves to only the initiated few, the original versions are coherent, comprehensible, and above all entertaining—much more so than watered-down modernized versions.

Why the First Folio?

In 1623, printer Isaac Jaggard and publisher Edward Blount produced a collected volume of Shakespeare's plays entitled "Mr. William Shakespeare's Comedies, Histories, & Tragedies" (now referred to as the "First Folio"). This publication was a risky venture, since plays were generally considered to hold about as much literary merit as comic books do now.[8] Prior to the Folio's publication, only about half of Shakespeare's plays had been printed in cheap quarto format.

The terms "quarto" and "folio" simply describe a book's printed size and structure. Books printed *in folio* are comprised of sheets of paper folded only once to form two leaves of equal size, or four printed pages (from L. *folium*: "leaf"). Works printed *in quarto* are comprised of sheets of paper folded twice to form four leaves of equal size, resulting in eight printed pages (from L. *quartus*: "fourth").

Shakespearean quartos exist in two forms: good and bad. A quarto is termed "good" (fairly accurate) if its printing was authorized by the acting company that owned the script (playwrights would sell their works outright to theatres). A quarto is termed "bad" (inaccurate or incomplete) if it is what is traditionally believed to be a pirated version.

In Shakespeare's time, acting companies guarded their scripts closely and were in no rush to publish a play so long as it could still turn a profit at the box office.[9] The concept of intellectual property was non-extant, so once a play was printed there wasn't much to prevent a rival theatre from staging it. Consequently, acting companies would seek to publish a play only if (a) it was old and no longer commercially viable in performance; or (b) there was pressing financial need to do so.[10]

The players' reluctance to publish their plays did not prevent opportunistic printers from doing so anyway: hence, the bad quartos. An unscrupulous publisher who wanted to capitalize on a play's success could obtain the script in a variety of ways. A simple avenue was to pay the price of admission, attend the play with paper and pencil in hand, and scribble down as much as could be caught by ear while the play was in progress.

Yet another way a printer could illicitly obtain a script was to enlist the aid of an actor or actors who had performed in the play. These actors would then attempt to reconstruct the whole from their own individual part-scripts and memory — quite a feat, since the part-scripts or cue-scripts employed by Elizabethan actors contained only the lines and cues for a single character. Here is the entire cue-script for the character of the *Captaine* in *The Tragedie of Hamlet, Prince of Denmarke*:

________________________ were ne're begun.
Enter Fortinbras with an Armie.
________________________ And let him know so.
I will doo't, my Lord.
________________________ Go safely on.
Exit.[11]

Cue-scripts had a twofold purpose: (1) to save time and expense, as paper was costly and copying-out had to be done by hand; and (2) to minimize the number of full copies and thus reduce the risk of a play's falling into undesirable hands. A greedy or disgruntled player with a complete script could sell it to either a printer or a rival playhouse; a player who had only a cue-script could do far less damage if he ever broke away from the fold.[12]

Whereas the quartos were quickly and cheaply produced, the Folio was an expensive volume intended to accurately preserve the plays. The cost of a play printed in quarto was sixpence; the original price of the First Folio was twenty shillings.[13] A book with such a price could not be shoddily produced, and great care was given to its printing and proofreading. Although the Folio appeared seven years after Shakespeare's death, two of his long-time colleagues and business partners, John Hemminge and Henry Condell, played a substantial role in its publication.[14] Printed by the reputable Isaac Jaggard, the Folio contains 36 of the 39 extant plays ascribed in full or in part to Shakespeare.[15]

The Folio's title page claims that it was "Published according to the True Originall Copies," and all evidence supports this. Of the 36 plays in the Folio, sixteen were previously printed as quartos (both good and bad). However, in only three cases does the Folio extensively follow earlier quartos.[16] This suggests that the majority of the Folio was compiled from original playhouse manuscripts supplied by Hemminge and Condell.

These handwritten manuscripts are termed either "Foul Papers" or "Fair Papers." "Foul Papers" are the author's original handwritten manuscripts; they are labeled "foul" because they include revisions and corrections and are therefore somewhat difficult to read.[17] "Fair Papers" were the official prompt-books copied out neatly, accurately, and legibly by the playhouse scribe (who would also have been tasked with making up cue-scripts).

The First Folio's source material, whether foul or fair, holds an impressive pedigree. The Foul Papers (albeit somewhat rough around the edges) are traceable directly to Shakespeare himself; the Fair Papers were actual prompt-books used in performance.[18] Hemminge and Condell's careful care and oversight of the Folio's printing must also be taken into account in assessing the First Folio's authority. In their introduction addressed "To the great Variety of Readers," Hemminge and Condell write,

> It had bene a thing, we confesse, worthie to have bene wished, that the Author himselfe had liv'd to have set forth, and overseen his owne writings; But since it hath bin ordain'd otherwise, and he by death departed from that right, we pray you do not envie his Friends, the office of their care, and paine, to have collected & publish'd them; and so to have publish'd them, as where (before) you were abus'd with diverse stolne, and surreptitious copies, maimed, and deformed by the frauds and stealthes of injurious impostors, that expos'd them : even those, are now offer'd to your view cur'd, and perfect of their limbes; and all the rest, absolute in their numbers, as he conceived them.

There is absolutely no reason to doubt that this is true.[19]

What's Wrong with Editing?

In addition to modernizing punctuation and spelling, the Shakespearean editor spends much time and effort "rectifying" the text. In an effort to produce *the* definitive version of any given play, he compares and amalgamates variant quarto and Folio readings and selects which individual passages, lines, and words he considers to be ultimately "correct."

There is a fundamental error in reasoning inherent in such comparative editing (if reason can truly be said to come into play at all). Unlike a novel, which is forever unchanging once printed, a play script continually evolves in performance. Lines, characters, and entire scenes that seemed flawless when the playwright committed them to paper may prove to have substantial defects when actually performed. It is certainly no secret that the modern playwright will continue to re-write a script while a play is in rehearsal, preview, or even after opening. Should a show close and several years lapse before a play's revival, considerable changes may be made to the script.

Take as an example the works of twentieth-century American playwright Tennessee Williams. Williams considered his plays to be ongoing works in progress and subjected them to constant revision. He did not consider a play finished or forever set simply because it had been produced on the stage or had appeared in print. Therefore, the hapless English or drama student told to pick up a copy of a Williams play for class may find that he has a text that differs extensively from that of his teacher or classmates.

Which of these differing versions of Williams' plays is ultimately "correct"? The answer, of course, is that they *all* are. An earlier version is "correct" in that it is a perfect reflection of the playwright's intent at the point in time it was produced. A variant later version is equally "correct"—in that it is a perfect reflection of the playwright's intent at the point in time when *it* was produced.[20]

In regards to which differing third act of *Cat on a Hot Tin Roof* is superior, Williams himself said that "the reader can, if he wishes, make up his own mind about it."[21] Good advice it is, too. The reader can compare both versions and simply decide which he likes best. (This advice, however, is not so practical for the producer who must ultimately pick only one version to stage.)

Now imagine if, some 400 years in the future, an editor attempted to "rectify" the variant third acts of *Cat on a Hot Tin Roof* in order to make multiple discrete texts into one "übertext." The editor would take a line from one and a line from the other; re-insert lines from the first version deleted in the second version; and freely intersperse dialogue from both while at the same time deleting lines of which he can make no sense in his new mongrel rendition.

Undeniably, such an attempt would be preposterous. Any self-respecting Williams scholar would balk at the mere suggestion, because the text would be adulterated to the point of being both unreadable and unperformable. Simply put, the resulting playscript would be mush.

Yet, incredibly, this is exactly what the modern Shakespearean editor does. He draws a line from a third quarto and follows it with a line from a second quarto. He re-inserts a dozen or so lines from a first quarto that don't appear in the Folio. He sets a line of verse using the third word from a second quarto and the fifth word from the Folio. To make matters worse, editors will frequently consult and incorporate material from the *bad* quartos. The result is that when the unsuspecting reader, student, teacher, actor, or director picks up an edited script of Shakespeare, he is served up page upon page of mixed-up, watered-down mush.

Shakespeare's good quartos are not "wrong" any more than the First Folio is "right"; but to attempt to marry quartos in an uneasy alliance with the Folio is unnecessary at best and ludicrous at worst. The quarto scripts may be considered valid in and of themselves but lose any such integrity when combined with each other and with the Folio. It is painfully ironic that, through the very act of editing, most editors who purport to clarify the intent of the deceased writer do exactly the reverse.[22]

Just as with the works of Tennessee Williams, everyone has the option of reading and examining all variant versions of Shakespeare's plays and deciding which he likes best. The quarto texts are readily available to those who wish to read, study, or stage productions from them. Common sense dictates, however, that the most recent version of a play reflects its highest point of evolution. These are the versions that were refined in the fire of performance before a living audience. These are the versions that the playwright himself, through benefit of experience and hindsight, considered to be the best, for otherwise no changes would have been made to earlier scripts. This in itself is reason enough to choose the Folio over the quartos.

The Importance of Spelling

In a quest for *the* definitive text, editors spend countless hours picking apart and putting back together the Folio and variant quartos. Similarly, they also standardize spelling in an attempt to find *the* definitive word. There is a fundamental flaw in this practice, because Shakespeare, the undisputed master of the English language, rarely uses a word in just one way or to mean just one thing.

Unfortunately for the editor who prefers his text clean, pat, and shallow, Shakespeare employs not only double but treble, quadruple, and quintuple entendre as well. Layer upon layer of meaning can be found in a single passage, a single word, or even a single syllable, and oftentimes the original spelling provides a vital clue to these multiple strata.

A somewhat straightforward example can be found in the first four lines of *The Life and Death of Richard III*. As printed in the First Folio, these lines appear as:

1. NOw is the Winter of our Discontent,
2. Made glorious Summer by this Son of Yorke:
3. And all the clouds that lowr'd upon our house
4. In the deepe bosome of the Ocean buried.

And in a text whose spelling has been "modernized":

1. Now is the winter of our discontent
2. Made glorious summer by this son of York,

3. And all the clouds that loured upon our house
4. In the deep bosom of the ocean buried.

The word "Son" (male child) in line two obviously carries the additional connotation of "sun" (heavenly body) on the evidence of the contextual words "Winter," "Summer," and "clouds." In this case, the editor has left the spelling of "son" intact (although the word has been robbed of its initial capital).

In the case of the word "lowr'd" in line three, the spelling has been changed to "loured" (probably because, unlike "lowr'd," "loured" will pass computerized spell-check). "Lour" is a verb meaning "to frown or scowl, to lurk, to look dark and angry" (OED), and this sense certainly is present. The word "lowr'd" is in all likelihood assonant and should be pronounced to rhyme with "clouds," "our," and "house"; but to remove the "w" erases the additional sense of "lower": "to descend or sink; to lessen the elevation of; to bring down in rank; to degrade or dishonor" (OED). A vital portion of this word's significance has disappeared by standardizing its spelling. Moreover, in removing the apostrophe from "lowr'd" and spelling it out as "loured," the editor has also erased Shakespeare's unmistakable intention that this word occupy one beat, not two, in the poetic meter.

A somewhat more extreme example of spelling change can be found in Act I, scene iv of *The Tragedie of Romeo and Juliet*, wherein *Mercutio* describes *Queene Mab*, "the Fairies Midwife," and how she travels nightly bringing dreams to men. Here is an excerpt as printed in the First Folio:

> ... her coullers of the
> Moonshines watry Beames, her Whip of Crickets bone,
> the Lash of Philome, her Waggoner, a small gray-coated
> Gnat...

And in the second (good) quarto of 1599:

> ... her collors
> of the moonshines watry beams, her whip of Crickets bone, the
> lash of Philome, her waggoner, a small grey coated Gnat...

In the First Folio and second quarto (the two primary authoritative texts), these lines, which are clearly written in prose, read "the Lash of Philome" and "the lash of Philome" respectively. Philome (a.k.a. Philomel or Philomela) is a character from Greek mythology. Her story is as follows:

> Philomel's sister, Procne, was the wife of King Tereus of Thrace. Procne bore Tereus a son, Itys, who over time developed an unhealthy sexual attraction for his aunt Philomel. Itys subsequently kidnapped Philomel, raped her, cut out her tongue so that she should not reveal what he had done, and then hid her among his slaves. Luckily Philomel was able to communicate with her sister Procne by weaving a tapestry that told the whole sordid story. Procne then killed Itys, and

> for additional revenge cooked his remains and fed them to his father, King Tereus. When Tereus discovered what had happened, he tried to kill Procne and Philomel. At this point, the gods of Olympus came to the women's aid, and Philomel, Procne, and Tereus were all turned into birds.

In some versions Philomel became a swallow; in others, a nightingale. The nightingale eventually won out, and in English, "Philomel" is a poetic term for a nightingale. Considering the imagery of the speech, in which *Mab* rides in a tiny hazelnut-shell coach driven by a gnat, it makes perfect sense that the fantastic little contraption should be pulled by a nightingale.

Even so, without exception, currently all commercially available edited versions emend these lines as follows[23]:

> Her collars of the moonshine's watt'ry beams:
> Her whip of cricket's bone, the lash of film:
> Her wagoner a small grey-coated gnat,

This transmutation both (a) obliterates the brutal tale of Philome and the imagery of her avian incarnation; and (b) reduces beautiful prose to mediocre verse. Incredibly, these changes are made on the spurious evidence of a single counterfeit quarto. The only possible source for the verse arrangement and the substitution of "film" for "Philome" is the first (bad) quarto of 1597[24]:

> The traces are the Moone-shine watrie beames,
> The collers crickets bones, the lash of filmes,
> Her waggoner is a small gray coated flie,

Although the first quarto is indisputably corrupt, for some reason editors always feel compelled to consult it when piecing together a textual hodge-podge.

Using material from the bad quartos to justify textual changes is damaging enough, but sometimes editors pluck words out of thin air with no textual justification at all. In these cases, the "corrections" cannot be supported by the Folio or any extant quarto, good or bad. This practice is usually rationalized with the done-to-death assertion that the Folio's compositors were inexperienced, incompetent, and/or negligent.

Such is the case in *The Tragedie of Macbeth,* the only source for which is the Folio. Consider this passage from Act V, scene iii, where *Macbeth* pointedly asks the *Doctor*:

> What Rubarb, Cyme, or what Purgative drugge
> Would scowre these English hence: hear'st thou of them?

And as printed in a modern edited version:

> What rhubarb, senna, or what purgative drug
> Would scour these English hence? Hear'st thou of them?

Editors collectively allege that "Cyme" is a typesetter's misreading of "Cynne" and therefore means "senna"—despite the fact that there is no evidence that "senna" was ever spelled with a "c" (OED gives only two spelling variants of the word as "senna" and "sena"). Moreover, changing the monosyllabic "Cyme" to the disyllabic "senna" completely upsets the line's poetic meter.

Since *Macbeth* considers the English to be just so much "shit" plugging up his kingdom, he seeks a "Purgative drugge" (a drug to cleanse the bowels) that will "scowre" ("evacuate the stomach or bowels," OED) them out. One such "Purgative" would be "Rubarb," defined in John Bullokar's 1616 dictionary as "A costly roote much used in Phisicke to purge choler." Another such "Purgative" would be "Cyme."

The OED's headword "cyme" is cross-referrenced to "cyma": "the young Sprout of Coleworts," and Thomas Thomas' 1587 Latin / English dictionary defines "Cyma" as "A young colewort."[25] "Colewort" is an old name for cabbage, known since ancient times as a highly effective "Purgative."

It is beyond belief that "Cyme" should be changed to "senna," especially as all that is required to accurately define this word is to look it up in the dictionary. With the understanding that such emendation is both unnecessary and misguided, original spelling is herein preserved intact.

The Importance of Punctuation

It can be argued that punctuation *is* meaning, as in the following well-known example:

> A woman without her man is nothing.
> A woman: without her, man is nothing.

In spite of this, Shakespearean editors freely alter punctuation and, in the process, also drastically alter meaning.

Since the living presence of the playwright is lacking, all editorial views as to Shakespearean punctuation must remain purely conjectural. However, evidence suggests that Shakespeare set great store by his punctuation and had great disdain for those players who did not follow it in speaking. Consider the prologue of "the most lamentable comedy, and most cruell death of *Pyramus* and *Thisbie*," the play-within-a-play in Act V, scene i of *A Midsommer Nights Dreame*. This prologue (supposedly written by the character *Peter Quince*) is delivered as follows:

> *Pro.* If we offend, it is with our good will.
> That you should thinke, we come not to offend,
> But with good will. To shew our simple skill,

> That is the true beginning of our end.
> Consider then, we come but in despight.
> We do not come, as minding to content you,
> Our true intent is. All for your delight,
> We are not heere. That you should here repent you,
> The Actors are at hand; and by their show,
> You shall know all, that you are like to know.

This speech might initially seem nonsensical, but it makes perfect sense when punctuated differently:

> *Pro.* If we offend: it is with our good will
> That you should thinke we come not to offend;
> But with good will, to shew our simple skill,
> That is the true beginning of our end.
> Consider then: we come, but in despight
> We do not come. As minding to content you,
> Our true intent is all for your delight.
> We are not heere that you should here repent you.
> The Actors are at hand, and (by their show)
> You shall know all that you are like to know.

This coherent (albeit not brilliant) speech is reduced to gibberish simply because the *Prologue* does not obey his punctuation in speaking. This is further made clear from the commentary quips of *Theseus* and *Lysander*, two of the play-within-a-play's spectators:

> *Thes.* This fellow doth not stand upon points.
> *Lys.* He hath rid his Prologue, like a rough Colt: he knowes not the stop. A good morall my Lord. It is not enough to speake, but to speake true.

This dialogue establishes that Shakespeare thought "points" (punctuation marks) and the "stop" (both a "mark or point of punctuation" and a "pause or breaking-off made by one speaking," OED) to be crucial to performance. It is therefore interesting to conjecture what Shakespeare would truly think of the armies of editors who, for the last four hundred years, have changed literally millions of commas, periods, colons, semi-colons, parentheses, periods, and dashes in an effort to "fix" his punctuation for him.

In Shakespeare's day, there was no "correct" way to punctuate, just as there was no "correct" way to spell. Moreover, it is very important to remember that Shakespeare was not an author but a playwright. He wrote plays intended to be spoken and acted before an audience, not books intended to be read quietly to oneself. This distinction is vital. Shakespeare employed not grammatical but elocutionary punctuation (punctuation as a tool for speaking). Grammatical correctness on the page might be paramount to an editor, but to Shakespeare it was completely inconsequential.[26]

In his preface to *The Tragedie of Anthonie and Cleopatra* (New Variorum edition, 1907), Dr. Horace Howard Furness states that in making changes to the Folio "the omission of punctuation, which at times makes the difference between sense and nonsense, may be censured as ill-advised." Nevertheless, over a century later, Shakespearean editors still routinely damage both punctuation and meaning.

Such disruption is evident in a speech by *Lady Percy* in *The Second Part of Henry the Fourth*, Act II, scene iii. This speech appears in the First Folio of 1623 as follows:

> He was the Marke, and Glasse, Coppy, and Booke,
> That fashion'd others. And him, O wondrous! him,
> O Miracle of Men! Him did you leave
> (Second to none) un-seconded by you,
> To looke upon the hideous God of Warre,
> In dis-advantage, to abide a field,
> Where nothing but the sound of *Hotspurs* Name
> Did seeme defensible: so you left him.

And as commonly printed in edited versions:

> He was the mark and glass, copy and book,
> That fashion'd others. And him — O wondrous him!
> O miracle of men! — him did you leave —
> Second to none, unseconded by you —
> To look upon the hideous god of war
> In disadvantage, to abide a field
> Where nothing but the sound of Hotspur's name
> Did seem defensible. So you left him.

In this example, no less than eleven punctuation changes have been made to eight lines of text. These eight lines do not occur in the quartos (all of which are bad anyway), so the editor's only guide for this passage is the Folio. In the Folio's "O wondrous!" *Lady Percy* sarcastically expresses her exasperated disbelief at her father-in-law's behavior. Moving the exclamation point from behind the word "wondrous" to behind the word "him" completely alters the sense of the line.

Dramatic characters reveal themselves through speech, and their essential nature is found not only in what they say but also in how they say it. Punctuation indicates the manner in which a character speaks and is thus as important as the words themselves. Consider these lines spoken by the bumbling constable *Dogberry* in Act III, scene v of *Much adoe about Nothing* as they appear in the First Folio:

> *Con.Dog.* A good old man sir, hee will be talking as
> they say, when the age is in the wit is out, God helpe us,
> it is a world to see: well said yfaith neighbour *Verges*,

> well, God's a good man, and two men ride of a horse, one
> must ride behinde, an honest soule yfaith sir, by my
> troth he is, as ever broke bread, but God is to bee wor-
> shipt, all men are not alike, alas good neighbour.

And as printed in a modern edited version:

> *Dogberry.* A good old man, sir, he will be talking. As they
> say, "When the age is in, the wit is out." God help us, it
> is a world to see! Well said, I'faith, neighbour Verges.
> Well, God's a good man. An two men ride of a horse,
> one must ride behind. An honest soul, I'faith, sir,
> by my troth, he is, as ever broke bread. But, God is
> to be worshipped, all men are not alike. Alas, good
> neighbour.

As evidenced by the Folio's seemingly interminable run-on sentence, the good constable has a very high opinion of himself and loves the sound of his own voice. When the grammar is "corrected" and the speech chopped up into nine separate sentences, the garrulous *Dogberry* becomes as measured and thoughtful as a schoolmaster. Punctuation, especially as manifested in speech, is essential to both meaning and character, and those who seek to get to the heart of Shakespeare's plays would do best to leave it alone.

Notes

1. Like most profane words, the "c-word" has an ancient pedigree. Its earliest recorded use is on a map of London from 1230 that shows a "Gropecunte Lane." Not surprisingly, this street was in a district where many brothels were in operation. The oh-so-proper OED omits to cite a single quotation of the word from the works of Shakespeare. However, on close examination it will often turn up, as in *Hamlet*, III.ii.:

> *Ham.* Ladie, shall I lye in your Lap?
> *Ophe.* No my Lord.
> *Ham.* I meane, my Head upon your Lap?
> *Ophe.* I my Lord.
> *Ham.* Do you thinke I meant Country matters?

2. Many theatre owners — including Philip Henslowe of *The Rose*, Ned Alleyn of *The Fortune*, Francis Langley of *The Swan*, and Aaron Holland of *The Red Bull*— also owned brothels; some invested in bear-baiting as well. To place "entertainment" prices in perspective: basic admission to the Globe Theatre cost one penny and the exclusive seats (on the stage) cost sixpence. The cheapest (and most squalid) prostitutes charged tuppence, although sixpence was the average rate.

3. The structural resemblance between the bear-baiting ring and the Elizabethan playhouse is no coincidence. Entrepreneur James Burbadge took considerable financial risk when he built the first permanent, dedicated theatre in London in 1576 (suitably named simply "The Theatre"). Burbadge, fearful of losing his investment, deliberately built in the design of a bear-baiting ring. If the theatrical venture failed, the building could easily be converted. Burbadge need not have feared: such was the theatre's widespread success that blood sport arenas such as *The Beare Garden* began to offer plays, and *The Cocke-pit* was later converted for exclusive use as a playhouse. It is interesting to note that today's populist sports arenas follow the same basic design as the bear-baiting ring while elitist theatre architecture has altered radically. The revolutionary Puritan Parliament shut down all the public playhouses in 1642; anyone caught performing was

judged a criminal, and anyone caught attending a play could be fined. The abandoned playhouses were torn down by order of Parliament in 1647. When the exiled King Charles II returned from France in 1660, theatre reappeared in England much transformed in style, content, and architecture.

4. A draconian form of execution not fully abolished in Great Britain until 1870. The punishment is described in the sentence passed on Thomas Howard, Fourth Duke of Norfolk, for the crime of High Treason: "this Bench judgeth thee be led backe from hence to the Tower, then to be layd uppon an Hurdle, and drawne through the middest of the City to the Gallowes, there to be hanged, and being halfe dead to bee taken downe, Bowelled, and after thy Head is cut off, to be quartered into foure parts, thy Head and Body to be done with according to the Queenes pleasure. And God have mercy on thy soule." Luckily for the Duke, his sentence was reduced to simple beheading. Not so lucky was a certain *Doctour Story,* whose execution is described in John Foxe's 1563 *Book of Martyrs*: "he being layde upon an hurdle, and drawne from the tower along the streetes to Tiborn, where he being hanged till he was halfe dead, was cut downe and stripped, & (which is not to be forgot) when the executioner had cut off his privy members, he rushing up upon a sodeine gave him a blow upon the eare, to the great wonder of all that stood by."

5. "Take Parsly, bruise it, and press out the Juice, and dip a Linnen-cloth in it, and put it up so dipped into the Mouth of the Womb, it will presently cause the Child to come away, tho' it be dead; and will bring away the After-burthen also" (Anonymous, *Aristotle's Compleat and Experience'd Midwife,* 1700).

6. The "red light" district outside the London city limits where the theatres were located. William Shakespeare both worked and resided there.

7. The volume appeared under Thomas' name alone in order to protect Harriet's reputation. The Bowdlers removed the more obvious vulgarities, but, alas, if they had truly known Shakespeare's depths of depravity they would never have undertaken the venture. If every single indecency were removed, nary a single line would be left.

8. Sir Thomas Bodley, founder of the famous library at Oxford University that bears his name, wrote to librarian Thomas James in 1612 that he should not collect "suche bookes, as almanackes, plaies & an infinit number, that are daily printed, of very unworthy maters & handling... some plaies may be worthy the keeping: but hardly one in fortie." The Bodleian unenthusiastically accepted a First Folio when Jaggard donated a copy in 1624. The volume was not granted the honor of listing in the catalogues and was sold as part of a lot for an unknown amount sometime around 1660–70. In 1905, when the Bodleian decided that a First Folio was perhaps "worthy the keeping" after all, it paid £10,000 (approx. $1,500,000 in modern currency) to Henry C. Folger to buy back its original copy.

9. In his preface to *The English Traveller*, author and playwright Thomas Heywood (c.1575–1650) complained that his plays were "not exposed unto the world in Volumes" partly because they were "still retained in the hands of some Actors, who thinke it against their peculiar profit to have them come in Print."

10. Such need arose when the London theatres were closed due to plague from June to December, 1592 and from April to December, 1593. As a result, roughly three times as many plays appeared in print in 1593–94 than in the previous eight years. A similar glut of plays flooded the market in 1600 when, due to pressure from conservative Puritans, the Lords of the Privy Council briefly threatened to permanently close all but two of the London theatres. Unable to earn an income from performing, the players had no option but to release their precious plays for sale in print.

11. In Act III, scene i of *A Midsommer Nights Dreame,* impresario *Peter Quince* scolds player *Francis Flute* for his inability to decipher a cue-script: "you speake all your part at once, cues and all." For more on the use of cue-scripts in the Elizabethan theatre, see Patrick Tucker's *Secrets of Acting Shakespeare: The Original Approach* (Oberon, 2002).

12. The infamous 1603 bad quarto of *Hamlet* was possibly assembled from memory by a supporting actor. It prints the play's most famous line, "To be, or not to be, that is the Question," as "To be, or not to be, I there's the point," but the minor part of *Marcellus* (one of the palace guards) is remarkably intact.

13. To place this sum in context: artisans earned about seven shillings per week. Incidentally, this wage was comparable to that of a hired actor, who earned between six and ten shillings per week.

14. Some theatres and acting companies were owned and managed outright by individuals, but both the Globe and Blackfriars theatres and their resident company, the Lord Chamberlain's (later King's) Men, were owned jointly by shareholders. Hemminge, Condell and Shakespeare were all Actor-Sharers, and all three are listed in the First Folio's "Names of the Principall Actors in all these Playes." Shakespeare and Hemminge were original founders of the Globe, and all three men were founders of the Blackfriars. In addition, Hemminge served as business manager and continued with the company right up until his death in 1630.

15. Those not included are *Pericles*, *Sir Thomas More*, and *The Two Noble Kinsmen*, all of which are collaborations of only partial Shakespearean authorship.

16. These are the "corrected and augmented" 1598 quarto of *Loves Labours Lost*, the 1600 quarto of *Merchant of Venice*, and the 1609 "corrected, augmented and amended" reprint of the 1599 quarto of *Romeo and Juliet*. The words "corrected" and "amended" usually appeared on a (good) quarto title page only when an inferior (bad) copy was already in circulation.

17. Edward Knight, a book-keeper (a.k.a. prompter) for the King's Men, may have originated the term when he apologized for the inferiority of his transcription of John Fletcher's play *Bonduca*: "the occasion. why these are wanting here. the booke where by it was first Acted from is lost: and this hath beene transcrib'd from the fowle papers of the Authors wch were found."

18. Some who question the integrity of the First Folio argue that the fair papers are suspect because they are not written out in the author's own hand; therefore, they are marred by copying errors made by the playhouse scribe. This argument is specious, since Shakespeare himself obviously thought the scribe's copies sufficiently accurate for use in staging his plays at the theatre in which he was part owner.

19. For the orthodox view of the publication and provenance of extant quartos and Folios, see Alfred W. Pollard's *Shakespeare Folios and Quartos* (Cooper Square Publishers, 1909).

20. E.g., the first quarto of *Richard III*, which differs significantly from later versions, probably reflects a practical adaptation for performance by a reduced cast while on tour.

21. "A Note of Explanation" to *Cat on a Hot Tin Roof* (Signet, 1958).

22. As Don Weingust observes in *Acting from Shakespeare's First Folio* (Routledge, 2006), "As any tinkerer knows, once something complex has been taken apart, it is nearly impossible to put it back together again just as it was."

23. All modern editions are so alike in both textual changes and annotation that one suspects them to be not original arrangements but rather mindless imitations of their forebears.

24. The source of this unauthorized quarto may have been a literary pirate who attended a performance and jotted down dialogue while the play was in progress.

25. The *Macbeth* quotation is inexplicably excluded from both the OED's entries for "cyma" n. and "cyme" n.1., which are dated as 1706 and 1877 respectively. Instead, it is offered as the first and only quotation under the completely separate headword "cyme" n.2., along with the somewhat feeble "definition" that the word is "supposed to be an error for cynne, SENNA." For more on the chronological unreliability of lexicons, see *Notes on the Annotation*, page 21 below.

26. For in-depth exploration of Shakespeare's use of elocutionary punctuation, see Percy Simpson's *Shakespearian Punctuation* (Oxford, 1911); Richard Flatter's *Shakespeare's Producing Hand* (Norton, 1948); Doug Moston's introduction to *The First Folio of Shakespeare 1623* (Applause, 1995); Patrick Tucker's *Secrets of Acting Shakespeare: The Original Approach* (Oberon, 2002); and Don Weingust's *Acting from Shakespeare's First Folio* (Routledge, 2006).

Notes on the Annotation

1 Traditionally, any lexicographical entry that post-dates Shakespeare is discarded in annotation. However, in *Explorations in Shakespeare's Language* (Longmans, Green and Co. 1962), Hilda Hulme ably demonstrates that even the most trustworthy lexicons misdate word usage by as much as four centuries.

Consider the word "pilcher" in the following line from Act III, scene i of *The Tragedie of Romeo and Juliet*:

> *Mer.* ...Will you
> pluck your Sword out of his Pilcher by the eares?

Because "pilcher" meaning "scabbard" has appeared nowhere else in the English language before or since, its usage here has proven highly puzzling to both lexicographers and annotators. The clearly perplexed editors of the OED offer only the following obtuse explanation for the above quotation:

> With use in quot. 1599 at sense 1 perh. cf. forms at PILCHARD n. (this use may perh. pun on this word), or perh. cf. PILCHER n.2

OED defines "pilchard" as "A small sea fish, Clupea pilchardus, closely allied to the herring, but smaller," and "pilcher" (n.2) as "A term of abuse for: a person considered worthless, contemptible, or insignificant."

A pun most certainly is in play, and the wordplay is indeed on "pilchard" (the fish), not "pilcher" (the term of abuse). The pilchard (pronounced with silent "d") is a small fish of the salmon family. The basic quibble is easily decipherable:

"pilcher" = "case" = "scabbard"

The OED dates "case" or "case-char" meaning "A fish of the family Salmonidæ" from 1751 but significantly can give no account of its etymology. The first supporting quotation under "case" (of only two total) reads: "There is a fish very much like it [the char] (but of another species supposed to be the case)." The OED's entry at "char" reads: "A small fish (*Salmo salvelinus*) of the trout kind, found in the lakes of mountainous districts in the north and in

Wales, and esteemed a delicacy." "Char" is dated from 1662, but the OED's etymological note states that the word is "Known in books only since 17th c.; but may have been in local use long before."

Shakespeare's punning use of "pilcher" is in and of itself suggestive that "case" meant "fish" far before 1751. Further evidence is arguably found in George Wilkins' *The Painfull Adventures of Pericles Prince of Tyre* (1608):

> the Fishermen... beganne to lewre and hallow to their Maister for more helpe, crying that there was a fish hung in their net, like a poore mans case in the Lawe...

And a further case for "case" can be made by Robert Herrick's poem entitled "Upon Case" (1648):

> *Case* is a Lawyer, that near pleads alone,
> But when he hears the like confusion,
> As when the disagreeing Commons throw
> About their House, their clamorous I, or No:
> Then *Case*, as loud as any *Serjant* there,
> Cries out, (my lord, my Lord) the Case is clear:
> But when all's hush't, *Case* then a fish more mute,
> Bestirs his Hand, but starves in hand the Suite.

The purpose of this work is to provide practical and sensible annotation to Shakespeare's Folio text, not to make comprehensive argument for each and every chronologically suspect lexicographic entry. Suffice to say that so-called "anachronistic" definitions are included "if the shoe fits." If "case" meaning "fish" were to be automatically discarded due to an 18th c. lexical date, then not much in terms of sense could be offered. All definitions herein are intended to posit, not prove, usage and content.

2 Period dictionaries commonly define a headword by a list of words and phrases with identical or overlapping shades of meaning. For example, John Florio's entry for "Porcile di venere" in his 1598 Italian / English dictionary is as follows:

> Porcile di venere, the hogs-stye of Venus, a womans privities or geare.

It can therefore safely be assumed that to Shakespeare's contemporaries "geare" meant "a womans privities." Consequently, "geare" is herein defined as "a woman's privities," with Florio's entry for "Porcile di venere" cited as the source. (N.B. that in this instance the OED's dating is off by at least 77 years, giving the first usage of "gear" meaning "organs of generation" as 1675.)

3 Words are sometimes herein defined by their synonyms. For example, the OED gives "luxury" as a definition for "deliciousness." The two can

therefore be considered synonyms, and "deliciousness" is herein defined as follows:

deliciousnesse ("luxury": "lasciviousness, lust," OED)

4 Play text is based on the 1876 J.O. Halliwell-Phillipps facsimile of the First Folio of 1623. Unless otherwise noted, quotations from other Shakespeare plays are from the same volume.

5 Quotations from Shakespeare's Sonnets are from the 1609 quarto.

6 Unless otherwise noted, biblical quotations are from the King James Bible, 1611 edition.

7 Greek words have been transcribed using the western alphabet.

8 When reference is made to an analogous character from Shakespeare's primary sources for *As you Like it* (the apocryphal Chaucerian *Tale of Gamelyn* or Thomas Lodge's *Rosalynde*), the character's name from the source work and the name of the corresponding character in *As you Like it* will be listed together separated by a slash; e.g., "Gamelyn / *Orlando*" or "Rosader / *Orlando*." Characters' names that have not been altered from the play's sources (e.g., "*Adam*" and "*Aliena*") will be listed only once.

Abbreviations of Key Reference Works

DPF ..... E. Cobham Brewer, *Dictionary of Phrase and Fable.*
EC ...... E.A.M. Colman, *The Dramatic Use of Bawdy in Shakespeare.*
EP....... Eric Partridge, *Shakespeare's Bawdy.*
F&H..... John S. Farmer and William E. Henley, *Slang and its Analogues.*
FG ...... Frances Grose, *Lexicon Balatronicum.*
FR....... Frankie Rubinstein, *A Dictionary of Shakespeare's Sexual Puns and Their Significance.*
GW...... Gordon Williams, *A Glossary of Shakespeare's Sexual Language.*
GW2..... Gordon Williams, *A Dictionary of Sexual Language and Imagery in Shakespearean and Stuart Literature.*
HC...... Henry Cockeram, *The English Dictionairie.*
HH...... Hilda M. Hulme, *Explorations in Shakespeare's Language.*
HK...... Helge Kökeritz, *Shakespeare's Pronunciation.*
JA....... J.N. Adams, *The Latin Sexual Vocabulary.*
JB .... John Bullokar, *An English Expositor.*
JF .... John Florio, *A worlde of wordes.*
JF2 ...... Jacques Ferrand, *Erotomania.*
JG....... John Garfield, *A Physical dictionary.*
JH....... James T. Henke, *Courtesans and Cuckolds.*
JH2...... James Hall, *Dictionary of Subjects and Symbols in Art.*
JM....... John Minsheu, *A dictionarie in Spanish and English.*
JP .... John Palsgrave, *Leclarcissement de la langue francoyse.*
LD ...... *Latin Dictionary and Grammar Aid.*
LS....... Lawrence Stone, *The Family, Sex and Marriage in England 1500–1800.*
ND...... *A New Dictionary of the Terms Ancient and Modern of the Canting Crew.*
OED..... *Oxford English Dictionary.*
OL ...... Ortensio Landi, *Delectable Demaundes.*
RC ...... Randle Cotgrave, *A dictionarie of the French and English tongues.*

RC2 . . . . . Robert Cawdrey, *A table alphabeticall.*
TB . . . . . . Thomas Blount, *Glossographia.*
TE. . . . . . . Thomas Elyot, *The Dictionary of syr Thomas Eliot knyght.*
TR . . . . . . Thomas W. Ross, *Chaucer's Bawdy.*
TT . . . . . . Thomas Thomas, *Dictionarium Linguae Latinae et Anglicanae.*
WT. . . . . . William Thomas, *Principal rules of the Italian grammer.*

As you Like it

First Folio Play-script
with Accompanying Annotation

Act I, scene i

Actus primus. Scœna Prima. [1]

Enter Orlando and Adam. [I.i.1]

Orlando. As I remember *Adam*, it was upon this fashion
bequeathed me by will, but poore a thousand
Crownes, and as thou saist, charged my brother [5]
on his blessing to breed mee well: and
there begins my sadnesse: My brother *Jaques* he keepes
at schoole, and report speakes goldenly of his profit:
for my part, he keepes me rustically at home, or (to speak
more properly) staies me heere at home unkept: for call [10]
you that keeping for a gentleman of my birth, that differs
not from the stalling of an Oxe? his horses are bred
better, for besides that they are faire with their feeding,
they are taught their mannage, and to that end Riders
deerely hir'd: but I (his brother) gaine nothing under [15]
him but growth, for the which his Animals on his

Notes I.i.

3. ***fashion.*** The *fashion* ("prevailing custom," OED) was to leave the bulk of an estate to the eldest son; see note: *courtesie of nations,* lines 47–48, below.

4–5. ***a thousand Crownes.*** At the time, the "crown" (the English name for the French *écu*) was valued at four shillings (J. Eric Engstrom, *Coins in Shakespeare*, p. 22). Thus, *a thousand Crownes* was equal to about nine months' salary for a skilled laborer but was not a grand inheritance for a gentleman.

5–6. ***charged my brother... breed mee well.*** *On his* father's *blessing*, *Orlando's brother* (whose name is *Oliver*, as a reader learns in line 27, below) was *charged* (enjoined) to *breed* (educate, rear) *Orlando* well. (Original audiences never learned *Oliver's* name; see note: *Sir Rowland de Boys*, lines 56–57, below.)

7. ***keepes.*** Supports, maintains.

8–10. ***at schoole... unkept.*** In Shakespeare's England, most young gentlemen went *to schoole* (i.e., university) at age fifteen or sixteen. *Orlando*, who is now seventeen (cf. II.iii.76), has been "stayed" (detained) *unkept* (unattended to or neglected) *at home* as if in a "stey" (variant of "sty": "a pigsty," OED). (*Orlando* may actually sleep in the barn; cf. and see notes: *the stalling of an Oxe*, line 12, below, and *lodging*, II.iii.26).

9. ***rustically.*** *Orlando* is "rusticall" ("Rude, ignorant"; "knowing nothing"; "untaught, not exercised or traded in a thing, nothing expert or cunning"; "rough, not fashioned, homely, simple, plaine, base," TT, s.v. "Rŭdis"). His lack of education causes him to "rust," both (a) "deteriorate, degenerate, spoil, esp. through inactivity or want of use" (OED); and (b) become affected with "rust," a disease that blights plants and trees; cf. II.iii.66–67.

11–12. ***differs not... the stalling of an Oxe.*** *Orlando* feels as impotent and stupid as an *Oxe* (both a castrated bull and a fool, OED) in a "stall" (stable). He is "stalled" (forestalled or prevented) from advancement like an *Oxe* that is "stalled" ("Of a draught animal: come to a halt because of mud or other impediment," OED). *Orlando* may also recall Proverbs 15:17: "Better is a dinner of herbes where love is, then a stalled oxe, and hatred therewith."

12–15. ***his horses... deerely hir'd.*** *His* (i.e., *Oliver's*) *horses* are *bred* (properly trained) and taught their "manége" ("The movements in which a horse is trained in a riding school," OED), and *to that end Riders* (horse trainers) are *deerely hir'd* (employed at great expense). By contrast, *Orlando* has been *bred* (brought up) as one of the "menage" ("meinie": "servants," "Common people," OED), and therefore lacks both (a) *mannage* ("a trade, an exercise," JF, s.v. "Maneggio"); and (b) *mannage* (behavior, deportment, conduct) becoming a gentleman. This deficiency places him even beneath *horses* (homonym of "whores," HK, pp. 115–116), who at least have *mannage* (sexual skill, EP) and can earn their *bred* (i.e., "bread") by "hiring" (renting out) their "ends" (genitals and "arse," GW2) to *Riders* (sexual partners; to "ride" is to copulate, F&H).

15–16. ***gaine nothing... but growth.*** *Orlando's* brother treats him "like shit," so he receives no *gaine* (benefit, advantage) except *growth* from *gaine* (i.e., manure; "Of old to Gain Land was as much as to Till and Manure it," OED). (For additional scatological wordplay in this scene, cf. and see notes: *dunghils*, line 17, below; *bound*, line 17, below; *countenance*, line 19, below; *mines*, line 21, below; *grieves*, line 23, below; *remedy*, *avoid*, and *it*, line 26, below; *reverence*, line 52, below; *elder*, line 54, below; *physicke your ranckenesse*, line 86, below; and *cleare* and *kindle*, line 168, below.)

dunghils are as much bound to him as I: besides this nothing that he so plentifully gives me, the something that
nature gave mee, his countenance seemes to take from
me: hee lets mee feede with his Hindes, barres mee the [20]
place of a brother, and as much as in him lies, mines my
gentility with my education. This is it *Adam* that
grieves me, and the spirit of my Father, which I thinke
is within mee, begins to mutinie against this servitude.
I will no longer endure it, though yet I know no wise [25]
remedy how to avoid it.

Enter Oliver. [I.i.2]

Adam. Yonder comes my Master, your brother.

Orlan. Goe a-part *Adam*, and thou shalt heare how
he will shake me up. [30]

---

17. ***dunghils.*** *Orlando* has been treated like a "dunghill" ("a stinking knave, a base brat," JF, s.v. "Sterquilinio") of the "dunghill" ("the lowest or most degraded situation," OED). His ignorance and idleness are a disgrace to his lineage, for "A slothfull man is compared to the filth of a dunghill: every man that takes it up, will shake his hand. An evil nurtured sonne is the dishonour of his father that begate him" (Sirach 22:2–3).

17. ***bound.*** *Bound* can mean (a) indebted; (b) fastened to, connected; (c) "constrained, subject, or slave unto" (TT, s.v. "Constringor"); and/or (d) "Confined in the bowels, costive" (OED).

17–20. ***nothing that he so plentifully gives me... take from me.*** Instead of being treated as *something* (a person of standing or regard), *Orlando* is treated as though he were "of nothing" ("of small worth," RC, s.v. "Dapoco"). *Oliver gives Orlando nothing* (i.e., screws him, FR; *nothing* was pronounced "noting," HK, p. 132; a "note" is "a pricke," RC, q.v.). This *Oliver* bestows *plentifully*—i.e., with his "horn of plenty" (penis, GW2, s.v. "horn") in *Orlando's* "horn" ("the fundament, the rectum," TR). Thus, *Orlando* loses the *something* (the "thing": "penis," EP) *that nature gave* him and ends up with *nothing* (i.e., with "no thing," or "lacking a thing, penis," GW).

19. ***countenance.*** Because *Oliver* does not *countenance* (look favorably upon, patronize) his youngest brother, *Oliver's countenance* (behavior, conduct) offers *Orlando* no *countenance* ("maintenance"; "standing, dignity," OED). *Oliver's countenance* (i.e., "continence": "The possession of normal voluntary control over excretory functions," OED) is the cause of *Orlando's* unhappy *countenance* ("continuance": "Retention in some position or state," OED; "retention" is "failure to eliminate a substance from the body," OED). I.e., *Oliver* treats *Orlando* "like shit."

20–21. ***hee lets mee feede with his Hindes... brother.*** *Orlando* is denied his *place* (social rank) and barred from a *place* ("space at the dining table," OED) in his brother's *place* ("mansion, a country house with its surroundings, the principal residence on an estate," OED). *Orlando* does not sleep in *Oliver's* house (II.iii.25–27), so he probably dines not with the *Hindes* (household servants) but with the *Hindes* (field hands; a "hind" is "a servant for husbandry," TB, s.v. "Heinsman"). Thus, *Oliver* makes "an ass" of *Orlando* ("hind" is "posterior," OED).

21. ***mines.*** *Oliver mines* (undermines; subverts or destroys) *Orlando's gentility* by sending it down the "mine" (i.e., sewer; literally "A ditch or drain," OED).

23. ***grieves.*** *Orlando's* brother *grieves* (i.e., "buggers"; to "grieve" is literally "To press heavily upon, as a weight; to burden," OED) him and gives him "griefs" (bowel pains, FR). Therefore, *Orlando* feels "Grievous" ("likelie to burst," RC, s.v. "Grevable").

23–24. ***the spirit of my Father... begins to mutinie.*** *The spirit* (vital force; also "semen," EP) of *Orlando's Father* causes his *spirit* ("penis," EC) *to mutinie* ("rise in revolt," OED). Cf. and see note: *villaine*, line 55, below.

25–26. ***I will no longer endure it... avoid it.*** *Orlando will no longer endure* (undergo, submit to) *this servitude* ("bondage, slavery, thraldom," TB, q.v.), but he can think of *no wise* (prudent, circumspect) *remedy* (redress, solution) *how to avoid* (escape, prevent) *it.*

Also, *Orlando* will no longer *endure* ("suffer," OED; to "suffer" is to "Be a pathic, one upon whom sodomy is practiced," FR) *this servitude* (i.e., "service," the passive role in sexual intercourse, JA, p. 163). Nonetheless, he must still put up with his brother's "shit" because he can think of *no wise remedy* ("phisicke," JF, s.v. "Medicamento"; a "physic" is "A cathartic, a purge, a laxative," JH) to *avoid* (empty; "eject by excretion," OED) *it* (with possible play on *it* as "A chamberpot," F&H).

29. ***Goe a-part.*** "To goe backe, aside, or out of company" (TT, s.v. "Sēcēdo").

30. ***shake me up.*** *Orlando* knows *Oliver* will (a) create a "shake-up" ("commotion, a disturbance," F&H); (b) *shake* him *up* (berate or abuse him); (c) "*shake* [him] *up*" ("rattle [his] chain," OED); and/or (d) *shake* him *up* (i.e., "fuck" him; to *shake* is "To possess carnally," F&H, s.v. "Ride").

Oli. Now Sir, what make you heere?

Orl. Nothing: I am not taught to make any thing.

Oli. What mar you then sir?

Orl. Marry sir, I am helping you to mar that which
God made, a poore unworthy brother of yours with [35]
idlenesse.

Oliver. Marry sir be better employed, and be naught
a while.

Orlan. Shall I keepe your hogs, and eat huskes with
them? what prodigall portion have I spent, that I should [40]
come to such penury?

Oli. Know you where you are sir?

Orl. O sir, very well: heere in your Orchard.

Oli. Know you before whom sir?

Orl. I, better then him I am before knowes mee: I [45]
know you are my eldest brother, and in the gentle condition of bloud you should so know me: the courtesie of
nations allowes you my better, in that you are the first

31–32. ***what make you... Nothing.*** *Oliver* uses *what make you* to mean "what are you doing," but *Orlando* interprets *make* literally as "construct."

33–34. ***What mar you... Marry.*** *Orlando* plays on the sound of *mar* and *Marry* and says that *Oliver* "mars" (hinders, impairs, or damages) him by keeping him in a "ree" ("A walled enclosure for sheep, cattle, or swine," OED; cf. and see notes: *staies*, line 10, above, and *stalling of an Oxe*, line 12, above).

36. ***idlenesse.*** Both (a) "loytering, sluggishnesse, languishing negligence" (RC, s.v. "Paresse"); and (b) "imbecility" (OED).

37. ***be naught.*** *Be naught* means (a) keep quiet, withdraw (OED); and (b) "fuck off" (to *be naught* is to copulate, GW2; *naught* is the female genitals, F&H).

39–41. ***keepe your hogs... penury.*** In the parable "Of the prodigall sonne" (Luke 15:11–32), the younger of two sons asks his father to give him "the portion of goods that falleth to me" (Luke 15:12); he then journeyed "into a farre countrey, and there wasted his substance with riotous living" (Luke 15:13). Reduced to *penury* ("scarcitie, necessitie," JF, s.v. "Inopia"), the *prodigall* worked feeding another man's *hogs* (a particularly demeaning task as swine are unclean as per Deuteronomy 14:7), and he was so hungry that he "would faine have filled his belly with the huskes that the swine did eate" (Luke 15:16). Humbled, he returned home in hopes that his father would hire him on as a servant, but his father instead welcomed him warmly and "killed for him the fatted calfe" (Luke 15:30).

Unlike the biblical *prodigall*, *Orlando* never came into possession of his *portion* (the "gift bestowed by a father on his younger sonnes, or on his daughters, for their preferment," RC, s.v. "Assene"). Nevertheless, his situation at home is worse than that of the *prodigall* son abroad.

42–44. ***sir... sir... sir.*** The repetition of the word *sir* sets up *Orlando's* insulting pun on "sir-reverence" (line 52, below). There is possible additional play on Fr. "Seur" ("An Elder tree," RC, q.v.); cf. and see note: *elder*, line 54, below.

43. ***your Orchard.*** An *Orchard* is (a) "A parke: a grove" (TT, s.v. "Arborētum"); or (b) "a garden" (JF, s.v. "Orto"), possibly here a kitchen-garden or herb-garden adjacent to the house (see note: *at the doore*, line 92, below). As the eldest son, *Oliver* has "The right, and prerogative of the eldest child," so his "portion due, by prime birth, unto him... is, the principall house, and garden, with the inclosure thereof" (RC, s.v. "Droict d'aisnesse").

46. ***eldest brother.*** See note: *elder brother*, line 54, below.

47–48. ***courtesie of nations.*** By *courtesie* ("by favour or indulgence; by common good will or allowance, as distinguished from inherent or legal right," OED), it was generally understood "that by the Law of Nature, or Nations, where there is no Will of the Father declared to the contrary, the Eldest Son ought to inherit. And this is the Judgment not only of Christian, but Heathen Writers. Thus Herodotus the most Antient Greek Historian, lays it down for a general Custom of all People, or Nations, that the Eldest Son should enjoy the Empire; and the Romans were likewise of this Opinion.... So that if this Right of Primogeniture be not absolutely Divine, yet it is at least most Natural, and Reasonable" (James Tyrrell, *Bibliotheca Politica*).

46–47. ***gentle condition of bloud... know me.*** Because *Oliver* and *Orlando* share the same *bloud* (family lineage), *Oliver should know Orlando* to be of *gentle condition* (i.e., "of a Gentlemanlie race, of gentle bloud," RC, s.v. "Noble").

48. ***my better.*** *Oliver* is *Orlando's better* (superior), so he should also be his *better* (variant of "[a]bettor": supporter, OED).

borne, but the same tradition takes not away my bloud,

were there twenty brothers betwixt us: I have as much [50]

of my father in mee, as you, albeit I confesse your comming

before me is neerer to his reverence.

Oli. What Boy.

Orl. Come, come elder brother, you are too yong in this.

Oli. Wilt thou lay hands on me villaine? [55]

Orl. I am no villaine: I am the yongest sonne of Sir

Rowland de Boys, he was my father, and he is thrice a vil-

laine that saies such a father begot villaines: wert thou

---

49. ***tradition.*** *Tradition* is (a) a generally accepted custom; and (b) "a teaching, a doctrine which is delivered to us from others" (TB, q.v.).

51–52. ***comming before me... his reverence.*** *Oliver* came into the world *before* (earlier than) *Orlando*, so as the elder sibling he holds a position *before* (of higher rank than) *Orlando's*. Nevertheless, *Orlando* thinks *Oliver is neerer* (closer in resemblance) *to his* father's "[sir-]*reverence*" ("excrement, a turd," F&H) than *his reverence* ("condition or state of being respected or venerated," OED).

53. ***Boy.*** A *Boy* is (a) a "male person of low birth or status" (OED); and (b) "a catamite" (FR; *Boy* is synonymous with "hind," "villein," and "peasant"; cf. and see notes: *Hindes*, line 20, above; *villaine*, line 55, below; and *pezant*, line 67, below).

54. ***elder brother.*** *Orlando* knows his *brother* to be *elder*, meaning (a) older; (b) hostile (superstition holds that the *elder* tree exerts a malevolent influence); and (c) an "ass[hole]" or "shitty": FR conjectures that *elder* plays on Fr. "aisne" ("Eldyst or first begotten," JP, q.v.) and "Asne" ("An Asse," RC, q.v.). In addition, the first "s" is silent in Fr. "Aisnesse" ("Eldership, eldestship, the being eldest, or first borne," RC, q.v.), which allows for possible play on "anus."

Because the *elder* ("alder tree," TE, s.v. "Sambucus") has a strong odor that repels flies, it was commonly planted around privies (according to tradition, the *elder* was afflicted with its pungent scent because "Judas was hang'd on an Elder," *Loves Labour's lost*, V.ii.). The *elder* has further scatological associations in that it was used to treat a variety of intestinal ailments. Martin Blochwich's *The Anatomie of the Elder-Tree* recommends an enema of *elder* flowers and elderberry stones "To dissipate wind, mittigate pain, and loosen the bound belly" and advises that there is "nothing more excellent to ease the pain of the Hemmorhoides, then a stove or fomentation made of the flowres of Elder." In addition, elderberries were used to relieve diarrhoea, and *elder* bark was used as a purgative (cf. the name of "Mistrisse Purge," "An Elder in the Family," in Thomas Middleton's *Familie of Love*).

54. ***elder... too yong in this.*** In striking (or attempting to strike) *Orlando*, *Oliver* has shown himself to be *yong* (childish, immature, infantile). Although *Oliver* is *elder* (older), he is nevertheless too *yong* (inexperienced) to beat *Orlando* in a fair fight, for proverbially "the Elder tree thoughe hee bee fullest of pith, is farthest from strength" (John Lyly, *Euphues*).

55. ***lay hands on.*** "To Seise" (RC, s.v. "Saisir"); cf. and see notes: lines 59–60, below.

55–56. ***villaine.... I am no villaine.*** *Orlando* denies being a *villaine*, which can mean (a) a "villein": "A servant, servitor, servingman; or (most properly) a thrall, slave, prentice, bondman" (JF, s.v. "Serf"); (b) "a raskal," "a base, vile, abject, skurvie fellow, a scoundrell" (JF, s.v. "Vigliacco"); (c) an impotent man (*villaine* is synonymous with "rascal": "a man without testicles, or an eunuch," FG); and/or (d) a pathic (*villaine* is synonymous with "hind"; see note: *pezant*, line 67, below).

56–57. ***Sir Rowland de Boys.*** *La Chanson de Roland* ("The Song of Roland") is one of the most celebrated of the early epic French poems known as *Les Chanson de Geste* ("The Songs of Heroic Deeds"). "The Song of Roland" inspired several centuries' worth of popular knock-off tales in which *Sir Rowland* carries an enchanted and indestructible sword named "Durandal" (similar to "Excalibur" of Arthurian legend) and embarks on a series of adventures with his best friend *Oliver*, whose bravery and strength rival his own (hence the English phrase, "to give a *Roland* for an *Oliver*": "to give as good as one gets, a quid pro quo or tit for tat," OED).

Although the names *Oliver*, *Sir Rowland*, and *Orlando* (the It. form of *Rowland*) suggest a connection between *As you Like it* and *Les Chansons de Geste*, this tie is tenuous in print and non-existent in performance (*Orlando's* eldest brother's name is never spoken within the play, so original audiences, who viewed the play without the benefit of a printed program, would never have learned it). Shakespeare evidently abandoned any aspirations of linking *Orlando* and *Oliver* to their epic French counterparts early on in the writing, but to early audiences *Sir Rowland's* name would nevertheless instantly conjure up images of chivalry and honor.

Sir Rowland's last name is here given as *de Boys* (or "DuBois," meaning "Of the Wood"), a name which may have been inspired by Ludovico Ariosto's narrative poem *Orlando Furioso* (or "Mad Roland," translated into English by John Harrington in 1591). In this tale, *Orlando* (a.k.a. *Sir Rowland*) finds the name of his beloved carved into a tree alongside that of his rival, goes mad with jealousy, and rages naked through the forest. Cf. *Orlando's* running through the forest and carving his lover's name on trees in III.ii.11–12.

57–58. ***thrice a villaine... begot villaines.*** Anyone who says that *Sir Rowland begot villaines* is *thrice a villaine* ("a traitor," "a deceiver, a betrayer," RC, s.v. "Proditore") because *Sir Rowland begot* (engendered) three sons, none of whom are *villaines* (see note: *villaine*, line 55, above).

not my brother, I would not take this hand from thy

throat, till this other had puld out thy tongue for saying [60]

so, thou hast raild on thy selfe.

Adam. Sweet Masters bee patient, for your Fathers

remembrance, be at accord.

Oli. Let me goe I say.

Orl. I will not till I please: you shall heare mee: my [65]

father charg'd you in his will to give me good educati-

on: you have train'd me like a pezant, obscuring and

59–60. ***this hand... thy throat.*** *Orlando* has seized *Oliver* by the *throat*, presumably because *Oliver* "lie[s] in [his] throat": "lie[s] foully or infamously" (OED).

59–60. ***this hand... this other.*** Cf. Matthew 5:30: "And if thy right hand offend thee, cut it off, and cast it from thee. For it is profitable for thee that one of thy members should perish, and not that thy whole body should be cast into hell."

60. ***puld out thy tongue.*** For his "puling" ("faultering in speech," RC, s.v. "Pepiement"), *Oliver* should have his *tongue puld out* (the traditional punishment for a "spreader of false rumours amongst the people," Edward Coke, *The Third Part of the Institutes of the Laws of England*).

61. ***raild on thy selfe.*** By his own "railing" ("defamation; injurious, opprobrious, or outragious language," RC, s.v. "Laidange"), *Oliver* has *raild on* himself—i.e., demoted himself from the rank of gentleman; to "rail" is "To bring (a person or thing) into (or out of, etc.), a certain state, condition, or place by railing" (OED). Cf. and see notes: lines 55–58, above.

66–67. ***good education.*** A *good education* was considered necessary for any gentleman, for "Learning... is an essentiall part of Nobilitie, as unto which we are beholden for whatsoever dependeth on the culture of the mind" (Henry Peacham, *The Compleat Gentleman*).

67. ***train'd me like a pezant.*** In Thomas Lodge's novel *Rosalynde* (one of Shakespeare's primary sources for *As you Like it*), Saladyne / *Oliver* decides to defraud his youngest brother Rosader / *Orlando* of his inheritance by suppressing "his wittes with a base estate, and though hee be a Gentleman by nature yet forme him a new, and make him a peasant by nourture: so shalt thou keepe him as a slave, and raign thy selfe sole Lord over al thy Fathers possessions."

Orlando has been *train'd* (taught, instructed) *like a pezant* (i.e., given no education at all), and *Oliver* treats *Orlando* like a lowly member of his "train" (attendants or servants). This "train" ("Treachery, guile, deceit, trickery," OED) causes *Orlando* to "train" (pass his time slowly and wearily, OED). *Orlando* has not received even the minimal "training" due to a horse (lines 12–15, above); instead, *Oliver* makes him a "train" (i.e., "a horse's ass"; the "traine" is "the hinder part of a beast," RC, s.v. "Trainer"). Thus, *Oliver* has *train'd* (i.e., "screwed"; "train" is Fr. for "prick," F&H, q.v.) his brother *like a pezant* (i.e., a "bugger"; "peisant" is "weighed down," HH, p. 237).

67. ***obscuring.*** *Orlando's* gentlemanly rank is "obscured" (hidden, concealed), so he appears as one who is "Obscure" ("of no gentill bloud, of no fame or bruite, of no credit, or estimation, nothing noble, base," TT, q.v.).

hiding from me all gentleman-like qualities: the spirit

of my father growes strong in mee, and I will no longer

endure it: therefore allow me such exercises as may be- [70]

come a gentleman, or give mee the poore allottery my

father left me by testament, with that I will goe buy my

fortunes.

Oli. And what wilt thou do? beg when that is spent?

Well sir, get you in. I will not long be troubled with [75]

you: you shall have some part of your will, I pray you

leave me.

---

68. ***gentleman-like qualities.*** Because *Orlando* has not been raised as a *gentleman* of "quality" ("The gentry," F&H), he does not think himself to be *gentleman-like* ("Like one of noble parentage, like one of a noble minde," JM, s.v. "Generosaménte"). Nevertheless, *Orlando* embodies the ideal *gentleman-like qualities* of kindness and honor, while *Oliver* has inherited his father's possessions but none of his *qualities* (character, abilities, and accomplishments). Cf. the fourth treatise of Dante's *Convito*: "Where Virtue is, there is / A Nobleman, although / Not where there is a Nobleman / Must virtue be also."

68–70. ***the spirit... no longer endure it.*** *Sir Rowland* was a knight who gained his title through extraordinary merit (knighthood was formerly bestowed for bravery in battle), and his noble *spirit* (character or temperament) would supposedly be transferred to his children via his *spirit* (semen; see note: *spirit*, line 23, above). Thus, gentility was an inherited trait: "The Noble, generous, and best Natures, are wonne by commendation, enkindled by Glory... Of which disposition for the most part, are most of our young Nobilitie and Gentlemen, well borne, inheriting with their being, the vertue of their Ancestors" (Henry Peacham, *The Compleat Gentleman*).

Orlando's redoubtable father's *spirit* (vigor, courage, or might as represented by sexual potency; see note: *spirit*, line 23, above) now *growes strong* ("Physically powerful; able to exert great muscular force," OED). Therefore he will *no longer endure* ("suffer patientlie," TT, s.v. "Perfero") *it* ("Sexual intercourse," EP)—i.e., he will *no longer* be a "patient" (i.e., a "pathic[us]" or "sodomite, one who submits to anal sex," LD) and "suffer" (i.e., allow himself to be "buggered"; see note: *endure*, line 25, above).

70–71. ***exercises as may become a gentleman.*** In order for *Orlando* to *become* (come to be) "gentlemanlike," he needs *exercises as may become* (befit) *a gentleman.* Among these were (a) "exercise" ("occupation, or studie," JF, s.v. "Essercítio"); (b) "exercise" ("Pastime, recreation," RC, s.v. "Apotherapic"); and (c) "exercise" (bodily exertion and improvement).

71. ***poore allottery.*** *Allottery*, a unique word of Shakespearean coinage, is constructed from the verb "allot" (to "appoint unto everie one his portion," RC, s.v. "Distribuer") and the noun "lottery" ("Something which comes to a person by lot or fortune," OED). *Orlando's* "lot" ("portion in an inheritance," TT, s.v. "Sors") is not "a lot" (a great amount), so his "lot" (destined condition) is to be *poore.*

72–73. ***by testament... buy my fortunes.*** With the "fortune" (money) left to him by his father, *Orlando* plans to *buy* ("abide": "watch for, expect, or await," OED) *his fortunes*, which can mean (a) success or prosperity; and/or (b) "things to come" (JM, s.v. "Agoréro").

The "Lady Fortune" (a.k.a. the ancient Roman goddess "Fortuna") was so inconstant that she was also known as "the whore Fortune" (Ben Jonson, *Catiline his conspiracy*). In order *to buy* (purchase) the Lady Fortune's "buy" (i.e., "bay" or vagina, GW; "buy" was pronounced "bay," HH, p. 210), *Orlando* will need that which was *left* him *by testament*—i.e., virility or "balls" inherited through blood: "*Testify* is Latin *testis*, witness, and *fio* (*ficare*), make. The same Latin *testis* appears, of course, in *testimony, testator, testament, testimonial,* and the diminutive *testicle.* The male genital glands have time out of mind been regarded as the basis of manhood. When, therefore, in ancient days an oath was taken, the right hand was placed on the testicles" (John Baker Opdycke, *Mark My Words*, p. 110). Cf. and see notes: *spirit*, lines 23 and 68, above, and *beg when that is spent*, line 74, below.

74. ***beg when that is spent.*** *When Orlando* has *spent* ("discharge[d] seminally," EP, s.v. "spend") the "spendings" ("semen," F&H, q.v.) from *that* ("The penis," F&H, s.v. "Prick"), he will have no choice but to *beg* (i.e., be a "beggar," used "euphemistically for bugger," OED). Cf. and see notes: *the spirit of my father*, lines 68–69, above; and *testament*, line 72, above.

75. ***get you in.*** This scene supposedly takes place outside in the *Orchard* (line 43, above), so *get you in* could mean "go inside." However, *Orlando* is barred from his brother's house (cf. lines 20–21, above, and II.iii.25–26), so *Oliver's* instruction to *get in* relates directly to contemporary theatre architecture. On the outdoor stage of an Elizabethan playhouse, an actor exited from audience view by going inside into the tiring house; cf. *goe in*, I.iii.145.

76. ***some part of your will.*** Perhaps *Oliver* means to give *Orlando some part of* his *will*, which can mean (a) a request or petition; (b) desire; (c) a person's written declaration of his desires as to the disposal of his property after death; and/or (d) "A piece of wilfulness" (OED). On the other hand, perhaps *Oliver* means to fulfill his own *will* (lust, libido, EC) by giving *Orlando's part* ("division in the buttocks," FR) his *part* (penis, testicles, and semen, JH)—i.e., to "fuck" him.

Orl. I will no further offend you, then becomes mee

for my good.

Oli. Get you with him, you olde dogge. [80]

Adam. Is old dogge my reward: most true, I have

lost my teeth in your service: God be with my olde ma-

ster, he would not have spoke such a word.

{*Exit Orlando and Adam.*} [I.i.3]

Oli. Is it even so, begin you to grow upon me? I will [85]

physicke your ranckenesse, and yet give no thousand

crownes neyther: holla *Dennis.*

Enter Dennis. [I.i.4]

Den. Calls your worship?

Oli. Was not *Charles* the Dukes Wrastler heere to [90]

speake with me?

78. ***offend.*** With possible play on *offend* as "commit sodomy" (an "offence" is "related to the buttocks," FR, q.v.; also see note: *offences*, III.ii.342).

79. ***good.*** For possible sexual implication, see notes: *good*, I.ii.28 and 65.

80–81. ***olde dogge... my reward.*** *Oliver* calls *Adam* a "dogged" ("Sullen, pouting, or in the Dumps," ND) *old dogge* ("lingering antique," F&H) because he "doggedly" (obstinately, stubbornly) "dogs" (fawns on) *Orlando*. As an *old dogge, Adam's* only *reward* ("what is given the Hounds, or Beagles by the Hands of the Huntsman or others, after they have finished their Chase, by the Death of what they pursu'd," ND) is that he is used like a *dogge* ("sodomite," FR) and "buggered" in the *reward* (variant of "rearward": "the buttocks," OED).

81–82. ***I have lost my teeth... service.*** *Adam*, who is almost eighty years old (II.iii.74–75), has *lost* his *teeth* in *Oliver's service* (employ) just like the old hound in the Aesop fable, related in a 1617 version as follows:

> A Master hastens on his hound, which was now waxen olde. He calls on him in vaine. His feet are slowe, hee maketh no haste. Hee had caught a wilde beast, the beast slips away from him being toothlesse. His master rates him with strokes and with words. The dogge answered that he ought of right to be pardoned; that now he was becomne olde, but that hee had been stout when he was young. But as I see, quoth hee, nothing pleaseth without commodity. You loved me being young; you hate me now becomne olde. You loved mee bringing in preies, you hate mee now slowe & toothlesse. But if you were thankful, whom you loved in times past, being young for your commodity sake you would love now beeing old for the cause of his profitable youth.

85. ***begin you to grow upon me.*** To *grow upon* means (a) to "increase so as to be more troublesome to"; (b) to "gain ground upon an enemy or rival"; and/or (c) to "come to take liberties with a superior" (OED). To "grow on" also means "to keep seedling plants in suitable situations or conditions as they develop to maturity" (OED); cf. *ranckenesse*, line 86, below.

86. ***physicke your ranckenesse.*** *Oliver* considers *Orlando* a "weed" ("An unprofitable, troublesome, or noxious growth," OED) that has become "rank" (of plants: "growing too luxuriantly or rampantly; thick and coarse," OED). Although *Orlando* is just a "weed" ("an animal lacking the points of a thoroughbred," F&H), he has become "rank" ("proud, haughty; insolent, arrogant," OED) regarding his "rank" (position in the social hierarchy). *Oliver* plans to *physicke* ("applie medecines unto," RC, s.v. "Penser") this *ranckenesse* with *physicke* ("Hard hitting; punishment," F&H) administered by a professional combatant (cf. lines 90–95, below).

Also, *Orlando's* "rank" ("worthless," F&H) *ranckenesse* (i.e., "shit"; *ranckenesse* is literally "Stench" or "rammishnesse," RC, s.v. "Virulence") is in need of *physicke* (a suppository, purgative, or laxative; see note: *remedy*, line 26, above).

87. ***Dennis.*** The part of *Dennis* may specifically have been written for one of the boy actors apprenticed to Shakespeare's company; cf. the *two Pages* in V.iii. Any name would serve for such a utilitarian character, but *Dennis* is probably named after Saint *Dennis*, the patron saint of France, in order to reinforce the play's French setting.

90. ***Charles.*** The name *Charles* derives from the Anglo-Saxon "ceorl" and English "churl" meaning "manly" or "strong" (literally, "full-grown").

90. ***the Dukes Wrastler.*** Like a jester, musician, or other paid entertainer, *Charles* is an official member of the *Dukes* retinue.

Den. So please you, he is heere at the doore, and im-

portunes accesse to you.

Oli. Call him in: 'twill be a good way: and to mor- {*Ex. Den.*} [I.i.5]

row the wrastling is. [95]

Enter Charles. [I.i.6]

Cha. Good morrow to your worship.

Oli. Good Mounsier *Charles*: what's the new newes

at the new Court?

Charles. There's no newes at the Court Sir, but the [100]

olde newes: that is, the old Duke is banished by his yon-

ger brother the new Duke, and three or foure loving

Lords have put themselves into voluntary exile with

him, whose lands and revenues enrich the new Duke,

therefore he gives them good leave to wander. [105]

Oli. Can you tell if *Rosalind* the Dukes daughter bee

banished with her Father?

Cha. O no; for the Dukes daughter her Cosen so

loves her, being ever from their Cradles bred together,

that hee would have followed her exile, or have died to [110]

92. ***heere at the doore.*** This scene was hitherto set outdoors in the *Orchard* (line 43, above) but here apparently shifts to the interior of the house.

94. ***a good way.*** *Oliver* believes that *a good way* (means) to rid himself of *Orlando* will be *Charles*, who is a "wey" ("One who fights; a fighting man," OED).

100–101. ***the olde newes... the old Duke is banished.*** This statement (together with lines 108–119, below, I.ii.5–6, and I.ii.252) suggests that the *old Duke* has recently been *banished*. However, if *Charles' newes* is *olde*, the events he recounts may have happened some time ago; cf. I.iii.71–76.

101–102. ***the old Duke... yonger brother the new Duke.*** The *new Duke* is named *Fredericke* (I.ii.79); the *old Duke* is simply tagged as "*Senior*" (II.i.2) to indicate that he is the elder of the two brothers. Just like *Orlando's* oldest brother, *Fredericke's* elder brother remains nameless to the audience (see note: *Sir Rowland de Boys*, lines 56–57, above).

104. ***lands... enrich the new Duke.*** These *Lords* are presumably guilty of treason for refusing to swear allegiance to *Fredericke*, for "if a man having an estate for life of himselfe or of another, commit Treason or Felony, the whole estate is forfeited to the Crowne" (Francis Bacon, *The Elements Of The Common Lawes Of England*).

105. ***good leave to wander.*** *Fredericke* grows rich from the banished *Lords'* estates, so he doesn't mind if they *wander* ("goe astray," RC, s.v. "Adirer"; also "depart farre off," TT, s.v. "Averro") and become "wanderers" ("vagabond[s]," RC, s.v. "Roder").

108–109. ***her Cosen... from their Cradles bred together.*** *Charles* may intimate that these "cousins" (harlots, FG) are *together* ("mutually engaged, as lovers," OED) and that they "breed" ("cherish, foster," OED) each other's *Cradles* (vaginas, F&H, s.v. "monosyllable"). Cf. I.ii.278–279 and I.iii.76–80.

110. ***hee.*** A possible typographical error for "she."

stay behind her; she is at the Court, and no lesse beloved
of her Uncle, then his owne daughter, and never two Ladies loved as they doe.

Oli. Where will the old Duke live?

Cha. They say hee is already in the Forrest of *Arden*, [115]
and a many merry men with him; and there they live
like the old *Robin Hood* of *England*: they say many yong
Gentlemen flocke to him every day, and fleet the time
carelesly as they did in the golden world.

Oli. What, you wrastle to morrow before the new [120]
Duke.

Cha. Marry doe I sir: and I came to acquaint you
with a matter: I am given sir secretly to understand, that
your yonger brother *Orlando* hath a disposition to come
in disguis'd against mee to try a fall: to morrow sir I [125]

---

115. ***Forrest of Arden.*** In Lodge's *Rosalynde*, *Orlando's* counterpart "Rosader" and the servant "Adam knowing full well the secrete wayes that led through the vineyards, stole away prively through the province of Bourdeaux, & escaped safe to the forrest of Arden." Therefore, the *Forrest of Arden* is probably the French *Forrest of* "Ardennes" situated northwest of Bordeaux (not the *Forrest of* "Ardennes" in what is now Belgium). However, Shakespeare's audiences (and Shakespeare himself) doubtless confused the continental "Ardennes" with the English *Forrest of Arden* in Warwickshire, a pastoral setting that figured prominently in sixteenth and seventeenth century literature. William Drummond's 1615 "Song I" epitomizes the idealized romantic view of this locale:

If living Eyes Elysian fields could see
This little Arden might Elysium bee.
Here Diane often used to repose Her,
And Acidalias Queene with Mars rejoyce her:
The Nymphes oft here doe bring their Maunds with Flowres,
And Anadeames weave for their Paramours,
The Satyres in those Shades are heard to languish,
And make the Shepheards Partners of their Anguish,
The Shepheards who in Barkes of tender Trees
Doe grave their Loves, Disdaines, and Jelousies,
Which Phillis when there by Her Flockes she feedeth
With Pitie whyles, sometime with laughter reedeth.

116. ***a.*** Possibly (a) an indefinite article; (b) "with" (OED); or (c) "at all times, on all occasions" (OED).

116–119. ***many merry men... the golden world.*** *As you Like it* is ostensibly set in *France*, but *Robin Hood* and his *many merry men* are, of course, a legend *of England* (although properly *Robin Hood's men* were not *merry* but "mǽra," Anglo Saxon for "exalted, illustrious, famous"; certainly at least one of the *old Duke's* followers is not *merry* but melancholy; cf. II.i.30). In likening *Duke Senior* and his band to *Robin Hood and* his *merry men, Charles* perhaps spins "a tale of Robin hood" ("a flimflam tale whether it be true or false," RC, s.v. "Buccisoffiola"), for many are led into a "fool's paradise" by those who "promise wonders, or golden worlds; (as some doe that either will not, or cannot, performe anything" (RC, s.v. "Promettre monts, & merveilles; ou, monts & vaux").

Perhaps the *Forrest of Arden* does in some small part resemble "the ancient golden world, The world that Adam held in Paradise" (George Peele, *The love of King David and fair Bethsabe*); cf. II.i.8. However, life in *Arden* is no *golden world* (state of extreme bliss and prosperity). It is bitter cold in winter (II.i.10–12, II.v.9–10, II.vi.17–18, II.vi.188–191, II.vii.196–199) and food is hard to come by (II.iv.66–88, II.iv.79–80, II.iv.91–92, II.v.42–43, II.vi.8–9, II.vi.19–20, II.vii.112, II.vii.137–140).

118. ***flocke... fleet.*** These *yong Gentlemen flocke* ("gather together in companies and multitude," JF, s.v. "Frottare") into a *fleet* ("number of persons," OED) and *fleet* ("passe away quickly," RC, s.v. "voler) *the time carelesly*, even though they are *fleet* (i.e., itinerant fugitives; OED omits any similar meanings, but cf. "a fugitive, a wandrer, a fleeter, a runnagate, one that flieth or is driven out of his countrie," JF, s.v. "Profugo").

123. ***secretly.*** Indirectly; through the grapevine.

124. ***a disposition.*** *Orlando* has a *disposition* (inclination) to test his *disposition* ("Physical aptitude"; "skill," OED) in the wrestling match.

125. ***disguis'd.*** *Orlando* plans to fight *disguis'd* because it was considered unseemly for a gentleman to wrestle in public. In *The Book of the Courtier*, Baldassarre Castiglione advises a young gentleman not to wrestle "in open syght of the people but privilye... emonge hys friendes and familiers," because "it is to ill a sight and to foule a matter and without estimation to see a Gentilman overcome by a Cartar and especially in wrastling. Therfore I beleve it is wel done to abstaine from it, at the leastwise in the presence of many, because if he overcome, his gaine is small, and his losse in being overcome very great."

125. ***a fall.*** Depending on which rules are followed, *a fall* occurs when (a) both of a wrestler's shoulders touch the ground; or (b) when both shoulders and one hip touch the ground.

wrastle for my credit, and hee that escapes me without
some broken limbe, shall acquit him well: your brother
is but young and tender, and for your love I would bee
loth to foyle him, as I must for my owne honour if hee
come in: therefore out of my love to you, I came hither [130]
to acquaint you withall, that either you might stay him
from his intendment, or brooke such disgrace well as he
shall runne into, in that it is a thing of his owne search,
and altogether against my will.

Oli. *Charles*, I thanke thee for thy love to me, which [135]
thou shalt finde I will most kindly requite: I had my
selfe notice of my Brothers purpose heerein, and have by
under-hand meanes laboured to disswade him from it;

126. ***credit.*** As a professional, *Charles* wrestles not only for *credit* ("glorie, praise, fame, renowne," JM, s.v. "Glória") but also for *credit* (i.e, money).

127. ***acquit him well.*** Prove himself commendably.

128–130. ***young and tender... out of my love to you.*** *Charles* most likely does not warn *Oliver out of love* (friendship, affection) but in search of *love* (i.e., a bribe; to *love* is to "offer something for sale for or at a price," OED). *Charles* hopes that *Oliver* will make him a *tender* ("offer of money," OED) not to hurt his brother.

Orlando is a *foyle* (variant of "fool") to challenge *Charles* because he will certainly be "foiled" ("overthrowne, set on the taile; that hath received an arse-posse, or fall on the arse," RC, s.v. "Culassé"). *Orlando* is *but young and tender* (thin, weak, frail), so *Charles* is *loth* (sorry) *to foyle him*, where *foyle* means (a) "wound, bruise, or hurt sore with blows" (RC, s.v. "Affoler"); (b) "shame, or steigne" (WT, s.v. "Violatione"); and/or (c) "fuck" (to *foyle* is literally "To dishonour; esp. to deflower a woman, to violate chastity," OED).

In addition, *young and tender* is a phrase commonly applied to new plant growth, so there may be play on *foyle* meaning "leaf" (OED); cf. *grow upon*, line 85, above, and *ranckenesse*, line 86, above.

130. ***come in.*** Should *Orlando come in* ("enter the field or arena," OED), he will "*come in for it*" ("incur punishment," OED).

132. ***intendment... brooke such disgrace.*** If *Orlando* persists in his *intendment* ("a purpose, an intent," JF, s.v. "Intendimento"), he will suffer *intendment* (i.e., "be screwed"; "tent" is "The penis," F&H; to "tent" is "To probe," OED). *Orlando* will *brooke* (bear or suffer) *disgrace* (sexual violation, JA, p. 170) in the *such* ("pubic-anal area," FR, who holds it to be a pun on L. "tale": "such"; "tail" means both the genitals and the posteriors). Also see note: *brooke*, II.i.46.

133. ***runne into.*** To *runne into* is (a) "to rush in, to fall or cast himselfe without consideration into" (TT, s.v. "Irruo"); and (b) to "procure unto himselfe; to undergoe a danger, disgrace, penaltie, &c" (RC, s.v. "Encourir").

133–134. ***his owne search... will.*** If *Orlando* does suffer *disgrace* (i.e., "get screwed"; see note: *disgrace*, line 132, above), it will not be due to *Charles' will* ("sexual desire," EP) but to *Orlando's search* (with "innuendo of sexual ingression and copulation," JH; to *search* is literally "To probe a wound," OED) for a *thing* (penis; see note: *something*, line 18, above).

135–136. ***thy love... I will most kindly requite.*** *Oliver* will (a) *kindly* (gratefully) *requite* (recompence, reward) *Charles* for his *love* (either his friendship or sale of his services; see note: *love*, line 130, above); and/or (b) *requite* ("Retaliate": "doe like for like," TB, q.v.) *Charles kindly* (i.e. "in kind": befittingly, appropriately). *Oliver* might offer *Charles* payment "in kind" ("in specie": "In the actual coin specified," OED), but he might instead offer payment "in kind" ("In the very kind of article or commodity in question... as opposed to money," OED)—i.e., with valuable information. Cf. *resolute*, line 139, below, and *payment*, line 156, below.

138. ***under-hand.*** Quiet or unobtrusive.

but he is resolute. Ile tell thee *Charles*, it is the stubbor-
nest yong fellow of France, full of ambition, an envious [140]
emulator of every mans good parts, a secret & villanous
contriver against mee his naturall brother: therefore use
thy discretion, I had as liefe thou didst breake his necke
as his finger. And thou wert best looke to't; for if thou
dost him any slight disgrace, or if hee doe not mightilie [145]
grace himselfe on thee, hee will practise against thee by
poyson, entrap thee by some treacherous devise, and never
leave thee till he hath tane thy life by some indirect
meanes or other: for I assure thee, (and almost with
teares I speake it) there is not one so young, and so vil- [150]
lanous this day living. I speake but brotherly of him,

---

139. ***resolute.*** *Resolute* means (a) "Obstinate; wilfull, selfewillie, opinionative; stiff-necked, stubborn" (RC, s.v. "Obstiné"); and (b) "A payment" (OED); cf. and see note: *kindly requite*, line 136, above.

139–140. ***stubbornnest.*** Both "intractable" and "wild."

140. ***fellow.*** *Fellow* can simply mean "a man" but is also (a) "One of the common people"; (b) "A person of no esteem or worth"; and/or (c) "the customary title of address to a servant or other person of humble station" (OED, which notes that "its application to one not greatly inferior was a gross insult").

140. ***ambition.*** The entire world, including human society, was believed to be a divinely ordained hierarchy. Therefore *ambition*, which means both "arogance" (JP,

q.v.) and "excessive desire of honor, preferment, or promotion" (RC, q.v.), was considered an affront to God. Christopher Harvey's 1647 *Schola Cordis* illustrates the typical view of *ambition*:

> The bane of kingdomes, worlds disquieter,
> Hells heire apparent, Satans eldest sonne,
> Abstract of ills, refined Elixir,
> And quintessence of sinne, Ambition,
> Sprung from th'infernall shades, inhabits here,
> Making mans heart its horrid mansion,
> Which, though it were of vast content before,
> Is now puft up, and swells still more and more.

140. ***envious.*** *Orlando* is (a) *envious* ("malicious, backbiting," TT, s.v. "Līvĭdus"); (b) "an envious fellow, or one that cannot endure another should be the better by him" (TB, s.v. "Stellion"); and/or (c) guilty of envy, one of the seven deadly sins.

141. ***emulator.*** An "imitator, or envier of another"; also "a competitor" (RC, s.v. "Emulateur").

142. ***contriver.*** A schemer or plotter; also an "inventor of falsehoods" (OED).

142. ***naturall brother.*** *Oliver* (a) describes himself as a *naturall* (affectionate, kind; also "Observant of familial obligations," OED) *brother* to *Orlando*; and (b) drops a hint that *Orlando* is a *naturall* ("a bastard," FG, q.v.).

142–143. ***use thy discretion.*** If *Charles* uses his *discretion* (wisdom, better judgment), he may find it best to *use discretion* (i.e., tear *Orlando* limb from limb; a *discretion* is "A separation," TT, s.v. "Discrētĭo"; "To discrete" is "To divide into discrete or distinct parts; to separate distinctly, dissever," OED).

143. ***I had as liefe.*** I.e., "I would just as soon prefer."

143. ***breake his necke.*** *Oliver's* spiteful wish is drawn directly from *The Tale of Gamelyn* (an apocryphal Chaucerian work and a source for both Lodge's *Rosalynde* and *As you Like it*) in which the evil oldest brother "bisoughte Jesu Crist that is heven king" that his youngest brother "mighte breke his nekke in that wrasteling." Even in the "Catch as Catch Can" wrestling popular in Shakespeare's day, it was considered foul for one wrestler to intentionally hurt another. However, as there were no real rules, injuries were common.

145–146. ***slight disgrace... grace himselfe on thee.*** If *Charles* offers *Orlando* the *slight disgrace* (small affront) of *slight* (trifling, unimportant) *disgrace* ("disfigurement," OED), *Orlando* will *mightilie* ("Vehemently, sharply: earnestly, egerly," TT, s.v. "Vehĕ menter") *grace himselfe* (i.e., advance his own *grace*: honor or esteem) at *Charles'* expense. There is possible additional pun on *disgrace* meaning castration (*grace* is the penis, FR; *dis-* is a prefix meaning to detach or separate; cf. and see notes: *devise*, line 147, below, and *tane thy life*, line 148, below).

147. ***entrap... devise.*** *Orlando* will (a) *entrap* (ambush or ensnare) *Charles by some treacherous devise* (stratagem or trick); and/or (b) *entrap* (i.e., "screw"; the "trap" is the "female pudendum," F&H) *Charles* and emasculate him (*de-* is a prefix meaning "to carry off," OED; "vice" means "penis," EC).

148. ***tane thy life.*** Another possible glance at emasculation; "life" is euphemistic for the penis (FR).

151. ***brotherly.*** *Oliver* speaks *brotherly* ("lovingly, kindlie," JM, s.v. "Fratérno") of *Orlando*. If *Oliver* were not *brotherly* (fraternally affectionate), he would say worse.

but should I anathomize him to thee, as hee is, I must
blush, and weepe, and thou must looke pale and
wonder.

Cha. I am heartily glad I came hither to you: if hee [155]
come to morrow, Ile give him his payment: if ever hee
goe alone againe, Ile never wrastle for prize more: and
so God keepe your worship.

Exit {*Charles*}. [I.i.7]

Farewell good *Charles*. Now will I stirre this Gamester: [160]
I hope I shall see an end of him; for my soule (yet
I know not why) hates nothing more then he: yet hee's
gentle, never school'd, and yet learned, full of noble
devise, of all sorts enchantingly beloved, and indeed
so much in the heart of the world, and especially of my [165]
owne people, who best know him, that I am altogether
misprised: but it shall not be so long, this wrastler shall
cleare all: nothing remaines, but that I kindle the boy
thither, which now Ile goe about.

Exit {*Oliver*}. [170]

152–153. ***anathomize him... blush, and weepe.*** *Oliver* says that he does not wish to "anathematize" ("curse," RC, s.v. "Anematiser") *Orlando*, but should he *anathomize* (dissect) his brother's character he would reveal *Orlando* as "Anathematized" ("cursed unto the pit of hell," RC, s.v. "Anathematisé"). However, should *Oliver* truly *anathomize* ("lay open," OED) *Orlando's* "anatomy" (the summation of his parts or character), *Oliver must blush* at (be ashamed of) his own deceit *and weepe*.

156. ***give him his payment.*** Both (a) beat the stuffing out of him (to "pay" is "To beat; to punish," F&H); and (b) "fuck" him (to "pay" is to copulate, GW).

157. ***goe alone.*** The word "one" was pronounced "own" (OED, q.v.; also see HK, p. 132). After the wrestling match, *Orlando* will therefore (a) not be able to *goe* (walk) *alone* (by himself); and (b) no longer be *alone* ("all one": in one piece). He will probably not be able to *goe* (copulate, EP), either.

160. ***stirre.*** To *stirre* is to "provoke: to encourage: to exhort: to perswade to the doing of a thing" (TT, s.v. "Adhortor"), with possible additional play on *stirre* meaning copulate (JA, p. 195) or sodomize (FR).

160. ***Gamester.*** A *Gamester* is (a) an athlete; (b) "a man fit and ready for anything" (F&H); (c) "a lewd person" (OED); and/or (d) a whore (EP).

163–164. ***noble devise.*** By *devise* ("The act of devising, apportioning, or assigning, by will; a testamentary disposition of real property; the clause in a will conveying this," OED), *Orlando* has not inherited his *noble* father's *devise* (i.e., coat of arms; a heraldic *devise* is "an invention or conceit in picture, with his Motto, or Word, born as well by Noble, and Learned Personages, as by Commanders in war," TB, q.v.). Nevertheless, he is full of *noble* (valiant, honorable) *devise* (opinion, purpose, intention). Cf. and see notes: lines 68–70, above.

164. ***of all sorts enchantingly beloved.*** *Oliver* does not believe that *Orlando* is *beloved of all sorts* (persons of different temperaments and social standing) for his genuinely good qualities. Instead, he thinks that *Orlando* is an "enchanter" ("a he witch, a charmer, a sorcerer," JF, s.v. "Incantatore") who knows how to "enchant" ("charme," "bewitch; "bleare the eyes, deceive the understanding," RC, s.v. "Enchanter").

165. ***the world.*** *The world* refers to (a) the public at large; and (b) those people who comprise the audience at *the world* (i.e., the Globe Theatre; cf. II.vii.147–154).

167. ***misprised.*** Both "underappreciated" and "misunderstood."

168. ***cleare all.*** *Oliver* hopes to (a) *cleare* (remove a burden or obstacle) *all* (i.e., *all* problems or impediments) by "clearing" (getting rid of) *Orlando*; and (b) rid himself of *Orlando's* "shit" and *cleare* ("purge the bowels," OED) *all* ("the whole," OED, with play on "hole" as "The rectum; short for arse-hole," F&H).

168. ***nothing remaines.*** *Nothing remaines* (i.e., there is nothing left to do) but to ensure that *Orlando* gets his "remain" ("balance or unpaid remainder of a sum of money," OED). Cf. and see note: *payment*, line 156, above.

168. ***kindle.*** Literally, to *kindle* is to "set on fire, ignite" (OED); figuratively, to *kindle* is to "provoke, or give boldnes to: to encourage" (TT, s.v. "Accendo"). *Kindle* is also another allusion to *Orlando's* being a "piece of shit": a "kandil" or "candle" is "A bougie; a suppository" (OED, which dates this sense from 1684, but cf. Thomas Adams' 1619 *The Happines of the Church*: "every frowne he makes, gives his Patron a vomite: and every candle of commendation a purge").

Act I, scene ii

SCŒNA SECUNDA. [1]

Enter Rosalind, and Cellia. [I.ii.1]

Cel. I pray thee *Rosalind*, sweet my Coz, be merry.

Ros. Deere *Cellia*; I show more mirth then I am mi-

stresse of, and would you yet were merrier: unlesse you [5]

could teach me to forget a banished father, you must not

learne mee how to remember any extraordinary plea-

sure.

Cel. Heerein I see thou lov'st mee not with the full

waight that I love thee; if my Uncle thy banished father [10]

had banished thy Uncle the Duke my Father, so thou

hadst beene still with mee, I could have taught my love

to take thy father for mine; so wouldst thou, if the truth

of thy love to me were so righteously temper'd, as mine

is to thee. [15]

Ros. Well, I will forget the condition of my estate,

to rejoyce in yours.

Notes I.ii.

4–5. ***mistresse of.*** "To be *mistresse of*" is the feminine analog of "To be master of" (to have something at one's command or control), with additional play on *mistresse* as a female tutor.

7. ***learne.*** To "teach, to instruct" (JF, s.v. "dottrinare").

9–10. ***full waight.*** The sixteen-ounce Norman "Avoir-du-pois" was "of full or due weight" (TB, q.v.), but the "troy weight" or "old London weight" consisted of only twelve ounces. *Cellia* implies that, even though *Rosalind* and *Cellia love* each other in "full measure" ("Amply, fully," RC, s.v. "À la grande laize"), they adhere to different standards. Cf. and see note: *righteously temper'd,* line 14, below.

14. ***righteously temper'd.*** *Cellia* is *temper'd* (endowed with a "temperament") that causes her to love *righteously* ("religiously," OED). By contrast, *Rosalind's* affection is not pure but *temper'd* ("toned-down"; "Modified by the admixture or influence of some other element," OED). During the Renaissance, coins were often not *temper'd* ("valued, rated," RC, s.v. "Mesuré") *righteously* (rightly, correctly) because the precious metal was *temper'd* (mixed or mingled with something else). Cf. and see note: *full waight,* lines 9–10, above.

16. ***the condition of my estate.*** The *condition* (state, standing) of *Rosalind's estate* (status or rank; also prosperity or fortune) is "debased" ("dejected, humbled, cast or sunke downe"; also "depressed; lessened or fallen in price; brought low," RC, s.v. "Ravallé"). Cf. *righteously temper'd,* line 14, above.

Cel. You know my Father hath no childe, but I, nor
none is like to have; and truely when he dies, thou shalt
be his heire; for what hee hath taken away from thy fa- [20]
ther perforce, I will render thee againe in affection: by
mine honor I will, and when I breake that oath, let mee
turne monster: therefore my sweet *Rose*, my deare *Rose*,
be merry.

Ros. From henceforth I will Coz, and devise sports: [25]
let me see, what thinke you of falling in Love?

Cel. Marry I prethee doe, to make sport withall: but
love no man in good earnest, nor no further in sport neyther, then with safety of a pure blush, thou maist in honor come off againe. [30]

Ros. What shall be our sport then?

Cel. Let us sit and mocke the good houswife *For-*
tune from her wheele, that her gifts may henceforth bee
bestowed equally.

Ros. I would wee could doe so: for her benefits are [35]
mightily misplaced, and the bountifull blinde woman
doth most mistake in her gifts to women.

18–20. ***no childe... thou shalt be his heire.*** A male *childe*, by virtue of its gender, would automatically supplant *Cellia* as her father's *heire. Duke Frederick* is unlikely to have any more children, however, and *Cellia* vows to return the throne to *Rosalind* upon her father's death.

21. ***perforce.*** Forcibly; violently.

21. ***render.*** "To restore, returne"; to "yeeld or give back" (RC, s.v. "Restituer").

23. ***turne monster.*** *Cellia* does not want to *turne monster* (which carries the same connotation as "turn Turk": "to turn renegade, to change for the worse," F&H). Should *Cellia* deprive *Rosalind* of her *monster* (i.e., "monstrance" or "monstrance of right": "a writ, issuing out of Chancery, for restoring a person to lands or tenements which legally belonged to him or her following the death of another person, but which had been seized by the Crown," OED), she would *turne* into a *monster* ("a monstrous example of evil," OED).

25–30. ***sports... come off againe.*** *Rosalind* suggests *falling in Love* in order to *make sport*, which means (a) entertaining diversion; (b) "Mischief; horseplay" (F&H); and/or (c) "sexual dalliance, copulation" (JH). *Cellia* advises loving a *man* only *in sport* (in jest) but not *in earnest* (sincerely; with "intense passion or desire," OED). If *Rosalind* is too *earnest* ("Of animals: Excited," OED), she may offer her lover an *earnest* ("A deposit in part of payment, to bind a bargain," FG)—i.e., consent to have sexual intercourse with him. If *Rosalind's* lover is a *good man* ("a vigorous fornicator," FG, s.v. "good"), she will *come off* (experience orgasm) *in* (during) *earnest* (i.e., copulation; "ornest" is Old English for "single combat," OED). However, she could not then *come off* (retreat) *in honour* (i.e., with her virginity intact).

29. ***a pure blush.*** Proverbially, "Many blush to hear what they are not ashamed to act." However, if *Rosalind* avoids becoming a *pure* (whore, F&H, s.v. "tart"), her *blush* will be *pure* (chaste, innocent).

32–34. ***houswife Fortune... bestowed equally.*** *Fortune* is here depicted as a *houswife* working at a spinning-*wheele* (mortals supposedly rode upon the "wheel of *Fortune*," and their prosperity went up or down according to the goddess' caprice). *Cellia* hopes to stop *Fortune's* arbitrary imparting of "weal" (prosperity, well-being, happiness) or "wheal" ("The ridge raised on the flesh by a blow," OED; cf. "stroake of Fortune," *Henry VIII*, II.ii.).

The goddess *Fortune* also had a reputation for being a *houswife* ("Hussy; light woman," EC; also "Cunt," F&H, s.v. "monosyllable"; cf. and see note: *buy my fortunes*, I.i.72–73). *Fortune's wheele* ("Female pudendum," JH) *bestowed her gifts* (i.e., granted sexual favors) to some, but others *Fortune bestowed* (i.e., "buggered"; to "bestow" is to "Engage in sexual bestiality or sodomy," FR). Cf. *misplaced*, line 36, below, and IV.iii.94.

35–37. ***her benefits... doth most mistake.*** The goddess *Fortune* was proverbially known to *mistake in her gifts* (see note: *properer man*, III.v.56). Because *Fortune* "mistakes" (i.e., "buggers"; to *mistake* is "to have anal intercourse," EC) those who least deserve it, her *benefits* ("profits": "sexual pleasure[s]," JH) are *misplaced* ("put... in a wrong place," OED—i.e., in the anus instead of the *place*: "female pudendum," F&H, s.v. "monosyllable").

36. ***the bountifull blinde woman.*** *Fortune* was *bountifull* ("free, liberall," "that yeeldeth fruit and commoditie," JF, s.v. "Munifico"), but she was also indiscriminate and therefore depicted blindfolded.

Cel. 'Tis true, for those that she makes faire, she scarce makes honest, & those that she makes honest, she makes very illfavouredly. [40]

Ros. Nay now thou goest from Fortunes office to Natures: Fortune reignes in gifts of the world, not in the lineaments of Nature.

Enter Clowne. [I.ii.2]

Cel. No; when Nature hath made a faire creature, [45] may she not by Fortune fall into the fire? though nature hath given us wit to flout at Fortune, hath not Fortune sent in this foole to cut off the argument?

Ros. Indeed there is fortune too hard for nature, when fortune makes natures naturall, the cutter off of natures [50] witte.

Cel. Peradventure this is not Fortunes work neither, but Natures, who perceiveth our naturall wits too dull to reason of such goddesses, hath sent this Naturall for

38–40. ***those that she makes faire... illfavouredly.*** *Fortune ill* (wrongfully, improperly) bestows her "favors" (privileges or gifts) when dispensing "favors" (appearances or looks). Therefore, women that *Fortune* makes *faire* (beautiful) *she scarce* (seldom) *makes honest* (chaste, sexually virtuous), while those that *Fortune makes honest* (reputable) *she makes very illfavouredly* (ill-looking, ugly). Even women whose "honesty" (chastity, purity) appears *honest* ("genuine," OED) might actually be "ill-favored" ("Filthie, unhonest, uncleane, all beraid, slutish, foule, naughtie, corrupt, base," TT, s.v. "sordĭdus").

41–43. ***Fortunes office... lineaments of Nature.*** Mother *Nature*, whose *office* (duty) is to oversee a person's *Nature* (personality, character, and physical qualities), determines a person's *lineaments* ("features, formes, proportions, draughts or shapes of a bodie or visage drawne out," JF, s.v. "Lineamenti"). By contrast, *Fortune reignes in* (rules over, governs) the *gifts of the world*, which she "reins in" (checks, holds back, restrains) according to the whim of her *reignes* (kidneys, which were regarded as the seat of sexual passion; cf. and see notes: *buy my fortunes*, I.i.72–73, and *houswife Fortune*, lines 32–33, above). However, both *Fortune* and *Nature* "shit on" people; *the world* is an *office* ("A privy, a lavatory," OED) where the *reignes* ("loins," OED) of both goddesses expel their *Nature* ("excrement," OED).

44. ***Enter Clowne.*** This character is tagged *Clowne* due to (a) his function within the play; and (b) his status as an all-licensed fool (a professional jester employed at court; cf. I.iii.138, II.ii.10–11, II.vii.40, III.ii.20–21, III.ii.34–72, and III.iii.77–78). Shakespeare never denotes this character by any other name (cf. and see note: *alias Touchstone*, II.iv.3).

45. ***creature.*** Both (a) human being; and (b) "whore" (GW).

46. ***fall into the fire.*** To *fall into the fire* can mean: (a) to become disfigured through mishap; (b) to be forced into adverse circumstances; (c) to be damned to *the fire* of Hell; (d) to *fall* ("fall from virtue, or from continence" EP) *into fire* (lust); and/or (e) to catch *fire* ("venereal infection," EC).

46–51. ***nature hath given us wit... natures witte.*** *Nature* has given the ladies *wit* (intelligence, good sense) to *flout at* (make fun of) *Fortune*, but *Fortune* has *sent in natures naturall* ("an idiot," FG) to *cut off* ("determine, conclude or bring a matter to a point or ende, to make agreement of a controversie," TT, s.v. "dēcīdo") *the argument.* This offers proof that the goddess *Fortune* is *hard* ("difficult to deal with, manage, control, or resist," OED) and is simply *too hard for* ("too much for," OED) Mother *nature* to withstand.

As *the cutter off of natures witte* (i.e., "whit" or "prick," FR), *Fortune* is a "ball-busting whore" who "cuts off" *the argument* (which possibly means "penis," GW). She thus proves herself *hard* (literally "Difficult to penetrate," OED) and demonstrates her mastery over *hard* ("allusive of penis erectus," EP) *nature* (the genitals; JA, p. 58) *Indeed* (i.e., in "the deed" or coïtus).

52. ***Peradventure.*** *Peradventure* (perhaps, perchance) the *Clowne* has not been sent *per* (by) the "venture" (whore, EC) *Fortune*, but instead represents an *adventure* ("hazard, danger, perill, jeopardie," JF, s.v. "Risco") *per* ("As laid down or stated by a judge," OED) the goddess *Nature.*

53–54. ***our naturall wits... goddesses.*** A similar notion is found in Lodge's *Rosalynde*: "*Fortune*, that sawe how these parties valued not her Deitie, but helde her power in scorne, thought to have about with them."

	our whetstone: for alwaies the dulnesse of the foole, is	[55]
	the whetstone of the wits. How now Witte, whether	
	wander you?	
Clow.	Mistresse, you must come away to your father.	
Cel.	Were you made the messenger?	
Clo.	No by mine honor, but I was bid to come for you	[60]
Ros.	Where learned you that oath foole?	
Clo.	Of a certaine Knight, that swore by his Honour	
	they were good Pan-cakes, and swore by his Honor the	
	Mustard was naught: Now Ile stand to it, the Pancakes	
	were naught, and the Mustard was good, and yet was	[65]
	not the Knight forsworne.	

55–56. ***the dulnesse of the foole, is the whetstone of the wits.*** A *whetstone* is literally a stone "whereon oyle being put, the gravers and carvers do whet their instruments" (JM, s.v. "Agazadéra)—i.e., a *whetstone* is a stone used to sharpen tools that shape other stones. Figuratively, therefore, a *whetstone* is anything used to sharpen the *wits.*

While in grammar school, the young William Shakespeare may have studied from Robert Recorde's 1557 book of arithmetic, *The Whetstone of Witte* (fully titled "The whetstone of witte whiche is the seconde parte of Arithmetike: containyng thextraction of Rootes: The cossike practise, with the rule of Equation: and the woorkes of Surde Nombers"). The book's title page contains the following poem:

Though many stones doe beare greate price,
The *whetstone* is for exersice
As neadefull, and in woorke as straunge:
Dulle thinges and harde it will so change,
And make them sharpe, to right good use:
All artesmen knowe, thei can not chuse,
But use his helpe: yet as men see,
Noe sharpenesse semeth in it to bee.

The *ground of artes* did brede this stone.
His use is greate, and moare then one.
Here if you lift your wittes to whette,
Moche sharpenesse therby shall you gette.
Dulle wittes hereby doe greately mende,
Sharpe wittes are fined to their full ende.
Now prove, and praise, as you doe finde,
And to your self be not unkinde.

(Shakespeare seemingly learned more about wordplay than "cossike practise," or algebra, from Recorde: a "Cos" is "A whetstone," TT, q.v.)

56–57. ***How now Witte, whether wander you?*** Both (a) "Where are you going?"; and (b) an allusion to the expression, *wit whether wil't* (IV.i.162). The phrase is "addressed to a person who is letting his tongue run away with him" (OED), for one whose *Witte* (intelligence, wisdom, judgment) "wanders" (goes astray) will *wander* ("ramble, rave, talk wildly," OED). The "will" of this expression means "Going or gone astray; that has lost his way, or has nowhere to go for rest or shelter; straying, wandering, 'lost'" (OED).

58–60. ***come away... No.*** The *Clowne* is a highly inappropriate *messenger*, for "every wyse man ought to take hede that he sende no folysshe servant upon a hasty message that is a mater of weyght" (Anonymous, *A Hundred Mery Tayls*; cf. "He that sendeth a message by the hand of a foole, cutteth off the feete, and drinketh dammage," Proverbs 26:6).

The *Clowne* may additionally quibble on *messenger* meaning a "Poursuivant," an official "sent upon any occasion or message; as for thee apprehending a party accused, or suspected of any offence committed" (TB, q.v.).

62. ***certaine.*** With play on *certaine* meaning (a) one in particular; and (b) having no doubt.

63–65. ***good Pan-cakes... the Mustard was good.*** "Pancake" means "The female pudendum; Cunt," as does "mustard-pot" (F&H, s.v. "monosyllable"); the burning sensation of *Mustard* was associated with both sexual excitement and venereal infection (GW2). The bawdy sense seems to be that the *Pan-cakes* (women or their genitals) *were good* ("sexually proficient," GW; also see note: *good*, line 28, above), but (a) the *Mustard* (i.e., the venereal diseases they carried) *was naught* (harmful or unlucky; also see note: *be naught*, I.i.37); and/or (b) the *Mustard* (regarded as an aphrodisiac) *was naught* (bad, inferior), so the *Knight's* ability to *stand to it* (i.e., achieve an erection and perform sexually) was hindered.

66. ***forsworne.*** One who is *forsworne* is "false of his word, that hath broken his oth" (TT, s.v. "Perjūrus").

Cel. How prove you that in the great heape of your knowledge?

Ros. I marry, now unmuzzle your wisedome.

Clo. Stand you both forth now: stroke your chinnes, [70] and sweare by your beards that I am a knave.

Cel. By our beards (if we had them) thou art.

Clo. By my knaverie (if I had it) then I were: but if you sweare by that that is not, you are not forsworn: no more was this knight swearing by his Honor, for he ne- [75] ver had anie; or if he had, he had sworne it away, before ever he saw those Pancakes, or that Mustard.

Cel. Prethee, who is't that thou means't?

Clo. One that old *Fredericke* your Father loves.

{*Cel.*} My Fathers love is enough to honor him enough; [80] speake no more of him, you'l be whipt for taxation one of these daies.

Clo. The more pittie that fooles may not speak wise- ly, what Wisemen do foolishly.

69. ***unmuzzle your wisedome.*** Should the *Clowne* attempt to speak *wisedome*, it would become clear that he is a "muzzle" ("one that assayeth and trieth to speake a toong, yet cannot," JM, s.v. "Boçál"). Were he to *unmuzzle* (remove the restraining bridle from) his "muss" (mouth, OED), his "musse" ("mumblings in speech," JF, q.v.) would just make a "muss" (mess).

A "muzzle" is also "a Barnacle" (RC, s.v. "Museliere"), a "kind of powerful bit or twitch for the mouth of horse or ass, used to restrain a restive animal" (OED). The implication is that the *Clowne* will show himself to be an "ass" if he is "unbridled" (speaks unrestrainedly). Cf. "There is one that keepeth silence and is found wise: and another by much babling becommeth hatefull" (Sirach 20:5); also cf. and see notes: lines 85–86, below, and IV.i.8–9.

70–71. ***your chinnes... your beards.*** The *Clowne* plays on *unmuzzle* (line 69, above) when he instructs the ladies to *sweare by* their *beards* (a "muzzle" is "a Beard, usually long and nasty," ND; cf. *not*, line 74, below). As women, *Cellia* and *Rosalind* do not have *beards* on their *chinnes* (the front part of their jaws), but they do have "mussels" (female genitals, GW2, s.v. "Oyster") and *beards* ("pubic hair," EP) on their *chinnes* (i.e., vaginas; a "chin[e]" is literally "An open fissure or crack in a surface; a cleft, crack, chink," OED).

72. ***if we had them.*** This parenthetical (a) reminds the audience that the boy actors playing *Rosalind* and *Cellia* are supposed to be females; and (b) comically points up the fact that *Rosalind* and *Cellia* as portrayed by male actors are not really women.

73–74. ***if you sweare... not forsworn.*** In swearing by his non-existent honor that *the Mustard was naught* (lines 63–64, above), the *Knight* swore by "nought" (nothing) so was therefore *not forsworn*. In swearing by their *beards* (lines 71–72 above), the male actors portraying *Rosalind* and *Cellia* are *not forsworn* because in order to play women they would need to *not* (clip or cut short a beard, OED) and thus would have no *beards* to swear by.

81. ***whipt for taxation.*** Either (a) *for* (because of, on account of) your *taxation* (accusation, censure) of others *you'l be whipt*; or (b) *for* ("as," OED) *taxation* ("imposition of any payment, an equall or like paine in recompence of a hurt," JF, s.v. "Taglione") *you'l be whipt*. To *be whipt* was a traditional punishment for fools; cf. "A whip for the horse, a bridle for the asse; and a rod for the fooles backe" (Proverbs 26:3).

83–84. ***The more pittie that fooles may not speak... foolishly.*** I.e., "since it is not safe for a wise man to speake truth, 'twere pitty fooles should loose their priviledge" (James Shirley, *The Bird in a Cage*, III.i.). Also see note: lines 85–86, below.

Cel.	By my troth thou saiest true: For, since the little	[85]
	wit that fooles have was silenced, the little foolerie that	
	wise men have makes a great shew; Heere comes Mon-	
	sieur the *Beu.*	
Enter le Beau.		[I.ii.3]
Ros.	With his mouth full of newes.	[90]
Cel.	Which he will put on us, as Pigeons feed their	
	young.	
Ros.	Then shal we be newes-cram'd.	
Cel.	All the better: we shalbe the more Marketable.	
	Boon-jour Monsieur le Beu, what's the newes?	[95]
Le Beu.	Faire Princesse,	
	you have lost much good sport.	
Cel.	Sport: of what colour?	
Le Beu.	What colour Madame? How shall I aun-	
	swer you?	[100]
Ros.	As wit and fortune will.	

85–86. ***since the little wit... silenced.*** An ostensible allusion to the proverb "Fooles are held wise as long as they are silent" (RC, s.v. "Fols sont sages quand ils se taisent"; cf. and see note: line 69, above).

Freedom of speech was by no means a recognized right in Renaissance society (the notable exception being the all-licensed fool, who was granted this valuable privilege; cf. and see notes: II.vii.52–54), so playwrights and players were in continual danger of saying the wrong thing and offending the wrong person. These lines may allude to any number of incidents that occurred in the late 1590s when *As you Like it* was written and first performed, including (1) the 1597 imprisonment of playwright Ben Jonson and players Gabriel Spencer and Robert Shaa for their respective roles in writing and staging the controversial play *The Isle of Dogs*; (2) the "bishop's ban" of June 1, 1599, which ordered that a number of satirical books be brought to the Bishop of London and burned; (3) the 1597 act of Parliament which dictated that "all fencers, bearwards, common players of enterludes, and minstrells, wandering abroad; all juglers, tinkers, pedlars, etc. shall be adjudged and deemed rogues, vagabonds, and sturdy beggers"; (4) the 1597 Privy Council order to tear down all playhouses within a three mile radius of London (luckily for William Shakespeare and posterity, this order was not enacted); and (5) the 1600 Privy Council order reducing the number of legally recognized acting companies to two.

86–88. ***the little foolerie... Monsieur the Beu.*** The implication is that *Monsieur the Beu* is just such a person (i.e., a supposedly wise man whose *foolerie makes a great shew*). In *Monsieur the Beu*, Shakespeare indulges the English penchant for French ridicule (*Monsieur le Beu* literally means "Mister Beautiful"; in English, a *Beau* is "a silly Fellow that follows the Fashions nicely," ND).

Although *As you Like it* is ostensibly set in France (and everyone in it is, therefore, French), *Monsieur the Beu* is unarguably treated as a foreigner in the court, with *Cellia* addressing the play's only line of French to him (line 95, below). Additional clues that *Monsieur the Beu* "out–Frenches the French" include (1) his perplexed literal interpretation of *colour* (lines 98–100, below), which suggests a lack of familiarity with English vernacular; (2) the substitution of *the* (line 88) for *le* (line 89), which mimics the idiom of French honorifics (cf. line 160, below, where *le Beu* addresses *Orlando* as *Monsieur the Challenger*, which is correct French syntax; in French translations of *As you Like it*, *le Beau* calls *Orlando* "Monsieur L'Aggressor"); (3) his pronounced French accent as evidenced by the spellings of *aunswer* (lines 99–100, below; a spelling unique to the First Folio) and *counsaile* (line 264, below); his pronunciation of *condition* as a four-syllable word (line 267, below); and his emphasizing the second syllable of *misconsters* (line 268, below) instead of the first and third, as is correct in English.

90–94. ***his mouth full of newes... the more Marketable.*** Just as *Pigeons put on* ("set an animal to feed solely or principally on a particular food," OED) *their young* with "pigeon milk" (half-digested regurgitated food from their stomachs), *Le Beu* seeks *Pigeons* ("dupe[s]," "gull[s]," F&H; cf. Fr. slang "pigeon": "sucker") on whom he can *put on* (impose, inflict) his *newes. Le Beu* will "cram" (fill up, stuff) the ladies with "cram" (both a "mass of dough or paste used for cramming fowls, etc.," OED, and "A lie... the idea is that of stuffing with nonsense," F&H). When "fed up to market" (fattened for sale) with the latest gossip, the ladies *shalbe the more Marketable* ("in demand," OED).

98–100. ***of what colour... aunswer you.*** *Cellia* uses *of what colour* to mean "of what kind," but *Le Beu* may be at a loss to *aunswer* because he interprets *colour* literally (see note: *Monsieur the Beu*, line 87–88, above).

101. ***wit and fortune.*** *Rosalind* ultimately decides that the match between *wit and fortune* is a draw; cf. lines 35–56, above.

Clo. Or as the destinies decrees.

Cel. Well said, that was laid on with a trowell.

Clo. Nay, if I keepe not my ranke.

Ros. Thou loosest thy old smell. [105]

Le Beu. You amaze me Ladies: I would have told
you of good wrastling, which you have lost the sight of.

Ros. Yet tell us the manner of the Wrastling.

Le Beu. I wil tell you the beginning: and if it please
your Ladiships, you may see the end, for the best is yet [110]
to doe, and heere where you are, they are comming to
performe it.

Cel. Well, the beginning that is dead and buried.

Le Beu. There comes an old man, and his three sons.

Cel. I could match this beginning with an old tale. [115]

Le Beu. Three proper yong men, of excellent growth
and presence.

Ros. With bils on their neckes: Be it knowne unto
all men by these presents.

Le Beu. The eldest of the three, wrastled with *Charles* [120]
the Dukes Wrastler, which *Charles* in a moment threw

102. ***the destinies decrees.*** *Destinies* is here a collective noun. The "three Ladies of destiny" who work as one are "Clotho, Lachesis, and Atropos. The first bears a Distaff, the second spins the thred of mans life, the third cuts off the same thred" (TB, s.v. "Parcae").

103–105. ***laid on with a trowell... thy old smell.*** *Cellia* thinks that the *Clowne* has *laid on* his words *with a trowell* ("an instrument that Masons and Plaisterers work with," TB, q.v.)—i.e., that he has "*layed* in *on* thick," or expressed himself clumsily or extravagantly (the "it" of this expression is euphemistic for "shit," dung being a traditional ingredient of plaster; cf. *render*, IV.iii.131). The *Clowne* has *ranke* ("pride," OED) in his *ranke* (hierarchical position, here with respect to his status as a professional jester) and thus denies being *ranke* ("excessive or superfluous," TT, s.v. "Luxŭriōsus," with further quibble on *ranke* as "a rew, ranke, lane, or course, of stones, or bricks, in building," RC, s.v. "Bauche"). Nevertheless, *Rosalind* finds him *ranke*, which means (a) "stinking like things vinewed or rotten" (JF, s.v. "Rancido"); (b) "luxurious, lustfull, wanton" (JF, s.v. "Lussurióso); and/or (c) "rotten": venereally infected.

106. ***amaze.*** *Le Beu* may be "amazed" (astonished, bewildered, or perplexed) due to a language barrier; see note: *Monsieur the Beu*, lines 87–88, above.

109–111. ***I wil tell you the beginning... the best is yet to doe.*** The additional wrestling matches described by *Le Beu* are treated fully in both *The Tale of Gamelyn* and *Rosalynde*. On the stage, however, multiple wrestling matches would make the match between *Charles* and *Orlando* somewhat anti-climactic.

112. ***performe.*** Execute; also finish.

113. ***dead and buried.*** I.e., moot because it is in the past.

114–119. ***an old man... by these presents.*** Many a *tale* (including *As you Like it*) employs the motif of *an old man and his three sons*, but *Cellia* my specifically recall the ballad of "The Old Man and his Three Sons" (which begins "Old Sir Robert Bolton had three sons"). The ballad's alternate title of "The Jovial Hunter of Bromsgrove" may inspire *Rosalind's* quibble on "bill" as (a) a "speare, a javelin, a forest bill, a long staffe with a pike in the end" (JF, s.v. "sarissa"), which was customarily carried "on the neck" (i.e., over the shoulder); (b) a "declaration made in form of Law" (TB, s.v. "Enditement"), which customarily began with the phrase *Be it knowne unto all men by these presents* (i.e., "by the present document or writing, or its contents," OED); and (c) a written or printed advertisement, the young men's good qualities serving to announce that they are *all men* (i.e., "manly": courageous, strong, virile) as well as would placards worn around *their neckes*.

The *Three yong men* possess the *presents* (gifts or endowments) of being *proper* ("beautifull, faire, gracefull, comely, seemely, welfavoured"; also "delectable, pleasant to the eie, sightly, having a good grace," JF, s.v. "Venusto") and *of excellent growth* (stature) *and presence* (demeanor, carriage; also "readines, courage," TT, s.v. "Praesentia"). Also, their *bils* (penises, GW2) announce that they are *proper* (i.e., genitally well endowed; a "prop" is literally a "stick, rod, pole, stake, beam, or other rigid support," OED); they posses *presents* ("genitals," FR) of *excellent growth* ("sexual erection," JH, s.v. "grow").

him, and broke three of his ribbes, that there is little
hope of life in him: So he serv'd the second, and so the
third: yonder they lie, the poore old man their Father,
making such pittiful dole over them, that all the behol- [125]
ders take his part with weeping.

Ros. Alas.

Clo. But what is the sport Monsieur, that the Ladies
have lost?

Le Beu. Why this that I speake of. [130]

Clo. Thus men may grow wiser every day. It is the
first time that ever I heard breaking of ribbes was sport
for Ladies.

Cel. Or I, I promise thee.

Ros. But is there any else longs to see this broken [135]
Musicke in his sides? Is there yet another doates upon
rib-breaking? Shall we see this wrastling Cosin?

Le Beu. You must if you stay heere, for heere is the
place appointed for the wrastling, and they are ready to
performe it. [140]

Cel. Yonder sure they are comming. Let us now stay
and see it.

122–123. ***broke three of his ribbes... little hope of life.*** These young men fare better than their counterparts in *The Tale of Gamelyn* and *Rosalynde*, in which they are all killed.

125. ***pittiful.*** Pitiable.

125. ***dole.*** *Dole* is (a) "griefe, sorrow, heavinesse; mourning, wayling, moaning, lamentation" (RC, s.v. "dueil"); and (b) "A funeral" (OED).

127. ***Alas.*** *Alas* is specifically "A lamentable voice used at the death and buriall of men, as we crie, alas" (TT, s.v. "Lessus").

132–133. ***breaking of ribbes... Ladies.*** The *Clowne* ironically references paradoxical social standards. Then as now, *Ladies* were not active participants in violent sports but were nevertheless ardent spectators; in 1561, Queen Elizabeth herself hosted a wrestling match in her chapel.

135. ***to see.*** With play on *see* as both (a) "allow"; and (b) "read music" (OED).

135–136. ***broken Musicke... sides.*** *Musicke* (melody) would be *broken* ("of sound: disjointed," OED) if (a) the *Musicke* (consort, company of musicians) was *broken* (not kept intact); and/or (b) the *Musicke* (musical instrument) was *broken* (shattered, separated into fragments). *Rosalind* likens a man's *broken* ribs to *Musicke* played on the *broken* "ribs" ("the curved pieces of wood forming the body of a lute or the sides of a violin," OED) of a "Ribé" ("a musicall instrument so called, a rebeck, or a croud, or a kit," RC, q.v.).

136. ***doates.*** To "dote" is (a) "to love to excess" (OED); and (b) to "do things against reason" (RC, s.v. "deliver"). "Dote" is also a variant of "dot": in music, "A point placed for various purposes after, over, or under a note, after a rest, or before or after a double bar" (OED).

139. ***appointed.*** Prefixed or predetermined, with play on "point" as both (a) a musical note; and (b) a "short strain or snatch of melody; a musical phrase" (OED)

Flourish. Enter Duke {Frederick}, Lords, Orlando, Charles, and Attendants. [I.ii.4]

{*Duke Fred.*} Come on, since the youth will not be intreated [145]
His owne perill on his forwardnesse.

Ros. Is yonder the man?

Le Beu. Even he, Madam.

Cel. Alas, he is too yong: yet he looks successefully

{*Duke Fred.*} How now daughter, and Cousin: [150]
Are you crept hither to see the wrastling?

Ros. I my Liege, so please you give us leave.

{*Duke Fred.*} You wil take little delight in it, I can tell you
there is such oddes in the man: In pitie of the challengers youth, I would faine disswade him, but he will not [155]
bee entreated. Speake to him Ladies, see if you can
moove him.

Cel. Call him hether good Monsieuer *Le Beu.*

{*Duke Fred.*} Do so: Ile not be by.

Le Beu. Monsieur the Challenger, the Princesse cals [160]
for you.

Orl. I attend them with all respect and dutie.

149. ***looks successefully.*** Appears likely to succeed.

150–152. ***Cousin... my Liege.*** *Frederick* addresses *Rosalind* with casual familiarity, but *Rosalind* responds with the utmost formality.

154–155. ***such oddes in the man... faine disswade him.*** *Such oddes* (probability of success) *is in the man* (i.e., *Charles*) that the *oddes* (in gambling, "the ratio between the amounts staked by the parties in a bet, based on the expected probability either way," OED) are greatly in his favor. By betting on *Charles*, *Frederick* stands to make a lot of money. Therefore, he may only "feign" ("counterfeit, to represent, to set a good face on the matter," TB, s.v. "Assimulate") that he *would faine* (prefer to) *disswade Orlando* from wrestling.

157. ***moove.*** Convince or persuade.

160–162. ***the Princesse... dutie.*** Strictly speaking, only *Cellia, the Princesse*, has called for *Orlando* (line 158, above), but *Orlando* offers his *respect and dutie* to both ladies.

Ros. Young man, have you challeng'd *Charles* the Wrastler?

Orl. No faire Princesse: he is the generall challenger, [165] I come but in as others do, to try with him the strength of my youth.

Cel. Yong Gentleman, your spirits are too bold for your yeares: you have seene cruell proofe of this mans strength, if you saw your selfe with your eies, or knew [170] your selfe with your judgment, the feare of your adventure would counsel you to a more equall enterprise. We pray you for your owne sake to embrace your own safetie, and give over this attempt.

Ros. Do yong Sir, your reputation shall not therefore [175] be misprised: we wil make it our suite to the Duke, that the wrastling might not go forward.

Orl. I beseech you, punish mee not with your harde thoughts, wherein I confesse me much guiltie to denie so faire and excellent Ladies anie thing. But let your [180] faire eies, and gentle wishes go with mee to my triall; wherein if I bee foil'd, there is but one sham'd that was never gracious: if kil'd, but one dead that is willing to

163–175. ***Young man... yong Sir.*** Forms of address corresponded to a strict social hierarchy. As of line 163, *Orlando's* social status is as yet unknown, so *Rosalind* addresses him simply as *Young man.* His demeanor subsequently convinces the ladies that he is a *Gentleman* and should thus be addressed as *Sir.*

166. ***come... in.*** See note: *come in,* I.i.130.

168–172. ***your spirits... a more equall enterprise.*** Proverbially, "excellent spirits are often lodged in exile, or small, bodies" (RC, s.v. "En petit champ croist bien bon bled"). *Orlando's spirits* (i.e., his "soule; Heart; breath, heat; mind, thought; opinion; wit, conceit; also, life, courage, mettall, stomacke, vivacitie, livelinesse, or smartnesse of humor; also, affection, fancie, disposition, inclination," RC, s.v. "Esprit") have grown *too bold* ("presumptuus, audacious," JF, s.v. "Audáce") for his *yeares* (age). Therefore, *Orlando* launches into a dangerous *enterprise* (undertaking, attempt) without *feare.*

171. ***feare.*** *Feare* means both (a) dread; and (b) peril, danger.

174. ***give over.*** Abandon.

174. ***attempt.*** Both (a) "triall" (JF, s.v. "sagiatta"); and (b) "intent or purpose" (JF, s.v. "Attento").

175–177. ***your reputation... not go forward.*** If *the Duke* cancels the "prise" (wrestling match, OED) on the ladies' behalf, then *Orlando's* manly *reputation* (honor, credit) will not be *misprised* ("scorned; unappreciated," OED).

182. ***foil'd.*** See note: *foyle,* I.i.129.

be so: I shall do my friends no wrong, for I have none to
lament me: the world no injurie, for in it I have nothing: [185]
onely in the world I fil up a place, which may bee better
supplied, when I have made it emptie.

Ros. The little strength that I have, I would it were
with you.

Cel. And mine to eeke out hers. [190]

Ros. Fare you well: praie heaven I be deceiv'd in you.

Cel. Your hearts desires be with you.

Char. Come, where is this yong gallant, that is so
desirous to lie with his mother earth?

Orl. Readie Sir, but his will hath in it a more modest [195]
working.

{*Duke Fred.*} You shall trie but one fall.

Cha. No, I warrant your Grace you shall not entreat
him to a second, that have so mightilie perswaded him
from a first. [200]

Orl. You meane to mocke me after: you should not
have mockt me before: but come your waies.

Ros. Now Hercules, be thy speede yong man.

186–187. ***fil up... emptie.*** When *Orlando* "empties" (voids, removes himself from) his *place* (worldly situation, position in the order of things), it *may be better supplied* (occupied) by someone else. In fact, *Orlando* considers his *place* (worldly situation or position) to be as "shitty" as a *place* ("A jakes, or house of ease," F&H) that needs to be "emptied" (drained or poured out). Also see note: *place*, II.i.68.

190. ***eeke out.*** Supplement, make up for the deficiency of.

191. ***Fare you well.*** Both (a) goodbye; and (b) good luck.

191. ***deceiv'd in you.*** Mistaken as to your abilities.

193–194. ***this yong gallant... lie with his mother earth.*** *Charles* thinks *Orlando* a *gallant* ("a boaster, a braver, a vaunter," "a swaggrer," JF, s.v. "Bravo") *that is desirous* (eager) *to lie with his mother earth* (i.e., in his grave). He also suggests that *Orlando* is a *gallant* (ladies' man, gigolo) and, quite obviously, a "motherfucker."

195–196. ***his will... a more modest working.*** *Orlando* does not make vulgar threats because his *will* (intention, determination; also character) has a *more modest* (moderate, unpretentious) *working* (construction, composition) than does *Charles'*. *Orlando* "modestly" (decently) rebuffs *Charles'* degrading insult (lines 193–194, above) and asserts that his *will* ("penis," EC; also sexual desire; see note: *will*, I.i.76) is *more modest* ("Conforming to the requirements of decency," OED) in its *working* (sexual intercourse, EP, s.v. "work").

198. ***your Grace.*** See note: *your Grace*, I.iii.48.

198–200. ***you shall not entreat... perswaded him from a first.*** *Frederick's* "might" (power) could not *perswade* (convince) *Orlando from* his determination to try *a first* fall. On the *first* fall, *Charles'* "might" (bodily strength) will injure *Orlando* so *mightilie* (to such a great degree) that there will be no "might" ("possibility," OED) of his making *a second* attempt. *Frederick* will therefore have no need to *entreat* ("prevail on," "persuade," OED) *Orlando to* try again.

201. ***after.*** I.e., *after* I have lost.

201–202. ***you should not have mockt me before.*** Because "Pride goeth before destruction: and an hautie spirit before a fall" (Proverbs 16:18).

203. ***Hercules, be thy speede.*** *Orlando* considers his match with *Charles* as a "Heraclio" ("a touch-stone to trie golde and silver," JF, q.v.; cf. lines 166–167, above), but *Rosalind* thinks it a "Herculean labor" ("a work of great difficulty, or almost impossible to be atchieved, which took beginning from the twelve labors of Hercules," TB, q.v.). The Greek hero *Hercules* was himself a fearsome wrestler who defeated such formidable opponents as Antaeus, the African giant; Cerberus, the three-headed hound of the underworld; and Death himself. *Rosalind* therefore appeals to both the demigod *Hercules* and the "lucky stars" of the constellation *Hercules* to be *Orlando's speede* (agent that assures success).

Notably, *Hercules'* madness was thought to be caused by epilepsy ("The falling sicknes" was also known as the "Herculeus morbus," TT, q.v.; cf. and see note: *quaile*, II.ii.22). Perhaps *Rosalind* fears that the only way *Orlando* can win is if *Charles* suffers an epileptic fit and falls down by himself.

Cel. I would I were invisible, to catch the strong fel-

low by the legge. [205]

Wrastle.

Ros. Oh excellent yong man.

Cel. If I had a thunderbolt in mine eie, I can tell who

should downe.

Shout. [210]

{*Duke Fred.*} No more, no more.

Orl. Yes I beseech your Grace, I am not yet well

breath'd.

{*Duke Fred.*} How do'st thou *Charles*?

Le Beu. He cannot speake my Lord. [215]

{*Duke Fred.*} Beare him awaie: {*Exit Lords with Charles.*} [I.ii.5]

What is thy name yong man?

Orl. *Orlando* my Liege, the yongest sonne of Sir *Ro-*

land de Boys.

{*Duke Fred.*} I would thou hadst beene son to some man else, [220]

The world esteem'd thy father honourable,

But I did finde him still mine enemie:

207–209. ***Oh excellent yong man... who should downe.*** *Rosalind's* and *Cellia's* contradictory comments indicate a change of advantage to each wrestler. In line 207, *Orlando* has momentarily gained the upper hand, but by lines 208–209, he is obviously at a disadvantage as *Cellia* calls for divine intervention in the form of a *thunderbolt* (the traditional weapon of Zeus, father to *Hercules* and king of the gods).

210. ***Shout.*** The *Shout* occurs when *Charles* is thrown at the end of the bout, which is now "all over but the shouting."

212–213. ***well breath'd*** *Well* exercised; out of breath.

220. ***some man else.*** I.e., any other *man* except that one.

222. ***still.*** Continually, on all occasions.

Thou should'st have better pleas'd me with this deede,

Hadst thou descended from another house:

But fare thee well, thou art a gallant youth, [225]

I would thou had'st told me of another Father.

{*Exeunt. Manet Orlando, Cellia, and Rosalind.*} [I.ii.6]

Cel. Were I my Father (Coze) would I do this?

Orl. I am more proud to be Sir *Rolands* sonne,

His yongest sonne, and would not change that calling [230]

To be adopted heire to *Fredricke.*

Ros. My Father lov'd Sir *Roland* as his soule,

And all the world was of my Fathers minde,

Had I before knowne this yong man his sonne,

I should have given him teares unto entreaties, [235]

Ere he should thus have ventur'd.

Cel. Gentle Cosen,

Let us goe thanke him, and encourage him:

My Fathers rough and envious disposition

Sticks me at heart: Sir, you have well deserv'd, [240]

If you doe keepe your promises in love;

But justly as you have exceeded all promise,

Your Mistris shall be happie.

225. ***gallant.*** Brave, strong.

229–231. ***I am more proud... heire to Fredricke.*** *Orlando* is not the *heire* ("the elder brother," JM, s.v. "Mayorázgo") and thus not his father's *heire* ("a succeeder in a mans goods or lands, an inheritour," JF, s.v. "Herede"). Nevertheless, he is *proud* of his *calling* (position, estate, or station in life) as *Sir Rolands yongest sonne* because he has inherited his father's *heire* (pronouned "air": "character," OED) along with his *calling* ("a name, a nomination, a title, an honor," JF, s.v. "nome"). Cf. and see note: *Sir Rowland de Boys*, I.i.56–57.

235. ***unto.*** In addition to.

239. ***My Fathers rough and envious disposition.*** *Cellia* is ashamed that her father is a "ruff" ("A blockhead," OED) with a *rough* ("harsh, rude; also, sturdie, fierce, cruell, difficile, rigorous, inflexible, unmercifull; also, dull, grosse, heavie, sottish, or slow of apprehension," RC, s.v. "dur") and *envious* (malicious, spiteful, odious) *disposition* (frame of mind, humor). *Frederick* cannot rival *Orlando* or his father *Roland* in character, but he has nevertheless "disposed" (i.e., "dispossessed": "deprived," RC, s.v. "depossedé") *Orlando* of his rightful prize with a "ruff" ("a trump at cards," JF, s.v. "Trionfo"; to "ruff" is "To trump (a card, etc.) when unable to follow suit," OED). Cf. and see note: *out of suites*, line 245, below.

240. ***well deserv'd.*** *Rosalind* thinks *Orlando* "well deserving, worthie of reward" (RC, s.v. "Meritoire").

242. ***justly... exceeded all promise.*** *Justly* (exactly) *as Orlando* has *exceeded* (surpassed) *all promise* (reasonable expectation of success) in the wrestling match, *Cellia* expects him to "exceed" (be better than) his *promises in love*. She also expects he will "exceed" ("Be virile, full of seed or semen," FR, with play on *ex-* meaning "out, forth" and "seed" meaning "semen," OED; OED also gives "exceed" = "issue") *justly* (i.e., in the "joust": "a familiar euphemism or substitute term for coition," TR, s.v. "juste"; cf. *quintine*, line 251, below).

243. ***happie.*** Fortunate and/or content.

Ros. Gentleman,

Weare this for me: one out of suites with fortune [245]

That could give more, but that her hand lacks meanes.

Shall we goe Coze?

Cel. I: fare you well faire Gentleman.

Orl. Can I not say, I thanke you? My better parts

Are all throwne downe, and that which here stands up [250]

Is but a quintine, a meere livelesse blocke.

Ros. He cals us back: my pride fell with my fortunes,

Ile aske him what he would: Did you call Sir?

Sir, you have wrastled well, and overthrowne

More then your enemies. [255]

Cel. Will you goe Coze?

Ros. Have with you: fare you well.

Exit {*Cellia and Rosalind*}. [I.ii.7]

Orl. What passion hangs these waights upon my toong?

I cannot speake to her, yet she urg'd conference. [260]

Enter Le Beu. [I.ii.8]

O poore *Orlando*! thou art overthrowne

Or Charles, or something weaker masters thee.

Le Beu. Good Sir, I do in friendship counsaile you

245. ***this.*** *Rosalind* gives *Orlando* her necklace (cf. III.ii.181) as a prize for victory in the wrestling match, but the gift is also a meaningful token of her personal affection which reveals to *Orlando*, *Cellia*, and the audience that she is seriously in love.

245–246. ***out of suites with fortune... lacks meanes.*** *Rosalind* either (a) is not in the "suit" (uniform, livery) *of Fortune*; or (b) does not hold *suites* (the four sets of cards in a pack; also "the whole number of cards belonging to such a set held in a player's hand at one time," OED) in her *hand* (the cards dealt to or held by a card-player) able to trump her ill *Fortune*. In either case, she is not "in suit with" ("in company with"; "in agreement or harmony with," OED) *Fortune*. She is therefore without *meanes* (ability) to give away *her hand* (i.e., in marriage) and thus cannot *give* (sexually bestow, EP) her *hand* (genitals, FR) or her "mean" ("Intercourse, fellowship; spec. sexual intercourse," OED).

249. ***Can I not say, I thanke you.*** *Orlando cannot say I thanke you* to the ladies, so this speech is obviously an aside to the audience.

249–251. ***My better parts... a meere livelesse blocke.*** A *quintine* was a training device for the joust that consisted of a cantilevered board with a sandbag attached to one end. A rider who rode at the *quintine* but "hit not the broad end of the Quintin with his Lance or Pole, was laughed at; and he that did, if he rid not the faster, had a good blow on his neck with a Bag full of Sand, which hung on the other end" (TB, s.v. "quintin"). *Rosalind* has struck *Orlando* as dumb as if he had been *throwne downe* by a *quintine*. His *better parts* ("the Soule and Minde," Sir John Davies, "Epigram 134") have deserted him, so he *stands up* like a *livelesse* (senseless) *blocke* ("stupid person," F&H) and *quintine* (i.e., blockhead; cf. IV.i.10–11).

Even though *Orlando's better parts* (i.e., his wits) have deserted him, his other *parts* (i.e., his reproductive organs; see note: *part*, I.i.76) have no trouble expressing themselves. His *quintine* (i.e., penis; literally, "a stout post or plank," OED) *stands up* just fine.

252. ***He cals us back.*** *Orlando* has done no such thing, but *Rosalind* creates an excuse to return and talk with him.

254. ***wrastled well... overthrowne.*** *Orlando* has *overthrowne* ("felled; beaten," "cast to the ground," RC, s.v. "Abbatu") *Charles*. He has also *overthrowne* ("besotted, or entangled in love," JF, s.v. "Guastato") *Rosalind*, who intimates that she would not mind being *overthrowne* ("Conquered, with innuendo of thrown over, onto [her] back," JH, q.v.) should *Orlando* "wrestle" (have sexual intercourse, JA, pp. 157–158) with her.

257. ***Have with you.*** I.e., "back off" or "cut it out."

259. ***passion... my toong.*** When hung with *waights*, a *toong* ("tryall, or cocke of a ballance," RC, s.v. "languette") will lose its "Aequilibrium" ("when the ballance doth hang neither on the one side, nor on the other," TT, q.v.) and "poise" ("Balance, equilibrium," OED). Similarly, *Orlando's passion* ("sexual love; physical desire," EP) has upset his "equilibrium" (balance of mind) and poise (self-possession). Thus, his tongue "waits" (disgraces, OED) him because it "waits" (remains stationary, delays) and makes him "tongue-tyed" ("silent, husht, as if his lips were frosen together," RC, s.v. "Avoir le bec gelé").

260. ***conference.*** With play on *conference* as (a) conversation; and (b) "copulation" (JH).

	To leave this place; Albeit you have deserv'd	[265]
	High commendation, true applause, and love;	
	Yet such is now the Dukes condition,	
	That he misconsters all that you have done:	
	The Duke is humorous, what he is indeede	
	More suites you to conceive, then I to speake of.	[270]
Orl.	I thanke you Sir; and pray you tell me this,	
	Which of the two was daughter of the Duke,	
	That here was at the Wrastling?	
Le Beu.	Neither his daughter, if we judge by manners,	
	But yet indeede the taller is his daughter,	[275]
	The other is daughter to the banish'd Duke,	
	And here detain'd by her usurping Uncle	
	To keepe his daughter companie, whose loves	
	Are deerer then the naturall bond of Sisters:	
	But I can tell you, that of late this Duke	[280]

266. ***commendation.*** "Glorie, fame, reputation, renowne, a great name" (RC, s.v. "Gloire").

269. ***The Duke is humorous.*** The Elizabethans believed that all matter, including the human body, was composed of four elements: earth, fire, air, and water. These four elements manifested in the human body as the four "humors" which determined a person's "complexion" ("making, temper, constitution of the bodie; also, the disposition, affection, humors, or inclination of the mind," RC, q.v.). These four humors were "Melancholy," which "resembles the earth, as Choler doth the fire; Blood the air;

Phleme the water" (TB, q.v.). A "Cholericke" person was "angrie, testie, fuming, chafing, pettish, irefull, in a rage, as hot as a toast" (RC, s.v. "Cholerique"). A person influenced by blood was of a "sanguine" humor and was "naturally, and by complexion, pleasant" (RC, s.v. "Jovian"). A "Phlegmatick" person was "cold and moist; full of, or subject to Fleam" (TB, q.v.) and thus subject to "Lethargie": "A disease contrarie to phrensie: for as phrensie is caused by hot humours inflaming the braine, so is a Lethargie by cold Phlegmaticke humours, oppressing the braine in such sort, that the Patient can doe nothing but sleepe, whereby he becommeth forgetfull, with losse (in a manner) of reason and all the senses of his body" (JB, q.v.). Finally, there was "Melancholy": "One of the fowre humours in the body, the grossest of al other, which if it abound too much, causeth heavinesse and sadnesse of minde" (TB, q.v.).

The Duke is humorous ("Full of humors," JB, q.v.) that make him *humorous* ("capricious; moodie, waspish; harebraind, giddie headed," RC, s.v. "Quinteux"). *Le Beu* is reluctant to *speake of* any specific humor, but by process of elimination the *condition* ("humor of a man," RC, s.v. "Qualibre") of *the Duke* must be "choleric." *Le Beu* implies that *The Duke* is either (a) in a "shitty" mood (a "choleric passion" is "a great pain in the Belly with pricking and shooting, and avoiding of choler, both by vomit and stool," JG, s.v. "Cholerica passio"); or (b) an "ass" or "asshole" ("choler" was pronounced "color," HK, pp. 98–99; Fr. "cul" is "An arse, bumme, tayle, nockandroe, fundament," RC, q.v.; "cul[e]" is "The rump," OED). *The Duke* demonstrates himself to be an "ass," for "Hee's but ill hid that shewes his taile; he is but a shallow dissembler that suffers the world to take notice of his worst humors" (RC, s.v. "Il est mal caché à qui le cul paroist").

270. ***conceive.*** I.e., "catch my meaning."

274. ***Neither his daughter... manners.*** Whereas *Cellia* is full of *manners* ("civilitie," JH, s.v. "Creanza"), her father is full of *manners* (i.e., "shit"; OED gives "maner" and "mannor" as spelling variants of "manure," which was pronounced "manner"; see HK, p. 271). Cf. and see notes: *humorous*, line 269, above, and *sodainly*, line 286, below.

275–276. ***the taller... The other.*** As *Rosalind* is the *taller* of the two ladies (cf. I.iii.123, IV.iii.93–96), *taller* may be an error and is often emended to "smaller."

276. ***banish'd.*** Exiled, with possible scatological play on "banished" as "cast out" (to "cast out" is "to void excrements," OED). Cf. and see note: *detain'd*, line 277, below.

277. ***detain'd by her usurping Uncle.*** *Rosalind* was forcibly *detain'd* ("withheld, stayed backe; restrained," RC, s.v. "Retenu") by her *Uncle* (cf. I.iii.71–74), who is (a) a "detainer" ("a wrongfull keeper of possession; a withholder of another mans right," RC, s.v. "detenteur"); and (b) as *detain'd* (i.e., "shitty"; to "detain" is "To constipate," OED) as an *Uncle* ("a necessary house," FG). Cf. I.i.17–19, wherein *Orlando*, who is also "treated like shit," is similarly *detain'd.*

279. ***deerer then the naturall bond of Sisters.*** *Le Beu* possibly hints that *Rosalind* and *Cellia* have a *bond* ("joyning together, a bonde or knot, affinitie, alliaunce, amitie, love, familiaritie, acquaintance," TT, s.v. "Conjunctĭo") that is "unnatural" (i.e., homosexual; "unnatural" is literally "Not in accordance or conformity with the physical nature of persons or animals," OED; "nature" means the "generative organs," F&H). Cf. I.i.112–113.

280. ***of late.*** *Of late* means "recently," which suggests that *Senior's* banishment is not itself recent. By contrast, I.i.100–119 seems to suggests the opposite.

Hath tane displeasure 'gainst his gentle Neece,
Grounded upon no other argument,
But that the people praise her for her vertues,
And pittie her, for her good Fathers sake;
And on my life his malice 'gainst the Lady [285]
Will sodainly breake forth: Sir, fare you well,
Hereafter in a better world then this,
I shall desire more love and knowledge of you.

Orl. I rest much bounden to you: fare you well.

{*Exit Le Beu.*} [I.ii.9] [290]

Thus must I from the smoake into the smother,
From tyrant Duke, unto a tyrant Brother.
But heavenly *Rosaline.*

Exit {*Orlando.*}

281–283. ***Hath tane displeasure... praise her for her vertues.*** *Frederick* may have detained *Rosalind* in hopes that he could solidify his claim to the throne by marrying her (cf. I.iii.73–74, and *Richard III*, wherein *Richard* seeks the hand of his *Neece Elizabeth* for exactly this reason). If so, *Frederick's displeasure* with *Rosalind* may stem from her "virtue" ("Female chastity," EP).

285–286. ***his malice... Will sodainly breake forth.*** *Duke Frederick* is full of *malice* (spite, ill-will), so *Rosalind* is in for some *malice* (i.e., some "bad shit"; *malice* is a variant of "malease," the prefix "*mal-*" means "ill, badly," and "to ease oneself" is "to relieve the bowels," OED). This *malice* will *breake forth* ("burst out, to leape or goe out of a place with violence," TT, s.v. "Prōrumpo") *sodainly* ("immediately, incontinently," RC, s.v. "Vistement"; "incontinent" is "Unable to retain natural evacuations," OED).

287. ***Hereafter in a better world then this.*** Perhaps the *better world* that *Le Beu* refers to is the *hereafter* (i.e., the afterlife). However, he might anticipate that *hereafter* ("in time to come," JF, s.v. "Infutúro") the *world* will be *better* when *Frederick* is no longer in a position of power.

288. ***love and knowledge.*** *Love and knowledge* are both euphemisms for sexual intercourse. Perhaps *Orlando's* athleticism aroused the *desire* (lust, sexual appetite) of *Le Beu* as well as *Rosalind*, for "The French enjoyed some reputation for homosexuality" (GW2, s.v. "French vice").

291. ***from the smoake into the smother.*** A variation of the proverb "from the frying-pan into the fire," which means "From ill to worse" (RC, s.v. "Braise"). Properly, the proverb here referenced is "out of the chimney into the fire" (a *smoake* is "A chimney," F&H, and a *smother* is "a smouldering or slow-burning fire," OED).

The "fire" is also "a symbol of sexual danger" (TR), so *Orlando* is imperiled not only from the *tyrant Duke* (line 292, below) but also from a *smoake* (variant of "smock": "A woman," F&H). *Orlando* is doubtless "inflamed" ("Passionately excited," OED) by *Rosaline*, and he hopes to create some *smoake* ("Copulation," JH) and *smother* ("fire": "Fierce sexual heat," EC) in her *smoake* ("chimney": "vagina," GW2).

Act I, scene iii

SCENA TERTIUS. [1]

Enter Celia and Rosaline. [I.iii.1]

Cel. Why Cosen, why *Rosaline*: *Cupid* have mercie,

Not a word?

Ros. Not one to throw at a dog. [5]

Cel. No, thy words are too precious to be cast away

upon curs, throw some of them at me; come lame mee

with reasons.

Ros. Then there were two Cosens laid up, when the

one should be lam'd with reasons, and the other mad [10]

without any.

Cel. But is all this for your Father?

Ros. No, some of it is for my childes Father: Oh

how full of briers is this working day world.

Notes I.iii.

4–5. ***Not a word... to throw at a dog.*** If *Rosaline* seems "not to have a word to throw at a dog," then she is "play[ing] at Mumbudget" or "at a Nonplus" (RC, s.v. "demeurer court"). Perhaps she is "at a Nonplus" ("a term often used, when a man can say no more, nor answer an objection," TB, q.v.) because she is "nonplust" ("at the end of [her] tether," F&H).

6–7. ***thy words are too precious... throw some of them at me.*** An allusion to Matthew 9:12: "Give not that which is holy unto the dogs, neither cast ye your pearles before swine: lest they trample them under their feete, and turne againe and rent you."

Celia suspects that *Rosaline* is being *precious* ("over-delicate, over-fastidious; affectedly refined in matters of taste, language," OED) and feels *cast away* ("rejected, cast off, refused, forsaken," JF, s.v. "Rigettato"). She hopes *Rosaline* will abandon her silent "throe" (anguish, agony) and "cast in [her] worts" (i.e., share her thoughts; "give [*Celia*] something to meditate upon or consider," OED). Cf. lines 109–110, below.

7–11. ***lame mee with reasons... mad without any.*** If *Rosaline's reasons* ("excuse[s]," TT, s.v. "Causa") amount to more than just a "Lame Excuse" ("a sorry Shift or Evasion," ND), then *Celia* invites *Rosaline* to *lame* ("lamme": "cudgell, bang, thwacke, belabor, beat," RC, s.v. "Estriller") her *with reasons* until she is *lame* (maimed, disabled). If *Rosaline* should "lay upon" (attack, beat) *Celia*, then one cousin (*Celia*) will be *laid up* ("ke[pt] indoors or in bed through illness," OED) *with reasons* (i.e., "raising[s]": "cut[s] or tear[s]," OED; "reason" was pronounced identically to "raising," HK, pp. 138–139).

The second cousin (*Rosaline*) is *mad* (sexually infatuated or excited, JH) because she is still a *mad* (i.e., a virgin; *mad* was a homophone of "maid," HK, pp. 126–127) *without reasons* (i.e., without "raisings": phallic erections). *Rosaline* has not been *laid* (i.e., "fucked") nor *lam'd* (i.e., "lime[d]": "impregnate[d]," OED; for pronunciation, see HK, pp. 174–175, 216, 221). Therefore, she will not be *laid up* (confined to bed due to pregnancy; cf. line 13, below).

13. ***some of it.*** With probable play on *it* meaning "The female pudendum" (F&H). Also see notes: *wholesome*, III.ii.56, and *summe*, III.ii.133.

14. ***how.*** Pronounced as, and with probable pun on, "ow" (i.e., "ouch!").

14. ***full of briers... working day world.*** "A workie-day" is "a weeke-day (which is no holy-day)" (RC, s.v. "Jour ouvrier"). *Rosaline* finds the *working day world* ("ordinary humdrum everyday life," OED; here specifically human love, which is, after all, a very ordinary thing) to be *full of briers* ("thornie, pricklie, crabbed, difficult," JF, s.v. "Spinoso"), for love has caused her to "sticke in the briars" (when someone ends up "in much trouble, to be so intangled that he can not get himselfe out," TT, s.v. "Hærĕo").

Perhaps *Rosaline* longs to be a "Sunday girl" ("a wanton, mistress," F&H, s.v. "tart") so that her *briers* (female pubic hair and pudenda, GW2) could *work* (copulate, JA, p. 156) and be *full* ("penetrate[d] genitally," GW, s.v. "fill") *of briers* (i.e., "pricks").

Cel. They are but burs, Cosen, throwne upon thee [15]
in holiday foolerie, if we walke not in the trodden paths
our very petty-coates will catch them.

Ros. I could shake them off my coate, these burs are
in my heart.

Cel. Hem them away. [20]

Ros. I would try if I could cry hem, and have him.

Cel. Come, come, wrastle with thy affections.

Ros. O they take the part of a better wrastler then
my selfe.

Cel. O, a good wish upon you: you will trie in time [25]
in dispight of a fall: but turning these jests out of service,
let us talke in good earnest: Is it possible on such a sodaine, you should fall into so strong a liking with old Sir
Roulands yongest sonne?

15–17. ***They are but burs... petty-coates will catch them.*** *Rosaline* can prevent *burs* (brambles, thistles) from ensnaring her *petty-coates* (skirts) by *walking in the* "trodden path" (i.e., "A usuall, beaten, or well-troden, way," JF, s.v. "Frayable").

Celia views the entanglements of love not as part of the *working day world* (line 14, above) but as "belonging to holy days" ("idle, vacant, unemployed," TB, s.v. "Ferial") and thus "idle" ("Sexually wanton," FR). Because "An idle maid is rarelie vertuous" (RC, s.v. "Fille oiseuse rarement vertuë use"), *Rosaline* should take care to stick to the *trodden paths* (i.e., the "straight and narrow"). Should *Rosaline very* (i.e., "vary":

waver, go astray) and indulge in *foolerie* ("folly": "Sexual folly: wantonness, promiscuity; wildness," EP), she will end up as a "petticoat" (whore, F&H, s.v. "tart"). Thus, her "petticoat" (vagina, GW2, s.v. "placket") will *catch burs* (i.e., "pricks"; also testicles; *burs* are literally the "sweet-bread of a Calfe," JF, s.v. "Leuisíni").

18–19. ***I could shake them off my coate... my heart.*** A *heart* torn by briars is a common metaphor for lovesickness or unrequited love (cf. *Loves pricke*, III.ii.113). *Rosaline* could easily *shake off* (cast off, get rid off) men's *burs* (i.e., genitals) from her *coate* (i.e., petticoat or vagina), but she finds it difficult to *shake off* ("abandon, quit, forsake, forgoe, waive or give over," RC, s.v. "Abandonner") the *burs* (briars, thorns) that stick in her *heart*.

20. ***Hem them away.*** If, as *Rosaline* asserts, the *burs* are not on her *Hem* ("skirt of any garment," WT, s.v. "Fimbria") but in her *heart* ("The region of the heart; breast, bosom," OED), then to dislodge them she can just *Hem* ("remove, clear away with a hem or cough," OED; cf. "My heart shall never have a wrinkle in it, so long as I can cry Hem with a cleare voice," Thomas Dekker, *The Second Part of the Honest Whore*).

21. ***cry hem, and have him.*** If *Rosaline* were able, she would *cry hem* (cough, clear her throat) and *have* (pronounced as "heave," HK, p.113) *him* (i.e., *Orlando*) from her heart.

Rosaline also wants to *have him* ("possess [him] carnally," F&H), but in order to *have* (i.e., marry) *Orlando*, she must legally *cry* ("proclaim the marriage banns of; to 'ask' in church," OED) *hem* (pronounced as "him," HK, p. 114).

22–24. ***wrastle with thy affections... a better wrastler then my selfe.*** *Celia* suggests that *Rosaline wrastle* ("struggle, or strive with," RC, s.v. "Luicter") *her* "affection," which means (a) state of mind or mental disposition; (b) passion, lust (EP); and (c) "An abnormal bodily state; a disease; a medical complaint or condition" (OED; cf. and see note: *madnesse*, III.ii.386). *Rosaline* has no desire to *wrastle* with her *affections*, because they *take the part of* ("side, bandie, be partiall, or factious," RC, s.v. "Partialiser") *a better wrastler*— i.e., *Orlando*, whom her *affections take the part of* ("adhere, or cleave unto," RC, s.v. "Participier"). *Rosaline* doubtless also wishes to *take* (carnally possess) his *part* (penis; see note: *part*, I.i.76). Also see note: *wrastled*, I.ii.254.

25. ***a good wish upon you.*** Either "good luck" or "may you get your wish."

25–26. ***you will trie... a fall.*** *In time* (sooner or later), *Rosaline will trie* (attempt, make an effort, endeavor) to "wrestle" *in dispight* (notwithstanding, regardless) *of a fall* (an overthrow or defeat in wrestling; see note: *fall*, I.i.125).

In time (at a suitable time), she *will trie* ("take the sexual measure of," JH) *Orlando* and his skills in "wrestling" (sexual intercourse; see note: *wrastled*, I.ii.254) *in dispight of* her own *fall* (loss of virginity; see note: *fall*, I.ii.46).

26. ***turning these jests... service.*** *Celia* wants *these jests* (jokes, pleasantries) turned *out of service* ("discharged and put out of paie," TT, s.v. "Ignominosa"). Cf. *out of suites*, I.ii.245.

27–28. ***sodaine.*** Of a "sudden," *Rosaline* has become "sodden" ("foolish, fantasticall"; full of "humorous toyes, fancies or conceites, giddines in the head, or qualmes over the stomacke," JF, s.v. "Capogirli") because she was struck by "love at first sight" (cf. and see note: *sodaine*, V.ii.34).

28. ***liking.*** *Liking* means "love, good will unto; a desire of, or longing after" (RC, s.v. "Affection"). EP defines "like" as "To be amorously fond of," but "passionate" or "lustful" would be closer to the mark; cf. "likorous," "likresse," or "lykerous": "Lecherous" (OED).

Ros. The Duke my Father lov'd his Father deerelie. [30]

Cel. Doth it therefore ensue that you should love his
Sonne deerelie? By this kinde of chase, I should hate
him, for my father hated his father deerely; yet I hate
not *Orlando.*

Ros. No faith, hate him not for my sake. [35]

Cel. Why should I not? doth he not deserve well?

Enter Duke {Frederick} with Lords. [I.iii.2]

Ros. Let me love him for that, and do you love him
Because I doe. Looke, here comes the Duke.

Cel. With his eies full of anger. [40]

{*Duke Fred.*} Mistris, dispatch you with your safest haste,
And get you from our Court.

Ros. Me Uncle.

{*Duke Fred.*} You Cosen,
Within these ten daies if that thou beest found [45]
So neere our publike Court as twentie miles,
Thou diest for it.

Ros. I doe beseech your Grace
Let me the knowledge of my fault beare with me:
If with my selfe I hold intelligence, [50]

30–33. ***deerelie... deerelie... hate... hate.*** The reiteration of these words is an example of a rhetorical "repeat," or "anaphora": "The repetition of the same word or phrase in several successive clauses" (OED). Cf. and see note: *chase,* line 32, below.

31. ***ensue.*** With play on *ensue* meaning (a) "follow as a logical conclusion" (OED); (b) "to inherite" (RC, s.v. "Succeder"); and (c) "To follow in a person's steps" (OED). Cf. and see note: *chase,* line 32, below.

32–34. ***By this kinde of chase... I hate not Orlando.*** A *chase* is a "Fugue": "a chase or report of Musick, as when two or more parts chase one another in the same point" (TB, q.v.), or "when one part beginneth and the other singeth the same, for some number of notes which the first did sing" (Thomas Morley, *A Plaine and Easie Introduction to Practicall Musicke*). *Celia* does not think it necessary for children to "sing the same song" ("repeat the same weakness," F&H) as their parents, nor are children and parents obliged to be "of the same sorte tunable, or musicall" ("Of one minde or wil, agreeable, of one assent," TT, s.v. "Concors").

Moreover, the musical "*Reports,* and *Fuges,* have an Agreement with the *Figures* in *Rhetorick,* of *Repetition,* and *Traduction*" (Francis Bacon and William Rawley, *Sylva Sylvarum*). "Traduction" is both (a) a "rhetorical figure consisting in the repetition of a word or its derivatives for some particular effect" (OED); and (b) "Transmission by generation to offspring or posterity" (OED). Therefore, if *Celia* follows this kind of *chase* (traduction), she *should hate Orlando.*

There may be an additional pun on "deer" and "chase" with allusion to the hunt; cf. and see notes: *seeke,* line 106, below, and *change,* line 109, below.

35–36. ***hate him not... deserve well.*** *Rosaline* asks *Celia* not to *hate Orlando* for her *sake* (with play on *sake* as a variant of "sack": vagina, F&H, s.v. "monosyllable"). *Celia* then inquires why she *should not,* because, according to *Rosaline's* own logic of line 30, above, *Orlando well* (justifiably, rightly) "deserves" (merits) *Celia's* hostility.

38. ***Let me love him for that.*** I.e., *Let me love* him because he is "well-deserving" of *love.* There is possible additional play on *that* meaning (a) "copulation" (JH); and (b) "The penis" (F&H, s.v. "prick").

41–44. ***Mistris... Cosen.*** As a Duke's daughter, *Rosaline* should properly be addressed as "My Lady." Thus, *Frederick's* use of *Mistris* is highly disrespectful, regardless of whether he intends *Mistris* to mean "whore" (F&H, s.v. "tart"). *Rosaline* attempts to appeal to *Frederick's* familial affection by addressing him as *Uncle,* but he blatantly rebuffs her with *Cosen* ("a nephew or niece," OED). He may additionally imply that she is a "cozener" ("a deceiver, an affronter," JF, s.v. "Cantoniére") or a *Cosen* ("A woman of the town, a harlot," FG).

41. ***dispatch you... safest haste.*** *Frederick* advises *Rosaline* to *dispatch* (prepare) to *dispatch* (depart). If she does not make "safe" ("certain," OED) *haste* to make herself "safe" (free from danger), she will be "dispatched" ("made an end of," RC, s.v. "Vuidé").

48. ***your Grace.*** *Rosaline* shifts from familiar entreaty (line 43, above) to the formal *your Grace,* "A courtesy-title now only given to a duke, a duchess, or an archbishop. Formerly used in addressing a king or queen" (OED). Here she appeals not to her Uncle's affection but to *Frederick's* sense of *Grace* (mercy, clemency) as a sovereign.

50. ***hold intelligence.*** Communicate with, have knowledge of.

Or have acquaintance with mine owne desires,
If that I doe not dreame, or be not franticke,
(As I doe trust I am not) then deere Uncle,
Never so much as in a thought unborne,
Did I offend your highnesse. [55]

{*Duke Fred.*} Thus doe all Traitors,
If their purgation did consist in words,
They are as innocent as grace it selfe;
Let is suffice thee that I trust thee not.

Ros. Yet your mistrust cannot make me a Traitor; [60]
Tell me whereon the likelihoods depends?

{*Duke Fred.*} Thou art thy Fathers daughter, there's enough.

Ros. So was I when your highnes took his Dukdome,
So was I when your highnesse banisht him;
Treason is not inherited my Lord, [65]
Or if we did derive it from our friends,
What's that to me, my Father was no Traitor,
Then good my Leige, mistake me not so much,
To thinke my povertie is treacherous.

Cel. Deere Soveraigne heare me speake. [70]

{*Duke Fred.*} I *Celia*, we staid her for your sake,

51. ***desires.*** Intentions.

52. ***franticke.*** *Franticke* means "witlesse, braine-sicke, braine-crackt" (RC, s.v. "Estropié de caboche")

53. ***deere Uncle.*** *Rosaline* here again changes tactics; cf. *Uncle*, line 43, above, and *your Grace*, line 48, above.

54. ***Never... in a thought unborne.*** Under the 1352 statute of Edward III (which was subsequently revised by both Henry VIII and his daughter, Elizabeth I), "When a man doth compass or imagine the death of our Lord the King, of my Lady his Queen, or of their eldest Son and Heir... it ought to be judged Treason" (Edward Coke, "Of High Treason"). Because the mere *thought* of deposing or assassinating a seated monarch was in itself treason, *Rosaline* protests her innocence by asserting that such a *thought* (dialectally pronounced "tot," HK, pp. 320–321) is as yet *unborne* ("unbegotten," JF, s.v. "Ingenerato").

56–58. ***Thus doe all Traitors... innocent as grace it selfe.*** *Rosaline* is an *innocent* (a "simpleton, an idiot," F&H) if she thinks she can achieve *purgation* ("cleering, expiation, justification, satisfaction; or the indeavor which a delinquent uses to purge himselfe," RC, s.v. "Purge") through mere *words* (pledges, guarantees). If *Traitors* needed only "graces" ("Ornaments of Speech," ND) to exonerate themselves, then *They* would be *as innocent* (blameless, free from sin) as *grace* (divinely inspired virtue; also "The source of grace, God," OED).

Additionally, *Frederick* may imply that *Rosaline* is "full of shit" (a *purgation* is an "emptying of the bowels" or "a laxative," OED; also "a glister," JM, s.v. "Aiúda").

57. ***consist.*** Depend upon, with possible play on "consistory": "court of judgement; a tribunal" (OED).

60. ***mistrust.*** Suspicion.

61. ***whereon the likelihoods depends.*** *Likelihoods* may be a collective noun as it was often used in the plural (cf. "To lay downe likely-hoods," *2 Henry IV*, I.iv.; and "poore likely-hoods Of moderne seeming," *Othello*, I.iii.).

62. ***thy Fathers daughter.*** Cf. lines 30–34, above.

65. ***Treason is not inherited.*** *Rosaline*'s argument, although heartfelt, is at odds with prevailing moral and legal opinion. High *Treason* was considered so heinous a crime that the family of the condemned suffered "attaint," or "corruption of the blood." Under this doctrine, the wife of a condemned man would "lose her Dower," and his children would "become base and ignoble... he shall lose his posterity, for his blood is stained and corrupted, and they cannot inherit to him or any other Ancestor" (Edward Coke, *The Third Part of the Institute of the Laws of England*).

66. ***derive.*** Obtain by descent.

66. ***friends.*** Kinsfolk, relatives (OED).

67. ***my Father was no Traitor.*** These are very dangerous words, because *Frederick*, who usurped *Rosaline's Father* (II.i.31–32), is by definition a *Traitor*.

68. ***my Leige.*** In addressing *Frederick* as *my Leige*, *Rosaline* attempts to make up for the dangerous intimation she made in line 67, above.

68–69. ***mistake me not... treacherous.*** If *Frederick* is so *treacherous* ("lewde, ungodlie, unnaturall," JF, s.v. "Sceleráto") as to *mistake* (i.e., "bugger"; see note: I.ii.37) his niece, she would be reduced to *povertie* (i.e., "beggary" or "buggery"; see note: *beg*, I.i.74).

71. ***staid.*** *Frederick staid* (trusted) *Rosaline* and *staid* her (kept her behind) as a "stay" ("A thing or a person that affords support; an object of reliance," OED) to *Celia*.

Else had she with her Father rang'd along.

Cel. I did not then intreat to have her stay,

It was your pleasure, and your owne remorse,

I was too yong that time to value her, [75]

But now I know her: if she be a Traitor,

Why so am I: we still have slept together,

Rose at an instant, learn'd, plaid, eate together,

And wheresoere we went, like *Junos* Swans,

Still we went coupled and inseperable. [80]

---

72. ***with her Father rang'd along.*** *Along* ("on account of," F&H) *her Father*, *Frederick* thinks that *Rosaline* should "range" ("rogue about, roame abroad, runne unsteadily from place to place, wander inconstantly up and downe," RC, s.v. "divaguer") *along* ("in company," OED) with him *along* ("At a distance, afar," OED). *Frederick* may additionally imply that *Rosaline* is a "ranger" (whore) and *her Father* a "ranger" (either a "whoremonger" or a "prick," F&H).

74. ***remorse.*** *Remorse* is (a) the "pricke of conscience; that part of the soule which opposeth it selfe unto sinne" (RC, s.v. "Synderese"); and (b) "mercie, compassion, commiseration or compunction of anothers harme" (JF, s.v. "Pietà").

75–76. ***too yong... now I know her.*** In contrast to I.i.101; I.i.108–109; I.ii.6; and I.ii.252, this line seems to suggest that *Duke Senior* was banished a long time ago.

For evidence of possible sexual double entendre on *know*, cf. lines 77–80, below, and I.ii.278–279.

76–77. ***if she be... so am I.*** I.e., "I am as much of a traitor as she is: none at all." *Celia* hints that, should *Rosaline* be judged a *Traitor*, as *Rosaline's* "spouse" she would also be "attainted." Cf. and see notes: line 65, above, and line 80, below.

76. ***Traitor.*** With possible play on "trader" as "whore" (a "trader" is a "trafficker," OED; "traffic" is "Sexual commerce," EP). Cf. and see notes: lines 77–80, below.

77. ***slept together.*** A very old euphemism for sexual intercourse. Also see note: *together*, I.i.109.

78. ***Rose at an instant.*** Ostensibly, "awoke at the same moment," with suggestion of a homoerotic relationship. The sexual imagery emphasizes the transsexual nature of the male actors who portrayed these female characters: even though the girls have

"roses" (vaginas, F&H), their sexual arousal is expressed in male terms ("rise" alludes to phallic erection, EP). *Instant*, which means "standing to a matter" (JM, s.v. "Instáncia"), reinforces the phallic imagery (cf. "If lust that's cal'd by th' sensuall Epicure, / The best of moving pleasures, and the lure, / That for the instance makes our organs rise," Richard Brathwait, "A Satyre called the Coni-borrowe"). As a synonym of "moment," *instant* may also mean "sexual climax" (GW).

78. ***learn'd.*** *Learn'd* ostensibly means "studied" or "went to school," but a "lesson" is a "coital act" (GW2). Women were expected to be virgins when they married, but that did not prevent homosexual experimentation: "the first sexual experiments of most boys and girls may well have taken the form of mutual masturbation with a member of one's own sex, or some other form of overt homosexual activity" (LS, p. 516).

78. ***plaid.*** To "play" is "to copulate" (F&H).

78. ***eate together.*** *Celia* invokes the ancient tradition of hospitality, in which a shared meal created a sacred and inviolable bond. *Eate together* is also a metaphor for sexual intercourse (EP).

79–80. ***Junos Swans... inseparable.*** *Swans* traditionally pulled the chariot of Venus, not *Juno*; typically, "the Peacock is a bird for none but *Juno*" (Robert Baron, *Erotopaignion*). Regarding the phrase *Junos Swans*, OED unequivocally states that the swan was "by Shakespeare, wrongly ascribed to Juno."

However, Venus and *Juno*, as the respective goddesses of love and marriage, were so closely associated that they were held to be interchangeable (cf. "Juno, Venus are but one," Samuel Wesley, *The life of Christ*), and if Shakespeare confused the two goddesses he was certainly not the only writer to do so (cf. "I should have deemd them *Junoes* goodly Swannes, Or *Venus* milke white Doves, so milde they are," Anonymous, *The Tragedye of Solyman and Perseda*).

Celia may purposefully substitute the "swan" (a symbol of "hermaphroditism, since in its movement and certainly in its long phallic neck it is masculine yet in its rounded, silky body it is feminine," Juan Edurado Cirlot, *A Dictionary of Symbols*) for the peacock (a symbol of lust, GW2) and *Juno* (goddess of marriage) for *Venus* (goddess of lust). Frankie Rubinstein (s.v. "Traitor") thinks the change deliberate, and Mario DiGangi agrees; in "Queering the Shakespearean Family," DiGangi asserts that "By assigning Venus's swans to Juno, Shakespeare has Celia peacefully 'couple' these often combative goddesses of love and marriage, just as she couples herself to Rosalind."

In any case, both "Venus' *Swans*" and "*Junos* Birds, the painted Jay" (Christopher Marlowe and George Chapman, *Hero and Leander*) are euphemisms for "whores."

80. ***coupled.*** *Celia* and *Rosaline* were *coupled* ("yoked together," JF, s.v. "Binato") like the birds that pull the chariot of *Venus* (see note: *Junos Swans*, line 79, above). There is possible implication that they were also *coupled* (married or mated; also "joined, in the act of intercourse," TR, s.v. "ycoupled").

Although *Celia* chooses to identify *Juno* with *Swans* instead of peacocks (see note: *Junos Swans*, line 79, above), *coupled* is a possible nod to *Juno's* "coppled" peacocks (a "copple" is a "crest on a bird's head. Hence an appellation for a crested fowl," OED). Cf. *Wedding is great Junos crowne*, V.iv.146; also see note: *crest*, IV.ii.17.

80. ***inseperable.*** *Celia* considers her bond to *Rosaline* as sacred as that of marriage, in which man and wife "are no more twaine, but one flesh. What therefore God hath joyned together, let not man put asunder" (Matthew 19:6). Cf. lines 77–80, above, and 103–104, below.

{*Duke Fred.*} She is too subtile for thee, and her smoothnes;

Her verie silence, and her patience,

Speake to the people, and they pittie her:

Thou art a foole, she robs thee of thy name,

And thou wilt show more bright, & seem more vertuous [85]

When she is gone: then open not thy lips

Firme, and irrevocable is my doombe,

Which I have past upon her, she is banish'd.

Cel. Pronounce that sentence then on me my Leige,

I cannot live out of her companie. [90]

{*Duke Fred.*} You are a foole: you Neice provide your selfe,

If you out-stay the time, upon mine honor,

And in the greatnesse of my word you die.

{*Exeunt. Manet Celia and Rosaline.*} [I.iii.3]

Cel. O my poore *Rosaline*, whether wilt thou goe? [95]

Wilt thou change Fathers? I will give thee mine:

I charge thee be not thou more griev'd then I am.

Ros. I have more cause.

Cel. Thou hast not Cosen,

Prethee be cheerefull; know'st thou not the Duke [100]

Hath banish'd me his daughter?

81. ***subtile... smoothnes.*** *Frederick* derides *Rosaline* for *her* disingenuous *smoothnes* ("gentlenesse, meekenesse," RC s.v. "Suavité") and for being a "smoother" (a "flattering sycophant, or claw-backe," RC, s.v. "Blandisseur"). He also accuses her of being *subtile* ("cunning, slye, shifting, deceitfull, false, full of tricks," RC, s.v. "Rusé").

84. ***name.*** *Name* means (a) "title of nobility"; and (b) "reputation" (OED).

87. ***Firme... is my doombe.*** *Frederick's doombe* ("A sentence pronounced: a judgement," JB, q.v.) is *Firme* ("Of a decree, law, or sentence: Immutable," OED). He has already "firmed" ("ma[de] a document valid by authoritative seal, indorsement, signature, stamp, or the like," OED) the *doombe* ("statute, law, enactment"; "ordinance, decree," OED) with his *Firme* ("Signature," OED).

90. ***out of her companie.*** *Companie* is (a) companionship; and (b) "Sexual connexion" (OED). Also see note: *out,* IV.i.81.

95. ***whether wilt thou goe.*** *Celia* twice contemplates this question (here and in line 108, below), so the ladies' ultimate destination (line 114, below) is not a foregone conclusion.

96. ***change... give.*** *Celia* first offers to *change* (exchange) *Fathers* with *Rosaline,* but then she decides that her own father is so worthless she would do better to simply *give* him away.

97–98. ***be not thou more griev'd... more cause.*** *Rosaline's cause* (ground) for grief is *more* (greater) because she has been banished along with her *more* (i.e., her father; "more" is literally "Forefathers, ancesters," OED).

Ros. That he hath not.

Cel. No, hath not? *Rosaline* lacks then the love

Which teacheth thee that thou and I am one,

Shall we be sundred? shall we part sweete girle? [105]

No, let my Father seeke another heire:

Therefore devise with me how we may flie

Whether to goe, and what to beare with us,

And doe not seeke to take your change upon you,

To beare your griefes your selfe, and leave me out: [110]

For by this heaven, now at our sorrowes pale;

Say what thou canst, Ile goe along with thee.

Ros. Why, whether shall we goe?

Cel. To seeke my Uncle in the Forrest of *Arden*.

Ros. Alas, what danger will it be to us, [115]

(Maides as we are) to travell forth so farre?

Beautie provoketh theeves sooner then gold.

Cel. Ile put my selfe in poore and meane attire,

And with a kinde of umber smirch my face,

The like doe you, so shall we passe along, [120]

And never stir assailants.

Ros. Were it not better,

104–105. ***thou and I am one... sundred.*** *Celia* uses the singular *am* because she considers herself and *Rosaline* to be *one*, and she will not allow them to be *sundred* (split in two). Cf. *inseperable*, line 80, above.

106. ***let my Father seeke another heire.*** *Frederick* is incapable of engendering another child (I.ii.18–19), so if he must *seeke* ("call to a dog to search for game," OED) *another heire* (i.e., "hare" or rabbit) he will be "made a hare" (made ridiculous, F&H, s.v. "hare"). Perhaps then he will "change his tune" (a *seeke* is a "series of notes upon a horn calling out hounds to begin a chase," OED; *heire* puns "air": a melody).

107. ***flie.*** Escape; but cf. line 79, above, where *Rosaline* and *Celia* are figured as birds.

109. ***doe not seeke to take your change upon you.*** *Celia* is "without chaunge" ("constant and stedfast," TT, s.v. "Empermutabile"), so she does not desire to be left out of *Rosaline's change* ("misfortune, case, parte, mischaunce, discommoditie, displeasure, adversitie. Also punishments that a misdoer hath for his offence," TT, s.v. "Vĭcis"). She holds *Rosaline* so "dear" (beloved, esteemed) that she will not allow her to be the only "deer" to endure the *seeke* (hunters' and hounds' pursuit; see note: *seeke*, line 106, above). *Celia* will hazard herself and force *Rosaline's* pursuers to *take change* (cause the "Hounds to riot, or to run riot; to flye out at a wrong Deere, and leave that which was first rowsed," RC, s.v. "Prendre le change").

111. ***by this heaven... our sorrowes pale.*** *Celia*, or the actor playing her, swears not just by actual *heaven* (God's abode) but by the theatre's *heaven* ("A ceiling, a canopy; *spec.* the covering over a stage," OED).

Celia suggests that *heaven* (the sky) grows *pale* (dim) in sympathy with their *sorrowes*. She assures *Rosaline* that, even though the situation now looks *pale* ("bleak," TB, s.v. "Pallid"), *heaven* (happiness, bliss) is right at the *pale* (boundary) of their *sorrowes*. As deer (see notes: lines 106 and 109, above), *Rosaline* and *Celia* will find *heaven* (pronounced "haven," HK, p. 113) once they leap the *pale* (fence) and fly *Frederick's pale* ("district or territory within determined bounds, or subject to a particular jurisdiction," OED).

114. ***Forrest of Arden.*** See note: *Forrest of Arden*, I.i.115.

116. ***Maides as we are.*** This parenthetical would have emphasized the fact that the male actors who originally portrayed *Rosaline* and *Celia* were not really *Maides* at all.

117. ***Beautie provoketh theeves.*** *Theeves* here means "rapists" (a "thief" is a "Perpetrator of illicit sexual acts," FR), who are "provoked" (enticed) by women's *Beautie* (fairness, attractiveness). *Beautie* also causes mens' *theeves* (i.e., their "pricks"; a "thief" is a "bramble," F&H; cf. *briers*, line 14, above, and *burs*, line 15, above) to be "provoked" ("stirre[d] up," TT, s.v. "Exăcerbātus"; also see note: *stir*, line 121, below).

118–119. ***poore and meane attire... smirch my face.*** *Celia* will *smirch* ("tan," OED) her *face with umber* (dirt, brown pigment) to simulate the complexion of a peasant woman. With *umber*, she can possibly disguise the fact that she is a "[h]umber" (variant of "hummer," "A man or a woman of notable parts," F&H), and she hopes that her *poore* ("needie, bare, beggerly," TT, s.v. "Pauper") and *meane* (low, humble) *attire* will render her sexually undesirable. Disguised thus, she will not *stir* (sexually arouse; to *stir* is literally to "raise up," OED) *assailants* (i.e., sexual predators; to "assail" is literally "To leap upon," "mount," OED).

Because that I am more then common tall,

That I did suite me all points like a man,

A gallant curtelax upon my thigh, [125]

A bore-speare in my hand, and in my heart

Lye there what hidden womans feare there will,

Weele have a swashing and a marshall outside,

As manie other mannish cowards have,

That doe outface it with their semblances. [130]

Cel. What shall I call thee when thou art a man?

Ros. Ile have no worse a name then *Joves* owne Page,

And therefore looke you call me *Ganimed.*

But what will you be call'd?

Cel. Something that hath a reference to my state: [135]

No longer *Celia*, but *Aliena.*

Ros. But Cosen, what if we assaid to steale

---

123. ***I am more then common tall.*** *Rosaline* is *more then common tall* because such an appearance befit the unfeminine height of William Hostler (or "Ostler"), the actor conjectured to have originated the role. (Shakespeare may have enjoyed more than a professional relationship with Hostler, who is believed by some scholars to be the enigmatic "Mr. W.H." who is credited as the "onlie begetter" of *Shake-Speares Sonnets* on the title page of the 1609 quarto.)

124. ***suite me all points like a man.*** To *suite* her purpose, *Rosaline* will *suite* (dress, attire) herself at *all points* (in every detail) *like a man*. Her *suite* (clothing) must therefore include a cod-piece to simulate a "point" (penis, EP).

125–126. ***A gallant curtelax upon my thigh... bore-speare.*** In order to look like a *gallant* ("a very fine Man; also a Man of Metal, or a brave Fellow," ND), *Rosaline* will wear a *curtleax* ("cutlass": "A short broad cutting sword," OED) *upon* her *thigh* (i.e., at her side). In addition, she will carry a *bore-speare* ("An hunting staffe, or javelin," TT, s.v. "Vēnābŭlum").

In order to pass for a *gallant* (virile man), *Rosaline* must appear to have a *spear* (i.e., penis) suitable for a *bore* (a type-figure of virility and lust, GW2) and disguise her *thigh* ("vagina," FR) as a *curtelax* ("cutlass": "penis," F&H, s.v. "prick").

128. ***a swashing and a marshall outside.*** *Rosaline* will assume an *outside* (appearance; also a suit of clothes, OED) that is *marshall* ("souldier-like," RC, s.v. "Militaire"). She will also assume an *outside* (aspect, character) that is *swashing* (swaggering, blustering) and *marshall* ("warlicke, valorous; borne under the Planet, or being of the humor, of Mars," RC, q.v.), even though such a demeanor is *outside* ("lacking internal substance, empty, superficial," OED).

129. ***mannish cowards.*** A "coward" is an impotent or effeminate man (FR; cf. RC's entry at "Pestri d'eau froide": "Effeminate, cowardlie, white-livered, without spirit, vigor, mettall"; also cf. JM's entry at "Pusilánimo": "a coward, a dastard, a meacoke"; a "meacock" is an effeminate man, GW2, s.v. "peacock").

OED cites this line as the first instance of *mannish* meaning "manly," but *mannish* was used derisively to describe masculine women from 1425. *Rosaline* is aware that, at best, her male disguise will make her appear as one of the "femalized gotish males, or mannish females, who out-stare the very Lawes of God, of Man, of Nature" (William Prynne, *Histrio-Mastix*)—i.e., she will come off as a homosexual. Cf. and see notes: line 130 and 133, below.

130. ***outface it with their semblances.*** With a manly *outface* ("outer or external face; the outside, surface," OED; cf. *outside*, line 128, above), *Rosaline* hopes to *outface* (brazenly maintain) her manly "semblance" ("shew, seeming appearance," TB, q.v.). She will be "lyke a Man, to see, in shape, in sho, That hath the Forme, and in effect is no" (Alexander Garden, "An Effoeminate Man").

132–133. ***no worse a name then Joves owne Page... Ganimed.*** *Rosaline* understands that she will never cut a very macho figure. Therefore, she selects *Ganimed*, the *name* of *Joves owne Page*, in hopes to at least pass for a *Ganimed* (i.e., a catamite; *Ganimed* was "the name of a Trojan boy, whom Jupiter so loved (say the Poets) as hee took him up to Heaven, and made him his Cup-bearer. Hence any boy that is loved for carnal abuse, or is hired to be used contrary to nature, to commit the detestable sin of Sodomy is called a Ganymede," TB, q.v.).

135–136. ***Something that hath a reference to my state... Aliena.*** *Celia* wishes to exchange her own name (which means "heavenly," from L. "caelum": "heaven") for *Something* that *hath a* more suitable *reference to* her *state* (both inner feelings and external situation). Because she is "alienated" ("estranged," RC, s.v. "Aliené") from her father, *Celia* chooses the name *Aliena*, a feminized form of "Alieno" ("an alien, a stranger, a forraine, a frenne," JF, q.v.). *Celia* plans to "alienate" ("go farre off or distant, to separate," JF, s.v. "Allontanare") herself from her father and to "alienate" ("sell, or make away [her] title to another," TT, s.v. "Emancĭpo") her *state* (high rank, throne); cf. line 106, above.

Celia's state is also "alien" ("strange": "against the course of nature," JF, s.v. "Mostruoso") because she is "coupled" (line 80, above) to *Rosaline*, a "mannish" woman (see note: *mannish*, line 129, above) and a "Ganymede" (see note: *Ganimed*, line 133, above).

The clownish Foole out of your Fathers Court:

Would he not be a comfort to our travaile?

Cel. Heele goe along ore the wide world with me, [140]

Leave me alone to woe him; Let's away

And get our Jewels and our wealth together,

Devise the fittest time, and safest way

To hide us from pursuite that will be made

After my flight: now goe in we content [145]

To libertie, and not to banishment.

Exeunt.

138. ***clownish.*** *Clownish* can mean (a) "Of the nature of a stage clown or jester" (OED); or (b) "dull, sottish, blockish" (RC, s.v. "Lourd").

139. ***travaile.*** Both (a) a journey; and (b) "trouble, molestation, care" (RC, q.v.).

145. ***flight.*** See note: *flie,* line 107, above.

145. ***goe in we content.*** Because *Rosaline* and *Celia* will no longer be *content* ("contained," OED), they will *goe* (depart) *in content* (satisfaction). Outside the constraints of court, they will have *libertie* ("sexual license," EC) to find *content* ("Sexual satisfaction," FR; JH notes that the "first syllable of this word could be pronounced so as to echo 'cunt'").

Also, the actors playing *Rosaline* and *Celia* will now *goe in*—i.e., exit from the theatre's open-air stage to the backstage, which was *in* (inside, within) the tiring house.

Act II, scene i

ACTUS SECUNDUS. SCŒNA PRIMA. [1]

Enter Duke Senior: Amyens, and two or three Lords
like Forresters. [II.i.1]

Duk.Sen. Now my Coe-mates, and brothers in exile:

Hath not old custome made this life more sweete [5]

Then that of painted pompe? Are not these woods

More free from perill then the envious Court?

Notes II.i.

4–5. ***Coe-mates... this life more sweete.*** *Senior* does not suggest to his *Coe-mates* (companions, comrades) that *life* in the woods is *sweete* (pleasant, easy) but rather that they have become inured to its hardships by *old* (familiar, longstanding) *custome* (habit; cf. "Necessity makes me suffer constantly, And custome makes it easie," John Webster, *The Tragedy Of The Dutchesse Of Malfy*). The lady *Fortune* may be an *olde* ("ugly," FG) *custome* (i.e., "customer": prostitute, GW), but her *life* ("vulva," FR) is nevertheless *sweete* ("filled with sexual pleasure," EP). Cf. and see notes: lines 6–15, below.

6–7. ***painted pompe... the envious Court.*** Traditionally, the *woods* are not *free from perill* (to be "in a wood" is to be "in a difficulty, trouble, or perplexity," OED), but the woods' *perill* is as nothing compared to the *envious* (malicious, backbiting) *Court*. The *perill* ("parel": "Ornament, decoration," OED) of the *Court* is *painted* ("garnished, gaily or trimly set forth," TT, s.v. "Pictus"), but its *pompe* ("sumptuousnesse, riches," JM, s.v. "Esplendidéza"; also "pride," WT, s.v. "Pompa") is *painted* ("Coloured so as to deceive; unreal, artificial; feigned, pretended," OED). In truth, the *Court* is a *pompe* (variant of "pump": literally "The well or sink of a ship, where bilge water collects and is pumped out; fig. a 'sink' of vice, filth, corruption, etc.," OED) that is *painted* (full of whoring and pandering, FR, s.v. "paint").

The figure is very old: Proverbs 30:28 warns that "the spider taketh hold with her hands, and is in kings palaces," and the "Whore of Babylon" herself, "With whom the kings of the earth have committed fornication" (Revelation 17:2), is *painted* as a "woman... arayed in purple and scarlet colour, and decked with gold, and precious stone & pearles, having a golden cup in her hand, full of abominations and filthinesse of her fornication" (Revelation 17:4).

Heere feele we not the penaltie of *Adam*,
The seasons difference, as the Icie phange
And churlish chiding of the winters winde, [10]
Which when it bites and blowes upon my body
Even till I shrinke with cold, I smile, and say
This is no flattery: these are counsellors
That feelingly perswade me what I am:
Sweet are the uses of adversitie [15]

8–9. ***Heere feele we not... The seasons difference.*** The greatest *penaltie* that God imposed upon *Adam* and Eve was expulsion from Eden (Genesis 3:24) and consequently mortality (Genesis 3:19). Another *penaltie* was strife: "I will put enmitie betweene thee and the woman, and betweene thy seed and her seed: it shall bruise thy head, and thou shalt bruise his heele" (Genesis 3:15). Yet another *penaltie* was God's injunction that "In the sweate of thy face shalt thou eate bread" (Genesis 3:19). Although the life of *Senior* and his followers is hard, they *feele* none of the above "penalties" because (1) *Senior* defies the adage that "exile is worse than death" (proverbial); (2) they have left enmity behind and now live in brotherhood as *Coe-mates* (line 4, above); and (3) *Senior* and his companions do not work for their food (cf. line 24, below, and II.v.42–43).

Although "Pardice... stil did florish, in eternal springe" (John Davies, *Wittes pilgrimage*), *The seasons difference* was not one of *Adam's* many "penalties"; rather, *The seasons difference* begins a new thought. *Senior* does not mind the *seasons difference* ("change, ficklenes, or unconstancie, diversitie, mutabilitie," RC, s.v. "Varietà") because the *seasons* ("spell[s] of bad or inclement weather," OED) "season" (fortify, improve, temper) him. Therefore, the *seasons* treats him with *difference* (variant of "deference": respect).

9–14. ***Icie phange... what I am.*** *Senior's* description of the *Icie* (freezing) *phange* (tooth) of the *cold winters winde* (along with II.v.10, II.vi.18, and II.vii.188–200) sets the scene as occurring in winter (probably March; see note: *velvet,* line 55, below). The timeline of *As you Like it* is imprecise, but by the end of the play spring has come in; cf. V.iii.18–35.

The *winde,* which is as mutable as the goddess *Fortune,* is the agent that traditionally delivers her *blowes* ("stripes, jerks with a whip leather, lashes, slashes," TT, s.v. "Staffilate"). Thus, a *cold winde* makes a man's *Fortune shrinke* (cf. "how the windes blew, and that the breath of his fortunes grew colder and colder," Thomas Dekker, *Penny-wise, Pound-foolish*). Although the *cold winters winde* seems *churlish* ("mercilesse, void of pitie," TT, s.v. "Inclēmens"; also "hard, grievous, fierce, stubborne, rigorous, rugged, stinging, biting," RC, s.v. "Aspero"), its *Icie phange* is not *churlish* ("without eloquence," TT, s.v. "Barbărus"). Thus, the *cold* and *winde* are trusted *counsellors* (advisors or confidents) who *perswade* ("put into the head, make sinke into the thought, or mind," RC, s.v. "Persuader") self-knowledge *feelingly,* which means (a) "Sensitively," "With emotion" (OED); (b) "Sencibly, palpably" (RC, s.v. "Sensiblement"); and/or (c) "by tryall, attemptingly, by assay," (JF, s.v. "Tentatamente").

Fortune is also a *cold* ("sexually frigid," EP) mistress with an *Icie* (unfriendly) *phange* (i.e., embrace and/or vagina; a *phange* is literally "a tight grasp, a grip," OED). Her "bite" ("Womans Privities," ND; also sexual intercourse, FR) and *blowes* (copulation or fellatio, JH) makes a man's *body* (penis, genitals, EP) *shrinke* ("wither or shrivel through withdrawal of vital fluid or failure of strength," "become reduced in size," OED; cf. *shrunke shanke,* II.vii.172, and see note: *shrunke,* III.iii.81).

13. ***flattery.*** *Flattery* is (a) "hypocrisie; a colour, or pretence; a fayning, or counterfeiting, of what one is, or meanes, not" (RC, s.v. "Simulation"); (b) "adulation, fauning, inticement, allurement, blandishment" (JF, s.v. "Lusinga"); and (c) an allusion to whoredom (to "flat" is to copulate, F&H, s.v. "greens"; to "flatter" is "To pimp or prostitute," FR). Cf. and see note: *painted pompe,* line 6, above.

15. ***Sweet are the uses of adversitie.*** This sentiment is both common and ancient. In "Of Adversity," Francis Bacon states that

> It was an high speech of Seneca, (after the manner of the Stoickes,) That the good things, which belong to Prosperity, are to be wished; but the good things, that belong to Adversity, are to be admired... Certainly, if Miracles be the Command over Nature, they appeare most in Adversity... The Vertue of Adveristy is Fortitude; which in Morals is the more Heroicall Vertue. Prosperity is the Blessing of the Old Testament; Adversity is the Blessing of the New; which carrieth the greater Benediction, and the Clearer Revelation of God's Favour.

Self-Knowledge is an especial *use* of *adversitie,* for "though the Lord give you the bread of adversitie, and the water of affliction, yet shall not thy teachers be remooved into a corner any more: but thine eyes shall see thy teachers" (Isaiah 30:20).

Senior finds the *uses of adversitie Sweet* (sexually satisfying; see note: *sweete,* line 5, above), despite the fact that *Fortune uses* (i.e., sexually *uses*) him for *adversitie* (i.e., buggery; "adversity" is literally "The state or condition of being contrary or opposed; opposition, contrariety," OED; the "contrary" is the anus, FR, because it is the sexual locus that is "contrary": "opposite to the proper or right one; the wrong," OED).

Which like the toad, ougly and venemous,

Weares yet a precious Jewell in his head:

And this our life exempt from publike haunt,

Findes tongues in trees, bookes in the running brookes,

Sermons in stones, and good in every thing. [20]

Amien. I would not change it, happy is your Grace

That can translate the stubbornnesse of fortune

Into so quiet and so sweet a stile.

Du.Sen. Come, shall we goe and kill us venison?

And yet it irkes me the poore dapled fooles [25]

Being native Burgers of this desert City,

Should in their owne confines with forked heads

Have their round hanches goard.

16–20. ***the toad... good in every thing.*** The Elizabethans thought the "toadstone" (which is actually a fossilized bit of bone or tooth) to be "a stone in the heades of olde and greate toades... which some affirme to be of power to repulse poysons" (Edward Fenton, *Certaine Secrete Wonders of Nature*). True toads (family *Bufonidae*) have *venemous* glands in their skin to deter predators, so *Senior* uses the toadstone as an example of finding *good in every thing* because the toadstone reputedly cures the "venom" of the self-same *toad* from which it came.

The *toad* is also emblematic of villainy and flattery, as well as lust and whoredom (GW2).

18. ***exempt from publike haunt.*** As exiles, *Senior* and his followers are *exempt* ("Priviledged from bearing office," HC, q.v.) *from publike* ("common, pertaining to every state of the people joyntly," TT, s.v. "Publĭcus") *haunt* ("meeting, resort, companie, assemblie," RC, s.v. "Frequence"). They are also *exempt* (free) from the *publike* (lewd, unchaste, JH) *haunt* (pronounced "aunt": "bawd or procuress," FG) of the court; cf. and see note: *painted pompe*, line 6, above.

21–23. ***happy is your Grace... so sweet a stile.*** *Senior's stile* ("manner or forme in speaking or writing," JF, q.v.) may be *quiet* and *sweet*, but it is nevertheless a powerful tool to combat fortune's adversity: a *stile* is (a) a writing implement; (b) a stabbing weapon; and (c) a ladder (OED). *Senior* is thus *happy* (fortunate), because his ability to *translate* ("interprete, expound, declare"; "tel or give the signification," "take and understand," TT, s.v. "Interprĕtor") *the stubbornesse* (implacability, ruthlesness, ferocity) *of fortune* allows him to *translate* (change, alter) his *stile* ("Condition with regard to external circumstances," OED).

24. ***venison.*** *Venison* is (a) "whatsoever Beast of the Forest is for the food of Man" (ND); and (b) "The action or practice of hunting; venery"; "venery" is both hunting and copulation (TR). This sets up the sexual metaphor of lines 25–28, below.

25. ***irkes.*** The verb "irk" ("To annoy; vex, trouble, disquiet, molest; discontent, grieve, afflict, offend; wearie, loath," RC, s.v. "Ennuyer") also exists in the compound form "forirk" ("To grow weary or disgusted," OED); cf. *forked,* line 27, below.

25. ***poore dapled fooles.*** The deer are *poore* (unfortunate) *dapled* (having mottled or spotted coats; cf. *motley,* II.vii.17) *fooles* (simpletons or innocents). They are also *poore* (i.e., "buggered"; *poore* puns L. "puer": boy, catamite, FR) and *dapled* (i.e., "screwed"; to "dabble" is to copulate, GW2).

26. ***native Burgers.*** *Native Burgers* can simply mean "indigenous citizens." However, *native* also means "born in servitude" (OED), and in German a "bürger" is specifically a member of the lower or middle class (as opposed to the ruling class).

In Elizabethan pronunciation, the pre-consonantal or final "r" was weakened (HK, pp. 261–262), so *burgers* may pun "buggers" ("burger" appears in only one other place in the Folio, where it carries similar pun; in Act I, scene ii of *Measure for Measure,* the *Clowne* relates that the city brothels "had gon down to, but that a wise Burger put in for them"). Cf. and see note: lines 27–28, below; also see note: *Citizens,* line 60, below.

26. ***desert.*** Uncultivated or uninhabited.

26. ***City.*** With possible allusion to the biblical "city of refuge" (Numbers 35:25–28 and 32; Joshua 21:13, 21, 27, 32 and 28; 1 Chronicles 6:57; and Psalms 48:2–3).

27–28. ***in their owne confines... round hanches goard.*** *Forked heads* might refer to "forked, or barbed arrow-head[s]" (RC, s.v. "Fer de fleiche à oreilles"), but arrows *with forked heads* were not typically used for hunting deer. *Forked heads* probably refers to the deer's antlers; in *The Gentleman's Recreation,* Nicholas Cox explains that "Heads having doubling Croches, are called Forked Heads, becase the Croches are planted on the top of the Beam like Forks."

A skilled hunter aims not for the *hanches* but to kill. However, the smell of blood from a wounded deer will excite the other animals in a herd, and they will "gore" ("pierce with the horns," OED) it with their *forked* ("Horned," OED) *heads* to drive it away (cf. *Jaques'* musings in lines 51–62, below). Thus, *in their owne confines* ("The borders of a City," HC, q.v.), the deer *have their round* (plump or plain) *hanches* ("thighs, hips," JF, s.v. "Coscie") *goard* ("pierced," "run through," RC, s.v. "Coufu") and *goard* (covered with blood).

The *forked heads* of the deer also symbolize cuckoldry (see note: *Citizens,* line 60, below). Because the deer have *forked heads* (i.e., are already impotent cuckolds), *Senior* thinks it a shame to also "bugger" them *in their owne confines* ("In the arse," FR). If a deer's *round* ("Homosexual," FR; also "heinous," OED, with possible play on "anus") *hanches* ("buttocks," JF, s.v. "Natiche") were *goard* (i.e., sexually penetrated), then it would indeed have a "head" ("prepuce," EP; "testes and scrotum," FR) in its "fork" ("nockandro," F&H).

"Gore" also means "Dung, fæces" (OED); this sets up the scatological imagery of lines 30 and 57, below (see notes).

1. Lord. Indeed my Lord
The melancholy *Jaques* grieves at that, [30]
And in that kinde sweares you doe more usurpe
Then doth your brother that hath banish'd you:
To day my Lord of *Amiens*, and my selfe,
Did steale behinde him as he lay along
Under an oake, whose anticke roote peepes out [35]
Upon the brooke that brawles along this wood,
To the which place a poore sequestred Stag
That from the Hunters aime had tane a hurt,
Did come to languish; and indeed my Lord
The wretched annimall heav'd forth such groanes [40]
That their discharge did stretch his leatherne coat

---

30. ***The melancholy Jaques grieves.*** *Jaques*, whom the audience will not meet until II.v., is under the influence of *melancholy* ("blacke choller, a humour of solitarinesse, or sadnesse," RC, q.v.). Like "choler" (see note: *humorous*, I.ii.269), *melancholy* was a "bowel disorder" (FR), "a malady associated... with the solitude of the close-stool" (EC, p. 110). Besides "fear and sorrow," symptoms of *melancholy* include "sharp belchings, fulsome crudities, heat in the bowels, wind and rumbling in the guts, vehement gripings, pain in the belly and stomack sometimes," and "much watering in the stomack" (RB). Consequently, a person suffering from *melancholy* would "grieve" (suffer intestinal problems or be "full of shit"; see note: *grieves*, I.i.23). *Jaques* is thus a very apt name for this *melancholy* character, who is "a pain in the ass"; his name puns "jakes": "A house of office, a cacatorium" (FG).

33. ***Amiens.*** The town of *Amiens* is located on the Somme river not far from the

Ardennes; the title of "vidame Amiens" was connected to the land of Picquigny. The *Lord of Amiens* is probably a "Vidame": "an honor in France, of which there are but four, [viz.] That of Chartres. 2. Amiens. 3. Chalons. And 4. of Gerbery. in Beauvois. A Vidame was originally the Judge of a Bishops Temporal Jurisdiction, or such an Officer to him, as the Viscount was to the Count or Earl, but in process of time, of an Officer, he became a Lord, by altering his Office into a Fief, held of the Bishoprick he belonged to; so that even to this day the Estate of all Vidames depends of some Bishoprick, or is annexed to the Temporalities thereof" (TB, q.v.).

34. ***Did steale.*** Either (a) crept; or (b) urinated ("steal" was a homonym of "stale," HK, p. 148; to "stale" is to urinate, JH).

34–35. ***lay along... oake.*** *Jaques* may *lay along* (lie prostrate) under *an oake* because (a) the tree was sacred to Jupiter (a.k.a. "Jove" or "Zeus") and was thus thought to provide protection from baleful influences; (b) the *oake* would provide shelter even in wintertime (the "French oake" is "a tree thats ever greene," RC, s.v. "Chesne vert"); or (c) *Jaques* is fatalistic and tempts fate as the *oake* proverbially draws lightning strikes. The *oake* is symbolically a suitable tree to shelter the *melancholy Jaques* (line 30, above) because "Almost every Part of the Oak is a Sovereign Medicine against Fluxes" (Thomas Ellis, *The Timber-Tree Improved*).

35. ***anticke.*** Both "ancient" and "grotesque."

35. ***peepes.*** To "peep" is "To protrude a very short distance into view" (OED).

36. ***brooke that brawles.*** *Jaques* is a "brawler" ("wrangler, contentious, or litigious person," RC, s.v. "Altercateur") who suffers *brooke* (variant of "broke": "affliction, trouble, misery," OED). Therefore, it is fitting that he should be found beside the *brooke that brawles* (roars; gushes noisily).

37. ***poore.*** See note: *poore dapled fooles*, line 25, above.

37. ***sequestred.*** Secluded or solitary; see note: *forked heads*, line 27, above.

38. ***Hunters aime.*** The *Hunters* took *aime* (directed their shots) at the deer and shot him in the *aime* (i.e., the ass; an *aime* is "a mark, or butt," OED; cf. and see note: lines 27–28, above).

39. ***languish.*** To "weare or waste away, to melt away: to draw to an ende" (TT, s.v. "Tābesco").

40–43. ***groanes... his innocent nose.*** This stag has recently lost his velvet (cf. and see note: *velvet*, line 55, below), and most male deer become sexually active shortly thereafter. Skilled "huntsmen knew venison was at its best when the stag was in 'pride of grease' immediately prior to the rut" (Malcolm Potts and Roger Short, *Ever since Adam and Eve: The Evolution of Human Sexuality*, p. 15; cf. *greazie*, line 60, below), so this stag *groanes* both in agony and in sexual excitement (*groanes* are "the Noise a Buck makes at Rutting time," ND, s.v. "growneth").

The stag's arduous death throes are expressed in terms of sexual ecstasy. *His leatherne coat did stretch* (echoic of the "leather stretcher": "penis," F&H, s.v. "prick") *Almost to bursting* (allusive to both lust and ejaculation, JA, pp. 150–151). *His coat* (scrotum, FR; *coat* plays on "cod": testicle, HK, p. 99) "discharged" (ejaculated, EC) *teares* (i.e., semen, JA, p. 142) that *cours'd downe his innocent* ("free from moral wrong," OED) *nose* (i.e., penis). Cf. and see note: *venison*, line 24, above.

41. ***leatherne coat.*** A *leatherne coat* was properly the apparel of servants and rustics and thus indicates the stag's inferior status (cf. and see note: *native Burgers*, line 26, above). This stag's fortunes have fallen since he was in "velvet"; cf. and see notes: *groanes*, line 40, above; and *velvet friend*, line 55, below.

Almost to bursting, and the big round teares
Cours'd one another downe his innocent nose
In pitteous chase: and thus the hairie foole,
Much marked of the melancholie *Jaques*, [45]
Stood on th' extremest verge of the swift brooke,
Augmenting it with teares.

Du.Sen. But what said *Jaques*?
Did he not moralize this spectacle?

1. Lord. O yes, into a thousand similies. [50]
First, for his weeping into the needlesse streame;
Poore Deere quoth he, thou mak'st a testament
As worldlings doe, giving thy sum of more
To that which had too must: then being there alone,
Left and abandoned of his velvet friend; [55]

---

42. ***big round teares.*** It was believed that "When the hart is arered, he fleethe to a ryver or ponde, and roreth cryeth and wepeth when he is take" (Stephen Batemen, *Batman uppon Bartholome*). Even though deer were "Supposed by poets to shed tears," the "drops, however, which fall from their eyes are not tears, but an oily secretion from the so-called tear-pits" (DPF, s.v. "Deer").

43–45. ***Cours'd... marked.*** Unlike the hunter who made the stag a "mark" or *aime* (line 38, above), *Jaques* "marks" (considers, remarks upon) the animal's plight as a victim of the "course" (pursuit) and *chase* (hunt).

44. ***pitteous.*** *Pitteous* is "Miserable, wretched, lamentable: pitiful, to be pitied"

(TT, s.v. "Mĭsĕrābĭlis"), with play on the stag's tears flowing copiously as from a "pit" ("a well, a waterhole; a pond, a pool," OED).

44. ***hairie.*** The deer is (a) *hairie* ("bushie, shaggie," JF, s.v. "Crinuto); (b) "harried" ("turmoiled, much troubled, or annoyed; and provoked, incensed," RC, s.v. "Harcelé"); and (c) "harried" ("ravish[ed], violate[d]," OED). Cf. and see notes: lines 27–28, above; and *groanes*, line 40, above.

44. ***foole.*** The deer is a *foole* because it wears a "mottled" or "motleyed" coat. Cf. *dapled*, line 25, above; and *motley*, II.vii.17.

46. ***th'extremest verge... brooke.*** The stag is "in the extremes" (at the very point of death), and *Jaques* must *brooke* ("bear or endure," ND) its *verge* ("end of life," OED) from *th'extremest* (outermost) *verge* (border of a river, edge of a precipice).

Jaques believes that the hunter has "brooked" (i.e., "broked": sexually violated, EP, s.v. "break") the deer's "extreme" ("extremity": "arse," FR) with his *verge* ("The male organ; the penis," OED). Cf. and see notes: lines 27–28, above.

49. ***moralize.*** To "expound morally, to give a moral sence unto" (TB, q.v.).

49. ***spectacle.*** A *spectacle* can simply be "a thing to be looked at" (RC2, q.v.) but is also "A piece of stage-display or pageantry, as contrasted with real drama" (OED). Whereas *Senior* considers the deer's agony to be an insubstantial *spectacle*, *Jaques* holds it to be very real.

51. ***weeping... needlesse streame.*** The *streame* was *needlesse* (not needy, not in want) of water, and therefore the water from the deer's *weeping* was *needlesse* ("vain, superfluous, not necessary," TB, s.v. "Suvervavuous").

53. ***worldlings.*** A "worldling" is "one that seeks after riches" (TB, s.v. "Mammonist"), "one thats throughly acquainted with, or gives himselfe wholly to, worldlie businesses" (RC, s.v. "Mondain"). The word had a decidedly negative connotation: "worldling-like" is "Prophanely; temporally; wickedly, ungodly" (RC, s.v. "Profanément").

54. ***too must.*** I.e., "too much," with play on "musch" as a variant of "must": "A reddish brown substance with a strong, persistent odour secreted by a gland of the male musk deer" (OED). An animal in *must* would be "in a condition marked by heightened aggression and unpredictable behaviour, usually occurring annually in association with a surge in testosterone level" (OED, s.v. "musth"). Cf. and see note: *groanes*, line 40, above.

54. ***then being there alone.*** I.e., "*Then*, *Jaques* drew morals from the deer's *being there alone*."

55. ***Left... of his velvet friend.*** The time at which individual deer lose their *velvet* (the thin layer of soft downy skin that covers a deer's antlers) varies by as much as a month. Stags are not generally hunted while in *velvet*, so those animals that still display it are safe from the hunters' arrows.

The stricken deer's *velvet* (i.e., rich or prosperous) *friend* have become "frenned" (strange, foreign, hostile, OED, s.v. "fren"). They now consider the wounded deer a *Left* ("A mean, worthless person," OED), so he is *Left* (neglected, forsaken) and *abandoned* ("given over; also, forgotten, overslipped, neglected, or let out, when good was t'have bene done," RC, s.v. "Delaissé").

Roebuck are in *velvet* during the winter, so this scene probably occurs sometime after the end of February; cf. "WHen you have hunted the Hare al winter... you may at the beginning of March give over the hunting thereof, and then begin to hunt the Roe" (Thomas Cockaine, *A Short Treatise of Hunting*).

'Tis right quoth he, thus miserie doth part
The Fluxe of companie: anon a carelesse Heard
Full of the pasture, jumps along by him
And never staies to greet him: I quoth *Jaques*,
Sweepe on you fat and greazie Citizens, [60]
'Tis just the fashion; wherefore doe you looke
Upon that poore and broken bankrupt there?
Thus most invectively he pierceth through
The body of Countrie, Citie, Court,
Yea, and of this our life, swearing that we [65]
Are meere usurpers, tyrants, and whats worse
To fright the Annimals, and to kill them up
In their assign'd and native dwelling place.

D.Sen. And did you leave him in this contemplation?

---

56. ***right.*** "True," with possible play on *right* as the rectum (FR). Cf. and see notes: lines 27–28, above; and *Fluxe of companie*, line 57, below.

56–57. ***miserie... Fluxe of companie.*** *Miserie* is (a) poverty; (b) sorrow; and (c) bodily pain, any of which will *part* (separate, divide) *the Fluxe* (flow, continuous stream) *of Companie* (fellowship, companionship; also a "Herd of Dear," ND). When a person is in *miserie* and his fortunes *Fluxe* (melt, dissolve, pass away), he is "treated like shit" (*Fluxe* is "laxativenesse in the bodie; the Squirt," RC, s.v. "Courance").

57. ***anon.*** Shortly thereafter.

57. ***carelesse.*** Carefree.

58. ***Full of the pasture.*** *Pasture* is "A pasture ground, or place where beasts feed" (TT, s.v. "Pascuum"). *The pasture* symbolizes wealth and plenty; as a verb, to *pasture* is "to delight, to please: to have his living by" (TT, s.v. "Pasco").

58. ***jumps along.*** The "jumped up" ("Conceited; arrogant," F&H) herd *jumps along* and abandons the wounded deer. In doing so, they "fuck" him (to "jump" is "To copulate," F&H).

60. ***Sweepe on... greazie Citizens.*** Upwardly-mobile *Citizens* were a figure of fun and were particularly associated with cuckoldry (GW2, s.v. "antlers" and "crest"). The "citizen" was figured as "a velvet-headed Cuckold" (Francis Beaumont and John Fletcher, *The Coxcombe*) and "A rascall-Deere" that "has his horns so high, they run through his hat" (Anonymous, *The Tincker of Turvey*). Cf. *forked heads*, line 27, above.

These *fat* (corpulent) and *greazie* ("very fat," JF, s.v. "Grassone") deer resemble *fat* ("indolent, self-complacent," OED) and *greazie* (fawning, flattering, F&H) *Citizens.* The arrogant herd ignores their distressed friend and "sweeps" (passes) *on* like a *Sweepe* ("The course of a river," OED; cf. *Fluxe of companie*, line 57, above). In "sweeping" (i.e., "fucking"; "sweep" is used of the male part in coition, GW2) their wounded comrade, the *Citizens* are *greazie* ("Filthy, obscene," OED) and *fat*, which means (a) "Ass-like" (FR); and (b) "shitty" (to "fat" is "to fertilize," OED)

61. ***just the fashion.*** I.e., "exactly the custom," with possible play on "fashioned" as "gelded or splayed" (FR; a *fashion* is a "cut," OED; to "cut" is "to gelde, or splaie any creature," JF, s.v. "Scoglionare"). The cuckold was held to be impotent or sexually inept; cf. and see note: *Citizens*, line 60, above.

62. ***poore.*** See note: *poore*, line 25, above.

62. ***broken.*** See note: *brooke*, line 46, above.

62. ***bankrupt.*** The *deer* is *bankrupt* in that he is both (a) "crackt in credit" (JF, s.v. "Fallito"); and (b) "buggered," because his *bank* ("seat": "posteriors," OED) is *rupt* (broken). Cf. and see notes: lines 25–28, above.

63. ***invectively.*** Using "An invective, a vehement, sore, sharpe, and bitter speaking against one, to defame his life and manners" (TT, s.v. "Invectiva").

63–64. ***pierceth through... Countrie, Citie, Court.*** *Jaques* is "piercing" ("smart; subtile, wittie, ingenious; eagre, vehement," RC, s.v. "Agu"). Therefore, he *pierceth* (minutely examines) the *body of Countrie, Citie, Court* (i.e., the entire "body politic"). The "piercing" *Jaques* is also a "jakes" (cf. RC's "Chaire percée": "A close stoole") whose "melancholy" (i.e., "shit"; see note: line 30, above) "pierceth" ("passe[s] through," RC, s.v. "Penetrer") the state's *body.*

66. ***meere.*** *Jaques* thinks *Senior* and his cohorts are (a) *meere* ("Notorious, infamous," OED; cf. and see note: *merry*, I.i.116); and (b) *meere* (i.e., "shitty"; "mire" is "Dung," and a "mere" is a "fen," OED).

67–68. ***fright the Annimals... native dwelling place.*** The hunters *fright* (scare) *and* "fret" (destroy and/or consume) *the Annimals* in the *place* that God has *assign'd* (granted) to them. They also "freight" (i.e., "bugger"; literally "burden") *the Annimals* in their *assign'd* (with play on "ass") *dwelling* (with play on "dwell" as "occupy" or "copulate") *place* ("anus," FR). Thus, *the Annimals* suffer "fret" ("Pain in the bowels, gripes, colic," OED).

69. ***contemplation.*** *Jaques* "contemns" (disdains, scorns) the exiles' forest life in his *contemplation* (musing, meditation).

2. Lord. We did my Lord, weeping and commenting [70]

Upon the sobbing Deere.

Du.Sen. Show me the place,

I love to cope him in these sullen fits,

For then he's full of matter.

1. Lor. Ile bring you to him strait. [75]

Exeunt.

73–74. ***I love to cope him... full of matter.*** *Senior* likes to *cope* ("to fight, to quarrell, to bicker, to combate," JF, s.v. "Azzuffare") *Jaques* when he is *sullen* ("melancholie, sad"; "solitarie, heavie, or pensive, full of black choler," JF, s.v. "Malincónico"), because *then he's full of matter* (topics for debate).

Senior also likes to *cope* (i.e., "fuck with"; to *cope* is "to coït with," EP) *Jaques then*, because he thinks it best to *cope* ("empty out," OED, s.v. "coup") *Jaques* (with play on "jakes") when *he's full of matter* (i.e., "shit"; literally "Faecal matter," FR; cf. and see note: *melancholy*, line 30, above).

75. ***strait.*** Immediately, with possible play on *strait* as the rectum (FR; a *strait* is literally "a narrow passage in the body," OED).

Act II, scene ii

Scena Secunda. [1]

Enter Duke {Frederick}, with Lords. [II.ii.1]

{*Duke Fred.*} Can it be possible that no man saw them?

It cannot be, some villaines of my Court

Are of consent and sufferance in this. [5]

1. Lo. I cannot heare of any that did see her,

The Ladies her attendants of her chamber

Saw her a bed, and in the morning early,

They found the bed untreasur'd of their Mistris.

2. Lor. My Lord, the roynish Clown, at whom so oft, [10]

Your Grace was wont to laugh is also missing,

Hisperia the Princesse Gentlewoman

Confesses that she secretly ore-heard

Your daughter and her Cosen much commend

The parts and graces of the Wrastler [15]

That did but lately foile the synowie *Charles*,

And she beleeves where ever they are gone

That youth is surely in their companie.

{*Duke Fred.*} Send to his brother, fetch that gallant hither,

If he be absent, bring his Brother to me, [20]

Notes II.ii.

5. ***consent and sufferance.*** Proverbially, "silence gives consent." *Frederick* thinks his attendants to be *of sufferance* (i.e., of tacit sanction) in *Celia's* flight. They have also caused *sufferance* ("Damage, injury," OED) by *sufferance* ("delay," OED) in delivering the news of her disappearance.

7–8. ***Ladies... in the morning early.*** A "lady of the chamber" is "A woman that makes profession of dressing, or decking of Brides; hence also, any waiting-woman, or chambermaid, that hath that office about hir Ladie, or mistresse" (RC, s.v. "Achemmeresse"). Because the *Ladies of* the *chamber* were tasked with dressing and undressing *Celia*, they would be the last to have seen her in the evening and the first to discover her absence *early in the morning.*

9. ***untreasur'd.*** *Celia* is herself a "treasure," but by running off she has severely compromised the "treasure" (honor, chastity, EP) of her "treasure" ("female pudendum," F&H).

10. ***roynish.*** *Roynish* means (a) "ill-favoured," "uncomelie, unhandsome" (JF, s.v. "Sfatata"); (b) morally tainted (cf. "an olde whoore, an over-ridden jade, a roynish rampe," JF, s.v. "Slandra"); (c) "Covered with scale or scurf; scabby, scurvy, coarse, mean, paltry, base" (OED), which implies being "poxed" (someone who is "Scabbed" is "Syphilitic," JH, q.v); and/or (d) "stump-legd" (JF, s.v. "Sgambo") and thus libidinous, for "men greatlie given to lecherie have for the moost parte so small and slender legges" due to the "aboundaunce of seede that maketh them so Lecherouse, which thing commeth ordinarilie to those, whose inferior parts of the bodie receive no great nourishment: Bicause all that which Nature taketh from the nether partes, is by Nature converted into superfluitie and seede" (OL).

12. ***Hisperia.*** *Hisperia* was properly one of the "Hesperides," the nymphs set to guard the tree that bore golden apples which was given by Jupiter to Juno as a wedding gift. Hercules managed to steal some of the golden apples in his eleventh labor, so this *Hisperia*, like her namesake, fails in her duty (cf. *untreasur'd*, line 9, above). Whereas the nymph *Hisperia* permitted the theft of a "golden apple" (i.e., an orange; cf. Gk. "chrysomelia" and L. "pomum aurantium"), the waiting-woman *Hisperia* lost an "orange" ("whore," GW, as *Celia* would certainly be considered if she were immodest enough to disappear from her bed in the middle of the night).

12. ***Gentlewoman.*** A woman from the lower classes was not considered a suitable companion for a lady of noble blood. Such an attendant was expected to herself be a *Gentlewoman* ("a maide or woman of good bringing up," JM, s.v. "Hijadálgo").

15. ***parts and graces.*** I.e., his manliness and virility; "grace" is the genitals (see note: *disgrace*, I.i.145) or "a sexual favour" (GW2); *parts* also alludes to the genitals (see note: *part*, I.i.76).

16. ***foile the synowie Charles.*** *Charles* has lots of "sinews" (muscles) and therefore great "Synnow" ("might, strength, force, power," RC, s.v. "Nerf"). Because *Orlando* was able to *foile* (see note: *foyle*, I.i.129) *Charles*, it can be assumed that *Orlando's* "sinew" ("Cord of the scrotum; penis," FR) is also great. Cf. and see notes: *spirit*, I.i.23, and *spirits*, I.ii.168.

19–20. ***that gallant... bring his Brother to me.*** The *gallant* ("very fine Man; also a Man of Metal, or a brave Fellow; also one that Courts or keeps, or is Kept by a Mistress," ND) is *Orlando. If he be absent, Frederick* instructs the *Lords* to fetch *his Brother* instead.

Ile make him finde him: do this sodainly;

And let not search and inquisition quaile,

To bring againe these foolish runawaies.

Exeunt.

22. ***search.*** Given the uncertain state of *Celia's* virginity, *Frederick* is especially eager that *search* ("examination, or questioning," RC, s.v. "Enqueste") should not fail to find his daughter, whom he probably plans to *search* ("to probe a woman's vagina to ascertain whether or not she is a virgin, i.e., whether or not she possesses a maidenhead," JH).

22. ***inquisition.*** Investigation; also "following, or hunting after by the foot" (RC, s.v. "Tracement").

22. ***quaile.*** To *quaile* is both (a) to fail; and (b) "to wither, to enfeeble," "to fade, to faint" (JF, s.v. "Amoscire"; supposedly "Hercules, is said to have faln into the Falling-sickness, by over much eating Quails, which disease has ever since been termed Hercules sickness," TB, s.v. "Hercules Pillars"). *Celia* has acted like a *quaile* (a "prostitute; a wanton girl or woman," EP) in running away, and *Frederick* fears that her "flight" (cf. I.iii.107 and 145) with *Orlando*, who is likened to Hercules when he pillaged the golden apples from the garden of the Hesperides (cf. and see note: *Hisperia*, line 12, above), has caused her to succumb to "falling sickness" (copulation, GW2). However, it is *Celia's* affection for *Rosalind*, not *Orlando*, that has drawn her away (I.iii.103–112).

23. ***runawaies.*** Because *Celia* and her companions have "run away" (fled) from *Frederick's* court, they are *runawaies* (renegades or traitors; a "runawaie" is one "that forsaketh his owne Captaine, runneth to the enemy, and serveth him," TT, s.v. "Perfŭga").

Act II, scene iii

Scena Tertia. [1]

Enter Orlando and Adam. [II.iii.1]

Orl. Who's there?

Ad. What my yong Master, oh my gentle master,

Oh my sweet master, O you memorie [5]

Of old Sir *Rowland*; why, what make you here?

Why are you vertuous? Why do people love you?

And wherefore are you gentle, strong, and valiant?

Why would you be so fond to overcome

The bonnie priser of the humorous Duke? [10]

Your praise is come too swiftly home before you.

Know you not Master, to seeme kinde of men,

Their graces serve them but as enemies,

No more doe yours: your vertues gentle Master

Are sanctified and holy traitors to you: [15]

Oh what a world is this, when what is comely

Envenoms him that beares it?

{*Orl.*} Why, what's the matter?

Ad. O unhappie youth,

Come not within these doores: within this roofe [20]

Notes II.iii.

5. ***memorie.*** *Orlando* is a living *memorie* ("memorial tomb, shrine, chapel, or the like; a monument," OED) of his father because he embodies his virtues.

7. ***vertuous.*** "Virtue" is both "Goodnes, honesty" (TT, s.v. "Prŏbitas") and "Physical strength" (OED); cf. lines 9–10, below.

9–10. ***fond... bonnie priser.*** *Orlando* was *fond* (foolish) to use the Duke's *bonnie* ("big-boned," RC, s.v. "Ossu") *priser* (prizefighter) as a *priser* ("estimator, valuer," "esteemer of things," RC, s.v. "Estimateur") to *fond* ("make trial of one's strength, skill," OED) his own abilities. Cf. I.ii.166–167.

10. ***humorous.*** See note: *humorous,* I.ii.269.

12–13. ***to seeme kinde of men... enemies.*** I.e., the *graces* (goodwill, favors) *of men* who *seeme* (appear) *kinde* (gentle, agreeable) become their own *enemies.* Cf. line 21, below; also see note: I.ii.35–37.

14–15. ***your vertues... holy traitors.*** *Vertues* are *sanctified* (endowed with saintly character) and *holy* (divine, sacred) because they are traditionally thought to bring blessings. *Orlando's vertues,* however, are merely *sanctified* ("sanctimonious": "Of pretended or assumed sanctity or piety, making a show of sanctity, affecting the appearance of sanctity," OED) and are "wholly" (entirely) *traitors* that bring him misfortune.

16–17. ***what is comely... beares it.*** "Venom" is literally snake poison, but figuratively "venom" is sin, the baleful influence wrought by "that old serpent, which is the devill and Satan" (Revelation 20:2); a sinner's "poison is like the poyson of a serpent" (Psalms 58:4) that *envenoms* his own soul.

Orlando beares (possesses) *what is comely* (i.e., virtue; cf. lines 7 and 14 above), but because he "bares" (reveals, manifests) this goodness in an evil world, it works as a "venom" against him (cf. lines 12–13, above).

19. ***unhappie.*** *Unhappie* can mean (a) poor; (b) unlucky; (c) suffering from misfortunes or evils; and/or (d) sad, miserable.

19. ***youth.*** *Orlando* is in his "*youth*-hood," or between the age of 14 and 22 (see note: *seven ages,* II.vii.154). This agrees with line 76, below, which suggests that *Orlando's* age is seventeen.

The enemie of all your graces lives
Your brother, no, no brother, yet the sonne
(Yet not the son, I will not call him son)
Of him I was about to call his Father,
Hath heard your praises, and this night he meanes, [25]
To burne the lodging where you use to lye,
And you within it: if he faile of that
He will have other meanes to cut you off;
I overheard him: and his practises:
This is no place, this house is but a butcherie; [30]
Abhorre it, feare it, doe not enter it.

{*Orl.*} Why whether *Adam* would'st thou have me go?

Ad. No matter whether, so you come not here.

Orl. What, would'st thou have me go & beg my food,
Or with a base and boistrous Sword enforce [35]
A theevish living on the common rode?
This I must do, or know not what to do:
Yet this I will not do, do how I can,
I rather will subject me to the malice
Of a diverted blood, and bloudie brother. [40]

Ad. But do not so: I have five hundred Crownes,

25–28. ***meanes... cut you off.*** *Oliver meanes* (intends) to "mean" (i.e., "fuck"; see note: *meanes*, I.ii.246) *Orlando* with "mean" ("Trickery; a trick," OED). *Oliver* will "meane" (variant of "main," which was "the 16th century form of maim," HK, p. 127) *Orlando* and "cut him off" (i.e., kill him or emasculate him).

26. ***burne the lodging... to lye.*** *Oliver* would hardly *burne* down his own house, so *Orlando* must "lodge" (abide, shelter) elsewhere. Possibly, he sleeps in a *lodging* ("a stable, a stall," JF, s.v., "Stallo") or in a "lodge" ("shed or out-house," OED). Cf. *staies*, I.i.10; *stalling*, I.i.12; and I.i.20–21.

30. ***This is no place... but a butcherie.*** *Oliver's* home is no *place* (stately residence; see note: *place*, I.i.21) *but* only *a butcherie* ("a slaughter house. Also a torturing place," JF, s.v. "Chianca").

31. ***Abhorre.*** Both (a) "to detest, to despise"; and (b) "to flie from" (TT, s.v. "Abhorrĕo").

32–33. ***whether... whether.*** Because *Oliver's* house is "wither" ("Hostile, adverse; fierce," OED), it does not matter *whether* (where, to what place) *Orlando* goes. If he enters here, he will end up a "wether" ("a eunuch," OED, derived from the original sense of "castrated ram"). Cf. *cut you off*, line 28, above.

35–36. ***base and boistrous... common rode.*** If *Orlando* takes the *common rode* (usual course of action) for one in his situation, he would "take to the road" ("turn highwayman," F&H). The *Sword* is a symbol of courage and justice, so as the son of *Sir Rowland de Boys* (cf. and see note: I.i.56–57) *Orlando* would be especially ashamed to use one for *base* (cowardly) *and boistrous* (violent, aggressive) purposes. Should he do so, he would prove *base* (illegitimate, bastard, OED) and *base* (unworthy) of his father's memory.

38–40. ***this I will not do... bloudie brother.*** *Rather* than stoop to crime, *Orlando* will *subject* himself to the *malice* (ill-will, spite) *of a diverted* ("alienated," "removed," RC s.v. "Destoué") *blood* (kindred, familial relationship).

Even though *Oliver* is *bloudie* ("Of good blood, well descended," OED), he is also *bloudie* ("cruell, fell, full of bloud, goarie, bloudthirstie, mercilesse," JF, s.v. "Sanguinoso"). Thus, *Orlando* is (a) *subject* to his brother's *malice* (i.e., "shit"; see note: *malice*, I.ii.285); and (b) *subject* (pathic, FR) *to* his brother's *diverted* ("perverted," JF, s.v. "Prevertito") *blood* (sexual appetite, lust, OED) and *malice* (i.e., his testicles and penis; FR derives the "testicle" sense from L. "malus": "apple," but L. "malus" is also "the mast of a ship; an upright pole," LD). Cf. *this nothing that he so plentifully gives me*, I.i.17–18.

41. ***five hundred Crownes.*** For the relative value of this amount, see note: *a thousand Crownes*, I.i.4–5.

The thriftie hire I saved under your Father,

Which I did store to be my foster Nurse,

When service should in my old limbs lie lame,

And unregarded age in corners throwne, [45]

Take that, and he that doth the Ravens feede,

Yea providently caters for the Sparrow,

Be comfort to my age: here is the gold,

All this I give you, let me be your servant,

Though I looke old, yet I am strong and lustie; [50]

For in my youth I never did apply

Hot, and rebellious liquors in my bloud,

Nor did not with unbashfull forehead woe,

The meanes of weaknesse and debilitie,

Therefore my age is as a lustie winter, [55]

Frostie, but kindely; let me goe with you,

Ile doe the service of a yonger man

---

42. ***thriftie hire.*** When *Adam* was *thriftie* ("strong and lustie," TT, s.v. "Bŏnus") and in *hire* (paid for his labor), he was *thriftie* ("parcimonious, pinching, frugall," JF, s.v. "Parsimonioso").

43. ***foster Nurse.*** A *foster Nurse* is a wet-nurse that suckles an infant. The toothless *Adam* (I.i.81–82) will need such a *foster Nurse* as he enters old age, or *second childishnesse* (II.vii.176).

45. ***unregarded age in corners throwne.*** *Age* (i.e., an elderly person) is often *unregarded* (unnoticed, unappreciated, and uncared for), so if *Adam* hadn't planned ahead, he would be "cornered" (in a fix, F&H).

46–47. ***he that doth the Ravens... Sparrow.*** In giving all he has to *Orlando*, *Adam* has faith that "providence" (God's divine care) will supply his "providence" (food, sustenance). Cf. Psalms 147:9: "He giveth to the beast his foode: and to the yong ravens which crie"; Luke 12:6: "Are not five sparrowes solde for two farthings, and not one of them is forgotten before God"; and Luke 12:24: "Consider the ravens, for they neither sow nor reape, which neither have storehouse nor barnes, and God feedeth them: How much more are yee better then the foules?"

52. ***Hot, and rebellious liquors.*** *Liquors* supposedly gave rise to *Hot* ("hastie, cholericke, fierce, furious; forward, hazardous, adventurous," RC, s.v. "Avoir le feu à la feste") "liquor" ("Humour," TT, q.v.) in the human body (see note: *humorous*, I.ii.269). Such *liquors* also caused "Rebellion in the flesh" ("the stirring of sexual appetite," JH, q.v.) and made men "rebel" (have an erection, GW; *rebellious* literally means "rising against," JF, s.v. "Ribellóso"). In *An introduction to wysedome*, Juan Luis Vives states that

> There is nothynge that can more hurte the bodies of yong men, than hotte meates and hote drynkes, for they inflame theyr lyvers, and sette on fyer theyr intrayles: And hereby mens myndes are made hotte, angry, prowde, impudent, and are thens so caryed with rashenesse, that lyke as they were madde, they seeke to accomplishe al their lustes, be they never so fylthy.

53. ***unbashfull forehead.*** The *forehead* was considered the vehicle by which *unbashfull* (immodest, intemperate) urges were translated into lewd and indulgent behaviors. In *The Contemplation of Mankinde*, Thomas Hill explains that

> Aristotle affirmeth, the forhead to be the seate or place of modestie, and honour: and the same for the neerenesse of the imaginative vertue, which with the common sence in the foreparte of the braine, is placed as principall of the heade, by force of whose vertue, either heavinesse or mirth, comelinesse or uncomelinesse, are sodenly caried unto the judgement of reason, & by the same judged. Of this we name such to have a shamelesse and brasen forehead, which put away or set aside all bashfulnesse and shame.

53. ***woe.*** *Woe* is a variant of "woo" (pursue), with possible play on *woe*: "Physical pain or distress; disease or infirmity" (OED).

54. ***The meanes of weaknesse and debilitie.*** *The meanes* is (a) sexual intercourse (see note: *meanes*, I.ii.246); and (b) masturbation (EP), both of which were thought to drain vitality and shorten the life span (GW2, s.v. "life shortened by coïtus"; this belief gave rise to the slang sense of "death" as "orgasm"). Such sexual immoderation, along with indulgence or intemperance of any kind, caused *weaknesse* ("Impotency," JB, q.v.) *and debilitie* ("faintnesse, feeblenesse, infirmitie, imbecilitie, decay of strength," RC, s.v. "Debilité"; cf. *disable*, IV.i.36, and *disabled*, V.iv.81).

55. ***lustie.*** *Adam* is no longer *lustie* ("in prime," "youthfull," JF, s.v. "Verde"). However, *Adam* did not indulge his carnal appetites in his youth (lines 51–54, above), so he remains both *lustie* ("lively, breathing, quicke, nimble, active, full of life, of long life, strong of nature, valiant," JF, s.v. "Vivace") and *lustie* ("Fertile"; "Full of lust or sexual desire," OED). Despite *Adam's* opinion of his own good health, he is nevertheless almost eighty (line 74, below), has no teeth (I.i.81–82), and is weak with age (II.vi.3–5; II.vii.137–140).

56. ***Frostie.*** A play on *Frostie* meaning (a) "Covered with or consisting of hoarfrost"; and (b) "Of the hair: Hoary, white" (OED).

56. ***kindely.*** *Adam* is still *lustie* (line 55, above), so he is also *kindely* (i.e., able to do "the deed of kind" or copulate, F&H).

In all your businesse and necessities.

Orl. Oh good old man, how well in thee appeares

The constant service of the antique world, [60]

When service sweate for dutie, not for meede:

Thou art not for the fashion of these times,

Where none will sweate, but for promotion,

And having that do choake their service up,

Even with the having, it is not so with thee: [65]

But poore old man, thou prun'st a rotten tree,

That cannot so much as a blossome yeelde,

In lieu of all thy paines and husbandrie,

But come thy waies, weele goe along together,

And ere we have thy youthfull wages spent, [70]

Weele light upon some setled low content.

Ad. Master goe on, and I will follow thee

To the last gaspe with truth and loyaltie,

From seaventie yeeres, till now almost fourescore

Here lived I, but now live here no more [75]

At seaventeene yeeres, many their fortunes seeke

But at fourescore, it is too late a weeke,

Yet fortune cannot recompence me better

Then to die well, and not my Masters debter.

Exeunt. [80]

60–61. ***constant service... meede.*** *Orlando* praises the *constant* (faithful) *service of the antique* (former) *world*, when those employed *sweate* (toiled, worked hard) *for dutie* ("good office, obligation," RC, s.v. "Debvoir"). Nowadays, he muses, those in *service* are only "desirous of *promotion*" ("Ambitious" and "greedie of honors," RC, s.v. "Ambitieux"; see note: *ambition*, I.i.140) and *sweate* only *for meede* ("a reward," "a guerdon, a recompence given to any man for his deserts," JF, s.v. "Prémio").

Orlando's view of "the good old days" is somewhat rosy. In the *antique Tale of Gamelyn* (written ca. 1350, approx. 250 years before *As you Like it*), *Adam*, "In hope of avauncement," agrees to help Gamelyn / *Orlando* only after Gamelyn promises to "parte with thee of my free lond" (i.e., give *Adam* some of his land).

66–67. ***thou prun'st a rotten tree... yeelde.*** Proverbially, "A tree is known by its fruit" (cf. III.ii.117), and "Every tree therefore which bringeth not foorth good fruit is hewen down, and cast into the fire" (Luke 3:9). *Adam* persists in a fool's errand, for *Orlando* considers himself *a rotten tree That cannot so much as yeelde* even *a blossome* (i.e., the hope or promise of achievement), let alone "fruit" (success, prosperity).

Orlando thinks himself *yeelde* (i.e., barren or impotent, FR; to "yeld" is literally "to make 'yell,' keep from breeding," OED). Therefore, *Orlando's* chances of bearing "fruit" (offspring, progeny) are as remote as those of a *tree* (an age-old phallic symbol) that (a) has been subjected to "pruning" ("A gelding, or cutting awaie of the stones," TT, s.v. "Castrātĭo"); and/or (b) is *rotten* ("Infected with venereal disease," EP; cf. III.ii.118–121).

68. ***In lieu of.*** In exchange for; as recompense for.

68. ***husbandrie.*** *Husbandrie* is a "seeding-cultivation-harvesting metaphor so common in Shakespeare when he wishes to speak of semen-sowing and sexual tillage" (EP). Cf. and see note: lines 66–67, above.

70–71. ***spent... low content.*** *Orlando* is certain that he and *Adam* will *light upon* (come upon by chance, unexpectedly discover) some *setled* (fixed, established) *low* (humble, unpretentious) *content* (state of material satisfaction).

73. ***last gaspe.*** The *last gaspe* is "the point of death" (JF, s.v. "Stare a pollo pesto"). RC gives the phrase as "A metaphor from hunting; wherein a Stag is sayd... when wearie of running he turns upon the hounds, and holds them at, or puts them to, a bay" (s.v. "Aux derniers abbois").

74–75. ***From seaventie... Here lived I.*** *Adam* has *lived Here* from the age of *seaventie* to *almost fourescore* (eighty). This short amount of time is an apparent contradiction to lines 41–42, above, but *Adam* may simply refer to the length of time that he has worked for *Oliver* as opposed to his father, *Sir Rowland*. Under *Oliver*, *Adam* has been beaten "livid" ("discoloured as by a bruise; black and blue," OED).

76. ***At seaventeene... fortunes seeke.*** *Orlando* is now *Seaventeene yeeres* old as he sets out to *seeke* his *fortunes*. This agrees with the age of *Orlando's* counterpart in *The Tale of Gamelyn*, which begins when Gamelyn / *Orlando* is in infancy. At the corresponding point in that story, *Adam* says that he "served thy brother this sixtene yeer," meaning that sixteen years ago the eldest brother took over the household upon his father's death.

77. ***too late a weeke.*** Because *Adam* is *too* "weak" (feeble), it is now *too late a weeke* ("Far too late," OED) for him to "lait" ("search for," "seek," OED) his fortune.

Act II, scene iv

Scena Quarta. [1]

Enter Rosaline for Ganimed, Celia for Aliena, and Clowne, alias *Touchstone.* [II.iv.1]

Ros. O *Jupiter,* how merry are my spirits?

Clo. I care not for my spirits, if my legges were not [5]
wearie.

Ros. I could finde in my heart to disgrace my mans
apparell, and to cry like a woman: but I must comfort
the weaker vessell, as doublet and hose ought to show it
selfe coragious to petty-coate; therefore courage, good [10]
Aliena.

Cel. I pray you beare with me, I cannot goe no further.

Clo. For my part, I had rather beare with you, then
beare you: yet I should beare no crosse if I did beare [15]
you, for I thinke you have no money in your purse.

Ros. Well, this is the Forrest of *Arden.*

Clo. I, now am I in *Arden,* the more foole I, when I

Notes II.iv.

2–3. ***Rosaline for Ganimed... alias Touchstone.*** The characters enter *for* ("in the character[s] of," OED) their false identities. The *Clowne* has assumed the *alias* (assumed name) of *Touchstone*, possibly to signify that he sharpens the wits of others (see note: *whetstone*, I.ii.56). The *Clowne*, who is himself a *Touchstone* ("one that hath a singular fine readie wit," JF, s.v. "Heraclio"), may also consider himself a standard by which to test the wits of others: a *Touchstone* is a dark piece of quartz or jasper that is rubbed against precious metals to determine their purity.

There is additional possible play on *Touch* meaning copulate (F&H) or masturbate (F&H, s.v. "touch up"), and on "stones" as the testicles.

4. ***Jupiter.*** *Rosaline*, who took on the name of *Joves owne Page* (I.iii.132), appeals to *Jupiter* (a.k.a. "Jove") as the patron god of hospitality and liberty, and as the protector of those in adversity.

4–10. ***how merry are my spirits... petty-coate.*** Line 4 evokes Matthew 26:41: "The spirit indeed is willing but the flesh is weake." *Rosaline's* confidence is waning, despite her conviction that she could conceal her womanly weakness under a mask of masculinity (I.iii.127–128). However, she makes a show of keeping up her own *spirits* (mood, frame of mind) like a man with *spirits* (i.e., with a penis and semen; see note: *spirit*, I.i.23).

Biblically, women are considered physically and spiritually inferior to men, who are charged to "give honour unto the wife as unto the weaker vessel" (1. Peter 3:7). *Rosaline* does not want to *disgrace* (dishonor) her *mans apparrell* (clothing) of *doublet and hose* (masculine attire of jacket and breeches), so she must show herself *coragious* (brave, valiant) *to petty-coate* ("the wearer of a petticoat; a woman or girl," OED). Otherwise, her masculine counterpart *Ganimed* would suffer *disgrace* (i.e., emasculation; see note: *disgrace*, I.i.145). If *Ganimed's doublet and hose* ("testicles and penis," FR) were not *coragious* (capable of "corage" or phallic erection, TR), it would betray *Rosaline's petty-coate* (vagina; see note: *petty-coates*, I.iii.17).

14–16. ***I had rather... no money in your purse.*** The *Clowne* must *beare* (support, uphold) *Celia*, who is on the point of collapse (lines 79–80, below). Given the Christian obligation to "take up the crosse" (i.e., follow Christ's example) and "give to the poore" (Mark 10:21), *Celia* is no "cross to bear" (trouble or affliction) because she *beares no crosse* ("coin generally," OED; many English coins were stamped with a *crosse*).

Even so, the *Clowne* would *rather beare* (engender children, bring forth young) *with Celia* than to *beare* (carry) her. *Celia*, however, was originally played by a male actor. Therefore, *if* the *Clowne did beare* ("bare": undress, unclothe) her/him, *Celia* would be revealed as an effeminate transvestite who (a) has "*no money in* the *purse*" (is impotent, F&H, s.v. "purse"); and/or (b) has a *purse* ("scrotum," EP) but *no money* ("female pudendum; Cunt," F&H, s.v. "monosyllable"). Therefore, the *Clowne* would *beare no crosse* (not have sex; to *crosse* is "To possess or 'cover' a woman," F&H).

18. ***now am I in Arden.*** To travel to *Arden*, the *Clowne* has disguised himself in a suit of "harden" (pronounced *Arden*, HK, p. 91), a "coarse fabric made from the hards of flax or hemp" (OED). However, the *Clowne* soon tires of his rustic "[h]arden" and resumes wearing his fool's motley; cf. II.vii.16–17.

was at home I was in a better place, but Travellers must
be content. [20]

Enter Corin and Silvius. [II.iv.2]

Ros. I, be so good *Touchstone*: Look you, who comes
here, a yong man and an old in solemne talke.

Cor. That is the way to make her scorne you still.

Sil. Oh *Corin*, that thou knew'st how I do love her. [25]

Cor. I partly guesse: for I have lov'd ere now.

Sil. No *Corin*, being old, thou canst not guesse,
Though in thy youth thou wast as true a lover
As ever sigh'd upon a midnight pillow:
But if thy love were ever like to mine, [30]
As sure I thinke did never man love so:
How many actions most ridiculous,
Hast thou beene drawne to by thy fantasie?

Cor. Into a thousand that I have forgotten.

Sil. Oh thou didst then never love so hartily, [35]
If thou remembrest not the slightest folly,
That ever love did make thee run into,
Thou hast not lov'd.
Or if thou hast not sat as I doe now,

19. ***place.*** Both (a) location; and (b) rank in the social hierarchy.

19–20. ***Travellers must be content.*** "Travel" and "travail" were interchangeably spelled. Therefore, (a) *Travellers* (those on a journey) must be *content* (satisfied) with adverse conditions; and (b) *Travellers* ("travailers": labourers, working people) must be *content* with their lot in life. Cf. III.ii.73–75.

21. ***Corin.*** A byword for a shepherd or shepherdess.

21. ***Silvius.*** *Silvius'* name is derived from L. "silva": "woods, forest" and literally means "of the forest" (Shakespeare may have first encountered this name in Virgil's *Aeneid*). The name of the analogous character in Lodge's *Rosalynde* is named "Montanus" (L. for "of the mountain").

22. ***I, be so.*** The ladies brought the *Clowne* along in hopes that he would lend moral support (I.iii.137–139), but instead they are forced to cheer him up.

24. ***scorne.*** To *scorne* is (a) "to abhorre, to mocke, to vilifie, to shame" (JF, s.v. "Scornáre"); (b) to "treat like shit" (to *scorne* is "to bid a turds on one," JF, s.v. "Incacáre"); and (c) to emasculate (FR; *scorne* is from either It. "scornare" or Old Fr. "escorner," both of which mean "to remove the horns").

29. ***sigh'd upon a midnight pillow.*** *Silvius* lies awake at night and imagines that his absent *lover* lies beside him; cf. "Nowe should I sighe; nowe my poore pillowe kisse / Entwinding it betweene my armes embrace / Ide hugg't as yf my deare duck were in place" (William Goddard, *A Satirycall Dialogue*). In *a true lover's* mind, the *pillow* becomes a *pillow* (a woman and her vagina, GW2). This is exactly the type of fetishism that the *Clowne* ridicules in lines 51–56, below.

33. ***fantasie.*** *Fantasie* is (a) sexual passion or desire; and (b) sexual intercourse (TR).

35. ***hartily.*** *Hartily* means "withall a mans hart and bowelles" (JF, s.v. "suiscer-atamente"); "entirely, from the verie inward parts" (JM, s.v. "Entrañableménte").

36. ***slightest.*** With play on "slight" meaning (a) small or flimsy; (b) foolish, unwise; and (c) loose in morals (OED).

36. ***folly.*** *Folly* means both (a) "indiscretion" (RC, s.v. "Gaillardeté"); and (b) a sexual escapade (EP).

Wearing thy hearer in thy Mistris praise, [40]

Thou hast not lov'd.

Or if thou hast not broke from companie,

Abruptly as my passion now makes me,

Thou hast not lov'd.

O *Phebe, Phebe, Phebe.* [45]

Exit {*Silvius*}. [II.iv.3]

Ros. Alas poore Shepheard searching of they would,

I have by hard adventure found mine owne.

Clo. And I mine: I remember when I was in love, I

broke my sword upon a stone, and bid him take that for [50]

comming a night to *Jane Smile*, and I remember the kiss-

ing of her batler, and the Cowes dugs that her prettie

chopt hands had milk'd; and I remember the wooing

of a peascod instead of her, from whom I tooke two

cods, and giving her them againe, said with weeping [55]

teares, weare these for my sake: wee that are true Lo-

---

40. ***Wearing thy hearer.*** Wearying the person listening to you.
43. ***passion.*** Sexual excitement or urgency (GW2).

45. ***Phebe.*** *Phebe* is "the Moone so called because she is Phebus sister" (JF, s.v. "Phebea") and is emblematic of both female chastity and inconstancy (cf. and see notes: *thrice crowned Queene of night*, III.ii.4, and *Diana in the Fountaine*, IV.i.149–150). *Silvius'* passion recalls that of *Endimion*, the shepherd in John Lyly's eponymous play, who in consumed by "melancholy passions, carelesse behaviour, untamed thoughts, and unbridled affections" for *Phebe*, the chaste and distant moon goddess.

47–48. ***searching of they would... mine owne.*** Based on the contextual evidence of *searching* ("prob[ing] a wound," OED), *they would* is a possible typesetter's error for "thy wound."

Silvius' and *Rosaline's hard adventure* (unfortunate circumstances, bad luck) spring from the same "venture" (pronounced "venter": womb, mother): their desire for *adventure* (copulation, JH, s.v. "venture"). *Silvius* is *hard* (i.e., has a phallic erection), which puts *Rosaline* in mind of her *owne* "wound" (vagina, GW). Also see note: *search*, I.i.133.

50. ***broke my sword... take that.*** In the *Clowne's* imagination, he casts a *stone* in the role of his rival and vigorously attacks it with his *sword*, bidding *him* (i.e., his *stone* rival) to *take that*. Additionally, the *Clowne* may have "broken his sword" (i.e., emasculated himself) by lavishing love on a *stone* ("a 'hard' or unfeeling person, or heart; also, a stupid person," OED).

51. ***comming a night.*** I.e., *comming* (having an orgasm) during sexual intercourse at *night* (which traditionally "afford[ed] secrecy for sexual activity," EC).

51. ***Jane Smile.*** *Jane*, like *Joan*, is a feminized form of "John." As the commonest of common names, it signifies "a Coarse Ord'nary Woman" (ND, s.v. "Joan") as well as a woman of loose morals (GW2, s.v. "Joan"; cf. *Jane Nightworke*, the name of a promiscuous woman in *2 Henry IV*). To *Smile* is "To look on or upon one with favour" (OED), which suggests that *Jane* readily "grant[ed] the favour" (consented to sexual intercourse, F&H, s.v. "ride").

52. ***batler.*** A *batler* is a club-like wooden tool used to beat laundry. However, *batler* might possibly be a variant or corruption of (a) "Batner": "an Oxe" (ND); or (b) "boulter": "sieve" (JF, s.v. "Buratto"); the sieve was a customary dairymaid's tool.

52–53. ***the Cowes dugs... milk'd.*** The *Clowne* worships the humble objects that his beloved has touched, including a *Cowes dugs* (udders, which he probably imagines as *dugs*: "woman's breasts," JH). Because his lady-love is a "cow" ("a coarse or degraded woman," OED; also a whore, F&H), the *Clowne* inverts the usual imagery of a lady's "milk-white breast" and "milk-white hand" (the white skin tone symbolized purity; cf. III.ii.382–383). *Jane Smile's hands* are *chopt* (chafed, cracked), which suggests that she is a "chopper" ("tart," F&H, q.v.) who "chops" ("exchange[s], barter[s]") her *hands* (genitals; see note: *hand*, I.ii.246). The *Clowne* probably also fantasizes about *Jane's* giving him a "milking" (i.e., a "hand job"; to "milk" is "to cause male ejaculation," EC).

53–56. ***wooing of a peascod... weare these for my sake.*** The *peascod* (peapod) is a "symbol of fecundity" (EC). A man would present a *peascod* to a woman as a token of his affection; if she accepted the gift, she granted him permission to woo her. The *Clowne* follows this custom and removes *two cods* (*peascods* or peapods) from the plant and presents them to his would-be lover (not *Jane* herself but her pea-plant stand-in). He hopes that *Jane* will accept them, for symbolically they represent his *cods* ("testicles," F&H) and *peas* ("piece": genitals, FR; N.B. that the word *peascod* is an inversion of "codpiece"). These, he hopes, she will *weare* (with "innuendo of genital friction in sexual intercourse," JH) *for* his *sake* (with play on "sake" / "sack": "scrotum," FR).

vers, runne into strange capers; but as all is mortall in
nature, so is all nature in love, mortall in folly.

Ros. Thou speak'st wiser then thou art ware of.

Clo. Nay, I shall nere be ware of mine owne wit, till [60]
I breake my shins against it.

Ros. *Jove, Jove,* this Shepherds passion,
Is much upon my fashion.

Clo. And mine, but it growes something stale with
mee. [65]

Cel. I pray you, one of you question yon'd man,
If he for gold will give us any foode,
I faint almost to death.

Clo. Holla; you Clowne.

Ros. Peace foole, he's not thy kinsman. [70]

Cor. Who cals?

Clo. Your betters Sir.

Cor. Else are they very wretched.

Ros. Peace I say; good even to your friend.

Cor. And to you gentle Sir, and to you all. [75]

Ros. I prethee Shepheard, if that love or gold

57. ***strange capers.*** *Capers* means activities or proceedings (OED). The *Clowne* might also imply that (a) *lovers runne into capers* (shrubs or flower beds) in order to *caper* ("fornicate," GW) with *strange* ("an adjective used to describe a sexually promiscuous woman," JH, s.v. "home-things") women; and/or (b) love is a "ball-busting" experience that "capers" (castrates, FR) a man and makes him "strange" (effeminate, FR). Cf. *tooke two cods*, lines 54–55, above, and *capricious*, III.iii.8. Also cf. and see note: *Aliena*, I.iii.136.

57–58. ***as all is mortall... mortall in folly.*** Those in *love* are *mortall* ("extreme, excessive," OED) *in* their *folly* (foolish or absurd ideas or actions), but their *nature* ("affection," "sexual desire," OED) *is mortall* (destined to die) because *all* (everything) *in nature is mortall.*

Also, *all nature* (the genitalia of both sexes; see note: *natures*, I.ii.50) *is mortall* ("long and tedious," OED) *in love* (i.e., sexual intercourse) and *folly* ("Lewdness, wantonness"; "lewd action or desire," OED).

59–61. ***wiser then thou art ware of... against it.*** *Rosaline* uses *ware* to mean "aware"; the *Clowne* plays on *ware* meaning "wary" and says that he will *nere* (never) *be ware* (be afraid of) his *owne wit* (awareness, intelligence) until he "breaks his shins" ("fall[s] against, or over," F&H) *it*—i.e., until it proves an impediment.

Neither will the *Clowne be ware of* his *owne wit* (i.e., penis; *wit* puns "whit" meaning "prick," FR) until *it* (sexual intercourse; see note: *it*, I.i.70; *it* can also signify the vagina; see note: *it*, I.iii.13) causes him to (a) *breake* his *shins* (suffer a sexual mishap, GW); or (b) *breake* his *shins* (i.e., contract venereal disease; the *shins* are "proverbially a site where pox produces painful nodes," GW).

62–65. ***this Shepherds passion... stale with me.*** *Rosaline* thinks that *this Shepherds* (i.e., *Silvius'*) *passion* ("harts bursting, harts griefe or sorrow," JF, s.v. "Crepacuore") *Is much upon* her *fashion*, meaning that (a) it is of the same sort or quality; or (b) she has "fassion" (knowledge, OED) of it.

The *Clowne* agrees, but adds that his own *passion* has grown *stale* (worn out, hackneyed) because it was wasted on a *stale* (whore, EP) whose infidelity made him a *stale* (a "lover... whose devotion is turned into ridicule for the amusement of a rival or rivals," F&H).

69–70. ***Clowne... kinsman.*** The *Clowne* calls *Corin* a *Clowne* ("a peasant, a countrie man, a swaine, a hinde," JF, s.v. "Contadino"), a decidedly rude form of address (cf. V.i.51). *Rosaline*, who wants to be civil, thinks the *Clowne* ("fool": jester) a *Clowne* ("fool": idiot) for behaving like a *Clowne* ("one very ill-bred or unmannerly," ND; "a loobie, a logger-head, a grosse fellow," JF, s.v. "Madarazzo").

72. ***Your betters Sir.*** The *Clowne* tells *Corin* that they are his *betters* (social superiors), but he adds a respectful *Sir* in deference to *Rosaline's* admonition.

74–75. ***your friend... gentle Sir.*** *Your* is "a dial[ectic] or vulgar pronunc[iation] of you" (OED, s.v. "yer"), so *your* may indicate *Rosaline's* attempt to disguise her refined accent. However, *Corin's* immediate assumption that [s]he is *gentle* (well-bred, educated) indicates that she does not imitate the local rustic speech very well; cf. III.ii.335–336.

76. ***love or gold.*** Equivalent to the modern phrase "love or money." *Love* here means human compassion or charity, as in Matthew 22:37–39: "Thou shalt love the Lord thy God with all thy heart, and with all thy soule, and with all thy minde. This is the first and great Commandement. And the second is like unto it, Thou shalt love thy neighbour as thy selfe." Cf. III.v.96.

Can in this desert place buy entertainment,

Bring us where we may rest our selves, and feed:

Here's a yong maid with travaile much oppressed,

And faints for succour. [80]

Cor. Faire Sir, I pittie her,

And wish for her sake more then for mine owne,

My fortunes were more able to releeve her:

But I am shepheard to another man,

And do not sheere the Fleeces that I graze: [85]

My master is of churlish disposition,

And little wreakes to finde the way to heaven

By doing deeds of hospitalitie.

Besides his Coate, his Flockes, and bounds of feede

Are now on sale, and at our sheep-coat now [90]

By reason of his absence there is nothing

That you will feed on: but what is, come see,

And in my voice most welcome shall you be.

Ros. What is he that shall buy his flocke and pasture?

Cor. That yong Swaine that you saw heere but erewhile, [95]

That little cares for buying any thing.

Ros. I pray thee, if it stand with honestie,

77. ***entertainment.*** Hospitable reception; also a meal.

79. ***travaile.*** Bodily hardship as well as journeying; see note: *Travellers*, line 19, above.

80. ***succour.*** Both (a) help or assistance; and (b) a place of shelter or refuge (OED).

81. ***Faire Sir.*** *Corin's* addressing *Rosaline* as *Faire Sir* confirms *Ganimed's* effeminate persona (OED notes the word *Faire* is used "almost exclusively of women"). Cf. IV.iii.83.

84–85. ***shepheard to another man... graze.*** *Corin* only grazes the sheep (tends to them in pasture); he does not *sheere* (shave off, remove) their *Fleeces* (wool) and thus does not *sheere* (pronounced "share," HK, pp. 206–208) the *Fleeces* ("A share of booty," OED) from their lucrative wool.

86. ***churlish.*** *Churlish* means (a) "Unnaturall," "unkind, without naturall affection" (RC, s.v. "Desnaturé"); and (b) "Uncivill; barbarous; uncourteous; ill-nurtured, rude, unmannerlie, clownish" (RC, s.v. "Incivil").

87. ***wreakes.*** *Wreakes* may be a variant of (a) "reck": "To take care or thought for or notice of something" (OED); or (b) "reak" or "reek" (variant of "reach," OED): to aim at or succeed in attaining.

87–88. ***the way to heaven... hospitalitie.*** Apparently, *Corin's* employer does not believe that "The liberall soule shalbe made fat: and he that watereth shall be watered also himselfe" (Proverbs 11:35). Neither does he heed the biblical advice to be "given to hospitalitie" (Romans 12:13); to "Use hospitalitie one to another without grudging" (Peter 4:9); or to "Bee not forgetfull to entertaine strangers, for therby some have entertayned Angels unawares" (Hebrews 13:2). Also see note: lines 14–16, above.

89. ***Coate.*** Both (a) "a sorry, slight Country-House or Hovel, now a Cottage" (ND); and/or (b) "A slight building for sheltering small animals, as sheep, pigs, fowls" (OED, s.v. "cote"). *Corin* makes reference to an additional *sheep-coat* (line 90, below), so *Coate* here probably means the former.

89. ***bounds of feede.*** The *bounds* (boundaries) *of feede* ("Feeding-ground; pasture land," OED) that provide *feede* (provender, fodder) for the animals.

90. ***sheep-coat.*** A "sheep-pen or fould" (RC, s.v. "Pecoreccio").

91–92. ***there is nothing... feed on.*** The obvious question is how there can be *nothing* to *feed on* when *Corin* has a whole flock of sheep. *Corin* cannot kill any of the sheep because they do not belong to him, but *Rosaline* and *Celia* bypass this problem by purchasing the flock (lines 98–99, below).

94. ***What is he.*** *Rosaline* inquires as to the identity and nature of the buyer in hopes of finding charity at the hands of the new owner.

95. ***Swaine.*** *Swaine* can mean (a) "a grasier, a drover, a flock-keeper, a heardgrome" (JF, s.v. "Pastore"); (b) "A freeholder within the forest" (OED); and/or (c) a lover ("swaining" is "Love-making; spooning," F&H); also see note: V.ii.85.

95. ***erewhile.*** A while ago.

96. ***That little cares... any thing.*** Presumably because *Silvius* is driven to distraction by unrequited love.

Buy thou the Cottage, pasture, and the flocke,

And thou shalt have to pay for it of us.

Cel. And we will mend thy wages: [100]

I like this place, and willingly could

Waste my time in it.

Cor. Assuredly the thing is to be sold:

Go with me, if you like upon report,

The soile, the profit, and this kinde of life, [105]

I will your very faithfull Feeder be,

And buy it with your Gold right sodainly.

Exeunt.

100. ***mend.*** *Rosaline* offers to hire *Corin* at a better rate of pay; *mend* can mean (a) improve in amount; and (b) raise the price of.

104. ***report.*** Investigation.

106. ***Feeder.*** *Corin* offers to be *Celia* and *Rosaline's Feeder* (the *Feeder* of a flock, shepherd, herdsman) as well as their *Feeder* (one who gives food to another). Cf. lines 76–78 and 90–93, above.

Act II, scene v

SCENA QUINTA. [1]

Enter, Amyens, Jaques, & others. [II.v.1]

Song.

{*Amy.*} *Under the greene wood tree,*

who loves to lye with mee, [5]

And turne his merrie Note,

unto the sweet Birds throte:

Come hither, come hither, come hither:

Heere shall he see no enemie,

But Winter and rough Weather. [10]

Jaq. More, more, I pre'thee more.

Amy. It will make you melancholly Monsieur *Jaques*

Jaq. I thanke it: More, I prethee more,

I can sucke melancholly out of a song,

As a Weazel suckes egges: More, I pre'thee more. [15]

Amy. My voice is ragged, I know I cannot please

you.

Jaq. I do not desire you to please me,

I do desire you to sing:

Come, more, another stanzo: Cal you 'em stanzo's? [20]

Notes II.v.

3. ***Song.*** The original melody for this *Song* has not survived. In *Shakespeare's Songbook*, Ross W. Duffin sets the lyrics to the traditional tune of "Sir Eglamore" on the basis that it shares an unusual seven-line stanza arrangement.

4. ***the greene wood tree.*** *The greene wood* is "taken as the typical scene of outlaw life, hence *to go to the greenwood*: to become an outlaw" (OED); cf. I.i.116–117. *The greene wood* also appears in bawdy songs as a scene of sexual assignation; cf. the double entendre of line 5, below.

The *greene* color of the foliage does not necessarily indicate that this scene takes place during the summer. See note: *oake*, II.i.35, and cf. line 10, below.

5. ***lye with.*** To *lye* is "To dwell or sojourn; esp. to sleep or pass the night in a place, to lodge temporarily" (OED). Also, to *lye with* means "to have sexual intercourse" (OED).

6–7. ***turne... the sweet Birds throte.*** The singer "turns" ("give[s] or send[s] back," "return[s]," OED) the *merrie Note* (happy song) given to him by the *sweet Birds throte.* Figuratively, "to sing a *merrie Note*" means to live a poor but carefree life: "He boldly chaunts it that hath naught to loose; wee say; and who doth sing so merrie a note as he that cannot change a groat?" (RC, s.v. "Asseurement chante qui n'a que perdre").

10. ***Winter and rough Weather.*** An indication that this scene takes place during the *Winter*; cf. and see notes: II.i.9–12 and 55; II.vi.18; and II.vii.188–200.

12. ***It will make you melancholly... Jaques.*** *Jaques* is apparently so hopelessly *melancholly* that even sure-fire remedies do nothing but worsen his condition. According to Robert Burton's *Anatomy of Melancholy*, music will "revive the languishing Soule, affecting not only the eares, but the very arteries, the vitall & animall spirits, it erects the mind, & makes it nimble... And this it will effect in the most dull, severe, and sorrowfull Soules, expell griefe with mirth, and if there be any cloudes or dust, or dregs of cares yet lurking in our thoughts, most powerfully it wipes them all away."

Also see note: *The melancholy Jaques*, II.i.30.

14–15. ***sucke melancholly... suckes egges.*** I.e., completely, for "the Weasell sucketh up the yolkes, but leaveth the shelles" (Austin Saker, *Narbonus*). In wishing to *sucke out melancholly* from *a song*, *Jaques* inverts the traditional medical terminology in which various remedies are used to "suck" *melancholly out* from the blood.

Because "egges are good against roughnes in the throat" (Thomas Twyne, *The Schoolemaster, or Teacher of Table Philosophie*), *Jaques* may also imply that *Amyens* suffers from an ailing *Weazel* ("flap of the throat," RC, s.v. "Epiglottide") and that his singing is not up to snuff.

16. ***ragged.*** *Ragged* is said "Of stone: having been roughly broken into smaller pieces" (OED). Thus, *Amyens* asserts that his voice is *ragged* ("harsh, discordant, rough," OED). Cf. *gravel'd*, IV.i.74.

20. ***stanzo's.*** A "stanzo" is (a) a "staffe of verses" (RC, s.v. "Stance"); and (b) an "Epigramme": "a title" (RC, q.v.). This sets up the wordplay on *names* in line 22, below.

Amy. What you wil Monsieur *Jaques.*

Jaq. Nay, I care not for their names, they owe mee
nothing. Wil you sing?

Amy. More at your request, then to please my selfe.

Jaq. Well then, if ever I thanke any man, Ile thanke [25]
you: but that they cal complement is like th' encounter
of two dog-Apes. And when a man thankes me hartily,
me thinkes I have given him a penie, and he renders me
the beggerly thankes. Come sing; and you that wil not
hold your tongues. [30]

Amy. Wel, Ile end the song. Sirs, cover the while,
the Duke wil drinke under this tree; he hath bin all this
day to looke you.

Jaq. And I have bin all this day to avoid him:
He is too disputeable for my companie: [35]
I thinke of as many matters as he, but I give
Heaven thankes, and make no boast of them.
Come, warble, come.

Song. Altogether heere.

Who doth ambition shunne, [40]

22–23. ***I care not... they owe mee nothing.*** *Jaques* does *not care* for the *names* of those who *owe* him *nothing* because he does not seek to recover their debts (the *names* of debtors were entered into account books; "Nomina facere," or "To make name," means "To borowe money and become debtour: or to lende money to one," Thomas Cooper, *Thesaurus linguae Romanae & Britannicae*).

25–26. ***if ever... Ile thanke you.*** Because *Jaques* never plans *to thanke any man*, he offers no thanks whatsoever.

26–27. ***complement... dog-Apes.*** "Dog-ape" can mean (a) "A Baboone, or Ape, thats faced like a dog" (RC, s.v. "Magot"); or (b) "Cynocephali": "A beast like unto an Ape, but having the face of a dogge" (TT, q.v.). The status of the Cynocephali as beast or human was hotly debated, but there was consensus as to their extremely ill nature. In *The Historie of Foure-Footed Beastes*, Edward Topsell explains that *dog-Apes* are "evill manered and natured," and that "they are as lustfull and venereous as goats, attempting to defile all sorts of women."

The deeply cynical *Jaques* thinks *complement* ("Civilitie, courtesie," RC, s.v. "Entregent") such as expressing thanks to be a thin veneer that barely conceals apathy or hostility. Men *encounter* (meet, behave towards) each other with *complement* when they truly desire an *encounter* ("an assault, a fight, a combat," JF, s.v. "Abbattimento"). This insincerity degrades a man into a "baboon" ("a stammering fellow, a foole, an asse, a doult," JF, s.v. "Babbuino"; also "a trifling, busie, or craftie knave; a crackrope, waghalter, unhappie rogue, retchlesse villaine," RC, s.v. "Baboin"). Cf. "that there should bee small love amongest these sweet Knaves, and all this Curtesie. The straine of mans bred out into Baboon and Monkey" (*Timon of Athens*, I.i.).

27–29. ***when a man thankes me hartily... beggerly thankes.*** When *a man thankes Jaques hartily* (pronounced "artily") or with "Art" ("craft, subtiltie, deceit, guile," RC), *Jaques* finds the *thankes beggerly* (mean, sordid). The gratitude is as *beggerly* ("false, counterfeit," RC, s.v. "Pietre"; also "rascallie, roguish," RC, s.v. "Truand") as the disproportionately large *thankes* offered by a "beggar" when given the *beggerly* ("scarce, little, paultrie, scantie, small," RC, s.v. "Chetif") gift of *a penie*. Thus, the *thankes* are *beggerly* ("Intellectually poor, destitute of meaning or intrinsic value," OED).

29–30. ***and you that wil not hold your tongues.*** *Jaques* tells those who do not want to sing to just shut up and not waste time giving him reasons why they won't.

31. ***cover the while.*** To *cover* is "To spread a cloth or the like over the upper surface of a table; *esp.* in preparation for a meal, to lay the cloth" (OED). If the *Lords* have no table, then they lay out a *cover* (tablecloth) on the ground, and *the while* (during that time) *Amyens* finishes his song. The *Lords* finish setting out the banquet by line 61, below.

35. ***He is too disputeable for my companie.*** *Duke Senior* seeks out *Jaques' companie* solely for the sake of argument (II.i.73–74), so it is no wonder that *Jaques* finds *Duke Senior disputeable* ("Ready or inclined to dispute; disputatious," OED).

36–37. ***I thinke of as many matters... no boast of them.*** *Jaques* keeps his deepest thoughts to himself; the speech that gives the greatest insight into the inner workings of his mind (II.i.50–68) is related second-hand by eavesdroppers who overheard him when he thought he was alone (II.i.33–35). By contrast, *Duke Senior's* stoic homily on the blessings of adversity (II.i.4–20) is delivered for the edification of his followers.

38. ***warble.*** To *warble* is "To sing, whistle, chirpe, as many birds together" (RC, s.v. "Gazouiller"). Cf. lines 6–7, above.

and loves to live i'th Sunne:

Seeking the food he eates,

and pleas'd with what he gets:

Come hither, come hither, come hither,

Heere shall he see. &c. [45]

Jaq. Ile give you a verse to this note,

That I made yesterday in despight of my Invention.

Amy. And Ile sing it.

{*Jaq.*} Thus it goes.

{*Amy.*} *If it do come to passe, that any man turne Asse:* [50]

Leaving his wealth and ease,

A stubborne will to please,

Ducdame, ducdame, ducdame:

Heere shall he see, grosse fooles as he,

And if he will come to me. [55]

What's that Ducdame?

Jaq. 'Tis a Greeke invocation, to call fools into a cir-

cle. Ile go sleepe if I can: if I cannot, Ile raile against all

the first borne of Egypt.

Amy. And Ile go seeke the Duke, [60]

His banket is prepar'd.

Exeunt

41. ***i'th Sunne.*** The exiles may live *i'the Sunne* ("free from care or sorrow," OED), but that does not necessarily mean it is warm. Cf. II.i.9–12; lines 9–10, above; and II.vii.196–198.

45. ***&c.*** An instruction to repeat the lyrics of lines 9–10, above.

46–47. ***a verse... in despight of my Invention.*** *In despight* (in contemptuous defiance of) *Jaques'* superior *Invention* (imagination; also "wit, arte, skill, knowledge," JF, s.v. "Ingégno"), he has purposely created an inferior *verse* (lyric) *to this note* (melody).

49–50. ***Thus it goes... {Amy.}*** In accordance with line 46, above, *Jaques* gives (delivers, hands over) the written verse to *Amyens* on the line *Thus it goes*. In line 50, *Amyens* sings it, as he said he would do in line 48, above.

50–52. ***turne Asse... stubborne will.*** *Jaques'* lyrics provide a very different perspective on the exiles' circumstances than *Amyens'* lyrics (lines 40–41, above). However, it is not clear whether those that *turne Asse* and leave their *wealth and ease* do so in order to satisfy their own *stubborne will* or *Duke Senior's.*

53–57. ***Ducdame... Greeke.*** In order to fill the meter established by "*Come hither*," *Ducdame* must be pronounced as three syllables. *Ducdame* is, as *Jaques* describes it, *Greeke* ("gibberish," FG), but textual critics have nevertheless proposed a wide variety of significations, including Latin "duc ad me" ("lead him from me") and Welch "Dewch da mi" ("come with me"). However, if the word is not Latin, Welch, or *Greeke,* it might be plain good English in the form of "duc" (variant of "duke," OED) and "dame" (variant of "damme": "Shortened form of *damn me!* used as a profane imprecation," OED).

57–58. ***invocation... a circle.*** In order to safely summon spirits or demons, a magician would draw two circles: one in which he himself stood, and another in which to confine the summoned specter (cf. V.iv.39 and 41). *Jaques'* verse is a magical *invocation* ("a calling upon any thing with trust in the same," RC2, q.v.) that has power to *call fools* (such as *Amyens* and the other *Lords*, who have quizzically gathered around) into a *circle.*

58–59. ***Ile go sleepe... the first borne of Egypt.*** As heirs to their fathers' estates, *all* the titled *Lords* who followed *Duke Senior* into exile are *the first borne* (cf. I.i.102–104 and lines 50–51, above). Nevertheless, they have ended up as "gypsies" ("A set of vagrants," FG).

Jaques stubbornly avoids *Duke Senior's* company (line 34, above), so if *Jaques* cannot *sleepe* it will probably be because the other *Lords* have awoken him to summon him to *Duke Senior's* banquet (cf. II.vii.10). Thus, *Jaques* threatens to *raile against* (curse) *all the first borne of Egypt* (i.e., the "sons of whores"; "gypsy" means whore, JH) who disturb his rest as mightily as "the LORD smote all the first borne in the land of Egypt... in the night" (Exodus 12:29–30).

61. ***banket.*** *Banket* is a variant of "banquet" and can mean (a) "A wine-drinking carousal" (OED; cf. line 32, above); (b) a feast; (c) a dessert; and/or (d) "a slight repast between meals" (OED). Whatever the *Duke's banket* contains, there is definitely fruit (II.vii.105) and also meat (cf. and see note: *Out-lawes*, II.vii.3).

Act II, scene vi

Scena Sexta. [1]

Enter Orlando, & Adam. [II.vi.1]

Adam. Deere Master, I can go no further:

O I die for food. Heere lie I downe,

And measure out my grave. Farwel kinde master. [5]

Orl. Why how now *Adam*? No greater heart in thee:

Live a little, comfort a little, cheere thy selfe a little.

If this uncouth Forrest yeeld any thing savage,

I wil either be food for it, or bring it for foode to thee:

Thy conceite is neerer death, then thy powers. [10]

For my sake be comfortable, hold death a while

At the armes end: I wil heere be with thee presently,

And if I bring thee not something to eate,

I wil give thee leave to die: but if thou diest

Before I come, thou art a mocker of my labor. [15]

Wel said, thou look'st cheerely,

And Ile be with thee quickly: yet thou liest

In the bleake aire. Come, I wil beare thee

To some shelter, and thou shalt not die

For lacke of a dinner, [20]

Notes II.vi.

4–5. ***Heere lie I downe... my grave.*** To "measure out one's grave" is a cynical variation of "to measure out one's length: to fall or lie prostrate" (OED) meaning to lie down with the intention of never getting up again. The prostrate person can no longer do anything useful, but at least his body can be used to *measure out* (determine the size of) his *grave.*

6. ***heart.*** *Heart* can mean (a) will; (b) strength; and/or (c) courage.

7. ***Live a little.*** I.e., *Live a little* longer.

8. ***uncouth.*** Both (a) "unknown, strange" (TB, q.v.); and (b) "solitary, desolate, wild, rugged, rough" (OED).

8–9. ***any thing savage... for foode to thee.*** In Lodge's *Rosalynde,* Rosader / *Orlando* unsuccessfully "ranged up and downe the woods, seeking to encounter some wilde beast with his rapier, that either he might carrie his friend Adam food, or els pledge his life in pawne of his loyaltie." *Orlando's* attempts at hunting *for foode* are similarly fruitless because he is armed only with a sword (II.vii.127), which is not the most effective weapon for hunting a *savage* ("untamed, wilde, cruell, fierce," JF s.v. "Immansueto") *savage* ("wild beast," OED).

Although this scene takes place in a different location than the scenes immediately prior (II.v.) and following (II.vii.), the acting space of the bare, multi-level Elizabethan stage permitted multiple locales to be depicted simultaneously. Therefore, in the original production, the *banket* laid out in II.v.31–61 would, ironically, have remained in audience view.

10. ***Thy conceite... powers.*** *Orlando* reassures *Adam* that he is only "near" to death in *conceite* (imagination), not in actual *powers* (bodily strength, vigor).

12. ***At the armes end.*** I.e., "at arm's length," at a distance.

12. ***I wil... be with thee presently.*** *Orlando* must leave *Adam* alone, but he will return *presently* (before long) with a "present" (a gift or offering) of food.

16. ***Wel said, thou look'st cheerely.*** *Orlando* commends himself for extracting a smile from *Adam.*

18. ***bleake.*** Cold. Cf. and see notes: II.i.9–12 and 55; II.v.10; and II.vii.188–200.

18. ***I wil beare thee.*** *Adam* is so weak that *Orlando* must carry him; cf. II.vii.178–180.

If there live any thing in this Desert.

Cheerely good *Adam*.

Exeunt

21. ***Desert.*** Uninhabited wilderness.

Act II, scene vii

Scena Septima. [1]

Enter {Duke Senior, Amyens, and Lords}, like Out-lawes. [II.vii.1]

Du.Sen. I thinke he be transform'd into a beast,

For I can no where finde him, like a man. [5]

1. Lord. My Lord, he is but even now gone hence,

Heere was he merry, hearing of a Song.

Du.Sen. If he compact of jarres, grow Musicall,

We shall have shortly discord in the Spheares:

Go seeke him, tell him I would speake with him. [10]

Enter Jaques. [II.vii.2]

1. Lord. He saves my labor by his owne approach.

Du.Sen. Why how now Monsieur, what a life is this

That your poore friends must woe your companie,

What, you looke merrily. [15]

Jaq. A Foole, a foole: I met a foole i'th Forrest,

A motley Foole (a miserable world:)

As I do live by foode, I met a foole,

Who laid him downe, and bask'd him in the Sun,

Notes II.vii.

2–3. ***like Out-lawes.*** A forest was "a place priviledged by Royal Authority and differs from Park, Warren, and Chase, and is on purpose allotted for the peaceable abiding and nourishment of the Beasts and Fowls thereto belonging" (Nicholas Cox, *The Gentleman's Recreation*). Hunting in a forest was strictly forbidden, and the *Duke* and his *Lords* here appear *like Out-lawes* because they carry a deer that they have killed for food. Cf. II.i.24 and I.i.115–117, where the elder *Duke* is described as living *in the Forrest of Arden... like the old Robin Hood of England.* The association between *Robin Hood* and poaching was so strong that leaders of Renaissance poaching gangs took on such aliases as "Friar Tuck" and "Robin Hood" (I.M.W. Harvey, "Poaching and Sedition in Fifteenth-Century England").

4. ***transform'd into a beast.*** *Senior* thinks *Jaques'* surliness and anti-social behavior have *transform'd* him *into a beast* ("anything unpleasant," F&H).

6. ***hence.*** *Hence* means "from here" and sets this scene as occurring in the same grove where *Amyens* and the *Lords* set out *Senior's* "banket" in II.v.

7–9. ***merry... discord in the Spheares.*** In the Earth-centered universe, the heavenly *Spheares* (planets and stars) were believed to circle the Earth on a series of concentric *Spheares* (transparent, hollow globes). The movement of these *Spheares*, which supposedly reflected the perfection of their Creator, produced the harmonious "music of the spheres." The orderly and hierarchical motion of the heavens was mirrored in the microcosm of human society, so in order to maintain "harmony" ("accord," "peace, agreement," RC, s.v. "Concorde") each person was expected to move only within his own "sphere" ("place, position, or station in society," OED).

Jaques is *compact* (made, comprised) of *jarres* ("Quarrels, Disputes, Contentions," ND). For *Jaques* to be *merry* and *grow Musicall* (fond of music; also "harmonious, delightsome, pleasing," RC, s.v. "Acroamatique") *hearing of* (listening to) *a song*, he would need to step far outside his usual melancholic "sphere" (quality, aspect). Therefore, *We shall shortly* (in a short time) *have discord* ("Warre; warfare," "strife, contention, debate," RC, s.v. "guerre") and *jarres* (wrong notes, want of harmony) *in the Spheares*—i.e., an apocalypse.

16–17. ***a foole i'th Forrest... a miserable world.*** *Jaques* thinks little of the inhabitants of "this wide forrest of fooles (the world)" (Thomas Dekker, *The Guls Horne-Booke*). Therefore, *Jaques* finds it incredible that he should meet a wise man *i'the Forrest* clad in a "Fool's Coat, or Colours, a Motley or incongruous Colours too near a Kin to match, as Red and Yellow, which is the Fool's Coat with us, as Blew and Green is with the French" (ND). *Jaques* thinks this *world* to be *miserable* ("wretched, lamentable: pitiful," TT, s.v. "Mĭsĕrābĭlis") because the *miserable* ("unworthy, inadequate," OED) *world* (pronounced "word," HH, p. 208) "fool" should be used of someone so *noble* and *worthy* (lines 37–38, below).

18. ***live by foode.*** Because "man doth not live by bread onely" (Deuteronomy 8:3), he also requires *foode* for his mind such as the intelligent conversation provided by the *Clowne*.

19. ***laid him downe.*** Both (a) fell prostrate; and (b) gave up, surrendered.

19. ***bask'd.*** To "bask" is (a) to bathe; and (b) "to be suffused with, or swim in, blood" (OED). Cf. and see note: *termes*, line 20, below.

19. ***in the Sun.*** See note: *i'th Sunne*, II.v.41.

And rail'd on Lady Fortune in good termes, [20]
In good set termes, and yet a motley foole.
Good morrow foole (quoth I:) no Sir, quoth he,
Call me not foole, till heaven hath sent me fortune,
And then he drew a diall from his poake,
And looking on it, with lacke-lustre eye, [25]
Sayes, very wisely, it is ten a clocke:
Thus we may see (quoth he) how the world wagges:
'Tis but an houre agoe, since it was nine,
And after one houre more, 'twill be eleven,
And so from houre to houre, we ripe, and ripe, [30]
And then from houre to houre, we rot, and rot,
And thereby hangs a tale. When I did heare
The motley Foole, thus morall on the time,

---

20. ***rail'd on Lady Fortune... termes.*** The *Lady Fortune* is not *good* even in the best of times (cf. I.ii.32–51), but she is especially inhospitable when in her *termes* ("Menses": "the flowers, fluxe, issue, or naturall purgation of women monthly," TT, q.v.). The *Clowne* knows he is not on *good termes* (friendly, in good standing) with the *Lady Fortune* because she has *rail'd on* him (i.e., bled on him; to "rail" is "Of blood, tears, etc.: to flow, to pour, to gush," OED; it was believed that "menstruall bloud is

venemouse," OL). Therefore, the *Clowne* "rails on" (derides, verbally abuses) the *Lady Fortune in termes* ("in express words, expressly, plainly," OED) that are *set*, meaning (a) elaborate, thorough; (b) grave, orderly; and/or (c) "Deliberately composed, not spontaneously arising" (OED).

23. ***Call me not foole... fortune.*** Proverbially, "fortune favors fools." The *Clowne* insists that he cannot be a *foole* because he is not fortunate; cf. line 20, above.

24. ***drew a diall from his poake.*** The fool *drew a diall* ("a clocke, an howerglasse, a watch," JF, s.v. "Horiólo") *from his poake* ("wallet, scrip, satchell, bag, pouch," RC, s.v. "Besace") in order to contemplate his mortality. The *diall* is a powerful memento mori, but the *diall* also puts the *Clowne* in mind of using his *diall* (penis, EP) and *poake* (scrotum, TR) to have a *poake* ("An act of coition," F&H) with a *diall* ("a metaphor for the pudend," EP; F&H are somewhat more direct with their definition of "clock" as "cunt," s.v. "monosyllable"). Cf. the double entendre in lines 25–32, below (see notes).

25. ***lacke-lustre eye.*** *Lacke-lustre* means (a) dull or depressed; and (b) lacking "lustre" or brightness. Traditionally, *lacke-lustre* eyesight was regarded as a consequence of sexual indulgence, for "Much use of Venus doth Dimme the Sight" (Francis Bacon and William Rawley, *Sylva Sylvarum*). Also see note: lines 42–44, below.

26–29. ***ten a clocke... eleven.*** The *Clowne's* musings on the *houre* (time) hold moral significance (cf. line 33, below). Traditionally, *ten* "is the perfection of all Numbers and conteineth in it selfe all numbers of perfection. And this is the opinion of the Pythagorians and Arithmetitians" (Helkia Crooke, *Mikrokosmographia*). *Nine* and *eleven* were held to be inherently evil numbers: *nine* signified defect because it fell short of *ten*, and *eleven* signified moral transgression because it went beyond *ten* (Christopher Butler, *Number Symbolism*, pp. 29–30).

Even though the fool is now at the *houre* of *ten* (i.e., in the "perfection" or prime of life), it seems like only an *houre* ago that it was *nine* (i.e., that he was a child in the womb; *nine* symbolizes the "period of gestation," GW); and in only an *houre* more *'twill be eleven* (symbolic of old age and decay; cf. George Rivers' *The Heroinae*: "her brest lanke as a quicksand, wasted as an hour-glasse at the eleventh use"). The *Clowne's* musings on the passage of time inspire *Jaques'* own contemplation of the "stages" of human life in lines 150–177, below.

27. ***wagges.*** To "wag" is (a) to travel or move along swiftly (OED); and (b) to copulate (GW). See note: *houre*, line 30, below.

30–31. ***from houre to houre... rot, and rot.*** *From houre to houre, we ripe* ("come to maturity" ND), *and ripe* ("be in the flower of age," TT, s.v. "Pŭbeo"), and then *from houre to houre, we rot* (grow old), *and rot* (decay in the grave).

A *ripe* is also "the bank of a river, such as the Bank in Southwark, where the brothels were" (FR), and the word *houre* was pronounced identically to "whore" (HK, pp. 117–118). Should a man *ripe* (have a phallic erection; literally "have the full bignes," TT, s.v. "Mātūresco") and *ripe* ("grope," OED) *an houre* (i.e., a whore) in a *ripe* (suburban whorehouse), then he will *rot* ("become faint, unlustie, and drooping," JF, s.v. "Marcire") *and rot* ("waste away from the effects of venereal disease," JH). Cf. III.ii.120.

32. ***thereby hangs a tale.*** *Thereby* (because of that, consequently) *a tale* (story, history) *hangs* (depends; also "remain[s] in consideration or attention," OED), and *thereby hangs a tale* ("about that there is something to tell," OED). Also, a venereally infected "tail" ("penis," F&H) *hangs* (droops, withers), so *thereby hangs a tale* ("a penis dangles because of that," EC).

My Lungs began to crow like Chanticleere,

That Fooles should be so deepe contemplative: [35]

And I did laugh, sans intermission

An houre by his diall. Oh noble foole,

A worthy foole: Motley's the onely weare.

Du.Sen. What foole is this?

Jaq. O worthie Foole: One that hath bin a Courtier [40]

And sayes, if Ladies be but yong, and faire,

They have the gift to know it: and in his braine,

Which is as drie as the remainder bisket

After a voyage: He hath strange places cram'd

With observation, the which he vents [45]

In mangled formes. O that I were a foole,

I am ambitious for a motley coat.

Du.Sen. Thou shalt have one.

Jaq. It is my onely suite,

---

34. ***Chanticleere.*** *Chanticleere* was the name of the rooster in the *Reynard the Fox* folktales, but in listening to the Fool *morall on the time* (line 33, above) *Jaques* recalls the "Chauntecleer" of Geoffrey Chaucer's *The Nonne Preestes Tale*, who

> In al the land of crowing nas his peer.
> His vois was merier than the mery orgon
> On messe-dayes that in the chirche gon;
> Wel sikerer [i.e., strong or confident] was his crowing in his logge,
> Than is a clokke, or an abbey orlogge.

36. ***sans intermission.*** *Jaques did laugh sans* (without) *intermission* ("pawse," "stop, ceasing; repose, resting," RC, s.v. "Pose").

40. ***Courtier.*** A *Courtier* is (a) "a man that haunteth, useth frequenteth, followeth, and keepeth at the court" (TT, s.v., "Aulĭcus"); (b) a play on "courter": "One who courts; a wooer" (OED; cf. line 41, below); (c) a "Broker" (RC, q.v.); and/or (d) a "pimp" (FR).

41–42. ***if Ladies... know it.*** The *Clowne* suggests that *yong and faire Ladies* who *know* the worth of their own "gifts" (endowments, qualities) always require a *gift* ("A fee for services rendered," OED) before they bestow their *gift* ("The sexual gift; genitals," FR).

42–44. ***his braine... After a voyage.*** *Bisket* ("Bread not well baked, or after other rough bread twise baked," TT, s.v. "Rudibus panis") kept very well, so it was commonly used for provisions on ships. *Bisket* was *drie* before *A voyage* even began, but the *remainder* (leftover) *bisket* would be especially so.

Perhaps *Jaques* praises the *Clowne* for his *drie* (ironic) *braine* (imagination, wit), but most likely he recognizes the *Clowne* as a kindred spirit. Melancholy was a *drie* humor (see note: *humorous*, I.ii.269), and men "will be soonest melancholy... by reason of the drinesse of their braines" (RB; also see note: *Schollers melancholy*, IV.i.12). Even so, a *drie braine* has its benefits: "the drie braine retaines more steadily" (John Davies, *Mirum in modum*), so those with a *drie braine* possess an excellent memory (cf. lines 44–45, below). Moreover, "melancholy men are witty, which Aristotle hath long since maintained in his Problems; and that all learned men, famous Philosophers, and Law-givers have still beene melancholy" (RB).

Sexual intemperance was thought to cause melancholy (see notes: *travells*, IV.i.19, and *Traveller*, IV.i.22), and the *Clowne* does have some experience with *Ladies yong and faire* (line 41, above). Therefore, his *braine* (scrotum or penis, FR) may be as *drie* (drained of semen, JH) as a *bisket* (sexual organ, GW2) *After a voyage* (copulation, GW).

44–45. ***strange places cram'd... formes.*** Like *Jaques* (IV.i.19–22), the *Clowne* is a traveler, and his brain is *cram'd* (stuffed full) with the *observation* (notice, perception) of *strange* (foreign) *places* (locations). However, the *Clowne* does not trouble himself with *observation* (obeying) of the traveler's solemn duty to relate "The Records of things done... in words most significant, phrases modestly elegant, and discourse most pertinent" (Richard Brathwait, *A Survey of History*). Instead, the *Clowne's formes* (styles of expression) are as *mangled* (corrupted, mutilated) as *formes* ("shape[s]": "sexual organs," OED) that have been *mangled* (castrated; to "mangle" is "to geld, to cut off," TB, s.v. "Castrate"). He *vents* (expresses, utters) his *cram'd* (nonsensical; see note: *cram'd*, I.ii.93) *observation* ("reckoning, account," RC, s.v. "Esgard") of *strange places* in much the same way that *strange* (i.e., homosexual; see notes: *strange*, II.iv.57, and *Aliena*, I.iii.136) *places* (i.e., "assholes"; see note: *place*, II.i.68) "vent" (fart, EP; Shakespeare "makes the association [of farting] with buggery," FR, s.v. "Fart").

48. ***Thou shalt have one.*** *Senior* thinks *Jaques* worthy of motley, for "The ideot likes, with bables for to plaie, / And is disgrac'de, when he is bravelie dreste: / A motley coate, a cockescombe, or a bell, / Hee better likes, then Jewelles that excell" (Geffrey Whitney, "Fatuis levia commitito").

49. ***suite.*** With play on *suite* meaning (a) a livery or uniform; and (b) the "pursuit of an object or quest" (OED). Cf. IV.i.86–87.

Provided that you weed your better judgements [50]
Of all opinion that growes ranke in them,
That I am wise. I must have liberty
Withall, as large a Charter as the winde,
To blow on whom I please, for so fooles have:
And they that are most gauled with my folly, [55]
They most must laugh: And why sir must they so?
The why is plaine, as way to Parish Church:
Hee, that a Foole doth very wisely hit,
Doth very foolishly, although he smart
Seeme senselesse of the bob. If not, [60]
The Wise-mans folly is anathomiz'd
Even by the squandring glances of the foole.
Invest me in my motley: Give me leave
To speake my minde, and I will through and through
Cleanse the foule bodie of th' infected world, [65]
If they will patiently receive my medicine.

Du.Sen. Fie on thee. I can tell what thou wouldst do.

50–52. ***weed... wise.*** *Jaques* thinks himself a *weed* ("generic for sorryness or worthlessness," F&H) unworthy of the *ranke* (title) of *wise*, so he yearns for a fool's *wise* ("mode, fashion," OED) and *weed* (dress, apparel). The *opinion* that he is *wise* is *ranke* ("monstrous, gross," OED) and must be "weeded" (cleared out) like a *ranke* (overgrown) *weed*. Cf. *ranckenesse*, I.i.86, and *ranke*, I.ii.104.

53–54. ***as large a Charter as the winde... for so fooles have.*** The *foole* was exempted from customary propriety due to his (supposedly) deficient intellect. Consequently, the *foole* had *liberty* (freedom) to voice what others knew but dared not say. If *Jaques* had the *foole's Charter* (privilege, legally recognized right) to "blow upon" ("tell tales of; to discredit; to defame," F&H) whomever he wished, his *winde* ("speech, talk," OED) would be *as large* (unrestricted, free) *as the winde*, which "bloweth where it listeth" (John 3:8).

55–60. ***they that are most gauled... the bob.*** *Although* the fool appears *senselesse* ("stupid, silly, foolish," OED) and his victims appear *smart* ("wittie, ingenious," RC, s.v. "Agu"), the opposite is in fact true (cf. V.i.35–36). Those hit by the fool's *bob* ("flout, scoffe, gird, nip, cut; also, a mischiefe, injurie, or ill turne, done," RC, s.v. "Coup de bec") do not *smart* (suffer, feel pain) because they are *senselesse* (unaware) that they have been "bobbed" (struck, hit; also "ma[d]e a fool of," OED). Therefore, those *that are most gauled* ("grieved with smarting of a wound or lash of a whip," JM, s.v. "Escozído") by *Jaques'* "gall" ("effrontery, cheek," F&H) are not *gauled* ("exasperated, aggravated, grieved," "incensed, provoked unto anger," RC, s.v. "Aigri"). Instead, they *most laugh* and reveal themselves as "fooles... whose propertie is to laugh most, when they have least cause" (Thomas Taylor, *Davids Learning*); cf. IV.i.3–9.

In addition, those whose "galls" (i.e., penises; a 'Gaule' is "A pole, big rod; long staffe, or pearch," RC, q.v.) *are gauled* (venereally infected, JH, s.v. "gall") *are most* in need of a *bob* (emasculation, FR) so as not to transmit their disease; cf. lines 64–65, below.

57. ***plaine... Parish Church.*** The *way* (course, direction) *to* a *Parish Church* would be *plaine* (evident, obvious) because (a) it was usually the tallest building in the village; and (b) the *way* (path) to it would be well-trodden.

61. ***anathomiz'd.*** Both (a) thoroughly analyzed; and (b) cursed. See note: *anathomize*, I.i.152.

62. ***squandring glances.*** *Glances* ("reproach[es], railing word[s], biting tearme[s], spightfull scoffe[s], despightfull gird[s]," "malicious taunt[s]," RC, s.v. "Convince") that are "squandered" ("scattered over a comparatively wide surface or area," OED).

63. ***Invest.*** *Jaques* wishes to be "invested" ("apparrelled, attired, suited, enrobed," RC, s.v. "Vestu") in *motley* (fool's clothing) with due "investiture" ("The action or ceremony of clothing in the insignia of an office; the ceremonial, official, or formal investing of a person with an office or rank," OED).

65. ***foule bodie... infected.*** A *bodie* that is *foul* (wicked, morally or spiritually polluted) and *infected* (tainted, contaminated) with the "foul disease" ("syphilis," GW). Cf. lines 55–60, above.

66. ***patiently.*** With play on *patiently* meaning (a) "with a quiet, peaceable, and contented minde" (TT, s.v. "Aēquānĭmĭter"); and (b) in a manner befitting a "patient": a sick person receiving medical treatment.

67. ***Fie.*** *Fie* expresses disapproval of something "Indecent" or "smutty" (F&H, s.v. "fie-fie"). *Senior* may also imply that *Jaques* is a "piece of shit" and/or an "asshole" (*Fie* means both "dung" and "the "orificium ana´le," DPF; FR gives the word as "akin to 'shit'").

Jaq. What, for a Counter, would I do, but good?

Du.Sen. Most mischeevous foule sin, in chiding sin:

For thou thy selfe hast bene a Libertine, [70]

As sensuall as the brutish sting it selfe,

And all th' imbossed sores, and headed evils,

That thou with license of free foot hast caught,

Would'st thou disgorge into the generall world.

---

68. ***for a Counter... good.*** *Jaques* anticipates *Senior's* allegations that he will do damage, so he moves to *Counter* (contradict, dispute) *Senior's* attack with his own *Counter* ("Encounter, hostile meeting, opposition," OED; in broadsword fighting, a *Counter* is an attack launched while one's opponent is attacking; "The stronger attack takes the advantage," OED). *Jaques* insists that he would provide a *Counter* (i.e., "cure"; a *Counter* is literally a contrary or opposing force) and *do good for a Counter* (i.e., a "cunter" or fornicator; *Counter* was pronounced "cunter" JH; cf. the OED spelling variant "cunter").

69. ***mischeevous foule sin... sin.*** *Chiding* is (a) "Blame, rebuke, a checke; a censure; a reproofe," "reprehension," "also, an imputation, ill report, or discommendation" (RC, s.v. "Blasme"); and/or (b) "bayting, schooling; and, a scoffing, mocking, deriding" (RC, s.v. "Vanneure").

Senior thinks that *in chiding* (rebuking or ridiculing) *sin, Jaques* would himself do *mischeevous* ("pernicious, wicked, deadly, hurtfull," "mortall, bringing death or destruction, dangerous," JF, s.v. "Pernicioso") *foule* ("filthie, dishonourable, unhonest," RC, s.v. "Turpe"; "disgustingly abusive," OED) *sin.* Just like *sin* (sexual intercourse, EP) spreads the "*foule* disease" (syphilis; cf. and see note: line 65, above), *Jaques* will spread *foule* ("physically loathsome; primarily with reference to the odour or appearance indicative of putridity or corruption," OED) "mischief" ("sickenes, disease, infection, paine," JF, s.v. "Male").

69–70. ***sin... a Libertine.*** A *Libertine* is one "loose in religion, one that thinks he may doe what he listeth" (RC2, q.v.); the "Libertines" were specifically "A sect of heretics in Holland... They maintained that nothing is sinful but to those who think it sinful" (DPF, q.v.). "Libertines" were thus understood to be "Pleasant and profuse

Livers, that Live-apace, but wildly, without Order, Rule, or Discipline, lighting the Candle (of Life) at both Ends" (ND, q.v.). By extension, a *Libertine* is "one unbound by (sexual) morality" (GW).

71. ***sensuall.*** As a *Libertine* (line 70, above), *Jaques* is both *sensuall* ("Excessively inclined to the gratification of the senses," OED) and *sensuall* ("lustfull," "lecherous, fleshly, baudie," TT, s.v. "Lĭbīdĭnōsus"). He therefore indulges in "Sensuality" ("libertinism, or epicurism, the pleasing of sence, contentment given to the appetite, satisfaction to the flesh," TB, q.v.).

71. ***brutish.*** *Brutish* is (a) "unreasonable," "without humane reason" (JF, s.v. "Irationale"); (b) "wild, rude, savage," "filthie" (RC, s.v. "Brutal"); and (c) "pertaining to the flesh, and bodily sence" (RC2, s.v. "sensuall").

71. ***sting.*** *Sting* is applied to "the fang or venom-tooth (and erroneously to the forked tongue) of a poisonous serpent" (OED). *Senior* implies that *Jaques* (a) has an "Adders-tongue" or "Serpents-tongue": "the venomous tongue of a Detractor" (RC, s.v. "Langue de Serpent"); and/or (b) is "Double tongued": "One who makes contrary declarations on the same subject at different times; deceitful" (DPF).

Sting is also used for (a) the "sting of sensual desire" (EP); (b) the "tail" or genitals (FR); and (c) the "stings of venereal infection" (GW); cf. line 72, below.

72. ***imbossed sores.*** *Imbossed sores* are "swellings caused by pox" (GW; a "Bosse" is "A bunch, or bumpe; any round swelling, uprising, or puffing up; hence, a wen, botch, bile, or plague sore," RC, q.v.).

72. ***headed evils.*** *Jaques* would be the "head" (source) of *evils* due to his *headed* (former, past; to "head" is "to go before, precede," OED) *evils* (sins, crimes); cf. and see note: *pride*, line 75, below.

Jaques "head" (penis; see note: *heads*, II.i.27) is also the source of *headed* ("That has come to a head or matured, as a boil," OED) *evils* ("pox sores," GW). *Senior* may further imply that *Jaques* is "full of shit" (a "head" is "a ship's latrine," OED; and *evils* means "perhaps privies," EC; cf. and see note: *melancholy Jaques*, II.i.30).

73. ***license of free foot.*** *Jaques* formerly had *license* ("Excessive liberty; abuse of freedom; disregard of law or propriety," OED) and was *free* (unrestricted, uninhibited, loose) of *foot* (action, motion). He is also guilty of *license* ("Licentiousness, libertinism," OED) with his *free* ("Sexually unrestrained," EC) *foot* ("penis," GW2; FR takes *foot* to mean a "small penis" because it is "only part of a yard," q.v.). When *Jaques* began his sexual escapades, he was *free* (free from venereal disease, EC, s.v. "Tainted Or Free"), but now he is highly contagious.

74. ***disgorge.*** In saying that *Jaques* will *disgorge* ("vomit, spue out, cast his gorge, unburthen his stomacke; to void, evacuate, emptie," RC, s.v. "desgorger") his wickedness, *Senior* possibly alludes to Proverbs 26:11: "As a dogge returneth to his vomite: so a foole returneth to his folly."

Disgorge may also play on "gurge" meaning "A whirlpool" (OED). The implication is that *Jaques'* evil is a dangerous vortex that engulfs all who come near (cf. TT's entry at "Gurges": "A swallow or deepe pitte in a water, a gulfe, a whirlepoole: sometime the streame, perillous daunger, or whirling rage of the sea: Also a naughtie wicked man flowing in mischiefe: an exceeding ryotour, & outragious waster: one that can not be satisfied").

74. ***generall world.*** If left to his own devices, *Jaques* would make the *generall* (whole) *world generall* ("Common: whore-like," FR; cf. F&H's "receiver-general," s.v. "tart").

Jaq. Why who cries out on pride, [75]

That can therein taxe any private party:

Doth it not flow as hugely as the Sea,

Till that the wearie verie meanes do ebbe.

What woman in the Citie do I name,

When that I say the City woman beares [80]

The cost of Princes on unworthy shoulders?

Who can come in, and say that I meane her,

When such a one as shee, such is her neighbor?

Or what is he of basest function,

That sayes his braverie is not on my cost, [85]

---

75. ***cries out.*** To "cry out" is (a) "To revile, reproach, raile at, or scould with, openly; to exclaime against" (RC, s.v. "Harauder"); (b) "to shent, to rate as we do dogs" (JF, s.v. "Sgridare"); and/or (c) to "make hue and cry" (RC, s.v. "Huer").

75. ***pride.*** *Pride,* or an exaggerated sense of one's own worth, is one of the "seven Capital sins," which, along with "Covetoviness, Lechery, Anger, Gluttony, Envy and Sloath" are "called Capital, because they are heads of many others, which proceed from them as Rivers from their source" (TB, s.v. "Capital"; cf. *headed evils,* line 72, above). *Pride* also means "Sexual desire" (EC).

76. ***taxe.*** To *taxe* is "to blame, to touch in credite, to slander, to disparage, or disable ones credite and reputation" (JF, s.v. "Tassare"). Cf. *taxation,* I.ii.81.

76. ***any private party.*** Any one particular person.

77–78. ***Doth it not... ebbe.*** *It* (i.e., pride) *Doth flow* (rises like the "flow": "ful tide," JF, s.v. "Piéna") as *hugely* as the *Sea* until pride's *verie meanes* (financial resources, which create occasion for pride) do *ebbe* (sink or recede as the tide; "Ebb-water" is "when there's but little Money in the Pocket," ND). Cf. these lines from John Donne's "Psalme 137":

> And, thou Babel, when the tide
> Of thy pride

Now a flowing, growes to turning;
Victor now, shall then be thrall,
And shall fall
To as low an ebbe of mourning.

79. ***woman in the Citie.*** *Woman in the Citie* may or may not bear a semantic link to "woman of the town" ("a prostitute," FG, s.v., "Town"), but *Citie* women were supposedly tempted to vanity and promiscuity by the "puttyng on of wanton and light aray, wherby they be entised rather to prid & whordome then to humilite, shamfastnes, & cleannes of life" (Thomas Becon, *Jewel of Joy*). Cf. "I marryed you out of the Countrie, but you have learn'd the Cittie fashions already: I am a Cuckold" (Edward Sharpham, *Cupids Whirligig*); also cf. "citizens fine wives undo their husbands (by their pride) within a yeare after they are married" (Thomas Dekker, *The Whore of Babylon*).

80–81. ***beares The cost... unworthy shoulders.*** England's sumptuary laws, which were first instituted in 1337 and not repealed until 1604, were a legally ordained dress code. These laws regulated every detail of a person's dress according to social rank. Restrictions extended not only to types of fabrics but also to trims, colors, the width of ruffs, the diameter of women's hoopskirts, hairstyles, and even the styles of men's beards and moustaches. Thus, the *shoulders* of anyone under the rank of a prince were, legally speaking, *unworthy* to "bear" (wear) the *cost of princes*— i.e., clothing that *cost* a princely sum (L. "sumptus" is "cost"; "sumpture" is "expense," as in "sumptuary law," OED).

Ultimately, however, these regulations proved unenforceable. In *Anatomie of Abuses*, Phillip Stubbes complains that "now there is such a confuse mingle mangle of apparell... and such preposterous excesse therof, as every one is permitted to flaunt it out, in what apparell he lust himselfe, or can get by anie kind of meanes." Therefore, *Jaques* could hold up for example many expensively (and illegally) dressed ladies in the audience.

82. ***come in.*** Enter into argument or battle (see note: *come in*, I.i.130), with possible additional play on *come in* meaning "to have carnal intercourse with" (OED). Cf. and see notes: *woman in the Citie*, line 79, above; and *neighbor*, line 83, below.

83. ***such is her neighbor.*** A *neighbor* (adulteress, FR) would be free with her *such* (L. "tale": "pubic-anal area," FR).

84. ***basest function.*** A person of *basest function* would be "of basest imployment": "one of the meanest ranke... or one that serves as a drudge" (RC, s.v. "Chambriere"). If such a person dressed above his station, his visible "function" ("qualitie, condition, sort, fashion, manner, degree," RC, s.v. "Qualité") would be "base" ("counterfeit," HH, p. 284).

Jaques continues to use elaborate clothing as a metaphor for faulty moral behavior. One of *basest function* would be of "base" (low) *function* ("virility or potency," EP) and would therefore be fit to serve only in *basest function* (i.e., as the passive partner in sodomy; "base" is "the lowest part" as well as "a socket," OED; *function* is copulation, JH). Cf. Fr. "baiser": "to fuck."

85. ***braverie.*** *Braverie* is (a) "gallantnesse, gorgeousnesse, or costlinesse in apparrell" (RC, q.v.); and (b) a possible play on "courage" ("sexual vigor, lust," JH, q.v.; also see note: *coragious*, II.iv.10).

85. ***That sayes... not on my cost.*** I.e., "that says I didn't pay for it, so it is none of my business."

Thinking that I meane him, but therein suites

His folly to the mettle of my speech,

There then, how then, what then, let me see wherein

My tongue hath wrong'd him: if it do him right,

Then he hath wrong'd himselfe: if he be free, [90]

why then my taxing like a wild-goose flies

Unclaim'd of any man. But who come here?

Enter Orlando. [II.vii.3]

Orl. Forbeare, and eate no more.

Jaq. Why I have eate none yet. [95]

Orl. Nor shalt not, till necessity be serv'd.

Jaq. Of what kinde should this Cocke come of?

Du.Sen. Art thou thus bolden'd man by thy distres?

Or else a rude despiser of good manners,

That in civility thou seem'st so emptie? [100]

86–87. ***suites His folly... speech.*** *Jaques'* statements cut like a "mettall" ("cord or lash of a whip," OED), but they are felt only by those who in *folly* "suit" ("match"; also "dress or attire," OED) their "suit" (dress, garb, clothing) *to the mettle* (substance or character) of his *speech*.

Such people would, presumably, also be guilty of *folly* (lewd thoughts or actions; see note: *folly*, II.iv.58) and would therefore "suit" (pronounced "shoot," HK, p. 145; to "shoot" is "To ejaculate," OED) their *mettle* ("semen," FG).

90. ***free.*** Innocent, guiltless.

91. ***wild-goose.*** A *wild-goose* belongs to no one, so if *Jaques'* victims are innocent he would be on a "*wild-goose* chase" ("The pursuit of anything unprofitable or absurd, a blind hunt," F&H). However, *Jaques* is certain that if he took aim he would hit a *wild* (licentious) *goose*, which means (a) a whore; (b) a venereal sore; and (c) "a person thus infected" (F&H).

96–100. ***shalt... this... thou.*** These are all clues that *Orlando* makes his threats at very close range. In line 96, *Orlando* threatens *Jaques* using the second person familiar form of the verb "shall" (i.e., "thou *shalt*," as opposed to the formal "you shall"). In line 97, *Jaques* responds by calling *Orlando this Cocke*; *this* is a demonstrative pronoun indicating close proximity. In lines 98 and 100, *Senior* also addresses *Orlando* with *thou*, the second person familiar pronoun.

Orlando's attack, although brave, is somewhat foolhardy as he is greatly outnumbered.

97. ***Of what kinde... come of.*** *Orlando* seems like a "*Cocke Of kinde*" (i.e., a swaggering bully; cf. "Now of these Cocks, some of them are made for nothing els but war and fighting, and never are they well but in quarrels, brawles, and fraies; and these be cocks of kind," Pliny the Elder, *The Historie of the World*). Therefore, *Jaques* asks of what *kinde* (condition, character, descent) *this Cocke* ("One who fights with pluck and spirit," OED) *should come of* (originate, belong to).

The *Cocke* was seen as the embodiment of both valor and sexual vigour, so *Cocke Of kinde* also means a sexually potent male (*Cocke*, quite obviously, means "penis," F&H, and *kinde* is both "The sexual organs" and "semen," OED). *Orlando* has a *kinde* ("nature": both innate disposition and manly vigor) inherited by descent (cf. *spirit*, I.i.23 and 68), so *Jaques* thinks that *Orlando* is either (a) a "big prick" descended from a long line of "big pricks" (see note: line 98, below); (b) a *Cocke* (heap of dung, OED); and/or (c) a "dunghill cock" ("a coward or spiritless fellow," OED).

98. ***bolden'd... by thy distres.*** *Orlando*, who has drawn his sword, is *bolden'd* (made audacious or shameless) *by* his *distres* ("perplexitie, or anguish: trouble and griefe of minde: scarcitie: adversitie or troublous state," TT, s.v. "angustiarium"). Given the customary link between courage and virility, *Orlando's* "sword" (penis, EP) may also be "bold" ("Strong, mighty, big"; "Well-filled, plump," OED). Thus, he suffers *distres* ("Physical discomfort from prolonged phallic erection," FR; *distres* is literally "painful exertion which puts a severe strain upon the physical powers," OED). Cf. *thorny point Of bare distresse*, lines 101–102, below.

99. ***rude.*** Both (a) "Fierce, cruell, in a rage" (TT, s.v. "Effĕrus"); and (b) "Uncourteous," "homely in maners: without honest civilitie" (TT, s.v. "Inurbānus").

100. ***emptie.*** *Senior* hints that *Orlando's* show of potency (both strength and sexual power) is really *emptie* ("impotent," JH).

Orl. You touch'd my veine at first, the thorny point

Of bare distresse, hath tane from me the shew

Of smooth civility: yet am I in-land bred,

And know some nourture: But forbeare, I say,

He dies that touches any of this fruite, [105]

Till I, and my affaires are answered.

Jaq. And you will not be answer'd with reason,

I must dye.

Du.Sen. What would you have?

Your gentlenesse shall force, more then your force [110]

Move us to gentlenesse.

Orl. I almost die for food, and let me have it.

Du.Sen. Sit downe and feed, & welcom to our table

Orl. Speake you so gently? Pardon me I pray you,

I thought that all things had bin savage heere, [115]

And therefore put I on the countenance

Of sterne command'ment. But what ere you are

That in this desert inaccessible,

Under the shade of melancholly boughes,

Loose, and neglect the creeping houres of time: [120]

If ever you have look'd on better dayes:

101–103. ***touch'd my veine... smooth civility.*** *Senior's first* supposition *touch'd* (guessed, hit upon) *Orlando's veine* (mood, condition); he was correct when he guessed that *Orlando* was a "vane" (an unstable person, OED; this sense derives from "vane" meaning "a vane to turn the wind; a weather-cock," OED; cf. *Cocke*, line 97, above). Because *Orlando's point* (condition or plight) is *thorny* (pricking, piercing) and he suffers *bare* (thorough) *distresse* (misery, want), he abandons *smooth* (polite, pleasant, friendly) *civility*. His predicament causes him to *bare* (unsheathe) his *thorny* (pricking, piercing) *point* (pointed weapon, point of a sword). In addition, *Orlando* is obviously not *smooth* ("effeminate," TB, s.v. "Liéve"; also "castrated," FR) because he "bears" (extends, stretches out, OED) his *veine* ("penis," JA, p. 35) to its *point* ("height, summit, zenith, acme," OED).

103–104. ***in-land bred... nourture.*** *Orlando* might mean that he was (a) *bred* (born and raised) within an *in-land* ("The inner part of an estate, feudal manor, or farm"; "the land around the mansion occupied by the owner or cultivated for his use, not held by any tenant," OED); or (b) *bred* (reared, trained) to "Hav[e] the refinement characteristic of the inlying districts of a country" (OED). In either case, *Orlando* would *know some nourture* ("manners, education, civilitie," JF, s.v. "Creanza").

105. ***fruite.*** There would not be much *fruite* available in the forest in wintertime, but there might be raisins. Cf. and see notes: *Forrest of Arden*, I.i.115, and *reason*, line 107, below.

107. ***answer'd with reason.*** *Jaques* hopes to *answere* ("satisfy"; also "give back in kind," "meet in fight," OED) *Orlando* with *reason* (logical thought, rational judgment). *Reason* and "raisin" were pronounced identically (HK, pp. 138–139; also cf. and see note: *reasons*, I.iii.10), so if *Jaques* answers *Orlando* with "raisin" ("a bunch, or cluster of Grapes," RC, q.v.), he might (a) give the "raisin" to *Orlando*; (b) throw the "raisin" at *Orlando*; or (c) eat the "raisin" himself.

110–111. ***Your gentlenesse shall force... to gentlenesse.*** *Orlando's gentlenesse* ("mildnesse, courtesie, humanitie, affabilitie, good nature," RC, s.v. "Bonnaireté") *shall force* (compel, convince) *Senior* and his band to offer help sooner than *force* (violence).

114. ***gently.*** Both (a) kindly, courteously; and (b) mildly, tenderly.

116–17. ***countenance... sterne.*** *Orlando* apologizes for his *sterne countenance* (behavior)—i.e., for being "an ass" (*sterne* is "The backside, the bum," F&H). Also see note: *countenance*, I.i.19.

118. ***desert inaccessible.*** Remote wilderness.

119. ***melancholly boughes.*** See note: *oake*, II.i.35.

120. ***Loose... time.*** To "loose time" is "To spend the time most vainely, idly, foolishly; to as little purpose as may be" (RC, s.v. "Chasser apres les mouches").

If ever beene where bels have knoll'd to Church:
If ever sate at any good mans feast:
If ever from your eye-lids wip'd a teare,
And know what 'tis to pittie, and be pittied: [125]
Let gentlenesse my strong enforcement be,
In the which hope, I blush, and hide my Sword.

Du.Sen. True is it, that we have seene better dayes,
And have with holy bell bin knowld to Church,
And sat at good mens feasts, and wip'd our eies [130]
Of drops, that sacred pity hath engendred:
And therefore sit you downe in gentlenesse,
And take upon command, what helpe we have
That to your wanting may be ministred.

Orl. Then but forbeare your food a little while: [135]
Whiles (like a Doe) I go to finde my Fawne,
And give it food. There is an old poore man,
Who after me, hath many a weary steppe
Limpt in pure love: till he be first suffic'd,
Opprest with two weake evils, age, and hunger, [140]
I will not touch a bit.

Duke Sen. Go finde him out,

123. ***sate.*** A variant spelling of "sat," with play on "sate" meaning "To fill or satisfy to the full" (OED).

126. ***gentlenesse... enforcement.*** Cf. lines 110–111, above.

140. ***weake evils.*** Afflictions that cause weakness.

And we will nothing waste till you returne.

Orl. I thanke ye, and be blest for your good comfort.

{*Exit Orlando.*} [II.vii.4] [145]

Du.Sen. Thou seest, we are not all alone unhappie:

This wide and universall Theater

Presents more wofull Pageants then the Sceane

Wherein we play in.

Ja. All the world's a stage, [150]

And all the men and women, meerely Players;

They have their *Exits* and their Entrances,

And one man in his time playes many parts,

His Acts being seven ages. At first the Infant,

Mewling, and puking in the Nurses armes: [155]

---

144. ***comfort.*** Relief, aid.

146. ***unhappie.*** See note: *unhappie*, II.iii.19.

147–149. ***This wide and universall Theater... we play in.*** *Senior* speaks of both (a) the *universall Theater* (i.e., the whole world; a *Theater* is "A place where some action proceeds," OED); and (b) the *universall Theater* (i.e., the Globe *Theater*) where the actors portraying *Senior* and his band *play in* a "pageant" ("a spectacle, a sight, a shewe," "a plaie, a thing to be seene and looked on," JF, s.v. "Spettácolo") and a *Sceane* ("A play, or Comody, a Tragedy, or the division of a play into certaine parts," JB, q.v.).

150–151. ***All the world's a stage... meerely Players.*** The Globe Theatre's sign purportedly depicted the subjugated Titan *Atlas* carrying the *world* on his back, and the theatre's motto was supposedly "Totus Mundus Agit Histrionem" (L. for *All the world's a stage*, or literally, "all the world acts the player"; the phrase is apparently drawn from the *Fragments* of Petronius: "quod fere totus mundus exerceat histrionem": "Almost the whole world are players").

If the entire *world* ("the whole earth," RC, s.v. "Terre") is a *stage* (the "part of a Theater wherein Players act," RC, s.v. "Poulpitre"), then each person is *meerely* ("Simply, singly, purely," RC, s.v. "Simplement") an "Actor" ("A stage-player, or one doing a thing," HC, q.v.) who plays to entertain (a) his "mere" (mother) *the world* (i.e., "Mother Earth"); and/or (b) the goddess Fortune, who oversees each *stage* ("degree or step in the 'ladder' of virtue, honour, etc.; a 'step' on Fortune's wheel," OED) of mortal existence; cf. *Rosalind's* and *Celia's* discussion in I.ii.32–51.

Also, every *stage* (period of development, step or degree of progress) that comprises the *world* ("Human existence; a period of this," OED) is *meerely* a *stage* ("A place in which rest is taken on a journey," OED). Ultimately, *all the* "play" (busy activity) of *men and women* will "play" ("move briskly," OED) towards a *stage* ("A scaffold for execution," OED).

152. ***their Exits and their Entrances.*** "Entrance" means (a) the coming of an actor onto the stage; (b) coming in, here specifically in reference to being born into the world; and (c) "The first part, the opening words of a chapter or book" (OED; cf. *Acts,* line 154, below).

Exits is italicized because the word was still considered foreign at the time the Folio was printed (L. "exit" is the third person singular indicative of "exīre": "to leave"; also to "die," LD). In English works, the word "exit" appeared only in stage directions until the mid-seventeenth century, at which time it properly entered the language with the sense "depart." OED dates "exit" meaning "Departure from the scene of life; death" from 1661, but this meaning is obviously in play here.

153. ***one man in his time playes many parts.*** It was not unusual for an Elizabethan actor to portray *many parts* (roles) within a single play. A "part" is also a "piece or section of something which together with another or others makes up the whole" (OED), and the *many parts* that *one man playes* together comprise his *time* (lifetime).

154. ***Acts.*** With play on "act" as (a) an "exploit, or deed" (RC, s.v. "Acte"); (b) "a part of a comedie or plaie," (TT, s.v. "Actus"); (c) a performance; and (d) the "external manifestation of any state" (OED).

154–176. ***seven ages... second childishnesse.*** According to Thomas Blount's *Glossographia* (s.v. "Age"),

> Proclus (a Greek Author) divides the life of man into seven ages. 1. Infancy, conteins four yeers. 2. Childhood continues ten yeers. 3. Youth-hood or Adolescency consists of eight yeers, that is, from fourteen to two and twenty. 4. Young man-hood continues fifteen yeers, that is, from two and twenty to forty one. 5. Ripe man-hood hath fifteen yeers of continuance, and therefore makes his progress to 56 yeers. 6. Old age, which, in adding 12 to 56, makes up 68. 7. Decrepit age is limited from 68 yeers to 88.

As described by *Jaques,* these *seven ages* correspond to the "parts" played by a single man as follows: (1) "Infancy": *the Infant;* (2) "Childhood": *the whining Schoole-boy;* (3) "Youth-hood": *the Lover;* (4) "Young man-hood": *a Soldier;* (5) "Ripe man-hood": *the Justice;* (6) "Old age": *the leane and slipper'd Pantaloone;* and (7) "Decrepit age": *second childishnesse.*

154–155. ***Infant, Mewling.*** "Mew" means (a) to "crie as a cat" (JF, s.v. "Gattillare"); and (b) to defecate ("mew" is used for "mewt" or "mute," "to discharge faeces," OED). Also, the tiny *Infant* in its swaddling clothes is *Mewling* ("chang[ing], transmut[ing]," OED) its form like a caterpillar in a cocoon.

155. ***Nurses.*** Children were commonly put out to wet *Nurses,* despite the fact that "the death rate of children fed by hired wet-nurses seems to have been about twice that of infants fed by their mothers" (LS, p. 107).

Then, the whining Schoole-boy with his Satchell
And shining morning face, creeping like snaile
Unwillingly to schoole. And then the Lover,
Sighing like Furnace, with a wofull ballad
Made to his Mistresse eye-brow. Then, a Soldier, [160]
Full of strange oaths, and bearded like the Pard,
Jelous in honor, sodaine, and quicke in quarrell,
Seeking the bubble Reputation
Even in the Canons mouth: And then, the Justice
In faire round belly, with good Capon lin'd, [165]
With eyes severe, and beard of formall cut,
Full of wise sawes, and moderne instances,
And so he playes his part. The sixt age shifts
Into the leane and slipper'd Pantaloone,

---

156. ***whining.*** To "whine" is (a) to complain; and (b) "to cry squeekingly" (ND).

156. ***Satchell.*** A bag for schoolbooks, with possible allusion to the boy's *Satchell* ("scrotum," GW2) governing his growth through puberty.

157. ***shining morning face.*** The boy's *face* is as *shining* ("cleane, neate, gay, trim, smugge, spruse, bright," JF, s.v. "Nitido") as the *morning* sun, and he looks "bright and *shining*" (cheerful). *Shining* also implies a ruddy complexion or rosy hue; cf. "as bright / As is the Mornings Face / With all her roseall Grace" (Joseph Beaumont, "Love"; "roseall" is "roseate": both "pink" and "happy," OED).

157–158. ***creeping like snaile... schoole.*** The *snaile* literally "creeps" (crawls on the ground), but the boy "creeps" in that he moves slowly. Cf. IV.i.53–55.

159. ***Sighing like Furnace.*** A *Furnace* is (a) an oven or cauldron; and (b) a volcano. If *Furnace* here means "oven," then the lover's *Sighing* resembles the wind from

the bellows; cf. "In vaine, my Hart, now you with sight are burnd, / With sighes you seeke to coole your hotte desire: / Since sighes (into mine inward fornace turnd) / For bellowes serve to kindle more the fire" (Philip Sidney, *The Countesse of Pembroke's Acradia*). If *Furnace* here means "volcano," then the *Sighing* of the lover represents violent volcanic eruption; cf. "Thus sayde, he gave a groane, as though his heart had broke, / And from the furnace of his breast, sent scalding sighes like smoke" (George Gascoigne, "The complaint of the greene Knight"). Either way, the *Lover* is extremely "hot": "Sexually eager, passionate" (JH).

159–160. ***a wofull ballad... Mistresse eye-brow.*** The fashion in *ballads* (songs, narrative poems) was to dissect the beauty of one's *Mistresse* and praise each separate part. In extolling a lady's virtues, a man "should write sonnets to her eyes, or call her brow the snow of Ida, or Ivorie of Corinth" (John Webster, *The White Divel*).

161. ***strange oaths.*** *Strange oaths* possibly means "foul language." However, *strange* can simply mean "exotic," and "to thinke to give assurance of faith by new and strange oathes, as many doe, is superfluous amongst honest men, and unprofitable, if a man will bee disloyall. The best way is to sweare by the eternall God, the revenger of those that vainlie use his name, and breake their faith" (Pierre Charron, *Of Wisdome*; cf. and see notes: *violated vowes*, III.ii.134, and *pretty oathes*, IV.i.182). The implication is that the *Soldier*, who was once a *Lover* (line 158, above), now only makes vows that he can easily break.

161. ***bearded like the Pard.*** The *Soldier* might (a) have a scruffy "beard" *like* a *bearded Pard* (panther or leopard); or (b) "beard" ("oppose openly and resolutely, with daring or with effrontery," OED) others as fiercely as a *Pard*.

162. ***Jelous in honor.*** Either (a) *Jelous* (furious, wrathful) when his *honor* has been offended; or (b) *Jelous* (eager for or devoted to) his *honor*.

162. ***sodaine, and quicke in quarrell.*** The *Soldier* may be *sodaine* ("sudden") and *quicke in quarrell* because he is (a) "sodden" (drunk); and/or (b) "sodden-brained" ("Dull, sottish, doltish, lumpish, blockish, heavie headed, grosse-witted," RC, s.v. "Goffe").

163–164. ***the bubble Reputation... Canons mouth.*** The *Soldier* is such a *bubble* ("dupe; gull," F&H) and so "canon" ("drunk," F&H) with the hope of *Reputation* ("Honour; renowne," "credit, praise, glorie, fame," RC, s.v. "Honneur") that he will seek it *even in the Canons mouth*.

164–165. ***the Justice... with good Capon lin'd.*** This *Justice* (constable or *Justice* of the Peace) is one of those corrupt "judges that judge for reward, and say with shame, Bring you; such as the Country calls Capon-Justices" (Samuel Ward, *Balme from Gilead*). Thus, *the Justice* has a *faire round belly lin'd* (filled) *with* the "fare" (food) of many a *good Capon* ("castrated cock," FG) that he has received as a bribe.

Roosters are made "capons" in order to fatten them, so the *Justice* is perhaps himself now a *Capon* ("an eunuch," FG) who has turned from lust to gluttony.

167. ***sawes.*** Both (a) old sayings or clichés; and (b) legal phrases.

167. ***moderne instances.*** Ordinary, everyday examples.

168. ***shifts.*** The man *shifts* (changes) as his *age shifts* (travels quickly) into a later "shift" ("share, a portion assigned on division," OED).

169. ***the leane and slipper'd Pantaloone.*** The *Pantaloone* of *Commedia dell'Arte* is a foolish old miser (hence the money *pouch on* his *side*, line 170, below). Despite the fact that *Pantaloone* is *leane* ("Worn thin by sexual excess," EP), he is still *slippered* (i.e., "slippery": "licentious," GW) and yearns for the "slipper" ("female pudendum," F&H).

With spectacles on nose, and pouch on side, [170]

His youthfull hose well sav'd, a world too wide,

For his shrunke shanke, and his bigge manly voice,

Turning againe toward childish trebble pipes,

And whistles in his sound. Last Scene of all,

That ends this strange eventfull historie, [175]

Is second childishnesse, and meere oblivion,

Sans teeth, sans eyes, sans taste, sans every thing.

Enter Orlando with Adam. [II.vii.5]

Du.Sen. Welcome: set downe your venerable bur-

then, and let him feede. [180]

Orl. I thanke you most for him.

Ad. So had you neede,

I scarce can speake to thanke you for my selfe.

Du.Sen. Welcome, fall too: I wil not trouble you,

As yet to question you about your fortunes: [185]

Give us some Musicke, and good Cozen, sing.

Song.

{*Amy.*} *Blow, blow, thou winter winde,*

Thou art not so unkinde, as mans ingratitude

Thy tooth is not so keene, because thou art not seene, [190]

170. ***spectacles.*** *Spectacles* were "part of the fool iconography, since the wearer is symbolically incapable of seeing the truth" (GW2).

Pantaloone is also a character who contributes to life's "spectacle" ("a publike sight, shew, pageant, play," RC, q.v.).

171–172. ***youthfull hose... shrunke shanke.*** The miserly *Pantaloone* would not throw anything away, and he has *sav'd* his *youthfull hose* (breeches, leggings) and wears them even though they are now *a world too wide* (large). The old man's "shanks" ("Leggs," ND) are *shrunke* ("growne leane, meagre, thinne, slender," RC, s.v. "Amaigri"), as is his *hose* (penis, FR). This is possibly due to a "shanker": "a little Scab or Pox on the Nut or or Glans of the Yard" (ND; cf. and see note: *whistles,* line 174, below).

172–174. ***his bigge manly voice... whistles in his sound.*** Whether through age, illness, or both, *Pantaloone* has lost his *bigge* (powerful, loud, full) *manly voice,* and his *pipes* (vocal cords) "turn" (return, revert) to the sound of *childish trebble* (high pitched, shrill) *pipes* (flutes or whistles). Presumably, the old man *whistles* because he has lost his teeth (cf. I.i.81–82), but *whistles* are also "symptoms of syphilis" (FR; a "siffle" is "a whistling," JF, s.v. "Fischio"). He may also "whistle" (fart, FR) in his *sound* (the "musical tone of the fart," TR).

174. ***Last Scene.*** The *Last Scene* is that in which the man is "last seen."

175. ***historie.*** A "true tale" (JF, s.v. "História"); also "a drama" (OED).

176. ***second childishnesse.*** I.e., second childhood, "for they say, an old man is twice a childe" (*Hamlet,* II.ii.).

176. ***oblivion.*** Either (a) forgetfulness; or (b) the "state or condition of being forgotten" (OED); cf. II.iii.45.

178. ***Enter Orlando with Adam.*** The word *with* indicates that *Orlando* carries *Adam.* This is confirmed by *Senior's* describing *Adam* as a *burthen* (lines 179–180, below).

179. ***venerable.*** Both (a) "reverend or honorable, worthie to be honored" (JF, s.v. "Venerabile"); and (b) "Ancient, antique, old" (OED).

184. ***fall too.*** Begin eating.

187–188. ***Song... winter winde.*** This *Song* about the *winter winde* (a) indicates the passage of time while *Orlando* relates his story; and (b) sets this scene as occurring during the *winter.* Cf. II.i.9–12 and 55; II.v.10; and II.vi.18.

189. ***unkinde.*** *Unkinde* is (a) hostile; (b) wicked; and/or (c) unnatural.

190. ***keene.*** Cruel; also biting or piercing.

although thy breath be rude.

Heigh ho, sing heigh ho, unto the greene holly,

Most frendship, is fayning; most Loving, meere folly:

The heigh ho, the holly,

This Life is most jolly. [195]

Freize, freize, thou bitter skie that dost not bight so nigh

as benefitts forgot:

Though thou the waters warpe, thy sting is not so sharpe,

as freind remembred not.

Heigh ho, sing, &c. [200]

Duke Sen. If that you were the good Sir *Rowlands* son,

As you have whisper'd faithfully you were,

And as mine eye doth his effigies witnesse,

Most truly limn'd, and living in your face,

Be truly welcome hither: I am the Duke [205]

That lov'd your Father, the residue of your fortune,

Go to my Cave, and tell mee. Good old man,

Thou art right welcome, as thy masters is:

Support him by the arme: give me your hand,

And let me all your fortunes understand. [210]

Exeunt.

191. ***breath.*** With probable play on *breath* meaning (a) "lack of decorum" (OED); and (b) "Ire, fury, rage" (OED, s.v. "breth").

191. ***rude.*** Violent or harsh; also uncivil or uncivilized.

192. ***Heigh-ho.*** *Heigh-ho* is the refrain of the song, but a *Heigh-ho* is also "a loud or audible sigh" (OED).

192. ***greene holly.*** *Holly*, one of very few evergreens native to England, is a symbol of hope and mirth.

193. ***fayning.*** *Fayning* means both (a) "gladsome, affectionate"; and (b) "dissembling, counterfeiting" (RC, s.v. "Desguisement").

196–198. ***bitter skie... the waters warpe.*** To *warpe* is (a) "to throw or cast" (TB, q.v.); (b) "To strike, hit, assail with a missile"; and/or (c) "to besprinkle with a liquid" (OED). The *bitter* ("bitingly cold," OED) *skie* "warps" (pelts down) *waters*, either as freezing rain, hail, sleet, or snow.

196. ***nigh.*** *Nigh* means "near," with possible play on "near": "meanly" (OED). Cf. "nighly": "avaritiously, greedily, covetously" (TT, s.v. "Avārē").

197. ***benefitts.*** Good deeds, kindnesses.

200. ***&c.*** An indication to repeat the chorus of lines 192–195, above.

201. ***Sir Rowlands.*** See note: *Sir Rowland de Boys*, I.i.56–57.

203. ***effigies witnesse.*** The *witnesse* (testimony, evidence) of *Sir Rowland's* "effigy" (likeness, portrait) is *limn'd* (painted, illuminated, or depicted) and *living in Orlando's face.*

205–206. ***the Duke That lov'd your Father.*** Cf. I.ii.232 and I.iii.30.

206. ***the residue.*** The rest.

208. ***masters.*** A possible typographical error for "master"; or possibly for "master's [son]."

Act III, scene i

Actus Tertius. Scena Prima. [1]

Enter Duke {Frederick}, Lords, & Oliver. [III.i.1]

{*Duke Fred.*} Not see him since? Sir, sir, that cannot be:

But were I not the better part made mercie,

I should not seeke an absent argument [5]

Of my revenge, thou present: but looke to it,

Finde out thy brother wheresoere he is,

Seeke him with Candle: bring him dead, or living

Within this twelvemonth, or turne thou no more

To seeke a living in our Territorie. [10]

Thy Lands and all things that thou dost call thine,

Worth seizure, do we seize into our hands,

Till thou canst quit thee by thy brothers mouth,

Of what we thinke against thee.

Ol. Oh that your Highnesse knew my heart in this: [15]

I never lov'd my brother in my life.

{*Duke Fred.*} More villaine thou. Well push him out of dores

And let my officers of such a nature

Make an extent upon his house and Lands:

Do this expediently, and turne him going. [20]

Exeunt

Notes III.i.

4. ***better part... mercie.*** *Frederick* alleges that he has a merciful *better part* (soul; see note: *better parts*, I.ii.249), but he has already demonstrated (I.ii.220–226, I.ii.264–270, and I.iii.44–47) that his *better part* is not *made* of *mercie*.

5. ***argument.*** *Argument* here means "object" or "example" (cf. "I doe much wonder, that one man seeing how much another man is a foole, when he dedicates his behaviours to love, will after hee hath laught at such shallow follies in others, become the argument of his owne scorne, by falling in love," *Much adoe about Nothing*, III.iii.).

8. ***Seeke him with Candle.*** *Seeke him with Candle* means "spare no expense or effort." There is possible allusion to Luke 15:8 ("what woman having ten pieces of silver, if she lose one piece, doth not light a candle, and sweepe the house, and seeke diligently till shee find it?"), but the contemporary phrase "to burn one candle to find another" meant to attempt to gain something of lesser value than the money, time and effort expended to obtain it. It is nevertheless in *Oliver's* best interest to find *Orlando*, whatever the cost, because in *Frederick's* eyes both brothers have equal worth as an object of revenge (lines 5–6, above).

Also see notes: *kindle*, I.i.168, and *Candle*, III.v.44.

8. ***bring him dead, or living.*** *Duke Frederick* here officially declares *Orlando* an outlaw. (In the *Tale of Gamelyn*, Gamelyn / *Orlando* is declared a "woolves-heed"; anyone could kill an outlaw to collect the bounty, which was exactly the same as that of a wolf.)

9–12. ***Within this twelvemonth... seizure.*** Accused offenders were expected to surrender themselves to the court "in person, or by Atturny, within a yeare after they have beene summoned" (RC, s.v. "Annotation de biens"). Those who failed to appear for trial could be declared outlaws: "At first outlawry was only applied to felony, but subsequently was used in civil cases where the defendant absconded; in a case of outlawry, foreiture of goods and lands followed" (Henry St. Clair Feilden, *A Short Constitutional History Of England*). *Frederick* perverts the usual course of law by seizing *Oliver's* lands at the beginning, as opposed to the end, of the customary *twelvemonth* grace period.

10. ***our.*** The plural pronoun *our* indicates that *Frederick* assumes royal authority and that his words have the force of law.

13. ***quit.*** Acquit.

19. ***extent.*** *Frederick* orders his officers to (a) value *Oliver's* property; and/or (b) confiscate *Oliver's* property. *Extent* "hath two significations, sometimes signifying a Writ or Commission to the Sheriff for the valuing of Lands or Tenements... Sometimes the act of the Sheriff or other Commissioner, upon this Writ" (TB, q.v.).

20. ***expediently.*** *Expediently* might mean "promptly" (OED, which cites this line as the only example). However, an "expedient" is "A helpe, fit meanes, device, tricke, shift, evasion, to avoid a mischiefe, or compasse any matter" (RC, q.v.). Therefore, *Frederick* tasks his *Lords* with inventing a convenient (albeit technically necessary) legal excuse in order to seize *Oliver's* property.

20. ***turne him going.*** I.e., "send him packing."

Act III, scene ii

Scena Secunda.

Enter Orlando. [III.ii.1]

Orl. Hang there my verse, in witnesse of my love,

And thou thrice crowned Queene of night survey

With thy chaste eye, from thy pale spheare above [5]

Thy Huntresse name, that my full life doth sway.

O *Rosalind*, these Trees shall be my Bookes,

And in their barkes my thoughts Ile charracter,

That everie eye, which in this Forrest lookes,

Shall see thy vertue witnest every where. [10]

Run, run *Orlando*, carve on every Tree,

The faire, the chaste, and unexpressive shee.

Exit {*Orlando.*}

Enter Corin & Clowne. [III.ii.2]

Co. And how like you this shepherds life Master *Touchstone*? [15]

Notes III.ii.

4. ***thrice crowned Queene... survey.*** The *thrice crowned Queene of night* is the moon goddess or "Hecate: called Cynthia to Heaven, Diana on earth, and Proserpina in hell: from whence she received the name of Trivia" (George Sandys, *Ovid's Metamorphosis Englished, Mythologized, And Represented in Figures*). *Orlando* believes *Rosalind's eye* (vagina) to be *chaste* and therefore invokes *Cynthia* as her "surveyor" ("guardian, overseer," TT, s.v. "Cūrātōrĭa"). However, the *Queene of night* was not always *chaste*; see note: *Diana in the Fountaine*, IV.i.149–150.

5. ***pale spheare.*** When the Earth was believed to be at the center of the universe, it was thought that the heavenly "spheres," which enclosed the Earth like the layers of an onion, each carried one of the seven known planets. The moon, which was considered a planet in its own right, resided in the first (and therefore perfect) *spheare.* The *pale* (enclosed area, realm, boundary) of the moon's *spheare* corresponded with the maidenly perfection of the virgin moon goddess, whose *pale* complexion symbolized her purity (cf. *chaste,* line 5, above; GW2 notes that the moon was "astrologically associated with the vagina," s.v. "Moon").

6. ***Huntresse.*** *Orlando* envisions *Rosalind* as one of the votary nymphs of Diana (virgin goddess of groves, forests, and the hunt). The "hunt" was also "symbolic of sexual pursuit" (TR); cf. 243–244, below, and IV.iii.21.

6. ***full life doth sway.*** *Rosalind* has power to *sway* (influence, govern, command) *Orlando's full* (entire) *life* (existence). In addition, she can "sway" (i.e., erect; a "sway" is a pump handle, and "Shakespeare's verb 'swayes' has reference to the smooth upward movement of some such lever," HH, p. 328) his *full* (virile; literally, "Of a fish: Charged with roe," OED) *life* (penis, FR). *Orlando* doubtless also hopes that *Rosalind* will subsequently cause his *life* (i.e., erect penis) to *sway* ("go down, fall," OED).

7–8. ***O Rosalind... charracter.*** *Orlando* will use the *Trees* as *Bookes* ("register[s] for memory of things," "paper journall[s]," "writing table[s]," TT, s.v. "Tăbella") and will *charracter* (write, engrave) his *thoughts in their barkes.* He also hopes to use his own "bark" (i.e., penis; literally the foreskin, JA, p. 74) to *charracter* ("imprint, stamp," RC, s.v. "Caracterer") his own *charracter* ("shape, resemblance, favor, figure," RC, s.v. "Forme") in *Rosalind's* "book" ("pudendum," JH; "The vaginal image is of a woman opening to receive a man, an idea sometimes reinforced by the phallic pen," GW2). Cf. I.iii.13, where *Rosalind* dreams of *Orlando* as father to her children.

9. ***everie eye... Forrest.*** A theatre's audience, of course, provides many "eyes" in this fictitious *Forrest.*

10. ***vertue.*** Chastity; womanly purity.

11. ***carve on every Tree.*** *Orlando's* father, *Sir Rowland,* would have been loosely associated with the *Orlando* (It. form of the name "Roland") in Ludovico Ariosto's *Orlando Furioso* (the story was dramatized by Robert Greene in 1594). In it, Medore, *Orlando's* rival for the love of a woman named Angelica, set about "in ev'ry stone or shadie tree, To grave their names with bodkin, knife or pin, *Angelica and Medore*" (John Harington, *Orlando Furioso in English Heroical Verse*). *Orlando,* upon finding the names "Medore" and "Angelica" carved together in a tree, went mad and raged naked through the forest.

12. ***unexpressive.*** Inexpressible; incapable of being justly represented through words.

15. ***this shepherds life Master Touchstone.*** *Touchstone* is not the *Clowne's* real name but the *alias* he assumed as a fugitive (II.iv.3). Given his *shepherds life,* the *Clowne's* assumption of the honorific *Master* (ancestor of the modern "Mister") is somewhat pretentious, for this title was reserved solely for a man who could "live without manuell labour, and thereto is able and will beare the post, charge, and countenance of a gentelman, he shall be called master, which is the title that men give to esquiers and gentlemen" (William Harrison, *Description of England*). The other working *shepherds* in this play (*Corin, Silvius,* and *William*) are never addressed as *Master.* By contrast, *Ganimed* and *Aliena,* who employ others to tend their flock for them, are respectively referred to as *Master* (line 86, below) and *Mistresse* (III.iv.47, V.i.66). Also cf. and see note: *good mans,* III.v.63.

Clow. Truely Shepheard, in respect of it selfe, it is a good life; but in respect that it is a shepheards life, it is naught. In respect that it is solitary, I like it verie well: but in respect that it is private, it is a very vild life. Now in respect it is in the fields, it pleaseth mee well: but in [20] respect it is not in the Court, it is tedious. As it is a spare life (looke you) it fits my humor well: but as there is no more plentie in it, it goes much against my stomacke. Has't any Philosophie in thee shepheard?

Cor. No more, but that I know the more one sickens, [25] the worse at ease he is: and that hee that wants money, meanes, and content, is without three good frends. That the propertie of raine is to wet, and fire to burne: That good pasture makes fat sheepe: and that a great cause of the night, is lacke of the Sunne: That hee that hath lear- [30] ned no wit by Nature, nor Art, may complaine of good breeding, or comes of a very dull kindred.

16–18. ***in respect of it selfe... naught.*** The *Clowne* finds nothing wrong with *a shepherds life* except that it is *naught*, which means (a) "altogither unprofitable" (TT, s.v. "Filicones"); (b) "sadde" (WT, s.v. "Tristo"); and/or (c) "wicked, impious" (RC, s.v. "Inique"; cf. lines 41–45 and 78–85, below). *A shepherds life* is also one of "nought" ("Poverty; low social status or position," OED), and therefore a shepherd is *naught* (i.e., "screwed"; see note: *naught*, I.i.37).

18–19. ***solitary... private.*** *Private* means (a) secluded or reclusive; and (b) "Deprived, bereft, or dispossessed" (OED).

The *Clowne* also thinks this life *private* (i.e.,"shitty"; a *private* is a "lavatory," OED; *solitary* is "Melancholike, full of black choler," TT, s.v. "Mĕlanchŏlicus"; cf. and see note: *melancholy*, II.i.30).

19. ***vild.*** A variant of "vile," which can mean (a) despicable; (b) filthy; (c) degrading; and/or (d) depraved.

20. ***the fields.*** "The country as opposed to a town" (OED).

21. ***tedious.*** Unpleasant or offensive; also "barren, voide or poore of wit, invention, or conceite" (JF, s.v. "Secco").

21–23. ***spare... against my stomacke.*** A shepherd's life is *spare* (frugal, temperate), which fits the *Clowne's humor* (mood, inclination). However, as it has *in it no more plentie* (wealth, luxury), it *goes much against* his *stomacke* ("disposition," F&H; "temper," OED).

Because a "spare diet maintaineth a good stomacke" (Nicholas Breton, *The Figure of Foure*), the *Clowne's* claim that a *spare life* goes *against* his *stomacke* directly contradicts accepted medical wisdom.

24. ***Philosophie.*** If *Corin* has *any Philosophie* ("love of learning, studie, knowledge, and wisedome," JF, s.v. "Philosofia"), he might be able to give the *Clowne* some lessons in patience. The "*Patientia Philosophica*, Is a Vertue obedient unto reason, in bearing wrongs, and suffering adversities; it moderates griefe, and bridles nature, so that it never rebells against Justice, Modesty, Constancy, or any other vertue" (Thomas Heywood, *Londini Sinus Salutis*).

26. ***the worse at ease.*** Less comfortable (*ease* is the "absence of pain," OED).

27. ***content.*** Satisfaction; also "Acceptance of conditions or circumstances" (OED). Cf. and see note: *Philosophie*, line 24, above.

28. ***propertie.*** Essential nature or characteristic.

31. ***no wit by Nature, nor Art.*** No wisdom by innate disposition or education.

31–32. ***good breeding... dull kindred.*** *Corin* considers the pampered gentry prone to dim-wittedness, and he finds those *of good breeding* ("polite education," OED) as dim-witted as those descended from *dull* (foolish, stupid) *kindred* (parents, ancestors). Cf. *too Courtly a wit*, line 70, below.

Clo. Such a one is a naturall Philosopher:

Was't ever in Court, Shepheard?

Cor. No truly. [35]

Clo. Then thou art damn'd.

Cor. Nay, I hope.

Clo. Truly thou art damn'd, like an ill roasted Egge,

all on one side.

Cor. For not being at Court? your reason. [40]

Clo. Why, if thou never was't at Court, thou never

saw'st good manners: if thou never saw'st good maners,

then thy manners must be wicked, and wickednes is sin,

and sinne is damnation: Thou art in a parlous state shep-

heard. [45]

Cor. Not a whit *Touchstone*, those that are good maners

at the Court, are as ridiculous in the Countrey, as

the behaviour of the Countrie is most mockeable at the

Court. You told me, you salute not at the Court, but

you kisse your hands; that courtesie would be uncleanlie [50]

if Courtiers were shepheards.

Clo. Instance, briefly: come, instance.

Cor. Why we are still handling our Ewes, and their

33–34. ***naturall Philosopher... in Court.*** In *An English Expositior*, John Bullokar explains that in

> Philosophy... There are three different kinds thereof. I. Rational Philosophie, including Grammer, Logick, and Rhetorick; and this dives into the subtilty of disputations and discourse. 2. Natural Philosophie, searching into the obscurity of natures secrets, containing besides, Arithmetick, Musick, Geometry, and Astronomy. 3. Moral Phylosophy, which consists in the knowledge and practise of civility and good behavior.

The *Clowne* ironically acknowledges *Corin's* skill in "naturall philosophie" ("the Arte or science of naturall things," JF, s.v., Fisica), but if *Corin* had been *in Court* he could also discuss "morall Philosophie" ("Ethicks," HC, q.v.). In this area, however, the *Clowne* finds *Corin* sadly deficient; cf. lines 41–45, below.

The *Clowne* thinks *Corin* a "Naturel," meaning (a) a "naturall Philosopher"; and (b) one of an "in-bred condition" (RC, q.v.; also see note: *nature*, II.iv.58). This makes him both a *naturall* ("An idiot, a simpleton," F&H) and a *naturall Philosopher* (i.e., "an ass" or a "shit-ass"; "A naturall Philosopher" is a "Physicien," RC, q.v.; a "physician" is "An arse," FR, and "Physic" is "A cathartic, a purge, a laxative," JH). The *Clowne* may additionally play on the pronunciation of *Philosopher*: cf. "a foolish philosopher, as wee say, a foolesopher" (JF, s.v. "Filosofastro").

36–40. ***thou art damn'd... your reason.*** The *Clowne*, who *vents* wisdom *In mangled formes* (II.vii.45–46), here makes oblique reference to the "First Satire" of Horace (Quintus Horatius Flaccus, 65–8 B.C.): "Est modus in rebus, sunt certi denique fines, Quos ultra citraque nequit consistere rectum" ("A meane there is in matters all, / and certaine bondes be pyghte [i.e., "fixed"], / On this syde or beyonde the whiche / nothyng thats good can lyghte," Thomas Drante, *Horace His arte of Poetrie*). Horace's adage may initially seem remote, but the link becomes clear in early Latin textbooks which idiomatically translate Horace's saying as "There is reason in rosting eggs" (Charles Hoole, *An easie entrance to the Latine tongue*).

Roasting *an Egge* directly in the fire requires *reason* ("wytte," "discretion," JP, q.v.) because the *Egge* must be constantly turned or it will be *roasted* only *on one side*. Roasting *an Egge* also requires *reason* ("Moderation," OED) lest it explode. As *an ill roasted Egge, Corin* has no *reason* (moderation) and is therefore *ill* ("evil," OED) and *damn'd* because he lacks the Christian virtue of "moderation" (a.k.a. "temperance"). Thus, *like an ill roasted Egge*, he is *damn'd* (i.e., "damnified": "spoiled," OED).

42. ***manners.*** Both (a) refined social behavior; and (b) morals.

44. ***parlous.*** *Parlous* is "Perillous": "dangerous, jeopardous, hazardous" (RC, s.v. "Perilleux").

46. ***Touchstone.*** *Corin* here drops the honorific "Master"; cf. and see note: *Master*, line 15, above.

49. ***salute.*** To *salute* is to "greete," "recommind, to all-haile, to bid good morrow or god speede, to do reverence" (JF, s.v. "Salutare").

52. ***Instance.*** Example.

53. ***still.*** Constantly.

Fels you know are greasie.

Clo. Why do not your Courtiers hands sweate? and [55]
is not the grease of a Mutton, as wholesome as the sweat
of a man? Shallow, shallow: A better instance I say:
Come.

Cor. Besides, our hands are hard.

Clo. Your lips wil feele them the sooner. Shallow a- [60]
gen: a more sounder instance, come.

Cor. And they are often tarr'd over, with the surgery
of our sheepe: and would you have us kisse Tarre? The
Courtiers hands are perfum'd with Civet.

Clo. Most shallow man: Thou wormes meate in re- [65]
spect of a good peece of flesh indeed: learne of the wise
and perpend: Civet is of a baser birth then Tarre, the
verie uncleanly fluxe of a Cat. Mend the instance Shepheard.

Cor. You have too Courtly a wit, for me, Ile rest. [70]

Clo. Wilt thou rest damn'd? God helpe thee shallow

54. ***Fels.*** Skins or fleeces.

54. ***greasie.*** *Corin* speaks of "Greasie woll, wooll unwashed and having the filth sticking unto it" (TT, s.v. "Lana succida"). In lines 56–58, below, the *Clowne* quibbles on *greasie* meaning "indecent" (see note: *greazie*, II.i.60).

56–57. ***grease of a Mutton... sweat of a man.*** The *grease* and *sweat* (substances "Produced by coital exertions," EC) *of a man* are as *wholesome* (healthful, salubrious) as those *of a Mutton* (whore). Additionally, *wholesome* might play on "hole" (vagina) and "sum" (phallic erection; see note: *summe*, line 133, below).

57–65. ***Shallow... shallow.*** The *Clowne* thinks *Corin's* "instances" (examples) *Shallow* (superficial) because they all have to do with his *Shallow* ("A drove, a flock," OED).

59–60. ***our hands are hard... the sooner.*** If a man's *hands* (i.e., genitals; see note: *hand*, I.ii.246) are *hard* (i.e., erect; see note: *hard*, I.ii.49), then *lips* (i.e., the labia pudendi) *will feele them the sooner.*

61. ***sounder.*** As a *sounder* ("A diligent searcher, examiner, inquirer," RC, s.v. "Recercheur"), the *Clowne* desires a *sounder* (more reasonable) example than anything relating to livestock or "sounders" ("A herd of swine," FG).

62. ***tarr'd... surgery.*** Sheep were *tarr'd* with a letter or symbol as an emblem of ownership. However, these sheep were *tarr'd* in *surgery*, so the probable allusion is to tar as a cure for "some scabbie diseases" (RC, s.v. "Tarc").

65–67. ***wormes meate... perpend.*** As a *peece of flesh* (human being), *Corin* is no more than *wormes meate* (i.e., damned and consigned to Hell; *Wormes* are one of Hell's torments as per Isaiah 66:34: "And they shall goe foorth, and looke upon the carkeises of the men that have transgressed against me: for their worme shall not die, neither shall their fire be quenched, and they shall be an obhorring unto all flesh"). *Corin* should *learne of the wise* (i.e., the *Clowne*) *and perpend* ("consider, advise upon, thinke of; examine; ponder," "revolve, or weigh in the mind," RC, s.v. "Considerer") his fate.

The *Clowne* thinks that *Corin's* arguments are as weak as a *peece* (penis, FR), *flesh* (genitals, F&H), and *meate* ("prick," F&H) that have contracted the "worm" (syphilis, FR). *Corin* must *learne of the wise* (the "Sexually experienced," FR) if he wishes to *perpend* (i.e., restore both his morals and his *peece of flesh* to a "perpendicular" or "upright" condition). If *Corin* can *Mend* (heal, correct) his *instance* (i.e., his virility; see note: *instant*, I.iii.78), then he can *Mend* (copulate; L. "coïtus" is used both for the mending of a wound and sexual intercourse).

67–68. ***Civet... fluxe of a Cat.*** *Civet*, "a sweet substance like Musk, which yet is but the turd of a little Beast like a Cat" (JG), was widely used in the manufacture of perfume. As *fluxe* (excrement; see note: *Fluxe*, II.i.57), *Civet* would indeed be of *baser* (lower) *birth* (origin) *then Tarre. Tarre* is extracted primarily from pine trees or coal, but *Civet* originates in the "base" (posteriors, anus; see note: *basest*, II.vii.84).

70. ***too Courtly a wit.*** The court was regarded as a place of refinement and learning, but *Courtly* also means "Characterized by the fair words or flattery of courtiers" (OED). *Corin* thinks that the *Clowne* has "one especiall Courtly quality; to wit, no wit at all" (Thomas Middleton, *Michaelmas Terme*).

70–71. ***rest... rest.*** *Corin* uses *rest* to mean "stop"; the *Clowne* quibbles on *rest* meaning (a) "repose"; and (b) "lie in death or in the grave" (OED).

man: God make incision in thee, thou art raw.

Cor. Sir, I am a true Labourer, I earne that I eate: get
that I weare; owe no man hate, envie no mans happinesse: glad of other mens good content with my harme: [75]
and the greatest of my pride, is to see my Ewes graze, &
my Lambes sucke.

Clo. That is another simple sinne in you, to bring the
Ewes and the Rammes together, and to offer to get your
living, by the copulation of Cattle, to be bawd to a Bel- [80]
weather, and to betray a shee-Lambe of a twelvemonth
to a crooked-pated olde Cuckoldly Ramme, out of all
reasonable match. If thou bee'st not damn'd for this, the
divell himselfe will have no shepherds, I cannot see else
how thou shouldst scape. [85]

---

72. ***God make incision... raw.*** *God make incision in thee* means "God save you." *Incision* is either (a) "cutting, in searching of a wound" (RC2, q.v.); or (b) "a graffing or sciencing" (TB, s.v. "Insition"). Both senses provided a favorite religious metaphor, so Shakespeare's audience would have been familiar with this expression from Sunday sermons. A person was sometimes seen as being in need of *God's* cleansing *incision* (cutting) to purify him from sin (cf. "God cures some by incision, by fire and torments," Jeremy Taylor, *The Rule and Exercises of Holy Dying*). Sometimes, however, a person attained salvation by being "grafted" into God's grace (cf. "such as are once truly regenerated and ingrafted into Christ by a lively faith, can neither finally nor totally fall from grace," William Prynne, *The Perpetuitie of a Regenerate Mans Estate*). Either sense of *incision* fits here, but the *Clowne's* assertion that *Corin* is *raw* favors the "cutting" sense. In medical terminology, a wound that is "raw" is "inflamed and painful" (OED) and therefore in need of *incision* (lancing); also see note: *simple*, line 78, below.

The *Clowne* has lowered his original opinion of *Corin* (that he is *an ill roasted Egge*, line 38, above) and now thinks him entirely *raw* ("not throughly baked," RC, s.v. "Encuict"; also "verie ignorant, unexpert," RC, s.v. "Neuf").

73–77. ***I am a true Labourer... my Lambes sucke.*** *Corin* refuses to believe the *Clowne's* assertion that he is *damn'd* (line 71, above) and enumerates his Christian virtues, albeit in a highly colloquial way. Being *a true Labourer* (an honest workman) is in itself a virtue, "For thou shalt eat the labour of thine handes: happie shalt thou bee, and it shall be well with thee" (Psalms 128:2). If *Corin envie*[s] *no mans happinesse*, then he keeps the Tenth Commandment: "Thou shalt not covet thy neighbours house, thou shalt not covet thy neighbours wife, nor his man servant, nor his maid servant, nor his oxe, nor his asse, nor any thing that is thy neighbours" (Exodus 20:17). If *Corin owe*[s] *no man hate* and is *glad of other mens good content with* his *harme*, then he heeds Christ's injunction to "Love your enemies, blesse them that curse you, doe good to them that hate you, and pray for them which despitefully use you, and persecute you" (Matthew 5:44). Lastly, *Corin* asserts that he is guilty of no greater *pride* (a deadly sin; cf. and see note: *pride*, II.vii.75) than *to see* his *Ewes graze, &* his *Lambes sucke*.

73–74. ***get that I weare.*** Like most working people in England, *Corin* probably wore wool (see notes: II.iv.85, II.vii.80–81). As a shepherd, he literally "gets" ("bring[s] in, gather[s], secure[s] a crop," OED) the wool for the clothing he wears.

78. ***simple sinne.*** *Corin* is very *simple* (foolish) to be guilty of such a *simple* (pitiful, wretched) *sinne*. *Corin* not only needs *incision* (line 72, above) but "must be cut of the Simples, Care must be taken to cure him of his Folly" (ND; "simples" are "Physical herbs; also follies," FG).

79. ***offer.*** To *offer* is (a) to attempt or make effort; and (b) to be inclined.

79–83. ***get your living... reasonable match.*** As someone who brings *Rammes* ("lecher[s]," GW) *together with Ewes* ("innocent female[s]," EC) and gets his *living by the copulation of Cattle* ("Whores," ND), *Corin* is no better than a pimp. The *Clowne's* estimation of husbandry is at odds with religious opinion, for man was given "dominion over the fish of the sea, and over the foule of the air, and over the cattell, and over all the earth" (Genesis 1:26).

80–81. ***Bel-weather.*** A *Bel-weather* is (a) the "leading sheep of a flock, on whose neck a bell is hung" (OED); and (b) "an aggressive cuckold" (EC; a "wether" is literally "a castrated ram," OED; also see note: *whether*, II.iii.33).

81–82. ***shee-Lambe of a twelvemonth... Cuckoldy Ramme.*** Horns were the symbol of the cuckold, so "the equating of the horned ram with the cuckold was a commonplace" (JH, s.v. "Ram"). This *olde Ramme* is destined to cuckoldry because his wife, a *shee-Lambe of a* mere *twelvemonth*, is so much younger than he. This *Ramme* is also *crooked-pated*, meaning (a) his "pate" (head) is *crooked* ("horned," TT, s.v. "Cornūātus"); (b) his "pate" (i.e., penis; see note: *heads*, II.i.27) is *crooked* ("wicked, lewde," TT, s.v. "Prāvus"); and/or (c) his "horns" ("erection[s] of the penis," F&H) are *crooked* ("Impotent," FR; *crooked* is literally "deformed," "bowed with age," OED).

83. ***bee'st... damn'd.*** *Corin* is *damn'd* to the *bee'st* (i.e., the "Beast" or Satan) because he mates "beasts" (animals) and makes a ram a "beast" (cuckold, JH; cf. line 82, above)

83–85. ***the divell himselfe... scape.*** The only way *Corin* can *scape* (escape) damnation is if *the divell himselfe* finds *shepherds* so thoroughly evil that he will not admit them to Hell.

Cor. Heere comes yong Master *Ganimed*, my new Mistris-
ses Brother.

Enter Rosalind. [III.ii.3]

Ros. *From the east to westerne Inde,*
no jewel is like Rosalinde, [90]
Hir worth being mounted on the winde,
through all the world beares Rosalinde.
All the pictures fairest Linde,
are but blacke to Rosalinde:
Let no face bee kept in mind, [95]
but the faire of Rosalinde.

Clo. Ile rime you so, eight yeares together; dinners,
and suppers, and sleeping hours excepted: it is the right
Butter-womens ranke to Market.

Ros. Out Foole. [100]

Clo. For a taste.
If a Hart doe lacke a Hinde,
Let him seeke out Rosalinde:
If the Cat will after kinde,

86. ***Master Ganimed.*** See note: *Master Touchstone,* line 15, above.

89–96. ***From the east... of Rosalinde.*** The italics used in lines 89–96 indicate that *Rosalind* reads written text.

89–95. ***east... Inde... winde... mind.*** *Inde* meant "India, the Indies" (RC, q.v.; "India" or the "East Indies" meant both India and Southeast Asia; the "West Indies" were the Caribbean Islands). *Inde* was pronounced to rhyme with *Linde* and *mind* (cf. "Among the greatest Oliphants in all the land of Inde, / A greater tush than had this Boare, ye shall not lightly finde," Arthur Golding, *The First Booke of Ovids Metamorphosis*). *Winde* was also pronounced in this way (cf. "But even some cruell Tiger bred in Armen or in Inde, / Or else the Gulfe Charybdis raisde with rage of Southerne winde," Ibid.).

The rhymes were slightly less forced in Elizabethan English because the vowel of *Inde, winde, Linde,* and *mind* was not pronounced identically to today's (HK, pp. 216–222). Nevertheless, as is subsequently remarked (lines 97–99, 114–115, 156–158, 166–168, 170–172, and 177–178, below), *Orlando's* love poems are inordinately bad. Shakespeare may intentionally mock the earnest but uninspired love poetry found in Lodge's *Rosalynde,* such as the "second Sonetto" of Rosader / *Orlando*: "When as I talke of Rosalynde, / The God from coynesse waxeth kinde, / And seemes in self flames to frie, / Because he loves as well as I."

89–90. ***Inde... jewel.*** *Inde* was renowned for fabulous jewels and wealth, but *Orlando* probably thinks of the *jewel* (chastity, EP) of *Rosalinde's jewel* ("female pudendum; Cunt," F&H).

91. ***worth... on the winde.*** *Rosalinde's worth* (excellence, high value) should be *mounted* ("Exalted," RC, s.v. "Exhaulsé"; "carried away by the wind," "vented, breathed, issued, or passed, out into the ayre," RC, s.v. "Essoré") and carried *through all the world.*

93–94. ***the pictures fairest Linde... blacke.*** *Pictures* that are *fairest* (best) *Linde* (drawn; cf. *limn'd,* II.vii.204) are *but* (only) *blacke* ("foul," OED) in comparison to *Rosalinde.* Apparently, *Orlando* is still preoccupied with *Rosalinde's blacke* (vagina, F&H). Also see note: *linde,* line 106, below.

95. ***face.*** *Face* means (a) visage; and (b) "pudendum" (FR).

97–98. ***dinners, and suppers.*** Dinner was the main meal eaten in the middle of the day; supper was a smaller meal eaten in the evening.

99. ***Butter-womens ranke to Market.*** *Orlando's* verses are *ranke* (unpleasant, rotten). The meter is as sing-song as the "Butter and Eggs Trot" ("A kind of short jogg trot, such as is used by women going to market, with butter and eggs," FG, q.v.) of "Butter women" (dairymaids) carrying their goods to *Market* in a *ranke* (consecutive line). *Orlando's* verses are also as *ranke* (sexually defiled or venereally infected; see note: *ranke,* I.ii.104) as a "Butter-woman" (whore, GW2, s.v. "Butter"; coital movements were likened to the churning of butter) who sells herself on the *Market.*

102–103. ***If a Hart... seeke out.*** *If a Hart* (male deer) with "heart" (i.e., in love) lacks a *Hinde* (female deer) to be his "dear" (beloved), he should *seeke out* ("hunt after," TB, s.v. "Vestigate") *Rosalinde.* The *Clowne* implies that *Rosalinde* is "game" (sexually promiscuous, EP). Also see notes: *seeke,* I.iii.106, and *Huntresse,* line 6, above.

104. ***Cat... after kinde.*** In gratifying its *will* (sexual urges; see note: *will,* I.i.76), the *Cat* who "Hunteth for his Kind" ("the Term for... Copulation," ND, s.v. "Otter") behaves *after* (according to) its *kinde* (nature, natural disposition). The implication is that *Rosalinde* is a *Cat* (whore) who seeks to do "the deed of kind" (copulate, F&H).

so be sure will Rosalinde: [105]

Wintred garments must be linde,

so must slender Rosalinde:

They that reap must sheafe and binde,

then to cart with Rosalinde.

Sweetest nut, hath sowrest rinde, [110]

such a nut is Rosalinde.

He that sweetest rose will finde,

must finde Loves pricke, & Rosalinde.

This is the verie false gallop of Verses, why doe you in-

fect your selfe with them? [115]

Ros. Peace you dull foole, I found them on a tree.

Clo. Truely the tree yeelds bad fruite.

106–107. ***Wintred garments... slender Rosalinde.*** *Garments* that are *slender* ("Of a thin consistency," OED) *must be linde* in order to be *Wintred* ("Adapted for or used in winter," OED). *Rosalinde*, who is *slender* (with allusion to her vaginal capacity), *must* also *be linde* ("Lined or padded on the inside: hence, = fucked," EC). If she is consequently *linde* (i.e., pregnant; literally "fill[ed]," OED), she will no longer be *slender*. The *Clowne* may also imply that *Rosalinde's garments* (i.e., "cloth": "female pudendum; Cunt," F&H) are *Wintred* (i.e., sexually frigid; see note: *cold*, II.i.12).

108–109. ***They that reap... to cart.*** *They that reap* (gather a crop) *must sheafe and binde* (i.e., tie it up into a bundle) and load it onto a *cart*. Those that *reap* (copulate, JA, p. 154) *must binde* (i.e., marry); otherwise, they will produce "sheaves" (i.e., a "Crop" or "illegitimate children," EC, q.v.) from the *sheafe* (i.e., vagina; the metaphor derives from threshing or beating sheaves to extract the grain; cf. "have you not threshing work enough, but children must be bang'd out oth' sheafe too," Francis Beaumont, *Wit Without Money*). Should *Rosalinde's sheafe* (i.e., vagina) produce "sheaves" (i.e., bastards), she *must* be brought *to cart* ("be flogged at the cart's a-se or tail," FG, a punishment for prostitutes).

110–113. ***Sweetest nut... Loves pricke.*** Like the expression "No Rose without a prickle" (RC, s.v. "Nulle rose sans espine"), *Sweetest nut hath sowrest rinde* is a proverb which means that nothing worthwhile can be gained without some difficulty. Because *Rosalinde* is a "hard nut to crack" (i.e., she doesn't easily "open" for sexual intercourse), her *nut* ("vulva... opened up to get at the sexual kernel," GW) will ultimately be very "sweet" (sexually satisfying; see note: *sweete*, II.i.5). The bawdy quibble on *rose* and *pricke* is obvious.

The *Clowne* may additionally imply that *Rosalinde* is a "sour" ("Crabbed, surly, ill-conditioned," F&H) *nut* ("something of trifling value," OED) who displays *rinde* ("Impudence, effrontery," OED).

114–115. ***false gallop of Verses... infect.*** A *false gallop*, also called a "canter," is the second fastest natural gait in a horse (the others being the walk, trot, and gallop; see note: lines 304–306, below). The jogging motions of the *false gallop* provide an apt metaphor for bad poetry: "I would trot a false gallop through the rest of his ragged Verses, but that if I should retort his rime dogrell aright, I must make my verses (as he doth his) run hobling like a Brewers Cart upon the stones, and observe no length in their feete" (Thomas Nashe, *Strange Newes*).

The *false gallop* is also a metaphor for coital movement, and these *Verses* are so *infect* ("Incomplete, imperfect," OED) that *Rosalind* will certainly be "infected" (contract venereal disease) if she allows them to *infect* (influence, take hold of) her. Also see note: *Verses*, line 167, below.

117. ***the tree yeelds bad fruite.*** "A good tree cannot bring forth evil fruit, neither can a corrupt tree bring forth good fruit" (Matthew 7:18), so *Orlando* must be as *bad* (rotten) as his poetry. Cf. II.iii.66–67.

Ros. Ile graffe it with you, and then I shall graffe it with a Medler: then it will be the earliest fruit i'th coun- try: for you'l be rotten ere you bee halfe ripe, and that's [120] the right vertue of the Medler.

Clo. You have said: but whether wisely or no, let the Forrest judge.

Enter Celia with a writing. [III.ii.iv]

Ros. Peace, here comes my sister reading, stand aside. [125]

Cel. *Why should this Desert bee,*
for it is unpeopled? Noe:
Tonges Ile hang on everie tree,
that shall civill sayings shoe.
Some, how briefe the Life of man [130]
runs his erring pilgrimage,
That the stretching of a span,
buckles in his summe of age.

118–121. ***Ile graffe it with you... the right vertue of the Medler.*** "Graffing" is "when a budde of one tree is cut of round with part of the barke, and set on an other: or when a hole is bored in a tree, and a kernell put in with a little lome" (TT, s.v. "Inŏcŭlātĭo"). *Rosalind* tells the *Clowne* that she will *graffe* the *bad tree* (line 117, above) *with you*— i.e., with "yew." As a "yew," the *Clowne* is indeed very bad, for the yew tree was considered "so venimous, as whosoever did but sleepe under the shade of this tree, or did eat of that mortiferous fruit, he forthwith died" (Pierre d'Avity, *The Estates, Empires, & Principallities Of The World*).

Then (afterwards), *Rosalind* will *graffe* this already doubly-bad tree with a *Medler*, a tree which yields "A fruit, vulgarly called an open a-se; of which it is more truly than delicately said, that it is never ripe till it is as rotten as a t--d, and then it is not worth a f--t" (FG). It is the *right* (proper) *vertue* (natural quality or characteristic) of the *Medler* to *be rotten* (decomposing) *ere* (before) it *bee ripe* (ready to harvest), but "As you may see in fruit-trees, whereof those that growe of a kernell are long ere they beare, but such as are grafted on a stocke a great deale sooner" (Francis Bacon, *The Wisdome of the Ancients*). As a grafted "meddler" (intrusive busybody), the *Clowne* will be *the earliest* (i.e., the soonest *rotten*) *fruit i'the country*, for he will *be rotten* (dead and decomposing in his grave) *before* he *is* even *halfe ripe* ("wise, discreet, considerate," JF, s.v. "Maturo").

If *Rosalind* "grafts" (sexually joins, JH, s.v. "Grafting") the *Clowne* with the aforementioned "bad" ("rotten" or venereally infected; see note: *rotten*, II.iii.66) "tree" ("woman regarded as a sex partner," JH), *then* (in that case) she will *graffe it* (the bad tree) *with a Medler* (the *Clowne,* who is a debauchee; to "meddle" is to copulate, F&H). As a *Medler*, the *Clowne* is already *rotten* (i.e., syphilitic) *before* he is even *halfe ripe* ("Sexually ripe; ready for sexual harvesting," JH), so his *fruit* (penis, GW2; also semen, JH) *will be the earliest* (i.e., the soonest syphilitic) *i'the country* (i.e., in the "cunt"). This is *right* (in accordance) with his *vertue* ("potency, virility," FR).

123. ***Forrest.*** The *Clowne* leaves final judgment of his sexual health not to just one "tree" (female sexual partner; see note: lines 118–121, above) but to the *Forrest* (female genitalia and pubic hair, FR) of an entire *Forrest* (i.e., the myriad sexual partners he is capable of servicing).

126–127. ***Why should this Desert bee... unpeopled.*** To maintain the poem's septenary meter, *bee* must be disyllabic with the first syllable unstressed ("be-YEE") and *unpeopled* quadrisyllabic ("UN-pee-OH-pled" or "UN-peep-OH-led").

128–129. ***Tongues... civill sayings shoe.*** By hanging his poems on *everie tree*, *Orlando* will turn them into "citizens" and give them *Tongues that shall shoe* (display, communicate) *civill* (of or pertaining to inhabitants or citizens; also civilized or courteous) *sayings.*

130–133. ***how briefe... summe of age.*** *The Life of man runs* (moves rapidly) through a *pilgrimage* (mortal journey) that is both *erring* ("wandring, roving," JF, s.v. "Errante") and *erring* ("going astraie, unskilful, false, spreading widly abroad, out of order," TT, s.v. "Errans"). This *briefe span buckles in* (limits, encloses) the *summe* (total amount) *of* a man's *age* (duration of life), and his *Life* "stretches" (achieves, reaches) *a span* (lifetime) that is only as *briefe* as *a span* ("the length of the hand from the wrist to the top of the litle finger," TT, s.v. "Orthodoron"; cf. "thou hast made my dayes as an hand breadth, and mine age is as nothing before thee," Psalms 39:5).

Even if a man's *Life* (penis; see note: *life*, line 6, above) "stretches" (rises to full height, extends) *a span* (literally, nine inches) at the *summe* ("highest attainable point," OED), the *summe* (conclusion, upshot) is that his "stretch" (i.e., penis; literally "A yard," FG) will *buckle* (bend, collapse). Thus, his *pilgrimage* ("journey": "sexual activity," GW2) is *briefe*, for he will no longer be able to "buckle" (copulate, GW) with a "buckler" (vagina, EP, s.v. "Sword").

Some of violated vowes,

twixt the soules of friend, and friend: [135]

But upon the fairest bowes,

or at everie sentence end;

Will I Rosalinda write,

teaching all that reade, to know

The quintessence of everie sprite, [140]

heaven would in little show.

Therefore heaven Nature charg'd,

that one bodie should be fill'd

With all Graces wide enlarg'd,

nature presently distill'd [145]

Helens cheeke, but not his heart,

Cleopatra's *Majestie:*

134–135. ***violated vowes... of friend, and friend.*** *Vowes* were held to be so sacred and inviolable that breaking them put the soul in mortal peril (see notes: *oaths*, II.vii.161, and *oathes*, IV.i.182). In Dante's *Inferno*, those guilty of betrayal are *soules* (i.e., "asses" or "assholes"; the "sole" is literally the "bottom") who fittingly occupy the deepest depth of Hell, or "Fundament of the world" (Canto XXXII).

If "friends" (lovers, JH) *violated* their *vowes*, then the woman would betray the man's "soul" (i.e., penis; a "sowel" is a "stout stick or staff" OED), and the man would betray the woman's "soul" ("vagina," ex the sense "bore of a cannon," GW). However, *Orlando* is certain that *Rosalind* could never be guilty of such disloyalty.

140–141. ***quintessence... heaven would in little show.*** The Elizabethans believed that all matter was made up of four elements (earth, air, fire, and water); these corresponded to the four bodily "humors" that determined a person's physical and mental temperament (see note: *humorous,* I.ii.269). Beyond these four earthly elements was a *quintessence* (from L. "quinta essentia": fifth essence) which was so "Exceedingly refined, or purified" (RC, s.v. "Quintessencé") that it was thought to be the physical manifestation of God. As the *quintessence* ("The fift substance, that which remaineth in any thing, after the corruptible elements are taken from it," HC, q.v.) inherent in *every sprite* ("spirit": each of the four elements, OED; also see note: *spirits,* I.ii.168), *Rosalind* embodies divine perfection and virtue. *Heaven* (God, divine creative power) would *show* (manifest) this perfection in very *little,* but *Rosalind,* as a microcosm of the larger world, manifests the *quintessence in little* (in miniature, with especial reference to painting; see note: lines 142–150, below).

Despite *Rosalind's quintessence* (virtue, purity), *Orlando* probably imagines the "essence" ("nature": "Semen," OED) of his *spirit* (erect penis, see notes: *spirit,* I.i.23 and 68) in her "quin" ("female pudendum," F&H).

142–150. ***heaven... one bodie... manie parts.*** An allusion to the fabled painting of Juno (or, in some accounts, Venus) by the Greek painter Zeuxis (born c. 464 B.C.). As Robert Albott relates in *Englands Parnassus,*

> When Zeuxis for the Goddesse Junos sake
> To paint a picture of most rare renowne
> Did many of the fayrest damsels make
> To stand before him bare from foote to crowne,
> A patterne of theyr perfect parts to take.

Zeuxis could assemble so *manie* perfect *parts* within one *bodie* only through artifice. In *Rosalind,* however, Mother *Nature* and the *Graces* (the sister goddesses who bestow charm and beauty) have *enlarg'd* ("bestow[ed] liberally," OED) *manie wide* (great, excessive) *Graces* (pleasing qualities). They have *distill'd* ("refined by distillation to the highest purity and exalted to its utmost degree of vertue," JG, s.v. "Elixar") her *parts* to the *quintessence* (line 140, above).

Orlando hopes that he will "charge" (sexually assault, EP) *Rosalind's heaven* ("female pudendum," F&H). He also hopes her *bodie* (vagina; TR) will be *fill'd* ("penetrate[d] genitally," GW) with his *enlarg'd* (extended) *Nature* (i.e., penis; see notes: *nature,* II.iv.58, and *natures,* I.ii.50) and *Graces* (i.e., genitals; see note: *disgrace,* I.i.145).

146. ***Helens cheeke... heart.*** *Helen* was the most beautiful woman in the world and the wife of King Menelaus of Sparta. Although beautiful, *Helen* was patently false; her elopement with Paris started the Trojan War. *Rosalinde* has *Helens cheeke* (beauty) but neither her *heart* (i.e., her fickleness) nor her "art" (cunning, deceit).

146. ***his.*** A possible typographical error for "her."

147. ***Cleopatra's Majestie.*** *Cleopatra* was "an Egiptian Queene, she was first beloved of J. Cæsar, after Marcus Anthonius was by her brought into such dotage, that he aspired the Empire, which caused his destruction" (HC, q.v.). *Cleopatra's* "majestick state begot an admiration in her beholders; a strong impression in the wounded hearts of her lovers... her eye reteyned a power to command love; and subdue the commandingst Conquerour with a look" (Richard Brathwaite, *The two Lancashire lovers*). (Shakespeare treats *Cleopatra's* story at length in *The Tragedie of Anthonie and Cleopatra*).

Attalanta's *better part,*

sad Lucrecia's *Modestie.*

Thus Rosalinde *of manie parts,* [150]

by Heavenly Synode was devis'd,

Of manie faces, eyes, and hearts,

to have the touches deerest pris'd.

Heaven would that shee these gifts should have,

and I to live and die her slave. [155]

Ros. O most gentle Jupiter, what tedious homilie of

Love have you wearied your parishioners withall, and

never cri'de, have patience good people.

Cel. How now backe friends: Shepheard, go off a lit-

tle: go with him sirrah. [160]

---

148. ***Attalanta's better part.*** *Attalanta* was "a warlike virgine" (Walter Raleigh, *The History of the World*) and a "Virago" (Thomas Heywood, *Gynaikeion*; a "virago" is "a manly woman," JF, s.v. "Andragone"). In *A Revelation of the Secret Spirit*, Giovan Battista Agnello describes *Attalanta* as

> a maid of most admirable swiftnes, in which gift she overpassed all mankind, [who] did covenant with her suters to runne for life and death, under condition of marriage; that whosoever of them were overrunne, should be put to death, but who did overrunne her, should live and marry her. Many did runne, many

were overrunne, many killed. Untill that Hippomanes running with her, and almost overcome, threw downe three golden Apples one after another, the gifts of Venus. Which, Atalanta stooping to take up, hindred her course, was wonne and obtained in marriage.

The *better part* was the soul or spiritual aspect of man (see note: *better parts,* I.ii.249). Females were considered inferior to men only in respect of their physical bodies, which their superior "male" souls inhabited for purposes of procreation: "Soules have no sexes, as Ambrose saith. In the better part they are both men. And if thy wives soule were freed from the frailty of her sexe, it were as manly, as noble, and every way as excellent as thine owne: Nay, and if it were possible for you to change bodies; hers would worke as manlily in thine, and thine as womanly in hers" (Robert Bolton, *Some Generall Directions for a Comfortable Walking With God*). Like *Attalanta, Rosalind* is that rare female whose physical body is strong enough to manifest her "manly" and "perfect" soul.

149. ***sad Lucrecia's Modestie.*** A "Lucrece" is "a chaste woman; so used from Lucretia, a chaste woman of Rome, the wife of Tarquinius Collatinus, who slew her self, because Sextus Tarquitus had ravished her" (TB, q.v.). (Shakespeare treats *Lucrecia's* story at length in *The Rape of Lucrece*).

150–153. ***Rosalinde of manie parts... deerest pris'd.*** *Rosalinde's manie parts* (personal qualities) were *devis'd* ("Fabricated, framed; built, forged, made; plotted, invented, contrived," RC, s.v. "Fabriqué") *by Heavenly Synode* ("A conjunction of two planets or heavenly bodies," OED; cf. "synodica": "The new moone or the conjunction of the moone and the sunne," TT, s.v. "Luna"). Because the "Sun and Moon do govern our body and spirit, and so moderate the Elements" (William Lilly, *The Starry Messenger*), this *Heavenly Synode devis'd* (ordered, determined) that *Rosalinde's* elements be astrologically distilled to the *quintessence* (cf. and see note: line 140, above). Each of *Rosalind's* features was selected from the best *faces, eyes, and hearts* (cf. and see notes: lines 142–149, above), so her *manie touches* (distinguishing characteristics) are *deerest pris'd* (most highly valued).

Orlando also hopes that *Rosalind* will be his *deerest* (beloved) and his "prize" ("The object of one"s love," JH). If so, he will win the "prize" (sexual achievement, JH) of *manie touches* (i.e., sexual caresses; see note: *Touchstone,* II.iv.3) from her *faces* (i.e., genitals; see note: *face,* line 95, above), *eyes* (vagina and vulva, JH) and *hearts* (pronounced "arts" and thus a pun on "arse").

150. ***manie parts.*** *Rosalind* has *manie parts,* including some that are "manny" ("Manlike, mannish," OED; cf. and see note: *Attalanta's better part,* line 148, above).

154. ***would.*** Intended.

156–158. ***Jupiter... have patience.*** *Rosalind* invokes *Jupiter* as the god of Oak trees and groves (cf. lines 233–235, below). *Orlando* has *wearied Jupiter's parishioners* (i.e., the trees themselves, whom *Orlando* has anthropomorphized as citizens of the forest; cf. and see notes: lines 126–129, above) with a *tedious* (tiresomely long) *homilie* (sermon) *of Love.* Moreover, he never once asked his listeners to *have patience* (cf. II.iv.40).

159. ***backe friends.*** *Rosalind, Corin,* and the *Clowne* have each acted like a "back friend" ("an enimie, a foe, an adversarie," JF, s.v. "Inimico"; a "pretended or false friend," OED) by listening to *Celia* behind her *backe.*

159–160. ***Shepheard... sirrah.*** *Celia* addresses *Corin* as *Shepheard;* she addresses the *Clowne* as *sirrah,* a condescending form of address used to social inferiors.

Clo. Come Shepheard, let us make an honorable retreit, though not with bagge and baggage, yet with
scrip and scrippage.

Exit {*Clowne and Corin*}. [III.ii.5]

Cel. Didst thou heare these verses? [165]

Ros. O yes, I heard them all, and more too, for some
of them had in them more feete then the Verses would
beare.

Cel. That's no matter: the feet might beare the verses.

Ros. I, but the feet were lame, and could not beare [170]
themselves without the verse, and therefore stood lamely in the verse.

Cel. But didst thou heare without wondering, how
thy name should be hang'd and carved upon these trees?

Ros. I was seven of the nine daies out of the wonder, [175]
before you came: for looke heere what I found on a
Palme tree; I was never so berim'd since *Pythagoras* time
that I was an Irish Rat, which I can hardly remember.

161–163. ***honorable retreit... scrippage.*** If an army in *retreit* was in possession of its *bagge and baggage* ("The cariage of an armie," "all t[h]ings necessarie to an host," TT, s.v. "Impĕdīmenta"), then the *retreit* was *honorable* because the force escaped *with bagge and baggage* ("safe and sound, scotfree; without the losse, wast, or expence, of any thing," RC, s.v. "Bague"). *Corin* and the *Clowne* have been "given the bag" (dismissed; this phrase is the ancestor of the modern "given the sack"), but their *retreit* is still *honorable* because each leaves with *scrip* (a "Shepheards scrip; or the bag, or poke, wherein he puts his victualls," RC, s.v. "Panetiere") and *scrippage* (a made-up word intended to echo *baggage*; according to OED, the usual phrase was "scrip and bourdon," a "bourdon" being a staff).

The *Clowne* and *Corin retreit* without *bagge and baggage* because they leave behind *Celia* and *Rosalind*, one of whom is a *bagge* (i.e., a "cunt"; *bagge* was used for the vagina, JA, p. 87) and the other of whom is a *baggage* ("Queane, Jyll, Punke, Flirt," RC, s.v. "Bagasse"; "Whore or Slut," ND). Nevertheless, their *retreit* is *honorable* because each is still in possession of his *scrip* (testicles, TR, s.v. "burdoun") and *scrippage* (i.e., his "burdoun" or penis, TR, q.v.).

Although the *scrip* (variant of "script," OED) calls for the *Clowne* to exit here, he may make a *scrip* ("scornful grimace," OED) at the ladies as he leaves.

167–172. ***more feete... stood lamely in the verse.*** These *Verses* (metrical lines of poetry) could not *beare* (hold, sustain) the *feete* (groups of syllables forming the basic unit of the poetic meter) because there were far *more feete* than there should be. Moreover, *the feet were lame* (metrically defective, halting) and could not *beare themselves without the verse* (the wordplay hinges on "staff" meaning both "A line of verse" and "a crutch," OED).

The *verses* (i.e., the "staff" or penis) might *beare* (sexually sustain) the "feat" (copulation, JH, s.v. "Done feats") if the *feete* (male genitalia; see note: *foot*, II.vii.73) could *beare the verses* (i.e., vagina; L. "versus" is a "furrow"; the furrow is "The female pudendum," F&H). However, the *feet were lame* (impotent, FR) and had *no matter* ("semen," EC). Thus, they *stood lamely in the verse* (i.e., "couldn't get it up" or were incompetent in the sex act; cf. "Fye, out upon't, this verses foote is lame, / Let it goe upright, or a mischiefe take it," John Davies, "To Mr. Tho. Bastard, and the Reader").

175. ***seven of the nine daies... wonder.*** A *wonder* (novelty, object of curiosity or admiration) proverbially lasts only *nine daies* ("nine days' wonder" is roughly equivalent to the modern "fifteen minutes of fame"). If *Rosalind* has been *seven of the nine daies out of the wonder*, then she has been wondering a long time but her interest has not yet abated.

177. ***Palme tree.*** A *Palme tree* ("date tree," TT, s.v. "Palme") could conceivably grow in the fairy-tale forest of Arden. However, *Palme tree* could mean "the paulme, or flower of a willow," (RC, s.v. "Chaton"; cf. "Willow braunches hallow, that they Palmes do use to call," Barnabe Googe, *The Popish Kingdome*). The *Palme* (a.k.a. "Willow") was a traditional symbol for unrequited or lost love. As such, it would be a particularly appropriate tree for *Orlando* to hang his love poetry on.

177–178. ***I was never so berim'd... Irish Rat.*** "Pythagoras the Phylosopher" held the "opinion of the transmigration of souls from one body to another" (TB, s.v. "Pythagorical"). *Rosalind* supposes that she was similarly *berim'd* back in *Pythagoras* lifetime (ca. 570–ca. 495 B.C.) *that* ("when" or "since," OED) she was incarnated as an *Irish Rat*. Then as now, she was *berim'd* "to death, as St. Patrick did the Rats in Ireland" (Edmund Hickeringill, *Gregory, Father-Greybeard, With his Vizard off*) with "Rat-Rhyme" ("Originally a rhyme or piece of poetry used in charming and killing rats. These rhymes were the merest doggerel," Joseph Wright, *The English Dialect Dictionary*, q.v.).

178. ***which I can hardly remember.*** I.e., "*which I can hardly* be expected to *remember*," because "rat rhyme," like *Orlando's* poetry, is utterly forgettable.

Cel. Tro you, who hath done this?

Ros. Is it a man? [180]

Cel. And a chaine that you once wore about his neck:
change you colour?

Ros. I pre'thee who?

Cel. O Lord, Lord, it is a hard matter for friends to
meete; but Mountaines may bee remoov'd with Earth- [185]
quakes, and so encounter.

Ros. Nay, but who is it?

Cel. Is it possible?

Ros. Nay, I pre'thee now, with most petitionary vehemence, tell me who it is. [190]

Cel. O wonderfull, wonderfull, and most wonderfull
wonderfull, and yet againe wonderful, and after that out
of all hooping.

Ros. Good my complection, dost thou think though
I am caparison'd like a man, I have a doublet and hose in [195]
my disposition? One inch of delay more, is a South-sea
of discoverie. I pre'thee tell me, who is it quickely, and
speake apace: I would thou couldst stammer, that thou

179. ***Tro.*** Know.

182. ***change you colour.*** Either "turn pale" or "blush." To "change one's color" can also mean to "change one's tune"; see note: *cattle of this colour*, line 399, below.

184–186. ***a hard matter for friends to meete... encounter.*** Proverbially, "Two men may often meet, but mountaines never" (RC, s.v. "Deux"). *Rosalind* and *Orlando* have *Mountaines* (i.e., seemingly insurmountable obstacles) dividing them, so *it is a hard* (difficult) *matter for friends* (lovers; see note: *friend*, line 135, above) *to meete.* However, even *Mountaines* can *bee remoov'd with Earthquakes, so friends* might *encounter* one another. Therefore, *Rosalind* can look forward to *Mountaines* (with play on "mountings" or sexual intercourse, HK, p. 131), for she may yet *encounter* (make love to, EP, with possible play on "count" as "cunt") *Orlando's hard* (i.e., erect) *matter* ("male genitals, especially the penis," JH; also see note: *matter*, line 169 above).

189–190. ***petitionary vehemence.*** *Rosalind* "petitions" (begs, entreats) *Celia* for information with *vehemence* ("eagarnesse, earnestnesse, violence, force, fierceness," RC, q.v.).

191. ***wonderfull.*** *Wonderfull* means (a) "passing admirable, horribly excellent" (RC, s.v. "Mirelifique"); and (b) "much to be wondered at" (RC, s.v. "Esmerveillable").

192–193. ***out of all hooping.*** *Celia* has hinted that *Orlando* is in the forest until she is *out of all hooping* ("whooping": "showting," RC, s.v. "Hopperie"). Out of all *hooping* (variant of "hoping"), *Rosalind* will shortly be *hooping* (copulating, GW2, s.v. "hoop") with *Orlando* and thus *out of* her *hooping* (hooped petticoats). However, despite *Celia's hooping* (i.e., "a great noise or troublesome dinne," "knock[ing] lowd and fast, like a Cooper in the hooping of caske," RC, s.v. "Tabouler"), her secret remains locked in as if by the "hoops" of a wine cask; cf. lines 198–202, below.

194–196. ***my complection... my disposition.*** *Rosalind* may blush or change *complection* ("The temperature of the humors in ones body, which causeth the colour," RC, q.v.), but *complection* was not just a person's appearance. It was also his "making, temper, constitution of the bodie; also, the disposition, affection, humors, or inclination of the mind" (RC, q.v.) as determined by the *complection* ("mixture of naturall humors," TT, s.v. "Crāsis"; also see note: *humorous*, I.ii.269). *Rosalind* wears *doublet and hose* and is thus *caparison'd* (attired in ornaments and trappings) *like a man*, but she does not have *doublet and hose* (a man's genitalia; see note: *doublet and hose*, II.iv.9) *in* her *disposition* ("Physical constitution, nature, or permanent condition," OED).

196–197. ***South-sea of discoverie.*** Either (a) every *inch of delay* takes as long as *discoverie* (investigation, exploration) *of* the *South-sea* (i.e., the *South* Pacific Ocean); or (b) every *inch* that *Celia* delays makes *discoverie* (revelation) feel as far *of* (variant of "off") as the *South-sea.*

198. ***apace.*** Swiftly; immediately.

might'st powre this conceal'd man out of thy mouth, as
Wine comes out of a narrow-mouth'd bottle: either too [200]
much at once, or none at all. I pre'thee take the Corke
out of thy mouth, that I may drinke thy tydings.

Cel. So you may put a man in your belly.

Ros. Is he of Gods making? What manner of man?
Is his head worth a hat? Or his chin worth a beard? [205]

Cel. Nay, he hath but a little beard.

Ros. Why God will send more, if the man will bee
thankful: let me stay the growth of his beard, if thou
delay me not the knowledge of his chin.

Cel. It is yong *Orlando*, that tript up the Wrastlers [210]
heeles, and your heart, both in an instant.

---

199. ***conceal'd.*** With possible play on *con* as "cunt" and "seal" the male genitals (see note: *seale*, IV.iii.64).

199–201. ***out of thy mouth... none at all.*** Beneath the obvious simile, there is indecent play on *mouth* as the vulva (FR). If a woman has *too much Wine* ("semen," FR) *or none at all* in her *bottle* ("vagina," GW), then she is either a slut or a saint (the former would have *Wine* coming out of her *bottle* because it was believed that "The diversitie of the seedes doeth lette conception, and causeth that the same can not be reteined," OL). Also, a woman with a *narrow* (i.e., morally constricted) *mouth* (i.e., vagina) might become insatiable once sexually active (cf. "hange her she lookes like a bottle of ale, when the corke flyes out and the Ale fomes at mouth, shee lookes my good button-breech like the signe of Capricorne," Thomas Dekker, *Satiro-mastix*).

201. ***Corke.*** To "draw a cork" is to copulate (F&H, s.v. "Greens"); *Corke* was also used to make pessaries. Cf. and see note: lines 199–201, above.

202–203. ***drinke thy tydings... belly.*** *Rosalind* wishes to *drinke* (eagerly absorb) *Celia's tydings* (news), but they are "tiding" ("That ebbs and flows; tidal," OED; cf. and see note: lines 196–201, above).

Also, if *Rosalind* "drinks" (a "copulation metaphor," GW) *Wine* (semen; see note: *Wine*, line 200, above), she will *put a man* (penis, GW2) *in* her *belly* (vagina, JH) and end up with *a man* (i.e., a child) *in* her *belly* (womb).

204–205. ***of Gods making... hat.*** *Rosalind* does not want an effeminate fop made by a tailor, but a man *of God's making* (i.e., a "man's man") who is capable in the *manner* (sex act, FR); cf. "there can be no kernell in this light Nut: the soule of this man is his cloathes" (*Alls Well, that Ends Well*, II.iv). She does not care what fashion of *hat* a man wears as long as *his head* is *worth a hat.* She also hopes that his *head* (penis; see note: *heads*, II.i.27) is *worth a hat* ("female pudendum," F&H; a *hat* is "a woman's privities: because frequently felt," FG).

205. ***chin worth a beard.*** *Rosalind* hopes that (a) this man's *chin* (jaw-line) is *worth a beard* (facial hair); and (b) his *chin* (penis, FR, who holds it a play on "mental": "Of or relating to the chin," OED, and "Mentule": "A man's yard," RC) is *worth a beard* (female pubic hair; see note: *beards*, I.ii.71).

206. ***but a little beard.*** Facial hair was considered a barometer of a man's virility: "those men that are hairy, are fuller of seed, & therefore more addicted to Venery, then those that are smooth... a woman cannot endure a man that hath but a little Beard; not so much, for that they are commonly cold and impotent, as that, so much resembling eunuches, they are for the most part inclined to baseness, cruelty, and deceitfulnesse" (JF2).

At age seventeen (II.iii.76), *Orlando* might have *but a little beard* because he is a late bloomer. However, *Orlando* probably has *but a little beard* because the actor who first played him had but *a little beard*, perhaps because he had recently shaved to portray a female character.

207–208. ***God will send more... thankful.*** A common sentiment; cf. Robert Hayman's poem "God rewards thankefull men" from *Quodlibets*:

> What part of the *Moon's* body doth reflect
> Her borrowed beames, yeeldeth a faire prospect;
> But that part of her, that doth not doe so,
> Spotty, or darke, or not at all doth show:
>
> So what wee doe reflect on *God the giver,*
> With thankefulnes: those *Graces* shine for ever:
> But if his *gifts* thou challeng'st to be thine,
> They'll never doe thee *Grace,* nor make thee shine.

208–209. ***stay the growth... knowledge of his chin.*** *Rosalind* is willing to *stay* (wait for) *the growth of his beard* as long as she eventually has *knowledge* (i.e., carnal *knowledge*) *of his chin* (penis; see note: *chin*, line 205, above).

210–211. ***tript up... in an instant.*** In the same *instant* that *Orlando tript up* ("foyle[d]," RC, s.v. "Supplanter") *the Wrastlers heeles*, *Rosalind's heart* was *tript up* ("overthrowne," RC, s.v. "Supplanté"). She is in love "head over heels" ("A tumbling tricke, or Sommersault, wherein the heeles are cast over the head; also, reciprocation of venerie," RC, s.v. "Combrecelle"), so she will perhaps be "light heeled" ("one who is apt, by the flying up of her heels, to fall flat on her back, a willing wench," FG). If *Rosalind* "trip[s]" ("succumb[s] sexually," EP), she might be *tript up* (i.e., become pregnant with an illegitimate child; a "Trip" is "a false step, a miscarriage, or a Bastard," ND). Cf. and see notes: *foyle*, I.i.129; and *overthrowne*, I.ii.254.

Ros. Nay, but the divell take mocking: speake sadde
brow, and true maid.

Cel. I'faith (Coz) tis he.

Ros. *Orlando*? [215]

Cel. *Orlando*.

Ros. Alas the day, what shall I do with my doublet &
hose? What did he when thou saw'st him? What sayde
he? How look'd he? Wherein went he? What makes hee
heere? Did he aske for me? Where remaines he? How [220]
parted he with thee? And when shalt thou see him a-
gaine? Answer me in one word.

Cel. You must borrow me Gargantuas mouth first:
'tis a Word too great for any mouth of this Ages size, to
say I and no, to these particulars, is more then to answer [225]
in a Catechisme.

Ros. But doth he know that I am in this Forrest, and
in mans apparrell? Looks he as freshly, as he did the day
he Wrastled?

Cel. It is as easie to count Atomies as to resolve the [230]
propositions of a Lover: but take a taste of my finding
him, and rellish it with good observance. I found him

212. ***the divell take mocking.*** *Rosalind* is so fed up with *Celia's mocking* that she utters a most un-maidenly curse. *Rosalind* is the only female character in the First Folio to use "The devil take," and her use of this imprecation puts her in company with such uncouth characters as *Thersites*, *Pandarus*, and *Falstaff*.

212–213. ***speake sadde brow, and true maid.*** *Rosalind* does not ask *Celia* to *speake* as a *true maid* with *a sadde brow*, but rather to *speake* of *Orlando's sadde brow* while he pined away in love for his own *true maid*— i.e., herself.

217–218. ***what shall I do with my doublet & hose.*** *Rosalind* is attired in *doublet and hose* (male clothing) and so presumably has *doublet and hose* (testicles and penis; see note: *doublet and hose*, II.iv.9). As a man, she cannot *do* (copulate with, F&H) *Orlando's what* ("penis," F&H).

219. ***Wherein.*** Either "into which place" or "in which condition."

220. ***Did he aske for me?*** *Rosalind* either (a) assumes that *Orlando* recognized *Celia*; or (b) forgets in her excitement that *Celia* is also in disguise.

222–223. ***Answer me in one word... Gargantuas mouth.*** *In one word* means either (a) concisely, briefly; or (b) "at one word": "without further ado" (OED). To literally *Answer Rosalind in one word*, *Celia* would need the incredibly large *mouth* of *Gargantua*, the giant invented by sixteenth-century novelist François Rabelais.

224. ***this Ages.*** The modern age as opposed to *Ages* past, for "There were Giants in the earth in those daies" (Genesis 6:4).

226. ***Catechisme.*** It was very tedious to learn a *Catechisme* ("an instruction or teaching by mouth or by the booke," JF, q.v.; "by the booke" means "by rote") such as the *Catechisme* ("An elementary treatise for instruction in the principles of the Christian religion, in the form of question and answer," OED).

228. ***freshly.*** *Freshly* means "flourishingly; youthfully, lustily, strongly, sturdily" (RC, s.v. "Verdement"). In addition, the word "fresh" is "so often associated with sexual prowess that it can almost be taken as a synonym" (TR).

230–231. ***as easie to count Atomies... a Lover.*** An "Atomie" is "Any thing so small, that it cannot bee made lesse" (JB, q.v.). Therefore, *to count Atomies* is a "proposition" (mathematical operation) that cannot be "resolved" (mathematically solved), and it is equally impossible to *resolve* ("answer," RC, s.v. "Respondre"; also "satisfie," RC2, q.v.) *Rosalind's* infinite *propositions* (questions).

It would also be impossible to *resolve* (fornicate, FR) every time *a Lover* ventures a "proposition" (an "invitation to engage in sexual activity," OED, which dates from 1937, but cf. "I know the wayes of pleasure, the sweet strains, / The lullings and the relishes of it; / The propositions of hot bloud and brains," George Herbert, "The Pearl").

231–232. ***a taste... observance.*** *Celia* will relate only a *taste* (tiny bit) of her encounter with *Orlando*, so *Rosalind* should *rellish* (savor, enjoy) this *rellish* (taste, flavor; also a small sample) with *good observance* (careful attention). *Rosalind* may want to *taste* (sexually enjoy, JH) *Orlando*, but she must imagine *rellish* (sexual intercourse, FG) with *Orlando's taste* (i.e., testes, FR) and *rellish* (i.e., erect penis; a *rellish* is literally "A projection; a piece which juts out," OED).

under a tree like a drop'd Acorne.

Ros. It may wel be cal'd Joves tree, when it droppes forth fruite. [235]

Cel. Give me audience, good Madam.

Ros. Proceed.

Cel. There lay hee stretch'd along like a Wounded knight.

Ros. Though it be pittie to see such a sight, it well becomes the ground. [240]

Cel. Cry holla, to the tongue, I prethee: it curvettes unseasonably. He was furnish'd like a Hunter.

Ros. O ominous, he comes to kill my Hart.

Cel. I would sing my song without a burthen, thou bring'st me out of tune. [245]

Ros. Do you not know I am a woman, when I thinke, I must speake: sweet, say on.

Enter Orlando & Jaques. [III.ii.6]

Cel. You bring me out. Soft, comes he not heere? [250]

Ros. 'Tis he, slinke by, and note him.

233–235. ***under a tree like a drop'd Acorne... fruite.*** *Orlando* lies *under* an oak *tree* (sacred to *Jove*, the ruler of the gods; cf. and see note: *Jupiter*, line 156, above) like a *drop'd Acorne* ("*Joves* nut" is the *Acorne*, OED). He looks as dejected as if (a) his

Acorne ("the nut of a mans yarde," TT, s.v. "Glans") had *drop'd* (fallen); or (b) his wife had *drop'd* (renounced) him and made him an *Acorne* (i.e., a cuckold; Fr. "Acorné" is "Horned; having hornes," RC, q.v.).

The oak is "most hard and durable" (RC, s.v. "Robre") and is thus an age-old emblem of masculitiy and stability (i.e., a phallic symbol). Perhaps *Orlando's Acorne* (penis) is "Acorné" (horned or erect; see note: *crooked-pated*, line 82, above) in imitation of his potent sire, *Jove* (cf. and see notes: *stretch'd along*, line 238, below, and *furnish'd like a Hunter*, line 243, below). Proverbially, "Great oaks from little acorns grow," so *Rosalind* expects the *fruit* (offspring) engendered from "*Jove's* nut" (i.e., *Orlando's* testicles and/or penis) to grow into an "oak" ("a man of good substance and credit," FG). Also cf. and see note: *fruit*, line 119, above.

236. ***audience.*** Hearing.

238. ***stretch'd along.*** *Orlando* is *stretch'd along* ("prostrate[d] at full length," "outstretched on the ground," OED, s.v. "lie along"). His "stretch" (i.e., penis; see note: *stretching*, line 132, above) is also *along* ("at length," OED).

242–243. ***Cry holla... unseasonably.*** *Rosalind* should *Cry holla* ("hoe there, enough, soft soft, no more of that if you love me," RC, s.v. "Holà") to her *tongue*, because it leaps about *unseasonably* (at an unfitting time) like the "curvettings, prauncings, or boundings of lustie horses" (RC, s.v. "Pannades").

Rosalind should also *cry holla to* her *tongue* (genitals or clitoris, FR) or she will "curvet" (move her hips up and down during copulation like curveting "horses" / "whores"). If *Rosalind* uses her *holla* ("hollow": vagina, F&H, s.v. "holloway") to "season" ("copulate," OED) *unseasonably* (i.e., inappropriately), then she will end up as a *holla* ("holler": "holour": "A fornicator," "debauchee," OED).

243–244. ***He was furnish'd like a Hunter... my Hart.*** *Rosalind* thinks it *ominous* ("that which signifieth som good or bad lucke to ensue," JB, q.v.) that *Orlando was furnish'd* (dressed, equipped) *like a Hunter*, for it signifies that *he comes to kill* her *hart* (a deer, with obvious play on "heart").

Orlando is also *furnish'd* ("Well-equipped sexually," FR) *like a Hunter* (lover or ladies' man; see note: *Huntresse*, line 6, above). Therefore, when *he comes* (has an orgasm, ejaculates) he can easily *kill* (i.e., provoke an orgasm; literally cause the "death" of) *Rosalind's Hart* ("Deer": "vagina," GW, q.v.).

245–246. ***sing my song... out of tune.*** *Celia* wishes to *sing her song* (i.e., tell her story) without *Rosalind's* continually interjecting *a burthen* (chorus of a song). If *Rosalind* continues to be a *burthen* (i.e., an "ass"; a "burdoun" is literally "a mule, a hinny," TR), she will make *Celia out of tune* ("out of temper," RC, s.v "Enchafouiné"; "ill at ease," RC, s.v. "Dehayté").

247–248. ***I am a woman... I must speake.*** *Rosalind's* opinion contradicts the traditional masculine viewpoint which held that "a womans heart and her tongue are not relatives; tis not ever true, that what the heart thinketh the tongue clacketh" (Robert Greene, *Greenes Never Too Late*).

The inherent irony of this line is that *Rosalind* was originally played by a male actor and therefore not *a woman* at all.

250. ***bring me out.*** *Rosalind* has brought *Celia out* ("into confusion, anger, or disturbance of feeling," OED). Therefore, *Celia* is now *out*, which means (a) "at a loss from failure of memory or confidence"; (b) "At variance, no longer friendly"; and/or (c) musically "out of tune" (OED); cf. line 246, above.

251. ***slinke.*** To *slinke* is to "slip aside" (RC, s.v. "Esquiver").

Jaq. I thanke you for your company, but good faith

I had as liefe have beene my selfe alone.

Orl. And so had I: but yet for fashion sake

I thanke you too, for your societie. [255]

Jaq. God buy you, let's meet as little as we can.

Orl. I do desire we may be better strangers.

Jaq. I pray you marre no more trees with Writing

Love-songs in their barkes.

Orl. I pray you marre no moe of my verses with rea- [260]

ding them ill-favouredly.

Jaq. *Rosalinde* is your loves name?

Orl. Yes, Just.

Jaq. I do not like her name.

Orl. There was no thought of pleasing you when she [265]

was christen'd.

Jaq. What stature is she of?

Orl. Just as high as my heart.

Jaq. You are ful of prety answers: have you not bin ac-

quainted with goldsmiths wives, & cond them out of rings [270]

252–255. ***I thanke you... societie.*** For the sake of *fashion* (good manners), *Orlando* has offered to accompany *Jaques*, but *Jaques had as lief* (would have preferred) to be *alone. Orlando* has likewise "had his fill" of *Jaques* to the point of *societie* (i.e., "satiety"; cf. "with sacietie seekes to quench his thirst," *Taming of the Shrew*, I.i.). However, *Orlando* has better *fashion* (manners) than *Jaques* and therefore thanks him *for* his *societie* (companionship).

256. ***God buy you.*** I.e., "God save you" (to *buy* is to "redeem from sin," OED). This phrase is the ancestor of the modern "goodbye."

257. ***I do desire... strangers.*** An inversion of the customary phrase expressing a *desire* to *be better* friends.

258–260. ***marre... marre.*** *Jaques* uses *marre* to mean "disfigure"; *Orlando* uses *marre* to mean "hurt" or "spoil."

261. ***ill-favouredly.*** See note: *illfavouredly*, I.ii.40.

262–267. ***Rosalinde is your loves name... What stature is she of.*** *Jaques* may ask about the *stature* (height, build, state, and/or condition) of *Orlando's* lady-love because he suspects that *Senior's* tall daughter named *Rosalinde* and *Orlando's* inamorata are one and the same.

263. ***Just.*** Exactly.

269. ***prety answers.*** *Prety* means (a) "wittie" (TT, s.v. "Scĭtus"); and/or (b) ready (cf. "pret": "ready," OED). *Jaques* also implies that *Orlando's answers* are *prety* (i.e., "prat-y" or asinine; the "prat" is "the buttocks," F&H).

269–270. ***bin acquainted with goldsmiths wives... rings.*** *Orlando* must have *bin acquainted* (familiar) *with goldsmiths wives*, for he has *cond* (learned) his *prety* ("mean, petty, insignificant," OED) *answers* from the glib phrases inscribed on *rings*.

Orlando's tongue is so *prety* ("cunning, crafty," OED) that he could even "con" (cheat) *goldsmiths wives out of rings*. This would be quite an accomplishment, because *goldsmiths wives*, who often worked alongside their husbands, were known to drive a particularly hard bargain. Moreover, *goldsmiths wives* were considered to be sexual mercenaries who demanded a very high price for their favors (cf. "Oh my Lord, I took him by weight, not fashion: Goldsmiths Wives taught me that way of bargain, and some Ladies swerve not to follow the example," Thomas Middleton, *Any Thing for a Quiet Life*). *Orlando* is so smooth that he could charm even *goldsmiths wives out of* their wedding *rings* and convince them to "acquaint" him with their "quaint[s]" ("womans privie parts," JF, s.v. "Conno") and *rings* ("Cunt[s]," F&H).

Orl. Not so: but I answer you right painted cloath,

from whence you have studied your questions.

Jaq. You have a nimble wit; I thinke 'twas made of

Attalanta's heeles. Will you sitte downe with me, and

wee two, will raile against our Mistris the world, and all [275]

our miserie.

Orl. I wil chide no breather in the world but my selfe

against whom I know most faults.

Jaq. The worst fault you have, is to be in love.

Orl. 'Tis a fault I will not change, for your best ver- [280]

tue: I am wearie of you.

Jaq. By my troth, I was seeking for a Foole, when I

found you.

Orl. He is drown'd in the brooke, looke but in, and

you shall see him. [285]

Jaq. There I shal see mine owne figure.

Orl. Which I take to be either a foole, or a Cipher.

Jaq. Ile tarrie no longer with you, farewell good sig-

nior Love.

Orl. I am glad of your departure: Adieu good Monsieur [290]

Melancholly.

271–272. ***I answer you right painted cloath... your questions.*** "Painted cloths" were cheap substitutes for tapestries and often portrayed moral fables with uninspired and didactic captions. Cf. Nicholas Breton's *No Whippinge, nor trippinge, but a kinde friendly Snippinge*:

> Reade what is written on the painted cloth;
> Doe no man wrong, be good unto the poore:
> Beware the Mouse, the Maggot, and the Moth;
> And ever have an eye unto the doore:
> Trust not a foole, a villaine, not a whore.
> Goe neat, not gaie; and spend but as you spare:
> And turne the Colte to pasture with the Mare.

Orlando has not *cond* his *prety answers out of rings* (lines 269–270, above) but rather responds in kind to *Jaques' questions*, which are mere "rime doggerels, fitter for a painted Cloth in an Ale-house" (Bruno Ryves, *Angliae Ruina*) than polite conversation. "Painted cloths" also depicted obscene subject matter (EC), and *Jaques'* indecent suggestions have seemingly been *studied* (learned) from a *painted cloath* (i.e., pornographic picture)—or perhaps directly from a *painted* (i.e., lewd; see note: *painted*, II.i.6) *cloath* ("Whore," FR; also see note: *garments*, line 106, above).

273–274. ***nimble wit... Attalanta's heeles.*** *Jaques* (a) compliments *Orlando* by saying that his *wit* (intellect, cleverness) is as *nimble* (quick, dexterous) as *Attalanta's heeles* (see note: *Attalanta's*, line 148, above); and (b) insults *Orlando* by saying that his *wit* disappears as quickly as *Attalantas heeles* (cf. "your wit ambles well, it goes easily," *Much adoe about Nothing*, V.i.).

275–278. ***raile against our Mistris the world... most faults.*** A man would commonly revere his *Mistris* (lady-love, paramour) as his *world* (entire existence). By contrast, *Jaques* wishes to *raile against* (curse) *the world* as a vacillating *Mistris* (cf. I.ii.32–34).

Orlando does not wish to *chide* (rebuke, scold) his *Mistris the world*, or anyone in it, because the *breather* (living thing) *against whom* he knows *the most faults* (moral failings) is himself. He can find no fault with his *Mistris'* "fault" (female reproductive organs, JH; a "fault" is literally a "crack," OED).

282–283. ***I was seeking for a Foole... you.*** *Jaques* implies that he did, indeed, find *a Foole* when he *found Orlando.*

286–289. ***mine owne figure... signior Love.*** *Jaques* protests that he is not truly *a foole* but a *figure* ("One acting a part," OED) who represents a fool's *figure* ("Represented character; part enacted," OED). Cf. II.vii.38, 46–47, and 49–66.

Foole and "full" were homonyms (HK, p. 108), so *Orlando* responds by saying that *Jaques' figure* (which means both "person" and "number") is *either* (a) the "full" (sum total) of *a foole*; or (b) only *a Cipher* ("A circle in Arithmetike like the letter O; which of it selfe is of no value," JB, q.v.; also "A person who fills a place, but is of no importance or worth, a nonentity," OED). If *Orlando* thinks *Jaques* a *Cipher* (nothing or "0"), *Jaques* similarly thinks *Orlando* is *Love* ("nothing, nil," OED; *Love* is from Fr. "l'oeuf," "the egg," the shape of which resembles "0").

291. ***Melanchولly.*** See notes: *humorous*, I.ii.269; and *melancholy*, II.i.30.

{*Exit Jaques.*} [III.ii.7]

Ros. I wil speake to him like a sawcie Lacky, and under that habit play the knave with him, do you hear Forrester.

Orl. Verie wel, what would you? [295]

Ros. I pray you, what i'st a clocke?

Orl. You should aske me what time o' day: there's no clocke in the Forrest.

Ros. Then there is no true Lover in the Forrest, else sighing everie minute, and groaning everie houre wold [300] detect the lazie foot of time, as wel as a clocke.

Orl. And why not the swift foote of time? Had not that bin as proper?

Ros. By no meanes sir; Time travels in divers paces, with divers persons: Ile tel you who Time ambles with- [305] all, who Time trots withal, who Time gallops withal, and who he stands stil withall.

Orl. I prethee, who doth he trot withal?

Ros. Marry he trots hard with a yong maid, between the contract of her marriage, and the day it is solemnizd: [310] if the interim be but a sennight, Times pace is so hard, that it seemes the length of seven yeare.

293. ***a sawcie Lacky.*** *Rosalind* will *speake to Orlando like a sawcie* (insolent) *Lacky* ("a boie, a lad, a youth, a yong man, a page," JF, s.v. "Garzone")—or possibly *like a sawcie* ("Wanton, lascivious," OED) *Lacky* (effeminate man or homosexual; cf. "Garzoneggiare, to play the boy, the lad, the lackie, the wagge or page. Also to followe boies," JF, q.v.).

294. ***play the knave.*** *Play the knave* can mean (a) "shew cunning, use tricks" (RC, s.v. "Clocher"); (b) "flowt, scoffe, deride, ride, mocke, gibe at" (RC, s.v. "Copier"); and (c) "put him down" or "get the better of him"; this sense derives from card games such as "Mawe" where the *knave* was trumps.

299–300. ***true Lover... groaning everie houre.*** Cf. "Lovers have in their hearts a clock still going; / For though Time be nimble, his motions / are quicker / and thicker / where Love hath his notions" (John Suckling, "That none beguiled be by times quick flowing"). For possible sexual pun, see notes: *groanes*, II.i.40, and *houre*, II.vii.30.

299–303. ***Lover... proper.*** Because "time flies," "Painters picture aged time / With wings at's heels, as if he always flew" (William Peaps, *Love In it's Extasie*). Therefore, it would be *as proper* to describe the *foote of time* as *swift.*

However, *Rosalind* hints that *time* is *lazie* for this *Lover* because (a) he has a *lazie* (i.e., impotent; *lazie* is literally "slacke, long in comming," JF, s.v. "Tardo") *foot* (penis; see note: *foot*, II.vii.73); and/or (b) he is a *lazie* ("worthless," OED) *foot* ("fuck," EP; cf. L. "futuo" and Fr. "foutre": "to fuck"). *Orlando* counters by asserting that *the foot of time* is both *swift* ("Hotte, burning: vehement: hastie in doing: quick," TT, s.v. "Ardens") and *proper* (i.e., virile; see note: *proper*, I.ii.116).

301. ***detect.*** Reveal, make known.

304–306. ***Time travels in divers paces... gallops.*** *Time travels in divers* (different) *paces* (rates of speed) like a horse's *paces* ("the various gaits of a horse," OED). According to Randle Holme's *Accademie of Armory*, to "Amble, is to go a fine easy pace"; a "Trot, or a Trotting Horse," "sets hard, and goes at an uneasy rate"; and a "Gallop" is "between full or high trot, and a swift running."

307. ***stands stil.*** Suggestive of "horses that are restie" who "stande and stop still" (JF, s.v. "Piantarsi").

309–311. ***trots hard... a sennight.*** A trotting horse moves quickly, but "the trotting of an horse" gives the rider "a hard shaking or jolting, a violent jogging" (TB, s.v. "Succussation"). A *young maid* is as eager to trot" (thrust her hips up and down during copulation, JH, s.v. "trotting horse") as a "trot" ("common prostitute," EP; "bawd," F&H). Therefore, *Times pace is hard* (difficult, arduous) even if the *interim* (interval) between *her contract* (betrothal) *and the day* that her *marriage is solemnized* (ratified by ceremony) is only a *sennight* (a "seven night," or one week). Cf. "Time goes on crutches, till Love have all his rites" (*Much adoe about Nothing*, II.i.).

Orl. Who ambles Time withal?

Ros. With a Priest that lacks Latine, and a rich man
that hath not the Gowt: for the one sleepes easily be- [315]
cause he cannot study, and the other lives merrily, because he feeles no paine: the one lacking the burthen of
leane and wasteful Learning; the other knowing no burthen of heavie tedious penurie. These Time ambles
withal. [320]

Orl. Who doth he gallop withal?

Ros. With a theefe to the gallowes: for though hee
go as softly as foot can fall, he thinkes himselfe too soon
there.

Orl. Who staies it stil withal? [325]

Ros. With Lawiers in the vacation: for they sleepe
betweene Terme and Terme, and then they perceive not
how time moves.

Orl. Where dwel you prettie youth?

Ros. With this Shepheardesse my sister: heere in the [330]
skirts of the Forrest, like fringe upon a petticoat.

Orl. Are you native of this place?

Ros. As the Conie that you see dwell where shee is
kindled.

314–318. ***a Priest that lacks Latine... wasteful Learning.*** A "Lack-Latin" ("An ingnoramus: specifically an unlettered priest," F&H) *cannot study* (meditate or think deeply) because he lacks the *burthen* (obligation) of *leane* (variant of "lone": "solitary," OED) and *wasteful* (causing "waste" or bodily decay) *Learning*. Therefore, he *sleepes easily*. Cf. *Schollers melancholy*, IV.i.12.

314–319. ***a rich man... tedious penurie.*** *A rich man* knows *no burthen* (affliction) of *heavie* (oppressive) *tedious* (troublesome) *penurie* (poverty, want), but he might suffer from *Gowt* (a.k.a. "the rich man's disease"). *Gowt* is "a pain in the joynts which comes for the most part by fits, stirred up by an influx of humors into the said joynts" (JG, s.v. "Arthritis"), and "There be foure causes of this superfluity of humors, the immoderat use of strong wine, Venery, crudities, and feeblenes of the parts" (Bruele Gualtherus, *Praxis Medicinae*). However, *a rich man that hath not the Gowt feeles no paine*, so he has no incentive to mend his self-indulgent ways. Therefore, he *lives merrily*.

323. ***softly.*** Slowly.

326–327. ***Lawiers... sleepe betweene Terme and Terme.*** *Lawiers* were as notoriously idle in *the vacation* ("the season wherein a Court sits not," RC, s.v. "Induce") as they were busy during *Terme* ("that time, wherein the Tribunals or places of Judgment are open for all that list to complain of wrong, or to seek their right by course of Law or Action," Thomas Blount, *Nomo-Lexicon: A Law-Dictionary*).

329. ***prettie.*** Possibly "clever" or "pleasing" (OED), but also see note: *prety*, line 269, above.

330–331. ***the skirts of the Forrest... petticoat.*** Either (a) *in the skirts* (edges, outlying territory) *of the Forrest* (wilderness, woods) *like fringe* (a decorative border or edging) *upon a petticoat* (skirt); or (b) *in the skirts* (lower portions of a gown) *of the Forrest* (a woman or her vagina; see note: *Forrest*, line 123, above) *like fringe* (i.e., pubic hair) *upon a petticoat* (female genitalia; see note: *petty-coates*, I.iii.17).

333–334. ***as the Conie... kindled.*** Perhaps (a) where the *Conie* (rabbit) *is kindled* (was born); or (b) where the "Coney, Kindleth a Litter, or Nest of Rabbets, or Kindlings" (Randle Holme, *The Academy of Armory*). Either way, the *Conie* both "dwells" and *is kindled* in "a conie hoale, a burrough for conies" (JM, s.v. "Madriguéra de conéjo"). Similarly, a *Conie* ("whore, wanton," GW2) "dwells" (i.e., fornicates; see note: *inhabited*, III.iii.9) *where she is kindled* (inflamed with passion or lust)—i.e., in the "cunny-burrow" ("The female pudendum, Cunt," F&H).

Rosalind here drops a hint that she has changed her gender, for "Hares are like Hermophrodites, one while Male, and another Female, and that which begets this yeare, brings young ones the next" (Richard Brome and Thomas Heywood, *The Late Lancashire Witches*).

Orl.	Your accent is something finer, then you could	[335]
	purchase in so removed a dwelling.	
Ros.	I have bin told so of many: but indeed, an olde	
	religious Unckle of mine taught me to speake, who was	
	in his youth an inland man, one that knew Courtship too	
	well: for there he fel in love. I have heard him read ma-	[340]
	ny Lectors against it, and I thanke God, I am not a Wo-	
	man to be touch'd with so many giddie offences as hee	
	hath generally tax'd their whole sex withal.	
Orl.	Can you remember any of the principall evils,	
	that he laid to the charge of women?	[345]
Ros.	There were none principal, they were all like	
	one another, as halfepence are, everie one fault seeming	
	monstrous, til his fellow-fault came to match it.	
Orl.	I prethee recount some of them.	
Ros.	No: I wil not cast away my physick, but on those	[350]
	that are sicke. There is a man haunts the Forrest, that a-	
	buses our yong plants with carving *Rosalinde* on their	
	barkes; hangs Oades upon Hauthornes, and Elegies on	

335. ***finer.*** More refined.
336. ***purchase.*** Acquire.

338. ***religious.*** Either (a) devout; or (b) in *religious* orders; see note: *Lectors*, line 341, below.

339. ***inland.*** See note: *in-land*, II.vii.103.

339. ***Courtship.*** *Courtship* is (a) "the humors, or fashions of Court"; and (b) the "courting, or wooing of a wench" (RC, s.v. "Court").

340–341. ***read many Lectors.*** *Ganimed's* uncle would *read* ("recite," OED) *many Lectors* ("lectures": sermons) against "lecture" (sexual misbehavior, GW2). The spelling of *Lectors* might simply reflect the pronunciation (cf. and see note: *features*, III.iii.6), but a "Lector" is "An ecclesiastic belonging to one of the minor orders, whose duty originally consisted in reading the 'lessons'" (OED).

341–342. ***not a Woman.*** The male actor who first portrayed *Rosalind / Ganimed* was truly *not a Woman*.

342–343. ***touch'd... their whole sex.*** The shepherd boy *Ganimed / Rosalind* likens *giddie* women to sheep with "gid" ("a brain-disease of sheep," OED). The *whole* (entire) female *sex* is *touch'd* (tainted, infected) *with giddie* (foolish, stupid) *offences* (moral failings). Every woman's *whole* ("hole": vagina) and *sex* ("female pudendum; Cunt," F&H) are *touch'd* (with play on "touch" as sexual intercourse; see note: *Touchstone*, II.iv.3) *with giddie* ("Lecherous," FR) *offences* (sexual transgressions, GW).

343. ***tax'd.*** See note: *taxe*, II.vii.76.

344–345. ***the principall evils... the charge of women.*** If a man *laid* (had sexual intercouse with) a woman and *laid a charge* ("load of semen," JH) to her, he risked contracting *evils* (sexually transmitted diseases; see note: *evils*, II.vii.72) from *the principall* ("pudend," EP).

347. ***halfepence.*** *Halfepence* are worth very little, so the word was used for anything "of contemptible value" (OED).

347–348. ***everie one fault seeming monstrous... match it.*** *Everie* woman's *fault* (vagina; see note: line 278, above) is *monstrous*—i.e., *everie one* will make an illicit *match* (sexual encounter, EP) and "make a monster of" ("cuckold," EP) her husband. There is additional play on *seeming* as (a) "copulating" (JH; to "seam" is literally "to join together"); (b) "seaming" or sexual defilement (GW, s.v. "enseam"); and (c) semen (*seeming* and "semen" were pronounced identically, HK pp. 269–270).

349. ***recount.*** Reckon or relate, with probable play on "count" / "cunt."

350–351. ***cast away... sicke.*** An allusion to both Matthew 9:12 ("They that be whole neede not a Physicion, but they that are sicke") and Matthew 7:6 (see note: *cast away*, I.iii.6).

351–352. ***haunts the Forrest... yong plants.*** *Orlando haunts* (frequents) *the Forrest* and *abuses* (mistreats) the *yong plants.* He also "aunts" (i.e., prostitutes; see note: *haunt*, II.i.18) *the Forrest* (with allusion to the female genitalia and pubic hair; see note: *Forrest*, line 123, above) and *abuses* ("violate[s] or pervert[s]," GW2) its *yong* (innocent) "trees" (i.e., women; see note: lines 118–121, above).

353. ***Oades... Elegies.*** An "ode" is a lyrical poem. An "Elegie" is "A mournefull song used in funerals, or other passions of sorrow" (JB, q.v.)

353. ***Hauthornes.*** Infusions of *Hauthornes* were thought to be "good for the trembling or passion of the heart" (Anonymous, *Philiatros*; cf. *Love-shak'd*, line 358, below).

Hauthornes have long been associated with Mayday fertility rites, and the blossoms are symbolic of the female reproductive organs and sexuality. The Hawthorn flower is also called "Lady's Meat" because its scent supposedly resembles that of the female genitalia (GW2, s.v. "moon").

brambles; all (forsooth) defying the name of *Rosalinde.*

If I could meet that Fancie-monger, I would give him [355]

some good counsel, for he seemes to have the Quotidian

of Love upon him.

Orl. I am he that is so Love-shak'd, I pray you tel

me your remedie.

Ros. There is none of my Unckles markes upon you: [360]

he taught me how to know a man in love: in which cage

of rushes, I am sure you art not prisoner.

Orl. What were his markes?

Ros. A leane cheeke, which you have not: a blew eie

and sunken, which you have not: an unquestionable spi- [365]

rit, which you have not: a beard neglected, which you

have not: (but I pardon you for that, for simply your ha-

---

354. ***brambles.*** *Ganimed* probably mentions *brambles* because of their "pricks." Cf. and see notes: *briers,* I.iii.14; *burs,* I.iii.15; and *Hauthornes,* line 353, above.

354. ***defying the name of Rosalinde.*** *Defying* is possibly a variant spelling of "deifying." However, by indiscriminately "*defying* out" ("eject[ing] as excrement," OED) *Rosalinde's name, Orlando* has made it "common as shit."

355–356. ***Fancie-monger... good counsel.*** This *monger* (trader, trafficker; particularly one of a disreputable nature) of *Fancie* (love, whims; also "delusive imagination," OED) is in need of *some good* (useful) *counsel* (advice). His *Fancie* (libido, lust, JA p. 57) has driven *him* to become a *monger* (i.e., whoremonger or pimp) of *Rosalind's Fancie* ("vagina," GW2; cf. and see note: *haunts the Forrest*, line 351, above).

If *Rosalinde could meet* ("have sexual intercourse with," OED) *him* (i.e., this *monger, Orlando*), she *would give him some good* (sexually eager or proficient; see notes: *good*, I.ii.28 and I.ii.65) *counsel* (with play on "coun sell" / "cunt sell").

356–359. ***the Quotidian of Love... remedie.*** *Love* was considered a bona-fide disease (see note: lines 364–365, below) whose symptoms were commonly likened to those of a *Quotidian* ("a daily Ague," JG, s.v. "Quotidiana"). Cf. these lines from Robert Heath's *Clarastella*:

> True lov's not like an Ague fit
> That doth of cold and heat admit;
> 'tis a quotidian feaver that
> With constant heat doth thirst create.

If *Orlando* is *Love-shak'd,* then he is indeed afflicted with a *Quotidian of Love*, for "a quotidian Fever shakes each part" (George Wither, *Britain's Remembrancer*). He is probably also eager for a "shake" (i.e., sexual intercourse; see note: *shake*, I.i.30) as a *remedie* (see note: *cure*, line 391, below).

360. ***my Unckles markes.*** Either (a) the *markes* (symptoms) of love described by *Rosalind's* uncle in his sermons; or (b) those he himself suffered. Cf. lines 337–341, above.

361–362. ***cage of rushes.*** Love is a *cage* (jail, prison) made *of rushes* (straw, twigs) that binds a man as weakly as a "rush" (a ring made *of rushes* used as a love token or in mock wedding ceremonies). Therefore, a woman had best not "rush" (hasten) to a *cage* ("bed; also breeding-cage," F&H) and surrender her "rush" ("rush-ring" or vagina; cf. "Tibs rush for Toms fore-finger," *Alls Well, that Ends Well,* II.ii.).

364–366. ***leane cheeke... unquestionable spirit.*** Love was considered "the most frequent, and most dangerous Disease that both sexes are subject to" (JF2). Among the tell-tale symptoms were *A leane cheeke, a blew eie,* and an *unquestionable* ("Not submitting to question; impatient," OED) *spirit.* According to Jacques Ferrand's *Erotomania,*

> the poore Inamorato thinkes of nothing but his dearely beloved Mistresse. All the Actions of his Body are in like manner quite out of tune, he growes pale withall leane, distracted, has no appetite, his eyes are hollow and quite sunke into his head. Then shall ye have him ever and anon weeping, sobbing, and sighing by himselfe, and in perpetuall Anxiety, avoiding all company, and choosing solitarinesse; that so he may entertaine his Melancholy thoughts with the greater freedome.

364–365. ***a blew eie and sunken.*** The lover's *eie* may be *blew* due to (a) lack of sleep; (b) weeping; and/or (c) thoughts that are *blew* ("indecent, 'smutty,' obscene," F&H).

366–367. ***a beard neglected... but I pardon you.*** Because *Orlando* has very little *beard* to neglect (cf. line 206, above), *Ganimed* pardons him for not neglecting his *beard.*

ving in beard, is a yonger brothers revennew) then your
hose should be ungarter'd, your bonnet unbanded, your
sleeve unbutton'd, your shoo unti'de, and everie thing [370]
about you, demonstrating a carelesse desolation: but you
are no such man; you are rather point device in your ac-
coustrements, as loving your selfe, then seeming the Lover of any other.

Orl. Faire youth, I would I could make thee beleeve I Love. [375]

Ros. Me beleeve it? You may assoone make her that
you Love beleeve it, which I warrant she is apter to do,
then to confesse she do's: that is one of the points, in the
which women stil give the lie to their consciences. But
in good sooth, are you he that hangs the verses on the [380]
Trees, wherein *Rosalind* is so admired?

Orl. I sweare to thee youth, by the white hand of
Rosalind, I am that he, that unfortunate he.

368–373. ***your hose should be ungarter'd... loving your selfe.*** If *Orlando* were truly in love, he would display *carelesse* (negligent) *desolation* (loneliness, grief) and "present himselfe a true Malecontent: with an hat without a band over-brimming his eyes, an unfashionable habit, as if he scorn'd to suit with time, and that unbrush'd: an head, as if newly fetterd with Medusa's locks, and that unkemb'd" (Richard Brathwait, *The Two Lancashire Lovers*). Instead, *Orlando* is *point device* (neat, fastidious; perfect in every particular) in his "Accoustrement" ("attire, bravery, provision: also habit or cloathing," TB, q.v.), which suggests that he is "one that loves himself, a selfish man" (TB, s.v. "Suist"; cf. and see note: *pride*, II.vii.75).

377–379. ***she is apter to do... consciences.*** A woman is not "apt" (inclined) to (a) *beleeve* that a man is truly in *Love* with her; and/or (b) *confesse* (reveal) that *she* herself is in *Love* and therefore "apt" ("Sexually willing or inclined," EC) to "do" (copulate; see note: *do,* line 217, above).

The widely accepted view of the sexes was that even if "Men appeare outwardly to be the more prone to Lust of the two: yet must we not therefore presently conclude women to be utterly free from the same desires, although they cunningly dissemble them as much as possibly they can" (JF2). On that "point" (subject), *women stil* (continually) *give the lie* ("speake falsely," JF, s.v. "Mentire") *to their consciences* (consciousness, inner awareness). Therefore, *women* are reluctant to *give the lie* (i.e., sexual intercourse) *to their consciences* (i.e., sexual organs; "conscience" is "a characteristically Shakespeare double entente on the pudend," EP). On that "point" (penis; see note: *points,* I.iii.124), *women* are reluctant *to confesse* (with bawdy quibble on *con* as "cunt," and *fesse* as "A buttocke; a haunch; a breech," RC, q.v.).

380. ***in good sooth.*** *In good sooth* means "Freely, frankely," "according to his conscience, gentilmanly: like one of honest condition" (TT, s.v. "Ingĕnŭē").

382–383. ***I sweare... by the white hand of Rosalind.*** Oaths were made by joining hands, so *Orlando* may actually grasp *Rosalind's white hand* (the fashionable pale color of which symbolized purity) when he "swears" his love.

Ros.	But are you so much in love, as your rimes speak?	
Orl.	Neither rime nor reason can expresse how much.	[385]
Ros.	Love is meerely a madnesse, and I tel you, de-	
	serves as wel a darke house, and a whip, as madmen do:	
	and the reason why they are not so punish'd and cured, is	
	that the Lunacie is so ordinarie, that the whippers are in	
	love too: yet I professe curing it by counsel.	[390]
Orl.	Did you ever cure any so?	
Ros.	Yes one, and in this manner. Hee was to imagine	
	me his Love, his Mistris: and I set him everie day	
	to woe me. At which time would I, being but a moonish	
	youth, greeve, be effeminate, changeable, longing, and	[395]
	liking, proud, fantastical, apish, shallow, inconstant, ful	
	of teares, full of smiles; for everie passion something, and	
	for no passion truly any thing, as boyes and women are	
	for the most part, cattle of this colour: would now like	
	him, now loath him: then entertaine him, then forswear	[400]

386–391. ***Love is meerely a madnesse... cure any so.*** It was thought that "Love is litle better then meere Madnesse" (JF2). Therefore, *Love* was considered a treatable medical condition like any other *madnesse*: "if the mind bee afflicted at all in Love; it is by reason of the mutuall Sympathy that there is betwixt it, and the body, as Aristotle proves plainly in his Physiognomy... diseases of the body doe infatuate and dull the mind, and draw the understanding also to Sympathize with it... We conclude then, that Love is not incurable" (JF2).

One accepted *cure* for those afflicted with the *madnesse* of *Love* was *a darke house, and a whip*: "Some Physitians counsell to take them and shut them up in Prison... and there give them correction... Many in this case use to whip and cudgell them; thinking by torturing the flesh and externall parts, to extinguish their inward flames. And of this opinion is Gordonius, who would have them whipped" (JF2.) *Ganimed / Rosalind*, however, "professes" (claims skill in) the alternate method of *curing Love by counsel.*

This approach assumed that "Lovers have so litle knowledge of the imperfections of their Ladies" because "Every Lover then beyng troubled in spirite, the judgement of his sence is impeached and letted in suche wise as he remeineth blind in the thing which he loveth" (OL). An effective method of treatment, therefore, was to *counsel* (advise) the lover about his mistress' faults, and "to reckon up all her Imperfections & vices, making them more, & greater then they are... as, in the opinion of all Physitians, that have written of the cure of this Malady, it is necessary to represent unto the party affected, the foulenes of his errour" (JF2).

However, *counsel* was not a sure-fire *cure*, and *Rosalind* knows there is a very good chance that this treatment will backfire, for "it so fals out oftimes, that these admonitions doe not worke any good at all upon them [the love-sick], but rather incense them, and make them the more headstrong and obstinate in their follies" (JF2). Ultimately, *Rosalind* hopes to *cure Orlando's Love* with the *cure* ("copulation," GW2; cf. and see note: *remedie*, V.ii.40).

394–395. ***moonish youth.*** *Moonish* is "influenced by the moon; acting as if so influenced, changeable, fickle" (OED). However, as a *Ganimed* (catamite; see note: *Ganimed*, I.iii.133), this *youth's* "moon" ("backside," GW2) would be *moonish* (i.e., sexually available like a woman's "moon" or vagina; see note: *pale spheare*, line 5, above).

395. ***greeve.*** *Ganimed* would *greeve* (lament) and *greeve* (vex, annoy) his lover by acting like a "grief" ("whore," FR) and "treating him like shit" (see note: *grieves*, I.i.23).

395. ***effeminate.*** *Ganimed* determines to *effeminate* ("gelde," TT, s.v. "Evĭro") *Orlando* by acting *effeminate* ("womanish," JF, s.v. "Infeminire"; also "unconstant, wavering, slipperie," JF, s.v. "Muliebre").

395. ***changeable.*** Unfaithful (see note: *change,* I.iii.109).

395. ***longing.*** I.e., *longing* for sex (*longing* is "sexual appetite," GW).

396. ***liking.*** Lecherous or lustful (see note: *liking*, I.iii.28).

396. ***proud.*** Both (a) "haughtie, disdainfull, or arrogant" (JF, s.v. "Superbire"); and (b) "Desirous of copulation" (FG); cf. and see note: *pride*, II.vii.75.

396. ***fantastical.*** Either (a) "toyish, odde, humorous, giddie headed, selfe conceited, haire braind" (RC, s.v. "Bizarre"); or (b) given to "fantasy" or lust (see note: *fantasie*, II.iv.33; also cf. and see note: *Fancie-monger*, line 355, above).

396. ***apish.*** *Apish* means "foolish, simple, doting" (JF, s.v. "Scimonito"). The "ape" was also a "figure of lust" (GW2, s.v. "monkey").

396. ***inconstant.*** I.e., "Unconstant": "Unfaithful in love or wedlock" (JH, q.v.).

397. ***passion.*** *Passion* means (a) pain and suffering; and (b) sexual desire. See notes: *passion*, I.ii.259 and II.iv.62.

398–399. ***boyes and women are... cattle of this colour.*** *Boyes* (young men; also homosexuals; see note: *Boy*, I.i.53) and *women are cattle* (livestock; also whores; see note: *Cattle*, line 80, above) *of this color* (kind, character) in that they constantly "change colour, as the Camelion is said to do" (TB, s.v. "Camelionize").

him: now weepe for him, then spit at him; that I drave

my Sutor from his mad humor of love, to a living humor

of madnes, which was to forsweare the ful stream of the world,

and to live in a nooke meerly Monastick: and thus I cur'd

him, and this way wil I take upon mee to wash your Li- [405]

ver as cleane as a sound sheepes heart, that there shal not

be one spot of Love in't.

Orl. I would not be cured, youth.

Ros. I would cure you, if you would but call me *Ros-*

alind, and come everie day to my Coat, and woe me. [410]

Orlan. Now by the faith of my love, I will; Tel me

where it is.

Ros. Go with me to it, and Ile shew it you: and by

the way, you shal tell me, where in the Forrest you live:

Wil you go? [415]

Orl. With all my heart, good youth.

Ros. Nay, you must call mee *Rosalind*: Come sister,

will you go?

Exeunt.

401. ***drave.*** A variant of "drove," with play on "drove" meaning "trouble[d], disturb[ed]" (OED).

402. ***living.*** Enduring.

403. ***the ful stream.*** *The ful stream* is "the entirety," with possible allusion to Proverbs 18:4: "The wordes of a wise mans mouth are lyke deepe waters: and the well of wisdome is lyke a full streame" (*The Bishop's Bible*).

404. ***to live in a nooke meerly Monastick.*** *Ganimed's* former patient decided *to live meerly* (entirely) *Monastick* (i.e., "monasticall," or "living solitarie," JF, s.v. "Monastico") *in a nooke* ("A lurking hole, or corner"; "secret place, hiding hole; also, a denne, or covert," RC, s.v. "Cachette"). This austere lifestyle provided excellent protection against a relapse of love, "For Prayer and Fasting are most Soveraigne Preservatives against this Love Divell" (JF2).

However, *Rosalind* really hopes that *Orlando* will live *meerly* ("lecherous[ly]," FR, who holds it a play on "merrily": "lustily," EP). Her true objective is not to cure *Orlando* but to drive him into her *nooke* (vagina, GW2, s.v. "notch") like a monk (monks had a lustful reputation; to "monk it" is to "copulate," GW2).

405. ***take upon mee.*** Despite *Rosalind's* supposedly male persona, she imagines herself in the supine female sexual position (to "undertake" is "To take a woman beneath one, for sexual intercourse," EC).

405–407. ***wash your Liver... one spot of Love in't.*** According to Leonard Mascall's *The First Booke of Cattell*, a "rotten sheepe or unsound" has "his liver... knottie and ful of blisters" and is prone to "Pockes" that "appeare on the skin, like red pimples or purples." To treat "Pockes of sheepe," Mascall advises that "it shalbe good to wash them in water."

Just like a "rotten" sheep, *Orlando* has a "Spotted liver" (a "'symptom' of lechery," JH), so his *Liver* (the seat of sexual passion, JH; also see note: *sight of two Rammes*, V.ii.34–35) is "unclean" (unhealthy; also morally impure). *Ganimed* proposes to treat *Orlano's* symptoms by "washing the liver" (a medical expression that meant to administer internal medicine which affected the patient's *Liver*). Thus, *Orlando's Liver* will be *as cleane* (healthy, pure) *as* the *heart* (genitals; see note: *Hart*, line 244, above) of a "sheep" ("whore," JH) who is *sound* ("Free from venereal disease," EP). His *heart* will have *not one spot* (moral blemish, EP), and his *heart* (i.e., his "arse"; *heart* was pronounced "art" which plays on L. "ars": "art," FR; cf. and see note: *hearts*, line 152, above) will have *not one spot* (pox sore, GW2, s.v. "Leopard"; hemorrhoids were "regarded by Elizabethans as a result of venereal disease," EC, s.v. "piled").

408. ***I would not be cured.*** Some thought "Love to be incurable, because that for the most part, he that is sicke of this disease, does not desire to be cured of it" (JF2). *Orlando's* case is not hopeless, however, "for there may be meanes found out of times to bring the Patient to desire and seeke out for cure of his Malady" (JF2).

410. ***Coat.*** See note: *Coate*, II.iv.89.

411. ***by the faith of my love.*** The fact that *Orlando* agrees to "treatment" for his "disease" by swearing *by the faith of* his *love* does not bode well for his recovery. He probably views *Ganimed's* offer of treatment as a challenge and a test of his *faith* in *love*.

Act III, scene iii

Scœna Tertia. [1]

Enter Clowne, Audrey, & Jaques. [III.iii.1]

Clo. Come apace good *Audrey*, I wil fetch up your

Goates, *Audrey*: and how *Audrey* am I the man yet?

Doth my simple feature content you? [5]

Aud. Your features, Lord warrant us: what features?

Clo. I am heere with thee, and thy Goats, as the most

capricious Poet honest *Ovid* was among the Gothes.

Jaq. O knowledge ill inhabited, worse then Jove in

a thatch'd house. [10]

Notes III.iii.

2. ***Audrey.*** Saint *Audrey* (a.k.a. "Saint Ethelreda") was a princess of the East Angles. Twice wed in dynastic alliances, she did not consummate either marriage due to a vow of perpetual chastity. After years of wedded un-bliss, she finally took the veil and founded the Abbey of Ely in 673. In 679, Saint *Audrey* died of a tumor on her neck, which she viewed as divine retribution for the extravagant necklaces she had worn as a young woman.

At the festival held in Ely on Saint *Audrey's* feast day (June 23), lace neckerchiefs were sold in commemoration of her death. These cheaply and shoddily produced necklaces were called "Saint Audrey lace," which became corrupted over time to "t'Audrey lace." Thus, the saint's name is the origin of the word "tawdry." It is unlikely that the *Audrey* of this play is appareled in a "tawdry" (cheap or gaudy) manner, but she is very likely "tawdry" ("Untidy; slovenly; ungraceful," OED; cf. V.iv.74–75).

Shakespeare might also have named this character *Audrey* (a) due to Saint *Audrey's* vow of chastity (cf. 16–17; 23–25, and 35, below); (b) because Saint *Audrey* was widely depicted as carrying a pastoral staff, a symbol of her status as abbess; and/or (c) for the name's rhyming possibilities; cf. lines 89–90, below.

3. ***apace.*** Quickly.

3. ***fetch up.*** "Overtake" or "bring back."

3–4. ***your Goates.*** As a goatherd, *Audrey* is probably smelly, "for as Kids grow to be Goats, their flesh acquireth a stinking savour" (Tobias Venner, *Via recta ad vitam longam*); "goatish" is "stinking of goates, of sweate or filth" (RC, s.v. "Lezzoso").

4. ***the man.*** I.e., "*the man* for you."

5–6. ***feature... features.*** *Feature* can mean (a) "proportion, shape, outward lineaments" (RC, s.v. "Pourfil d'un homme"); or (b) "Hansomnesse, comelinesse, beautie" (JB, q.v.). *Feature* was pronounced "FATE-er" (HK, p. 106; cf. *Lectors*, III.ii.341), and a "faitour" is "A vagabond, roamer," "wandering idlesbie, ranging or gadding rogue" (RC, s.v. "Vagabond"). *Audrey's* alarmed outcry might be caused by fear that these disreputable "faitours" will steal her livestock.

7–8. ***thy Goats... the Gothes.*** In A.D. 8, the Roman emperor Augustus (Gaius Julius Caesar Augustus, 63 B.C.–A.D. 14) banished the poet *Ovid* (Publius Ovidius Naso, 43 B.C.–A.D. 17 or 18) to Constanta in what is now Romania. There, he lived among the *Gothes*, an East Germanic tribe that inhabited the banks of the Black Sea. *Ovid* was probably banished for political reasons, but the pretext for his banishment was the licentiousness of his verses. Therefore, *Ovid* was understood to be not *honest* (chaste, pure) but *capricious* ("lecherous," GW; cf. "Give me a sceane of venery, that will make a mans spirrits stand on theyr typtoes, and die his bloode in a deepe scarlet, like your *Ovids Ars Amandi*," John Day, *The Ile of Guls*).

The *Clowne*, like the *capricious* ("humorous, fantasticall," RC, s.v. "Capricieux") *Ovid*, lives in exile among the *Gothes* (i.e., the *Goats*; these two words were "pronounced alike or very nearly so," HK, p. 109). Also like *Ovid*, the *Clowne* is *capricious* (the word stems from L. "capro" or "caper": goat; *Goats* symbolized "A favorite type of bestial lechery," JH; also see note: *capers*, II.iv.57).

9–10. ***knowledge ill-inhabited... a thatch'd house.*** *Jaques* finds it *ill* (unfortunate) that the *Clowne's* commendable *knowledge* should "inhabit" (reside in) a "Habit" ("A garment, raiment, vestiment, or vesture; apparell, or a sute of apparell," RC, q.v.) and *house* ("A covering of textile material," OED) so *ill* (of poor or inferior quality)—i.e., a fool's motley uniform (cf. and see note: *motley*, II.vii.17). For this wise man to wear fool's clothing is more incongruous than *Jove*, the mighty king of the gods, inhabiting *a thatch'd house* ("a countrie cottage, a hovell," JF, s.v. "Cascina").

The ostensible allusion is to the ancient Greek tale of Philemon and Baucis, a poor old couple who lived in "A small thatch't Cottage" (George Sandys, *Ovid's Metamorphoses*). When *Jove* and Mercury (a.k.a. "Zeus" and "Hermes") visited their village disguised as humble travelers, no one granted them hospitality except Philemon and Baucis. *Jove* destroyed the rest of the village in a flood, but he transformed the couple's *thatch'd house* into an opulent temple in which Philemon and Baucis served as *Jove's* own consecrated priest and priestess. *Jove* also granted them each one wish, and the pair were so in love that they both asked to die at the same moment so that one would never know the pain of losing the other. When they died, *Jove* turned them into intertwining trees (Baucis into a linden, a symbol of fertility, and Philemon into an oak; see note: *Acorne*, III.ii.233) standing at the door to the temple that had once been their home.

On a different note, *Jove inhabited* many different shapes (such as a bull when he raped Europa, and a swan when he raped Leda) in order to have *ill* ("immoral," OED; "sexually bestial," FR) *knowledge* (i.e., carnal *knowledge*) of his lovers. Thus, *Jove inhabited* ("occupied" or copulated with, F&H) many a *thatch'd house* ("female pudendum," F&H, s.v. "monosyllable").

Clo. When a mans verses cannot be understood, nor
a mans good wit seconded with the forward childe, understanding: it strikes a man more dead then a great reckoning in a little roome: truly, I would the Gods hadde
made thee poeticall. [15]

Aud. I do not know what Poetical is: is it honest in
deed and word: is it a true thing?

Clo. No trulie: for the truest poetrie is the most faining, and Lovers are given to Poetrie: and what they
sweare in Poetrie, may be said as Lovers, they do feigne. [20]

Aud. Do you wish then that the Gods had made me
Poeticall?

Clow. I do truly: for thou swear'st to me thou art honest: Now if thou wert a Poet, I might have some hope
thou didst feigne. [25]

11–13. ***When a mans verses... understanding.*** *The Clowne* seeks to win *Audrey* with his *verses* (poetry), but *Audrey* is "without understanding" ("Luskish, slow," "witles," TT, s.v. "Sŏcors"). Therefore, his *verses cannot be understood* ("made known or patent," OED) to her, and his *good wit* ("conceit, understanding; or, a good utterance, a ready tongue, a quicke deliverie," RC, s.v. "Bon boute-hors") is not *seconded* (followed, succeeded, or accompanied) *with the forward* ("Principal, foremost, chief," OED) *childe* (consequent result) of her *understanding* (comprehension, knowledge).

It is therefore unlikely that the *Clowne's verses* (i.e., "staff of *verses*" or penis; "staff" is "verse," OED) can compel *Audrey* to "understand" (be in a supine coital position "under" his "stand," or phallic erection, FR; cf. and see note: *take upon*, III.ii.405). Neither will his *good* (sexually adept; see notes: *good*, I.ii.28 and 65) *wit* (penis; see note: *wit*, II.iv.60; also "semen," GW) *be seconded* (succeeded) *with a forward child* (a child that continues its parents' lineage into the future; cf. "his poore neighbours comfort their servile lives with the sight of their forward Children," Christopher Middleton, *Chinon of England*).

13–14. ***it strikes a man more dead... a little roome.*** A *reckoning* is a "statement of something" and also a "Thought, idea" (OED); a *roome* is a "particular portion of space; a certain space" (OED). Therefore, *a great reckoning in a little roome* means "a great amount of import in a small space of words." *Audrey's* vapidity *strikes* the *Clowne* more *dead* (silent) than had she subdued him with "Pith": a "jest, or Sentence, that couches a great deal in a little room" (ND, q.v.).

Unlike *Rosalind*, whose *white* (III.ii.382) person contains all the world's shining wonder *in little* (III.ii.141), the coarse, tan, and very dirty and smelly *Audrey* cannot be said to possess "white riches in a little roome" (Christopher Marlowe, *The Famous Tragedy of the Rich Jew of Malta*). Nevertheless, the *Clowne* is "stricken" (love-smitten) with *Audrey*, and the very sight of her *strikes* him *dead* (cf. and see note: *murder in mine eye*, III.v.13).

The Marlovian echo suggests oblique allusion to Marlowe's own *reckoning* (death, day of judgment): he was stabbed to death by Ingram Frizer in an upstairs *roome* of a Deptford inn on May 30, 1593, supposedly in an argument over the *reckoning* (bill). Also cf. and see note: III.v.86–87.

There is probable additional play on "strike" as "copulate" (F&H), "death" as "sexual orgasm" (JH), *reckoning* as "counting" (i.e., "cunting"), and *roome* as "vagina" (GW2).

14–45. ***truly... Amen.*** The repetition of the word "true" (or a variant thereof) in lines 17, 18, 23, 27, 33, and 45 ironically underpins the discussion of honesty. In addition, there may be play on "trou" (Fr. for "hole" and slang for the vagina).

15. ***poeticall.*** *Poeticall* is (a) "having the sensibility of a poet"; (b) "fond of poetry"; and/or (c) "worthy to be celebrated in poetry" (OED).

16–17. ***honest in deed and word.*** The naïve *Audrey* does not know that "Deeds and words dwell farre asunder: either because many things that are spoken are not intended to be done; or because few things will so quickly, or can so easily be done, as they are spoken" (RC, s.v. "Du dire au faict y a grand traict"). Cf. and see note: lines 18–20, below.

18–20. ***truest poetrie... they do feigne.*** *What Lovers sweare in Poetrie, they do feigne* (desire), and the *truest* (most sincere) *poetry is the most faining*, which means (a) "longing, wistful" (OED); (b) "gladsome, affectionate" (OED); and/or (c) "imaginative" (OED, s.v. "feigning"). Also, the *truest* (most proper or genuine) *poetry is the most faining* ("fibbing, lying," "meere imagination, forged stuffe," RC, s.v. "Controuvement"), so *what Lovers sweare in Poetrie, they do feigne* (pretend, falsify).

23–25. ***for thou swear'st... some hope thou didst feigne.*** If *Audrey* were *a Poet* and swore herself *honest* (chaste), then there would be *some hope* that she did *feigne* (lie). Consequently, the *Clowne* might have *some hope* of having sex with her without first having to marry her.

Aud. Would you not have me honest?

Clo. No truly, unlesse thou wert hard favour'd: for honestie coupled to beautie, is to have Honie a sawce to Sugar.

Jaq. A materiall foole. [30]

Aud. Well, I am not faire, and therefore I pray the Gods make me honest.

Clo. Truly, and to cast away honestie uppon a foule slut, were to put good meate into an uncleane dish.

Aud. I am not a slut, though I thanke the Goddes I am foule. [35]

Clo. Well, praised be the Gods, for thy foulnesse; sluttishnesse may come heereafter. But be it, as it may bee, I wil marrie thee: and to that end, I have bin with Sir *Oliver Mar-text*, the Vicar of the next village, who hath [40] promis'd to meete me in this place of the Forrest, and to couple us.

26–27. ***Would you not have me honest... truly.*** The *Clowne* might say that (a) he *truly* seeks to *have* (i.e., sexually) *Audrey honest* (once; "onest" is a variant of "once," OED; also see note: *alone*, I.i.157); or (b) he could *not have* (sexually possess) *Audrey* if she were *truly honest* (chaste, pure). Also see note: *honestie*, line 33, below.

27. ***hard favour'd.*** Either (a) ugly; or (b) *hard* (unyielding) with her "favor" (sexual preferment, F&H).

28–29. ***honestie... a sawce to Sugar.*** Because the *beautie* ("female pudendum; Cunt," F&H) of a *beautie* (beautiful woman) is generally not "honest" (chaste), a woman who possesses both *beautie* and *honestie* (sexual virtue) would simply be too "sweet" (precious); cf. I.ii.38–40. The *Clowne's* viewpoint differs from the moral ideal, "for as meat pleaseth better in a cleane dish, so vertue in comely persons is more amiable" (Andrew Willet, *Hexapla in Genesin & Exodum*; cf. lines 33–34, below). There may be additional play on *sauce* as "semen" (FR), and on *Honie* as both "semen" (F&H) and "sexual pleasure" (EP).

30. ***A materiall foole.*** *Jaques* thinks the *foole materiall* ("Full of sense," OED); he is only a *foole* in his *materiall* (clothing). Cf. and see note: *knowledge ill inhabited*, line 9, above.

33–34. ***cast away honestie... an uncleane dish.*** Ostensibly, the *Clowne* says that to *cast away* (waste) *honestie* (chastity) *uppon a foule* ("ill favoured," TT, s.v. "Squaleo") *slut* ("an awkward person or thing," F&H) would be to *put good meate into an uncleane dish* (i.e., be a complete waste; cf. and see note: lines 28–29, above).

Also, to *cast away honestie* (i.e., marriage; "To marry a woman with whom one has cohabitated as a mistress, is termed, making an honest woman of her," FG, s.v. "Honest Woman") *uppon a foule slut* ("a whore, a flurt, a strumpet," JF, s.v. "Paltrocca"), *were to put good meat* (male genitalia; see note: *meate*, III.ii.65) *into an uncleane* (impure, morally tainted) *dish* ("vagina," FR).

35–36. ***I thanke the Goddes I am foule.*** *Audrey* is thankful that she is *foule* (unattractive) because her appearance helps preserve her chastity. Cf. I.ii.38–40 and V.iv.66–68.

39. ***to that end.*** "For that purpose," but cf. and see note: *end*, line 50, below.

39–40. ***Sir Oliver Mar-text.*** "Clergymen had at one time *Sir* prefixed to their name. This is not the *Sir* of knighthood, but merely a translation of the university word *dominus* given to graduates" (DPF). Nevertheless, the title *Sir* "denoted that the priest had not graduated in a university" (OED).

Oliver is "a name fetched from the peace bringing Olive" (TB, q.v.) and is thus appropriate for a religious man (for a possible explanation as to why there are two characters named *Oliver* in this play, see note: *Sir Rowland de Boys*, I.i.56–57). The name *Mar-text* is self-explanatory.

40. ***Vicar.*** A *Vicar* is "a curate, a parson, a countrie priest, a sir John lack-latine" (JF, s.v. "Piovano"; also see note: *a Priest that lacks Latine*, III.ii.314). DPF notes that "At the Reformation many livings which belonged to monasteries passed into the hands of noblemen, who, not being in holy orders, had to perform the sacred offices vicariously. The clergyman who officiated for them was called their vicar or representative" (q.v.). Parishioners usually did not highly esteem vicars who were "Gadding, raunging, roaming, trotting up and downe the countrey" (RC, s.v. "Vicariant").

42. ***couple.*** To *couple* is literally "To yoake or joine too" (TT, s.v. "Adjŭgo"). Once the *Clowne* and *Audrey* are "yoked" ("married," FG), then they can *couple* (copulate; see note: *coupled*, I.iii.80).

Jaq. I would faine see this meeting.

Aud. Wel, the Gods give us joy.

Clo. Amen. A man may if he were of a fearful heart, [45]
stagger in this attempt: for heere wee have no Temple
but the wood, no assembly but horne-beasts. But what
though? Courage. As hornes are odious, they are necessarie. It is said, many a man knowes no end of his goods;
right: Many a man has good Hornes, and knows no end [50]
of them. Well, that is the dowrie of his wife, 'tis none
of his owne getting; hornes, even so poore men alone:

45. ***Amen.*** *Amen* continues the *Clowne's* string of wordplay on "truly": *Amen* as "Retained in the Bible from the original Gr. or Heb." means "Truly, verily" (OED).

45. ***A man.*** A play on the sound of *Amen.*

45–46. ***A man may... stagger in this attempt.*** For fear of being made a "Staggerd" ("a red Male Deer four years old," TB, q.v., with obvious play on "stag" as "a cuckold," EP), *A man of fearful* (apprehensive, anxious) *heart* (courage, with play on "hart" as a male deer) *might stagger* (begin to doubt, become less determined, waiver) *in* his *attempt* (aim, purpose) of marriage.

Also, if *A man* lacks *heart* ("courage" or sexual capability; see note: *coragious,* II.iv.10), he might *stagger* (i.e., not be able to "get it up"; to *stagger* is to "be readie to fall," TT, s.v. "Collābāsco"; "to totter as a thing that is loose," JF, s.v. "Traballare") *in* his *attempt* (i.e., sexual *attempt,* EP).

46–47. ***no Temple... horne-beasts.*** The *Clowne* questions the validity of a marriage not consecrated in a *Temple* ("a church or a chappell, a place consecrated to devine service," JF, s.v. "Tempio"); cf. lines 83–86, below. In the forest, the only *Temple* (i.e., model or standard; a *temple* is a "template," OED) for his marriage is *the wood* ("branchwood; also, branches collectively," OED), which reminds him that he might be "Branch'd" ("Horned, cuckolded," JH, q.v.). The *Horne-beasts* (animals with horns) who comprise the *assembly* (gathering, company) at his wedding likewise suggest that his *assembly* ("sexual union," FR) will make him a "horned beast" ("A cuckold," RC, s.v. "Cornard"). As such, he will wear a *Temple* (a headdress or ornaments worn on the forehead, OED) of "horns" on his "Temples" ("the sides of the head betweene the eyes, and eares," RC, q.v.).

47–48. ***what though?*** I.e., "So what?"

48–49. ***hornes are... necessarie.*** Because men have *hornes* (phallic erections; see note: *crooked-pated,* III.ii.82), marriage is *necessarie.* Therefore, *hornes* (i.e., cuckolds) are also *necessarie,* for "who e're is borne / To marry, likewise must possesse the horne" (Lodovico Ariosto, "The Fourth Satyre").

49–51. ***many a man knowes no end... the dowrie of his wife.*** *Many a man has good Hornes* (i.e., "horns of plenty" or "cornucopiae") due to *the dowrie of his* rich *wife.* Such *a man* is so wealthy that he *knowes no end* (limit) *of his goods* (possessions).

Also, *a man* with *good* (sexually capable; see notes: *good,* I.ii.28 and 65) *Hornes* (phallic erections; see note: *crooked-pated,* III.ii.82) still might not "know" (have carnal knowledge of) the *end* ("pudendum," JH) *of his goods* (i.e., his wife, who was considered the *goods* or property of her husband). Instead, his wife's *dowrie* (i.e., her "cunny" or "cunt"; a "dower" is "A burrow of rabbits," OED; cf. and see note: *Conie,* III.ii.333) gives him a "Horn of plenty" ("the horns of the cuckold," JH; also see note: *plentifully,* I.i.18).

52. ***hornes... poore men alone.*** *Poore men* living *alone* do not wear a cuckold's *hornes,* but they lack the convenient means of a wife to relieve their *hornes* (phallic erections; see note: *crooked-pated,* III.ii.82).

No, no, the noblest Deere hath them as huge as the Rascall: Is the single man therefore blessed? No, as a wall'd
Towne is more worthier then a village, so is the fore- [55]
head of a married man, more honourable then the bare
brow of a Batcheller: and by how much defence is better then no skill, by so much is a horne more precious
then to want.

Enter Sir Oliver Mar-text. [III.iii.2] [60]

Heere comes Sir *Oliver*: Sir *Oliver Mar-text* you are
wel met. Will you dispatch us heere under this tree, or
shal we go with you to your Chappell?

{*Mar.*} Is there none heere to give the woman?

Clo, I wil not take her on guift of any man. [65]

{*Mar.*} Truly she must be given, or the marriage is not
lawfull.

Jaq. Proceed, proceede: Ile give her.

53–54. ***the noblest Deere... the Rascall.*** The *noblest Deere* has a *nob* (head) *blest* with "knobs" (i.e., antlers; cf. "knobbler": "A male deer in its second year," OED). However, even a *Rascall* ("a lean, worthless deer," DPF) has horns. Therefore, a man who wears the cuckold's horns is not necessarily a *Rascall* (i.e., impotent or castrated; see note: *villaine*, I.i.56); he could very well be a *Deere* (i.e., a "dear" or lover) *blest* with a good "knob" ("penis," OED).

54. ***Is the single man therefore blessed?*** For centuries, the Catholic Church held that a *single* and celibate life in imitation of Christ was more *blessed* than married life. However, after the Protestant Reformation, many condemned "the errour of the Moonkes and Nunnes amongest the Christians: who doe seeme to reject and contemne the blessing of God, by leading a single life, and not observing the commandement given by GOD unto man at his creation when hee willed him to encrease and multiply: by the which (as they say) all men are bounden to marrie" (Giles Fletcher, *The Policy of the Turkish Empire*).

There may be additional play on "blessed" / "blast": to sound a horn (OED). To "blast" also means "To curse" (FG), a possible play on Gk. "keras": "horn" (FR).

54–57. ***a wall'd Towne... a Batcheller.*** The *Clowne* uses a *wall'd Towne* and a small *village* as an analogy to extol married life over single life. A *village* is not "worthy" ("Strong, powerful," OED) and thus quite "indefensible" ("Incapable of being defended by force of arms," OED). By contrast, a *wall'd Towne* is highly "defensible" ("fortified," OED) on account of its "horn-works" (outer defensive fortifications; cf. *defence*, line 57, below). Similarly, *a married man* is "worthy" ("Capable of justifying," OED) the *brow* ("Brow-antler," OED) on his *forehead*, so his "horn-works" (cuckold's horns) are "defensible" (justifiable). Conversely, *the bare brow of a Batcheller* is quite "indefensible" (unjustifiable, inexcusable).

57–58. ***defence is better then no skill.*** It *is better* for a man to have *skill* (ability, expertise) than "to want *skill*" ("be ignornant," RC, s.v. "Ignorer") in *defence* (knowledge of how to defend himself). Just as a *wall'd Towne* (lines 54–55, above) needs "horn-works" for *defence* ("fortification, provided for the safegard of those that make good a Place beleaguered," RC, s.v. "Defense"), it is better for a man to marry and have "horn-works" (i.e., cuckold's horns) than to remain unmarried and have *no skill* (i.e., no "skell" or "shell," OED; the "shell" is "The female pudendum; Cunt," F&H, s.v. "Monosyllable").

58–59. ***a horne... to want.*** An allusion to the "horn of plenty"; cf. and see note: lines 49–51, above.

62. ***dispatch.*** The *Clowne* wants *Mar-text* to *dispatch* ("conclude or settle a business," OED) because he is eager to *dis-* ("undo or spoil," OED) *Audrey's patch* ("female pudendum," F&H) and *dispatch* (copulate, JH).

63. ***your Chappell.*** *Mar-text* probably does not have *a Chappell*; see note: lines 77–78, below.

65. ***I will not take her... any man.*** The *Clowne* has no interest in *Audrey* if she is a second-hand *guift* from another *man* to whom she has already given her *guift* (sexual favor; see note: *gift*, II.vii.42).

66–67. ***she must be given... not lawfull.*** This *marriage is not lawfull* anyway, because to be *lawfull* (1) the "banns" announcing the *marriage* must be read in church for three consecutive weeks prior to the wedding; and (2) at least two witnesses must attend the ceremony. Paradoxically, even an illegal *marriage* was binding for life once consummated (LS, p. 32), but the *Clowne* hopes that he can later opt out of his *marriage*; cf. lines 83–86, below.

68. ***Proceed.*** If *Mar-text* follows this spoken stage direction, he will here begin to speak the marriage ceremony and continue until the *Clowne* interrupts him in line 91, below. *Jaques* may also here give *Mar-text* his fee for performing the ceremony, which was customarily laid down on the Bible along with the ring.

Clo. Good even good Master what ye cal't: how do you

Sir, you are verie well met: goddild you for your last [70]

companie, I am verie glad to see you, even a toy in hand

heere Sir: Nay, pray be cover'd.

Jaq. Wil you be married, Motley?

Clo. As the Oxe hath his bow sir, the horse his curb,

and the Falcon her bels, so man hath his desires, and as [75]

Pigeons bill, so wedlocke would be nibling.

Jaq. And wil you (being a man of your breeding) be

married under a bush like a begger? Get you to church,

and have a good Priest that can tel you what marriage is,

this fellow wil but joyne you together, as they joyne [80]

Wainscot, then one of you wil prove a shrunke pannell,

and like greene timber, warpe, warpe.

---

69. ***Good even.*** I.e., "Good evening," a greeting used any time after noon.

69. ***Master what ye cal't.*** The *Clowne* addresses *Jaques* as *Master what ye cal't* (a) to avoid saying *Jaques'* name, which sounds like "jakes" ("A privy," OED, of which "jaques" is a variant spelling; cf. and see note: *melancholy Jaques*, II.i.30); and/or (b) because *Jaques'* name resembles "Jack" meaning "the penis" and/or "erection" (F&H; "what you call it" is both "a mans or womans privities," JF, s.v. "Cotale"; also "a dildo," GW2, s.v. "what d'ye callum").

70. ***goddild you.*** A contraction of "God yield you" meaning "God reward you." The phrase was "a common expression of gratitude or goodwill" (OED)—unless "yield" is taken to mean "yeld" or "geld" (see note: *yeelde*, II.iii.67).

71. ***toy.*** The *Clowne* hopes to take *Audrey's toy* ("maidenhead," F&H) and *toy* (copulate, EP) with her *toy* ("female pudendum," F&H).

72. ***pray be cover'd.*** Hats were customarily doffed in greeting (see note: *Cover thy head*, V.i.19), so the *Clowne* might tell *Jaques* (a) to *be cover'd* (put his hat on);

and/or (b) follow his example and find a "prey" ("sexual quarry," SG) so that he may *be cover'd* (i.e., have sex; to "cover" is to copulate, F&H, s.v. "ride").

73. ***Motley.*** See note: *motley*, II.vii.17.

74. ***the Oxe hath his bow.*** Just like an *Oxe* must have *his* "oxbow" (the collar that goes around the *Oxe's* neck and attaches to the yoke), a man must marry, be an *Oxe* ("A cuckold," EP), and bear the "yoke" (a traditional symbol of marriage). There may be additional play on the "yoke" as "antlers (resembling a plough-yoke) allusive of cuckoldry" (GW2). Cf. and see notes: lines 45–59, above.

74. ***the horse his curb.*** A *curb* is "a bridle," "a restraint, a bit" (JF, s.v. "Freno"), and the *Clowne* is a *horse* ("stallion": "Whore-Master," ND) who needs a "bit" (copulation, GW2) from the "horse-collar" ("female pudendum," F&H).

75. ***the Falcon her bels.*** *Bels* were attached to a *Falcon's* claws to help locate the bird if she went astray. A *Falcon* ("hawk": whore, GW2) also needs *bels* (the male genitals, particularly the testicles, GW2).

76. ***Pigeons bill.*** *Pigeons bill* ("stroke bill with bill," OED). Also, a "pigeon" (whore, GW2) will *bill* ("kisse like a Pigeon," "give long, and lascivious kisses," RC, s.v. "Pigeonner") and also *bill* (copulate, GW2). Also see note: *bils*, I.ii.118.

76. ***wedlocke... nibling.*** The *Clowne* "nibbles" ("consider[s] a bargain, or an opportunity, eagerly but carefully: as a fish considers bait," F&H) *wedlocke* because he wants to "nibble" ("copulate," F&H).

77. ***breeding.*** With play on *breeding* as (a) upbringing and education; and (b) mating.

77–78. ***be married... like a beggar.*** The *Clowne* is about to *be married* by a "hedge-priest" ("A poor or vagabond parson," DPF) and "go by beggar's bush, or Go home by beggar's bush" ("go to ruin. Beggar's bush is the name of a tree which once stood on the left hand of the London road from Huntingdon to Caxton; so called because it was a noted rendezvous for beggars," DPF). *Jaques* may also imply that (a) *Audrey* is a "buss-beggar" (a "Tart," F&H, s.v. "Tart"); or (b) the *Clowne* is a *beggar* (i.e., a "bugger": "A blackguard, a rascal," FG) to marry *Audrey* simply for her *bush* (pubic hair and vagina, JH).

80–82. ***joyne you together... warpe.*** *Wainscot* ("A pane, peece, or pannell of a wall," RC, s.v. "Pan") is traditionally constructed using a "frame and *pannell*" system in which each *pannell* is set into a slightly larger frame. If the *timber* (wood) is *greene* (not properly dried), it will *warpe* (shrink or shrivel, bend or twist).

If the *Clowne* and *Audrey* are "joined" (fastened, united) only by their "joints" (genitals, FR), then they will only be "joined" *together as they joyne Wainscot* (i.e., with a tongue-and-groove system, in which the joints have "male" and "female" ends). Both of them are *greene* ("Young, inexperienced, unacquainted; ignorant," FG) and lack control of their "greens" ("longings, desires," F&H), so they might "shrink" (shun one another) and *warpe* (i.e., be sexually unfaithful; to *warpe* is to "reject, renounce" as well as "To pervert," OED). If *Audrey* over-indulges her "greens" (vagina, F&H, s.v. "monosyllable") and the *Clowne* his *timber* (i.e., penis; *timber* is literally "a beame, a prop," JF, s.v. "Assuto"), then they will "shrink" (lose vitality; the vital spirits were thought to be "overpowered and altered by... immoderate indulgence of the sexual appetite," Francis Bacon, *Historia Vitae et Mortis*; also see note: *shrinke*, II.i.12). Thus, *Audrey* will become a *pannell* (loose woman, whore, F&H, s.v. "Tart") and the *Clowne* a *pannel* ("a weak or effeminate man," OED, s.v. "parnel"; for the dropping of the pre-consonantal "r," see HK, pp. 261–262).

Clo. I am not in the minde, but I were better to bee
married of him then of another, for he is not like to marrie me wel: and not being wel married, it wil be a good [85]
excuse for me heereafter, to leave my wife.

Jaq. Goe thou with mee,
And let me counsel thee.

{*Clo.*} Come sweete *Audrey*,
We must be married, or we must live in baudrey: [90]
Farewel good Master *Oliver*: Not O sweet *Oliver*, O brave
Oliver leave me not behind thee: But winde away, bee
gone I say, I wil not to wedding with thee.

{*Exit Clowne, Audrey, and Jaques.*} [III.iii.3]

{*Mar.*} 'Tis no matter; Ne're a fantastical knave of them [95]
all shal flout me out of my calling.

{*Exit Mar-text.*}

84–86. ***not like to marrie me wel... leave my wife.*** *Mar-text* is part of the "brisk trade carried on by unscrupulous clergymen, operating in districts which were immune from superior ecclesiastical supervision, who would marry anyone for a fee, no questions asked" (LS, p. 33). Should the *Clowne* later deny his marriage, *Mar-text* would be hard to track down because he is itinerant. However, the presence of *Jaques* as a witness would complicate matters somewhat; see note: IV.i.120–124.

90. ***baudrey.*** *Baudrey*, which means "leacherie" (JF, s.v. "Lenocinio") and also "filthines, uncleannes, baudines" (JF, s.v. "Puttaneggio), concludes a string of rhymes that began in line 87, above.

91. ***O sweet Oliver.*** A ballad entitled "O swete Olyver, Leave me not behind the" was entered into the Stationer's Register on August 6, 1584. Many contemporary references to this popular song survive, but the music and lyrics (except those here quoted by the *Clowne*) do not. However, the c. 1690 "Leyden Lute Manuscript" (also known as the "Thysius Lute Book") includes the traditional tune "The Hunt Is Up" under the name "Soet Oliver," so *O sweet Oliver* might share this melody.

If the theatre's musicians here joined in to accompany the *Clowne*, *O sweet Oliver* might have originally been an all-out production number.

95. ***fantastical.*** See note: *fantastical,* III.ii.396.

96. ***flout.*** Mock, deride.

96. ***calling.*** A *calling* is a "summons, invitation, or impulse of God to salvation or to his service; the inward feeling or conviction of a divine call" (OED). The "allusion is to the calling of the apostles by Jesus Christ to follow Him" (DPF).

Act III, scene iv

SCŒNA QUARTA. [1]

Enter Rosalind & Celia. [III.iv.1]

Ros. Never talke to me, I wil weepe.

Cel. Do I prethee, but yet have the grace to consider,

that teares do not become a man. [5]

Ros. But have I not cause to weepe?

Cel. As good cause as one would desire,

Therefore weepe.

Ros. His very haire

Is of the dissembling colour. [10]

Cel. Something browner then Judasses:

Marrie his kisses are Judasses owne children.

Ros. I'faith his haire is of a good colour.

Cel. An excellent colour:

Your Chessenut was ever the onely colour: [15]

Notes III.iv.

3–22. ***I wil weepe... and comes not.*** *Rosalind* here genuinely displays the womanly behavior she made fun of in III.ii.395–401: she *weepe*[s] *for* (III.ii.401) *Orlando* one moment, *loath*[es] *him* (III.ii.400) the next, and after that is *longing, and liking* (III.ii.395–396).

5–6. ***teares do not become a man... cause to weepe.*** "The Stoyckes say, that it becommeth not a man of courage to weepe, for that it is a signe of a weak & effeminate mind. But the holy scriptures teach otherwise, for in them there are many examples not onely of women: but of most valiaunt men who by teares have testified theyr sorrow, and are not yet accounted to have offended therein" (Ludwig Lavatar, *The Book of Ruth Expounded in Twenty Eight Sermons*). Therefore, *Ganimed's teares* are not dishonorable because "he" has *cause to weepe.*

9–11. ***haire... browner then Judasses.*** *Judas* was traditionally depicted with "Judas-coloured" ("Fiery-red," DPF) hair because "They that have red haire, byn commonly yreful and lacke wyt, and ben of litle truth" (Robert Copland, *The Shepardes Kalender*). *Orlando's* hair is *browner then Judasses,* but every *haire* on his head is *dissembling* (hypocritical, deceiving). Therefore, *Rosalind* has "be[en] done brown" ("be[en] roasted, deceived, taken in," DPF).

12. ***his kisses are Judasses owne children.*** *Judas* kissed Jesus in the Garden of Gethsemane to identify him for arrest (Matthew 26:48–49; Mark 14:44–45; Luke 22:47–48). Therefore, a "Judas kiss" is "A deceitful act of courtesy" (DPF).

13. ***a good colour.*** *Orlando's* brown hair (lines 9–11, above) is a "sign of amorousness" (GW, s.v. "Brown") that indicates he is *good* (virile; see notes: *good,* I.ii.28 and 65).

14–15. ***An excellent colour... Chessenut.*** The *Chessenut* is an emblem of saintly purity, for "The chestnut in its husk is surrounded by thorns, but is unharmed by them. For this reason it is a symbol of chastity, because this virtue is a triumph over the temptations of the flesh" (George Wells Ferguson, *Signs and Symbols in Christian Art,* s.v. "Chestnut"; cf. lines 16–17, below). In Lodge's *Rosalynde, Aliena* muses that "in elder time (as Coridon hath tolde me) the Shepheards Love-gifts were apples and chestnuts, & then their desires were loyall and their thoughts constant."

The *Chessenut,* also known as "Jovis Glans" (TT, q.v.), the "Gland de Jupiter" (RC, q.v.), or "God's Acorn" (GW2), was thought to assist phallic erection (GW2; cf. and see notes: *Acorne,* III.ii.233, and *nut,* line 27, below). Thus, *Chessenut was ever the onely colour* for an *excellent* ("Lewd... From L. cellare, to raise high... it puns on 'sellary,' a lewd person," FR) *colour* (i.e., a well-endowed man; "culls" are the testicles, F&H; cf. Fr. "Couillatris": "Well hangd betweene the legs," RC, q.v.).

Celia might also imply that *Orlando* is a "cul" (i.e., an "asshole"; "cul" is "An arse, bumme, tayle, nockandroe, fundament," RC, q.v.) who is "full of shit," because (a) "the Chestnut is a purgation very gentle" (Nicholas Monardes, *Joyfull Newes out of the Newfound World*); (b) "The bark of the Chestnut-tree is dry and binding, and stops fluxes" (Nicholas Culpeper, *A Physicall Directory*); and/or (c) a "Glans" is "a suppositorie made like an acorn, & put into the fundament to cause solublenesse" (TT, q.v.; cf. TT's "Bălănus": "All kinde of mast, or Acornes: a great chestnut, which is called Marron: a suppositorie").

Ros. And his kissing is as ful of sanctitie,

As the touch of holy bread.

Cel. Hee hath bought a paire of cast lips of *Diana*: a

Nun of winters sisterhood kisses not more religiouslie,

the very yce of chastity is in them. [20]

Rosa. But why did hee sweare hee would come this

morning, and comes not?

Cel. Nay certainly there is no truth in him.

Ros. Doe you thinke so?

Cel. Yes, I thinke he is not a picke purse, nor a horse- [25]

stealer, but for his verity in love, I doe thinke him as

concave as a covered goblet, or a Worme-eaten nut.

Ros. Not true in love?

Cel. Yes, when he is in, but I thinke he is not in.

Ros. You have heard him sweare downright he was. [30]

Cel. Was, is not is: besides, the oath of Lover is no

stronger then the word of a Tapster, they are both the

confirmer of false reckonings, he attends here in the for-

rest on the Duke your father.

16–17. ***as ful of sanctitie... holy bread.*** *Rosalind* might say that (a) *Orlando's kissing is as ful of sanctitie* ("Holinesse," JB, q.v.) *as* the "Holie-bread, used in Popish Churches" (RC, s.v. "Pain benist"); or (b) *Orlando's kissing is as ful of sanctitie* (i.e., "holy" or full of holes) *As holy bread* (i.e., "bread full of holes like a spunge," TT, s.v. "Spongiosus"); cf. and see note: *sanctified*, II.iii.15. She may also imagine *Orlando's bread* (i.e., penis; *bread* is "The staff of life," OED, s.v. "staff"; the "staff of life" is "The penis," F&H, s.v. "staff") *kissing* (copulating with, F&H, s.v. "Ride") her "hole" (vagina).

18–20. ***Hee hath bought... yce of chastity.*** Instead of kissing with his own lips, *Orlando* is so *cast* (variant of "chaste," OED) that *Hee hath bought a paire of lips cast* ("cast in a mould," "made after the fashion," JM, s.v. "Formádo") *of* those of the virgin goddess *Diana*. Even the *kisses* of a *Nun* ("A vestall virgin," TT, s.v. "Săcerdōtissa") of the *sisterhood* of "winter" (i.e., sexual frigidity; cf. and see notes: *Icie*, II.i.9; *cold*, II.i.12; and *Wintred*, III.ii.106) could not rival *Orlando's* for *the yce of chastity*. (This would make *Orlando* entirely unsatisfying as a lover, but *Rosalind* doesn't seem to notice *Celia's* sarcasm.)

25–26. ***not a picke purse, nor a horse-stealer.*** *Orlando* may be inconstant, but he would not *picke* (illicitly open) a woman's *purse* ("female pudendum," F&H), nor would he make her a *horse* (i.e., "whore"; see note: *horses*, I.i.12) or a "stale" ("common whore," F&H; also see note: *steale*, II.i.34).

26–27. ***as concave... a Worme-eaten nut.*** *Orlando* is *as concave* ("hollow": "not answering inwardly to outward appearance; insincere, false," OED) as a *covered* ("Gilded" or "overlaid with golde," TT, s.v. "Inaūrātus") *goblet*. It is impossible to see into *Orlando's* heart, for *a covered* (gilded) *goblet* is not transparent and therefore *covered* ("close, secret, secretly kept, hard to be knowne," TT, s.v. "Rĕcondĭtus"; cf. "For gilded gobblet hides the harmes, that glasse will soone bewraie," Thomas Churchyard, "A letter to maister Cressie"). *Celia* surmises that *Orlando's* "vessel" (human body as enclosing the soul) is merely *covered* (used of base metal "Overlaid or plated with precious metal," OED), so in spite of his lustrous appearance he is "base" ("counterfeit," OED) and of "base" (cowardly, worthless) "mettle" (character).

At the core, *Orlando* is as *Worme-eaten* ("faultie, naughtie, imperfect, corrupted, diseased, blemished, offensive, full of vices, wicked, lewde, corrupt, full of errours, false," JF, s.v. "Vitioso") and as *concave* ("hollow": "empty, vain," OED) as a *nut* that has fallen pray to "A kinde of wormes... that eates the Nutte, And leaves the shell as bare as bare maie bee" (Thomas Churchyard, "A Letter sent from the noble Erle of Ormondes house at Kilkennie, to the honourable sir Henry Sidney, then Lorde Deputie, and liyng at Korke, in Irelande"). He is also as *concave* (i.e., corrosive; *concave* can mean "hollow ulcers," JG) as an "ulcer" ("a purulent sore frequently associated with pox," GW2) in a *cover'd* (i.e., wanton; see note: *cover'd*, III.iii.72) *goblet* (i.e., "cup" or "vagina," GW2), *or a Worme-eaten* (i.e., syphilitic; see note: *wormes*, III.ii.65) *nut* ("glans penis," OED).

31–33. ***the oath of Lover... false reckonings.*** A *Tapster* (bartender) "confirms" (asserts, maintains) *false* (sham, spurious) *reckonings* (accounts, tavern bills), and a *Lover* "confirms" *false* (deceitful, treacherous) *reckonings* (accounts of his conduct or actions). A *Lover* also resembles a *Tapster* (pimp, JH, s.v. "Lay") in that both of them "confirm" ("encourage," OED) *false* (illicit, adulterous) *reckonings* (sexual intercourse; see note: *reckoning*, III.iii.13–14).

Ros. I met the Duke yesterday, and had much que- [35]

stion with him: he askt me of what parentage I was; I

told him of as good as he, so he laugh'd and let mee goe.

But what talke wee of Fathers, when there is such a man

as *Orlando*?

Cel. O that's a brave man, hee writes brave verses, [40]

speakes brave words, sweares brave oathes, and breakes

them bravely, quite travers athwart the heart of his lo-

ver, as a puisny Tilter, that spurs his horse but on one side,

breakes his staffe like a noble goose; but all's brave that

youth mounts, and folly guides: who comes heere? [45]

Enter Corin. [III.iv.2]

Corin. Mistresse and Master, you have oft enquired

After the Shepheard that complain'd of love,

Who you saw sitting by me on the Turph,

Praising the proud disdainfull Shepherdesse [50]

35–36. ***I met the Duke... with him.*** The ladies came to *Arden* to find *the Duke* (I.iii.114), but after having *some question* (conversation) *with* her father, *Rosalind* appears to have lost interest in joining him.

36. ***he askt me of what parentage I was.*** *Senior* may have immediately noticed *Ganimed's* resemblance to *Rosalind*; cf. V.iv.32–33.

40–42. ***brave... bravely.*** *Orlando* is not "of a brave humor" ("Generous; noble, gentle, worthie, gallant," "of an excellent race, of the right stampe, of a good kind;

also, valiant, couragious, hardie, stout," RC, s.v. "Genereux") but merely "brave[s] it, or play[s] the Gallant" (RC, s.v. "Se braver"). *Orlando breakes* his *oathes bravely* (fearlessly, showily, gallantly), and he is such a "braver" ("affronter, abuser of people to their faces; a common swaggerer, an impudent, or bold companion; also, an open, or publique deceiver, beguiler, cheater, cogging mate; cousening merchant," RC, s.v. "Affronteur") that he will *brave* ("wrong, abuse; cosen, gull, deceive, impudently, openly, or to the face of," RC, s.v. "Affronter") anybody without compunction.

41–42. ***breakes them... travers athwart the heart.*** In jousting, it was extremely "dishonourable to break a lance traverse, or across the breast of an opponent, without striking him with the point; for as it could only occur from the horse swerving on one side, it showed unskillful riding... 'To break across,' the phrase for bad chivalry, did not die with the lance. It was used by the writers of the Elizabethan age to express any failure of wit or argument" (Charles Mills, *The History of Chivalry; or Knighthood and Its Time*).

The joust was also a metaphor for the rites of love and sexual intercourse (see note: *justly*, I.ii.242). *Celia* therefore implies that *Orlando* is both romantically and sexually inept; see notes through line 45, below.

43. ***a puisny Tilter.*** A *puisny* ("novice," OED) *Tilter* (jouster) is an unskillful rider, but *Orlando* is a *puisny* ("ineffectual, weak," OED) *Tilter* ("male copulator," JH) and an unskillful "rider" (sexual partner, F&H). This is perhaps because (a) his *Tilter* (i.e., penis; a *Tilter* is literally "a Sword," ND) is *puisny* ("puny": tiny, weak); and/or (b) his "Puisne" ("Puinne": "Prick-wood, Prick-timber," RC, q.v.) is infected with "The noysome, and stinking worme, or vermine called, a Punie" (RC, s.v. "Punaise"; cf. *Worme-eaten nut*, line 27, above).

43. ***spurs his horse but on one side.*** *Orlando spurs* (i.e, "pricks") *his horse* (i.e., whore; see note: *horses,* I.i.12) *but on one side*, which will cause both *horse* and rider to "swerve" ("Be sexually unfaithful," FR). *Orlando* eagerly *spurs* (i.e., copulates with) the *side* (loins, organs of generation, OED) of *his horse* (i.e., whore), but he has absolutely no intention to "spur" ("publish the banns of marriage in church," OED).

44. ***breakes his staffe... goose.*** *Orlando breakes his staffe* ("tilt[s] or contend[s] with an antagonist," OED) *like a noble goose* (simpleton, idiot) and ineptly *breakes his staffe* ("shaft of a spear or lance," OED; cf. lines 41–43, above). He also *breakes* the vows he made in his *staffe* (verses; see note: *verses*, III.iii.11) and offers only a "broken staff" (literally a "broken crutch" but figuratively a false assurance; cf. "poore deceived man, who stands and trusts / Upon the broken staffe of his false lusts," Francis Quarles, *The Historie of Samson*; in Lodge's *Rosalynde*, Coradin / *Corin* advises Montanus / *Silvius* that love is merely "A broken staffe which follie doth upholde").

Celia may also suggest that *Orlando* puts his *staffe* ("penis," F&H) into the "brakes" (pubic hair, EP) *like a noble goose* ("a Passionate Coxcomb," ND).

44–45. ***all's brave that... folly guides.*** *Orlando* is a *brave* (i.e., a worthless liar; see note: *brave*, line 40, above), but *Rosalind* nevertheless admires him because *all's brave* (worthy, good) *that youth mounts* ("raise[s] in honour" or "exalt[s]," OED) and *folly guides*. There is additional play on "mount" meaning "copulate" (F&H) and on *folly* as lust (see note: *foolerie*, I.iii.16).

47. ***Mistresse and Master.*** See note: *Master Touchstone*, III.ii.15.

48. ***complain'd.*** *Complain'd* means (a) "Claymed; challenged; accused, appeached" (RC, s.v. "Calengé"); and (b) "lamented" (RC, s.v. "Guementé"),

50. ***disdainfull.*** See note: *disdaine*, line 55, below.

That was his Mistresse.

Cel. Well: and what of him?

Cor. If you will see a pageant truely plaid

Betweene the pale complexion of true Love,

And the red glowe of scorne and prowd disdaine, [55]

Goe hence a little, and I shall conduct you

If you will marke it.

Ros. O come, let us remove,

The sight of Lovers feedeth those in love:

Bring us to this sight, and you shall say [60]

Ile prove a busie actor in their play.

Exeunt.

53. ***pageant.*** See note: *Pageants*, II.vii.148.

54. ***pale complexion of true love.*** According to Jacques Ferrand's *Erotomania*,

> The Palenesse of the Colour, is a thing so Proper to those that are deeply in Love, that Diogenes, one day meeting a young Man that looked very pale, guessed him to be either a very Envious person, or else that he was in Love... It is the proper Colour & Badge of Love... which colour is for the most part the signe of a distempered Liver, according to Galen: which being caused by reason of the great abundance of yellow Choler, mixt with the crude Humors, and dispersed all over the body, it infecteth with its colour the skinne.

Also see notes: *Liver*, III.ii.405–406; *complection*, III.ii.194; and *leane cheeke*, III.ii.364.

55. ***red glowe.*** Allusive to a fire that is "glowing red, firie hot, red hot" (JF, s.v. "Rouénte"); "red-hot" is "violent, extreme" (F&H).

55. ***disdaine.*** *Phebe* is guilty of *disdaine* ("Hawtinesse of minde, pride," "arrogancie with proude wordes," TT, s.v. "Fastus") and "disdains" (despises) *Silvius*. Therefore, she causes him to "distaine" ("To discoulour," "to make pale, wanne, lew; to take away the hue of," RC, s.v. "Descoulorer"); cf. *pale complexion*, line 54, above.

59. ***The sight of Lovers... in love.*** In order to "feed" (provide support, comfort) herself, *Rosalind* seeks *The sight* ("spectacle," "a shewe, a pageant, a plaie, a thing to be seene and looked on," JF, s.v. "Spettácolo"; cf. *pageant*, line 53, above, and *play*, line 61, below) *of* other *Lovers*.

61. ***prove.*** Attempt to be.

61. ***busie.*** Either "diligent" or "meddlesome" (OED).

61. ***play.*** Both (a) "A dramatic or theatrical performance" (OED); and (b) "Amorous sport" (EP).

Act III, scene v

Scena Quinta. [1]

Enter Silvius and Phebe. [III.v.1]

Sil. Sweet *Phebe* doe not scorne me, do not *Phebe*

Say that you love me not, but say not so

In bitternesse; the common executioner [5]

Whose heart th' accustom'd sight of death makes hard

Falls not the axe upon the humbled neck,

But first begs pardon: will you sterner be

Then he that dies and lives by bloody drops?

Enter Rosalind, Celia, and Corin. [III.v.2] [10]

Phe. I would not be thy executioner,

I flye thee, for I would not injure thee:

Thou tellst me there is murder in mine eye,

'Tis pretty sure, and very probable,

That eyes that are the frailst, and softest things, [15]

Who shut their coward gates on atomyes,

Notes III.v.

3. ***scorne.*** See note: *scorne*, II.iv.24, and cf. and see note: *sterner*, line 8, below.

3–4. ***do not Phebe Say that you love me not.*** This is a run-on sentence. In strictly correct modern punctuation, there would be a full stop after *do not Phebe.*

5–8. ***the common executioner... begs pardon.*** Although an *executioner* ("a headsman," JF, s.v. "Carnefice") was an instrument of justice, in performing his duties he nevertheless violated the sixth commandment ("Thou shalt not kill," Exodus 20:13). Therefore, before carrying out an execution, the *executioner* would *first* beg *pardon* from the condemned.

7. ***humbled.*** *Humbled* is "prostrated; bent, or brought downe; made, or growne low; decreased, fallen, stooping" (RC, s.v. "Abbaisse"). Cf. *sterner*, line 8, below.

8. ***sterner.*** *Phebe* is so "stern" ("Cruell, fierce, curst, untractable; hard-hearted," RC, s.v. "Feroce") that she "sterns" ("cast[s] down," OED) her would-be lover. She also "sterns" (i.e., emasculates; to "stern" is literally "To cut off the tail of a dog," OED; see note: *tale*, II.vii.32) him, and in doing so she acts like (a) an "ass" (see note: *sterne*, II.vii.117); and/or (b) a "ball-busting whore" ("stern" is "the Tail of a Wolf," ND; a "wolf" is a "whore," FR); cf. and see note: line 40, below.

9. ***dies and lives by bloody drops.*** An executioner *dies* ("cause[s others] to die or come to an end," OED) and *lives* (gets his living or livelihood) by *bloody drops* (the *drops* of blood that fall when he beheads his victim). Also, to "die and live" (a common inversion of the phrase "live and die") means to devote oneself entirely to someone or something (cf. "ye are in our hertes to dye and live with you," *The Byble in Englyshe*, "The Seconde Epystle of S. Paule the Apostle to the Corinthians").

In addition, *Silvius* suffers *bloody drops* (i.e., grief) like an executioner suffers *bloody drops* (i.e., guilt); a "heart dropping blood" or a "bleeding heart" symbolized guilt, grief, or both.

12–13. ***I flye thee... murder in mine eye.*** The eyes were thought to hold real physical power, so *Phebe* avoids *Silvius* because she does not want to unwittingly *injure* or *murder* him with her *eye*. In *Erotomania*, Jacques Ferrand describes the eyes as

> the passages indeed, by which Love enters into our Heads, and so seazeth on the braine, the Cittadell of Pallas: and are the conduicts by which it is conveighed into our hearts, and most secret parts... the ancient Poet Musaeus, who in his excellent Poëm of the Love of Hero and Leander, speakes thus. The excellent beauty, saith he, of a woman, that is without all contradiction perfectly faire, wounds the heart more swiftly, then the swiftest flying arrow, and through the eyes is conveighed into the most inward parts, and there festers into a cruell wound, and hard to be cured.

Therefore, "The eyes of the Ladie have... suche force upon the harte of the Lover, as the beames of the Sunne have uppon thinges on earthe," but only "yf the lookes be amorouse, otherwise it is cleane contrarie" (OL).

14. ***pretty.*** *Pretty* can mean (a) cunning; (b) insignificant; and/or (c) asinine (see note: *prety*, III.ii.269).

14. ***probable.*** Plausible.

15. ***frailst.*** "Frail" means (a) easily destroyed; (b) weak; (c) "Tender" (OED); and/or (d) "easily tempted to succumb to carnal delights" (JH; also see note: *sight*, V.ii.34).

15. ***softest.*** Weakest.

15–16. ***eyes... gates on atomyes.*** *Eyes shut their coward* (with play on "cowered": lowered) *gates* (i.e., eyelids) *on atomyes* (motes, small particles; see note: *Atomies*, III.ii.230).

Should be called tyrants, butchers, murtherers.

Now I doe frowne on thee with all my heart,

And if mine eyes can wound, now let them kill thee:

Now counterfeit to swound, why now fall downe, [20]

Or if thou canst not, oh for shame, for shame,

Lye not, to say mine eyes are murtherers:

Now shew the wound mine eye hath made in thee,

Scratch thee but with a pin, and there remaines

Some scarre of it: Leane upon a rush [25]

The Cicatrice and capable impressure

Thy palme some moment keepes: but now mine eyes

Which I have darted at thee, hurt thee not,

Nor I am sure there is no force in eyes

That can doe hurt. [30]

Sil. O deere *Phebe,*

If ever (as that ever may be neere)

You meet in some fresh cheeke the power of fancie,

Then shall you know the wounds invisible

That Loves keene arrows make. [35]

Phe. But till that time

Come not thou neere me: and when that time comes,

25. ***Leane upon a rush.*** With possible play on *Leane* as copulation (to *Leane* is literally to "lie down, rest," OED; also see note: *leane*, II.vii.169) and *rush* as the female genitalia (see note: *rushes*, III.ii.362).

26–27. ***The Cicatrice... some moment keepes.*** The *palme* of the hand is *capable* ("able to receive or containe," JF, s.v. "Capace") *The Cicatrice* ("a skarre, a marke or signe of a sore or hurt," JF, q.v.) for *some moment* (space of time).

28. ***darted.*** *Darted* means "flung, hurled, cast, throwne, as a dart; also, hit, hurt, strucken, wounded with a dart" (RC, s.v. "Dardé"). A "dart" is "an arrow"; cf. lines 34–35, below, and see note: *murder in mine eye*, line 13, above.

29–30. ***there is no force in eyes... hurt.*** *Phebe's* statement is contrary to prevailing opinion. See notes: lines 12–13, above, and *sight*, V.ii.34.

32. ***as that ever may be neere.*** *That ever* (occasion) is, in fact, very *neere* (shortly forthcoming, close by) in the person of *Ganimed / Rosalind.* Even though *Ganimed* acts like an *ever* ("wild boar," OED) to *Phebe* (the "wild boar" is "An emblem of warlike fury and merciless brutality," DPF), "he" whets *Phebe's* sexual appetite like a "boar" (a "Type of bestial lust," EC). Thus, *Ganimed* stimulates *Phebe's* "neer" ("loin" and also "kidney," OED; the kidneys were regarded as the seat of sexual desire, JA, p. 92).

33. ***fresh.*** *Fresh* is (a) "New," "straunge, not seene afore" (TT, s.v. "Nŏvus"); (b) "lustie, in prime, lively, youthfull, strong" (RC, s.v. "Verde"); and/or (c) sexually attractive or virile (see note: *freshly*, III.ii.228).

33. ***cheeke.*** *Phebe* falls in love with *Ganimed's cheeke* (face) and *cheeke* ("Insolence; jaw," F&H) without knowing that "he" is really a "cheke" (variant of "chick," OED).

33. ***fancie.*** *Fancie* means "affection," but also see note: *Fancie* III.ii.355.

34–35. ***the wounds invisible... keene arrows make.*** *Love* (i.e., Cupid) has shot *Silvius* with one of his *keene* (sharp-pointed; also "cruel; harsh," OED) *arrows*, so *Silvius'* "arrow" ("penis," OED) is *keene* (i.e., erect; literally "Sexually ardent or excited," EP). Also see note: lines 12–13, above.

Afflict me with thy mockes, pitty me not,

As till that time I shall not pitty thee.

Ros. And why I pray you? who might be your mother [40]

That you insult, exult, and all at once

Over the wretched? what though you hav no beauty

As by my faith, I see no more in you

Then without Candle may goe darke to bed:

Must you be therefore prowd and pittilesse? [45]

Why what meanes this? why do you looke on me?

I see no more in you then in the ordinary

Of Natures sale-worke? 'ods my little life,

I thinke she meanes to tangle my eies too:

No faith proud Mistresse, hope not after it, [50]

'Tis not your inkie browes, your blacke silke haire,

---

40. ***who might be your mother.*** It "grew to a common adage concerning cruell men, that they had sucked a Hircanian Tiger" (Peter Heylyn, *Mikrokosmos*); it was also said of merciless people that "like the Wolfe they sucke cruelty from their mothers breasts" (William Hampton, *A proclamation of Warre from the Lord of Hosts*). Thus, *Rosalind* hints that *Phebe's mother* was either (a) a "tiger" (used of "agressive female[s]" and "masculine women," FR); or (b) a "wolf" (a "figure of devouring, destructive sexuality," GW; also see note: *sterner*, line 8, above). *Phebe* absorbed her *mother's* cruel and heartless nature while suckling, for "the manners of the nurse are participated unto

the infant together with the milke. For the welpes of dogges, if they doe sucke Wolves or Lionesses, will become more fierce and cruell than other-wise they would" (Ambroise Paré, *The Workes of that famous Chirurgion Ambrose Parey*).

41. ***insult, exult, and all at once.*** *Phebe* does not hesitate to *insult* ("leap on the prostrate body of a foe," DPF) and *exult* ("jump for joy," DPF) *all at once* ("At one stroke"; also "At one and the same time," OED).

44. ***without Candle... darke to bed.*** If *Rosalind* went *to bed* in the *darke without* a *Candle*, she would see nothing at all (which is exactly what she sees in *Phebe*). Because *Phebe* is not "fair" (of light complexion) but *darke* (dark-haired and dark-eyed; cf. lines 51–52 and 137, below), by the standards of the day she would not be considered "fair" (beautiful). No man who had to look at *Phebe* would want to put his *Candle* (penis, F&H, s.v. "prick") into her *darke* ("female pudendum; Cunt," F&H, s.v. "monosyllable"). Indeed, no man would ever *goe to bed* with *Phebe* unless "By candle-light; in extremitie, or at the point of death, when a man is readie to give up the ghost... for then the Romanists light candles, upon a conceit that evill spirits are driven away thereby" (RC, s.v. "À la chandelle").

47–48. ***the ordinary Of Natures sale-worke.*** As a piece *Of sale-worke* (ready-made goods of inferior quality, OED), *Phebe* is an extremely *ordinary* (common, unremarkable) *ordinary* (commonplace object, OED). Therefore, she should be grateful for the opportunity to be an *ordinary* ("A wife," F&H) instead of a piece of *sale-worke* (i.e., a prostitute; *sale-worke* is literally something "sold or intended for sale," OED; cf. line 65, below). Even if *Phebe* were a "ship" ("a whore," FR) who tried to "sell" her *worke* (sexual intercourse, F&H, s.v. "ride"), she is such an *ordinary* piece of *sale-worke* (i.e., "sail-work") that she would undoubtedly be an *ordinary* ("a ship out of commission, not in service," OED, which dates from 1754). *Rosalind* additionally suggests that *Phebe* is as common as the "nature" (i.e., "shit"; see note: *Nature*, I.ii.43) found in an "ordinarie" ("privie, close stoole, or jakes," JF, s.v. "Oridnario").

48. ***'ods.*** A corruption of "God save."

49. ***tangle my eies.*** This line is a verbal stage direction for *Phebe* to "make eyes" at *Rosalind*; cf. line 74, below. Also see note: *eye*, line 13, above, and *sight*, V.ii.34.

As an *eies* (i.e., an "eyas," or young hawk), *Ganimed* must take care not to be "entangled" (ensnared, OED) in *Phebe's* "tangle" (a trap for catching birds; "The Anglo-Saxon tan means a twig, and twigs smeared with birdlime were used for catching small birds, who were 'entangled' or twigged," DPF, s.v. "Entangle"; "This birdcatcher's device provides a common metaphor for whoring or bawding," GW, s.v. "limed twig"). The implication is that *Phebe* is a "twigger" (whore, F&H, s.v. "Harlot") who can *tangle* (ensnare, entrap) a man's *eies* ("Eyeballs or testes," "penis," FR) in her *tangle* (i.e., pubic hair).

50. ***proud.*** Both (a) haughty; and (b) amorous or lustfull (see note: *pride*, II.vii.75).

50. ***Mistresse.*** In addressing *Phebe* as *Mistresse*, *Rosalind* is either (a) ironically respectful (cf. and see notes: *Master*, III.ii.15, and *good mans*, line 63, below); or (b) openly disrespectful (see note: *Mistris*, I.iii.41).

51. ***inkie browes.*** A possible suggestion that *Phebe's browes* (pubic hair and genital area, FR) are *inkie* (where "ink" is semen, HH, p. 136).

51. ***blacke silke haire.*** *Silke* was used "of whores" (FR), and *blacke* alludes to the female genitalia (see note: *blacke*, III.ii.94). *Haire* plays on "hare" meaning "prostitute, light wench" (EP; also see note: *Hare*, IV.iii.21).

Your bugle eye-balls, nor your cheeke of creame

That can entame my spirits to your worship:

You foolish Shepheard, wherefore do you follow her

Like foggy South, puffing with winde and raine, [55]

You are a thousand times a properer man

Then she a woman. 'Tis such fooles as you

That makes the world full of ill-favourd children:

'Tis not her glasse, but you that flatters her,

And out of you she sees her selfe more proper [60]

Then any of her lineaments can show her:

But Mistris, know your selfe, downe on your knees

---

52. ***bugle eye-balls.*** *Phebe* has *eye-balls* as black as a *bugle* ("A tube-shaped glass bead, usually black," OED). Additionally, her *bugle* (i.e., vagina; literally "A tube," OED) traps a man's *eye-balls* (testicles; see note: *eies*, line 49, above).

52. ***cheeke of creame.*** If the shepherdess *Phebe* has a *cheeke of creame* (i.e., a pale complexion), then she most definitely puts on airs (and/or make-up; see note: *umber*, I.iii.119). There is possible indecent play on *cheeke*[s] as "Buttocks" (FR) and *creame* as "The seminal fluid" (F&H).

53. ***entame my spirits.*** Both (a) *entame* (subdue, subjugate) the *spirits* (heart and mind); and (b) *entame* ("Castrate, make impotent; effeminate," FR, s.v. "tame"; to "entame" is literally "To make a cut into," OED; to "tame" is "to temper, soften," OED) the *spirits* (genitals and semen; see note: *spirit*, I.i.23). Cf. *scorne*, line 3, above.

53. ***worship.*** With possible play on "warship"; cf. and see note: *ordinary*, line 47, above.

55. ***foggy South... winde and raine.*** *Phebe* is *puffing* ("swelling with anger; or, in a great chafe, in a monstrous fume," RC, s.v. "Bouffard"), but *Silvius* moons for her like "a puffing fellow" ("a gull, a foole," JF, s.v. "Soppiatone"). *Silvius'* judgment is

decidedly *foggy* (dull, bemuddled, confused) if he "follows" (devotes himself to) *Phebe* and weeps for her like "the south wind bringing much raine" (TT, s.v. "Pincerna pluviarum"). Perhaps he has been "infected" by the *South winde*, the "feeder of foule carnall Vice" and the "Nurse of blacke thoughts, south-Fogg, which rots the minde" (Nathaniel Richards, "The Flesh").

Silvius' "rane" ("prolonged or repeated cry or utterance," OED), *winde* (empty talk), and "puff" ("false praise," F&H) is *foggy* (literally "Of food: Apt to puff up the body," OED). *Phebe* "puffs up" (fills with conceit, F&H) because *Silvius* serves as her "puffer" ("A person who praises or extols the merits of someone or something, esp. in an exaggerated manner," OED; also "A person employed to bid at an auction in order to raise the price or to encourage others to bid," OED; cf. line 65, below).

Silvius is wholly under the *raine* (i.e., "rein" or "reign": control or governance) of his *raine* ("rein," the kidneys and loins regarded as the seat of sexual desire). Thus, he is *puffing* (i.e., has an erection; to "puff" is literally "to swell, bulge," OED) and desires to *winde* (copulate, *JH*). Moreover, in likening *Silvius* to the *foggy South*, *Rosalind* suggests that he is an "ass" or "asshole" (*South* is the "buttocks" or "rump," EP; *foggy* is "Boggy," OED, and "bog" means "anus," GW).

56. ***properer man.*** *Properer* means (a) more attractive; (b) worthier; and/or (c) more respectable. Being a "proper man" is no guarantee of *Silvius'* success in love, however, because proverbially "Faire men come often to foule ends; the properer the men the worse their lucke" (RC, s.v. "Les beaux hommes au gibbet"). There is possible additional play on "prop" as the penis (see note: *proper*, I.ii.116, and cf. *puffing*, line 55, above).

59. ***'Tis not her glasse... that flatters her.*** In *Anatomy of Melancholy*, Robert Burton remarks that

> Love is like a false glasse which represents every thing fairer then it is. Love is blind as the saying is, Cupids blind, and so are all his followers... Every lover admires his mistris, though she be very deformed of her selfe, ill favoured, crooked, bald, goggle-eyed, or squint-eyed, sparrow mouthed, hookenosed or have a sharpe foxe nose, gubber-tussed, rotten teeth, beetle-browed, her breath stinke all over the roome, her nose drop winter & summer with a Bavarian poke under her chin, lave eared, her dugges like two double ingges, bloodi-falne-fingers, scabbed wrists, a tanned skinne, a rotten carkasse, crooked backe, lame, splea-footed, as slender in the middle as a cowe in the waste, goutie legges, her feete stinke, she breeds lice, a very monster, an aufe imperfect, her whole complection savours, and to thy judgement lookes like a marde in a lanthorne, whom thou couldest not fancy for a world, but hatest, lothest, & wouldest have spit in her face, or blow thy nose in her bosome... to another man a doudy, a slut, a nasty, filthy beastly queane, dishonest peradventure, obscene, base, beggerly, foolish, untaught, if he love her once, he admires her for all this, he takes no notice of any such errors or imperfections, of body or mind, he had rather have her then any woman in the world.

Rosalind also hints that *Phebe* is a "piece of shit" who would have no trouble finding a likeness of herself in a *glasse* ("looking-glass": "A chamber pot, jordan, or member mug," FG). Cf. and see note: *ordinary* and *Natures*, lines 47–48, above.

61. ***lineaments.*** "Lineament" is the "feature, of the face, or of any other part" (RC, q.v.).

62. ***Mistris.*** See note: *Mistresse*, line 50, above.

And thanke heaven, fasting, for a good mans love;
For I must tell you friendly in your eare,
Sell when you can, you are not for all markets: [65]
Cry the man mercy, love him, take his offer,
Foule is most foule, being foule to be a scoffer.
So take her to thee Shepheard, fareyouwell.

Phe. Sweet youth, I pray you chide a yere together,
I had rather here you chide, then this man wooe. [70]

Ros. Hees falne in love with your foulnesse, & shee'll
Fall in love with my anger. If it be so, as fast
As she answeres thee with frowning lookes, ile sauce
Her with bitter words: why looke you so upon me?

Phe. For no ill will I beare you. [75]

Ros. I pray you do not fall in love with mee,
For I am falser then vowes made in wine:
Besides, I like you not: if you will know my house,
'Tis at the tufft of Olives, here hard by:
Will you goe Sister? Shepheard ply her hard: [80]
Come Sister: Shepheardesse, looke on him better
And be not proud, though all the world could see,
None could be so abus'd in sight as hee.

63. ***thanke heaven... for a good mans love.*** The religious would both *thanke heaven* and expiate their sins through *fasting* (abstinence from food). *Phebe* should *thanke heaven* for the possibility of *fasting* (i.e., marriage; to "fast" is "To make fast in wedlock; to betroth, wed," OED) with a "good man," even though she thinks him beneath her because he is only a "goodman" ("a yeoman," OED; "Goodman" was the usual title used for men below the rank of gentry, and "Goodwife" was correspondingly used for women; cf. *Mistris*, line 62, above, and see note: *Master*, III.ii.15).

65. ***Sell when you can... markets.*** *Phebe's* "market" ("vulva," GW2, s.v. "marketplace") would not be very desirable for "market" ("copulation," JH) even if available on the "market" (i.e., if she were a prostitute). *Phebe* would therefore do best to *Sell when* she *can*. Cf. *sale-worke*, line 48, above.

66. ***Cry the man mercy.*** Beg his forgiveness.

67. ***Foule is most foule... scoffer.*** *Phebe* is *foule* ("Ouglie, deformed," "loathsome to looke on," RC, s.v. "Soudre"), so she *is most foule* ("Dishonest, vile, reprocheable, sluttish, naughtie, lewd," TT, s.v. "Impūrus") *to be a scoffer* ("a railer, reprocher, or mocker," TT, s.v. "Dīcax"). There is further implication that *Phebe* is (a) a "fowl" (wench, whore, JH; also "a grosse woman," WT, s.v. "Feminaccia"); and/or (b) "shitty" (to *foule* is "to drop ordure," OED).

68. ***take her to thee.*** To *take to* is (a) to apply oneself diligently; (b) to attack; and/or (c) to take charge of or "undertake" (see note: *take upon*, III.ii.405).

68. ***fareyouwell.*** I.e., "good luck."

73–74. ***sauce... bitter.*** *Rosalind* will give *Phebe* the *bitter* (sour) *sauce* (seasoning) of *bitter* ("spitefull, malitious," RC, s.v. "Amarulente") *sauce* (impudence, abuse).

77. ***falser then vowes made in wine.*** *Vowes* of love *made in wine* (i.e., while intoxicated) are untrustworthy, for "Wine is hote and full of vapours, and therfore provoketh lust, his heat dissolveth seede, and with his ventositie causeth the courage to ryse" (OL).

78. ***like.*** See note: *liking*, I.iii.28.

78–79. ***if you will know my house... Olives.*** A *tufft* ("grove of trees," RC, s.v. "Embellissment") *of Olives* could possibly grow in Arden, for "Both the tame and the wilde Olive trees grow in very many places of Italy, France, and Spaine" (John Gerard, *The Herball or Generall Historie of Plantes*). *Olives* are symbolic of both peace and chastity (DPF), so *Ganimed* may signal to *Silvius* that he has no desire to pursue *Phebe's tufft* (pubic hair and vagina, GW2).

79–80. ***hard by... hard.*** *Hard by* means "close by," but *hard* is also used "Of the erected penis" (JH). Thus, *Silvius* should *ply* ("woo," EP; also "attack or assail," OED) *Phebe hard* (with obvious pun) in order to *ply her* (i.e., have sex with her; to "apply" is "To connect one thing with another physically," OED).

81. ***looke on him better.*** I.e., "Think better of him," but *Rosalind* also instructs *Phebe* to give *Silvius* more encouraging (and therefore less harmful) looks. Cf. and see note: *murder in mine eye*, line 13, above.

83. ***abus'd in sight.*** Love was believed to be engendered by *sight* (see note: *sight*, V.ii.34), so *Silvius' sight* (eyesight) causes him "site" ("Care or sorrow; grief," OED). Love (i.e., Cupid) was "most commonly painted with his eyes bound up" because "he blindeth poore Lovers and maketh them so like unto beastes, that they cannot at all deserne the imperfections of their Ladies" (OL). In causing *Silvius* to fall in love with *Phebe*, Cupid has both (a) *abus'd* (misguided, deceived) his *sight* (vision); and (b) *abus'd* (i.e., "screwed" or "buggered"; "abuse" is used of illicit or unlawful sexual acts, FR) his *sight* ("site" or anus, FR; a "site" is literally a "seat," OED). Cf. IV.i.207–208.

Come, to our flocke,

Exit {*Rosalind, Celia, and Corin*}. [III.v.3] [85]

Phe. Dead Shepheard, now I find thy saw of might,

Who ever lov'd, that lov'd not at first sight?

Sil. Sweet *Phebe.*

Phe. Hah: what saist thou *Silvius*?

Sil. Sweet *Phebe* pitty me. [90]

Phe. Why I am sorry for thee gentle *Silvius.*

Sil. Where ever sorrow is, reliefe would be:

If you doe sorrow at my griefe in love,

By giving love your sorrow, and my griefe

Were both extermin'd. [95]

Phe. Thou hast my love, is not that neighbourly?

Sil. I would have you.

Phe. Why that were covetousnesse:

Silvius; the time was, that I hated thee;

And yet it is not, that I beare thee love, [100]

But since that thou canst talke of love so well,

Thy company, which erst was irkesome to me

I will endure; and Ile employ thee too:

But doe not looke for further recompence

Then thine owne gladnesse, that thou art employd. [105]

86–87. ***Dead Shepheard... at first sight.*** The *Dead Shepheard* (i.e., author of pastoral poetry) is probably Christopher Marlowe, who died in 1593. Marlowe's "Hero and Leander" contains the line "Who ever lov'd that lov'd not at first sight," and *Phebe* now finds his *saw* (saying, maxim) *of might* (strength, force). Cf. and see note: *great reckoning in a little roome,* III.iii.13–14.

92. ***reliefe.*** *Silvius* seeks *Phebe's reliefe* (aid, assistance) to gain *reliefe* ("release for pent-up desires," EC; "easing of sexual desire in coitus," GW2). Cf. *cure,* III.ii.391, and *remedie,* V.ii.40.

94. ***love.*** I.e., sexual intercourse.

95. ***extermin'd.*** I.e., "Exterminated": "driven forth, cast out, chaced away; &, ruined, undone, destroyed" (RC, q.v.).

96–98. ***Thou hast my love... covetousnesse.*** *Phebe* abides by Christ's injunction to "love thy neighbour as thy selfe" (Mark 12:31), but for *Silvius* to expect anything greater than *neighbourly* (friendly) *love* would be *covetousnesse* ("greedines, avarice," JF, s.v. "Cupidità"; also "lust, desire, dishonest love," TT, s.v. "Cŭpĭdĭtās"). Such *covetousnesse* would place him in violation of the Tenth Commandment: "Thou shalt not covet thy neighbours house, thou shalt not covet thy neighbours wife, nor his man servant, nor his maid servant, nor his oxe, nor his asse, nor any thing that is thy neighbours" (Exodus 20:17). Cf. III.ii.74–75.

97. ***have.*** I.e., sexually.

102. ***erst.*** "Not long ago, a little while since" (OED).

103–105. ***employ... employd.*** *Phebe* will *employ* (use the services of) *Silvius,* but he should expect neither *recompence* ("Love-making," FR) nor "employment" ("copulation," JH).

Sil. So holy, and so perfect is my love,
And I in such a poverty of grace,
That I shall thinke it a most plenteous crop
To gleane the broken eares after the man
That the maine harvest reapes: loose now and then [110]
A scattred smile, and that Ile live upon.

Phe. Knowst thou the youth that spoke to mee yere-while?

Sil. Not very well, but I have met him oft,
And he hath bought the Cottage and the bounds
That the old *Carlot* once was Master of. [115]

Phe. Thinke not I love him, though I ask for him,
'Tis but a peevish boy, yet he talkes well,
But what care I for words? yet words do well
When he that speakes them pleases those that heare:
It is a pretty youth, not very prettie, [120]
But sure hee's proud, and yet his pride becomes him;
Hee'll make a proper man: the best thing in him
Is his complexion: and faster then his tongue
Did make offence, his eye did heale it up:
He is not very tall, yet for his yeeres hee's tall: [125]
His leg is but so so, and yet 'tis well:

106–107. ***holy... poverty of grace.*** *Silvius* is in *poverty* (want, lack) *of holy* (sacred, divine) *grace* (favor, goodwill). *Silvius* also lacks *Phebe's holy* (with play on "hole": vagina) *grace* ("vulva," FR; "sexual favor," GW2). This makes him feel "poor" (i.e., buggered; see notes: *poore*, II.i.25, and *povertie*, I.iii.69) and deprived of *grace* (i.e., his manhood; see note: *disgrace*, I.i.145).

108–110. ***plenteous crop... maine harvest reapes.*** As one in *poverty* (line 107, above), *Silvius* would be happy to *gleane* ("picke up eares of corne after reapers," RC, s.v. "Glaner") *the broken eares* ("the hose or cod of corne," TT, q.v.) *after the maine harvest.* Cf. Leviticus 23:22: "And when ye reape the harvest of your land, thou shalt not make cleane riddance of the corners of the field, when thou reapest, neither shalt thou gather any gleaning of thy harvest: thou shalt leave them unto the poore, and to the stranger"; also cf. Deuteronomy 24:19: "When thou cuttest downe thine harvest in thy field, and hast forgot a sheafe in the field, thou shalt not go againe to fetch it: it shalbe for the stranger, for the fatherlesse, and for the widdow."

Even if another *man reapes* (sexually claims; see note: *reap*, III.ii.108) *Phebe's maine crop* (sexual harvest of virginity, GW2) during the *harvest* (sexual intercourse, JA, p. 154), *Silvius* will be content with her *broken* (devirginated, EP, s.v. "Break") *eares* (i.e., genitals; "vagina" is L. for "sheath, case; the husk of grain," LD; cf. and see note: *sheafe*, III.ii.108). There is possible additional play on *maine* as the vagina (a "main" is literally "A principal channel, duct, or conductor for conveying water," OED; the "main avenue" is the "Cunt," F&H, s.v. "monosyllable"), and on *plenteous* as copulation (FR, who holds it a pun on "copia" and "copulate"; also see note: *plentifully*, I.i.18).

110. ***loose.*** "To shoot, let fly" (OED), with possible play on *loose* meaning "in animal husbandry... [to] release the female to the male" (GW2).

111. ***scattred smile... live upon.*** Even though *Phebe* treats *Silvius* like "scat" (i.e., "shit"; cf. Gk. "skat": "dung"), her *scattred* ("discarded; throwne abroad," RC, s.v. "Escarté"; also "carelesse," RC, s.v. "Desbandé") *smile* would serve as "scat" (i.e., fertilizer) for *Silvius* to *live upon.* To him, it would be "scat" ("Treasure," OED).

112. ***yere-while.*** I.e., "erewhile," or a little while earlier. The "y" spelling of "yere" might indicate that *Phebe* speaks in a rustic dialect; cf. *your*, II.iv.74.

115. ***Carlot.*** The italics indicate that *Carlot* is a proper name. *Carlot* is derived from Fr. "carle" meaning (a) a "churle, chuffe, clusterfist, hind, boore" (RC, s.v. "Franc-topin"); and/or (b) "a miser, micher, pinch-pennie, pennyfather" (RC, s.v. "Vilain"). Cf. II.iv.86–88.

117. ***peevish.*** *Peevish* is (a) "wayward, curst, perverse, skittish, snappish, saucie, malapert, prowd, foolish, knavish, fierce, arrogant, impudent" (RC, s.v. "Protérvo"); and/or (b) silly (OED).

120. ***pretty.*** See note: *prety*, III.ii.269.

121. ***proud.*** See note: *pride*, II.vii.75.

122. ***proper.*** See note: *proper*, I.ii.116.

122–123. ***the best thing... complexion.*** *The best thing* about *Ganimed*, besides his *thing* ("penis," F&H), is his *complexion* (i.e., everything altogether; see note: *complection*, III.ii.194).

There was a pretty rednesse in his lip,

A little riper, and more lustie red

Then that mixt in his cheeke: 'twas just the difference

Betwixt the constant red, and mingled Damaske. [130]

There be some women *Silvius*, had they markt him

In parcells as I did, would have gone neere

To fall in love with him: but for my part

I love him not, nor hate him not: and yet

Have more cause to hate him then to love him, [135]

For what had he to doe to chide at me?

He said mine eyes were black, and my haire blacke,

And now I am remembred, scorn'd at me:

I marvell why I answer'd not againe,

But that's all one: omittance is no quittance: [140]

Ile write to him a very tanting Letter,

And thou shalt beare it, wilt thou *Silvius*?

Sil. *Phebe*, with all my heart.

Phe. Ile write it strait:

The matter's in my head, and in my heart, [145]

I will be bitter with him, and passing short;

Goe with me *Silvius*.

Exeunt.

128. ***lustie.*** See note: *fresh*, line 33, above.

130. ***constant.*** Uniform.

130. ***mingled Damaske.*** *Ganimed's* lip resembles (a) *mingled* ("Diversified, varied," RC, s.v. "Bigarré") *Damaske* ("damask rose," a variety of rose with pink or light red flowers); or (b) *mingled* ("Of textile fabrics: woven in mixed colours," OED) *Damaske* (varigated silk from Damascus).

Also, *Phebe* wishes to surrender her *Damaske* (i.e., her "rose" or "maidenhead," EP) and "mingle" (have sexual intercourse, JA, p. 180) with *Ganimed.*

131–132. ***markt him In parcells.*** *Phebe* both (a) *markt* (noticed or considered) *Ganimed's* person "By parts and parcells, by peeces, by members, peece meale, particularly" (TT, s.v. "Partĭcŭlātim"); and (b) *markt him* (singled him out as a "mark" or sexual target, EP) because "many small parcells joyned together make up a great bodie, or bulke" (RC, s.v. "Les petis ruisseaux font les grandes rivié res"). Cf. *complexion*, line 123, above.

132. ***gone neere.*** To "go near" is "to be on the point of" (OED). Also see note: *neere*, line 32, above.

136. ***what had he to doe.*** I.e., "What business was it of his?"

139. ***answer'd.*** An "answer" is a return thrust in fencing. Cf. *tanting*, line 141, below.

140. ***all one.*** All the same.

140. ***omittance is no quittance.*** A variation of the proverb "suffrance is no quittance" (John Heywood, "Of mine acquayntance with a certaine yong man") or "forbearance is no quittance" (Henry Porter, *The Two Angry Women of Abington*). Just because *Phebe* has "omitted" ("not spoken of," JB, s.v. "Paralipomenon") *Ganimed's omittance* ("omission," OED; an "omission" is "A fault; a sinne, vice, delict, offence, trespasse, transgression; also, an error, slip, misse, fayle, default," RC, s.v. "Faulte"), she has not necessarily issued a *quittance* ("An Acquitance, Release, discharge," RC, s.v. "Quitance") for *Ganimed's ommittance* (i.e., "omission" or "defaults of payment," RC, s.v. "Reblandir le Seigneur"). She is therefore entitled to "payback" (i.e., revenge, retaliation).

141. ***tanting.*** *Phebe* is *tanting* ("Haughty; 'high and mighty'; '"stuck-up,'" OED, s.v. "taunt"), so she will "tant" ("answer back in equivalent terms," OED) *Ganimed* with a *letter* that is *tanting* ("biting, nipping, pinching, snipping, detracting, backbiting," "satiricall, stinging, sharp, be it with teeth or words," RC, s.v. "Mordace"). Thus, she will give "Tint for tant" ("hit for hit," ND, q.v.). *Phebe* also hopes that *Ganimed* will find her letter *tanting* (i.e., sexually stimulating; to "tant" is literally "To hoist, raise, elevate," OED).

145. ***matter's.*** *Matter* can mean (a) a topic; and (b) a "subject of contention" (OED).

146. ***passing short.*** Extremely irascible.

Act IV, scene i

Actus Quartus. Scena Prima. [1]

Enter Rosalind, and Celia, and Jaques. [IV.i.1]

Jaq. I prethee, pretty youth, let me better acquainted

with thee.

Ros They say you are a melancholly fellow. [5]

Jaq. I am so: I doe love it better then laughing.

Ros. Those that are in extremity of either, are abho-

minable fellowes, and betray themselves to every mo-

derne censure, worse then drunkards.

Jaq. Why, 'tis good to be sad and say nothing. [10]

Ros. Why then 'tis good to be a poste.

Jaq. I have neither the Schollers melancholy, which

is emulation: nor the Musitians, which is fantasticall;

Notes IV.i.

5–8. ***melancholy fellow... abhominable.*** Those in *the extremity* (utmost excess) *of laughing* reveal themselves as witless simpletons (cf. and see note: II.vii.55–56).

Someone in *the extremity of melancholy* is equally *abhominable* ("worthie to be forsaken and refused," TT, s.v. "Aversandus"), because "folly [and] Melancholy madnesse are but one disease; Delirium is a common name to all" (RB).

Moreover, both types of *fellowes are in the extremity* (i.e., "ass"; see note: *extremest*, II.i.46) and thus *abhominable* (gulity of "abhomynable synne" or sodomy, TR, q.v.; *abhominable* alludes to the anus, JA, p. 116). Cf. and see notes: lines 8–11, below.

8–9. ***betray themselves... worse then drunkards.*** The fool and the drunkard *betray themselves to every moderne* (commonplace, everyday) *censure* ("Blame, rebuke, a checke," "a reproofe, chiding, reprehension," RC, s.v. "Blasme") because they share a tendency for unreserved honesty. Both are thus exposed as "asses," for "Wine ever goes bare breeched; the drunkard discovers all thats within, or about, him; any man may see his hart, and (if he have a mind) his arse" (RC, s.v. "Le vin n'a point de chaussure"). Similarly, the melancholic with "a broken or crackt heart can hold no good thing in; applyable also to a heart that pierced with griefe, cannot hold but must utter it" (RC, s.v. "Un sac percé ne peut tenir le grain").

10–11. ***'tis good to be sad... a poste.*** *Jaques* says it is *good to be sad* (sorrowful, regretful) *and say nothing*, because Christian doctrine teaches that "in all our miseries and adversities, we must be silent in our hearts, by quieting our wills in the good will of God" (William Perkins, *A Commentarie or Exposition, upon the Five First Chapters of the Epistle to the Galatians*). In response, *Rosalind* quips that (a) it is *good* for a *poste* (support beam) to be *sad* ("Strong, firm," OED); and (b) it is *good* for a *poste* ("block": "blockhead," OED) to be *sad* ("Solid; dense," OED). She also hints that *Jaques* is a *poste* (i.e., "an ass"; L. *poste* is "behind, in the rear," LD).

12–13. ***the Schollers melancholy... emulation.*** Robert Burton's *Anatomy of Melancholy* gives "Aemulation" ("desire to exceede another," RC2, q.v.) as a specific cause of *melancholy.* Burton devotes an entire section to "Love of Learning, or overmuch study. With a Digression of the misery of Schollers," and explains that *Schollers melancholy* is caused by "contemplation, which dries the braine, and extinguisheth naturall heat; for whilst the spirits are intent to meditation about in the head, the stomacke and litter are left destitute, and thence comes black blood, & crudities, for want of concoction, & for want of exercise, the superfluous vapors cannot exhale." Cf. and see note: II.vii.42–44.

13. ***the Musitians... fantasticall.*** Music was thought to help cure melancholy (see note: *melanchollly*, II.v.12), but *Musitians* themselves were especially prone to the disease (melancholy was so much associated with *Musitians* that Thomas Nabbes' allegorical *Masque of Microcosmus* personifes "Melancholy" as "A Musician. His complexion haire and clothes black: a Lute in his hand. He is likewise an amorist").

Musitians were vulnerable because they were *fantasticall*, which means (a) "fantastic": "Having a lively imagination; imaginative" (OED); and/or (b) subject to "fantasy" or amorous inclination (see note: *fantasie*, II.iv.33). RB asserts that

> great is the force of Imagination, and much more ought the cause of melancholy to be ascribed to this alone, then to the distemperature of the body... And although this Phantasie of ours be a subordinate faculty to reason, and should be ruled by it, yet in many men, through inward or outward distemperatures, defect of organs, which are unapt or hindred, or otherwise contaminated, it is likewise unapt, hindred and hurt.

(In modern terms, the *Musitians* melancholy perhaps translates as an "artistic temperament.")

nor the Courtiers, which is proud: nor the Souldiers,
which is ambitious: nor the Lawiers, which is politick: [15]
nor the Ladies, which is nice: nor the Lovers, which
is all these: but it is a melancholy of mine owne, compounded of many simples, extracted from many objects,
and indeed the sundrie contemplation of my travells, in
which by often rumination, wraps me in a most humo- [20]
rous sadnesse.

14–15. ***the Courtiers... the Souldiers, which is ambitious.*** RB groups the *Courtiers* "pride" together with the *Souldiers* "ambition" under the heading "Concupiscible appetite" and attributes the *Souldiers* melancholy to

> Ambition, a proud covetousnesse, or dry thirst of Honor, a great torture of the mind, composed of envy, pride, and covetousnes, a gallant madnes... if he cannot satisfie his desire, as Bodine observed, he runs mad. So that both wayes, hit or misse, he is distracted so long as his Ambition lasts, he can looke for no other but anxiety and care, discontent and griefe in the meane time, and madnesse it selfe, or violent death in the end.

Similarly, RB explains that *Courtiers*

> clime and clime still, with much labour, but never make an end, never at the top. A Knight would be a Baronet, and then a Lord, and then an Earle... for a courteour's life, as Budaeus describes it, is a gallimaufry of ambition, lust, fraud, imposture, dissimulation, detraction, envy, pride, the Court a common conventicle of flatterers, time-servers, polititians &c. If you will see such discontented persons, there you shall likely find them.

15. ***the Lawiers, which is politick.*** *Jaques'* melancholy does not derive from his nation's *Lawiers* (lawgivers or lawmakers, OED). In *Anatomy of Melancholy*, Robert Burton opines that *Lawiers* are "generally noxious to a body politicke" and the cause of

> ill government, which proceeds from unskilfull, slothfull, griping, covetous or tyrannising magistrates, when they are fooles, idiots, children, proud partiall, undiscreet, oppressors, tyrants, not able or unfit to manage such offices, many noble Citties and florishing Kingdomes by that meanes are desolate, the whole body grones under such heads, and all the members must needs be misaffected.... where there be many diseases, many discords, many lawes, many law suits, many lawyers, and many Physitians, it is a manifest signe of a distempered Melancholy

state, as Plato long since maintained: for where such kind of men swarme, they will make worke for themselves, and make that body Politike diseased, which was otherwise sound.

16. ***the Ladies, which is nice.*** *Nice* can mean (a) ignorant, foolish, silly, simple; (b) dissolute, wanton, lascivious; (c) lazy, sluggish, slothful; and/or (d) pampered, luxurious (OED). *Nice Ladies* would therefore be prone to melancholy because "There is no greater cause of Melancholy then idlenesse" (RB). As long as people "are idle, they shall never be pleased. Well they may build castles in the aire for a time, and sooth up themselves with phantasticall humors, but in the end they will prove as bitter as gall" (RB).

16–17. ***the Lovers, which is all these.*** According to RB's meticulous analysis of "Love Melancholy," the *Lovers* affliction encompasses: (a) the emulation of the scholar (lines 12–13, above) because there is "No love without a mixture of Jealousie"; (b) the fantasy of the musician (line 13, above) because passion "proceed[s] first from the eyes to bee carried by our spirits, and kindled with imagination in the liver and heart"; (c) the pride of the courtier (line 14, above) because *Lovers,* "if once they be in love, they will be most neat & spruce and beginne to trick up, and to have a good opinion of themselves"; (d) the ambition of the soldier (lines 14–15, above) in that a man who loves a woman "desires... with all intention and egernesse of mind, to compasse or injoy her"; (e) the policy of the lawyer (line 15, above) in that *Lovers* can be "Saints in shew," but "cunningly can they dissemble," and "counterfeit... til they have satisfied their owne ends"; and (f) the niceness of the lady (line 16, above) in that just as "Idlenesse overthrowes all... love tyranniseth in an idle person."

17–18. ***compounded of many simples... objects.*** *Jaques* was formerly a *Libertine* (II.vii.70), and this has contributed to his present melancholy condition (see notes: lines 19 and 22–23, below). His consciousness of his former faults causes him to "object" ("reproach; disgrace, blemish, taint," "impute unto, charge or upbraid with, lay in ones dish, cast in his teeth, a fault or error committed," RC, s.v. "Reprocher") himself with *objects* ("objections": "charge[s] or accusation[s]," OED). Thus, *Jaques' many simples* ("Foolish or silly behaviour[s] or conduct; foolishness, folly," OED) and *objects* ("obstacles"; cf. *travells,* line 19, below) are the *simples* (individual ingredients) which "compound" (comprise, mix together to form) his melancholy.

19. ***sundrie.*** *Sundrie* is (a) "Consisting of different elements, of mixed composition" (OED); and (b) a play on "sun-dry." *Jaques* has spent some time in the hot Italian sun (lines 39–40, below), and RB notes that "hote countries are most troubled with melancholy," and that "many Venetian woemen are melancholy" because "they tarry too long in the Sun." Cf. and see note: II.vii.42–44.

19. ***travells.*** "Travel" and "Travail" were interchangeably spelled (HK, p. 151; cf. and see note: *Travellers,* II.iv.19). *Jaques'* melancholy is occasioned by (a) his *travells* (journeys); (b) his "travails" (suffering, painful troubles, hardships); and (c) his "travail" ("the physical exertion of copulation," JH), for melancholy is brought on by "Love of Gaming, &c. and pleasures immoderate" (RB). Cf. and see notes: II.vii.70–71; *Traveller,* line 22, below; and *Travellor,* line 35, below.

20. ***wraps.*** To "wrap" is "To cover or envelop" (OED); to "rap" is "To affect with rapture, ravish; to transport to or into a state of bliss, joy, etc." (OED). There may be additional play on "rap" as "An act of breaking wind" (OED; see note: *melancholy,* II.i.30).

20–21. ***humorous sadnesse.*** See notes: *humorous,* I.ii.269, and *melancholy,* II.i.30.

Ros. A Traveller: by my faith you have great rea-

son to be sad: I feare you have sold your owne Lands,

to see other mens; then to have seene much, and to have

nothing, is to have rich eyes and poore hands. [25]

Jaq. Yes, I have gain'd my experience.

Enter Orlando. [IV.i.2]

Ros. And your experience makes you sad: I had ra-

ther have a foole to make me merrie, then experience to

make me sad, and to travaile for it too. [30]

Orl. Good day, and happinesse, deere *Rosalind.*

Jaq. Nay then God buy you, and you talke in blanke

verse.

{*Exit Jaques.*} [IV.i.3]

Ros. Farewell Mounsieur Travellor: looke you [35]

22–23. ***A Traveller... sold your owne Lands.*** In *Anatomy of Melancholy*, Robert Burton unreservedly derides travelers who

> with a wanton eye, a liquorish tongue, and a gamesome hand, when they have indiscreetly impoverished themselves, mortgaged their wits together with their lands, and entombed their ancestors' fair possessions in their bowels, they may lead the reast of their days in prison, as many times they do; they repent at leisure, and then all is gone... ttis then too late to look about; their end is misery, sorrow, shame, and discontent.

Cf. II.vii.70–71.

23–25. ***Lands... poore hands.*** *Jaques* has *seene* (copulated with, JH, s.v. "Seen in it") the *Lands* (vaginas, FR; cf. F. "Landie": "The deaw-lap in a womans Privities," RC, q.v.) of *other mens* wives. Thus, he has "had" (i.e., sexually) *rich* (amorous, bawdy, F&H) *eyes* (genitals; see note: *eyes*, III.ii.152), but now his *hands* (sexual organs; see note: *hand*, I.ii.246) are *poore* (i.e., impotent; "poverty" is "Impotence, effeminacy," FR; cf. and see note: *disable*, line 36, below).

Rich also means "Of soil, lands, etc.: Abounding in the qualities necessary to produce good vegetation or crops" (OED); cf. *gain'd*, line 26, below.

26. ***I have gain'd my experience.*** *Jaques* sold his lands to pursue *experience* ("sexual intercourse," TR), so now he has no lands to "gain" (cultivate). However, his *experience* (i.e., the "shit" he has endured; *experience* is literally "A proofe, tryall," RC, s.v. "Preuve") has served as "gain" (fertilizer; see note: *gaine*, I.i.15) to "gain" (improve) his *experience* (knowledge, wisdom).

28. ***experience makes you sad.*** *Jaques* is "sadder and wiser" ("having gained wisdom from sad or bitter experience," OED). His *experience* (sexual misbehavior; see note: *experience*, line 26, above) has also made him *sad* (i.e., impotent; *sad* is literally "Of pastry, dough, etc.: that has failed to rise," OED).

29. ***a foole to make me merrie.*** For possible sexual pun, see notes: *foolerie*, I.iii.16, and *meerly*, III.ii.404.

31–33. ***Good day... blanke verse.*** *Jaques* finds *Orlando's* "verses" of love *blanke* ("Void of interest or event; vacant," "simple," OED; cf. III.ii.258–261).

Technically speaking, *blanke verse* is iambic pentameter, a meter consisting of five feet of alternating unstressed and stressed syllables. The line *Good day, and happinesse, deere Rosalind* employs this meter (see *Textual Preparation*, p. 390, note 17). The actor playing *Jaques* hastily exits from a love scene that he assumes will be spoken in *blanke verse*. He is wrong in this assumption: line 31 is the only line of *blanke verse* in this entire scene, which continues and concludes entirely in prose.

35. ***Mounsieur Travellor.*** *Rosalind* finds *Jaques* a *Travellor* (i.e., an annoying person who inflicts her with "travaile": "Wearinesse, tediousnesse," RC, s.v. "Fatigue").

As you Like it is ostensibly set in France, so all gentlemen would be addressed as *Monsieur*. However, the French title here points up the corrupting foreign influence on the English *Travellor* (cf. *Monsieur le Beu*, I.ii.95; *signior Love*, III.ii.288–289; and *Monsieur Melancholly*, III.ii.290–291).

The "o" spelling of *Travellor* (as opposed to the "e" spelling which occurs at II.iv.19 and line 22, above) may indicate that the word should be pronounced to approximate the Fr. "travailleur" (the sound [œ] as used in Fr. "eur" has no exact equivalent in English). This suggests play on *Travellor* as (a) Fr. "travailler" (to copulate, F&H, s.v. "ride"); and/or (b) Fr. "travailleur" as a possible male analog to Fr. "travailleuse" (whore, F&H, s.v. "Tart").

lispe, and weare strange suites; disable all the benefits
of your owne Countrie: be out of love with your
nativitie, and almost chide God for making you that
countenance you are; or I will scarce thinke you have
swam in a Gundello. Why how now *Orlando*, where [40]
have you bin all this while? you a lover? and you
serve me such another tricke, never come in my sight
more.

Orl. My faire *Rosalind*, I come within an houre of my
promise. [45]

Ros. Breake an houres promise in love? hee that

---

36. ***lispe.*** In *The Arte of Rhetorique*, Thomas Wilson laments that
Some farre journeid gentilman, at their retourne home, like as thei love to go in forrein apparell, so thei will pouder their talke, with oversea language, He

> that cometh latelie out of Fraunce, will talke Frenche Englishe, and never blushe at the matter. An other choppes in with Englishe Italianated, and applieth the Italian phrase, to our Englishe speaking.

A *lispe* was also indicative of licentiousness (TR, s.v. "nekke") and thus suggests the dissolution of the continent. Cf. and see note: *Monsieur Travellor*, line 35, above.

36. ***strange suites.*** Proverbially, an "Englishman Italianate is a devil incarnate." Italy was considered a highly immoral place (as well as the "source of VD" and one of the "breeding grounds of sodomy," FR); France shared this reputation (see note: *knowledge*, I.ii.288). To an Englishman, *strange* (foreign, alien) *suites* (clothing, fashions) symbolized the vice of the *strange* (sexually depraved or homosexual; see note: *Aliena*, I.iii.136) continental lifestyle. Cf. "Italian Fashion" (homosexuality or sodomy, GW); "French Velvet" (a "patch of velvet used in treating syphilis, to cover lanced chancres," EC), and these lines describing a wearer of *strange suites* from John Marston's "Satyre IX":

> For (sadly truth to say) what are they els
> But imitators of lewd beastlines?
> Farre worse then Apes; for mow, or scratch your pate,
> It may be some odde Ape will imitate.
> But let a youth that hath abus'd his time,
> In wronged travaile, in that hoter clime,
> Swoope by old Jack, in clothes Italienate:
> And I'le be hang'd if he will imitate
> His strange fantastique sute shapes.
> Or let him bring or'e beastly luxuries,
> Some hell-devised lustfull villanies,
> Even Apes & beasts would blush with native shame,
> And thinke it foule dishonour to their name,
> Their beastly name, to imitate such sin
> As our lewd youths doe boast and glory in.

36–37. ***disable... your owne Countrie.*** The Englishman who traveled abroad might *disable* ("disparage," JF, s.v. "Dishabilitare") his *owne Countrie.* Also, he might come home *disable* ("impotent," OED; cf. *debilitie*, II.iii.54) and thus not able to enjoy the *benefits* (i.e., "favors" or sexual gifts; see note: *favour'd*, III.iii.27) of his *owne* native *Countrie* (with play on "cunt").

40. ***swam.*** To "swim" is to "float along on the surface of the water, as a ship" (OED).

40. ***Gundello.*** I.e., "A Gundola, or Venetian Wherrie" (RC, s.v. "Gondole"). The cabin of the *Gundello* was a convenient place for sexual assignations and thus symbolized the depraved and dissolute nature of the Venetian lifestyle.

41–43. ***and you serve me... my sight more.*** *And* (if) *Orlando* "serves" (assaults) *Rosalind with such another tricke* ("an affront, a wrong, an injurie," JF, s.v. "Arlasso"), he will never *serve* her ("render [her] sexual service," GW) with a *tricke* ("a copulation," JH). If *Orlando* isn't careful, he will lose the opportunity to (a) *come* ("come into bodily contact or sexual connexion," OED) with *Rosalind*; and (b) *come* (achieve orgasm, ejaculate) *in Rosalind's* "site" (synonymous with "place": the "female parts," TR).

46. ***Breake an houres promise.*** Because *Orlando* has not kept his appointment, his *promise* is no better than *an houres* (i.e., "a whore's"; see note: *houre*, II.vii.30).

will divide a minute into a thousand parts, and breake
but a part of the thousand part of a minute in the affairs
of love, it may be said of him that *Cupid* hath clapt
him oth' shoulder, but Ile warrant him heart hole. [50]

Orl. Pardon me deere *Rosalind.*

Ros. Nay, and you be so tardie, come no more in my
sight, I had as liefe be woo'd of a Snaile.

Orl. Of a Snaile?

Ros. I, of a Snaile: for though he comes slowly, hee [55]
carries his house on his head; a better joyncture I thinke
then you make a woman: besides, he brings his destinie
with him.

Orl. What's that?

Ros. Why hornes: which such as you are faine to be be- [60]
holding to your wives for: but he comes armed in his
fortune, and prevents the slander of his wife.

Orl. Vertue is no horne-maker: and my *Rosalind* is
vertuous.

47–49. ***divide a minute... affairs of love.*** Cf. III.ii.297–301.
49–50. ***Cupid hath clapt him oth' shoulder... heart hole.*** *Orlando* is "*heart*

whole" ("Uninjured at the heart," OED) because *Cupid's* arrow has *clapt* (hit, struck) him on the shoulder instead of making a *hole* (wound) in his *heart. Orlando's* affection is therefore not "*heart* whole" ("Whole-hearted; free from hypocrisy or affectation; sincere, genuine," OED), and his vows of love are "whole" ("Wholly," OED) *heart* (pronounced "art": artificial pretence).

Cupid acts as a "Shoulder-clapper" ("a Sergeant or Bailiff," ND, q.v.) sent to arrest debtors and issues a *warrant* (order of arrest) to "arrest" (capture; also entrance) lovers. However, *Orlando* is "whole" ("sound": "Financially solid or safe," OED) and thus free from "debt" ("sexual obligation," GW). (The legal puns continue through lines 193, below).

Rosalind also implies that *Orlando* is an insincere *heart hole* (i.e., "asshole"; "hole" is the "arse-hole," F&H; for *heart,* see note: III.ii.406) whose idea of love is to visit a *warrant* (i.e., a "warren" or "Bawdy-house," ND). Therefore, *Cupid* has *clapt him* (i.e., given him the "clap," or "venereal taint," FG) *oth' shoulder* (i.e., on his "ass" and/or testicles; in leatherworking, the *shoulder* is "The portion of a hide between the butt and the cheeks," OED; in metalworking, the *shoulder* is "The projection between the blade and the tang of a knife, chisel, etc. which abuts on the handle," OED).

52–53. ***so tardie... a Snaile.*** *Orlando* is a *Snaile* ("Exceptionally tardy or slow," OED). He is also "a great snaile, a gull, a loggerhed, a joulthead, a patch, a lubie, a sneaker, a lurking companion" (RC, s.v. "Lumacone") who "comes tardy off" ("falls[s] short," OED) when he "comes" (has an orgasm, ejaculates). Cf. line 55, below.

55–56. ***Snaile... a better joyncture.*** "In England, brides... were expected to bring with them as a dowry a substantial cash sum, called a 'portion.' In the sixteenth and early seventeenth centuries, this money went directly to the father of the groom... In return, the father of the groom guaranteed the bride an annuity, called a 'jointure,' if she survived her husband as a widow" (LS, p. 88).

Rosalind thinks that a *Snaile* could make *a better joyncture* than *Orlando* because he at least *carries* a *house.* By contrast, as a younger son *Orlando* cannot guarantee his wife any real estate as part of her *joyncture* (see note: *your Orchard,* I.i.43).

The *Snaile* is also "a traditional symbol of sexual power" (JH); thus, he *carries* ("gain[s] sexual mastery or possession of a woman," EP) a woman's *house* ("vagina," GW) on his *head* (testicles and penis; see note: *heads,* II.i.27). Because the *Snaile comes* (i.e., achieve orgasm) *slowly,* he makes a *woman a better joyncture* (i.e., is a more satisfying sexual partner; *joyncture* literally means "Joining, conjunction, union," OED; also see note: *joyne,* III.iii.80).

57–62. ***his destinie... the slander of his wife.*** *Rosalind* expresses the cynical view that all married men share the same *destinie*: to wear a cuckold's *hornes* (cf. III.iii.48–49). A snail has *hornes* before he is married, so he (a) *prevents* (anticipates) the *slander* (disgrace) *of his wife*; and (b) *prevents* (avoids) *slander* (scandal).

63–64. ***Vertue is no horne-maker... vertuous.*** *Rosalind* is *vertuous* (righteous, just, good) and is therefore *no horne-maker*—i.e., she is not one to belittle or berate her husband. To "make horns" is a vulgar gesture implying cuckoldry in the party at which it is aimed. The gesture is made by holding the "Index and little finger extended, the remaining middle and ring fingers folded and pressed on the thumb... When the hand is posed in the manner described and raised vertically, it gives an approximation of the contour of the head of a horned animal" (Andrea de Jorio, *Gesture in Naples and Gesture in Classical Antiquity,* pp. 140–141). *Rosalind* is also *vertuous* (chaste) and therefore *no horne-maker* ("one who 'horns' or cuckolds," OED).

Ros. And I am your *Rosalind.* [65]

Cel. It pleases him to call you so: but he hath a *Rosa-*
lind of a better leere then you.

Ros. Come, wooe me, wooe mee: for now I am in a
holy-day humor, and like enough to consent: What
would you say to me now, and I were your verie, verie [70]
Rosalind?

Orl. I would kisse before I spoke.

Ros. Nay, you were better speake first, and when you
were gravel'd, for lacke of matter, you might take occasion to kisse: verie good Orators when they are out, [75]
they will spit, and for lovers, lacking (God warne us)
matter, the cleanliest shift is to kisse.

Orl. How if the kisse be denide?

Ros. Then she puts you to entreatie, and there begins
new matter. [80]

66–67. ***a Rosalind of a better leere then you.*** *Orlando* has a *Rosalind* of *a better leere*, meaning (a) face or appearance; (b) "Temper, disposition" (OED); and/or (c) "ass" (literally "flank or loin," OED). *Leere* is also the "Colour of sheep or cattle, due to the nature of the soil" (OED), so *Celia* hints that *Rosalind* is a "cow" or "sheep" (i.e., slut; see notes: *Cowes*, II.iv.52 and *sheepes*, III.ii.406). *Orlando* "lears" (i.e., worships; "lear" is "doctrine, religion," OED) an idealized *Rosalind*, but the actual *Rosalind*, who is now "leering" (making eyes) at *Orlando*, is guilty of "leer" ("immodest desire," OED).

69. ***holy-day humor.*** See note: *holiday*, I.iii.16.

69. ***consent.*** *Consent* contains a possible pun on "con" (i.e., "cunt"). Also see note: *consenting*, V.ii.9.

70. ***verie, verie.*** *Ganimed* wishes *Orlando* to speak to him as though he were *Orlando's verie* (genuine, actual) *Rosalind*, a woman who "varies" (vascilates; cf. III.ii.394–401). The transsexual boy actor playing the girl *Rosalind* playing the boy *Ganimed* also "varies" (is bisexual or sexually deviant, FR; to "vary" is literally "to differ from some standard," OED).

74–76. ***gravel'd... will spit.*** An "orator" (public speaker) who suffers a *lacke of matter* ("Material for expression"; "a theme, a topic, a subject of exposition," OED) will (a) be *gravel'd* ("put to silence, or to a Nonplus," RC, s.v. "Demeurer court"); and (b) "be gravelled" ("sticke fast on ground, or in the gravell," RC, s.v. "Aggraver"). When a *good* orator is thus *out* ("In error or at a loss from failure of memory or confidence," OED), he *will spit* (expectorate, eject saliva).

An "orator" is also a vigorous fornicator ("whore" was pronounced "or"; "-ator" is a L. suffix that turns a verb into a masculine noun which indicates someone who does something; therefore, an "orator" is "one who does a whore"). *Good Orators* (i.e., sexual performers) *will spit* ("emit semen," GW2) *when they are out* (an allusion to *coïtus interruptus*)—i.e., *good Orators* know when they are about to *spit* and thus pull *out*. However, if an "orator" is *gravel'd* ("sicke or troubled with the stone or gravell in the bladder," JF, s.v. "Arrenato"), he might suffer a *lacke of matter* (semen; see note: *matter*, III.ii.169). If so, he could not *take* (i.e., sexually) a woman's *occasion* (vagina, FR; an *occasion* is literally "a case," OED), but he *might* at least *take occasion* (opportunity) *to kisse*.

76–77. ***lacking (God warne us) matter... kisse.*** When a lover lacks *matter* (a subject for discussion), the *cleanliest* (most clever or adroit) *shift* (evasion, stratagem) *is to kisse*, but *Rosalind* hopes that *God* will *warne* (protect, defend) them from such an event.

Rosalind also hopes that *God* will *warne* ("fortify": "impart strength or vigour to," OED) *Orlando's God* (i.e., penis; a "gaud" is literally a "pointed rod or stick," OED) so that it will never lack *matter* (virility; see note: *matter*, III.ii.169).

A *shift* ("a woman's smock," OED; also the woman herself, JH, s.v. "Shifts") will stay "clean" (unsoiled; also morally pure) if all a woman's lover does is *kisse*, but if a woman gives a man a *kisse* it might encourage him to *shift* (i.e., have an erection; literally "bestir [him]self," OED) and *shift* ("succeed," OED) in *shift* (copulation, JH, s.v. "Make a shift").

78–80. ***denide... new matter.*** If a man's request for a *kisse* is *denide*, he must then "entreat" ("beg amorously," EP). The woman's denial gives him (a) *new matter* (something *new* to talk about); and (b) *new matter* (i.e., sexual vigour or appetite; see notes: III.ii.169 and 184).

Orl. Who could be out, being before his beloved

Mistris?

Ros. Marrie that should you if I were your Mistris,

or I should thinke my honestie ranker then my wit.

Orl. What, of my suite? [85]

Ros. Not out of your apparrell, and yet out of your

suite:

Am not I your *Rosalind*?

Orl. I take some joy to say you are, because I would

be talking of her. [90]

Ros. Well, in her person, I say I will not have you.

Orl. Then in mine owne person, I die.

Ros. No faith, die by Attorney: the poore world is

almost six thousand yeeres old, and in all this time there

was not anie man died in his owne person (*videlicet*) in [95]

81–84. ***Who could be out... ranker then my wit.*** *Orlando* thinks that a man who is *before* (in the presence of) his *beloved Mistris* would never be *out*, meaning (a) at a loss for words; and (b) barred from sexual entry. If *Rosalind's wit* (vagina, FR; "whit" is synonymous with "bit": "Female pudendum," F&H, s.v. "monosyllable") were so "rank" (wanton, lascivious; see note: *ranke*, I.ii.104) that she could not keep *Orlando out* (i.e., sexually), then her *honestie* (sexual virtue) would be more "rank" ("rotten, addle," JF, s.v. "Magagnoso") than her *wit* (intelligence).

86–87. ***Not out of your apparrell... suite.*** If *Rosalinde* put *Orlando out* (made him silent and/or expelled him), he would be *out of* (excluded from) his *suite* (courtship, wooing) but not be *out of* his *apparrell* (i.e., not undressed for sex). *Suite* (litigation) also continues the string of legal puns.

90. ***talking of her.*** In *talking of Rosalind*, *Orlando* risks worsening his "disease"; see note: III.ii.386–391.

91. ***in her person.*** "On her behalf," with possible play on *person* as the "human genitals" (OED, which dates from 1824).

91. ***have.*** I.e., sexually.

92–93. ***in mine owne person... by Attorney.*** *In* his *owne person* (on his own behalf), *Orlando* protests that he will *die* if *Rosalind* will not have him. *Rosalind* thinks it imprudent for *Orlando* to *die in person* ("Corporally, bodily, personally," RC, s.v. "Corporellement") and instead recommends that he *die by Attorney* ("an agent for another, a factor, one that seeth to another mans affaires, or that hath the charge of a thing committed to him," JF, s.v. "Procuaratore").

If *Rosalind* will not sleep with *Orlando*, he could easily find an *Attorney* ("Procurer": pimp or bawd). Thus, he would *die* (i.e., achieve orgasm, ejaculate) *by Attorney* (i.e., "by a tourney" or sexual intercourse; "tourney" is synonymous with "joust"; see note: *justly*, I.ii.242; "tourn" is also "Copulation of Roes," ND).

93–96. ***the poore world... a love cause.*** At the time *As you Like it* was written (circa 1600), theologians reckoned that God created the *world* "betweene five thousand and sixe thousand yeares agoe. For Moses hath set downe exactly the computation of time from the making of the world to his owne daies: and the Prophets after him have with like diligence set downe the continuance of the same to the very birth of Christ" (William Perkins, *A Golden Chaine*). Using a similarly obtuse method of biblical computation, *all time* was divided into three 2000 year periods (the flood of Noah occurring 2000 years after the Creation, the birth of Christ occurring 2000 years after the flood, and the Apocalypse set to occur 2000 years after the birth of Christ). Therefore, the devout believed that "the second comming of Christ shall be about sixe thousand yeares from the beginning of the worlde" (Ibid.). Because *the poore world is* now *almost six thousand yeeres old*, it is about to end. Therefore, *Rosalind* expresses the belief that not only *has* no man ever *died* for *love* but that no man ever will.

Rosalind's belief that *not anie man* ever *died in his owne person* (in actual existence; in real life as opposed to fiction) by pursuing a *cause* (synonymous with "suit": both "wooing" and "lawsuit") *of love* is at odds with prevailing opinion, for "It is so well knowne in every village, how many have either died for love or voluntary made away themselves, that I not need such labor to prove it" (RB). However, the *cause* (reason) for a man's demise may sometimes have been his *cause* ("Sexual needs; sexual business," JH).

95. ***videlicet.*** Like any good *Attorney* (line 93, above), *Rosalind* intersperses her arguments with Latin phrases such as *videlicet* ("To wit, that is to say," JB, q.v.).

a love cause: *Troilous* had his braines dash'd out with a
Grecian club, yet he did what hee could to die before,
and he is one of the patternes of love. *Leander*, he would
have liv'd manie a faire yeere though *Hero* had turn'd
Nun; if it had not bin for a hot Midsomer-night, for [100]
(good youth) he went but forth to wash him in the Hellespont, and being taken with the crampe, was droun'd,
and the foolish Chronoclers of that age, found it was
Hero of Cestos. But these are all lies, men have died
from time to time, and wormes have eaten them, but not [105]
for love.

Orl. I would not have my right *Rosalind* of this mind,
for I protest her frowne might kill me.

Ros. By this hand, it will not kill a flie: but come,

96–97. ***Troilous... to die before.*** In Greek legend, *Troilous* was a son of King Priam and Queen Hecuba of Troy (although the god Apollo may actually have been his father). Medieval authors transformed *Troilous* from a Trojan soldier into a courtly lover who was smitten with Criseyde (or Cressida), the daughter of the *Grecian* priest Calchas. Criseyde abandoned *Troilous* in favor of the *Grecian* general Diomedes, but *Troilous* remained steadfast. In matters of love, *Troilous* was therefore considered "a Patterne, or Touchstone whereby the goodnesse of things is tryed" (RC, s.v. "Paragon"), and in the vernacular "all constant men be *Troylusses*, all false women *Cressids*" (*Troylus and Cressida*, III.ii).

There are varying accounts of *Troilous'* death: in one version, the *Grecian* warrior Achilles beheads him; in another, Achilles strangles him; and in yet another, Achilles drags *Troilous* under his chariot. Therefore, love did not cause *Troilous'* death, *yet he did what hee could to die before*, meaning (a) to *die* of love *before* he actually died; or (b) to have sex and *die* (achieve orgasm) *before* he lost his life.

No existing story relates that *Troilous* had *his braines dash'd out with a Grecian club*, but there is an intriguing fourth century A.D. account of *Troilous'* demise written by Servius Maurus Honoratus. In this version, Achilles falls in love (or lust) with *Troilous*, and *Troilous* dies in Achilles' arms from the sheer exhaustion of making love. In this case, *Troilous* could indeed be said to have had his *braines dash'd out* (i.e., had the "shit fucked out of him"; to "dash" is "to strike vehemently, to thrust into," TT, s.v. "Illīdo"; *braines* is "Excrement," FR; cf. RC's "Bran": "A turd") *with* the *club* ("penis," F&H) of *a Grecian* (homosexual, FR; the ancient Greeks were infamous for their homo-eroticism). Even so, it was not love but lovemaking that caused *Troilous to die*.

98–104. ***Leander... Hero of Cestos.*** *Hero of Cestos* (or "Sestus," an ancient Greek town situated on the Gallipoli peninsula in what is now Turkey) was a priestess of Aphrodite who lived atop a high tower on the *Hellespont* (the "Sea of Helle"). *Leander*, her clandestine lover, lived on the opposite shore. Every night, *Hero* would light a beacon atop the tower to guide *Leander* as he swam out to her. The wind blew out the light one night, and *Leander*, unable to find his way in the stormy sea, *droun'd*. When his body washed ashore, *Hero* killed herself by jumping from the summit of the tower. However, neither *Hero* nor *Leander* technically died of love: *Leander droun'd* because he was *taken with the crampe* while swimming across the *Hellespont*, and *Hero* died of a fall from a great height.

99–100. ***liv'd... though Hero had turn'd Nun.*** Paradoxically, as a *Nun* (consecrated virgin; see note: *Nun*, III.iv.19) of Aphrodite, *Hero* had already taken a vow of chastity. That, however, did not prevent her sleeping with *Leander*. *Rosalind* perhaps means that *Leander* would have *liv'd* if (a) *Hero* had actually honored her vows of chastity as a *Nun*; or (b) *Hero* abandoned *Leander* and *turn'd Nun* ("whore," JH).

100–102. ***a hot Midsomer-night... the Hellespont.*** *Leander* ventured into the *Hellespont* because he was *hot* ("randy," F&H) for *Hero*. He wanted to *wash* ("fuck," EC) her so badly that he was driven to "*Midsomer* Moon Madness" ("Madness is supposed to be affected by the moon, and to be aggravated by summer heat; so it naturally follows that the full moon at midsummer is the time when madness is most outrageous," DPF). However, *Rosalind* posits an innocent explanation for *Leander's* nocturnal swim: the *Midsomer-night* was *hot*, and he simply wanted to *wash* (swim, bathe) to cool off.

103. ***Chronoclers.*** *Rosalind* thinks that the *Chonoclers* ("historie writer[s]," RC2, q.v.) of such "chronicles" ("yearelie relations of the chiefe matters acted, or happening, in a countrey," RC, s.v. "Chroniques") are "chronicles" (asses or assholes, FR; "chronicles" plays on "annual" / "anal": "Annalls" are "brief histories or Chronicles of things done from yeer to yeer," TB, q.v., and an "Annalist" is "he that makes or writes such Annals or yeerly Chronicles," TB, q.v.).

104–106. ***men have died... but not for love.*** *Men have died* (expired, lost their lives) *from time to time* (from age to age, continuously through *time*), and *wormes have eaten them* (either in their graves or in Hell; see note: *wormes*, III.ii.65), *but not for love*. Also, *men have died* (experienced orgasm) *from time to time, and wormes* (venereal diseases such as syphilis; see note: *wormes*, III.ii.65) *have eaten them, but* this was due to lust, not *love*.

108. ***her frowne might kill me.*** See note: *murder in mine eye*, III.v.13.

109. ***it will not kill a flie.*** *Rosalind's* frown cannot even *kill a flie*, let alone *Orlando*. Cf. III.v.18–19 and 27–30.

	now I will be your *Rosalind* in a more comming-on dis-	[110]
	position: and aske me what you will, I will grant it.	
Orl.	Then love me *Rosalind.*	
Ros.	Yes faith will I, fridaies and saterdaies, and all.	
Orl.	And wilt thou have me?	
Ros.	I, and twentie such.	[115]
Orl.	What saiest thou?	
Ros.	Are you not good?	
Orl.	I hope so.	
Rosalind.	Why then, can one desire too much of a	
	good thing: Come sister, you shall be the Priest, and	[120]
	marrie us: give me your hand *Orlando*: What doe you	
	say sister?	
Orl.	Pray thee marrie us.	
Cel.	I cannot say the words.	
Ros.	You must begin, will you *Orlando.*	[125]
Cel.	Goe too: wil you *Orlando*, have to wife this *Ro-*	
	salind?	
Orl.	I will.	
Ros.	I, but when?	
Orl.	Why now, as fast as she can marrie us.	[130]

110–111. ***comming-on disposition.*** *Rosalind* will be of a *comming-on* ("sexually forward," GW2) *disposition* (frame of mind) like "Coming-women" ("such as are free of their Flesh; also breeding Women," ND). She will also be of a *disposition* ("sexual inclination," JH) more suitable for achieving *comming-on* ("The sexual orgasm," JH).

111. ***aske me what you will... grant it.*** *Rosalind* will *grant Orlando* anything, even if he asks her to *grant* him her *what* ("pudend," EP).

112–113. ***love me... fridaies and saterdaies.*** *Rosalind* will *love Orlando* whether she is "Friday-faced" ("melancholy," "sour-featured," F&H) or indulging in "Saturday wit" ("lewd or bawdy talk," OED). *Fridaes and saterdaies* were the days appointed by the church for fasting, but *Rosalind* would agree to make *love* to *Orlando* anytime, despite an injunction to "fast" ("abstain sexually," JH).

114. ***have.*** Both (a) *have* in marriage; and (b) *have* sexually; *Rosalind* plays on the latter meaning in line 115, below.

119–120. ***can one desire... a good thing.*** Proverbially, "A man may take too much of a good thing" (RC, s.v. "On se saoule bien de manger tartes"), because "In striving to take too much of a thing we spoyle it, and despoyle ourselves of all further use of it" (RC, s.v. "Avarice rompt le sac"). Hence, "We have a prettie saying in our Englishe tongue, too much of one thing, is good for nothing" (Thomas Rogers, *The anatomie of the minde*). Cf. *ill roasted Egge*, III.ii.38.

The specific *thing Rosalind* desires is a *good* (virile, sexually potent; see notes: *good*, I.ii.28 and 65) *thing* (penis; see note: *thing*, III.v.122).

120–124. ***you shall be the Priest... I cannot say the words.*** *Celia* has good reason to hesitate, for *Rosalind* is essentially tricking *Orlando* into marriage. Even without a *Priest*, "The contract *per verba de praesenti*... by which the pair exchanged before witnesses such phrases as 'I do take thee to my wife' and 'I do take thee to my husband,' was regarded in ecclesiastical law as an irrevocable commitment which could never be broken, and which nullified a later church wedding to someone else" (LS, p. 32). Moreover, "sexual intercourse was permitted to take place immediately after the formal public betrothal" (LS, p. 628), so a verbal contract would allow *Orlando* and *Rosalind* to immediately consummate their union.

Ros. Then you must say, I take thee *Rosalind* for wife.

Orl. I take thee *Rosalind* for wife.

Ros. I might aske you for your Commission,
But I doe take thee *Orlando* for my husband: there's a [135]
girle goes before the Priest, and certainely a Womans
thought runs before her actions.

Orl. So do all thoughts, they are wing'd.

Ros. Now tell me how long you would have her, after you have possest her? [140]

Orl. For ever, and a day.

Ros. Say a day, without the ever: no, no *Orlando*, men
are Aprill when they woe, December when they wed:
Maides are May when they are maides, but the sky changes when they are wives: I will bee more jealous of [145]

134–136. ***I might aske you... before the Priest.*** *Celia* began the ceremony somewhat unwillingly in her role as *the Priest* (line 124, above) and has since not participated as she should. *Orlando* has now usurped the priest's role by speaking *before the Priest* (the priest customarily dictates the words of the ceremony and the bride and groom repeat them). Therefore, *Rosalind might aske Orlando for* his *Comission* ("A writing, shewing that one or many have some authority in matters of trust committed to their charge," HC) to perform a wedding ceremony. However, *Rosalind* also *goes before* (i.e., does not wait for) *the Priest* (i.e., *Celia*) and speaks her own vows without prompting. (In any event, a *Priest* with a *Commission* was not necessary for a marriage to be valid; see note: lines 120–124, above).

136–137. ***a Womans thought... actions.*** *Rosalind*, like *Orlando* (line 133, above), has jumped her cue to speak in the wedding ceremony. She is perhaps anxious to proceed because her *thought* (i.e., of consummating the marriage) *runs before* (anticipates) her "action" ("Sexual intercourse," EP).

138. ***all thoughts... wing'd.*** *All thoughts* fly on "wings," "For nimble thought can jumpe both sea and land, / As soone as thinke the place where he would be" (Sonnet 44).

139–140. ***how long you would have her... possest her.*** *Rosalind* asks *Orlando* (a) *how long* he *would have* ("keep, hold"; also "cherish" and "esteem," OED) *Rosalind after he* has *possest* (obtained, won) *her*; and (b) *how long Orlando would have her* (i.e., sustain sexual intercourse; to *have* is literally to "keep up," OED) *after he* has *possest her* (i.e., sexually).

142–143. ***men are Aprill... December when they wed.*** Perhaps an "allusion to April as a month in spring... or to its changeable weather" (OED). *Men are* as "warm" ("Sexually ardent," EP) as *Aprill when they woe*, but they become as "cold" (adverse, distant, and/or frigid) as *December* after *they wed. Rosalind* may also describe *men* as *Aprill when they woe* because their eagerness to *wed* makes them utter fools ("My April morn" is "my wedding day; the day when I was made a fool of," DPF, s.v. "April"; an "April Gentleman" is "a foolish man; *spec.* a newly-married husband, considered as a fool," OED).

144–145. ***Maides are May... the sky changes when they are wives.*** *Maides* (young women) are *May* (in their "bloom or prime," OED) *when they are maides* (unmarried). Once *they are wives*, however, *the sky changes* as quickly as it does during *May*, a month traditionally associated with changeable weather (cf. the proverb "Cast not a clout ere May be out"; i.e., don't discard your warm clothing in *May* because the weather can easily turn cold again). In referring to *Maides* as *May*, *Rosalind* again asserts that women are extremely capricious. Cf. III.ii.395–401, and lines 145–152, below.

thee, then a Barbary cocke-pidgeon over his hen, more
clamorous then a Parrat against raine, more new-fangled then an ape, more giddy in my desires, then a monkey: I will weepe for nothing, like *Diana* in the Fountaine, & I wil do that when you are dispos'd to be merry: [150]
I will laugh like a Hyen, and that when thou art inclin'd
to sleepe.

Orl. But will my *Rosalind* doe so?

Ros. By my life, she will doe as I doe.

---

146. ***Barbary cocke-pidgeon... hen.*** The *Barbary pidgeon* is a fancy *pidgeon* thought to have originated in *Barbary* (the middle and western coastal regions of North Africa). Pigeons mate for life, but the *hen* (female bird) might still copulate with another *cocke* (male bird) if given the opportunity. For this reason, a *cocke-pidgeon* often "drives" *his hen*—i.e., herds her away from other male birds (Richard F. Johnston and Marián Janiga, *Feral Pigeons*, pp. 65–67). All varieties of pigeons display similar behavior, but *Rosalind* perhaps chooses the *Barbary* variety because *Barbary* alludes to Saracen culture (OED) and thus evokes a harem.

The "Guinea Hen" (a variety of turkey native to Africa) is also termed a *Barbary Hen*. Thus, *Barbary cocke-pidgeon* might allude to the *cocke* ("cuckold," GW2) and *pidgeon* (dupe; see note: *Pigeons*, I.ii.91) of a "Guinea Hen" ("courtezan," F&H).

146–147. ***more clamorous... against raine.*** *A Parrat* is *clamorous* ("out-crying, full of noise; that does nothing but bawle, bray, and crie out," RC, s.v. "Criard") and whistles and preens *against* (before, in expectation of) *raine.* Because *a Parrat* simply repeats what it hears, it is also an emblem for empty and mindless talk.

The *Parrat* was also reputedly lecherous (FR, s.v. "Delicate"), so *Rosalind* hints that she will be *clamorous* for *Orlando's raine* (seminal emission, JH, s.v. "Rain showers"; also see notes: *reignes,* I.ii.42, and *raine,* III.v.55).

147–148. ***more new-fangled then an ape.*** *Rosalind* will be *more new-fangled* ("fantasticall, humorous," "giddie-headed," RC, s.v. "Mercure"; also "skittish; inventive, conceited," RC, s.v. "Fantastique") *then an ape* (i.e., a vain and mindless imitator of new fashion trends; see note: *strange suites,* line 36, above). She will also be *more new-fangled* ("nat constante and stedy of purpose," JP, s.v. "muable") *then an ape* (i.e., a nymphomaniac; see notes: *apish,* III.ii.396, and *monkey,* lines 148–149, below).

148–149. ***more giddy... then a monkey.*** *Rosalind* will be *more giddy* ("dizie, madde, foolish, frantike, raving in the head," JF, s.v. "Stordito") *in* her *desires* (wishes, requests) *then a monkey* ("a gull, a ninnie, a mome, a sot," JF, s.v. "Caparrone"). Her *desires* (lust, sexual appetite, GW) will make her *more giddy* (lustful, wanton; see note: *giddie,* III.ii.342) with her *monkey* ("The female pudendum," F&H) *then a monkey* (a symbol of monstrous lechery, JH).

149–150. ***I will weepe... Diana in the Fountaine.*** *Rosalind* will *weepe* so much that she will gush as much as a *Fountaine* decorated with a statue of *Diana. Diana* was a popular figure in fountains (probably due to the fact that the ancient tale of *Diana* bathing *in the Fountaine* provided a convenient excuse to depict a nude woman). *Rosalind* also hints at the changes that *Diana* ("The Moon," TB q.v.) will effect *in* her *Fountaine* ("vagina," GW2)—i.e., at the "Pre-Menstrual Syndrome" that will make her *weepe for nothing.* In *Withcraft in the Middle Ages* (pp. 47–48), Jeffrey Burton Russell describes *Diana* as

> an unusally schizonphrenic deity. Her best-known characteristics are those of the maiden huntress, the cold and pale virgin of the moon who transforms would-be lovers into animals and slays them. But, as those will recognize who remember St. Paul's encounter with Diana of the Ephesians, the many-breasted fertility goddess of Asia Minor, Diana did not always choose to be maidenly. The virgin huntress was also the protector of animals... and consequently the guarantor of their fertility. It was Diana's proclivities for procreation that made her the goddess of the moon, whose crescent phase symbolizes increase, and whose horns in that stage symbolize (among other things) the strange lunar pull upon animals; the moon was also associated with the monthly period of fertility of women as well as that of animals.

Also see note: *pale spheare,* III.ii.5.

151–152. ***laugh like a Hyen... inclin'd to sleepe.*** When *Orlando* is tired and *inclin'd to sleepe, Rosalind* will *laugh like a* "Hyena, a beast like a woolf having a main and long hairs over all the body. It is the subtillest (as some say) of all beasts, and will counterfeit the voice of a man, to draw shepheards out of their houses in the night, to the end he may kill them. It is written that he changeth sex often, being sometimes male, and sometimes female" (TB, q.v.).

Even if *Orlando* is *inclin'd* ("disposed to love-making," EP) *to sleepe* (i.e., have sex), *Rosalind* will still *laugh* ("Make love," FR) adulterously *like a Hyen* (i.e., an unfaithful wife; the *Hyen* symbolized adultery and fornication, GW2, s.v. "Hyena").

Orl.	O but she is wise.	[155]
Ros.	Or else shee could not have the wit to doe this:	
	the wiser, the waywarder: make the doores upon a wo-	
	mans wit, and it will out at the casement: shut that, and	
	'twill out at the key-hole: stop that, 'twill flie with the	
	smoake out at the chimney.	[160]
Orl.	A man that had a wife with such a wit, he might	
	say, wit whether wil't?	
Ros.	Nay, you might keepe that checke for it, till you	
	met your wives wit going to your neighbours bed.	
Orl.	And what wit could wit have, to excuse that?	[165]
Rosa.	Marry to say, she came to seeke you there: you	
	shall never take her without her answer, unlesse you take	
	her without her tongue: ô that woman that cannot	
	make her fault her husbands occasion, let her never nurse	
	her childe her selfe, for she will breed it like a foole.	[170]

155–157. ***she is wise... the waywarder.*** *Orlando* asserts that *Rosalind,* unlike *Ganimed, is wise* ("In one's right mind, sane," OED). *Ganimed* agrees that *Rosalind* does indeed have *wit* ("reason," "right mind," "sanity," OED) and alleges that a woman who is not *wise* ("Sexually experienced," FR) *could not have the wit* (vagina; see note: *wit,* line 84, above) *to doe this*—i.e., to be "wayward" ("froward, hard to rule, ill to intreat; out of all order," RC, s.v. "Dyscole"). A "wayward" woman will go in search of another man's "warder" (i.e., penis; a "warder" is literally "a staffe," JP, q.v.), but to her husband she will be a "warder" ("One who wards off," OED) and bar him from her "way" ("vagina," GW).

157–160. ***make the doores upon a womans wit... out at the chimney.*** As described in Walter Hilton's *The Scale of Perfection*, the "five wits," or five bodily senses, are

> five windows, by which sin cometh into thy soul, as the Prophet saith: Death cometh in by our windows. These are the five senses by which the soul goeth out of herself, and fetcheth her delight, and seeketh her feeding in earthly things, contrary to the nobility of her own nature. As by the eye to see curious and fair things, and so of the other sense. By the unskilful using of these senses willingly to vanities, thy soul is much letted from the sweetness of the spiritual senses within; and therefore it behoveth thee to stop these windows, and shut them, but only when need requireth to open them... therefore, turn home again into thyself, and hold thee within.

Woman is "the weaker vessel" (1. Peter 3:7), so it is all but impossible to restrain her *wit* (i.e., her five wits, or temptations of the flesh). A man cannot *make* (close, shut, make secure) his wife's *doores* (vagina and anus, JA, p. 89) simply by "making" ("mat[ing] with," OED) her. If *out at the casement* (i.e., if "out the window": given an opportunity or occasion, OED), *a womans* "wit" (vagina; see note: line 156, above) will *out* (copulate, FR; cf. F&H's "to play at in and out" and "to get outside of": "to copulate").

In folklore, the *key-hole* and the *chimney* were seen as a means of egress for witches, demons, and the devil, so *Rosalind* implies that a wife will prove harder to control than a supernatural fury. Any man who attempts to *make the doores upon a womans wit* will find that she "Shut[s] the door" ("Of the woman, to refuse to copulate with the man; not to permit his sexual entry," JH, q.v.), and her *wit* (sexual urges, genitals) *will* still *out* (i.e., fornicate) *at the key-hole* ("female pudendum," F&H, where *key* is the "penis," F&H). Any attempt to *stop* (close up or obstruct; also "allusive of penis as vaginal plug," GW2) *that* (i.e., her *key-hole* or vagina) will make a woman *flie out* (get angry, scold, F&H), and her *wit* will still *flie* (i.e., be "fly": "wanton," F&H) *with the smoake* (copulation; see note: *smoake*, I.ii.291) *out at the chimney* ("vagina," GW2).

162. ***wit whether wil't.*** See note: I.ii.56–57.

163. ***checke.*** Rebuke.

164. ***wit.*** With play on *wit* as the vagina (see note: *wit*, line 84, above).

166–167. ***you shall never take her... answer.*** It is "commonly spoken; that a woman is never to seeke for an answer; and though it be the weaker Sexe, yet is their wit more quicke and nimble then that of men" (Fernando de Rojas, *The Spanish Bawd*). Therefore, a man *shall never take* (catch in wrongdoing; also rebuke, OED) his wife *without* her having a ready *answer* (an explanation to clear herself).

Also, should a man *take* (marry) a woman, she will *never* be *without* an *answer*—i.e., her "goose" (fool) of a husband, who is an "anser" ("A goose or a gander," TT, q.v.) for marrying her in the first place.

168. ***tongue.*** With possible play on *tongue* as the clitoris (see note: *tongue*, III.ii.242).

168–170. ***that woman that cannot make her fault... foole.*** When a woman's *husband* finds *fault* with *her*, he gives *her occasion* (opportunity) to "treat him like shit" (an *occasion* is "An act of defecation," OED). A woman's husband is always the *occasion* (cause) of any *fault* (defect; also sexual transgression) in *her fault* (vagina; see note: *faults*, III.ii.278). Any *woman that cannot make* it so is *a foole*, so she should *never nurse her child her selfe*, for *she will breed* ("feede," "nourish," JF, s.v. "Allevare"; also "cause [it] to become," OED) *a foole*; see note: III.v.40.

Orl. For these two houres *Rosalinde*, I wil leave thee.

Ros. Alas, deere love, I cannot lacke thee two houres.

Orl. I must attend the Duke at dinner, by two a clock
I will be with thee againe.

Ros. I, goe your waies, goe your waies: I knew what [175]
you would prove, my friends told mee as much, and I
thought no lesse: that flattering tongue of yours wonne
me: 'tis but one cast away, and so come death: two o'
clocke is your howre.

Orl. I, sweet *Rosalind.* [180]

Ros. By my troth, and in good earnest, and so God
mend mee, and by all pretty oathes that are not dangerous, if you breake one jot of your promise, or come one
minute behinde your houre, I will thinke you the most
patheticall breake-promise, and the most hollow lover, [185]
and the most unworthy of her you call *Rosalinde*, that
may bee chosen out of the grosse band of the unfaithfull: therefore beware my censure, and keep your promise.

177–178. ***that flattering tongue... cast away.*** *Rosalind* consented to grant *Orlando* anything (line 111, above), so she has supposedly behaved like a *cast away* (i.e., a "cast-off": "Tart," F&H, q.v.) and allowed *Orlando* to *cast* ("throw [her] down... for the purpose of copulation," GW2). *Orlando wonne* (sexually enjoyed, JH, s.v. "Win") *Rosalind* with his *flattering* (copulating; see note: *flattery*, II.i.13) *tongue* (penis; see note: *tongue*, III.ii.242). However, now that she is no longer *cast* ("chaste," OED), she is *cast away* (i.e., "treated like shit"; to *cast* is to "void excrements," OED).

178. ***come death.*** *Rosalind's* melodramatic assertion that she will die because *Orlando* has abandoned her is completely at odds with the opinion she expressed in lines 104–106, above.

181–183. ***By my troth... not dangerous.*** *Oathes* were taken very seriously and were thus *dangerous* to break: "Oathes must not be made but by the name of God, and then are they as dangerous to be broken, as if you should rebell against him... Oathes are the more dangerous, by how much God is most holy, and cannot endure to have his name unhallowed at any time, much lesse by ordinary and audacious custome" (Thomas Gainsford, *The Rich Cabinet*).

By contrast, *pretty* (polite) *oathes* not made in God's name were not truly binding. Should *Rosalind* break her *oathes* (i.e., not think badly of *Orlando* if he fails to arrive on time), she invokes no more *dangerous* consequence than for *God* to *mend* her ("free [her] from sin or fault," OED).

Oathes were, in fact, so sacred that many people considered their casual stage use by fictitious characters such as *Rosalind* to be blasphemous. In *A Second and Third Blast of Retrait from Plaies and Theaters*, Anthony Munday judges that "Hearers of plaies are accessarie to the wickednes of plaiers," for at the theatre "we can heare, without stopping our eares, so manie counterfet othes uttered of plaiers! which, as light as they seeme in our eies, are great reproches, and injuries to the Majestie of God." Under growing pressure from religious conservatives, in May 1606 Parliament passed an act "For the preventing and avoyding of the great abuse of the holy Name of God in Stage-playes, Interludes, Maygames, Shewes and such like"; the statute imposed a hefty ten-pound fine on persons that "doe or shall in any Stage-play, Interlude, Shew, Maygame, or Pageant, jestingly, and prophanely speake, or use the holy Name of God, or of Christ Jesus, or of the holy Ghost or of the Trinitie, which are not to bee spoken but with feare and reverence." Under this statute, even *Rosalind's* seemingly innocuous *God mend mee* became *dangerous*, especially for a hired player for whom ten pounds represented about half a year's wages.

185. ***patheticall breake-promise.*** Although *Orlando* is a *patheticall* (miserable, unworthy) *breake-promise*, he is nevertheless *patheticall* ("passionate; persuasive, affection-moving," RC, s.v. "Pathetique").

185. ***hollow lover.*** I.e., a *lover* who is "Hollow-hearted": "False, Base, Perfidious, Treacherous" (ND). Also see notes: *holla*, III.ii.242, and *concave*, III.iv.27.

187–188. ***chosen... the unfaithfull.*** *The grosse* ("Lewd, obscene," EP) *band* ("company of men, or an assembly," RC2, q.v.) who are *unfaithfull* and break their *band* ("bond" or promise) is *grosse* (large). *Rosalind* here echoes religious rhetoric: "To be the peculiare people of God, is to be chosen out of the company of the unfaythful and wycked people" (Thomas Becon, *A new yeares gyfte more precious than golde*). This prompts *Orlando's* promise of "religion" in line 190, below.

188. ***censure.*** A *censure* is "a judgement, a sentence" (JF, s.v. "Arbitrio); also see note: *censure*, line 9, above. Given the surrounding religious wordplay, *censure* (pronounced "censer"; cf. and see notes: *Lectors*, III.ii.341, and *feature*, III.iii.5) might pun "censer": "A vessel in which incense is burnt" (OED). If *Orlando* doesn't keep his promise, *Rosalind* will be "incensed" (furious).

Orl. With no lesse religion, then if thou wert indeed [190]

my *Rosalind*: so adieu.

Ros. Well, Time is the olde Justice that examines all

such offenders, and let time try: adieu.

Exit {*Orlando*}. [IV.i.4]

Cel. You have simply misus'd our sexe in your love-prate: [195]

we must have your doublet and hose pluckt over

your head, and shew the world what the bird hath done

to her owne neast.

Ros. O coz, coz, coz: my pretty little coz, that thou

didst know how many fathome deepe I am in love: but [200]

it cannot bee sounded: my affection hath an unknowne

bottome, like the Bay of Portugall.

Cel. Or rather bottomlesse, that as fast as you poure

affection in, it runs out.

---

190. ***religion.*** With play on *religion* as (a) "Strict fidelity or faithfulness" (OED); (b) "Awe, dread" (OED); and/or (c) "the worship of God, or of things held sacred; a reverend, and conscientious affection unto them, or feare of offending them" (RC, q.v.).

192–193. ***Time is the olde Justice... let time try.*** An allusion to the proverb "Time tries all things." *Rosalind* depicts *Time* as an *Olde Justice* (judge, magistrate) *that examines* (tries, investigates the guilt or innocence of) *all such offendors* ("defendant[s] in a criminall action," RC, s.v. "Criminel"). Also see note: *offences*, III.ii.342.

195. ***You have simply misus'd... love-prate.*** In her *prate* (variant of "prat": "A trick; a piece of trickery or fraud; a prank or practical joke," OED), *Rosalind* has made *prate* (idle or foolish talk) that has *simply* (completely; also stupidly) *misus'd* ("sp[oken]

falsely of, misrepresent[ed]," OED) her *sexe*. She has also *misus'd* (i.e., "buggered"; cf. and see note: *mistake*, I.ii.37) the "prat[e]" (backside; see note: *prety*, III.ii.269) of her own *sexe*.

196–198. ***your doublet and hose... her owne neast.*** Shakespeare drew this delightful bit of bawdy from Lodge's *Rosalynde*: "And I pray you (quoth Aliena) if your roabes were off, what mettall are you made of that you are so satyricall against women? Is it not a foule bird defiles the owne nest?"

Even though *Rosalind* looks like a man with *doublet and hose* (testicles and penis; see note: *doublet and hose*, II.iv.9), she is really a *bird* ("Tart," F&H, q.v.) with a *neast* ("female pudendum," F&H). Therefore, if her *doublet* (jacket) *and hose* (breeches, leggings) were *pluckt* (pulled off) *over* her head, then *the world* could see that she has "nested" ("defecate[d]," F&H) in her own *neast* (i.e., "shit on" her own sex, for proverbially "It's an ill bird that fouls its own nest").

There is additional play on "pluck" meaning "to strip a bird of feathers" (OED), the implication being that *Rosalind* is dressed in "false feathers" (i.e., pretends to be what she is not; the phrase derives from Aesop's fable in which a crow adorns itself with peacock feathers).

200–202. ***how many fathome deepe... Bay of Portugall.*** *Rosalind* loves *Orlando* "from the bottom of her heart," and it is just as impossible to "sound" (give voice to, express) how *deepe* she is *in love* as it is to "sound" (ascertain the depth of) *the Bay of Portugall* (which in parts is more than 1400 *fathome*, or 8400 feet, *deepe*).

Because *Rosalind's affection* ("lust, desire," TT, s.v. "Cupiditas") is so *deepe*, she cannot "sound" (restore to health, heal) her *affection* ("An abnormal bodily state; a disease; a medical complaint or condition," OED; cf. and see note: III.ii.386–391). *Rosalind* is "of no Bottom" ("of no Basis of Principles," ND) where *Orlando* is concerned, and in order to win him she will not scruple to behave like a "deep one" ("A thorough-paced rogue, a sly designing fellow," FG).

The Bay of Portugall is also a metaphor for extremely great sexual capacity (cf. "Look to your stern deer Mistress, and steer right, / Here's that will work, as high as the Bay of Portugal," Philip Massinger, *A Very Woman*). *Rosalind* wants *Orlando* to *fathome* ("clasp or embrace," OED) her and *fathome* ("penetrate," OED) her *bay* ("vagina," GW), but his "depth" (i.e., penis size; "depth" is literally "Measurement or distance from the top downwards," OED) is still *unknowne* to her. Nevertheless, she supposes he could sink *deepe* ("A play on sexual ingression," JH) enough to "sound" ("pierce, or goe deepe into," RC, s.v. *Profonder*) the *bottome* ("pubic region," GW2; also "posteriors," F&H).

203–204. ***bottomlesse... it runs out.*** *Rosalind* believes her *affection* (love) to be *bottomlesse* ("Inexhaustible, unfathomable," OED), but *Celia* thinks it *bottomlesse* ("Without foundation, baseless," OED). *Orlando* is a *bottomlesse* ("That has no bottom," OED) "vessel" (container, person), so as fast as *Rosalind* pours *affection in*, *it runs out* (leaks, escapes). Therefore, *Rosalind's* incessant talk of love is just "A Tale of a Tub with the Bottom out, a sleeveless frivolous Tale" (ND, s.v. "Bottom").

Celia also hints that *Rosalind's* own "bottom" (vagina; see note: *bottome*, line 202, above) is *bottomlesse* ("unsatiable," RC, s.v. "Profond") due to her "affection" (lust; see note: *affection*, line 201, above). So much "bottom" (i.e., semen; "bottom" is literally "the last portion of the wine in a cask," OED; see note: *Wine*, III.ii.200) has been "poured" *in* to *Rosalind's* "Bottomless Pit" ("the female pudenda," F&H) that it *runs out again*; cf. and see note: III.ii.200–201.

Ros. No, that same wicked Bastard of *Venus*, that was [205]
begot of thought, conceiv'd of spleene, and borne of
madnesse, that blinde rascally boy, that abuses every
ones eyes, because his owne are out, let him bee judge,
how deepe I am in love: ile tell thee *Aliena*, I cannot be
out of the sight of *Orlando*: Ile goe finde a shadow, and [210]
sigh till he come.

Cel. And Ile sleepe.

Exeunt.

---

205. ***wicked.*** *Wicked* is (a) "Roguish, mischievous"; and/or (b) "amorous, wanton" (F&H).

205. ***Bastard of Venus.*** *Venus,* the goddess of love and most beautiful of all the gods, was married to the deformed and ugly Vulcan, god of fire. Needless to say, *Venus*

did not find the marriage particularly satisfying, so she had an affair with Mars, the god of war. The result was the *Bastard* (illegitimate child), Cupid. (The figure was common: in *Orlando Furioso*, Robert Greene terms Cupid "the bastard brat of Mars.")

Because Cupid is a *Bastard* (a play on Fr. "Bastardeau": "A damme, or water-stop," RC, q.v.; OED notes that the word was "considered by Littré and Scheler to be a dim[inutive] of *bastard* 'a dike,'" s.v. "batardeau"), *Rosalind* thinks it impossible for her love to "run out" like "bastard, a kinde of sweete wine" (JF, s.v. "Bastardo"). Cf. lines 203–204, above.

206–207. ***begot of thought... madnesse.*** *Rosalind* here speaks not of the god "Cupid" but of "Cupid" (physical desire, EP) and recounts the successive steps to its birth: (1) the man "begets" it; (2) the woman "conceives" it; (3) it *is borne.*

206. ***thought.*** With possible play on *thought* as "mind": "physical passion" (FR). Also see note: *braine*, II.vii.42.

206. ***spleene.*** *Spleene* is (a) a sudden whim, impulse, or caprice; (b) eagerness or impetuosity; (c) delight or amusement; (d) passion, lust (EC, s.v. "Spleenful"); and/or (e) the "Penis and semen" (FR; *spleene* is literally "The milt of man or beast," HC, q.v.).

206. ***borne.*** With play on *borne* meaning (a) created; (b) carried; and/or (c) "Limited in scope, outlook, mental equipment" (OED, s.v. "borné"; OED dates from 1725, but the noun "bourn" meaning "A boundary" is dated from 1523; cf. RC's "Borner": "To limit, bound").

207. ***madnesse.*** Infatuation or sexual frenzy (JH, s.v. "Mad"). Also see note: III.ii.386.

207–208. ***blinde rascally boy... his owne are out.*** Because "love is *blinde*," Love (a.k.a. "Cupid") *abuses* (misguides, deceives) everyone else's *eyes* (eyesight, vision). Cupid also *abuses every ones eyes*—i.e., he "buggers" everyone in the "Blind Eye" ("podex," F&H; cf. and see note: *abus'd in sight*, III.v.83). Because Cupid is capable of such "rascalities" ("knaveries, rogueries, villanies," JF, s.v. "Furfanterie"), he is *rascally*, which means (a) "base, filthie" (JF, s.v. "Facchinarie"); (b) "untrustworthy" (OED); and/or (c) "paultrie, not worth an old shoo" (JF, s.v. "Ciabattarie").

207. ***boy.*** When Cupid was born, he did not mature but remained a *boy*. His mother *Venus* was alarmed, but Themis, the goddess of justice, told her that love could not grow without passion. *Venus* took the hint, conceived another child by Mars (she'd apparently completely given up on her husband Vulcan), and gave birth to Anteros (the "Anti-Eros" or "Anti-Cupid," who represents Reciprocal Love). Cupid thereafter thrived, but in popular tradition he is often represented as the small *boy* that he was before the birth of his brother. As a match-maker, Cupid can also be considered a *boy* (pander, FR).

208. ***judge.*** *Time* will *try Orlando* (lines 192–193, above), but *Cupid* will be *Rosalind's judge.*

210–211. ***shadow... sigh till he come.*** *Rosalind* is under a *shadow* (gloom, depression) and seeks a *shadow* (shady place) in which to "sye" ("collapse," OED). She has "no man," so she will *sigh* ("while away time by sighing," OED) like "the know-man or gnow-man of a diall; the shadow whereof pointeth out the howers" (JF, s.v. "Gnomone"); cf. III.ii.297–301. *Rosalind* plans to *sigh* until such time as *Orlando's shadow* ("gnomen": "cock of a diall," RC2) will *shadow* (sexually cover, JH) her. Then, she will *come* (achieve orgasm) beneath a *shadow* ("tester or canopy for a bed," OED). Cf. and see note: *diall*, II.vii.24.

Act IV, scene ii

Scena Secunda. [1]

Enter Jaques and {Amyens,} Lords, Forresters. [IV.ii.1]

Jaq. Which is he that killed the Deare?

Lord. Sir, it was I.

Jaq. Let's present him to the Duke like a Romane [5]

Conquerour, and it would doe well to set the Deares

horns upon his head, for a branch of victory; have you

no song Forrester for this purpose?

Lord. Yes Sir.

Jaq. Sing it: 'tis no matter how it bee in tune, so it [10]

make noyse enough.

Musicke, Song.

What shall he have that kild the Deare?

His Leather skin, and hornes to weare:

Then sing him home, the rest shall beare this burthen; [15]

Notes IV.ii.

5–7. ***Romane Conquerour... branch of victory.*** In *The boke named the Governour*, Thomas Elyot explains that "the Romanes... in the huntyng of redde dere and falowe... to them, whiche in this huntynge doo shewe moste prowesse and activitie, a garlande, or some other lyke token, [is] to be gyven in sygne of victory, and with a joyfull maner to be brought in the presence of him that is chiefe in the companye, there to receyve condygne [i.e., "deserved"] prayse for theyr good endevour."

As a sign *of victory, a Romane Conquerour* would customarily wear a garland *upon his head* and carry a *branch* of "Palme," for "The branches of this tree, were wont to be carried as a token of victory, because they are of that nature, that they will still shoot upward, though oppressed with never so great weight, the leaves thereof never fall" (JB, q.v.). Therefore, the "Palm" ("the Attire of a Buck," ND, q.v.; "Attire" is "The 'head-gear' of a deer," OED) makes an appropriate *branch of victory* for a man who wears a "horn"—i.e., for a man who is "branched" or cuckolded (see note: *wood*, III.iii.47).

13–14. ***kild the Deare... hornes to weare.*** The *Leather skin, and hornes* of the deer were prized trophies of the hunt: "The Horns, the Skin, and the right Shoulder, are the Keepers, or chief Huntsman's Fee" (Randle Holme, *Accademie of Armory*). In Thomas Lodge's *Rosalynde*, a teasing *Ganimede* challenges a love-sick and sullen Rosader / *Orlando* with "What newes Forrester? hast thou wounded some deere, and lost him in the fall? Care not man for so small a losse, thy fees was but the skinne, the shoulder, and the hornes: tis hunters lucke, to ayme faire and misse: and a woodmans fortune to strike and yet goe without the game."

When a *Deare* is *kild*, the horn call termed the "Mort, or Death" is "Blown at the Death of the Deer" (ND, q.v.). An effective "hunter" (ladies' man; see note: *Huntresse*, III.ii.6) brings about the "mort, or death, of the deer (or dear one)," "the sexual 'dying'... that is caused by the orgasm" (EP, s.v. "Mort o' the deer"). A hunter's *skin* ("Scrotum," FR) might be skilled with the *Leather* ("The female pudendum," F&H), but he is nevertheless a "Leather-head" ("a Thickskull'd, Heavy-headed Fellow," ND, q.v.) if he marries, for a married man cannot escape the cuckold's *hornes*. Cf. III.iii.48–49 and IV.i.57–62.

15. ***sing him home.*** To *sing* is "To make one's way with singing" (OED); to *sing home* means to rejoice triumphantly or revel carelessly (cf. "The Conny-catchers they shard the purchase, and went singing home as winners doe that have leave and leisure to laugh at the spoile of such wealthie and honest marchants," Robert Greene, *The Second part of Conny-catching*).

15. ***the rest shall beare this burthen.*** In *Shakespeare's Songbook*, Ross W. Duffin notes that these words do not appear in the earliest surviving music for this song, a circa 1625 handwritten manuscript. For this reason, along with the fact that stage directions in the First Folio are usually set in italics, this line is often interpreted as a stage direction calling for *the rest* (i.e., the *rest* of the *Lords* and *Forresters*) to join in the *burthen* (chorus, refrain).

However, the early music manuscript mentioned by Duffin has no established connection with Shakespeare or with any performance of *As you Like it*. Therefore, the line could have been cut by the manuscript's composer to more easily adapt the song to a "round" arrangement. Also, the Folio usually sets lyrics and words that are read in italics (cf. II.v.3–10, 40–45, and 50–55; III.ii.89–96 and 126–155; and IV.iii.45–46, 50–54, and 56–69); the stage directions within or adjacent to a block of such italicized lines are generally set in regular roman typeface (cf. line 12, above; II.v.3; II.vii.187; IV.iii.44 and 49; and V.iii.17). Therefore, this line was probably intended to be sung or spoken. The words certainly fit contextually, for *the rest* (i.e., the other men) *shall* also *beare* (suffer, endure) the same *burthen* (burdensome fate) of being made a cuckold.

Take thou no scorne to weare the horne,

It was a crest ere thou wast borne,

Thy fathers father wore it,

And thy father bore it,

The horne, the horne, the lusty horne, [20]

Is not a thing to laugh to scorne.

Exeunt.

16–19. ***Take thou no scorne... thy father bore it.*** A man wears *the horne* ("A horn-like appendage or ornament worn on the head," OED) as a *crest* (a heraldic device "originally borne by a knight on his helmet," OED) inherited from his *father*, and his *fathers father*. Thus, a man should not *Take scorne* ("be indignant," OED; "fret, fume, chafe, stomacke extreamely," RC, s.v. "Despiter"), because it is *no scorne* (shame, disgrace) *to weare the horne* (with obvious "allusion to the horns of the cuckold," JH).

A man would never have been *borne* if his *father*, and his *fathers father*, did not have such a *crest* (the "combe of a cocke," JM, s.v. "Crésta"; also the penis, GW, which notes that "The cock symbolism is apt since the crest is always erect while the male bird is in good health"). If a man's paternal ancestors had not worn *the horne* (i.e., experienced phallic erection; see note: *crooked-pated*, III.ii.82), then they would never have worn *the horne* (i.e., gotten married and doomed themselves to cuckoldry; cf. III.iii.48–49 and IV.i.57–62). Therefore, a man should not allow himself to be made a *scorne* (i.e., impotent; see note: *scorne*, II.iv.24) because he wears *the horne*. Instead of being "crestfallen" ("Langourous, languishing, dejected," RC, s.v. "Elangoré"), he should be "crest-risen" ("lustie, proud, stately, highminded," RC, s.v. "Acresté").

Moreover, a man who was *borne* when *the horne* (the stars that comprise the constellations of Aries and Taurus, OED) was at its *crest* (summit, zenith) is astrologically destined to *weare the horne* (be a cuckold; the "Ram" or Aries is associated with the cuckold's horns, JH, q.v.; "Taurus" carries the same associations, EC, q.v.).

21. ***a thing.*** With probable play on *thing* as penis (see note: *thing*, III.v.122).

21. ***to laugh to scorne.*** *To laugh to scorne* is to "to mock, flowt, frump, scoffe, deride, jeast at" (RC, s.v. "se Mocquer"). Also see notes: *laugh*, IV.i.151, and *scorne*, II.iv.24.

Act IV, scene iii

SCŒNA TERTIA. [1]

Enter Rosalind and Celia. [IV.iii.1]

Ros. How say you now, is it not past two a clock?

And heere much *Orlando.*

Cel. I warrant you, with pure love, & troubled brain, [5]

Enter Silvius. [IV.iii.2]

He hath t'ane his bow and arrowes, and is gone forth

To sleepe: looke who comes heere.

Sil. My errand is to you, faire youth,

My gentle *Phebe*, did bid me give you this: [10]

I know not the contents, but as I guesse

By the sterne brow, and waspish action

Which she did use, as she was writing of it,

It beares an angry tenure; pardon me,

I am but as a guiltlesse messenger. [15]

Ros. Patience her selfe would startle at this letter,

And play the swaggerer, beare this, beare all:

Shee saies I am not faire, that I lacke manners,

She calls me proud, and that she could not love me

Notes IV.iii.

5–8. ***with pure love... gone forth To sleepe.*** To distract himself from love, *Orlando* may have *t'ane his bow and arrowes* and *gone* hunting: he then grew exhausted and fell asleep. However, a man *with pure* (genuine, true, real) *love* would have a *troubled brain* and thus not *sleepe* easily, for "It is an ordinary thing in melancholike men and such as are troubled in the braine, not to sleepe and to continue in that estate many dayes and nights" (Simon Goulart, *Admirable and Memorable Histories*).

Celia hints that *Orlando's love* cannot be so *pure* as to *trouble* his *brain*, for he has entirely abandoned his courtship and *t'ane his bow and arrowes and gone forth To sleepe* (an expression meaning "to give up an ardent pursuit"; cf. "one business more will make me take my Bow and Arrows, and then lye down to sleep, with the Proverb," Thomas Killigrew, *The Second Part of Thomaso, or The Wanderer*). Either that, or *Orlando* is merely a man of *bow and arrowes* (i.e., of falsehood and lies; the *bow and arrowes* "are put for an ill-speaking and lying tongue," Thomas De Laune, *Tropologia*; cf. "Their tongue is as an arrowe shot out, it speaketh deceit: one speaketh peaceably to his neighbour with his mouth, but in heart he layeth his waite," Jeremiah 9:8).

Celia also intimates that *Orlando's* feelings are (a) *pure* (entirely) *love* (nothing; see note: *Love*, III.ii.289); and/or (b) *pure brain* (i.e., "complete shit"; "pure" is dung, HH, p. 131; also see note: *braines*, IV.i.96).

9. ***errand.*** *Silvius* has agreed to deliver an *errand* ("A message," OED) for *Phebe*, but he is unaware that she is forcing him to "run errands" ("pimp," FR) on her behalf.

10. ***My gentle Phebe.*** Because "love is blind" (see note: III.v.59), *Silvius* hasn't noticed that *Phebe* is not particularly *gentle* (courteous, kind, or refined).

11–14. ***I know not the contents... an angry tenure.*** *Phebe* appeared *waspish* ("Peevish," ND) and assumed an *angry tenure* (variant of "tenor": tone) when writing her letter to *Ganimed.* Therefore, *Silvius* assumes that the *contents* (subject matter) will cause "content" ("contention, dispute, quarrel," OED). In reality, *Phebe's* letter is not *angry* but *waspish* (amorous, EP; cf. lines 45–69, below). She hopes that her letter will establish *tenure* ("hold, or manner of holding a possession," RC2, q.v.) over *Ganimed* and bring about her own "content" (sexual fulfillment; see note: *content*, I.iii.145).

12. ***sterne brow.*** See notes: *sterner*, III.v.8; *sterne*, II.vii.117; and *browes*, III.v.51.

16–17. ***Patience her selfe... swaggerer.*** *Phebe* would *startle* (arouse, provoke) the gentle and silent goddess *Patience* (a.k.a. "Angerona," who was depicted with her mouth bound and with her finger to her lips, enjoining silence) to be a *swaggerer* ("A Martialist, or Warrior; also a fray-maker," RC, s.v. "Guerroyeur"; "A braver, affronter, abuser of people to their faces," RC, s.v. "Affronter").

In Christian tradition, *Patience* ("suffrance, endurance, forbearing, constancie in abiding evill, aptnes to suffer or abide," JF, s.v. "Patienza") is one of the seven heavenly virtues, so *Phebe* would apparently "try the *Patience* of a saint."

17. ***beare this, beare all.*** A variation of "take this and take all," a proverb akin to "If I suffer this I shall have worse." In *Paroemiologia Anglo-Latina*, John Clarke translates the phrase as "post folia cadunt arbores" ("First the leaves fall, then the trees"), meaning that to allow even a slight affront is to open oneself up to all manner of further abuse.

18–19. ***Shee saies... she could not love me.*** As will shortly be made clear (lines 45–69, below), *Phebe's* letter says no such thing.

Were man as rare as Phenix: 'od's my will, [20]

Her love is not the Hare that I doe hunt,

Why writes she so to me? well Shepheard, well,

This is a Letter of your owne device.

Sil. No, I protest, I know not the contents,

Phebe did write it. [25]

Ros. Come, come, you are a foole,

And turn'd into the extremity of love.

I saw her hand, she has a leatherne hand,

A freestone coloured hand: I verily did thinke

That her old gloves were on, but twas her hands: [30]

She has a huswives hand, but that's no matter:

I say she never did invent this letter,

This is a mans invention, and his hand.

Sil. Sure it is hers.

Ros. Why, tis a boysterous and a cruell stile, [35]

20. ***Were man as rare as Phenix.*** I.e., "If I were the only man alive." In *The English Dictionairie*, Henry Cockeram describes the *Phenix* as

> the rarest bird in the world, living onely in Arabia, there was never but one at a time in the world, it is of the bignes of an Eagle, of colour purple, with a bright coller of golde about his necke, a goodly taile, and a tuft of feathers on his head, he liveth above 600. yeares, and being olde, buildeth him an nest of Cinamon, and the twigges of Frenkincense, which he filleth with Spices, and with the labouring of his wings in the Sunne, setteth it on fire, and is there consumed in it, out of whose ashes there groweth a worme, and of the worme another Phenix.

20. ***'od's.*** A contraction of "God save."

21. ***the Hare that I doe hunt.*** Proverbially, "He who hunts two hares leaves one and loses the other. No one can do well or properly two things at once" (DPF). *Rosalind*, who is now in hot pursuit of *Orlando*, is herself a *Hare* (transsexual; see note: *Conie*, III.ii.333). She therefore has no interest in "hunting" (sexually pursuing; see note: *Huntresse*, III.ii.6) *Phebe* for her *Hare* (female genitalia; see note: *Conie*, III.ii.333). Also see note: *haire*, III.v.51.

26–27. ***a foole... the extremity of love.*** *Silvius* is *a foole* ("an asse," JF, s.v. "Bambaro") that has (a) been *turn'd into* (become) *the extremity* (paramount desperation) *of love*; and (b) been *turn'd* (driven) *into* love's *extremity* (i.e., "ass"; see note: *extremest*, II.i.46). Cf. *straights of Fortune*, V.ii.68.

28. ***I saw her hand.*** A possible allusion to *Phebe's* "showing her cards," or revealing her intentions.

28. ***a leatherne hand.*** *Phebe's* (a) *hand* is *leatherne* (brown or coarse, resembling leather); (b) *hand* (handwriting) is *leatherne* (awkward; OED records *leatherne* as an adverb meaning "clumsily"); (c) *hand* (style of expression) *is leatherne* (abusive; to "leather" is "to beat," FG); and/or (d) *hand* (vagina; see note: *hand*, I.ii.246) is *leatherne* (i.e., "loose" or pliant like "leather": "The female pudendum," F&H; also see note: *leatherne*, II.i.41).

29. ***freestone coloured hand.*** *Phebe's hand* is the color of *Freestone* (brownish-gray). *Freestone* was widely used in fortifications, so if *Phebe's hand* (handwriting, style of expression) is *coloured* (has the character or tone) of *freestone*, then her heart must be just as impenetrable.

31. ***a huswives hand.*** *Phebe* (a) has the weathered *hand of* a "huswife": "a housholde or kitching woman servant, a kitching drudge" (JF, s.v. Massára); and (b) has both the *hand* (writing style) and the *hand* (vagina; see note: *hand*, I.ii.246) of a "huswife" (whore; see note: *houswife*, I.ii.32).

33. ***invention.*** With play on *invention* as (a) a literary composition; (b) in rhetoric, the "finding out or selection of topics to be treated, or arguments to be used" (OED); and/or (c) excrement (see note: *invention*, line 38, below).

35. ***boysterous.*** *Boysterous* is (a) "vehement, violent, raging, furious, most forcible" (RC, s.v. "Impetueux"); and (b) unskillful or indelicate (OED).

A stile for challengers: why, she defies me,

Like Turke to Christian: womens gentle braine

Could not drop forth such giant rude invention,

Such Ethiop words, blacker in their effect

Then in their countenance: will you heare the letter? [40]

Sil. So please you, for I never heard it yet:

Yet heard too much of *Phebes* crueltie.

Ros. She *Phebes* me: marke how the tyrant writes.

Read.

Art thou god, to Shepherd turn'd? [45]

That a maidens heart hath burn'd.

---

36. ***A stile for challengers.*** *Phebe's stile* (literary composition, OED) has the *stile* (manner of expression) of a "challenger" ("provoker in any combat or quarrell," JF, s.v. "Attore").

36–37. ***she defies me, Like Turke to Christian.*** The "defiance" ("Renunciation of faith, allegiance, or amity," OED) between *Turke* and *Christian* dates back to A.D. 380 when Emperor Theodosius I declared Christianity the official religion of the Byzantine Empire. Squabbles between *Turke* and *Christian* continued for the next millenia, and the Crusades did nothing to improve relations.

To the Elizabethan Englishman, the *Turke* symbolized all that was ruthless and barbaric. A *Turke* was a "cruel, hard-hearted man" (FG), and Turks were "reputed to be lechers, castrators, ambisexuals, sodomites" (FR). *Phebe* subjects *Ganimed* to "Turkish treatment" ("barbarous usage," FG, s.v. "Turk"), and her abusive "defiance" ("challenge, for a single combat," RC, s.v. "Cartée") is as unpleasant as being "put to death with a stake as the Turkes do the Christians, putting a stake or sharpe pole in at the fundament, and out at the mouth" (JF, s.v. "Impalare").

There is possible additional play on *Turke* as a synonym of "Tartar" (both an inhabitant of Asia and a purgative, FR) and "defy" meaning "defecate" (see note: *defying*, III.ii.354). Cf. *braine, drop forth, rude invention, blacker*, and *countenance*, lines 37–40, below.

37–38. ***womens gentle braine... rude invention.*** Renaissance physicians were firmly rooted in the concept of man as microcosm (see note: *in little*, III.ii.141). Thus, they believed that the anatomy and functions of the human *braine* mirrored that of the larger body. The hemispheres of the *braine*, because of their suggestive shape, were "called according to their figure clunes, the haunches or buttockes. Betwene which lyeth that hole [i.e., the latter foramen], whiche... seemeth like unto the fundament" (John Banister, *The Historie of Man*). Just like the buttocks and fundament of the body, the *braine* expelled "excrements" which manifested themselves, among other things, as tears, phlegm, hair, migraine headaches, and ideas (cf. "Our Religion in England is no newe excrement of the braine of man, but drawne out of the fountaine of all trueth, God himselfe," Thomas Nashe, *The First parte of Pasquils Apologie*).

Ganimed thinks that the *gentle braine* of a woman *Could not drop* ("mute, or drop, as birds doe," RC, s.v. "Esmeutir") *forth* such "droppings" ("dung," OED). This *invention* (i.e., "shit"; cf. "his invention had a hard stoole, and yet it was for his ease," Thomas Nashe, *Strange Newes*) is simply too *giant* (enormous; also stupid and cruel; the traditional giants of folklore "are cannibals of vast stature and immense muscular power, but as stupid as they are violent and treacherous," DPF) and *rude* (large or inexpert; also "offensive through reference to or representation of sexual or excretory organs or functions," OED, which dates from 1961, but cf. Henry More's 1651 *The second lash of Alazonomastix*: "I have beat thee from the Bung-hole, and that rude expression borrowed thence"). Also see note: *braines*, IV.i.96.

39–40. ***Ethiop words... their countenance.*** If written in black ink, *Phebe's words* would be *blacker* in their *countenance* (appearance) and *effect* ("outward manifestation," OED) than an *Ethiop* ("a blacke Moore, or man of Ethiope," TT, s.v. "Ethiopo"). Her words are also *blacker* (more wicked or deadly) in their *effect* (the impression produced on a reader) *Then in their countenance* (i.e., "continence": "Tenor, contents," OED).

Rosalind suggests that *Phebe* is a "blacker" (a "blackener; bleacher, darkener, obscurer," RC, s.v. "Noircisseur") who "blackens" (i.e., slanders or "throws shit" at) her enemies (cf. and see note: *countenance*, I.i.19). However, as will shortly be revealed (lines 45–69, below), *Phebe's words* are not actually "black" (destructive). Instead, they convey the *effect* ("affect": "desire; amorous desire," EP; "lust," GW) of her "black" (vagina; see note: *blacke*, III.ii.94) and *countenance* (with play on "cunt," JH).

43. ***She Phebes me.*** *She Phebes* (i.e., "Ephebes") *Ganimed*, or idolizes him like an "Ephebe," an ancient Greek statue depicting a beautiful and nude adolescent boy. Although *Ganimed* is young, *Phebe* nevertheless considers him an "Ephebe" ("A mariageable youth or stripling; one thats foureteene and upwards," RC, q.v.). Cf. lines 65–67, below, and III.v.117, 120, and 122; also see note: *youth*, II.iii.19.

43. ***tyrant.*** As a bird, a "Phebe" is a *tyrant* flycatcher (OED, which dates this usage from 1700); the "Fly-catcher" is "The female pudendum" (F&H).

45–46. ***Art thou god... heart hath burn'd.*** Even though *Ganimed* has treated *Phebe* with "heart-burning" ("ill-will," "spite," TB, s.v. "Malovolence"), he has set her heart aflame. *Phebe* imagines *Ganimed* as the human incarnation of either (a) the *god* Cupid, whose arrows were commonly pictured with flaming heads; or (b) the *god* Jupiter (a.k.a. "Jove" or "Zeus"), whose "thunderbolts" were figured as flaming arrows from heaven. Jupiter may be the better candidate because (a) Jupiter pursued many lovers, while Cupid had only one ill-fated affair with Psyche; and (b) *Phebe* alludes to Jupiter's pursuit of Nemesis, the goddess of *vengeance* (lines 53–54, below).

Can a woman raile thus?

Sil. Call you this railing?

Ros. Read.

Why, thy godhead laid a part, [50]

War'st thou with a womans heart?

Did you ever heare such railing?

Whiles the eye of man did wooe me,

That could do no vengeance to me.

Meaning me a beast. [55]

If the scorne of your bright eine

Have power to raise such love in mine,

Alacke, in me, what strange effect

Would they worke in milde aspect?

Whiles you chid me, I did love, [60]

How then might your praiers move?

He that brings this love to thee,

Little knowes this Love in me:

And by him seale up thy minde,

Whether that thy youth and kinde [65]

50. ***thy godhead laid a part.*** *Ganimed*, as a god in human form (lines 45–46, above), has *laid a part* ("put off, given over, abandoned, forsaken, omitted, forgone," RC, s.v. "Laissé") his *godhead* (divinity).

51. ***War'st thou with a womans heart.*** The arrow is a weapon of war employed by both Cupid and Jove (see note: lines 45–46, above). *Ganimed* has started a "war" ("amorous struggle," FR) with *Phebe*, and it looks as though *Ganimed* will *Wars't* (i.e., "worst": "defeat, overcome, get the better of," OED) her *womans heart.*

53–55. ***the eye of man... a beast.*** When a person gave another the "evil *eye*" (looked upon him with envy), his *eye* "darted noxious rays on objects which they glared upon" (DPF). The *eye of* a mortal man such as *Silvius*, who looked upon *Phebe* with *covetousnesse* (III.v.98), could do her *no vengeance* (i.e., not arouse reciprocal love; *vengeance* is literally "retributive injury"; cf. and see notes: *murder in mine eye*, III.v.13; *consenting*, V.ii.9, and *sight*, V.ii.34). However, *Ganimed*, a god in human form (lines 45–46, above), has proven to be her "Nemesis" ("the Goddess of Revenge," TB, q.v.).

Nemesis (a.k.a. *vengeance*) dwelt among men during the golden age, but she ultimately despaired of humanity's wickedness and withdrew to the heavens where she now wields thunderbolts to smite the arrogant (cf. and see note: line 45, above). She also asserts a baleful influence as the planet Kronos (a.k.a. "Saturn" or the "Nemesis Stella; by Astrologers term'd Infortuna Major," Marcus Manilius, *Astronomica*; cf. and see note: *milde aspect*, line 59, below).

Phebe clearly considers *Ganimed* divine (lines 45–46, above), but *Rosalind* purposely misconstrues *Phebe's* verses to mean that *Ganimed*, as Jove's incarnation, is not a *man* but *a beast* ("A god or a man, the former behaving like a sex-driven animal, the latter behaving with the sexual appetite of an animal," EP). In *Rosalind's* deliberate misinterpretation, *Phebe* is figured as *vengeance* (a.k.a. "Nemesis"), whom Jove (a.k.a. "Jupiter" or "Zeus") ardently pursued in "all shapes of every animal" (Athanaeus, *The Deipnosophists*). Cf. and see note: *Jove in a thatch'd house*, III.iii.9–10.

56–59. ***bright eine... milde aspect.*** *Eine* is (a) an archaic plural of "eye"; (b) poetically used for heavenly bodies (OED, s.v. "eye"); and (c) "The groine, or grine; the part thats next about our privities," RC, s.v. "Eine"). *Ganimed's eine* (eyes) are *bright* (shining and lustrous as stars), but *Phebe* is also attracted by his *bright* (i.e., testicles; L. "polimen" means both "testicle" and "brightness," JA, p. 69) and *eine* (groin, genitals; cf. and see note: *eies*, III.v.49).

Aspect means "beholding or viewing, sight, presence or beauty. In Astronomy it signifies the distance between the Planets and heavenly signes" (TB, q.v.). In regards to *Phebe*, *Ganimed's aspect* is now *bright* ("Burning, flaming, verie hotte," TT, s.v. "Flāgrans"), but *Phebe* hopes it will change to a *milde* ("Of light or a luminous body: shining softly, lambent"; also "gracious, clement," OED) *aspect* (influential planetary position). With luck, *Ganimed* will no longer emit baleful *vengeance* (line 54, above) but exert the salutatory astrological power of the all-powerful god and planet Jupiter (a.k.a. the "fortuna major"). Cf. and see notes: lines 45–46, above.

64. ***seale up thy minde.*** *Phebe* wants *Ganimed* to *seale up* ("decide irrevocably," OED) his *minde* (feelings, intentions) and then *seale up* (fasten *up* with a *seale* of wax) his *minde* (written opinion) and return it via *Silvius*. Hopefully, *Ganimed's minde* ("physical passion," FR) will *seale up* ("consummate a marriage by sexual congress," JH, q.v.). If so, he will *up* (raise) his *seale* (penis, JH) and affix his *seale* ("testes," F&H) to *Phebe's seale* ("maidenhead," GW2; "female pudendum; cunt," F&H, s.v. "monosyllable").

65. ***kinde.*** See notes: *kinde,* II.vii.97, and *kindely*, II.iii.56.

Will the faithfull offer take

Of me, and all that I can make,

Or else by him my love denie,

And then Ile studie how to die.

Sil. Call you this chiding? [70]

Cel. Alas poore Shepheard.

Ros. Doe you pitty him? No, he deserves no pitty:

wilt thou love such a woman? what to make thee an in-

strument, and play false straines upon thee? not to be en-

dur'd. Well, goe your way to her; (for I see Love hath [75]

made thee a tame snake) and say this to her; That if she

love me, I charge her to love thee: if she will not, I will

never have her, unlesse thou intreat for her: if you bee a

true lover hence, and not a word; for here comes more

company. [80]

Exit {*Silvius*}. [IV.iii.3]

Enter Oliver.

Oliv. Good morrow, faire ones: pray you, (if you know)

Where in the Purlews of this Forrest, stands

A sheep-coat, fenc'd about with Olive-trees. [85]

66–67. ***the faithfull offer take... make.*** *Phebe* makes *Ganimed* an *offer* ("proposal of marriage," OED). If *Ganimed* will *take* (marry) her, he will be entitled to *all that* she *can make*, meaning (a) do; (b) become; (c) provide; (d) "give birth to, conceive" (OED); and/or (e) earn (a married woman's income legally belonged to her husband; English law did not grant married women the right to separate earnings until 1870). Also see note: *make*, IV.i.157.

68–69. ***my love denie... studie how to die.*** If *Ganimed* "denies" (refuses) *Phebe's* love, she *will studie* (meditate upon; decide) *how to die*— i.e., decide the manner of her suicide. Cf. and see note: IV.i.94–96.

73–74. ***an instrument... false straines upon thee.*** Like a musician who plays *false* (not in pitch, out of tune) *straines* (notes, music) on an *instrument*, *Phebe* has "played false" (deceived, betrayed) *Silvius* and used him as an *instrument* (tool, weapon). *Phebe*, who is of a *false* (deceitful, faithless) "strain" ("kind, class, or sort of persons," OED), has "strained" (compelled) *Silvius* into "strain" ("Constraint, bondage," OED). By exploiting *Silvius'* desire to "strain" ("copulate," F&H), *Phebe* forces him to make *straines* ("Extreme or excessive effort[s]," OED) on her behalf.

Phebe has also (a) made *straines upon Silvius* (i.e., "shit on him"; "strain" is literally "Something strained or squeezed out"; to "strain" is to "make efforts to evacuate the bowels," OED); and (b) made him into an *instrument* (i.e., a "pussy"; literally the "female pudendum," F&H); cf. *tame snake*, line 76, below

74–75. ***not to be endur'd.*** See note: *endure*, I.i.25; and cf. *instrument*, lines 73–74, above, and *tame snake*, line 76, below.

75–76. ***Love hath made thee a tame snake.*** *Love* is indeed powerful if it can *tame* a *snake*, for in popular tradition the *snake* is the only creature that cannot be made *tame*: "It is also to be considered, how untame by nature these vipers (for the most part) are; in so much as they be not by mans industrie or cunning to be made familiar, or traind to doo anie thing" (Reginald Scot, *Discoverie of Withcraft*).

Silvius' Love for *Phebe* has (a) made him a *tame* ("weak, spiritless, insipid, dull," OED) *snake* ("a wretched or miserable fellow," RC, s.v. "Haire"); and (b) made his *snake* (penis, GW) *tame* (impotent, emasculated; see note: *entame*, III.v.53).

Rosalind additionally hints that *Phebe* is a "viper" (a "false or treacherous person," OED; also an "emblem of destructive lust," GW); it was believed that when vipers "engender, the male putteth his head into the females mouth, which she biteth off" (HC, s.v. "Viper").

78–79. ***unlesse thou intreat... not a word.*** *Rosalind* fears that *Silvius* is so devout in his love that he will actually *intreat* on *Phebe's* behalf. Thus, she instructs him to go *hence* and *not* speak *a word*.

82. ***Enter Oliver.*** An audience unfamiliar with the plot of *As you Like it* would doubtless feel apprehensive upon seeing *Oliver* at this point. Up until now, he has been one of the play's villains, and he was last seen setting out to bring *Orlando* back *dead, or living* (III.i.8).

83. ***faire ones.*** A "fair one" is either a "well favoured chylde" or a "praty mayden" (TE, s.v. "Bellatulus"); "fair one" is also used to address a "litle sweete hart" (TT, s.v. "Bellātŭlus").

84. ***Purlews.*** The *Purlews* are the "skirts, of forrests; the places that be next, or neere adjoyning, unto them" (RC, s.v. "Rain de forests"). Cf. *skirts of the Forrest*, III.ii.331.

85. ***Olive-trees.*** See note: *Olives*, III.v.79.

Cel. West of this place, down in the neighbor bottom
The ranke of Oziers, by the murmuring streame
Left on your right hand, brings you to the place:
But at this howre, the house doth keepe it selfe,
There's none within. [90]

Oli. If that an eye may profit by a tongue,
Then should I know you by description,
Such garments, and such yeeres: the boy is faire,
Of femall favour, and bestowes himselfe
Like a ripe sister: the woman low [95]
And browner then her brother: are not you
The owner of the house I did enquire for?

Cel. It is no boast, being ask'd, to say we are.

Oli. *Orlando* doth commend him to you both,
And to that youth hee calls his *Rosalind*, [100]
He sends this bloudy napkin; are you he?

Ros. I am: what must we understand by this?

Oli. Some of my shame, if you will know of me
What man I am, and how, and why, and where
This handkercher was stain'd. [105]

Cel. I pray you tell it.

86–87. ***West of this place... ranke of Oziers.*** The *place* (location) that *Oliver* seeks is to the *West, down in the neighbor* (close by, adjoining) *bottom* ("a low dale," "a vale, a valley," RC, s.v. "Bassa"). To find it, *Celia* directs him to the *ranke* (row) *of Oziers* (willow trees).

Oziers are indeed *ranke* (smelly): taken internally, the bark and leaves are "cold and moist flourishing very late, and causing ventosities" (Pierre de La Primaudaye, *The French Academie*). These *Oziers* are thus appropriately located in the *West* ("Buttocks," FR, who links the semantics to "Postīca": "that part which is toward the West, or behind us," TT; cf. and see note: *poste,* IV.i.11).

Celia might also imagine her *place* (vagina; see note: *misplaced,* I.ii.36) *down* (in "the supine position of sexual intercourse," JH) under *Oliver's* "neighborly" ("Friendly, Kind, Loving, Obliging," ND) *bottom* (genitals and posteriors; see note: *bottome,* IV.i.202). If *Celia* is *ranke* (sexually excited; see note: *ranke,* I.ii.104), she needs *Oziers* (willows, whose blossoms were used as an antaphrodisiac).

87–88. ***The ranke of Oziers... right hand.*** Perhaps *Celia* means (a) *The ranke of Oziers* (willows) will be on the *right hand,* and to find the place you should follow the *murmering streame* on the *Left*; or (b) you will find the place after you have *Left* (departed from) *The ranke of Oziers by the murmuring streame* and headed towards the *right hand* side. Either way, her directions would be difficult to follow.

91–92. ***If that an eye... know you by description.*** *Oliver's eye* (sight) has "profited" (gained, benefited) *from a tongue* (i.e., the spoken *description* of the pair that he presumably received from *Orlando*). However, in order to locate *Celia, Duke Frederick* sent *Oliver* to find *Orlando* (II.ii.12–21 and III.i.7–10). Therefore, *Oliver* might readily note the resemblance of *Aliena* and *Ganimed* to *Celia* and *Rosalind* and draw the logical conclusion (cf. lines 176–177, 182–184, 186–187, 192–193, below, and V.ii.22).

In addition, *profit* is "Sexual pleasure"; for possible bawdy wordplay, see notes: *eies,* III.v.49, and *tongue,* III.ii.242.

93. ***boy.*** *Boy* is not necessarily pejorative, but see note: *Boy,* I.i.53.

93–96. ***the boy is faire... browner.*** *Faire* here means "light-skinned." *Rosalind,* who took on masculine attire as a disguise, did not worry much about her ladylike complexion (cf. III.ii.382–383). *Celia,* however, attempted to make herself *browner* (more tan, darker skinned; cf. I.iii.119). Also see note: *a good colour,* III.iv.13.

94–95. ***Of femall favour... ripe sister.*** *Ganimed* has a *femall favour* (face, appearance) and *bestowes* (presents, carries) *himselfe* not *like Aliena's* brother but like *a sister* who is *ripe*: either (a) knowledgeable or studious; (b) prone to mischief; (c) "fine, excellent" (OED); (d) mature; or (e) of marriageable age. *Ganimed* also *bestowes* (grants his [homo-]sexual favors; see note: *bestowed,* I.ii.34) *himself like a ripe* (shamelessly wanton; see note: *ripe,* II.vii.30) *sister* (whore, JH).

95. ***low.*** *Low* can mean (a) short; (b) humble or meek; (c) ordinary or commonplace; and/or (d) coarse or vulgar.

101. ***napkin.*** Handkerchief.

Oli. When last the yong *Orlando* parted from you,

He left a promise to returne againe

Within an houre, and pacing through the Forrest,

Chewing the food of sweet and bitter fancie, [110]

Loe what befell: he threw his eye aside,

And marke what object did present it selfe

Under an old Oake, whose bows were moss'd with age

And high top, bald with drie antiquitie:

A wretched ragged man, ore-growne with haire [115]

Lay sleeping on his back; about his necke

A greene and guilded snake had wreath'd it selfe,

Who with her head, nimble in threats approach'd

The opening of his mouth: but sodainly

Seeing *Orlando*, it unlink'd it selfe, [120]

And with indented glides, did slip away

Into a bush, under which bushes shade

---

109. ***Within an houre.*** An apparent inconsistency; cf. IV.i.171–172.

109. ***pacing.*** Walking, especially "as an expression of anxiety, frustration, etc" (OED).

110. ***Chewing the food.*** *Orlando* is given to "Ruminate," or "To chew over againe

as beasts doe, that chew the cud: wherfore it is often taken for to studie and thinke much of a matter" (JB, q.v.).

110. ***fancie.*** See note: *Fancie*, III.ii.355.

111. ***Loe.*** "Looke, see"; "behold, there" (RC, s.v. "Voilà).

112. ***object.*** *Oliver* presented himself to *Orlando* as an *object* ("something placed before or presented to the eyes or other senses," OED). He was also an *object* (variant spelling of "abject," OED), meaning (a) a "base minded, fall-hearted coward" (TB, s.v. "Niding"); (b) a "skurvie fellow, a scoundrell" (JF, s.v. "Vigliacco"); and/or (c) "A person cast off or cast out; an outcast, exile; a degraded or downtrodden person" (OED).

113–124. ***Under an old Oake... cowching.*** This speech contains many allusions to armorial bearings and terms, but the significance (if any) is unclear. These are, in order, *Under* or "beneath," line 113; *Oake*, line 113; *ragged* or "raguly," line 115; *haire* (or possibly "hare"), line 115; *sleeping* or "dormant," line 116; *greene* or "vert," line 117; *guilded* or "Or," line 117; *snake* or "serpent," line 117; *wreath'd*, line 117; *unlink'd* ("link" alludes to either the "shackle" or "chain"), line 120; *indented*, line 121; *glides*, line 121; and the *Lyonnesse cowching* or "lion couchant," lines 123–124.

113–114. ***an old Oake... drie.*** In contrast to the thriving *Oake* under which *Orlando* sleeps that *droppes forth fruite* (III.ii.232–235), this *Oake* is *bald* ("Leafless" or "barren," OED) and *drie* (impotent and/or venereally infected, JH). Thus, it symbolizes *Oliver's* "impotency" (i.e., helplessness). Cf. *ragged*, line 115, below, and the threat imposed by female creatures in lines 117–118 and 123–124, below.

115. ***ragged.*** *Ragged* means (a) "tattered; poore, needie, beggerlie in array" (RC, s.v. "Loqueteux"); (b) "Of an animal or its coat: rough, shaggy, unkempt; with fur hanging in tufts" (OED); and/or (c) impotent or emasculated (a "rag" is "a castrated scrotum," FR; in heraldry, *ragged* is "raguly": "Any bearing that is ragged, like the trunk or limbs of a tree lopped of its branches," Anonymous, *The Manual of Heraldry*).

115. ***ore-growne with haire.*** *Oliver's* proliferation of *haire* is not a symbol of virility but of stagnation; cf. the image of the moss enveloping the tree in line 113, above.

116–119. ***Lay sleeping on his back... The opening of his mouth.*** According to Edward Topsell's *The Historie of Serpents*,

> Serpents doe sometimes creepe into the mouthes of them that are fast asleepe, where-uppon a certaine Poet saith...
>
> Then would I not upon the grasse,
> Lye on my back where Serpents passe.
>
> For if a man sleepe open-mouthed, they slilie convey themselves in, and wind & role them round in compasse, so taking up their lodging in the stomacke, and then is the poore wretched man, miserably and pittifully tormented; his life is more bitter then death.

117. ***A greene and guilded snake.*** The *snake* symbolizes both sin and redemption; the dual symbolism arose because the same *snake* that was "a female symbol of the renewal of the earth's vegetation" later "became the serpent of the Garden of Eden in Hebrew mythology" (JH2, s.v. "Snake").

The *greene* and *guilded* ("glistering like gold," JB, s.v. "Deaurate") colors of the *snake* suggest that even though *Oliver's* own *snake* (penis) was *guilded* (i.e., "gelded"), he yet has hope of again being *greene* (fertile, virile; also see note: *greene*, III.iii.82).

121. ***indented.*** *Indented* means "That hath many turnings, windings, or bendings, crooked, full of crinkle crankles" (TT, s.v. "Sĭnuōsus").

A Lyonnesse, with udders all drawne drie,
Lay cowching head on ground, with catlike watch
When that the sleeping man should stirre; for 'tis [125]
The royall disposition of that beast
To prey on nothing, that doth seeme as dead:
This seene, *Orlando* did approach the man,
And found it was his brother, his elder brother.

Cel. O I have heard him speake of that same brother, [130]
And he did render him the most unnaturall
That liv'd amongst men.

Oli. And well he might so doe,
For well I know he was unnaturall.

Ros. But to *Orlando*: did he leave him there [135]
Food to the suck'd and hungry Lyonnesse?

Oli. Twice did he turne his backe, and purpos'd so:
But kindnesse, nobler ever then revenge,
And Nature stronger then his just occasion,
Made him give battell to the Lyonnesse: [140]
Who quickly fell before him, in which hurtling
From miserable slumber I awaked.

Cel. Are you his brother?

123. ***A Lyonnesse with udders all drawne drie.*** Shakespeare draws this episode from Lodge's *Rosalynde*, but the lion of Lodge's novel is unquestionably male. Shakespeare perhaps changed the animal's sex due to (a) the mother lion's reputation for ferocity when nursing her young; (b) the slang sense of *Lyonnesse* as "harlot" (F&H); or (c) the belief that in the "Lion Year" (the one year in seven when the *Lyonesse* supposedly whelped) other creatures become infertile. Superstition ascribed "sterility to the lioness. The women of antiquity, when they met a lioness, considered it as an omen of sterility... under the sign of the lion, the earth also becomes arid, and consequently unfruitful" (Angelo De Gubernatis, *Zoological Mythology*). Cf. *bald* and *drie*, line 114, above; *ragged*, line 115, above; and *guilded*, line 117, above.

124. ***cowching.*** A *cowching* lion (or, in heraldry, a "lion couchant") is "Lying down; head erect, and tail beneath him" (DPF, s.v. "Lion")—i.e., in a position ready to pounce.

126–127. ***royall disposition... seeme as dead.*** The lion is commonly known as the "King of Beasts," and according to popular belief "Lions hate to pray on dead carkasses" (Thomas Lodge, *Rosalynde*). In *The Historie of Foure-Footed Beastes*, Edward Topsell explains that if lions

> leave of their meate, they returne not to it againe to eate it afterwardes, whereof some assigned the cause to bee in the meate, because they can endure nothing which is unsweete, stale, or stinking; but in my opinion they do it throgh the pride of their naturs, resembling in al things a Princely majesty, and therefore scorne to have one dish twice presented to their own table.

Topsell also notes that lions' "clemencie in that fierce and angry nature is also worthy commendation, and to be wondered at in such beastes, for if one prostrate himselfe unto them as it were in petition for his life, they often spare except in extremitie of famine... the Lyon will spare a prostrate suppliant, making confession unto him that hee is overcome."

131–134. ***render... unnaturall.*** *Orlando* "rendered" (depicted, portrayed) his brother's "nature" (character, temperament) as *unnaturall* ("treacherous, villainous, knavish, wicked, cruel, bad, lewde, ungodlie," JF, s.v. "Sceleráto"). *Orlando* thus "rendered" (covered) *Oliver* as with a coat of "render" (plaster, of which dung was a principal ingredient). Also see notes: *Nature*, I.ii.43, and *naturall*, I.ii.279.

138. ***kindnesse, nobler ever then revenge.*** An ancient sentiment with many variations; cf. "Thou canst nat revenge thy wronge in nobler wyse / Than whan of thy foes / thou mayst have thyne intent / To pardon theyr trespas and theyr malyce dispyse" (Dominicus Mancinus, *The Myrrour of Good Maners*).

Orlando's kindnesse ("Natural inclination"; also "Kinship; near relationship; natural affection arising from this," OED) and *nature* (temperament) were *nobler* (greater) than his *revenge* ("desire to be revenged," OED). Thus, he did not take advantage when his *just* (righteous) *occasion* (opportunity) arose.

141–142. ***in which hurtling... I awaked.*** *In* (during) *which* (that) *hurtling* ("conflict," OED), *Oliver awaked From miserable slumber.*

Ros. Was't you he rescu'd?

Cel. Was't you that did so oft contrive to kill him? [145]

Oli. 'Twas I: but 'tis not I: I doe not shame
To tell you what I was, since my conversion
So sweetly tastes, being the thing I am.

Ros. But for the bloody napkin?

Oli. By and by: [150]
When from the first to last betwixt us two,
Teares our recountments had most kindely bath'd,
As how I came into that Desert place.
In briefe, he led me to the gentle Duke,
Who gave me fresh aray, and entertainment, [155]
Committing me unto my brothers love,
Who led me instantly unto his Cave,
There stript himselfe, and heere upon his arme
The Lyonnesse had torne some flesh away,
Which all this while had bled; and now he fainted, [160]
And cride in fainting upon *Rosalinde*.
Briefe, I recover'd him, bound up his wound,
And after some small space, being strong at heart,
He sent me hither, stranger as I am

147. ***conversion.*** *Oliver* relates his *conversion* ("A turning from evill to good," JB, q.v.) in quasi-religious terms (cf. and see note: line 152, below). In Lodge's *Rosalynde,* Saladyne / *Oliver* undergoes a genuine *conversion,* but Shakespeare's re-working of the story leaves open the possibility that *Oliver* is just following through on *Duke Frederick's* orders in order to win back his lands (III.i.11–14).

152. ***Teares our recountments... bath'd.*** "Recountment" is synonymous with "recount" meaning "An account, a narrative; narration" (OED). As a verb, "recount" means "recounter," both (a) "To offer or give a pledge in return for another"; and (b) "To meet, to encounter by chance; to come upon or fall in with" (OED). Therefore, upon their "recountment" (chance re-encounter), *Orlando* and *Oliver* exchanged *recountments* (accounts of themselves and pledges of friendship).

Not in the "bath of birth" ("The female pudendum; Cunt," F&H, s.v. "monosyllable") but in a "bath" ("The immersion or washing of baptism," OED) of *Teares* were *Oliver* and *Orlando* "recounted" (i.e., re-born as brothers from the "count" or "cunt").

152. ***kindely.*** See note: *kindnesse,* line 138, above.

155. ***aray, and entertainment.*** Clothing and food.

161. ***And cride... upon Rosalinde.*** *Orlando* completely forgot his appointment with *Ganimed* due to his battle with the lioness and his reunion with his brother. When he remembered, he *cride Rosalinde's* name.

164. ***stranger.*** *Oliver* is a *stranger,* meaning (a) "one with whom we have no familiaritie" (RC, s.v. "Estrangier"); and (b) "a newborn child" (OED). Cf. and see notes: lines 147 and 152, above.

To tell this story, that you might excuse [165]

His broken promise, and to give this napkin

Died in this bloud, unto the Shepheard youth,

That he in sport doth call his *Rosalind.*

Cel. Why how now *Ganimed*, sweet *Ganimed.*

Oli. Many will swoon when they do look on bloud. [170]

Cel. There is more in it; Cosen *Ganimed.*

Oli. Looke, he recovers.

Ros. I would I were at home.

Cel. Wee'll lead you thither:

I pray you will you take him by the arme. [175]

Oli. Be of good cheere youth: you a man?

You lacke a mans heart.

Ros. I doe so, I confesse it:

Ah, sirra, a body would thinke this was well counterfei-

ted, I pray you tell your brother how well I counterfei- [180]

ted: heigh-ho.

Oli. This was not counterfeit, there is too great te-

stimony in your complexion, that it was a passion of ear-

nest.

Ros. Counterfeit, I assure you. [185]

169–170. ***Why how now... Many will swoon.*** In the absence of a written stage direction to *swoon*, the actor playing *Rosalind* will not do so until he hears the spoken stage direction in line 170.

170–171. ***Many will swoon... more in it.*** At this point, *Rosalind* has been looking at the bloody handkerchief for fully 70 lines, so it cannot be the sight of *bloud* that causes her to *swoon*. Rather, her *swoon* is caused by sympathy (see note: *consenting*, V.ii.9) with *Orlando's fainting* (line 161, above).

171. ***Cosen Ganimed.*** In her distress, *Aliena / Celia* forgets that *Ganimed / Rosalind* is supposed to be her brother (*Cosen* was used for "A collateral relative more distant than a brother or sister," OED, and nowhere in the Folio does any character describe or address an actual sibling as *Cosen*). Cf. the use of "brother" and "sister" when *Rosalind* and *Celia* are in the company of others under their assumed disguises of *Ganimed* and *Aliena* (III.ii.86–87, III.ii.125, III.ii.330, III.ii.417, III.v.80–81; IV.i.120; and V.ii.36) with the use of *Cosen* when they are undisguised or speaking privately (I.ii.3 and 25; I.ii.228; I.ii.237; I.ii.247; I.ii.256; I.iii.3, 9, 15, 99, and 137; III.ii.214; and IV.i.199).

177. ***heart.*** Courage.

179. ***sirra.*** *Rosalind* attempts to reassume the irreverent persona of *Ganimed* by addressing *Oliver* as *sirra* (see note: *sirrah*, III.ii.160).

179–181. ***counterfeited... heigh-ho.*** In an attempt to convince *Oliver* that her anguish was *counterfeited* (feigned), *Rosalind* utters a *heigh-ho* (a loud sigh; see note: *Heigh ho*, II.vii.192). By now, however, *Oliver* has probably figured out the truth; cf. and see notes: lines 91–92, above; *Rosalind*, line 193, below; V.ii.22; and V.ii.30–32.

182–183. ***testimony in your complexion.*** *Ganimed's complexion* (appearance) gives *testimony* ("witnesse, deposition, evidence," RC, s.v. "Tesmoignage") that there is *mony* (i.e., "money" or a vagina; see note: *money*, II.iv.16) but no *test* (i.e., testicles; see note: *testament*, I.i.72) in his/her *complexion* (bodily constitution or makeup). Cf. and see note: *doublet and hose in my disposition*, III.ii.195–196.

183. ***passion.*** Literally "A fit or seizure; a faint" (OED).

183–184. ***earnest.*** Sincere, with possible play on *earnest* as "money." Cf. *Counterfeit*, line 185, below, and the "mony" of *testimony*, lines 182–183, above.

Oli. Well then, take a good heart, and counterfeit to

be a man.

Ros. So I doe: but yfaith, I should have beene a wo-

man by right.

Cel. Come, you looke paler and paler: pray you draw [190]

homewards: good sir, goe with us.

Oli. That will I: for I must beare answere backe

How you excuse my brother, *Rosalind.*

Ros. I shall devise something: but I pray you com-

mend my counterfeiting to him: will you goe? [195]

Exeunt.

193–194. ***How you excuse... devise something.*** *Oliver* does not want to know "if" *Rosalind* will *excuse Orlando*, but rather *how* (in what manner). In their mock-chivalric wooing ritual, *Rosalind* is expected to *devise* (invent) a worthy response.

193–195. ***Rosalind... commend my counterfeiting.*** In addressing *Ganimed* as *Rosalind*, *Oliver* may drop a veiled hint that her cover has been blown. Thus warned, *Rosalind* entreats him to *commend* her *counterfeiting* to *Orlando*. Cf. V.ii.22 and 30–32.

Act V, scene i

Actus Quintus. Scena Prima. [1]

Enter Clowne and Awdrie. [V.i.1]

Clow. We shall finde a time *Awdrie*, patience gentle *Awdrie*.

Awd. Faith the Priest was good enough, for all the [5]
olde gentlemans saying.

Clow. A most wicked Sir *Oliver, Awdrie*, a most vile
Mar-text. But *Awdrie*, there is a youth heere in the
Forrest layes claime to you.

Awd. I, I know who 'tis: he hath no interest in mee [10]
in the world: here comes the man you meane.

Enter William. [V.i.2]

Clo. It is meat and drinke to me to see a Clowne, by
my troth, we that have good wits, have much to answer
for: we shall be flouting: we cannot hold. [15]

Will. Good ev'n *Audrey*.

Aud. God ye good ev'n *William*.

Will. And good ev'n to you Sir.

Clo. Good ev'n gentle friend. Cover thy head, cover
thy head: Nay prethee bee cover'd. How olde are you [20]

Notes V.i.

5–6. ***the olde gentlemans.*** A possible implication that *Jaques* is *the olde gentleman* ("The devil," DPF).

6. ***saying.*** *Awdrie* found *Jaques' saying* ("speaking, a speech, a proverb, a motto," JF, s.v. "Detto") to be a mere *saying* ("flim-flam tale," JF, s.v. "Diceria"). Cf. *Jaques'* own disdainful description of a man in the "fifth age" (i.e., between 41 and 56 years old) who is *Full of wise sawes, and moderne instances* (II.vii.167).

7. ***vile.*** *Vile* means "base, abject, skornefull, cowardly, craven, faint harted, base minded, contemptible, of no woorth, of no value or account, little woorth or set by, good cheape, of little price, dogge cheape" (JF, s.v. "Vil").

9. ***layes claime.*** To "lay claim" is (a) to "aime at, sue, stand, lay or put in, for" (RC, s.v. "Pretendre"); and (b) to "pretend a title unto" (RC, s.v. "Clamer").

10. ***no interest in mee.*** Although *Awdrie's* other suitor has *interest* (concern or curiosity; regard) for her, he nevertheless has no *interest* (right or title to a share) *in* her. She reassures the *Clowne* that she does not owe any other man *interest* (i.e., sexual intercourse; *interest* is literally "the occupation of a thing; Also money or moneys worth given above the principal sum for the lone of it," TB, s.v. "Usury"; see notes: *money*, II.iv.16, and *inhabited*, III.iii.9).

13. ***meat and drinke.*** "Delight" (F&H).

13. ***a Clowne.*** Cf. and see note: *Clowne*, II.iv.69.

15. ***flouting.*** *Flouting* is "mocking," "scoffing at; a deriding, or laughing to scorne" (RC, s.v. "Irrision").

16–19. ***Good ev'n... gentle friend.*** *Good ev'n* was a greeting used any time after noon. *William's* repetition of this phrase prompts the *Clowne's* mocking description of him as *gentle*, meaning (a) "courteous, gracious, in words" (RC, s.v. "Affable"); and (b) "of a gentle, or gentlemanlie humour; he hath no one jot of ill breeding in him" (RC, s.v. "Jamais mauvaise poule ne le couva"). The *Clowne* may also imply that *William* is a *gentle* ("A maggot," F&H).

19–20. ***Cover thy head... bee cover'd.*** *William* has apparently doffed his hat as a sign of respect. The *Clowne*, who is presumably the social superior, "may either acknowledge the salutation or do nothing at all — for in such hierarchical exchanges it is the party of lower status who does the moving" (John Anthony Burrow, *Gestures and Looks in Medieval Narrative*, p. 28).

If *William* obeyed the *Clowne's* first command to *Cover* his *head* (i.e., put his hat back on), then the *Clowne* would have no reason to repeat the order unless there were some comic business. Perhaps the *Clowne* repeatedly doffs his own hat, or knocks *William's* hat off again.

For possible bawdy wordplay, see notes: *heads*, II.i.27, and *cover'd*, III.iii.72.

Friend?

Will. Five and twentie Sir.

Clo. A ripe age: Is thy name *William*?

Will. *William*, sir.

Clo. A faire name. Was't borne i'th Forrest heere? [25]

Will. I sir, I thanke God.

Clo. Thanke God: A good answer:

Art rich?

Will. 'Faith sir, so, so.

{*Clo.*} So, so, is good, very good, very excellent good: [30]

and yet it is not, it is but so, so:

Art thou wise?

Will. I sir, I have a prettie wit.

22–23. ***Five and twentie... A ripe age.*** In Shakespeare's England, *Five and twentie* was indeed a *ripe* (marriageable) *age*, for it was the mean age of marriage for men such as *William* who were "yeomen, husbandman, and tradesman" (LS, p. 40). Also see note: *ripe*, II.vii.30.

23–25. ***William... A faire name.*** In England, *William* was considered so *faire* (pleasing, attractive) a *name* that it ranked among the three most common male names in every decade between 1570 and 1700 (Scott Smith-Bannister, *Names and Naming Patterns in England 1538–1700*, p. 136). Therefore, *William* could obviously be said to be *A faire* ("of tolerable though not highly excellent quality," "pretty good," OED) *name*. Cf. *So, so*, lines 29–31, below.

29. ***so, so.*** "Fairish, reasonably faire, passable" (RC, s.v. "Bellastre").

33. ***prettie.*** See note: *prety*, III.ii.269.

Clo. Why, thou saist well. I do now remember a saying: The Foole doth thinke he is wise, but the wiseman [35]
knowes himselfe to be a Foole. The Heathen Philosopher, when he had a desire to eate a Grape, would open
his lips when he put it into his mouth, meaning thereby, that Grapes were made to eate, and lippes to open.
You do love this maid? [40]

Will. I do sir.

34–37. ***a saying... The Heathen Philosopher.*** The *wiseman* knowing *himselfe to be a Foole* is an ancient maxim with many variations. Among them is that found in the Epistle entitled "On Our Blindness" by *The Heathen Philosopher* Seneca (Lucius Anneus Seneca the younger, ca. 4 B.C.–A.D. 65): "si quando fatuo delectari volo, non est mihi longe quaerendus: me rideo" ("whenever I wish to enjoy the quips of a clown, I am not compelled to hunt far; I can laugh at myself").

Many a *Heathen Philosopher*, including Socrates, expressed similar sentiments, but at the time *As you Like it* was written the adage appears to have been particularly associated with Seneca: cf. "He that thinkes himselfe wise, is a Foole ipso facto. It was a modest speech that fell from the Philosopher. Si quando fatuo delectari volo, non est mihi longe quaerendus; me [r]ideo" (Thomas Adams, *The Happines of the Church*). Also cf. and see note: lines 36–39, below.

The *Clowne* thinks *William* a *Foole* because *William doth thinke himselfe wise* (but the *Clowne doth* also *thinke himselfe wise*; cf. lines 14–15, above). Moreover, *William* is a *Heathen Philosopher* ("a sorry poor tatter'd Fellow, whose Breech may be seen through his Pocket-holes," ND; "this saying arose from the old philosophers, many of whom despised the vanity of dress to such a point, as often to fall into the opposite extreme," FG). Cf. *naturall Philosopher*, III.ii.33.

36–39. ***The Heathen Philosopher... lippes to open.*** In *The Happines of a Religious State*, Girolamo Piatti summarizes the belief of *The Heathen Philosopher* Seneca that truth is best communicated not by argument but by example:

> Wherefore, as we use to say, that pictures are the books of unlearned people, so are examples also books written with great Roman letters, which a bodie cannot choose but see and reade, be he never so negligent and carelesse.
>
> Seneca in few words pithily expresseth two other fruits of Example.
>
> One word of a man's mouth (sayth he) and daylie conversation, wil benefit thee more, then a whole Oration penned; first, because men believe their eyes before their eares; secondly, because it is a long busines to goe by precepts; example is a shorter way, and more effectual... Seneca sayth; first, because, whatsoever the matter is, when we see a thing done by an other, we learne that it is not so hard, but we likewise may doe the same... if there should be question, whether ther be anie passage over a high hil, there could not be a more certain proofe of it, then to shew that manie have passed already, and to see them stand on the top of it.

Therefore, if *The Heathen Philosopher* Seneca had *desire to eate a Grape* and *open*[ed] *his lips* and *put it into his mouth*, he thereby would succinctly demonstrate by example the *meaning* ("underlying truth," OED) *that Grapes were made to eate, and lippes to open*.

Metaphorically, "Chast wives are as the grapes, which we may see / To hang upon the Vine" (William Fennor, *Pasquils Night-Cap*; in the 1591 tract *A Preparative to Mariage*, Henrie Smith cautions the potential husband that "when he takes a wife he takes a Vineyard, not grapes, but a vineyard to beare him grapes: therfore he must sow it, and dresse it, and water it, and fence it, and thinke it a good vineyard if at last it bring forth grapes"). The origin of the figure is unknown, but there is a distant echo in Deuteronomy 28:30: "Thou shalt betrothe a wife, and another man shall lie with her: thou shalt build an house, and thou shalt not dwell therein: thou shalt plant a vineyard, and shalt not gather the grapes thereof."

William is a *mouth* ("A silly fellow. A dupe," FG). Therefore, the best way for the *Clowne* to teach him that *Grapes* (i.e., a wife and her "fruitful vine": "woman's private parts, i.e. that has flowers every month, and bears fruit in nine months," FG) *were made to eate* (i.e., be consumed sexually) would be for the *Clowne* to marry *Awdrie*, *open* her *lippes* (i.e., labia), and fulfill his *desire* (i.e., consummate his marriage).

Clo. Give me your hand: Art thou Learned?

Will. No sir.

Clo. Then learne this of me, To have, is to have. For

it is a figure in Rhetoricke, that drink being powr'd out [45]

of a cup into a glasse, by filling the one, doth empty the

other. For all your Writers do consent, that *ipse* is hee:

now you are not *ipse*, for I am he.

Will. Which he sir?

Clo. He sir, that must marrie this woman: Therefore [50]

you Clowne, abandon: which is in the vulgar, leave the

societie: which in the boorish, is companie, of this fe-

male: which in the common, is woman: which toge-

ther, is, abandon the society of this Female, or Clowne

thou perishest: or to thy better understanding, dyest; or [55]

(to wit) I kill thee, make thee away, translate thy life in-

to death, thy libertie into bondage: I will deale in poy-

42. ***Give me your hand.*** The *Clowne* perhaps takes *William's* hand because *William's* wit has impressed him; the gesture would "indicate a relationship of equality, with any superiority of status disclaimed" (John Anthony Burrow, *Gestures and Looks in Medieval Narrative*, p. 28; cf. and see note: *Cover thy head*, line 19, above). However, by taking *William's hand* the *Clowne* also gives his subsequent threats (lines 51–61, below) the force of formal oath.

42–44. ***Art thou Learned... to have.*** *Learned* is (a) educated; and (b) "Said of one 'learned in the law'; hence applied by way of courtesy to any member of the legal profession" (OED). *William* readily confesses he is not *Learned*, so the *Clowne* gives him a quick legal lesson in the precept that possession is "the surest poynt of all the Law" (Anonymous, *Edward III*).

45–47. ***a figure in Rhetoricke... empty the other.*** It is a common *figure* ("A metaphor or metaphorical mode of expression," OED) *in Rhetoricke* ("the Art and Science of Eloquence, or of speaking well and wisely," TB, q.v.) *that drink being powr'd out of a cup into a glasse, by filling the one, doth empty the other* (cf. the similar *figure* in *Richard II*, IV.i.: "Now is this Golden Crowne like a deepe Well, / That owes two Buckets, filling one another, / The emptier ever dancing in the ayre, / The other downe, unseene, and full of Water"). Just as two vessels cannot contain the same *drink*, *one* woman's *glasse* (i.e., vagina; literally "the membrane constituting her maidenhead," EP, s.v. "crack") can be "filled" (sexually possessed or impregnated; see note: *fill'd*, III.ii.143) when the *cup* ("penis," GW2) of only *one* man "empties" (ejaculates, GW). Cf. a "little of one with t'other": copulation (F&H, s.v. "Greens").

47–48. ***all your Writers do consent... I am he.*** *All your* learned *Writers* would *consent that ipse is hee*, for in Latin *ipse* literally means "he" (as well as meaning "shee, the same, himselfe, or his owne selfe: the very," TT, q.v.). Moreover, if *William* thinks that *hee* is *ipse* (the very) man to marry *Awdrey*, then *hee* is *not ipse* ("in his right mind," OED).

51–55. ***abandon... dyest.*** *William* is *vulgar* ("vile, base," JF, s.v. "Volgare"), *boorish* ("hoblike, lumpish, loblike; blunt, blockish, brutish, barbarous, unmannerlie, uncivill, ignorant, home-bred, untaught," RC, s.v. "Rude"), and *common* ("verie humble," TT, s.v. "Infimus"). Therefore, the *Clowne* translates his learned phrases into *vulgar* ("Common or much used of the common people," TB, q.v.) and *common* ("manifest, evident, apparent," RC, s.v. "Public") language that *William* can understand.

56. ***to wit.*** Either (a) "'To be sure,' as one may know, truly, indeed"; or (b) "That is, namely" (OED).

56. ***make thee away.*** I.e., "do away with you."

56–57. ***translate... thy libertie into bondage.*** By threatening to *translate* ("convert; alter, change, transforme, turne," RC, s.v. "Convertir") *William's libertie* (i.e., life) *into* the *bondage* of death, the *Clowne* inverts a common religious figure. Contemporary religious tracts frequently describe God (or Christ) as delivering mankind from the *bondage* of death into the *libertie* of everlasting life. This line is one of several that evokes religious imagery and vocabulary and suggests that the *Clowne's* invective heats up to the fury of a hellfire sermon. Cf. and see notes: lines 60–61, below.

57. ***deale.*** To *deale* is (a) "To deliver blows"; and (b) "To contend or fight about" (OED).

son with thee, or in bastinado, or in steele: I will bandy

with thee in faction, I will ore-run thee with police: I

will kill thee a hundred and fifty wayes, therefore trem- [60]

ble and depart.

Aud. Do good *William.*

Will. God rest you merry sir.

Exit {*William.*} [V.i.3]

Enter Corin. [65]

Cor. Our Master and Mistresse seekes you: come a-

way, away.

Clo. Trip *Audry*, trip *Audry*, I attend,

I attend.

Exeunt [70]

58. ***bastinado.*** "A staffe: a cudgell" (TB, q.v.)

58–59. ***bandy... in faction.*** The *Clowne* will *bandy* ("discuss from mouth to mouth," OED) *William's* treachery openly. Consequently, others will *bandy* ("be partial, or factious, to take parts," TB, s.v. "Partiary") and *bandy* ("give and take blows," OED) *in faction* ("A factious quarrel or intrigue," OED). Moreover, the *Clowne* will "bandy against" *William*—i.e., "pursue [him] with all insolencie, rigour, extremitie" (RC, s.v. "Jouër à bander & à racler contre").

59. ***ore-run thee with police.*** The *Clowne* plans to *ore-run* ("overpower, overcome, defeat comprehensively," OED) *William* with *police* ("policy": "A device, a contrivance, an expedient; a stratagem, a trick," OED).

60. ***kill thee a hundred and fifty wayes.*** A play on the phrase, "a hundred ways to death." The source is Horace's "Ode 13," in which the Hell-Hound Cerberus is termed "Bellua centiceps" (the "hundred headed beast") to symbolize the manifold *wayes* that death claims the living. By threatening to *kill William* in *a hundred and fifty wayes*, the *Clowne* therefore threatens to *kill* him in every way possible — with an additional *fifty wayes* thrown in for good measure.

60–61. ***tremble and depart.*** *Tremble and depart* evokes language commonly found in sermons and religious tracts, such as Arthur Dent's 1607 *The Ruine of Rome*: "And as all the beastes of the forrest doo tremble and couch in their dennes when the Lyon roareth: And as that subject doth hide himselfe, and dare not shewe his head, with whom the King is displeased: So here it is saide, that the whole earth doth tremble, and all the celestiall creatures are amazed and confounded with beholding the angry face of God against the worlde." The origin is Proverbs 20:2 ("The feare of a king, is as the roaring of a Lion: who so provoketh him to anger, sinneth against his owne soule") and Amos 3:8 ("The lyon hath roared, Who will not feare? the Lord God hath spoken, Who can but prophecie?").

66. ***Our Master and Mistresse seekes you.*** *Corin* uses the singular verb *seekes* because he accounts his *Master and Mistresse* as a unit.

68. ***Trip, Audry, trip.*** The *Clowne* calls for *Audry* to *trip* (caper, move along quickly) and bring along her *trip* ("A heard or flocke of goates," TB, q.v.; cf. III.iii.3–4). The none-too-graceful *Audry* may also *trip* (stumble, fall down).

The *Clowne* also looks forward to the time that *Audry* will *trip* (consent to his sexual advances; see note: *tript*, III.ii.210).

Act V, scene ii

SCŒNA SECUNDA. [1]

Enter Orlando & Oliver. [V.ii.1]

Orl. Is't possible, that on so little acquaintance you
should like her? that, but seeing, you should love her?
And loving woo? and wooing, she should graunt? And [5]
will you persever to enjoy her?

Ol. Neither call the giddinesse of it in question; the
povertie of her, the small acquaintance, my sodaine woing, nor sodaine consenting: but say with mee, I love
Aliena: say with her, that she loves mee; consent with [10]
both, that we may enjoy each other: it shall be to your
good: for my fathers house, and all the revennew, that
was old Sir *Rowlands* will I estate upon you, and heere
live and die a Shepherd.

Enter Rosalind. [V.ii.2] [15]

Orl. You have my consent.
Let your Wedding be to morrow: thither will I
Invite the Duke, and all's contented followers:
Go you, and prepare *Aliena*; for looke you,
Heere comes my *Rosalinde*. [20]

Notes V.ii.

3–4. ***Is't possible... you should love.*** *Oliver* and *Aliena / Celia like* (lust after; see note: *liking*, I.iii.28) each other even though they have very *little acquaintance. Love* upon *seeing* (i.e., at first sight) was accepted as physiological fact; cf. and see notes: *murder in mine eye*, III.v.13, and lines 34–38, below.

6. ***persever to enjoy her.*** *Oliver* will *persever* (persist in a course of action) *to enjoy* (obtain, possess) *Aliena*. In order *to enjoy* ("take sexual pleasure of," GW) her, he must also *persever*— i.e., have an erection; to *persever* is to "stand to" (RC, s.v. "Persister"); DPF notes that *persever* "comes from an obsolete Latin verb, severo (to stick rigidly); hence severus (severe or rigid)" (q.v.).

7. ***Neither call the giddinesse... in question.*** *Oliver* asks *Orlando* not to *call in question* (cast doubt upon or closely inquire into) his *giddinesse*, meaning (a) rapid or thoughtless actions; and (b) passion or lust (see note: *giddie*, III.ii.342).

8. ***povertie.*** *Oliver* loves *Aliena* even though "When *povertie* comes in at the door, love flies out of the window" (proverbial). *Oliver* may or may not truly believe *Aliena* to live in *povertie*; see notes: IV.iii.91–92 and 147.

8–9. ***sodaine woing... sodaine consenting.*** *Oliver* became instantly *sodaine* (i.e., "sodden" or "besotted"; see note: *sodaine*, II.vii.162) with *Aliena*, so his *woing* was *sodaine* ("sudden": quick). *Aliena's sodaine consenting* (i.e., accepting and reciprocating *Oliver's* affections) was likewise due to "love at first sight," a physical reaction caused by "Consent, as one Sore Eye infects the other, (unseen) because they are both strung with one Optic Nerve: As in two Strings set to an Unison, upon the Touch of One, the other will Sound" (ND, s.v. "Consent"). Thus, they are now both *sodaine* (lustful or unable to contain their passion, FR). Cf. and see notes: *murder in mine eye*, III.v.13, and lines 34–38, below.

11. ***enjoy.*** See note: *enjoy*, line 6, above.

12–14. ***my fathers house... die a Shepherd.*** *Oliver's* offer to *estate* (bestow or settle) *old Sir Rowlands house* and its *revennew* upon *Orlando* is perhaps not as generous as it seems; cf. III.i.11–14 and 18–19, and see note: IV.iii.147.

18. ***Invite... all's contented followers.*** Either (a) *Invite all* of *Duke Senior's followers* who are *contented* ("Willing, ready," OED) to attend; or (b) *Invite all of Duke Senior's followers* who are *contented* ("not disposed to complain; marked by contentment," OED), which would pointedly exclude *Jaques*. *Orlando* need not fear *Jaques'* gloomy influence, however, for *Jaques* will absent himself from the wedding of his own accord (V.iv.200–205).

Ros. God save you brother.

Ol. And you faire sister.

{*Exit Oliver.*} [V.ii.3]

Ros. Oh my deere *Orlando*, how it greeves me to see
thee weare thy heart in a scarfe. [25]

Orl. It is my arme.

Ros. I thought thy heart had beene wounded with
the clawes of a Lion.

Orl. Wounded it is, but with the eyes of a Lady.

Ros. Did your brother tell you how I counterfeyted [30]
to sound, when he shew'd me your handkercher?

Orl. I, and greater wonders then that.

Ros. O, I know where you are: nay, tis true: there

21–22. ***brother... faire sister.*** *Aliena* and *Ganimed* are supposedly *brother* and *sister* (cf. III.ii.86–87, III.ii.125, III.ii.330, III.ii.417, III.v.80–81, IV.i.120, and line 36, below). By marrying *Aliena*, *Oliver* will therefore become *Ganimed's brother* (i.e., brother-in-law).

Oliver presumably calls *Ganimed* his *faire sister* (i.e., sister-in-law) because *Ganimed* has come to visit *Orlando* in his "assumed" persona of *Rosalind*. However, it is also possible that *Oliver* has guessed *Ganimed's* true identity (cf. and see notes: IV.iii.91–92, and *Rosalind*, IV.iii.193). Also cf. and see note: *ripe sister*, IV.iii.95.

25–26. ***weare thy heart... my arme.*** The lion injured *Orlando's arme* (IV.iii.158–159), but because *Orlando* "wears his heart on his sleeve" his *heart* is equally mangled.

29. ***Wounded... with the eyes of a Lady.*** *Orlando* does not speak poetically but recounts medically established fact. Cf. and see notes: *murder in mine eye*, III.v.13, and lines 34–38, below.

30–32. ***I counterfeyted to sound... greater wonders then that.*** *Ganimed's* "sounding" (fainting) at the sight of *Orlando's* blood is a "wonder" (surprising or astonishing event). The "greater wonder" that *Orlando* refers to may be (a) *Oliver's* falling in love with *Aliena* on their first encounter; or (b) *Ganimed's* fainting because [s]he is actually *Rosalind*, who as a boy/girl would indeed be a "wonder" (i.e., a "Monster," JP, q.v.; a "monster" is "any deformed creature, or misshapen thing that exceedeth, lacketh or is disordred in natural form," JF, s.v. "Móstro").

was never any thing so sodaine, but the sight of two
Rammes, and *Cesars* Thrasonicall bragge of I came, saw, [35]
and overcome. For your brother, and my sister, no sooner met, but they look'd: no sooner look'd, but they
lov'd; no sooner lov'd, but they sigh'd: no sooner sigh'd
but they ask'd one another the reason: no sooner knew
the reason, but they sought the remedie: and in these [40]
degrees, have they made a paire of staires to marriage,
which they will climbe incontinent, or else bee incontinent before marriage; they are in the verie wrath of
love, and they will together. Clubbes cannot part
them. [45]

Orl. They shall be married to morrow: and I will
bid the Duke to the Nuptiall. But O, how bitter a thing
it is, to looke into happines through another mans eies:

34–35. ***never any thing so sodaine... the sight of two Rammes.*** "Love at first *sight*" occurred "when the beames which procede from the hart do unite & conforme them selves to the thing viewed and loked upon" (OL). In *Erotomania*, Jacques Ferrand describes Love as a physical event that follows a predictable course in the body:

> Love, having first entred at the Eyes, which are the Faithfull spies and intelligencers of the soule, steales gently through those sluces, and so passing insensibly through the veines to the Liver, it there presently imprinteth an ardent desire of the Object, which is either really lovely, or at least appeares to be so. Now this desire, once enflamed, is the beginning and mover of all the sedition. But distrusting its owne strength, and fearing it is not able to overthrow the Reason; it presently layeth siege to the Heart: of which having once fully possest it selfe, as being the strongest fort of all it assaults so violently the Reason, and all

the noble forces of the Braine, that they are suddenly forced to yeeld themselves up to its subjection.

Thus, *Oliver* and *Celia* are *sodaine* (i.e., besotted; cf. lines 8–9, above; also see notes: *sodainly*, I.ii.286, and *sodaine*, II.vii.162). They have become "rammish" ("Lustful," F&H) just as "suddenly" as the *sight of two Rammes* (symbolic of a "type of potent lechery," EC, s.v. "Ram"; also see note: *Rammes*, III.ii.79). Consequently, the pair now desire a "ram" ("An act of coition," F&H).

34–43. ***sight... a paire of staires... incontinent before marriage.*** *Sight* (looking, beholding) was the first *degree* ("one of a flight of steps," OED) on the *paire of staires* ("flight of stairs or steps," OED) *to* love and subsequently *marriage*. However, "the staires that lead up to this palace [of love and marriage] are of a very slippery substance. The three first steps are, the immodest cast of the eyes, superfluity of words, & the violence of the hands" (JF2). *Oliver* and *Celia* have ensnared each other with *a paire of staires* (i.e., "stares" or loving looks), so they must *climbe the staires to marriage incontinent* (quickly), *or else* they will *bee incontinent* (unable to resist their sexual appetites, EP). If they don't marry soon, *Oliver* will "climb" (sexually mount, EP) *Aliena's* "downstairs" ("female pudendum; Cunt," F&H) *before marriage*.

35–36. ***Cesars Thrasonicall bragge... overcome.*** Upon his victory over King Pharnaces II of Pontus (d. 47 B.C.), Julius Cæsar (100–44 B.C.) described his entire campaign only as "Veni, vidi, vici" ("I came, I saw, I conquered"). This terse *bragge* ("vante, a boaste, a glory," JF, s.v. "Vanto") was generally considered *Thrasonicall* ("Vain-glorious, full of boasting as Thraso was," JB, q.v.; "Thraso" is the name of a braggart soldier found in Terence's play *Eunuchus*).

Oliver's bragge (penis, FR; a "Braguette" is "A codpeece," RC, q.v.) is also *sodaine* (quick) to "come" (yield to sexual temptation, JH, q.v.), "see" (copulate, F&H, s.v. "Ride"), and *overcome* ("achieve an orgasm while in the superincumbent position," JH; cf. *Don Armatho's* use of *overcome* and "overcame" in his love letter to *Jaquenetta* in *Loves Labour's lost*, IV.i.)

39–40. ***reason... remedie.*** *Oliver's reason* (i.e., phallic erection; see note: *reasons*, I.iii.10) makes him want to "do *reason*" (copulate, GW2, q.v.) with *Celia*, who likewise seeks love's *remedie* (i.e., sexual intercourse; see note: *cure*, III.ii.391). Since ancient times, sex was understood as a *remedie* for love; in *Erotomania*, Jacques Ferrand relates that

> Diogenes going one day to the Oracle at Delphos, to aske counsell, what was the most soveraigne and speediest Remedy for the cure of his sonne, that was growne mad for Love: received this answere, that he must enjoy Her, that was the cause of his Madnesse... This opinion is also set downe in expresse tearmes by Hippocrates... saith he, that all young wenches, when once they begin to bee taken with this disease, should presently bee married out of hand.

43–45. ***wrath of love... part them.*** *Clubbes* can *part* (separate) those in *wrath* (anger, fury), but *Oliver* and *Aliena* are in such *wrath* ("ardour of passion, love," OED) that *Clubbes cannot part them*.

46–47. ***They shall be married... bid the Duke to the Nuptiall.*** *Orlando* perhaps emphasizes the fact that *Duke Senior* will attend *Oliver* and *Aliena's Nuptiall* because he suspects (or knows) that *Ganimed* is really *Rosalind*. He therefore drops a hint that *Rosalind's* father will be conveniently available to give her away *to morrow* should she be inclined to *be married* herself.

48. ***happines.*** Both (a) felicity; and (b) good fortune.

by so much the more shall I to morrow be at the height
of heart heavinesse, by how much I shal thinke my bro- [50]
ther happie, in having what he wishes for.

Ros. Why then to morrow, I cannot serve your turne
for *Rosalind*?

Orl. I can live no longer by thinking.

Ros. I will wearie you then no longer with idle talking. [55]
Know of me then (for now I speake to some pur-
pose) that I know you are a Gentleman of good conceit:
I speake not this, that you should beare a good opinion
of my knowledge: insomuch (I say) I know you are: neither do I labor for a greater esteeme then may in some [60]
little measure draw a beleefe from you, to do your selfe
good, and not to grace me. Beleeve then, if you please,

49–50. ***height of heart heavinesse.*** Someone at the *height of heart heavinesse* would not be at the *height* (utmost point of exaltation) but would instead be very "low" (dejected, depressed).

51. ***having what he wishes for.*** With obvious sexual implication; also see note: *what*, IV.i.111.

52–53. ***cannot serve your turne for Rosalind.*** *Orlando* feels that *Ganimed* is no longer enough to "serve his turn" (satisfy his needs). Only the real *Rosalind* can *serve* (sexually *serve*; see note: *serve*, IV.i.42) him a *turne* ("act of coition," F&H).

54. ***live... by thinking.*** *Orlando* can no longer *live* (exist, continue, or subsist) nor *live* (variant of "leve": "exercise faith," OED) *by thinking* ("supposing, imagining, deeming; presuming," RC, s.v. "Cuidant").

55–57. ***idle talking... to some purpose.*** *Ganimed's idle* (wanton or promiscuous; see note: *holiday*, I.iii.16) *talking* has hitherto been *idle* (useless, frivolous, empty), but now he plans to speak *to some purpose* (to the point or with a definite end in mind)—which is probably *some purpose* (fornication, FR).

57. ***of good conceit.*** *Orlando* is *of good conceit* ("readie judgement, ripe wit, quicke understanding," RC, s.v. "Bon-enten-tu"). Hopefully, he will also have a *good conceit* ("liking, upon the first essay, of a thing," RC, s.v. "Goust") to effect some *good* (sexually satisfying; see notes: *good*, I.ii.28 and 65) *conceit* (conception of offspring, OED, with play on "con" as "cunt").

58–59. ***I speake not this... I know you are.*** *Ganimed* does not tell *Orlando* he is *of good conceit* (line 57, above) to flatter him into bearing *a good opinion of Ganimed's* own *knowledge*. Instead, *Ganimed* simply states the truth, *insomuch* ("considering that," RC, s.v. "Car") he knows *Orlando* to be intelligent.

59–61. ***neither... in some little measure.*** *Ganimed* exerts himself in order to *do Orlando good*, not to *grace* (bring credit or praise upon) himself. *Neither* does *Ganimed labor* (exert himself, seek) for any *greater esteeme* (regard, favorable opinion) than that which will *in some little measure* (small degree) *draw* (elicit) *a beleefe* ("Confident anticipation, expectation," OED) *from Orlando*.

Rosalind also hopes to *labor* (exert herself sexually, GW) for the *esteeme* (i.e., "standing" or phallic erection; also a sexual embrace, JA, p. 81) of *Orlando's little* ("with innuendo of poor sexual performance," JH, q.v.) *measure* (penis, EP). This she will do for *Orlando's good* (sexual satisfaction; see notes: *good*, I.ii.28 and 65), not to indulge her own *grace* (vagina; see note: *grace*, III.v.107).

62. ***if you please.*** With possible play on *please* meaning "gratify sexually" (JH).

that I can do strange things: I have since I was three
yeare old converst with a Magitian, most profound in
his Art, and yet not damnable. If you do love *Rosalinde* [65]
so neere the hart, as your gesture cries it out: when your
brother marries *Aliena*, shall you marrie her. I know into what straights of Fortune she is driven, and it is not
impossible to me, if it appeare not inconvenient to you,
to set her before your eyes to morrow, humane as she is, [70]
and without any danger.

Orl. Speak'st thou in sober meanings?

Ros. By my life I do, which I tender deerly, though
I say I am a Magitian: Therefore put you in your best a-
ray, bid your friends: for if you will be married to mor- [75]
row, you shall: and to *Rosalind* if you will.

63–64. ***do strange things... a Magitian.*** Ever *since Ganimed was three yeare old,* he has had opportunity to "converse" ("be much conversant, associate, or keepe much companie, with," RC, s.v. "Converser avec") *a Magitian* ("one using witchcraft," RC2, q.v.). For this reason, *Ganimed* can *do strange things* ("worketh wonders," TB, s.v. "Portentifical").

Perhaps it was this "conversation" ("sexual intercourse," JH, s.v. "Converse") with a *Magitian* (hermaphrodite, bisexual, FR, s.v. "Witch") that made the androgynous *Ganimed* a "strange thing" (a "thing that commeth against nature, or otherwise then nature giveth: a monster," TT, s.v. "Ostentum"; cf. and see note: *wonders,* line 32, above).

64–65. ***profound in his Art... not damnable.*** Shakespeare's contemporaries classified magic into various categories. TB (s.v. "Conjuration") explains that the

> difference between Conjuration and Witchcraft is, that the Conjurer seems by prayers and invocation of Gods powerful names, to compel the Devil to say or do what he commands him: The Witch deals rather by a friendly and voluntary conference or agreement between him or her, & the Devil or Familiar, to have his or her turn served for soul, blood, or other gift offered him: So that a Conjurer compacts for curiosity to know secrets, and work marvels; and the Witch of meer malice to do mischief.

During the reign of Elizabeth I, both conjuration and witchcraft were *damnable* ("Liable to judicial condemnation," OED), but only witchcraft was held to be *damnable* (causing the soul's condemnation to Hell). Conjuration was widely considered benign, so conjurers were not subject to the same punishment as witches until James I's 1604 "Acte againste Conjurations Inchantments and witchcraftes" decreed that any person who "shall use practise or exercsise any Invocation or Conjuration of any evill and spirit... shall suffer pains of deathe as a Felon or Felons, and shall loose the priviledge and benefit of Cleargie and Sanctuarie."

66. ***so neere the hart... cries it out.*** *Orlando's* earlier demeanor has changed somewhat (cf. III.ii.360–374), for now his *gesture* ("posture, behavior, carriage," RC, s.v. "Contenance") *cries out* (proclaims) that he holds *Rosalind neere the hart* ("closest to [his] affection," OED). Additionally, *Orlando* may (a) "cry out" (make a cloud or impassioned exclamation); and/or (b) make a specific *gesture* ("making of signes, or countenances; a motion, or stirring of any part of the bodie," RC, s.v. "Geste") to indicate that *Cupid's* arrow has struck him very *neere the hart*; cf. IV.i.49–50.

68. ***straights of Fortune... driven.*** *Fortune* is a capricious whore (cf. and see note: *houswife Fortune*, I.ii.32–33) who has *driven* (i.e., "screwed"; a "drive" is a "coital thrust," GW2) *Rosalind* and *driven* her into her *straights* (i.e., vagina, "Ex the standard sense of a narrow waterway between two large bodies of water," GW2; cf. to "rush up the straight": to copulate, F&H)—or possibly into her "straight" (rectum; see note: *strait*, II.i.75).

69. ***if it appeare not inconvenient to you.*** If it does not *appeare* (seem) an *inconvenient* ("improper, unfittting, misbecomming,," RC, s.v. "Inconvenable") way for *Orlando* to acquire a "convenient" ("mistress," FG), *Ganimed* will magically make *Rosalind appeare* ("come forth into view, as from a place or state of concealment, or from a distance; to become visible... esp. of angels, disembodied spirits, and visions," OED).

70–71. ***humane as she is... danger.*** Although a conjurer sought to subjugate the supernatural beings he summoned (see note: *not damnable*, line 65, above), a single misstep could cause him to lose control and thus fall into both physical and spiritual *danger*. Conjurers would dictate to summoned spirits the form in which they should appear, but *Ganimed* offers to produce the real, *humane* (variant spelling of "human") *Rosalind*, not a spirit or demon in her form. Thus, there is no risk of *danger*.

72. ***sober.*** *Sober* can mean (a) "serious"; (b) "sensible; free from exaggeration; not fanciful or imaginative"; and/or (c) "Guided by sound reason; sane, rational" (OED).

73–74. ***By my life... a Magitian.*** The practice of magic in the form of witchcraft was a capital offence; see note: *not damnable*, line 65, above.

74–76. ***put you in your best aray... to morrow.*** Most Elizabethan brides and bridegrooms did not buy new clothing but simply wore their *best aray* (clothing) to the wedding ceremony. *Ganimed* tells *Orlando* to put on his *best aray* out of certainty that *Rosalind* will appear, and that *Orlando* will therefore *be married to morrow*.

75. ***friends.*** Both (a) acquaintances; and (b) kinsfolk (OED).

Enter Silvius & Phebe. [V.ii.4]

Looke, here comes a Lover of mine, and a lover of hers.

Phe. Youth, you have done me much ungentlenesse,

To shew the letter that I writ to you. [80]

Ros. I care not if I have: it is my studie

To seeme despightfull and ungentle to you:

you are there followed by a faithful shepheard,

Looke upon him, love him: he worships you.

Phe. Good shepheard, tell this youth what 'tis to love [85]

Sil. It is to be all made of sighes and teares,

And so am I for *Phebe.*

Phe. And I for *Ganimed.*

Orl. And I for *Rosalind.*

Ros. And I for no woman. [90]

Sil. It is to be all made of faith and service,

And so am I for *Phebe.*

Phe. And I for *Ganimed.*

Orl. And I for *Rosalind.*

Ros. And I for no woman. [95]

79. ***ungentlenesse.*** By revealing *Phebe's* letter to *Silvius, Ganimed* has shown himself to be "Ungentle, rude, rusticall, clownish, without nurture or civilitie, feirce, in whome is neither love nor humilitie" (TT, s.v. "Agrestus"). *Ganimed's* failure to appreciate *Phebe's* superior literary efforts also demonstrates *ungentlenesse* ("ignorance of good letters," TT, s.v. "Inhūmānĭtas"). *Phebe* perhaps also accuses *Ganimed* of *ungentlenesse*— i.e., of being *un*-("without," OED) *gentle* (with play on "genital")— i.e., of having "no balls."

81. ***studie.*** Endeavor or aim.

82. ***despightfull.*** *Despightfull* is "reproachfull," "outragious or most injurious, in words" (RC, s.v. "Contumelieux").

84. ***Looke upon.*** To "regard favourably, hold in esteem" (OED).

85. ***shepheard... what 'tis to love.*** Although *Phebe* does not reciprocate *Silvius'* affection, she recognizes his eloquence on the subject (cf. III.v.101–103). As a *shepheard, Silvius* is a highly appropriate messenger of *love*, who is "painted by some in forme of a Shepherd" because "they which pursue and followe love be more lyker beastes then men" (OL).

86–91. ***sighes and teares... faith and service.*** *Silvius* expresses old chivalrous notions of courtly love, which held that "the meate of perfecte Lovers" is "Sighes and teares" (OL). In his 1528 *The Book of the Courtier*, Baldassarre Castiglione describes a true lover as one who declares "all his tokens of love & faithfull service" and endures "the teares, sighes, vexations and tourmentes of lovers: Bicause the soule is alwayes in affliction and travaile."

87–106. ***And so am I for Phebe... blame you me to love you.*** Elizabethan actors presented plays with a bare minimum of rehearsal, and they worked from cue-scripts that contained only their own cues and lines (see *Introduction*, p. 9, and *Textual Preparation*, p. 386). Given these performance conditions, there must have been simple guidelines for blocking and action, and one such guideline was for the actor to direct his speech to the person that he named in it (e.g., *my deere Orlando*, line 24, above, and *Good shepheard*, line 85, above). In the absence of spoken titles indicating to whom a speech should be addressed, the common-sense rule of thumb would be for the actor to respond to the character who delivered his cue line (Patrick Tucker, *Secrets of Acting Shakespeare: The Original Approach*, p. 263).

As per *Phebe's* spoken stage direction (line 85), *Silvius* would address his first speech (lines 86–87) to *Ganimed*. He would thereafter also address his protestations of love (lines 91–92, 96–101, and 106) to *Ganimed* because *Ganimed* gives him his cues. For the same reason, *Phebe* would address lines 88, 93, 102, and 106 to *Silvius*; *Orlando* would address lines 89, 94, and 103 to *Phebe*; and *Ganimed / Rosalind* would address lines 90, 95, and 104 to *Orlando*. Thus, each of *Rosalind's* avowals that she loves *no woman* becomes a veiled declaration of love to *Orlando* (who may already know the truth of her identity: cf. and see notes: lines 32 and 46–47, above). The comic repetition culminates in line 106 when *Phebe, Silvius*, and *Orlando* cry out simultaneously (see *Textual Preparation*, VI.i.) and place *Rosalind* at the center of a confused and noisy stage huddle.

Sil. It is to be all made of fantasie,

All made of passion, and all made of wishes,

All adoration, dutie, and observance,

All humblenesse, all patience, and impatience,

All puritie, all triall, all observance: [100]

And so am I for *Phebe.*

Phe. And so am I for *Ganimed.*

Orl. And so am I for *Rosalind.*

Ros. And so am I for no woman.

Phe.	*Sil.*	*Orl.*
If this be so, why blame you me to love you?	If this be so, why blame you me to love you?	If this be so, why blame you me to love you? [106]

Ros. Why do you speake too, Why blame you mee to love you.

Orl. To her, that is not heere, nor doth not heare.

Ros. Pray you no more of this, 'tis like the howling [110]

of Irish Wolves against the Moone: I will helpe you

96. ***all made of fantasie.*** *Silvius* is subject to *fantasie* ("wanton lusts of bodie, lecherie," TT, s.v. "Libido") because his *all* (i.e., his "awl" or penis, JH; an "awl" is literally a "slender, cylindrical, tapering, sharp-pointed blade, with which holes may be pierced," OED) is *made* (i.e., erect, EP, s.v. "mar"). Also see notes: *fantasie*, II.iv.33, and *Fancie*, III.ii.355.

96–100. ***all... all.*** *Silvius* repeats *all* nine times in the course of five lines. This points up the irrational mind of the lover, for it is impossible to be *all* (entirely) *made* (comprised) of eleven different things.

97–100. ***passion... triall.*** *Silvius* describes romantic love in customary quasi-religious terms: *passion* (sexual desire; see note: *passion*, I.ii.259) involves *passion* (suffering and martyrdom; see note: *passion*, II.iv.62).

97. ***wishes.*** A "wish" is "An imprecation, a malediction" (OED), which suggests that the lover curses himself with his *wishes* (lust, wantonness, JA, p. 57; L. "libido" is used both for desires and sexual passions).

98. ***adoration.*** Like God, a lover requires *adoration* ("worshipping," JB, q.v.).

98. ***dutie, and observance.*** A man owes his lover *dutie* (sexual service, JH, s.v. "to do Duty") and *observance* ("Diligent heede, or attendance," JB, q.v.) just as he owes God both *dutie* ("Performance of the prescribed services or offices of the church," OED) and *observance* ("worship," RC, q.v.). Cf. *religion*, IV.i.190.

99. ***humblenesse.*** Unrequited love demands (a) *humblenesse* ("lowlinesse," RC, s.v. "Basenesse") of spirit; and (b) that a man's "humbles" ("genitals," GW2; "humbles" are literally the "loins of a hart," OED, s.v. "numbles") remain "humbled" ("the opposite of proud... not elevated," JH).

99. ***patience, and impatience.*** A lover's desire for *patience* (i.e., for his lady-love to be "patient," "the technical term of the passive role in intercourse," JA, p. 189) is marked by *impatience* ("Impatient desire," OED).

100. ***puritie.*** Just as religion demands *puritie* ("sinlessness," OED), a "pure" ("a Mistress," ND) demands *puritie* ("chastity, honesty, cleanness of life," TB, s.v. "Pudicity").

106–109. ***If this be so... nor doth not heare.*** *Orlando* probably addresses this question to *Ganimed* (see note: line 87, above). This suggests that he has guessed *Ganimed's* true identity, and his subsequent explanation that he speaks *To her, that is not heere, nor doth not heare* is an effort to save face. Cf. and see notes: lines 30–32 and 46–47, above.

110–111. ***howling... against the Moone.*** In their passionate outcries, *Phebe, Silvius,* and *Orlando* are *howling against the Moone* ("crav[ing] for the impossible," F&H, s.v. "cry for the moon"). The full *Moone* supposedly causes madness in love, and *Phebe, Silvius,* and *Orlando* suffer the extreme "lunacy" of *Wolves,* who "are more subject to madnesse then any other Beast... because their bodies are chollerick, and their braines encrease and decrease with the Moone" (Edward Topsell, *The Historie of Foure-Footed Beastes*). Although they are human beings endowed with reason, they now resemble the *Irish* who "were once a yeare turned into Wolves" (Edmund Campion, *Two histories of Ireland*).

The three of them "howl" (i.e., clamor for sexual intercourse; "howleth" is "the Noise a Wolf maketh at Rutting time," ND, q.v.) just like (a) a "wolf" ("A sexually aggressive male," OED) for *the Moone* (female genitalia; see note: *pale spheare*, III.ii.5); and/or (b) a "wolf" (whore; see note: *sterner*, III.v.8) for *Moone* (variant of "mone": "Sexual intercourse," OED).

if I can: I would love you if I could: To morrow meet
me altogether: I wil marrie you, if ever I marrie Woman, and Ile be married to morrow: I will satisfie you,
if ever I satisfi'd man, and you shall bee married to mor- [115]
row. I wil content you, if what pleases you contents
you, and you shal be married to morrow: As you love
Rosalind meet, as you love *Phebe* meet, and as I love no
woman, Ile meet: so fare you wel: I have left you com-
mands. [120]

Sil. Ile not faile, if I live.

Phe. Nor I.

Orl. Nor I.

Exeunt.

114–117. ***I will satisfie... contents you.*** The lines *I will satisfie you* and *I will content you* both make sense whether addressed to *Orlando* or *Silvius.* Because Shakespeare does not provide a clear verbal clue to whom these lines should be directed (see note: lines 87–106, above), the actor playing *Rosalind* is free to choose.

Whether addressed to *Orlando* or *Silvius, Rosalind* promises him that he will be *satisfi'd*: both (a) have his desires fulfilled, be made happy (OED); and (b) have his sexual desires fulfilled (EP).

Whether addressed to *Orlando* or *Silvius, Rosalind* promises that she will (a) *content* ("satisfy so as to stop complaint," OED) him with *what pleases* (gives pleasure or happiness to) him; and (b) *content* (sexually satisfy; see note: *content,* I.iii.145) him with *what pleases* (sexually gratifies; see note: *please,* line 62, above) him.

121. ***Ile not faile, if I live.*** I.e., "The only reason that I won't be there is if I'm dead."

Act V, scene iii

SCŒNA TERTIA. [1]

Enter Clowne and Audrey. [V.iii.1]

Clo. To morrow is the joyfull day *Audrey*, to morow will we be married.

Aud. I do desire it with all my heart: and I hope it is [5] no dishonest desire, to desire to be a woman of the world? Heere come two of the banish'd Dukes Pages.

Enter two Pages. [V.iii.2]

1.Pa. Wel met honest Gentleman.

Clo. By my troth well met: come, sit, sit, and a song. [10]

2.Pa. We are for you, sit i'th middle.

1.Pa. Shal we clap into't roundly, without hauking, or spitting, or saying we are hoarse, which are the onely prologues to a bad voice.

2.Pa. I faith, y'faith, and both in a tune like two [15] gipsies on a horse.

Song.

It was a Lover, and his lasse,

With a hey, and a ho, and a hey nonino,

That o're the greene corne feild did passe, [20]

Notes V.iii.

6. ***dishonest desire... woman of the world.*** *Audrey* hopes it is not a *dishonest* ("filthy, unclean, unchast," TB, s.v. "Obscene") *desire* (longing) to be a *woman of the world* ("A married woman," DPF)—or to have *longing* (sexual *longing*) and to become a *woman of the world* (one who is "sexually experienced," GW2).

8. ***two Pages.*** A professional Elizabethan acting company included a number of boy apprentices who were learning the acting trade. Shakespeare therefore went out of his way to include parts such as these *two Pages* for the young apprentices to play.

12–13. ***clap into't roundly... hoarse.*** The *Pages* plan to *clap* ("burst foorth," JF, s.v. "Scoccare") *into* their song *roundly* ("without dalliance, or delay," RC, s.v. "À certes") and without any *hauking* ("labouring to void fleame out of the lunges by retching," TT, s.v. "Screātus"). There is possible additional play on (a) "hawk" as the bird of prey, and *clap* as "The lower mandible of a hawk" (OED); and (b) *clap* as venereal infection (see note: *clapt*, IV.i.49), and being *hoarse* as a symptom "of syphilis... or its mercury treatment" (GW2).

13. ***the onely.*** I.e., "only the."

15. ***I faith.*** I.e., "Aye, faith."

15. ***y'faith.*** I.e., "in faith."

15–16. ***both in a tune like two gipsies on a horse.*** A possible allusion to *two gipsies* "canting" or "chanting" *on* ("about," OED) *a horse*. "Chanting a horse" means "to get one or more independent persons apparently, to give him a good name, swear to his perfections and make a bidding—by way of teazer" (John Badcock, *Slang*, s.v. "Chant"), and *gipsies* were notoriously deceitful horse-traders who could easily pass off an inferior *horse* as first-rate. Just like *two gipsies in a tune* (in agreement) "cant" ("enhance by competitive bidding," OED) or "chant" (falsely praise) *a horse*, the *two Pages* will "cant" or "chant" (sing) *in a tune* (in pitch, in harmony, or in unison).

19. ***hey nonino.*** *Hey nonino* was "A refrain once used to cover indelicate allusions" (F&H). Thus, it came to denote the female genitalia (FR; cf. JF's entry at "Fóssa": "a grave, a pit, a ditch, a trench, any fosse digging or mote about a house. Used also for a womans pleasure-pit, nony-nony or pallace of pleasure").

20. ***greene.*** *Greene* (a) is the "Colour of love and copulation" (FR); (b) is euphemistic for the vagina (cf. and see note: *greene*, III.iii.82); and (c) denotes "virility" (OED).

20. ***corne.*** *Corne* (a grain or cereal plant) commonly symbolizes fertility and has "various sexual significations" (GW2), including semen and the male genitalia (*corne* is "a horn," OED; a "horn" is "an erection of the penis," F&H).

20. ***feild.*** An age-old metaphor for the female genitalia (JA, pp. 82–83).

In the spring time, the onely pretty rang time.

When Birds do sing, hey ding a ding, ding.

Sweet Lovers love the spring,

And therefore take the present time.

With a hey, & a ho, and a hey nonino, [25]

For love is crowned with the prime.

In spring time, &c.

Betweene the acres of the Rie,

With a hey, and a ho, & a hey nonino:

These prettie Country folks would lie. [30]

In spring time, &c.

This Carroll they began that houre,

With a hey and a ho, & a hey nonino:

How that a life was but a Flower,

In spring time, &c. [35]

Clo. Truly yong Gentlemen, though there was no

great matter in the dittie, yet the note was very untunable

21. ***spring time.*** The plot of *As you Like it* follows a rather loose timeline, but this lyric suggests that it is now *spring time*. Therefore, some time has elapsed since the *Clowne* and his companions first arrived in Arden; cf. II.i.9–12 and II.vii.188–200.

21. ***spring.*** With possible play on *spring* as (a) the vagina (GW2; cf. *Fountaine*, IV.i.149–150); and/or (b) phallic erection (to "spring" is literally "To arise, to grow... also to grow or increase in height," TT, s.v. "Surpo").

21. ***spring time... rang time.*** *Rang time* is usually emended to "ring time" on the evidence of (a) a possible rhyme with *spring* and with *sing* and *ding* (line 22, below); and (b) *Carroll* (line 32, below), which can mean "A ring-dance with accompaniment of song" (OED). However, *the spring* is just as readily a *time* to *rang* (i.e., "range" or wander; cf. and see note: *rang'd*, I.iii.72), and this *Lover and his lasse* certainly "range" because they *passe o're the greene corne feild* (lines 18–20, above). A *rang* is also "A range, rank, row" (OED), and these lovers *lie Betweene the acres of the Rie* (lines 28–30, below).

26. ***love is crowned with the prime.*** *Love* (affection) *is crowned* (most perfect or abundant) *with the prime*, meaning (a) the season of spring; and/or (b) the time when one is "in youth, in ones flower" (JF, s.v. "Infiore").

Also, *love* (sexual intercourse) *is crowned* (with play on "crown" as the genitals, FR) *with the prime*, which means (a) "sexual excitement" (JH); and/or (b) orgasm (*prime* is "the state of full perfection," OED; "perfection" alludes to sexual climax, JA, pp. 143–144).

27–35. ***&c.*** An instruction to repeat the song's refrain of lines 21–23, above.

28–30. ***Betweene the acres of the Rie... would lie.*** *These prettie* (i.e., "pret" or "ready"; "ready" is "prepared to perform sexually," GW2) *Country folks* ("ordinary People, as Country-folks, Harvest-Folks, Work-folks, &c," ND, q.v.) *would lie* (i.e., have sexual intercourse) *Betweene the acres* (tilled fields) *of the Rie* (a staple grain in the English diet). There is possible additional pun on *Rie* as (a) "waggerie, good roguerie; a merrie pranke, a pleasant, and knavish part; good-fellowship" (RC s.v. "Drolerie"); and/or (b) sexual intercourse (a "wry" is literally "A twisting or tortuous movement," OED).

30. ***prettie Country.*** With possible play on *prettie* as the "female pudendum" (F&H), and on *Country* as "cunt."

32. ***Carroll.*** A *Carroll* is (a) "a song. Also a kinde of dance" (JF, s.v. "Caróla"); and (b) "Diversion or merry-making" (OED). *Carroll* thus possibly alludes to sexual intercourse (to "sing" is "to coit with," EP; to "dance" is to "copulate," JH; and "merry" is "Sexually wanton," FR).

34. ***a life was but a Flower.*** A common sentiment; cf. Psalms 103:15–16: "As for man, his dayes are as grasse, as a flower of the field, so he flourisheth. For the wind passeth over it, and it is gone, and the place therefof shall know it no more."

There may be additional play on *Flower* as (a) "The female pudendum; Cunt" (F&H, s.v. "monosyllable"); and/or (b) the penis (GW2).

36–37. ***no great matter in the dittie... untunable.*** The *matter* (subject, composition, or written words) *in the dittie* ("the matter of a song," RC2, q.v.) held *no great matter* (i.e., *no* objectionable subject *matter*). Nevertheless, the *dittie* was a *dittie* (variant of "dite": loud cacophony or clamorous outcry, OED). Therefore, the *note* (pitch or melody; also "piece of work," "Handiwork," OED) was a *note* ("An object of censure," OED) that was *very untunable* ("disagreeing, repugnant, contrarie; most harsh," TT, s.v. "Discordant").

1.Pa. you are deceiv'd Sir, we kept time, we lost not

our time.

Clo. By my troth yes: I count it but time lost to heare [40]

such a foolish song. God buy you, and God mend your

voices. Come *Audrie.*

Exeunt.

38. ***you are deceiv'd.*** The *Page* does not accuse the *Clowne* of lying but merely of being *deceiv'd* (mistaken). See note: *Upon a lye*, V.iv.74.

38–39. ***lost not our time.*** I.e., stayed in the same rhythm or kept the beat.

40. ***time lost.*** See note: II.vii.120.

41. ***mend.*** To *mend* is to (a) improve; and (b) repair.

42. ***voices.*** A possible play on *voices* and "vices" (HK, p. 151).

Act V, scene iv

SCENA QUARTA. [1]

Enter Duke Senior, Amyens, Jaques, Orlan-
do, Oliver, Celia. [V.iv.1]

Du.Sen. Dost thou beleeve *Orlando*, that the boy

Can do all this that he hath promised? [5]

Orl. I sometimes do beleeve, and somtimes do not,

As those that feare they hope, and know they feare.

Enter Rosalinde, Silvius, & Phebe. [V.iv.2]

Ros. Patience once more, whiles our compact is urg'd:

You say, if I bring in your *Rosalinde*, [10]

You wil bestow her on *Orlando* heere?

Du.Se. That would I, had I kingdoms to give with hir.

Ros. And you say you wil have her, when I bring hir?

Orl. That would I, were I of all kingdomes King.

Ros. You say, you'l marrie me, if I be willing. [15]

Phe. That will I, should I die the houre after.

Ros. But if you do refuse to marrie me,

You'l give your selfe to this most faithfull Shepheard.

Phe. So is the bargaine.

Ros. You say that you'l have *Phebe* if she will. [20]

Notes V.iv.

6–7. ***I sometimes do beleeve... know they feare.*** *Orlando* knows that his optimistic expectations are just "hopes" (empty desires), and he hopes that his doubts are only "fears" (groundless anxieties).

9. ***our compact is urg'd.*** *Rosalind* will "repeat, or urge a thing often, thereby to make it the better understood, or remembred" (RC, s.v. "Calcioler") a *compact* ("bargaine, agreement," JB, q.v.). This *compact* requires that certain people be *compact* (i.e., married; *compact* is "joyned together," RC2).

10–29. ***You say... If she refuse me.*** This seemingly redundant clarification of who is to marry whom gives *Audrey* and the *Clowne* time to change into their wedding clothes after their exit in V.iii.43 (see note: *best array*, V.ii.74–75). Similarly, the *Clowne's* description of courtly manners (lines 74–106, below) gives *Rosalind* and *Celia* time to change their costumes before they re-enter in line 111, below.

12–14. ***had I kingdoms... were I of all kingdomes King.*** *Duke Senior* thinks *Orlando* so deserving that he would willingly bestow *kingdoms* along with his daughter. *Rosalind* has no dowry at all due to her father's exile, but even so *Orlando* thinks her so valuable that he would marry her *were* he *of all kingdomes King.*

Sil. Though to have her and death, were both one thing.

Ros. I have promis'd to make all this matter even:
Keepe you your word, O Duke, to give your daughter,
You yours *Orlando*, to receive his daughter: [25]
Keepe you your word *Phebe*, that you'l marrie me,
Or else refusing me to wed this shepheard:
Keepe your word *Silvius*, that you'l marrie her
If she refuse me, and from hence I go
To make these doubts all even. [30]

{*Exit Rosalind and Celia.*} [V.iv.3]

Du.Sen. I do remember in this shepheard boy,
Some lively touches of my daughters favour.

Orl. My Lord, the first time that I ever saw him,
Me thought he was a brother to your daughter: [35]
But my good Lord, this Boy is Forrest borne,
And hath bin tutor'd in the rudiments
Of many desperate studies, by his unckle,
Whom he reports to be a great Magitian.

Enter Clowne and Audrey. [V.iv.4] [40]

Obscured in the circle of this Forrest.

23. ***matter.*** Both (a) business; and (b) "sexual intrigue" (GW). There is possible additional play on "mater": "one who mates."

23. ***even.*** "Equal towards all"; also "Just, true" (OED).

33. ***lively touches of my daughters favour.*** In *Ganimed, Senior* notices *Touches* (qualities or characteristic traits) that are *lively* ("done or drawen to the life," JF, q.v.; also "striking," OED) in that they resemble *Rosalind's favour* (face, features, or family likeness, OED).

37–39. ***tutor'd... great Magitian.*** Cf. III.ii.337–338 and V.ii.63–65.

37. ***rudiments.*** "The first grounds or principles of an art or any knowledge" (JB, q.v.).

38. ***desperate studies.*** *Studies* that are (a) reckless or careless; (b) dangerous (see note: *not damnable*, V.ii.65); and/or (c) undertaken in a wretched state or condition.

41. ***Obscured in the circle of this Forrest.*** *Ganimed's* magical uncle remains *Obscured* ("Hidden, concealed," RC, s.v. "Occulté") because he dabbles in the "occult" (magical arts). Magicians would protect themselves from summoned spirits by standing within a magical *circle*, and this man similarly shields himself *in the circle* (region; literally the "circuit or compass of a place," OED) *of this Forrest*. Thus, he is as well hidden as *the circle* ("female pudendum," F&H, s.v. "Monosyllable") within the *Forrest* (public hair; see note: *Forrest*, III.ii.123). Cf. *fringe upon a petticoat*, III.ii.331.

Jaq. There is sure another flood toward, and these couples are comming to the Arke. Here comes a payre of verie strange beasts, which in all tongues, are call'd Fooles. [45]

Clo. Salutation and greeting to you all.

Jaq. Good my Lord, bid him welcome: This is the Motley-minded Gentleman, that I have so often met in the Forrest: he hath bin a Courtier he sweares.

Clo. If any man doubt that, let him put mee to my [50] purgation, I have trod a measure, I have flattred a Lady, I have bin politicke with my friend, smooth with mine enemie, I have undone three Tailors, I have had foure quarrels, and like to have fought one.

Jaq. And how was that tane up? [55]

Clo. 'Faith we met, and found the quarrel was upon the seventh cause.

42–44. ***another flood toward... verie strange beasts.*** In Genesis 6:14, God commanded Noah to "Make thee an Arke" and to preserve specimens of all the *beasts* of the earth: "Of every cleane beast thou shalt take to thee by sevens, the male and his female: and of beastes that are not cleane, by two, the male and his female" (Genesis 7:2). So many "pairs" are now appearing that *Jaques* thinks another *flood* must be *toward* (imminent). Apparently, *Jaques* considers this *payre* of *beasts* (i.e., *Audrey* and the *Clowne*) to be of the *strange* (i.e., unnaturally libidinous; see note: *strange*, II.iv.57) and "unclean" (unchaste, obscene) variety. Also see note: *beast*, IV.iii.55.

44–45. ***verie strange beasts... call'd Fooles.*** *In all tongues* (languages), lovers were (and still are) commonly likened to *Fooles* and *beasts* due to their general lack of good sense. In *Anatomy of Melancholy*, Robert Burton explains that

> The major part of lovers are carried headlong like so many brute beasts, reason counsels one way, their friends, fortunes, shame, disgrace, danger, and an Ocean of cares that will certainely follow; yet this furious lust, praecipitates counter-poiseth, waighes downe on the other: though it be their utter undoing, perpetuall infamy, losse, yet they will doe it, and become at last, insensati void of sence; degenerate into dogs, hogges, asses, brutes, as Jupiter into a Bull, Apuleius an Asse, Lycaon a Wolfe, Tereus a Lap-wing, Calisto a Beare, Elpenor and Grillus into Swine by Circe. For what els may we thinke those ingenious Poets to have shadowed in their witty fictions and poemes, but that a man once given over to his lust... is no better then a beast.

Also see note: *shepheard*, V.ii.85.

48. ***Motley-minded.*** Because a person's outward appearance supposedly reflects his inner qualities, "the Apparell oft proclaimes the man" (*Hamlet*, I.iii.). The *Clowne* thus not only wears a fool's *Motley* but is *Motley-minded.* (The outer and inner man did not always agree, however; cf. the jester *Feste's* defense of his intellect in Act I, scene v of *Twelfe Night, Or what you will*: "*Cucullus non facit monachum*: that's as much to say, as I weare not motley in my braine.")

49. ***Courtier.*** See notes: *Courtier*, II.vii.40, and *Courtly*, III.ii.70.

50–51. ***put mee to my purgation.*** I.e., "put me to the proof." In order to prove that he is not "full of shit" (see note: *purgation*, I.iii.57), the *Clowne* volunteers to undergo *purgation* (a trial by ordeal).

51–54. ***trod a measure... like to have fought one.*** According to Baldassarre Castiglione's *The Book of the Courtier*, the ideal courtier should "daunce well without over nimble footinges"; try "with women to be alwayes gentle, sober, meeke, lowlie, modest, serviceable, comelie, merie"; not "geve himselfe so for a prey to friend how deere and loving so ever he wer, that without stoppe a manne shoulde make him partaker of all his thoughtes, as he woulde his owne selfe"; "Not to be stubborne, wilfull nor full of contention: nor to contrary and overtwhart men after a spiteful sort"; "be handesome and clenly in his apparaile"; and "knowe what is to be done in quarrels whan they happen."

The Clowne parodies these commendable qualities and represents the courtier as an extravagant, deceitful, vain, shallow, short-tempered and cowardly fop. Cf. and see notes: *Courtly*, III.ii.70; and *Courtiers*, IV.i.14.

51. ***trod a measure... flattred a Lady.*** With possible play on "tread" as sexual intercourse (OED), *measure* as the penis (see note: *measure*, V.ii.61), and "flat" as copulation and/or pandering (see note: *flattery*, II.i.13).

55. ***tane up.*** I.e., "made up" or settled amicably.

56–57. ***we met... the seventh cause.*** According to the code of the duello, there were only two "causes" for which a man could legitimately challenge another to combat: (1) if his adversary accused him of a crime deserving the death penalty; and (2) if his adversary insulted his honor (being called a liar constituted such an insult; see note: *Upon a lye*, line 74, below). When the *Clowne* and his opponent *met* to fight their duel, they *found the quarrel was upon the seventh cause*—i.e., that a duel could not be justified because their *cause* (reason for fighting) ranked far beneath either of the accepted two.

Jaq. How seventh cause? Good my Lord, like this fellow.

Du.Se. I like him very well. [60]

Clo. God'ild you sir, I desire you of the like: I presse in heere sir, amongst the rest of the Country copulatives to sweare, and to forsweare, according as mariage binds and blood breakes: a poore virgin sir, an il-favor'd thing sir, but mine owne, a poore humour of mine sir, to take [65] that that no man else will: rich honestie dwels like a miser sir, in a poore house, as your Pearle in your foule oyster.

Du.Se. By my faith, he is very swift, and sententious

Clo. According to the fooles bolt sir, and such dulcet [70] diseases.

---

61. ***God'ild you.*** See note: *goddild you*, III.iii.70.

61. ***I desire you of the like.*** The *Clowne* says that (a) he desires *Duke Senior* to have *the like* (a fondness or liking) for him; and (b) he "likewise" desires to *like Duke Senior* (which suggests that he doesn't, even though he wants to).

61–62. ***presse in.*** *Presse in* can mean (a) to push one's way through a crowd; (b) to intrude presumptuously; (c) to take upon oneself; and/or (d) to eagerly pursue an undertaking.

62. ***Country copulatives.*** As a part of speech, a "copulative" is a conjunction that connects words or phrases (from L. "Copulativus": "that coupleth, or may cowple," TE, q.v.). The *Clowne* wants to be a *copulative* (i.e., one with a "copulative," or "conjunction by marriage," OED) in order to form a "copula" ("Sexual union," OED) and, of course, to "copulate." There is probable additional play on *Country* and "cunt."

63–64. ***to sweare, and to forsweare... blood breakes.*** The *Clowne* plans to *sweare* the nuptial vows (including the one to forsake all others except his wife) *according* ("accordingly," OED) *as marriage binds*. Nevertheless, the *Clowne* suspects that *blood* (sexual appetites or urges; see note: *blood*, II.iii.40) might cause him to *forsweare* (repudiate or renounce) his marriage vows and "break" (violate his promise, OED; commit adultery, GW). Cf. the *Clowne's* attitudes on spousal fidelity in III.iii.45–59 and 83–86.

64–65. ***an il-favor'd thing... but my owne.*** According to "Adage 15" of Desiderius Erasmus, "Suuam ciuque pulchrum" (or "What is one's own is beautiful") is a

> proverbial saying about people who prefer what is their own, whatever it may be like, and rather out of prejudice than judgment. It arises from the usual attitude of mind among the human race, with whom philautia, or self-love, is so deeply rooted that you will find no one so modest, so thoughtful, or so clear-sighted that he will not be blind or suffer from delusions, misled by some mental bias, when it comes to putting a value on something of his own... Even today there is a shrewd and common saying, 'there's no such thing to be found as an ugly sweetheart,' because to him who loves them even homely things must seem very beautiful.

Cf. and see note: III.v.59.

65–66. ***a poore humour... to take that that no man else will.*** The *Clowne* had to fend off at least one of *Audrey's* other suitors (V.i.44–61), so this is not strictly true.

66–68. ***rich honestie dwels... as your Pearle in your foule oyster.*** The *Pearle in your foule oyster* was "regarded as a symbol of the Soul or Spirit lying encased within the human body" (Harold Bayley, *Lost Language of Symbolism*). The saying was proverbial; cf. III.ii.110, and this lyric from "Fine knacks for ladies": "It is a precious Jewell to bee plaine, / Sometimes in shell th'orienst pearles we finde" (John Dowland, *The Second Booke of Songs or Ayres*).

Audrey's "shell" (human body as encasing the soul) may be *foule*, but within her *oyster* ("female pudendum," F&H) she holds a *Pearle* (symbol of purity and virginity, GW2).

69–71. ***swift... dulcet diseases.*** Proverbially, "a Fooles Bolt is soone shot" (*Henry V*, III.vii.), meaning that "Simpletons cannot wait for the fit and proper time, but waste their resources in random endeavours... The allusion is to the British bowmen in battle; the good soldier shot with a purpose, but the foolish soldier at random" (DPF). If the *Clowne* indulges his *swift* (quick, nimble) *and sententious* ("full of sentences, pitthy, full of matter," TB, q.v.) *wit According to the fooles bolt*, then he indiscriminately fires off his quips at anything or anybody in a *swift* (rapid-fire) manner. Cf. Proverbs 29:11: "A foole uttereth all his mind: but a wise man keepeth it in till afterwards."

Other people may consider the *Clowne's* shooting off his mouth to be a *disease* ("evil affection or tendency," OED), but the *Clowne* thinks his witticisms *dulcet* ("prettie and sweet," RC, s.v. "Doucet"). In view of the fact that the *Clowne* has acquired many scraps of wisdom which he *vents In mangled formes* (II.vii.45–46), his use of *dulcet* here suggests that he "mangles" the phrase "Abundat dulcibus vitiis" ("He abounds with agreeable vices"), a criticism of the attractive but fallacious views of Seneca found in the *Institutio Oratortia* by Roman orator and rhetorician Quintilian (Marcus Fabius Quintilianus, A.D. 35–100).

The *Clowne* also hints that a "fool" who indiscriminately "shoots" his *bolt* (i.e., ejaculates; see notes: *suites*, II.vii.86, and *arrows*, III.v.35) will end up with *diseases* of the *dulcet* (i.e., scrotum; "Doucets" are literally the "stones of a Deere," RC, s.v. "Daintiers"; "doucet" and "dulcet" were interchangeably spelled, OED).

Jaq. But for the seventh cause. How did you finde
the quarrell on the seventh cause?

Clo. Upon a lye, seven times removed: (beare your
bodie more seeming *Audry*) as thus sir: I did dislike the [75]
cut of a certaine Courtiers beard: he sent me word, if I
said his beard was not cut well, hee was in the minde it
was: this is call'd the retort courteous. If I sent him
word againe, it was not well cut, he wold send me word
he cut it to please himselfe: this is call'd the quip modest. [80]
If againe, it was not well cut, he disabled my judgment:

74–95. ***Upon a lye... good manners.*** The *Clowne's* parody of the *good manners* demanded by the code of honor is not far from the truth. Many a *booke in print* instructed gentlemen (or would-be gentlemen) how to *quarrel in print* ("In a precise and perfect way or manner; with exactness, to a nicety," OED) and *by the booke* (according to formal rules). A gentleman who was given the *lye* (i.e., called a liar) was expected to defend his honor in combat, and Vincentio Salviolo's 1594 *Of Honor and Honorable Quarrels* expounds on "the manner and diversitie of Lies," including "Lies Certaine," "conditionall Lyes," "the Lye in generall," "the Lye in particular," "foolish Lyes,"

"The lye before the other speakes," "A lye that giveth meanes to be repented," "A lye at pleasure," "A lye given without cause," "A lye given after an ill sorte," and "the returning back of the lye." Despite the gravity of *a lye*, Salviolo nevertheless enjoins "That straightwaies upon the Lye, you must not take armes." As Edward Muir explains in *Ritual in Early Modern Europe* (p. 150):

> When one party insulted or accused another of a dishonorable deed, the accused had to respond by 'giving the lie,' that is by stating loudly and clearly, 'You lie in the throat.' The original speaker then denied the lie by formally challenging the other to a duel... [The] preliminary stages could become quite complex with the exchange of challenges and counter challenges, the publishing of extended justifications printed on large sheets of paper suitable for posting, and minute disputes about honor and etiquette. The complexity of the rituals allowed the actual violence to be delayed indefinitely, even for years, and always gave someone who did not want to risk his hide an honorable way out, since it was virtually impossible to follow the ritual script perfectly, and any slip brought a gentleman's honor into question.

74–75. ***beare your bodie more seeming Audry.*** The *Clowne* has hitherto had no objection to *Audry's* deportment, so he may here admonish her because her bearing (a) is not in keeping with her posh wedding clothes (see note: lines 10–29, above); or (b) is not *seeming* (befitting) her position as the wife of a grand "courtier" such as the *Clowne* imagines himself to be.

75–76. ***dislike the cut of a... beard.*** To insult a man's *beard* might be considered an insult to his (a) virility (see note: *beard*, III.ii.206); and/or (b) social status (see note: II.vii.81). Also see note: *bearded*, II.vii.161.

76–106. ***if I said... much vertue in if.*** In *Of Honor and Honorable Quarrels*, Vincentio Salviolo describes "Conditionall lyes" as lies

> such as are given conditionally: as if a man should saie or write these woordes. If thou hast saide that I have offered my Lord abuse, thou lyest: or if thou saiest so heerafter, thou shalt lye. And as often as thou hast or shalt so say, so oft do I and will I say that thou does lye. Of these kinde of lyes given in this manner, often arise much contention in words, and divers intricate worthy battailes, multiplying wordes upon wordes whereof no sure conclusion can arise: the reason is, because no lye can bee effectuall or lawefull, before the condition is declared to bee true, that is, before it be justified that such words were certainly spoken.

The *Clowne* avoids combat because he dares not provoke his opponent beyond *the Lye with circumstance* (Salviolo's "conditional lie"), and his opponent *durst not* give him *the lye direct* (the *lye* classified by Salviolo as the "lye certaine," one "given uppon wordes spoken affirmatively, as if anie man should saie or write unto another. Thou has spoken to my discredit, and in prejudice of my honour and reputation, and therefore doost lye").

Therefore, the word *if* (with play of *if* / "F": euphemistic for "fuck") holds much *vertue* (strength, power) in a *Quarrell* (an "Innuendo of the vagina, perhaps suggested by 'quarrel' = 'quarry,'" JH, s.v. "Woman's quarrel"; "quarry" is "the female pudendum," F&H;), especially for a "man's man" preoccupied with the *vertue* (sexual potency; see note: *vertue*, III.ii.121) of his *peace-maker* ("penis," F&H).

81. ***disabled.*** Belittled, with play on *disabled* meaning "unfit for Venerie" (RC, s.v. "Esrené") or "unable to performe nuptiall rites" (RC, s.v. "Maleficié"). Cf. *vertue*, line 106, below.

this is called, the reply churlish. If againe it was not well
cut, he would answer I spake not true: this is call'd the
reproofe valiant. If againe, it was not well cut, he wold
say, I lie: this is call'd the counter-checke quarrelsome: [85]
and so to lye circumstantiall, and the lye direct.

Jaq. And how oft did you say his beard was not well
cut?

Clo. I durst go no further then the lye circumstantial:
nor he durst not give me the lye direct: and so wee mea- [90]
sur'd swords, and parted.

Jaq. Can you nominate in order now, the degrees of
the lye.

Clo. O sir, we quarrel in print, by the booke: as you
have bookes for good manners: I will name you the de- [95]
grees. The first, the Retort courteous: the second, the
Quip-modest: the third, the reply Churlish: the fourth,
the Reproofe valiant: the fift, the Counterchecke quarrelsome: the sixt, the Lye with circumstance: the sea-
venth, the Lye direct: all these you may avoyd, but the [100]
Lye direct: and you may avoide that too, with an If. I
knew when seven Justices could not take up a Quarrell,

90–91. ***measur'd swords.*** In order to be certain that one duelist did not have an unfair advantage over the other, *swords* would be *measur'd* to ensure that both were the same length. Given the manly posturing of the *Clowne* and his opponent, each also wanted to "take the measure" (assess the abilities or worth) of the other. To demonstrate that one was not a "bigger man" than the other, they wanted to be sure that their *swords* (i.e., penises) were of the same "measure" (length).

92. ***nominate.*** Both "name" and "remember" (RC, s.v. "Mentionner").

98. ***Counterchecke.*** To *Counterchecke* is "to blame or check one againe, that telleth us of our fault" (TT, s.v. "Rĕtaxo"); Elisha Coles' 1676 *English Dictionary* defines *Counterchecke* as "blame him that blames you" (q.v.).

100. ***avoyd.*** To "make void or of no effect; to refute, disprove"; also "to invalidate" (OED).

102. ***take up.*** See note: *tane up*, line 55, above.

but when the parties were met themselves, one of them
thought but of an If; as if you saide so, then I saide so:
and they shooke hands, and swore brothers. Your If, is [105]
the onely peace-maker: much vertue in if.

Jaq. Is not this a rare fellow my Lord? He's as good
at any thing, and yet a foole.

Du.Se. He uses his folly like a stalking-horse, and under the presentation of that he shoots his wit. [110]

Enter Hymen, Rosalind, and Celia. [V.iv.5]

Still Musicke.

{*Hymen.*} *Then is there mirth in heaven,*
When earthly things made eaven
attone together. [115]
Good Duke receive thy daughter,
Hymen from Heaven brought her,
Yea brought her hether.

---

105. ***shooke hands, and swore brothers.*** The two *shooke hands* (a gesture made by grasping each other by the wrist) and vowed to be "sworn brothers," who "in the Old English law, were persons who by mutual oath covenanted to share each other's fortune" (DPF, q.v.).

107. ***rare.*** The *Clowne* is "A rare thing seldome seene, which signifieth that some strange matter shall after follow" (JB, s.v. "Prodigie"; cf. lines 42–43, above). There

is possible additional play on *rare* meaning "arse" (FR; "rear," which means both "rare" and "The buttocks or backside," was also spelled "rare," OED).

109–110. ***He uses his folly like a stalking-horse... shoots his wit.*** A *stalking-horse* is a "horse made of canvas or such like, to gather within fowle to shoote at them with a fowling peece" (JM, s.v. "Boezuélo"); "Fowlers used to conceal themselves behind horses, and went on stalking step by step till they got within shot of the game" (DPF). Figuratively, a *stalking horse* is "A masque to conceal some design" (DPF), so the *Clowne's folly* is merely a deceptive *presentation* (appearance) under which *he shoots his wit* (with allusion to the *fooles bolt* of line 70, above). Although "presented" under the pretence of *folly*, the *Clowne's* account of his duel nevertheless offers cutting commentary on courtly manners (see note: lines 74–95, above).

111. ***Hymen.*** *Hymen* is "the God of marriages, or a song sung at marriages. The Greeks at their marriages were wont to sing Hymen, Hymenæe" (TB, q.v.). The god *Hymen* is a particularly fitting catalyst to transform *Ganimed* into *Rosalind*, for while still in human form *Hymen* donned female clothing in order to gain access to his lover.

The presence of the god *Hymen* (a.k.a. "Hymenaios") indicates that the music and dancing in this scene take the form of a stately masque. Masques, which were elaborate participatory theatrical events centered on classical themes, were popular entertainments at weddings.

The song of lines 113–120 is not assigned to a specific singer, but it makes sense that *Hymen* should sing it. In modern productions, the marriage song (and/or the portrayal of *Hymen* himself) is often assigned to *Amyens* because he sings other songs in the play. However, *Amyens* is currently on stage attending *Duke Senior* (line 2, above). Furthermore, it is unclear how *Ganimed / Rosalind* and *Aliena / Celia* could possibly recruit *Amyens* to perform in their amateur theatricals.

If the role of *Hymen* is doubled by another character, the logical person to do so is *Corin* because (a) he has not appeared on stage since V.i.; and (b) he works for *Ganimed* and *Aliena*, so he could plausibly be recruited to perform in their masque. Moreover, if *Corin* is doubled by the same actor who plays *Adam* (who has not appeared on stage since II.vii.), then *Hymen's* appearance would be decidedly comical: both *Corin* and *Adam* are old and thus physically not the right "type" for the role of *Hymen*, who was depicted as young, nubile, and nude or scantily clad.

112. ***Still Musicke.*** Musicians may here enter with *Hymen*, *Rosalind*, and *Celia*, but there is no stage direction for them to do so. In the original production, the *Still* (either "soft" or "continuous") *Musicke* may have been provided by musicians seated backstage or in one of the upper boxes behind the stage. *Hymen* himself might have appeared on the upper level, or perhaps he was lowered onto the stage on the throne that descended from the heavens (cf. *mirth in heaven*, line 113, below).

113–114. ***heaven... eaven.*** *Heaven* and *eaven* were pronounced identically. Therefore, *earthly things* (affairs) are made not just *eaven* (equitable) but also "heaven" (i.e., heavenly).

114–115. ***earthly things... attone together.*** All *things* (events, occurrences) on earth *attone* (harmonize, come into concord) *together*. Now that *Rosalind* has been restored to her true gender, *earthly things* (genitals, EP) may *attone* (become "at one," with implication of sexual intercourse, TR) *together* (see note: *together*, I.i.109).

116–117. ***daughter... brought her.*** *Brought her* was pronounced "brought 'er," thus rhyming with *daughter*.

118. ***Yea.*** *Yea* can mean (a) yes; (b) truly; and/or (c) indeed.

	That thou mightst joyne his hand with his,	
	Whose heart within his bosome is.	[120]
Ros.	To you I give my selfe, for I am yours.	
	To you I give my selfe, for I am yours.	
Du.Se.	If there be truth in sight, you are my daughter.	
Orl.	If there be truth in sight, you are my *Rosalind.*	
Phe.	If sight & shape be true, why then my love adieu	[125]
Ros.	Ile have no Father, if you be not he:	
	Ile have no Husband, if you be not he:	
	Nor ne're wed woman, if you be not shee.	
Hy.	Peace hoa: I barre confusion,	
	'Tis I must make conclusion	[130]
	Of these most strange events:	
	Here's eight that must take hands,	
	To joyne in *Hymens* bands,	
	If truth holds true contents.	
	You and you, no crosse shall part;	[135]
	You and you, are hart in hart:	

119–120. ***That thou mightst joyne his hand... within his bosome is.*** As *Rosalind's* father, *Duke Senior* is expected to give her away (cf. and see note: V.ii.46–47). *Hymen* invites the *Duke* to *joyne his* (i.e., *Orlando's*) *hand with his* (i.e., *Rosalind's*, with allusion to her assumed masculine persona of *Ganimed*). *Ganimed / Rosalind* has already given away *his*/her *heart* to *Orlando* and plighted *his*/her troth to him (IV.i.120–135). Because *Ganimed's / Rosalind's heart* is already *within his* (i.e. *Orlando's*) *bosom*, the *Duke* must also give *Orlando* the rest of him/her.

121–123. ***To you I give my selfe... If there be truth.*** *Rosalind* says the same thing twice because she (a) speaks once to her father and once to *Orlando*; (b) speaks once to *Phebe* and once to *Orlando*; or (c) speaks once to her father and once to *Phebe.*

A repeated line generally indicates simultaneous dialogue (see *Textual Preparation*, VI.i.), but this is not the case here. Given the rapid-fire production schedule of an Elizabethan theatre (see *Textual Preparation*, pp. 381–382), actors did not waste precious time rehearsing "talking only" segments. By contrast, scenes that contained special production elements (like dancing and fights) were thoroughly rehearsed and blocked, and the dialogue was set to time out with the choreography and music. Therefore, the actor playing *Duke Senior* would have learned in rehearsal that his cue for line 123 would be repeated. Consequently, he would not speak until after his cue had been spoken for the second time.

123–124. ***If there be truth in sight.*** "Seeing is believing," but the *Duke* and *Orlando* "can't believe their eyes." Even the *sight* of the transformed *Ganimed* is not enough to procure their "Oculate Faith, that is, confirmed by the eye-sight, or such a Faith as represents the thing believed, as it were to the eye; a seeing Faith" (TB, q.v.).

125. ***If sight & shape be true... adieu.*** If *Ganimed's sight* (appearance) *& shape* (both bodily form and "Fashion of dress," OED) *be true* (in accordance with reality), then he is a *shape* ("an ill-made Man," ND, s.v. "Shapes"). Because *Ganimed's sight* (i.e., genitals; see note: *sight*, IV.i.42) *& shape* ("sexual organs," OED) are *true* (i.e., a "trou" or vagina; see note: *truly*, III.iii.14), *Phebe* must bid him/her *adieu*. Cf. line 134, below.

129. ***Peace hoa: I barre confusion.*** *Hymen* calls for *Peace* in order to *barre* ("to prohibite, to forbid, to restraine," JH, s.v. "Interdire") *confusion* (disorderly commotion, tumult). This indicates that the other characters are speaking together cacophonously.

130–131. ***make conclusion... strange events.*** *Hymen* will *make conclusion* (settle) these *strange* (unusual) events, and therefore these *strange* (sexually deviant; see notes: *Aliena*, I.iii.136, and *strange*, II.iv.57) couples can *make conclusion* ("coitus," TR; also see note: *Epilogue*, line 212, below).

132–134. ***Here's eight... If truth holds true contents.*** *If* the *truth* ("troth": the solemn promise to wed) of these *eight* (*Rosalind* and *Orlando*; *Celia* and *Oliver*; *Phebe* and *Silvius*; and *Audrey* and the *Clowne*) *holds true contents* ("Acceptance of conditions or circumstances, acquiescence," OED, s.v. "content"), then they *must* all *take hands* ("the symbol of troth-plight in marriage," OED) *To joyne* (combine two things in one, unite) in *Hymens bands* (the bond of wedlock).

135–136. ***You and you... are hart in hart.*** *Hymen* delivers one of these lines to *Rosalind* and *Orlando*; the other line he delivers to *Celia* and *Oliver*. Line 136 is probably addressed to the former because *Rosalind's hart* is already *within Orlando's bosome* (lines 119–120, above).

You, to his love must accord,

Or have a Woman to your Lord.

You and you, are sure together,

As the Winter to fowle Weather: [140]

Whiles a Wedlocke Hymne we sing,

Feede your selves with questioning:

That reason, wonder may diminish

How thus we met, and these things finish.

Song. [145]

Wedding is great Junos crowne,

O blessed bond of boord and bed:

'Tis Hymen peoples everie towne,

High wedlock then be honored:

Honor, high honor and renowne [150]

To Hymen, God of everie Towne.

Du.Se. O my deere Neece, welcome thou art to me,

Even daughter welcome, in no lesse degree.

Phe. I wil not eate my word, now thou art mine,

Thy faith, my fancie to thee doth combine. [155]

Enter Second Brother. [V.iv.6]

2.Bro. Let me have audience for a word or two:

I am the second sonne of old *Sir Rowland*,

137–138. ***You... a Woman to your Lord.*** These lines are obviously addressed to *Phebe* and *Silvius*, because if *Phebe* does not *accord* (agree) to *Silvius'* love, she must instead marry *Rosalind* and *have a Woman* as her *Lord* (husband).

139–140. ***You and you... fowle Weather.*** The *Clowne* and *Audrey* are *sure* ("joined in wedlock, married," OED) *together* as *sure* (certain) *As Winter* goes hand in hand with *fowle Weather*. In *Weather* lore, "If the Sunne shine hote in winter, it bee-tokeneth foule weather" (Austin Saker, *Narbonus*). Therefore, even though the *Clowne* and *Audrey* are now "hot" for one another, their love is *sure* to cool off. Cf. *Venus and Adonis*: "Lusts winter comes, ere sommer halfe be donne: / Love surfets not, lust like a glutton dies / Love is all truth, lust full of forged lies." Also cf. lines 199–200, below.

141–142. ***Whiles a Wedlocke Hymne... questioning.*** *Whiles Hymen* sings *a Wed-locke Hymne*, the other characters undertake *questioning* (conversation) to bring each other up to date on their adventures.

141–151. ***a Wedlocke Hymne... God of everie Towne.*** *Hymen's Wedlocke Hymne* imitates those found in marriage masques, which themselves imitate the *Hymen* or "Hymenaios" sung by the ancient Greeks in their bridal processions (see note: *Hymen*, line 111, above). *Hymen's Wedlocke Hymne* is remarkably similar to those found in clas-sical Greek drama; cf. this example from Aristophane's *The Birds*:

> Once upon a time the Fates
>   Queenly Hera thus did bring
> To the most august of mates,
>   The high-thron'd Olympian king;
> Sounding their praise even so,
> Hymen Hymenaeus O!

146–147. ***Wedding is great Junos crowne... bed.*** *Great Juno* (Gk. Hera) was the goddess of marriage and the wife of Jupiter (Gk. Zeus). Her *crowne* ("crowning, con-summation, completion, or perfection," OED) *is Wedding*, the *blessed bond of boord and bed* (i.e., "bed and board"), the "full connubial relations" (OED) that allow the couple to *boord* (copulate, EP) in *bed* ("a bridal bed, or a bed of love-making," EP).

148. ***'Tis Hymen peoples everie towne.*** *Hymen peoples everie towne* because *Hymen* (i.e., marriage) allows for rupture of the *Hymen* ("A skinne in the secret partes of a maide broken when shee is defloured," TT, q.v.).

149. ***High.*** *High* can mean: (a) "Of exalted rank, station, dignity, position"; (b) "Of great consequence; important"; and/or (c) "Far advanced into antiquity" (OED).

152–153. ***O my deere Neece... in no lesse degree.*** *Hymen's* song ends while the other characters are filling each other in on their exploits. *Senior* has already welcomed his own *daughter* (line 123, above), and in lines 152–153 he welcomes his *Neece Celia*, whom he holds *Even* as *deere* and *in no lesse degree* (rank, relation) than a *daughter*. *Senior's* consoling words may be prompted by hearing that *Celia* has renounced her own father (I.iii.106).

155. ***Thy faith... doth combine.*** I.e., *Thy faith* "combines" (joins or binds) *my fancie* (affection) *to thee*. For possible sexual pun, see note: *Fancie-monger*, III.ii.355.

156–158. ***Enter Second Brother... sonne of old Sir Rowland.*** This is *Orlando's Second Brother Jaques*, who has been away at school (I.i.7). The audience would not necessarily remember the *Second Brother's* name as it was mentioned only once at the very beginning of Act I. Therefore, Shakespeare helpfully has this character introduce himself as *the second sonne of old Sir Rowland* (as opposed to "*Jaques de Boys*").

That bring these tidings to this faire assembly.
Duke Frederick hearing how that everie day [160]
Men of great worth resorted to this forrest,
Addrest a mightie power, which were on foote
In his owne conduct, purposely to take
His brother heere, and put him to the sword:
And to the skirts of this wilde Wood he came; [165]
Where, meeting with an old Religious man,
After some question with him, was converted
Both from his enterprize, and from the world:
His crowne bequeathing to his banish'd Brother,
And all their Lands restor'd to him againe [170]
That were with him exil'd. This to be true,
I do engage my life.

Du.Se. Welcome yong man:
Thou offer'st fairely to thy brothers wedding:
To one his lands with-held, and to the other [175]
A land it selfe at large, a potent Dukedome.
First, in this Forrest, let us do those ends
That heere were well begun, and wel begot:
And after, every of this happie number

160–169. ***Duke Frederick... his banish'd Brother.*** *Duke Frederick's* conversion allows for a happier ending than that of Lodge's *Rosalynde.* In Lodge's novel, the "middle brother" appears to inform the exiles that the usurping Torismond / *Duke Frederick* has *Addrest* (dispatched) *a mightie power* (army), but he then enjoins King Gerismond / *Duke Senior* to "shew thy selfe in the field to encourage thy subjects." In *Rosalynde,* the exiled King Gerismond recovers his kingdom by force of arms, with "Torismonds armie put to flight, & himselfe slaine in battaile."

163. ***conduct.*** *Conduct* is a "guiding or leading, a leading of Souldiers, as Commanders do" (TB, q.v.)

163. ***purposely.*** *Purposely* is "determinately" (TT, s.v. "Præcīsē").

166. ***an old Religious man.*** This *old Religious man* is a hermit ("One dwelling solitarie in the wildernesse attending onely to devotion," JB, q.v.). Cf. III.ii.404.

170. ***all their Lands restor'd to him.*** I.e., *all* those who lost *their Lands* will each have them *restor'd to him.*

171–172. ***This to be true... engage my life.*** The *Second Brother* realizes that his serving as *Duke Frederick's* emissary could be perceived as suspicious, which is why he offers to *engage* (give as surety, pledge) *his life. Duke Frederick* sent *Oliver* in quest of *Orlando* (see note: IV.iii.91–92), and if *Oliver* failed to return *Frederick* may also have recruited the services of *Orlando's Second Brother.* If this is the case, it would certainly explain how the *Second Brother* knows the details of both *Frederick's* campaign and his conversion.

174–176. ***Thou offer'st fairely... a potent Dukedome.*** The *Second Brother* "offers" (presents a gift) *to* his *brothers wedding fairely* (becomingly; also "favourably, gently, mildly; faithfully, uprightly, sincerely, without fraud, malice, or envie," RC, s.v. "Candidement"). In delivering the news that *Senior* has been restored to his dukedom, the *Second Brother* also gives to *Orlando a potent* (powerful) *Dukedome* (which as *Rosalind's* husband he will inherit upon *Senior's* death), and to *Oliver his lands with-held.*

176. ***at large.*** *At large* means "in great measure" (RC, s.v. "Copieusement") or "As a whole, as a body; in general; taken altogether" (OED).

177. ***do those ends.*** Finish what we have begun.

179. ***happie.*** Fortunate.

That have endur'd shrew'd daies, and nights with us, [180]

Shal share the good of our returned fortune,

According to the measure of their states.

Meane time, forget this new-falne dignitie,

And fall into our Rusticke Revelrie:

Play Musicke, and you Brides and Bride-groomes all, [185]

With measure heap'd in joy, to'th Measures fall.

{*Dance.*}

Jaq. Sir, by your patience: if I heard you rightly,

The Duke hath put on a Religious life,

And throwne into neglect the pompous Court. [190]

2.Bro. He hath.

Jaq. To him will I: out of these convertites,

There is much matter to be heard, and learn'd:

---

180. ***shrew'd.*** Difficult, harsh.

180. ***with us.*** *Senior's* use of *us* to mean solely himself indicates that he has reassumed royal prerogative. He speaks of himself in the plural from this point forward (lines 181, 184, and 206–207, below).

181–182. ***Shal share the good of our returned fortune... their states.*** The wheel of the goddess *fortune* has *returned* ("turn[ed] again," OED), and thus the *fortune* (good luck, prosperity) of *Senior* and his followers has *returned* (come back).

Fortune, who is a capricious whore, judges men's worth not with *measure* ("Restraint in conduct; modesty, discretion; prudence," OED) but with her *share* ("pubic region, groin," OED). Thus, the goddess deals *good fortune* to men *According to their measure* (i.e., genital endowment; see note: *measure*, V.ii.61) and "state" ("suggestive of the erected penis," JH, s.v. "stately"; *state* is literally "the height or chief stage of a process; the condition of full vigour," OED); cf. I.ii.32–40. Now that *Senior* has regained his "potency" (both "authority" and "Ability to achieve erection or ejaculation in sexual intercourse," OED; cf. *potent Dukedome*, line 176, above), he attempts to compensate for *fortune's* abuses. His followers *Shal share* his *good fortune*, but only *According to the measure* ("proportion, rate," also "quantitie, size; an equallnesse, or answerablenesse," RC, s.v. "Proportion") of *their* respective *states* (social positions).

183. ***new-falne dignitie.*** *Senior's* current *dignitie* ("honour; authoritie, superioritie; greatnesse of estate, or in office; great estimation, or worthinesse; Nobilitie, or noblenesse," RC, s.v. "Dignité") is not just *new-falne* (newly come about); it is also a "new fall" ("A recidivation, relapse," RC, s.v. "Recheute") into the former state of *dignitie* that he enjoyed prior to his exile.

184–185. ***fall into our Rusticke Revelrie... Musicke.*** *Senior* decides to *fall* (descend from a high social position) and abandon his *new-falne dignitie* (line 183, above). Thus, his companions can *fall into* (swiftly or vigorously undertake) their *Rusticke* ("uplandish, homelie, of the field or countrey, rurall, clownish, rude," JF, s.v. "Selvaggio") *Revelrie* ("boisterous mirth or merrymaking," OED). Up until now, the wedding festivities have resembled a stately masque, but the tone of the *Musicke* and dancing here changes to a decidedly less dignified style.

186. ***With measure heap'd in joy... fall.*** *Senior* enjoins his followers to *fall to* (begin, undertake) the *Measures* (music and dancing) with "heaped measure" ("Fulnesse, aboundance," RC, s.v. "Comble") of *joy*.

187. {***Dance.***} According to *Senior's* spoken stage directions of lines 184–186, above, the characters here perform a rustic dance (and possibly even dance off stage when they exit in line 208, below). The dialogue of lines 188–207 is spoken concurrently.

189. ***The Duke hath put on a Religious life.*** In seeking verification that *Duke Frederick hath put on* (assumed, adopted) a *Religious life*, *Jaques* takes a stab at *Duke Senior*, whose *Religious life* was merely *put on* (feigned, simulated). *Senior* affected religious zeal for his ascetic *life* (II.i.4–20) but adopted it only out of constraint. By contrast, *Frederick* undergoes a sincere conversion and chooses a *Religious life* of his own free will, which may be why *Jaques* seeks *Frederick's* company but eschewed *Senior's* (II.v.32–37).

190. ***throwne into neglect.*** Forgotten or forsaken.

190. ***the pompous Court.*** *Pompous* can mean "stately, majesticall, proude" (JF, s.v. "Pomposo") but can also mean "boastful, vainglorious; arrogant; presumptuous, pretentious" (OED). Cf. *Duke Senior's* likening *the pompous Court* to the "Whore of Babylon" (II.i.6–7); the *Clowne's* description of the courtier (lines 50–54, above); and *convertites* (line 192, below).

192–193. ***convertites... much matter to be heard, and learn'd.*** A "convertite" is (a) "one that hath turned to the Faith; or is woon unto a religious profession; or hath abandonned a loose to follow a godlie, a vicious to lead a vertuous, life" (RC, s.v. "Convers"); and (b) "A reformed Magdalen" (OED; cf. *Senior's* likening of courtly life to whoredom in II.i.6–7). *Jaques*, who thinks little of *Senior's* "potency" and his *potent Dukedome* (line 176, above), believes *Frederick* to have better *matter*, which means (a) topics of discussion; and (b) the male genitals and semen (see notes: *matter*, III.ii.169 and 184). Also see note: *learn'd*, I.iii.78.

you to your former Honor, I bequeath

your patience, and your vertue, well deserves it. [195]

you to a love, that your true faith doth merit:

you to your land, and love, and great allies:

you to a long, and well-deserved bed:

And you to wrangling, for thy loving voyage

Is but for two moneths victuall'd: So to your pleasures, [200]

I am for other, then for dancing meazures.

Du.Se. Stay, *Jaques*, stay.

Jaq. To see no pastime, I: what you would have,

Ile stay to know, at your abandon'd cave.

Exit {*Jaques*}. [V.iv.7] [205]

Du.Se. Proceed, proceed: wee'l begin these rights,

As we do trust, they'l end in true delights.

{*Exeunt. Manet Rosalind.*} [V.iv.8]

Ros. It is not the fashion to see the Ladie the Epi-

logue: but it is no more unhandsome, then to see the [210]

194–200. ***you to your former Honor... two moneths victuall'd.*** *Still* (continuous) *Musicke* has been playing since line 112, above, and the dancers fell *to'th Measures* in line 186, above. By speaking over the music and dancing, *Jaques* takes on a de facto role in the masque. He addresses the lovers in imitation of *Hymen's* speech (lines 135–140, above), but *Jaques'* benedictions contain a decidedly pragmatic, material element. His solemn prognostications are in stark contrast to the upbeat tune over which he speaks (see note: *Rusticke Revelrie*, line 184, above).

194–195. ***you to your former Honor... well deserves it.*** These lines are delivered to *Duke Senior*, who, after much *patience* (i.e., "getting screwed"; see note: *patience*, V.ii.99) has now been restored to his *former vertue* (i.e., "potency"; see note: *vertue*, III.ii.121).

196–198. ***you to a love... well-deserved bed.*** Lines 196 and 198 could be addressed to either *Orlando* or *Silvius*; delivery of either line to either character works both logically and dramatically. However, given the Elizabethan respect for hierarchy, line 196 is probably delivered to *Orlando* because he is *Duke Senior's* (male) heir and thus the second highest ranking person present.

Line 197 is delivered to *Oliver*. Now that *Aliena* has resumed her rightful identity as *Celia*, *Oliver* has no reason to *live and die a Shepherd* (V.ii.14). Therefore, he can return to his *land* and *great* (aristocratic) *allies* (relatives, kinsfolk).

199–200. ***And you to wrangling... victuall'd.*** These lines are delivered to the *Clowne*, who *Jaques* is sure will fall to *wrangling* ("brabling, brawling," RC, s.v. "Altercation") with his wife. The *Clowne* is eager to undertake a *loving voyage* (i.e., sexual intercourse; see note: *voyage*, II.vii.44), but he has only enough "love" for *Audrey* to provide "victuals" ("food": "sexual sustenance," GW) for *two moneths*. Therefore, he is sure to be unfaithful and end up "rangling" ("Intriguing with a variety of women," FG).

201–203. ***I am for other... no pastime.*** *Jaques* has renounced *pastime* ("recreation, anie thing that withdraweth the minde from heavines, releasing from studie," TT, s.v. "Avŏcāmentum") and "pastimes" ("Sexual play," EC); cf. and see notes: II.vii.70 and IV.i.17–30. He therefore has no interest in *dancing meazures* (i.e., "fucking around"; *dancing* alludes to copulation, JH; also see note: *measure*, V.ii.61).

204. ***Ile stay to know... abandon'd cave.*** This line suggests that *Jaques* intends to take up the life of a hermit. Cf. III.ii.403–404.

206. ***Proceed, proceed.*** *Senior* abandoned the dancing in order to talk to *Jaques* but here turns his attention back to the revelers.

206–207. ***begin these rights... true delights.*** *Senior* will begin *these rights* (i.e., the marriage ceremony), and he trusts they will end in *true* (legitimate, rightful; also see note: *true*, line 125, above) *delights* (sexual pleasures, EP).

209–210. ***It is not the fashion... the Epilogue.*** It was *not the fashion* (prevailing custom) *to see the Ladie the Epilogue*, but the practice was not unheard of: a *Ladie* also serves as *the Epilogue* in Francis Beaumont's *Knight of the Burning Pestle*, and in Thomas Dekker and John Ford's *The Witch of Edmonton*.

210. ***unhandsome.*** *Unhandsome* is "unproper, unfit" (JF, s.v. "Mas destro").

Lord the Prologue. If it be true, that good wine needs
no bush, 'tis true, that a good play needes no Epilogue.
Yet to good wine they do use good bushes: and good
playes prove the better by the helpe of good Epilogues:
What a case am I in then, that am neither a good Epi- [215]
logue, nor cannot insinuate with you in the behalfe of a
good play? I am not furnish'd like a Begger, therefore
to begge will not become mee. My way is to conjure
you, and Ile begin with the Women. I charge you (O
women) for the love you beare to men, to like as much [220]
of this Play, as please you: And I charge you (O men)
for the love you beare to women (as I perceive by your
simpring, none of you hates them) that betweene you,
and the women, the play may please. If I were a Woman, I would kisse as many of you as had beards that [225]
pleas'd me, complexions that lik'd me, and breaths that
I defi'de not: And I am sure, as many as have good
beards, or good faces, or sweet breaths, will for my kind
offer, when I make curt'sie, bid me farewell.

Exit {*Rosalind*}. [230]

FINIS.

211–213. ***good wine needs no bush... good bushes.*** "An ivy-bush was once the common sign of taverns, and especially of private houses where beer or wine could be obtained by travelers" (DPF). "Good wine draws customers without any help of an ivy-bush" (RC, s.v. "À bon vin il ne faut point d'enseigne") was a proverbial saying which meant that a good product would sell well even without advertising.

There is additional bawdy play on *wine* as both an aphrodisiac and semen (see notes: *wine*, III.v.77 and *Wine*, III.ii.200), and on *bush* as the female genitalia and pubic hair (see note: *bush*, III.iii.78).

212–214. ***a good play needes no Epilogue... good Epilogues.*** *A good play* (dramatic performance) *needes no Epilogue* ("a Speech made after an Interlude or Play ended," TB, q.v.), but *good playes* (dramatic performances) *prove the better by the helpe of good Epilogues.*

Also, *a good play* (i.e., "a good fuck"; see note: *plaid*, I.iii.78) will *prove the better by the helpe* of *a good Epilogue* (i.e., orgasm; an *Epilogue* is literally "A conclusion, or finall end," TT, s.v. "Epĭlŏgus"; "conclusion" alludes to orgasm, JA, pp. 143–144; also see note: *conclusion*, line 130, above).

215–217. ***What a case am I in... a good play.*** The male actor playing *Rosalind* is in *a case* (plight) because he is not *a good Epilogue.* Moreover, because the *play* was not very *good,* he *cannot insinuate* (i.e., make an "Insinuation": "A cunning speech to creepe into ones favour," JB, q.v.) *in* its *behalfe.*

The male actor playing *Rosalind* is also in a *case* because his feminine *case* ("clothes or garments," OED) places him in sexual limbo. His appearance suggests that he has *a case* (vagina, EP), but as a male he is physically unequipped to provide men with *good play* (i.e., sexual intercourse; see note: *plaid*, I.iii.78). As a transvestite, he is equally useless to women because he cannot *insinuate* (with play on L. "insinuare": "to penetrate," LD).

217–218. ***I am not furnish'd... to begge will not become mee.*** It would not *become* (be suitable for) the actor playing *Rosalind to begge* because he is *furnish'd* (dressed) like a *Ladie* (line 209, above), not *a Begger.* The male/female *Rosalind's* blurred gender places him/her in a sexually inconvenient position. Although he is *furnish'd* (well-hung or sexually potent; see note: *furnish'd*, III.ii.243), his feminine dress suggests he is *a Begger* (i.e., a "bugger"; see note: *beg*, I.i.74).

218–224. ***My way is to conjure you... the play may please.*** This male/female actor claimed to be *a Magitian* (V.ii.74), so he/she hopes to *conjure* (influence by magic) *the Women* and the *men* to *conjure* (come together in sexual congress, FR). Although the boy/girl *Rosalind's* indeterminate gender excludes him/her from the *way* ("natural, sexual fulfilment," GW), he/she attempts to *conjure* ("beseech earnestly, intreat vehemently," RC, s.v. "Conjurer") *the* actual *Women* and *men* in the audience to effect *play* (sexual intercourse; see note: *plaid*, I.iii.78) that will *please* (be sexually satisfying; see note: *please*, V.ii.62).

223. ***simpring.*** *Simpring* is (a) inane grinning; and/or (b) ingratiating behavior.

224–225. ***If I were a Woman.*** The male actor who originally portrayed *Rosalind* was, of course, not *a Woman.*

225. ***beards.*** See note: *beard*, III.ii.206.

226. ***lik'd.*** *Lik'd* means "delighted" or "pleased, satisfide" (JF, s.v. "Piaciuto").

226. ***complexions.*** See note: *complection*, III.ii.194.

226–227. ***that I defi'de not.*** I.e., that I did not disapprove of.

FINIS.

Textual Preparation

The First Folio of 1623 preserves Shakespeare's work intact with a bare minimum of errors.[1] Typesetter's errors (such as backwards, inverted, or upside-down letters, spacing inconsistencies, etc.) are easily recognizable and have been corrected in this transcription.[2] Only categorically obvious typesetting errors are emended; no other textual errors (including errors in punctuation, spelling, or lineation) are assumed. Detection of any other errors as may occur is left to the capable discernment of the individual reader.

Enter Boy and Watch.
Match. Lead Boy,which way?

An obvious typographical error in the First Folio.

Given the overall integrity of the First Folio, all dialogue is preserved fully intact: the spelling, punctuation, capitalization and verse lineation (except in the case of simultaneous delivery) have not been altered in any way.

Minimal contextual adjustments have been made to present the First Folio text in a user-friendly format. These modifications exclusively address the following:

(I) Variant character tags and speech prefixes;
(II) Discrepancies in entrances and exits;
(III) Act and scene division;
(IV) Font and
  i. Interchangeable vowels and consonants;
  ii. Ligatures;
(V) Abbreviations;
(VI) Dual column format and
  i. Simultaneous dialogue;
  ii. Turned-up and turned-under lines.

(I) Variant character tags and speech prefixes.

Shakespearean characters often turn up in the First Folio under multiple aliases. For example, in *The Life and Death of Richard III*, a character appears whose full historical name and title is "Sir Thomas Stanley, Earl of Derby." This character's lines are sometimes assigned to *Derby* and sometimes to *Stanley*. Similarly, the historical character "Anthony Woodville, Lord Rivers" is tagged as both *Woodville* and *Rivers*.

In *The Tragedie of Romeo and Juliet*, *Juliet's* father is variously tagged as *Father, Capulet,* and *Old Capulet*; the comic servant as *Servant, Peter,* and *Clowne*; and *Juliet's* mother as *Mother, Madam, Wife, Lady, Old Lady*, and *Lady of the house*. Such a plethora of titles can be confusing to both reader and producer, because it is not immediately apparent that they belong to one single character. Therefore, for purposes of clarity, any character who appears under multiple names is assigned a uniform character tag. For example, in *Romeo and Juliet*, any lines spoken by *Juliet's* mother will be assigned to *Lady Capulet*.[3]

Sometimes, instead of the name of the character, the name of the actor who originally played the part is used in the Folio.[4] An example of this can be found in Act V, scene i of *A Midsommer Nights Dreame*:

Tawyer with a Trumpet before them.
Enter Pyramus and Thisby, Wall, Moone-shine, and Lyon.

Pyramus, Thisby, Wall, Moone-shine, and *Lyon* are all character names, but the mysterious "*Tawyer*" is the actual personage William Tawyer (or Tawier), a bit player and musician employed at the Globe Theatre.[5]

The names of two more prominent players turn up in *Much adoe about Nothing*:

Kem. Gods my life, where's the Sexton? let him write
downe the Princes Officer *Coxcombe*: come, binde them
thou naughty varlet.
Couley. Away, you are an asse, you are an asse.

"*Kem*[*p*]" and "*Couley*" are William Kemp (or Kempt) and Richard Couley (or Cowly); both are included in the Folio's list of "Principall Actors." The appearance of Kemp and Couley's names in print allows scholars to identify them as the actors who originated the roles of *Dogberry* and *Borachio* respectively. However, to a reader trying to follow the story or to a company staging the play, this information is of no practical value whatsoever. Consequently, where they occur, actors' names are replaced with those of the characters.

(II) Discrepancies in entrances and exits.

In the First Folio, all entrances that will occur within a scene are sometimes lumped together at the beginning. In *The Merry Wives of Windsor*, the following characters are listed in the entrance at the top of Act I, scene i:

Enter Justice Shallow, Slender, *Sir* Hugh Evans, *Master* Page, Falstoffe, Bardolph, Nym, Pistoll, Anne Page, *Mistresse* Ford, *Mistresse* Page, Simple.

However, for the first 69 lines of dialogue, only *Shallow*, *Slender*, and *Evans* speak. Moreover, these three characters talk about *Master Page, Falstoffe*, and *Anne Page* as if they are not actually present. *Master Page* does not speak until line 70, in dialogue that runs as follows:

Evan. ... I will peat the doore for Mr.
Page. What hoa? Got-plesse your house heere.[6]
M.Page. Who's there?

It is therefore reasonable to assume that *Master Page* does not enter onto the scene until he says "Who's there" after *Evans* "peats the door." Common sense is the largest factor in assigning an exact point for entrances and exits; if a character speaks a line of greeting or farewell, it is safe to assume that his entrance or exit falls at that point.

Sometimes a character is never assigned an entrance to a scene but is clearly present, as in Act I, scene iii of *The Life and Death of Richard III*:

Q.M. *Rivers* and *Dorset*, you were standers by,
And so wast thou, Lord *Hastings*, when my Sonne
Was stab'd with bloody Daggers: God, I pray him,
That none of you may live his naturall age,
But by some unlook'd accident cut off.

Queene Margaret clearly speaks directly to other characters present: *Rivers*, *Dorset*, and *Lord Hastings*. However, *Hastings* is not given an entrance in the First Folio. Since *Hastings* also speaks during this scene, he obviously must be on stage. Therefore, his omission from the list of entering characters must be an error.[7] Similarly, sometimes a character is clearly absent from the stage but has not been instructed to exit.

Such inaccuracies are hardly noticeable to the reader but can prove greatly inconvenient for the producer. In order to make the scripts viable for production, every character has been assigned clear and precise entrance and exit cues.[8]

Other than entrances and exits, very few stage directions have been added. Such insertions are invasive and unnecessary; all that is truly required to grasp the stage business is simple attention to a line's content. *Hamlet*'s advice to "sute the Action to the Word, the Word to the Action" is tremendously apt.

Most stage directions are embedded in the dialogue itself. This system was highly practical, especially considering that the professional actor did not have the modern luxury of performing a single play for weeks or months on end. A public playhouse in Shakespeare's England had to continually serve up fresh fare in order to draw an audience. On average, ten different plays were presented in a two-week period. Old plays were revived and new plays introduced on an ongoing basis, and almost never was the same play repeated on two consecutive days. A leading actor would have as many as seventy-one different roles in his repertoire; a supporting actor would of necessity have even more, as he would be expected to portray multiple characters within a single play.[9]

Under such circumstances, a prompter (or "book-holder") was always at hand to assist a player if he had trouble recalling his lines. Likewise, a player could not reasonably be expected to recall his blocking without some readily available memory aid. It is hardly difficult to recall the accompanying action to such lines as "I do embrace thee," "I kisse your Highnesse Hand," "poore gyrle she weepes," and so on.[10]

(III) Act and scene division.

Act and scene division of plays in the First Folio occurs somewhat haphazardly. Some plays are clearly broken down into acts and scenes; some into acts only; some are wholly lacking this division. Any act and scene division that appears in the Folio has been retained.

In addition, for the benefit of those staging the plays, scenes are further divided into French scenes (so named because of their use by 17th century French Dramatists). A new French scene begins each time a character or set of characters enters or leaves the stage. Act and scene numbers are printed in Roman numerals (in upper and lower case respectively); French scenes are printed in Arabic numerals. For example: Act three, scene two, French scene seven will appear in the right margin as [III.ii.7].

(IV) Font.

The original font(s) employed in the First Folio differ in some significant ways from contemporary fonts. Some alphabetical symbols (such as the long "s") are wholly obsolete and have been replaced with their modern equivalents:

As printed in the Folio	*Herein transcribed as*
ſiſters	sisters
kiſſe	kisse
ſoule	soule

i. Interchangeable vowels and consonants

The glyphs U, V, I, and J present much unnecessary confusion in direct transcription. Although their descendents still survive in modern typeface, these letters are not used in exactly the same way as were their Renaissance predecessors.

"U" and "V" did not originally represent different letters and came to be considered as such only comparatively recently in the evolution of the modern alphabet. The "U" form derives from the black letter tradition that originated in handwritten calligraphy; the "V" form is older and dates all the way back to Roman usage. The earliest printed texts employed one or the other exclusively, but over time both began to appear together.

When the First Folio was printed, the convention was to use "V" in the initial position and "U" in the median and terminal positions.[11] For the convenience of the modern reader, these transcriptions use "U" to designate the vowel and "V" to designate the consonant:

As printed in the Folio	*Direct transcription*	*Herein printed*
vn-vrg'd	vn-vrg'd	un-urg'd
vſe	vse	use
loue	loue	love

In addition, a modern "W" (double U) is substituted for "VV" (double V):

As printed in the Folio	*Direct transcription*	*Herein printed*
vvould	vvould	would

Likewise, "I" and "J" originated as the same letter, and in the First Folio "I" represents both vowel and consonant. In updating the font, "I" has been used for the vowel and "J" for the consonant:

As printed in the Folio	*Direct transcription*	*Herein printed*
iniurious	iniurious	injurious
Iuie	Iuie	Ivie
Iuſtice	Iustice	Justice

ii. Ligatures

Seventeenth century printers employed ligatures (glyphs representing a combination of two or more characters) because they took less time to set and took up less room on the printed line. In modern usage, only a few ligatures (such as the "æ" in "Cæsar") have survived. Obsolete glyphs can therefore create something of a puzzle in direct transcription.

The most common enigma presented by these obsolete glyphs involves the letter "Y" and its predecessor, the Anglo-Saxon thorn. The thorn was a phonetic symbol that represented the "th" sound, both voiced (as in "*th*at") and unvoiced (as in "*th*ink"). By the late Renaissance, the thorn had disappeared except in ligatures employing its nearest equivalent in the standard typeset: the letter "Y."[12] The similarity between the two is clearly discernable in early Black Letter fonts.

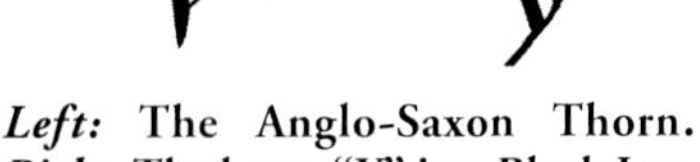

***Left:* The Anglo-Saxon Thorn. *Right:* The letter "Y" in a Black Letter font.**

Words in the Folio that employ "Y" / thorn ligatures have been fully spelled out using modern typeface:

As printed in the Folio	*Direct transcription*	*Herein printed*
yͭ	yt	that
yͧ	yu	thou
yͤ	ye	the (or thee)

Other enigmatic ligatures involve the use of a tilde (~) over vowels; the tilde stands for either "M" or "N" (exactly which must be determined from context):

As printed in the Folio	*Direct transcription*	*Herein printed*
thẽ	thẽ	them (or then)
mã	mã	man
thẽſelues	thẽselues	themselves

Only the most commonly used ligatures have been updated to modern font. Any other deviation has been retained, for any indiscriminate change can severely damage content. Consider the following lines from Act V, scene i of *A Midsommer Nights Dreame* as printed in modern editions:

Pir. O grim-look'd night! O night with hue so black!
O night, which ever art when day is not!
O night, O night! alack, alack, alack,
I fear my Thisby's promise is forgot!
And thou, O wall, O sweet, O lovely wall,
That stand'st between her father's ground and mine!
Thou wall, O wall, O sweet and lovely wall,
Show me thy chink, to blink through with mine eyne!

This speech as printed in the First Folio contains an important (and easily discernable) difference in the typeface:

Pir. O grim lookt night, ô night with hue so blacke,
O night, which ever art, when day is not:
O night, ô night, alacke, alacke, alacke,
I feare my *Thisbies* promise is forgot.
And thou ô wall, thou sweet and lovely wall,
That stands between her fathers ground and mine,
Thou wall, ô wall, o sweet and lovely wall,
Shew me thy chinke, to blinke through with mine eine.

The circumflex (^) over the "o" is not necessarily attributable to the typesetter's negligence or error. *Nick Bottome*, the character who portrays the role of *Piramus* in the play-within-a-play, is the consummate ham. It therefore follows that the "^" over the "o" could just as easily demonstrate *Bottome's* highly melodramatic inflection. Instead of substituting "O," the original "ô" is preserved in the belief that the original glyph far better reflects the substance of both speech and speaker.

(V) Abbreviations

As with ligatures, commonly used abbreviations are spelled out as full words:

As printed in the Folio	*Direct transcription*	*Herein printed*
Mr	Mr	Master
S.	S.	Saint
L.	L.	Lord

(VI) Dual column layout and simultaneous dialogue.

The First Folio was printed in a two-column format, a space-saving textual arrangement favored by many printers in an age when paper was highly expensive. Many books from the period, including the 1611 King James Bible, are laid out in this way.

i. Simultaneous dialogue

Isaac Jaggard and his employees were scrupulous in their composition and proofreading of the First Folio.[13] However, the printed work failed its original handwritten sources in one highly significant respect: all simultaneous dialogue was inadvertently erased.

It is a readily observable phenomenon in everyday life that two or more people will speak at once. It follows that dramatists, who seek, in Hamlet's words, to "hold as 'twer the Mirrour up to Nature," should also adopt overlapping speech as a theatrical device.

In modern scripts, simultaneous dialogue is easily recognizable because it is arranged in multiple columns across the width of the entire page. This multicolumn arrangement was not unknown to Elizabethan dramatists. It is found in the 1616 Folio of Ben Jonson's works, where, in Act IV, scene v of *The Alchemist*, fully sixteen lines of concurrent dialogue are printed in two discrete columns. To remove any doubt whatsoever as to the congruity of these speeches, this dialogue is prefaced by the stage direction "*They speake together.*"

If we could look over the shoulder of Shakespeare's book-holder, we would undoubtedly find numerous places where multiple characters speak at once. The apparent absence of simultaneous dialogue in the Folio is wholly attributable to its layout.

When Jaggard chose a dual-column layout for the Folio, he created a conundrum for his typesetters. Since the main body of sequential dialogue was already printed in side-by-side columns, it was impossible to further break down simultaneous dialogue into additional columns. In this situation, the compositors had no choice but to eliminate the multiple columns. When a compositor came upon multi-column (a.k.a. simultaneous) dialogue in a handwritten manuscript, he took the leftmost speech and placed it first in order in the column. Next, he took the speech immediately to its right and placed it underneath. This continued until all multiple columns had been distilled down into one. As a result, concurrent speeches deceptively appear as consecutive in the First Folio.

When the use of cue-scripts is taken into account, the most readily apparent clue as to simultaneous dialogue lies in what appears to be a "repeated" cue line. Consider the following lines from Act V, scene ii of *As you Like it* as printed within a single First Folio column:

Phe. If this be so, why blame you me to love you?
Sil. If this be so, why blame you me to love you?
Orl. If this be so, why blame you me to love you?
Ros. Why do you speake too, Why blame you mee to love you.

The actor who originally played *Rosalind* would not have the entire prompt-script in hand. Instead, he would have only a part script in which his line and cue would run as follows:

________________________________ to love you?
Why do you speake too, Why blame you mee to love you.

Since the actor playing *Rosalind* will begin to speak as soon as he hears the cue "to love you," it follows that *Phebe*, *Silvius*, and *Orlando* deliver their lines simultaneously.

In passages where the dialogue doesn't make sense when delivered sequentially, the lines are probably overlapping. Take, for example, the following excerpt from Act I, scene i of *The Tragedie of Romeo and Juliet*:

Enter old Capulet in his Gowne, and his wife.
Cap. What noise is this? Give me my long Sword ho.
Wife. A crutch, a crutch: why call you for a Sword?
Cap. My Sword I say: Old *Mountague* is come,
and flourishes his Blade in spight of me.
Enter old Mountague, & his wife.

Moun. Thou villaine Capulet. Hold me not, let me go
2. Wife. Thou shalt not stir a foote to seeke a Foe.

Upon critical examination, something seems amiss. If *Mountague* is not yet on stage, why should *Capulet* claim that "Old *Mountague* is come"? How can *Capulet* describe his enemy's actions if he is not yet in sight? The simple answer is, of course, that the patriarchs of the rival families enter onto the scene at the same time.

Sadly, no handwritten promptbook pages from Shakespeare's Folio plays survive, but the above lines would probably have been laid out in the original handwritten prompt-copy as follows:

Enter old Capulet in his Gowne, and his wife.	*Enter old Mountague, & his wife.*
Cap.	*Moun.*
What noise is this? Give me my long Sword ho.	Thou villaine Capulet. Hold me not, let me go
Wife.	*2. Wife.*
A crutch, a crutch: why call you for a Sword?	Thou shalt not stir a foote to seeke a Foe.
Cap.	
My Sword I say: Old *Mountague* is come And flourishes his Blade in spight of me.	

Admittedly, this textual arrangement is conjectural. However, it is absurd to slavishly and unquestioningly follow the columnar format set down by Jaggard and his associates in 1623. Such a practice serves only to preserve the mechanical limitations of the First Folio's printer, not the intentions of its author.[14] Many passages that initially seem redundant, nonsensical, or melodramatic make perfect sense when delivered simultaneously.[15] In order to restore working viability to Shakespeare's play scripts, some attempt must be made to accurately arrange dialogue as originally delivered in performance.[16]

ii. Turned-up and turned-under lines

The First Folio's columns were of limited width and accordingly limited the width of the text that could be placed within them. Consequently, lines that were too long were either turned up (had part of the text placed on the row above), as in *Measure for Measure*, Act V, scene i:

Isab. Oh that it were as like as it is true. (speak'st,
Duk. By heaven (fond wretch) thou knowst not what thou

Or turned under (had part of the text placed on the row beneath), as in Act I, scene ii of *Comedie of Errors*:

E.Dro. What meane you sir, for God sake hold your
Nay, and you will not sir, Ile take my heeles. (hands:

In the two examples above, the typesetter has inserted an opening parenthesis to indicate that the fractured text is truly one single line of iambic pentameter.[17] In all cases where parentheses mark a fracture, the text is herein adjusted to a single row. Therefore, the example immediately presented above will appear as:

E.Dro. What meane you sir, for God sake hold your hands:
Nay, and you will not sir, Ile take my heeles.

Parentheses are not universally employed to identify turned-up and turned-under lines in the Folio. They primarily occur on pages with tightly packed type, because there was simply no room to spill over a long line's excess text onto a row of its own. When the Folio's typesetters had the luxury of space, an extra-long line could be readily accommodated on two rows, as in *Alls Well, that Ends Well*, Act II, scene iii:

King. Why then young Bertram take her shee's thy
wife.

Although this speech is broken up onto two rows, scrutiny will reveal the line to be ten beats with a meter suspiciously akin to a regular line of iambic pentameter. Therefore, this is probably a turned under verse line. Most editions would therefore place this line onto one single row, as follows:

King. Why, then, young Bertram, take her; she's thy wife.

Such changes to lineation are not made herein, because such evidence, although suggestive, is not unarguably conclusive. Systematic "fixing" of fractured verse lines is ill-advised, because characters often switch back and forth between prose and verse, as in Act IV, scene I of *Twelfe Night, Or what you will*:

Enter Sebastian and Clowne

Clo. Will you make me beleeve, that I am not sent for you?

← *The Clowne begins the scene in prose and continues in prose throughout.*

Seb. Go too, go too, thou art a foolish fellow,
Let me be cleere of thee.

← *Sebastian begins the scene in verse.*

Clo. Well held out yfaith: No, I do not know you, nor I am not sent to you by my Lady, to bid you come speake with her: nor your name is not Master *Cesario,* nor this is not my nose neyther: Nothing that is so, is so.

Seb. I prethee vent thy folly some-where else, thou know'st not me.

← *Sebastian switches to prose in mid-speech.*

Clo. Vent my folly: He has heard that word of some great man, and now applyes it to a foole. Vent my folly: I am affraid this great lubber the World will prove a

Cockney: I prethee now ungird thy strangenes, and tell me what I shall vent to my Lady? Shall I vent to hir that thou art comming?

Seb. I prethee foolish greeke depart from me, there's money for thee, if you tarry longer, I shall give worse paiment. ← *Sebastian continues the scene in prose.*

It is important to know that such switches between verse and prose occur and to understand their dramatic purpose: Shakespeare uses these switches to mark important emotional transitions for the character.[18] Consequently, it is often difficult to determine whether an initial lowercase letter indicates a fractured verse line or a switch between verse and prose. Consider the following example from Act III, scene i of *The Life and Death of Richard III*:

Yorke. I would that I might thanke you, as, as, you
call me.

The words "call me" placed on a line of their own might be a sign that *Yorke* lapses into prose. On the other hand, the lineation could just as easily denote a turned-under alexandrine (an extra-long verse line consisting of twelve beats). In this case, it is simply impossible to tell which was originally intended. Because such ambiguity frequently occurs, the lineation is left intact. In such cases, the ultimate determination as to Shakespeare's intent justly lies with the individual.

Notes

1. In his preface to *Loves Labours Lost* (New Variorum edition, 1904), Dr. Horace Howard Furness estimates that in the entire canon "there is only one obstinately refractory line, or passage, in every eight hundred and eighty." In a play of approx. 3,000 lines, this equates to 3.4 significant errors. Compare this to the thirty-one "corrections" (eleven to punctuation, ten to spelling, and ten to capitalization) made to eight lines of *2 Henry IV* illustrated above (*Introduction*, page 17).

2. For a list of textual corrections, see Appendix I. This textual preparation is intended to be helpful to actors, directors, producers, students, teachers, and general readers. Those researching the process and mechanics of 17th century printing in general, and of the First Folio in particular, will find little of interest herein and will be better served by consulting original Folios or facsimiles thereof.

3. Since these variant titles did not appear in the cue-scripts used by Shakespeare's players, they are completely non-essential to an actor's character interpretation. For those who may find them of interest, however, variant character titles are preserved in Appendix IV.

4. Shakespeare was part owner of an established theatre with a long-standing resident company. Consequently, he often wrote parts with specific actors in mind.

5. From his appearance in *Midsommer Nights Dreame*, Mr. Tawyer's employment with the King's Men can be dated from as early as 1594. When he died in 1625, William Tawyer was entered into the sexton's register of St. Savior's Church, Southwark, as "Mr. Heminges man." Apparently, despite this long tenure, Tawyer never rose very high in the ranks of the theatrical profession. Even with over thirty years' experience with Shakespeare's company, his name is not among the First Folio's list of "Principall Actors."

6. The phonetic spellings are here indicative of *Evans'* Welsh accent.

7. Such omissions are easily explained when the "Foul Papers" are taken into account as source material. A Playwright scribbling away in a white heat would be most concerned with setting down dialogue as it played out in his head. Minor points, like precise moments for entrances and exits, could be added in later when a clean prompt-book was prepared.

8. For a list of emended entrances and exits, see Appendix II.

9. Based on Bernard Beckerman's analysis of Philip Henslowe's 1594–1597 box office records from *The Rose* (*Shakespeare at the Globe,* Collier, 1962).

10. For more on Shakespeare's embedded stage directions and the performing style of his company, see Ronald Watkins' *On Producing Shakespeare* (Citadel Press, 1950).

11. The earliest printed book to use "U" and "V" to delineate vowel from consonant respectively was printed in Italy in 1524 and was written by Gian Giorgio Trissino (1478–1550), a fervent orthographic reformer. Trissino even appealed to Pope Clement VII for the introduction of new letters into the Italian alphabet. As with all revolutionaries, it took time for his views to become widely adopted. The First Folio was printed, 99 years later, according to older convention.

12. The substitution of "Y" for the thorn also appears on Shakespeare's gravestone. His epitaph reads:

GOOD FREND FOR IESVS SAKE FORBEARE,
TO DIGG THE DVST ENCLOASED HEARE:
BLEST BE YE MAN YT SPARES THES STONES
AND CVRST BE HE YT MOVES MY BONES

Shakespeare's family obviously thought it more important to prevent his crypt from re-use (a very real possibility when demand exceeded supply for prime chapel burial space) than to extol his earthly accomplishments. Incidentally, Shakespeare had the honor of burial in Stratford-on-Avon's Holy Trinity Church not because of his fame but because he was a lay-rector of the parish. Tradition holds that he died on his 52nd birthday, April 23, 1616, after drinking too much with fellow-poets Ben Jonson and Michael Drayton. His true memorial was raised in the First Folio. In his dedication, Ben Jonson speaks of Shakespeare as "a Moniment, without a tombe, / And art alive still, while thy Booke doth live, / And we have wits to read, and praise to give," for "He was not of an age, but for all time!"

13. For illustration of the proofreading of the First Folio, see the Norton Facsimile, Appendix A.

14. At the time of writing (Fall 2010), not one single commercially available edition of any Shakespearean play has yet attempted to restore simultaneous dialogue.

15. For an in-depth exploration of simultaneousness in Shakespeare, see Richard Flatter's *Shakespeare's Producing Hand* (Greenwood Press, 1948).

16. Since this text restores simultaneous dialogue, for obvious reasons the "through" line numbering system established by Dr. Charlton Hinman is not herein employed.

17. A poetic meter frequently used by Shakespeare. Iambs are feet of poetry composed of an unstressed syllable followed by a stressed syllable; "pentameter" indicates there are five such feet in a verse line (from Gk. *penta,* five). The resulting verse line will therefore consist of ten alternating stressed and unstressed syllables. By no means does Shakespeare limit himself exclusively to regular iambic pentameter; departures from the norm indicate both rhythmic and expressive variation. For more on Shakespeare's irregular verse as reflective of a character's emotional state, see Flatter, pp. 25–54.

18. For more on Shakespeare's use of verse versus prose, see Doug Moston's introduction to *The First Folio of Shakespeare 1623* (Applause Books, 1995).

Appendix I

Typographical Errors Corrected from the First Folio of 1623

Act, scene, line	*Herein printed*	*Originally printed*
I.ii.58	father	farher
I.iii.82	her	per
II.ii.12	Gentlewoman	Centlewoman
II.ii.24	*Exeunt.*	*Exunt.*
II.vii.42	braine	braiue
II.vii.92	of any man.	of any. man
III.ii.29	good	pood
III.ii.177	berim'd	berim d
III.ii.293	Lacky, and	Lacky. and
V.ii.50	heavinesse, by	heavinesse. by
V.iv.86	to	ro
V.iv.178	were	wete

Appendix II

Stage Directions, Entrances and Exits Emended from the First Folio of 1623

Act, scene, line	*Herein printed*	*First Folio text*
I.i.84	*Exit Orlando and Adam.*	*Ex. Orl. Ad.*
I.i.94	*Ex. Den.*	No exit given
I.i.159	*Exit* {*Charles*}.	*Exit.*
I.i.170	*Exit* {*Oliver*}.	*Exit.*
I.ii.143–144	*Enter Duke* {*Frederick*}, *Lords, Orlando, Charles, and Attendants.*	*Enter Duke, Lords, Orlando, Charles, and Attendants.*
I.ii.216	*Exit Lords with Charles.*	No exit given
I.ii.227	*Exeunt. Manet Orlando, Cellia, and Rosalind.*	*Exit Duke.*
I.ii.258	*Exit* {*Cellia and Rosalind*}.	*Exit.*
I.ii.290	*Exit Le Beu.*	No exit given
I.ii.294	*Exit* {*Orlando.*}	*Exit*
I.iii.37	*Enter Duke* {*Frederick*} *with Lords.*	*Enter Duke with Lords.*
I.iii.94	*Exeunt. Manet Celia and Rosaline.*	*Exit Duke, &c.*
II.ii.2	*Enter Duke* {*Frederick*}, *with Lords.*	*Enter Duke, with Lords.*
II.iv.46	*Exit* {*Silvius*}.	*Exit.*
II.vii.2–3	*Enter* {*Duke Senior, Amyens, and Lords*}, *like Out-lawes.*	*Enter Duke Sen. & Lord, like Out-lawes.*
II.vii.145	*Exit Orlando.*	No exit given
III.i.2	*Enter Duke* {*Frederick*}, *Lords, & Oliver.*	*Enter Duke, Lords, & Oliver.*
III.ii.13	*Exit* {*Orlando.*}	*Exit*
III.ii.164	*Exit* {*Clowne and Corin*}.	*Exit.*
III.ii.292	*Exit Jaques.*	No exit given
III.iii.94	*Exit Clowne, Audrey, and Jaques.*	No exit given
III.iii.97	{*Exit Mar-text.*}	*Exeunt*

Act, scene, line	***Herein printed***	***First Folio text***
III.v.85	*Exit {Rosalind, Celia, and Corin}.*	*Exit.*
IV.i.34	*Exit Jaques.*	No exit given
IV.i.194	*Exit {Orlando}.*	*Exit.*
IV.ii.2	*Enter Jaques and {Amyens,} Lords, Forresters.*	*Enter Jaques and Lords, Forresters.*
IV.iii.81	*Exit Silvius.*	*Exit. Sil.*
V.i.64	*Exit {William.}*	*Exit*
V.ii.23	*Exit Oliver.*	No exit given
V.iv.31	*Exit Rosalind and Celia.*	*Exit Ros. and Celia.*
V.iv.187	*Dance.*	No stage direction given
V.iv.205	*Exit {Jaques}.*	*Exit.*
V.iv.208	*Exeunt. Manet Rosalind.*	*Exit*
V.iv.230	*Exit {Rosalind}.*	*Exit.*

Appendix III

Lineation Emended from the First Folio of 1623

Act, scene, line	*Originally printed*
I.i.83–84	Both on line 83
I.ii.205–206	Both on line 205
I.ii.209–210	Both on line 209
I.ii.257–258	Both on line 257
I.ii.293–294	Both on line 293
I.iii.146–147	Both on line 146
II.i.75–76	Both on line 75
II.ii.23–24	Both on line 23
II.iii.18	Attached contiguously to lines 4–17
II.iii.79–80	Both on line 79
II.iv.107–108	Both on line 107
II.v.50	Attached contiguously to line 49
II.v.61–62	Both on line 61
II.vi.22–23	Both on line 22
II.vii.210–211	Both on line 210
III.i.20–21	Both on line 20
III.ii.12–13	Both on line 12
III.ii.163–164	Both on line 163
III.ii.262–263	Both on line 262
III.ii.418–419	Both on line 418
III.iii.96–97	Both on line 96
III.iv.61–62	Both on line 61
III.v.147–148	Both on line 147
IV.i.193–194	Both on line 193
IV.i.212–213	Both on line 212
IV.ii.21–22	Both on line 21
IV.iii.49–50	Both on line 49

Act, scene, line	*Originally printed*
IV.iii.80–81	Both on line 80
V.i.63–64	Both on line 63
V.i.69–70	Both on line 69
V.ii.105–106	Printed sequentially: (1) *Phebe's* line; (2) *Silvius'* line; (3) *Orlando's* line.
V.ii.123–124	Both on line 123
V.iii.42–43	Both on line 42
V.iv.30–31	Both on line 30
V.iv.204–205	Both on line 204
V.iv.207–208	Both on line 207
V.iv.229–230	Both on line 229

Appendix IV

Character Tags Emended from the First Folio of 1623

Act, scene, line	*Herein printed*	*Originally printed*
I.ii.80	*Cel.*	*Ros.*
I.ii.145	*Duke Fred.*	*Duke.*
I.ii.150	*Duke Fred.*	*Du.*
I.ii.153	*Duke Fred.*	*Du.*
I.ii.159	*Duke Fred.*	*Duke.*
I.ii.197	*Duke Fred.*	*Duk.*
I.ii.211	*Duke Fred.*	*Duk.*
I.ii.214	*Duke Fred.*	*Duk.*
I.ii.216	*Duke Fred.*	*Duk.*
I.ii.220	*Duke Fred.*	*Duk.*
I.iii.41	*Duke Fred.*	*Duk.*
I.iii.44	*Duke Fred.*	*Duk.*
I.iii.56	*Duke Fred.*	*Duk.*
I.iii.62	*Duke Fred.*	*Duk.*
I.iii.71	*Duke Fred.*	*Duk.*
I.iii.81	*Duke Fred.*	*Duk.*
I.iii.91	*Duke Fred.*	*Duk.*
II.ii.3	*Duke Fred.*	*Duk.*
II.ii.19	*Duke Fred.*	*Duk.*
II.iii.18	*Orl.*	No tag; speech attached contiguously to line 17
II.iii.32	*Orl.*	*Ad.*
II.v.4	*Amy.*	No tag
II.v.49	*Jaq.*	*Amy.*
II.v.50	*Amy.*	No tag; speech

Act, scene, line	***Herein printed***	***Originally printed***
		attached contiguously to line 49
II.v.56	No tag; speech attached contiguously to line 55	*Amy.*
II.vii.188	*Amy.*	No tag
III.i.3	*Duke Fred.*	*Du.*
III.i.17	*Duke Fred.*	*Duke.*
III.iii.64	*Mar.*	*Ol.*
III.iii.66	*Mar.*	*Ol.*
III.iii.89	*Clo.*	*Ol.*
III.iii.95	*Mar.*	*Ol.*
V.i.30	*Clo.*	*Cle.*
V.iv.113	*Hymen.*	Hymen.

Bibliography

Key Reference Works

Adams, J.N. *The Latin Sexual Vocabulary*. Baltimore: Johns Hopkins University Press, 1982.

Blount, Thomas. *Glossographia, or A dictionary, interpreting all such hard words, whether Hebrew, Greek, Latin, Italian, Spanish, French, Teutonick, Belgick, British or Saxon; as are now used in our refined English tongue*. London: Tho. Newcomb, 1656.

Brewer, E. Cobham. *Dictionary of Phrase and Fable*, 4th ed. Philadelphia: Claxton, Remsen, and Haffelfinger, 187–.

Bullokar, John. *An English Expositior: teaching the interpretation of the hardest words in our language*. London: John Legatt, 1616.

Burton, Robert. *The Anatomy of Melancholy, what it is*. Oxford: John Lichfield and James Short for Henry Cripp, 1621.

Cawdrey, Robert. *A table alphabeticall, conteyning and teaching the true writing, and understanding of hard usuall English wordes, borrowed from the Hebrew, Greeke, Latine, or French, &c.* London: J.R. for Edmund Weaver, 1604.

Cockeram, Henry. *The English Dictionarie*. London: For Edmund Weaver, 1623.

Colman, E.A.M. *The Dramatic use of Bawdy in Shakespeare*. London: Longman, 1974.

Cotgrave, Randle. *A dictionarie of the French and English tongues*. London: Adam Islip, 1611.

Elyot, Thomas. *The Dictionary of syr Thomas Eliot knyght*. London: Thomas Berthelet, 1538.

Farmer, John S., and William E. Henley. *Slang and its Analogues*. New York: Scribner & Welford, 1890.

Ferrand, Jacques. *Erotomania or A treatise discoursing of the essence, causes, symptomes, prognosticks, and cure of love, or erotique melancholy*. Translated by Edmund Chilmead. Oxford: L. Lichfield, 1640.

Florio, John. *A worlde of wordes, or most copious, dictionarie in Italian and English, collected by John Florio*. London: Arnold Hatfield for Edw. Blount, 1598.

Garfield, John. *A Physical dictionary, or, An Interpretation of such crabbed words and terms of arts, as are deriv'd from the Greek or Latin, and used in physick, anatomy, chirurgery, and chymistry: with a definition of most diseases incident to the body of man, and a description of the marks and characters used by doctors in their receipts*. London: By G.D. for John Garfied, 1657.

Grose, Frances. *Lexicon Balatronicum: A Dictionary of Buckish Slang, University Wit, and Pickpocket Eloquence*. London: For C. Chappell, 1811.

Hall, James. *Dictionary of Subjects and Symbols in Art*, 2nd ed. Oxford: Westview, 2007.

Henke, James T. *Courtesans and Cuckolds: A Glossary of Renaissance Dramatic Bawdy (exclusive of Shakespeare)*. New York: Garland, 1979.
Hulme, Hilda M. *Explorations in Shakespeare's Language*. London: Longmans, Green, 1962.
Kökeritz, Helge. *Shakespeare's Pronunciation*. New Haven, CT: Yale University Press, 1953.
Landi, Ortensio. *Delectable Demaundes*. London: John Cawood for Nicholas Englande, 1566.
Latin Dictionary and Grammar Aid. Notre Dame, IN: University of Notre Dame. http://archives.nd.edu/latgramm.htm (accessed October 2007).
Minsheu, John. *A dictionarie in Spanish and English, first published into the English tongue by Ric. Percivale Gent*. Edited by Richard Percivale. London: Edm. Bollifant, 1599.
A New Dictionary of the Terms Ancient and Modern of the Canting Crew, in its several Tribes of Gypsies, Beggers, Thieves, Cheats, &c. London: For W. Hawes, P. Gilbourne and W. Davis, 1690[?].
Palsgrave, John. *Lesclarcissement de la langue francoyse compose par maistre Johan Palsgrave Angloyse natyf de Londres, et gradue de Paris*. London[?]: Richard Pynson and Johan Haukyns, 1530.
Partridge, Eric. *Shakespeare's Bawdy*. London: Routledge and Kegan Paul, 1947.
Ross, Thomas W. *Chaucer's Bawdy*. New York: E. P. Dutton, 1972.
Rubinstein, Frankie. *A Dictionary of Shakespeare's Sexual Puns and Their Significance*. London: Macmillan, 1984.
Simpson, J. A., and E.S.C. Weiner, eds. *Oxford English Dictionary*, 2nd ed. Oxford: Clarendon, 1989.
Stone, Lawrence. *The Family, Sex and Marriage in England 1500–1800*. New York: Harper and Row, 1977.
Thomas, Thomas. *Dictionarium Linguae Latinae et Anglicanae*. Canterbury: Richard Boyle, 1587.
Thomas, William. *Principal rules of the Italian grammer, with a dictionarie for the better understandyng of Boccace, Petrarcha, and Dante: gathered into this tongue by William Thomas*. London: In Fletestrete, in the house of Thomas Berthelet, 1550.
Williams, Gordon. *A Dictionary of Sexual Language and Imagery in Shakespearean and Stuart Literature*. London: Athlone, 1994.
_____. *A Glossary of Shakespeare's Sexual Language*. London: Athlone, 1997.

Other Reference Works

Adams, Joseph Quincy. *Shakespearean Playhouses: A History of English Theatres from the Beginnings to the Restoration*. Boston: Houghton Mifflin, 1917.
Adams, Thomas. *Diseases of the Soule: A Discourse Divine, Moral, and Physicall*. London: George Purslowe for John Budge, 1616.
_____. *The Happines of the Church*. London: G.P. for John Grismand, 1619.
Albott, Robert. *Englands Parnassus*. Edited by Charles Crawford. Oxford: Clarendon, 1913.
Alighieri, Dante. *Il Convito: The Banquet of Dante Alighieri*. Translated by Elizabeth Price Sayer. London: Routledge, 1887.
_____. *The Divine Comedy: Hell*. Edited and translated by Dorothy L. Sayers. London: Penguin, 1950.

Anglo, Sydney. *The Martial Arts of Renaissance Europe*. New Haven, CT: Yale University Press, 2000.

Anthon, Charles. *A Classical Dictionary*. New York: Harper and Brothers, 1869.

Apperson, George Latimer, and M. Manser. *Wordsworth Dictionary of Proverbs*. Ware, Hertfordshire: Wordsworth, 2006.

Ariosto, Lodovico. *Ariostos seven planets governing Italie, or, His satyrs in seven famous discourses*. Translated by Robert Tofte. London: William Stansby for Roger Jackson, 1611.

Aristophanes. *Scenes from the Birds of Aristophanes*. Translated by Isaac Flagg. Berkeley: The University Press, 1903.

Aristotle's Compleat and Experience'd Midwife: In Two Parts. London: 1700.

Atsma, Aaron J., ed. "Theoi Greek Mythology." Auckland, New Zealand: The Theoi Project. http://www.theoi.com/ (accessed 2009–2010).

Augustine, Saint. *St. Augustine, Of the citie of God*. Translated by John Healey. London: George Eld, 1610.

Ayre, John, ed. *The Catechism of Thomas Becon, S.T.P.* Cambridge: The University Press, 1894.

Bacon, Francis. *Bacon's Essays*. Edited by Alfred S. West. Cambridge: Cambridge University Press, 1908.

_____. *A Declaration of the Practices and Treasons Attempted and Committed by Robert late Earle of Essex and his Complices*. London: By Robert Barke, 1601.

_____. *The Elements of the Common Lawes of England*. London: By the Assignes of J. More, 1636.

_____, and William Rawley. *Sylva Sylvarum: or A Naturall Historie*. London: John Haviland for William Lee, 1635.

_____. *The Wisedome of the Ancients, London 1619*. Amsterdam: Theatrum Orbis Terrarum, 1968.

Badcock, Thomas. *Slang. A Dictionary of the Turk, the Ring, the Chase, the Pit, of Bon-Ton, and the Varieties of Life*. London: For T. Hughes, 1823.

Baldwin Smith, Lacey, ed. *Horizon Book of the Elizabethan World*. New York: Houghton Mifflin, 1967.

Bancroft, Thomas. *Two Books of Epigrammes, and Epitaphs*. London: J. Okes for Matthew Walbancke, 1639.

Banister, John. *The Historie of Man*. London: John Day, 1578.

Baron, Robert. *Erotopaignion, or, The Cyprian Academy*. London: By W.W., 1647.

Bateman, Stephen. *Batman uppon Bartholome*. London: Thomas East, 1582.

Bath, Jo, and John Newton, eds. *Witchcraft and the Act of 1604*. Leiden: Brill, 2008.

Bayley, Harold. *Lost Language of Symbolism Vols. 1 and 2 (1912)*. Whitefish, MT: Kessinger, 2003.

Beaumont, Francis. *Wit without money*. London: For Andrew Crooke, 1661.

Beaumont, Francis, and John Fletcher. *Comedies and Tragedies Written by Francis Beaumont and John Fletcher*. London: For Humphrey Robinson and Humphrey Moseley, 1647.

_____. *Fifty comedies and tragedies written by Francis Beaumont and John Fletcher, Gentlemen*. London: J. Macock for John Martyn, Henry Herringman, and Richard Marriot, 1679.

_____. *The Scornful Ladie*. London: J. Beale for Myles Partrich, 1616.

Beckerman, Bernard. *Shakespeare at the Globe 1599–1609*. New York: Collier, 1962.

Becon, Thomas. *A new yeares gyfte more precious than golde*. London: John Mayler for John Gough, 1543.

Bell, Robert, ed. *Early Ballads Illustrative of History, Traditions, and Customs; also Ballads and Songs of the Peasantry Of England*. London: George Bell and Sons, 1885.

Bellamy, John G. *The Tudor Law of Treason: An Introduction*. London: Routledge and Kegan Paul, 1979.

Bentham, William Gurney. *A Book of Quotations, Proverbs, and Household Words*. Philadelphia: J.B. Lippincott, 1907.

Bernstein, Theodore Menline, and Jane Wagner, eds. *Bernstein's Reverse Dictionary*. London: Routledge & Kegan Paul, 1976.

Berry, Edward Wilber. *Tree Ancestors: A Glimpse Into the Past*. Baltimore: Williams and Wilkins, 1923.

Berry, Herbert. *The Boar's Head Playhouse*. Cranbury, NJ: Associated University Presses, 1986.

_____, William Ingram, and Glynne Wickham, eds. *English Professional Theatre, 1530–1660*. Cambridge: Cambridge University Press, 2000.

Blochwich, Martin. *Anatomia Sambuci: Or, The Anatomie of the Elder*. London: For Thomas Heath, 1655.

Blount, Thomas. *Nomo-Lexikon, A Law Dictionary*. Clark, NJ: Lawbook Exchange, 2005.

Blurt Master Constable. London: Edward Allde for Henry Rockytt, 1602.

Boaistuau, Pierre. *Certaine Secrete Wonders of Nature*. Translated by Edward Fenton. London: Henry Bynneman, 1569.

Boas, Frederick S., ed. *The Poetical Works of Giles Fletcher and Phineas Fletcher*. Vol. 2. Cambridge: Cambridge University Press, 1909.

Bohn, Henry G. *A Hand-Book of Proverbs*. London: H.G. Bohn, 1855.

Bolton, Robert. *Some generall directions for a comfortable walking with God*. London: Felix Kyngston for Edmund Weaver, 1626.

The Booke of common praier and administration of the sacramentes and other rites and ceremonies in the Churche of Englande. London: Richard Jugge and John Cawode, 1559.

Boorde, Andrew. *A compendyous regyment or a dyetary of healthe*. London: William Powell, 1547.

Bowdler, Thomas. *The Family Shakespeare in Ten Volumes*. London: For Longman, Hurst, Rees, Orme, and Brown, 1818.

Brathwait, Richard. *A Strappado for the Divell*. London: John Beale for Richard Redmer, 1615.

_____. *A Survey of History: Or, A Nursery for Gentry*. London: By N. and J. Okes for Jasper Emery, 1638.

_____. *The Two Lancashire Lovers*. London: Edward Griffin For R. Best or his Assignes, 1640.

Breton, Nicholas. *The Figure of Foure, or A Handfull of sweet Flowers*. London: For John Wright, 1631.

_____. *No Whippinge, nor Tripping: but a kind friendly Snippinge*. Edited by Charles Edmonds. London: Elkin Mathews, 1895.

_____. *Wits Private Wealth*. London: Edward Allde for John Tappe, 1612.

Brome, Alexander. *Songs and Poems*. London: For Henry Brome, 1661.

Brome, Richard, and Thomas Heywood. *The late Lancashire witches*. London: Thomas Harper for Benjamin Fisher, 1634.

Brooke, C.F. Tucker, ed. *The Shakespeare Apocrypha*. Oxford: Clarendon, 1918.

Broughton, Richard. *The First Part of the Resolution of Religion, Devided Into Two Bookes*. London: English secret press, 1603.

Browne, William. *The Whole Works of William Browne.* 2 vols. Edited by William Carew Hazlitt. London: Printed for The Roxburghe Library, 1868.
Bruele, Gualtherus. *Praxis Medicinae, Or, The Physicians Practice.* London: John Horton for William Sheares, 1632.
Brunet, Stephen, R. Scott Smith, and Stephen M. Trzaskoma, eds. and trans. *Anthology of Classical Myth.* Indianapolis, IN: Hackett, 2004.
Brydall, John. *Decus & Tutamen, or a prospect of laws of England.* London: G. Sawbridge, W. Rawlins, and S. Roycroft, 1679.
Burford, E.J. *The Orrible Synne: A Look at London Lechery from Roman to Cromwellian Times.* London: Calder and Boyars, 1973.
Burke, David. *More Street French: Slang, Idioms, and Popular Expletives.* New York: John Wiley and Sons, 1990.
Burrow, John Anthony. *Gestures and Looks in Medieval Narrative.* Cambridge: Cambridge University Press, 2002.
Butler, Christopher. *Number Symbolism.* London: Routledge and Kegan Paul, 1970.
The Byble in Englyshe. London: Thomas Petyt and Robert Redman for Thomas Berthelet, 1540.
Camden, William. *Annales: The True and Royall History of the famous Empresse Elizabeth.* London: For Benjamin Fisher, 1625.
Campion, Edmund. *Two Histories of Ireland.* Dublin: Thomas Harper, 1633.
Cerasano, S.P., ed. *Medieval and Renaissance Drama in England.* Vol. 20. Cranbury, NJ: Associated University Presses, 2007.
Chapman, George, and Christopher Marlowe. *Hero and Leander: Begun by Christopher Marloe; and finished by George Chapman.* London: Felix Kingston for Paule Linley, 1598.
Chappel, William, and Harry Ellis Woodbridge. *Old English Popular Music.* Vol. 1. London: Chappell and Macmillan, 1893.
Charron, Pierre. *Of Wisdome.* Translated by Samson Lennard. London: Edward Blount and William Aspley, 1608.
Chaucer, Geoffrey. *The Complete Works of Geoffrey Chaucer.* Edited by Walter W. Skeat. Oxford: Clarendon, 1900.
Christy, Robert. *Proverbs, Maxims, and Phrases of All Ages.* New York: G.P. Putnam's Sons, 1904.
Churchyard, Thomas. *A Generall Rehearsall of Warres.* London: Edward White, 1579.
_____. *A Pleasaunte Laborinth called Churchyardes Chance.* London: Jhon Kyngston, 1580.
Ciesla, William M. *Non-Wood Forest Products From Temperate Broad-Leaved Trees.* Rome: Food and Agriculture Organization of the United Nations, 2002.
Cirlot, Juan Eduardo. *A Dictionary of Symbols.* Translated by Jack Sage. Mineola, NY: Dover, 2002.
Clarke, John. *Paroemiologia Anglo-Latina in usum scholarum concinnata.* London: Felix Kyngston for Robert Mylbourne, 1639.
Classe, Olive. *Encyclopedia of Literary Translation into English.* Vol. 1. Chicago: Fitzroy Dearborn, 2000.
Clegg, Cyndia Susan. *Press Censorship in Elizabethan England.* Cambridge: Cambridge University Press, 1997.
Cockaine, Thomas. *A Short Treatise of Hunting.* London: Thomas Orwin for Thomas Woodcocke, 1591.
Coke, Edward. *The First Part of the Institutes of the Laws of England, Or, A Commentary Upon Littleton.* 2 vols. London: For J. & W. T. Clarke (etc.), 1832.

_____. *The Fourth Part of the Institutes of the Laws of England.* London: For E. and R. Brooke, 1797.
_____. *The Selected Writings and Speeches of Sir Edward Coke.* 3 vols. Edited by Steve Sheppard. Indianapolis: Liberty Fund, 2003.
_____. *The Third Part of the Institutes of the Laws of England: Concerning High Treason, and other Please of the Crown, and Criminal Cause,* 4th ed. London: For A. Crooke (etc.), 1669.
Colburn, Forrest D., ed. *Everday Forms of Peasant Resistance.* Armonk, NY: M.E. Sharpe, 1989.
Coles, Elisha. *An English Dictionary, 1676.* Menston, England: Scolar Press, 1971.
Collier, John Payne, and William Carew Hazlitt, eds. *Shakespeare's Library.* Vol. 2, *As You Like It.* London: Reeves and Turner, 1875.
La conusaunce damours. London: Rycharde Pynson, 1528[?].
Cooper, Clyde Barnes. *Some Elizabethan Opinions of the Poetry and Character of Ovid.* Menasha, WI: Collegiate Press, 1914.
Cooper, Thomas. *Thesaurus Linguae Romanae & Britannicae.* London: Henry Denham, 1578.
Copland, Robert. *The Shepardes Kalender.* London: Thomas Este for John Wally, 1570.
Cox, John D., and David Scott Kastan, eds. *A New History of Early English Drama.* New York: Columbia University Press, 1997.
Cox, Nicholas. *The Gentleman's Recreation In Four Parts, Viz. Hunting, Hawking, Fowling, Fishing,* 3rd ed. London: Joseph Phillips and Henry Rodes, 1686.
Cressey, David. *Birth, Marriage, and Death: Ritual, Religion, and the Life-Cycle in Tudor and Stuart England.* Oxford: Oxford University Press, 2002.
Crooke, Helkiah. *Mikrokosmographia: A Description of the Body of Man.* London: William Jaggard, 1615.
Culman, Leonhard. *Sententiæ Pueriles, Anglo-Latinæ.* Tranlsated by Charles Hoole. London: C. Ackers, 1744.
Culpeper, Nicholas. *The English Physitian, Or An Astrologo-Physical Discourse of the Vulgar Herbs of this Nation.* London: Peter Cole, 1652.
_____. *A Physicall Directory, or, A translation of the London Dispensatory made by the Colledge of Physicians in London.* London: For Peter Cole, 1649.
Dallimore, William, and Thomas Moore. *Holly, Yew, & Box.* London: John Lane, 1908.
Davies, John. *The Complete Works of John Davies of Hereford.* 2 vols. Edited by Alexander B. Grosart. Blackburn, Lancashire: Chertsy Worthies' Library, 1878.
_____. *Mirum in Modum.* London: For William Aspley, 1602.
_____. *Wits Bedlam.* London: G. Eld, 1617.
Davison, Peter, ed. *The First Quarto of King Richard III.* New York: Press Syndicate of the University of Cambridge, 1996.
Day, John. *The Ile of Guls.* London: John Hodgets, 1606.
de Givry, Grillot. *Witchcraft, Magic & Alchemy.* Translated by J. Courtenay Locke. New York: Dover, 1971.
De Gubernatis, Angelo. *Zoological Mythology: or, The Legends of Animals.* 2 vols. London: Trubner, 1872.
de Jorio, Andrea. *Gesture in Naples and Gesture in Classical Antiquity.* Translated by Adam Kendon. Bloomington: Indiana University Press, 2000.
de La Primaudaye, Pierre. *The French Academie.* London: John Legat, 1618.
De Laune, Thomas. *Tropologia.* London: John Richardson and John Darby for Enoch Prosser, 1681.
de Rojas, Fernando. *The Spanish Bawd Represented in Celestina.* London: J.B., 1631.

Dekker, Thomas. *The Guls Hornbook and The Belman of London In Two Parts.* Edited by Oliphant Smeaton. London: J. N. Dent, 1904.
_____. *Penny-Wise, Pound Foolish.* London: A. M. for Edward Blackmore, 1631.
_____. *Satiro-Mastix: or, The Untrussing of the Humorous Poet.* Edited by Hans Scherer. London: David Nutt, 1907.
_____. *The second part of the honest whore, with the humors of the Patient Man, the Impatient Wife.* London: Elizabeth All-de, for Nathaniel Butter, 1630.
Dekker, Thomas, and Philip Massinger. *The Virgin Martir.* London: B.A. for Thomas Jones, 1622.
Dekker, Thomas, and John Webster. *West-Ward Hoe.* London: To be sold by John Hodgets, 1607.
_____. *The Whore of Babylon.* London: For Nathaniel Butter, 1607.
Dekker, Thomas, John Ford, and William Rowley. *The Witch of Edmonton.* J. Cottrel for Edward Blackmore, 1658.
Dent, Robert William. *Proverbial Language in English Drama Exclusive of Shakespeare.* Berkeley: University of California Press, 1984.
Diamond, A.S. *Primitive Law, Past and Present.* London: Routledge, 2004.
DiGangi, Mario. "Queering the Shakespearean Family." *Shakespeare Quarterly* 47 no. 3 (Autumn 1996): 269–290.
Donne, John. *Poems, By J. D.: With Elegies on the Authors Death.* London: M. F. for John Marriot, 1633.
Douce, Francis. *Illustrations of Shakespeare.* Vol. 10. London: For Thomas Tegg, 1839.
Dowland, John. *The Second Booke of Songs or Ayres.* London: Thomas Este, 1600.
Drante, Thomas, trans. *Horace His arte of Poetrie.* London: Thomas Marshe, 1567.
Drummond, William. *The Poetical Works of William Drummond of Hawthornden.* Edited by L. E. Kastner. Manchester: Manchester University Press, 1913.
Dryden, John. *The Works of John Dryden.* 18 vols. Edited by George Saintsbury and Walter Scott. Edinburgh: For William Paterson by T. and A. Constable, 1882–1893.
Duffin, Ross W. *Shakespeare's Songbook.* New York: W.W. Norton, 2004.
Dyer, T.F. Thistelton. *Folk-Lore of Shakespeare.* New York: Harper Brothers, 1884.
Edwards, Richard. *The excellent Comedie of two the moste faithfullest Freendes, Damon and Pithias.* London: Richard Johnes, 1571.
Ellis, Robert Leslie, Douglas Denon Heath, and James Spedding, eds. *The Works of Francis Bacon.* Vol. 10. Taggard and Thompson, 1864.
Ellis, William. *The Timber-Tree Improved.* Vol. 5. London: For T. Osborne and M. Cooper, 1744.
Elyot, Thomas. *The boke named the Governour.* London: Thomas Berthelet, 1537.
Engstrom, J. Eric. *Coins in Shakespeare.* Hanover, NH: Dartmouth College Museum, 1964.
Estienne, Henri. *A World of Wonders.* London: For John Norton, 1607.
Facaros, Dana, and Michael Pauls. *Turkey.* London: Cadogan Guides: 1986.
Fennor, William. *Cornu-Copiae, Pasquils Night cap: Or, Antidot for the Head-ache.* London: For Thomas Thorp, 1612.
Ferguson, George Wells. *Signs & Symbols in Christian Art.* New York: Oxford University Press, 1966.
Firth, C.H., and R.S. Rait, eds. *Acts and Ordinances of the Interregnum, 1642–1660.* London, Pub. by H.M. Stationery Off., printed by Wyman and Sons, 1911.
Fitzgerald, Percy. *A New History of the English Stage.* 2 vols. London: Tinsley Brothers, 1882.

Flatter, Richard. *Shakespeare's Producing Hand: A Study of His Marks of Expression to be Found in the First Folio*. New York: W.W. Norton, 1948.
Fletcher, Giles. *The Policy of the Turkish Empire. The First Booke*. London: John Windet for W.S., 1597.
Folkard, Richard. *Plant Lore, Legends, and Lyrics*. London: Sampson Low, Marston, Searle, and Rivington, 1884.
Fontenrose, Joseph Eddy. *Python: A Study of Delphic Myth and its Origins*. New York: Biblo and Tannen, 1974.
Fowler, William Chauncey. *English Grammar*. New York: Harper and Brothers, 1881.
Foxe, John. *Actes and monuments*. London: John Day, 1563.
Franceschina, John Charles. *Homosexualities in the English Theatre: From Lyly to Wilde*. Westport, CT: Greenwood, 1997.
Frieze, Henry S., and Walter Dennison, eds. *Virgil's Aeneid: Books I–XII*. New York: American Book, 1902.
Furnivall, Frederick, ed. *Harrison's Description of England in Shakespeare's Youth*. London: N. Trubner, 1877.
Garden, Alexander. *Characters and Essayes*. Aberdeen: Edward Raban, 1625.
Garriot, Edward Bennet. *Weather Folk-Lore and Local Weather Signs*. Washington, DC: Government Printing Office, 1903.
Gascoigne, George. *The Complete Works of George Gascoigne*. 2 vols. Edited by John W. Cunliffe. Cambridge: Cambridge University Press, 1907.
Gerard, John. *The Herball or Generall Historie of Plantes*. London: Adam Islip, Joice Norton, and Richard Whitakers, 1633.
Goddard, William. *A satirycall dialogue or a sharplye-invective conference, betweene Allexander the great, and that truelye woman-hater Diogynes*. Dordrecht: George Waters, 1616[?].
Golding, Arthur, trans. *The. XV. Bookes of P. Ovidius Naso, entytuled Metamorphosis*. London: By Willyam Seres, 1567.
Gomme, George Laurence, and Henry Benjamin Wheatley, eds. *Chap-Books and Folk-Lore Tracts*. London: Printed for the Villon Society, 1885.
Googe, Barnabe. *The Popish Kingdome*. London: Henrie Denham for Richard Watkins, 1570.
Gosson, Stephen. *The Schoole of Abuse (1579)*. London: For the Shakespeare Society, 1841.
Goulart, Simon. *Admirable and Memorable Histories Containing the wonders of our time*. London: George Eld, 1607.
Graves, Robert. *The Greek Myths*. 2 vols. London: Penguin, 1960.
Greaves, Richard L. *Society and Religion in Elizabethan England*. Minneapolis: University of Minnesota Press, 1981.
Greeley, William, and Theodore S. Woolsey. *Studies in French Forestry*. New York: John Wiley and Sons, 1920.
Green, Thomas A., ed. *Folklore: An Encyclopedia of Beliefs, Customs, Tales, Music, and Art*. 2 vols. Santa Barbara, CA: ABC-CLIO, 1997.
Greene, Robert. *The Historie of Orlando Furioso 1594*. Edited by Robert McKerrow. Oxford: Printed for the Malone Society by Horace Hart at the Oxford University Press, 1907.
_____. *The Life and Complete Works in Prose and Verse of Robert Greene*. 15 vols. Edited by Alexander B. Grosart. London: Hazell, Watson, and Viney, 1881–1886.
_____. *The Second Part of Conny-Catching*. London: John Wolfe for William Wright, 1591.

Grimal, Pierre. *The Dictionary of Classical Mythology*. Translated by A.R. Maxwell-Hyslop. Oxford: Blackwell, 1996.

Grummere, Richard, trans. *The Epistles of Seneca*. 3 vols. London: Heinemann, 1917.

Guerber, Hélène Adeline. *Myths of Greece and Rome*. New York: American Book, 1921.

Guizot, François Pierre Guillaume, trans. *Oeuvres Complètes de Shakspeare*. Vol. 4. Paris: Didier, 1863.

Hageneder, Fred. *The Meaning of Trees: Botany, History, Healing, Lore*. San Francisco, CA: Chronicle, 2005.

Hake, Edward. *Newes out of Powles Churchyarde*. Edited by Charles Carrington. London: Henry Sotheran, Baer, 1872.

Hall, John. *The Court of Virtue*. Edited by Russel A. Fraser. London: Routledge and Kegan Paul, 1961.

Hall, Joseph. *The Works of the Right Reverend Father in God, Joseph T. Hall*. 10 vols. Edited by Josiah Pratt. London: C. Whittingham, 1808.

Halliwell-Phillipps, J.O. *Outlines of the Life of Shakespeare*, 3rd ed. London: Longman, 1883.

_____, ed. *The Tinker of Turvey, or Canterbury Tales: An Early Collection of English Novels*. London: Thomas Richards, 1859.

_____, ed. *The works of William Shakespeare: in reduced facsimile from the famous first folio edition of 1623*. London: Chatto and Windus, 1876.

Hampton, William. *A proclamation of warre from the Lord of Hosts*. London: John Norton for Mathew Lawe, 1627.

Harington, John, trans. *Orlando Furioso in English Heroical Verse*. London: Richard Field, for John Norton and Simon Waterson, 1607.

Harvey, Christopher. *Schola Cordis*. London: For H. Blunden, 1647.

Harvey, I.M.W. "Poaching and Sedition in Fifteenth-Century England." In *Lordship and Learning: Studies in Memory of Trevor Aston*, edited by Ralph Evans, 169–182. Woodbridge, Suffolk: Boydell, 2004.

Hay, Peter. *Theatrical Anecdotes*. New York: Oxford University Press, 1989.

Hazlitt, William Carew, ed. *The Doubtful Plays of William Shakespeare*. Glasgow: Routledge, 1887.

_____, ed. *Shakespeare Jest-Books; Reprints of the Early and Very Rare Jest-Books Supposed to Have Been Used by Shakespeare*. London: Willis and Sotheran, 1864.

Heath, Robert. *Clarastella: together with Poems occasional, Elegies, Epigrams, Satyrs (1650)*. Gainesville, FL: Scholar's Facsimiles & Reprints, 1970.

Herbert, George. *The Poems of George Herbert*. Edited by Arthur Waugh. London: Oxford University Press, 1913.

Herrick, Robert. *The Poetical Works of Robert Herrick*. Edited by George Saintsbury. Vol. 2. London: George Bell and Sons, 1893.

Heylyn, Peter. *Mikrokosmos: A little description of the great world*. Oxford: John Lichfield and William Turner, 1625.

Heywood, John. *The Proverbs and Epigrams of John Heywood (A.D. 1562)*. Charleston, SC: BiblioLife, 2008.

Heywood, Thomas. *The Dramatic Works of Thomas Heywood*. Vol. 4. London: John Pearson, 1874.

_____. *The English Traveller*. London: Robert Raworth, 1633.

_____. *Gynaikeion*. London: Adam Islip, 1624.

Hickeringill, Edmund. *Gregory, Father-Greybeard, With his Vizard off*. London: Printed by Robin Hood, 1673.

Hilton, Walter. *The Scale (or Ladder) of Perfection*. London: Westminster Art and Book, 1908.
Hinman, Charlton, ed. *The Norton Facsimile: The First Folio of Shakespeare*. New York: Norton, 1968.
Hoby, Thomas, trans. *The Book of the Courtier from the Italian of Count Baldassare Castigliore: Done Into English by Sir Thomas Hoby Anno 1561*. London: David Nutt, 1900.
Holme, Randle. *The Academy of Armory*. Chester: Printed for the Author, 1688.
The Holy Bible, King James Version, a reprint of the edition of 1611. Peabody, MA: Hendrickson, 2003.
Hoole, Charles. *An easie entrance to the Latine tongue*. London: William Dugard for Joshuah Kirton, 1649.
Horace. *The Odes of Horace Literally Translated into English Verse*. Translated by Henry George Robinson. London: Longman, Brown, Green, and Longmans, 1846.
Hornum, Michael B. *Nemesis, the Roman State and the Games*. Leiden, the Netherlands: E.J. Brill, 1993.
Hughes, Paul L., and James F. Larkin, eds. *Tudor Royal Proclamations*. Vol. 2, *The Later Tudors*. New Haven, CT: Yale University Press, 1969.
Hyll, Thomas. *The Contemplation of Mankinde*. Henry Denham for William Seres, 1571.
Ingleby, Clement Mansfield, and Lucy Toulmin Smith. *Shakespeare's Centurie of Prayse*. London: N. Trubner, 1879.
Irish, David. *Levamen Infirmi*. London: Printed for the Author, 1700.
Jameson, Anna. *Legends of the Monastic Orders*. Edited by Estelle M. Hurll. Boston: Houghton, Mifflin, 1896.
Janiga, Marián, and Richard F. Johnston. *Feral Pigeons*. Oxford: Oxford University Press, 1995.
Jonson, Ben. *The Workes of Benjamin Jonson*. London: Will. Stansby, 1616.
_____. *The Workes of Benjamin Jonson*. London: Richard Bishop, 1640.
Keach, Benjamin. *Preaching from the Types and Metaphors of the Bible*. Grand Rabids, MI: Kregel, 1972.
Kenner, T.A. *Symbols and Their Hidden Meanings: The Mysterious Significance and Forgotten Origins of Signs and Symbols in the Modern World*. New York: Thunder's Mouth, 2006.
Kesserling, Krista J. *Mercy and Authority in the Tudor State*. Cambridge: Cambridge University Press, 2003.
Killigrew, Thomas. *Comedies, and Tragedies. Written by Thomas Killigrew, Page of Honour to King Charles the First and Groom of the Bed Chamber to King Charles the Second*. London: Henry Herringman, 1664.
Knight, Charles. *Studies of Shakespeare*. London: George Routledge and Sons, 1868.
Kurz, Doriane, and Seymour Resnick. *Embarrassing Moments in French and How to Avoid Them*. New York: Frederick Ungar, 1953.
Laslett, Peter. *The World We Have Lost: England Before the Industrial Age*. New York: Scribner's, 1965.
Lavater, Ludwig. *The Book of Ruth expounded in twenty eight Sermons*. London: Robert Waldgrave, 1586.
Leader, Damian Riehl. *A History of the University of Cambridge*. Vol. 1. Cambridge: Cambridge University Press, 1994.
Lean, Vincent Stuckey. *Lean's Collectanea*. Vol. 4. Bristol: J.W. Arrowsmith, 1904.
Lee, Sydney. *A Life of William Shakespeare*. New York: Macmillan, 1916.
Lemprière, John. *Bibliotheca Classica*. Edited by Lorenzo L. Da Ponte and John D. Ogilby. New York: W.E. Dean, 1851.

Lilly, William. *The Starry Messenger*. London: For John Partridge and Humphry Blunden, 1645.
Little Giant Encyclopedia of Superstitions. New York: Sterling, 1999.
Lounsbury, Thomas Raynesford, ed. *The Canterbury Tales by Geoffrey Chaucer*. New York: Thomas Crowell, 1903.
Lust's Dominion; Or, The Lascivious Queen. London: Printed for F.K., 1657.
Lyly, John. *The Complete Works of John Lyly*. 3 vols. Edited by R. Warwick Bond. Oxford: Clarendon, 1902.
Madden, Dodgson Hamilton. *The Diary of Master William Silence: A Study of Shakespeare and of Elizabethan Sport*. London: Longmans, Green, 1907.
Mancinus, Dominicus. *The myrrour of good maners*. London: Rychard Pynson, 1518[?].
The Manual of Heraldry. Edinburgh: John Grant, 1904.
Marlowe, Christopher. *The Famous Tragedy of The Rich Jew of Malta*. London: John Beale for Nicholas Vavasour, 1633.
_____. *Hero and Leander (1598)*. London: For Frederick Etchells and Hugh Macdonald, 1924.
Marston, John. *The Poems of John Marston*. Edited by Arnold Davenport. Liverpool: Liverpool University Press, 1961.
Marston, John, and John Webster. *The Malcontent*. London: V.S. for William Aspley: 1604.
Marvin, Dwight Edwards. *The Antiquity of Proverbs*. New York: G.P. Putnam's Sons, 1922.
Mascall, Leonard. *The First Booke of Cattell*. London: For John Wolfe, 1587.
Massinger, Philip. *Three New Playes; Viz The Bashful Lover. The Guardian, The Very Woman*. London: For Humphrey Moseley, 1655.
Maus, Katharine Eisaman. *Inwardness and Theater in the English Renaissance*. Chicago: University of Chicago Press, 1995.
McKerrow, Ronald Brunlees, and Wentworth Smith, eds. *The Tragedy of Locrine, 1595*. Oxford: Oxford University Press, 1908.
Medwall, Henry. *Nature*. London: William Rastell, 1534[?].
Melnikoff, Kirk. "The 'Extremities' of Sumptuary Law in Greene's Friar Bacon and Friar Bungay." In *Medieval and Renaissance Drama in England*, Vol. 19, edited by S.P. Cerasano, 227–234. Cranbury, NJ: Associated University Presses, 2006.
Middleton, Christopher. *The Famous Historie of Chinon of England*. London: John Danter for Cuthbert Burbie, 1597.
Middleton, Thomas. *No {Wit, Help} Like A Womans*. London: For Humphrey Moseley, 1657.
_____. *"Michaelmas Term" and "A Trick to Catch the Old One": A Critical Edition*. Edited by George R. Price. The Hague: Mouton, 1976.
Mills, Charles. *The History of Chivalry, Or, Knighthood and Its Times*. Philadelphia: Lea and Blanchard, 1844.
Monardes, Nicolás. *Joyfull Newes out of the newfound world*. London: William Norton, 1580.
More, Henry. *The second lash of Alazonomastix, laid on in mercie upon that stubborn youth Eugenius Philalethes*. Cambridge: By the printers of the University of Cambridge, 1651.
Morley, Thomas. *A plaine and easie introduction to practicall musicke set downe in forme of a dialogue*. London: Peter Short, 1597.
_____. *Of Thomas Morley the first booke of canzonets to two voyces*. London: Thomas Este, 1595.

Moston, Doug, ed. *The First Folio of Shakespeare 1623*. New York: Applause, 1994.

Mountfort, Walter. *The Launching of the Mary*. Edited by W.W. Greg and John Henry Walter. Oxford: For the Malone Society by John Johnson at the Oxford University Press, 1933.

Muir, Edward. *Ritual in Early Modern Europe*, 2nd ed. Cambridge: Cambridge University Press, 2005.

Nabbes, Thomas. *Works of Thomas Nabbes*. 2 vols. Edited by A.H. Bullen. London: Wyman and Sons, 1887.

Narcissus. London: D. Nutt, 1893.

Nashe, Thomas. *The works of Thomas Nashe*. Vol. 1. Edited by Ronald B. McKerrow. London: A.H. Bullen, 1904.

Natura Exenterata, Or Nature Unbowelled By the most Exquisite Anatomizers of Her. London: For H. Twiford, G. Bedell, and N. Ekins, 1655.

Norrick, Neal R. *How Proverbs Mean: Semantic Studies in English Proverbs*. Berlin: Mouton, 1985.

Opdycke, John Baker. *Mark My Words: A Guide to Modern Usage and Expression*. New York: Harper and Brothers, 1949.

Opie, Iona, and Moira Tatem. *A Dictionary of Superstitions*. New York: Barnes and Noble, 1999.

Orr, D. Alan. *Treason and the State: Law, Politics and Ideology in the English Civil War*. Cambridge: Cambridge University Press, 2002.

Palmer, Abram Smythe. *The Ideal of a Gentleman, or, A Mirror for Gentlefolks*. London: George Routledge and Sons, 1908.

Paré, Ambroise. *The workes of that famous chirurgion Ambrose Parey translated out of Latine and compared with the French. by Th: Johnson*. Translated by Thomas Johnson. London: Th: Cotes and R. Young, 1634.

Parker, Matthew, et al., eds. *The holie Bible, conteynyng the Olde Testament and the newe*. London: Richard Jugge, 1568.

Parliamentary Debates, House of Lords, July 16, 1963, columns 189–190.

Partlicius, Simeon. *A new method of physick*. Translated by Nicholas Culpeper. London: Peter Cole, 1654.

Peacham, Henry. *The Compleat Gentleman*. London: For Francis Constable, 1634.

Peaps, William. *Love In it's Extasie: Or, The large Prerogative*. London: W. Wilson for Mercy Meighen, Gabriell Bedell, and Thomas Collins, 1649.

Pechet, John. *The Compleat Midwife's Practice*. London: For H. Rhodes, J. Philips, and K. Bentley, 1698.

Peele, George. *The historie of the two valiant knights*. London: Thomas Creede, 1599.

_____. *The Love Of King David And Fair Bethsabe*. London: Adam Islip, 1599.

Pepin, Ronald E. *The Vatican Mythographers*. New York: Fordham University Press, 2008.

Perkins, William. *A Commentarie or Exposition, upon the five first Chapters of the Epistle to the Galatians*. Cambridge: John Legat, 1604.

_____. *A golden Chaine: Or, The Description of Theologie*. Cambridge: John Legat, 1600.

Piatti, Girolamo. *The Happines Of A Religious State Divided into three Bookes*. Translated by Henry More. Rouen: J. Cousturier, 1632.

Planche, James Robinson. *A Cyclopedia Of Costume*. Vol. 2. London: Chatto and Windus, 1879.

Pliny the Elder. *The Historie of the World: Commonly called, The Naturall Historie of C. Plinius Secundus*. Translated by Philemon Holland. London: Adam Islip. 1634.

Plummer, Alfred. *The London Weavers' Company, 1600–1970*. London: Routledge and Kegan Paul, 1972.

Pollard, Alfred W. *Shakespeare Folios and Quartos*. New York: Cooper Square, 1909.

Porter, Henry. *The Pleasant History of the two angry women of Abington*. London: William Ferbrand, 1599.

Potts, Malcolm, and Roger Valentine Short. *Ever Since Adam and Eve: The Evolution of Human Sexuality*. Cambridge: Cambridge University Press, 1999.

Powell, Thomas. *Humane industry, or, A history of most manual arts*. London: For Henry Herringman, 1661.

The Problemes of Aristotle, with other Philosophers and Phisitions. Edinburge: By Robert Waldgrave, 1595.

Prynne, William. *Histrio-Mastix*. London: E.A. and W.J. for Michael Sparke, 1633.

_____. *The Perpetuitie of a Regenerate Mans Estate*. London: William Jones, 1626.

Rahner, Hugo. *Greek Myths and Christian Mystery*. Translated by Brian Battershaw. New York: Biblo and Tannen, 1971.

Raleigh, Walter. *The History of the World*. William Stansby for Walter Burre, 1617.

Recorde, Robert. *The whetstone of witte: whiche is the seconde parte of Arithmetike: containyng thextraction of rootes: the cossike practise, with the rule of equation: and the woorkes of surde nombers*. London: Jhon Kyngstone, 1557.

Ribton-Turner, Charles James. *A History of Vagrants and Vagrancy, and Beggars and Begging*. London: Chapman and Hall, 1887.

Richards, Nathaniel. *Poems Sacred and Satyricall*. London: Felix Kyngston for Roger Michell, 1641.

Rivers, George. *The Heroinae*. London: R. Bishop for John Colby, 1639.

Robinson, Eloise, ed. *The Minor Poems of Joseph Beaumont*. Vol. 2. Boston: Houghton Mifflin, 1914.

Rogers, Thomas. *A philosophicall discourse, Entituled, The Anatomie of the minde*. London: by John Charlewood for Andrew Maunsell, 1576.

Rolfe, William J., ed. *Shakespeare's Comedy of As You Like It*. New York: Harper and Brothers, 1899.

Roud, Steve, and Jacqueline Simpson. *A Dictionary of English Folklore*. Oxford: Oxford University Press, 2003.

Rowlands, Samuel. *The Knave of Clubbs*. London: Edward Allde, 1611.

Rowlett, Russ. "How Many? A Dictionary of Units of Measurement." Chapel Hill, NC: University of North Carolina at Chapel Hill. http://www.unc.edu/~rowlett/units/ (accessed October 2009).

Russell, Jeffrey Burton. *Witchcraft in the Middle Ages*. Ithaca, NY: Cornell University Press, 1984.

Ryves, Bruno. *Angliae Ruina: or, Englands Ruine*. London: 1648[?].

St. Clair Feilden, Henry. *A Short Constitutional History of England*, 3rd ed. Edited by W. Gray Etheridge. Boston: Ginn, 1895.

Saker, Austin. *Narbonus*. London: Richard Jones, 1580.

Salgādo, Gāmini. *The Elizabethan Underworld*. London: J.M. Dent, 1977.

Sandys, George, trans. *Ovid's Metamorphosis Englished, Mythologiz'd And Represented in Figures*. Oxford: John Lichfield, 1632.

Saviolo, Vincentio. *Vincentio Saviolo his practise: In two bookes. The first intreating of the use of the rapier and dagger. The second, of honor and honorable quarrels*. London: Thomas Scarlet for John Wolfe, 1595.

Sayle, Charles, ed. *The Works of Sir Thomas Browne*. Vol. 2. London: Grant Richards, 1904.

Schelling, Felix E. *English Literature During The Lifetime Of Shakespeare.* New York: Henry Holt, 1910.
Schimmel, Annemarie. *The Mystery of Numbers.* Oxford: Oxford University Press, 1993.
Schouler, James. *A Treatise on the Law of the Domestic Relations*, 5th ed. Boston: Little, Brown, 1895.
Scot, Reginald. *Discoverie of Witchcraft.* London: William Brome, 1584.
Segar, William. *The Booke of Honor and Armes (1590) and Honor Military and Civil (1602).* Delmar, NY: Scholars Facsimilies and Reprints, 1975.
Shakespeare, William. *An excellent conceited Tragedie of Romeo and Juliet.* London: John Danter, 1597.
_____. *Anthony and Cleopatra.* Edited by Horace Howard Furness. Philadelphia: J.B. Lippincott, 1907.
_____. *As You Like It.* Edited by Horace Howard Furness. Philadelphia: J.B. Lippincott, 1890.
_____. *Loves Labour's Lost.* Edited by Horace Howard Furness. Philadelphia: J.B. Lippincott, 1904.
_____. *The most excellent and lamentable Tragedie, of Romeo and Juliet.* London: Thomas Creede, for Cuthbert Burby, 1599.
_____. *Shake-Speares Sonnets.* London: G. Eld for T. T., 1609.
_____. *The Tragicall historie of Hamlet Prince of Denmarke by William Shake-speare.* London: For NL and John Trundell, 1603.
_____. *Venus and Adonis.* London: Richard Field, 1594.
_____. *The Works of William Shakespeare.* 6 Vols. Edited by Alexander Dyce. London: Edward Moxon, 1857.
Sharpham, Edward. *Cupid's Whirligig.* Edited by Allardyce Nicoll. Waltham Saint Lawrence: Golden Cockerel, 1926.
Shaw, Peter, ed. *The Philosophical Works of Francis Bacon.* Vol. 2. London: For J.J. and P. Knapton (etc.), 1733.
Sherburne, Edward, trans. *The sphere of Marcus Manilius made an English poem with annotations and an astronomical appendix.* London: For Nathanial Brooke, 1675.
Sherry, Richard. *A Treatise of the Figures of Grammer and Rhetorike.* London: Robert Caly[?], 1555.
Shirley, James. *The Bird in a Cage.* London: B. Alsop and T. Fowcet for William Cooke, 1633.
Sidney, Philip. *The Countesse of Pembroke's Acradia.* Edited by Albert Feuillerat. Cambridge: Cambridge University Press, 1912.
Simpson, Percy. *Shakespearian Punctuation.* Oxford: Clarendon, 1911.
Singman, Jeffrey L. *Daily Life in Elizabethan England.* Westport, CT: Greenwood, 1995.
Smith, Charles G. *Shakespeare's Proverb Lore: His Use of the Sententiae of Leonard Culman and Publilius Sysrus.* Cambridge, MA: Harvard University Press, 1968.
Smith, D. Nichol, ed. *Eighteenth Century Essays on Shakespeare.* Glasgow: Maclehose and Sons, 1903.
Smith, Henrie. *A Preparative to Mariage.* London: Thomas Orwin for Thomas Man, 1591.
Smith-Bannister, Scott. *Names and Naming Patterns in England, 1538–1700.* Oxford: Oxford University Press, 1997.
Solyman and Perseda. London: Edward Allde for Edward White, 1592.
Spenser, Edmund. *The Works of Edmund Spenser.* Edited by R. Morris. New York: Macmillan, 1902.

Starr, Brian. *Calendar of Saints*. North Charleston, SC: BookSurge, 2006.
Sternfeld, F.W. *Music in Shakespearean Tragedy*. Routledge and Kegan Paul, 1963.
Stockton, Lewis. *Marriage Considered from Legal and Ecclesiastical Viewpoints*. Buffalo, NY: Huebner-Bleistein Patents, 1912.
Stubbes, Phillip. *Anatomie of Abuses*. London: Richard Jones, 1583.
Suckling, John. *The Works of Sir John Suckling*. 2 vols. Edited by L.A. Beurline and Thomas Clayton. Oxford: Clarendon, 1971.
Taylor, Jeremy. *The Rule and Exercises of Holy Dying*. London: For R.R., 1651.
Taylor, John. *All The Workes Of John Taylor The Water Poet*. London: J.B. for James Boler, 1630.
Taylor, Richard. *How to Read a Church: A Guide to Symbols and Images in Churches and Cathedrals*. London: Rider, 2003.
Taylor, Thomas. *Christ Revealed: or The Old Testament Explained*. London: Miles Flesher for R. Dawlman and L. Fawne, 1635.
_____. *Davids Learning, or The Way to True Happinesse*. London: William Stansby for Henrie Fetherstone, 1617.
Tegetmeir, William Bernhard. *Pigeons: their Structure, Varieties, Habits, and Management*. London: George Routledge and Sons, 1868.
Toller, T. Northcote, ed. *An Anglo-Saxon Dictionary Based on the Manuscript Collections of the Late Joseph Bosworth*. Oxford: Clarendon Press, 1882.
Topsell, Edward. *The Historie of Foure-Footed Beastes*. London: William Jaggard, 1607.
_____. *The Historie of Serpents; or, the Second Book of Living Creatures*. London: William Jaggard, 1608.
Tresidder, Jack, ed. *The Complete Dictionary of Symbols*. San Francisco: Chronicle, 2005.
Tucker, Patrick. *Secrets of Acting Shakespeare: The Original Approach*. New York: Routledge, 2002.
Turner, James, ed. *Sexuality and Gender in Early Modern Europe: Institutions, Texts, Images*. Cambridge: Cambridge University Press, 1995.
Turner, William. *The Names of Herbes, A.D. 1548*. Edited by James Britten. London: N. Trubner, 1881.
Twyne, Thomas. *The Schoolemaster, or Teacher of Table Philosophie*. London: Richarde Jones, 1576.
Venner, Tobias. *Via recta ad vitam longam*. London: Edward Griffin for Richard Moore, 1620.
Vives, Juan Luis. *An introduction to wysedome*. Translated by Richard Morison. London: Thomas Berthelet, 1544.
Voegelin, Eric. *The Collected Works of Eric Voegelin*. Vol. 19, *History of Political Ideas, vol. I, Hellenism, Rome, and Early Christianity*. Edited by Athanasios Moulakis. Columbia: University of Missouri Press, 1997.
_____. *The Collected Works of Eric Voegelin*. Vol. 22, *History of Political Ideas, vol. IV, Renaissance and Reformation*. Edited by David L. Morse and William M. Thompson. Columbia: University of Missouri Press, 1997.
Walsh, William Shepard. *Handy-book of Literary Curiosities*. Philadelphia: J.B. Lippincott, 1909.
Ward, Samuel. *Balme from Gilead to recover conscience*. London: by Thomas Snodham for Roger Jackson and William Bladen, 1618.
Watkins, Ronald. *On Producing Shakespeare*. London: Michael Joseph, 1950.
Watson, George. *The Roxburghshire Word Book*. Cambridge: Cambridge University Press, 1923.

Watt, Francis. *The Law's Lumber Room.* London: John Lane, By Francis Watt, 1895.
Webster, John. *The Complete Works of John Webster.* Edited by Frank Laurence Lucas. London: Chatto and Windus, 1928.
_____. *The Tragedy Of The Dutchesse Of Malfy.* London: Nicholas Okes for John Waterson, 1623.
_____. *The White Divel.* London: Nicholas Okes for Thomas Archer, 1612.
Weingust, Don. *Acting from Shakespeare's First Folio: Theory, Text and Performance.* New York: Routledge, 2006.
Werness, Hope B. *The Continuum Encyclopedia of Animal Symbolism in Art.* New York: Continuum, 2006.
Wesley, Samuel. *The Life of Our Blessed Lord & Saviour Jesus Christ: An Heroic Poem.* London: For Charles Harper and Benjamin Motte, 1693.
Wheatley, Henry Benjamin. *Shakespeare's editors 1623 to the Twentieth Century.* London: Blades, East, and Blades, 1919.
Whitney, Geffrey. *A choice of emblemes, and other devises.* Leyden: In the house of Christopher Plantyn by Francis Raphelngius, 1586.
Wilkins, George. *The Painfull Adventures of Pericles Prince of Tyre.* London: T. Purfoot for Nathanial Butter, 1608.
Willet, Andrew. *Hexapla in Genesin & Exodum.* London: John Haviland, 1633.
Williams, Tennessee. *Cat on a Hot Tin Roof.* New York: Signet, 1955.
Wilson, Thomas. *The Arte of Rhetorique.* London: John Kingston, 1560.
Wither, George. *Britain's Remembrencer.* Manchester: Charles E. Simms for the Spenser Society, 1880.
_____. *Wither's Motto.* London: For John Marriott, 1621.
Wood, John George. *The Illustrated Natural History.* London: George Routledge, 1855.
Wright, Joseph, ed. *The English Dialect Dictionary.* Vol. 5. London: Oxford University Press, 1904.
Wright, Thomas. *Dictionary of Obsolete and Provincial English.* Vol. 1. London: George Bell and Sons, 1904.
Yonge, C.D., trans. *The Deipnosophists: or, Banquet of the Learned of Athanaeus.* Vol. 2. London: Henry G. Bohn, 1854.
Youngs, Frederick A. *The Proclamations of the Tudor Queens.* Cambridge: Cambridge University Press, 1976.